THE RISE AND FALL OF D.O.D.O.

THE **RISE** AND **FALL** OF

D.O.D.O.

NEAL STEPHENSON
AND NICOLE GALLAND

THE BOROUGH PRESS

I

Copyright © Neal Stephenson 2017

Neal Stephenson asserts the moral right to
be identified as the author of this work

A catalogue record for this book
is available from the British Library

ISBN: 978-0-00-813256-9

This novel is entirely a work of fiction.
The names, characters and incidents portrayed in it are
the work of the author's imagination. Any resemblance to
actual persons, living or dead, events or localities is
entirely coincidental.

Designed by Jamie Lynn Kerner

Printed and bound in Great Britain by
Clays Ltd, St Ives plc

MIX
Paper from
responsible sources

FSC
www.fsc.org   FSC™ C007454

FSC™ is a non-profit international organisation established to promote
the responsible management of the world's forests. Products carrying the
FSC label are independently certified to assure consumers that they come
from forests that are managed to meet the social, economic and ecological
needs of present and future generations, and other controlled sources.

Find out more about HarperCollins and the environment at
www.harpercollins.co.uk/green

FOR LIZ DARHANSOFF

CONTENTS

———

AUTHORS' NOTE

———

To the reader:

For your convenience we have included a list of characters as well as a glossary of acronyms and terms that are unique to the D.O.D.O. world. Because the lists contain many spoilers, we have placed them at the back of the book.

N. S. and N. G.

THE RISE AND FALL OF D.O.D.O.

PART ONE

Diachronicle

MY NAME IS MELISANDE STOKES and this is my story. I am writing in July 1851 (Common Era, or—let's face it—Anno Domini) in the guest chamber of a middle-class home in Kensington, London, England. But I am not a native of this place or time. In fact, I am quite ~~fucking~~ desperate to get out of here.

But you already knew that. Because when I'm done writing this thing—which, for reasons that will soon become clear, I'm calling Diachronicle—I am going to take it to the very discreet private offices of the Fugger Bank, Threadneedle Street, lock it up in a safe deposit box, and hand it over to the most powerful banker in London, who is going to seal it in a vault, not to be opened for more than one hundred and sixty years. The Fuggers, above all people in this world, understand the dangers of Diachronic Shear. They know that to open the box and read the document sooner would be to trigger a catastrophe that would wipe London's financial district off the map and leave a smoking crater in its place.

Actually, it would be much worse than a smoking crater . . . but a smoking crater is how history would describe it, once the surviving witnesses had been sent off to the madhouse.

I'm writing with a steel-nibbed dip pen, model number 137B, from Hughes & Sons Ltd. of Birmingham. I requested the Extra Fine Tip, partly to save money on paper, and partly so that I could jab my thumb with it and draw blood. The brown smear across the top of this page can be tested in any twenty-first-century DNA lab. Compare the results to what is on file in my personnel record at DODO HQ and you will know that I am a woman of your era, writing in the middle of the nineteenth century.

I intend to write everything that explains how I came to be here, no matter how far-fetched or hallucinatory it may sound. To quote Peter Gabriel, a singer/songwriter who will be born ninety-nine years from now: This will be my testimony.

I DO ATTEST that I am here against my will, having been Sent here from September 8, 1850, and from the city of San Francisco, California (the day before California was granted statehood).

I do attest that I belong in Boston, Massachusetts, in the first quarter of the twenty-first century. There, and then, I am part of the Department of Diachronic Operations: a black-budget arm of the United States government that has gone rather badly off the rails due to internal treachery.

In the time in which I write this, 1851, magic is waning. The research that DODO paid me to perform indicates that magic will cease to exist at the end of this month (July 28). When that happens, I will be trapped here in a post-magic world for the rest of my days. The only way anyone will ever know what became of me is through this deposition. While I have managed to land myself in comfortable (by 1851 standards) quarters with access to pen, ink, leisure time, and privacy, it has been at the expense of freedom; my hosts would not consider allowing me out of the house alone for an evening constitutional, let alone to seek out witches who might help me.

One comment before I begin. If anyone from DODO ever reads this, for the love of God please add corset-makers to the list of abettors we need to recruit in any Victorian DTAPs. Corsets are intended to be custom-made to conform to the actual shape of a lady's body, and it's uncomfortable to have to borrow one or buy one "off the rack," although servants and poorer women generally do that (but do not lace them tightly, as they must engage in manual labor). Being here entirely on charity, I prefer not to ask my hosts to extend credit for a custom-fit one, but wearing this one (borrowed from my hostess) is just awful. It makes a Renaissance bodice feel like a bikini, I'm not even kidding.

Diachronicle
DAY 33 (LATE AUGUST, YEAR 0)

*In which I meet Tristan Lyons and immediately agree to get into
more trouble than I could possibly realize at the time*

I MET TRISTAN LYONS IN the hallway outside the faculty offices of the Department of Ancient and Classical Linguistics at Harvard University. I was a lecturer, which means that I was given the most unpopular teaching assignments with no opportunity for university-supported research and no real job security.

On this particular afternoon, as I was walking down the hallway, I heard voices raised within the office of Dr. Roger Blevins, Department Chair. His door was slightly ajar. Usually it gaped open, so that anyone walking by might glance at his ego-wall, upon which hung every degree, honor, and accolade he'd ever collected, honestly or otherwise. When not yawning thus, the door was tightly closed, advising "Do Not Disturb" in 48-point

Lucida Blackletter to make sure we all understood how exclusive his company was.

But here it was, uncharacteristically a quarter open. Intrigued, I glanced in, just as a clean-cut man was making a decisive exit, looking back at Blevins with an expression somewhere between disgust and bemusement. His biceps smacked into my shoulder as he ploughed into me with enough force to throw me off balance. I pivoted backward and landed sprawled on the floor. He retreated instinctively, his backpack smacking into the doorjamb with a hard thump. From within the office, Blevins's voice was hurling a stream of invective.

"Apologies," the man said at once, turning red. He was about my age. He slipped out into the hallway and began to reach toward me to help me up.

The door swung farther open, quite forcefully—right into my shin. I made a noise of pained protest and the pompous voice from within the room went silent.

Blevins—thick grey hair perfectly immobile, dressed as if he expected at any moment to be sworn in to give expert testimony—emerged from his office and peered down at me disapprovingly. "What are you doing there?" he asked, as if he'd caught me spying.

"My fault, I'm sorry, miss," said the young man, again holding his hand toward me.

Blevins grabbed the edge of the door and began pulling it closed. "Watch where you're going," he said to me. "If you'd been in the *middle* of the hall you'd have avoided a collision. Please collect yourself and move on."

He gave the young man a look I could not make out from where I was, then turned back into his office, closing the door hard behind him.

After a second of stunned silence, the young man extended his hand closer to me and I took it, with a nod of thanks, to rise. We were standing quite close to each other.

"I am . . ." he began again. "I am so very sorry—"

"It's fine," I said. "If you've annoyed Roger Blevins, how bad can you be?"

At that he looked startled—as if he'd come from someplace where speaking ill of the brass simply wasn't done. We kept staring at each other. It seemed a perfectly normal thing to do. He was nice to look at in an ROTC sort of way, and his expression implied he didn't mind looking at me either, although I am not the sort the ROTC boys ever took an interest in.

Suddenly he held out his hand. "Tristan Lyons," he said.

"Melisande Stokes," I rejoined.

"You're in the Ancient and Classical Linguistics Department?"

"I am," I said. "I'm an exploited and downtrodden humanities lecturer."

Once again, that startled, wary look. "I'm treating you to coffee," he said.

That was presumptuous, but I was so pleased with him for upsetting Blevins that it would have been churlish to turn him down.

He wanted to take me to the Apostolic Café in Central Square, which was perhaps ten minutes by foot down Mass Ave. It was that time of year in Boston when the summer feels definitely over, and the city's seventy-odd colleges and universities are coming back to life. Streets were jammed with parental minivans from all over the Northeast, moving their kids into their apartments and dorm rooms. Sidewalks were clogged with discarded sofas and other dump-bound furniture. Add that to the city's baseline traffic—people, cars, bikes, the T—and it was all very loud and bustling. He used that as an excuse to cup my elbow in one hand, keeping me close to him as we walked. Presumptuous. As was the very idea that you could walk two abreast in such a crowded place. But he kept making a path through the crowd with expectant looks and crisp apologies. Definitely not from around here.

"Can you hear me clearly?" he said almost directly into my ear, my being half a step ahead of him. I nodded. "Let me tell you a couple of things while we're walking. By the time we get to the café, if you think I'm a creep or a nutcase, just tell me, and I'll simply buy you a coffee and be on my way. But if you don't think I'm a creep or a nutcase, then we're going to have a very serious conversation that could take hours. Do you have dinner plans?"

In the society I inhabit currently, such an approach would be considered so outrageous that when I think on it, it is hard to believe I did not instantly excuse myself and walk away from him. On the contrary, at the time I found his awkward inappropriateness, his bluntness, rather compelling. And I confess, I was curious to hear what he had to say.

"I might," I said. (Confession: I did not.)

"All right, listen," he began. "I work for a shadowy government entity, you've never heard of it, and if you try to Google it, you won't find any reference to it, not even from conspiracy-theory nuts."

"Conspiracy-theory nuts are the only ones who would use a term like 'shadowy government entity,'" I pointed out.

"That's why I use it," he retorted. "I don't *want* anyone to take me seriously, it would get in the way of my efficiency if people were paying attention to me. Here's what we need. Tell me if you're interested. We have a bunch of very old documents—cuneiform, in one case—and we need them translated, at least roughly, by the same person. You'll be paid very well. But I can't tell you where we got the documents, or how we got them, or why we're interested in them. And you cannot ever tell anyone about this. You can't even say to your friends, 'Oh, yeah, I did some classified translating for the government.' Even if we publish your translation of it, you can't take ownership of it. If you learn something extraordinary from translating the material, you can't share it with the world. You're a cog in a piece of machinery. An anonymous cog. You'd have to agree to that before I say another word."

"That's why Blevins threw you out," I said.

"Yes, he's strongly committed to academic freedom."

Dear reader, give me credit for not ~~going LOL on~~ mocking him. "No he isn't."

This startled Tristan, who looked at me like a puppy after you've stepped on his tail. On second thought, given his ROTC bearing, let's make that a mature German shepherd.

"He was pissed off that he'd never get any glory or royalties," I explained. "But he knew he couldn't say that. So, academic freedom or whatever."

Tristan seemed to actually think about this as we crossed Temple Street. His type are trained to respect authority. Blevins was nothing if not authoritative. So, this was a little test. Was his straight-arrow brain going to explode?

Through all the bustle, in the golden light of early autumn, I could see the entrance to the Central Square T stop. "What's your position?" he asked me.

"On academic freedom? Or getting paid?"

"You haven't kicked me to the curb yet," he said. "So, I guess we're talking about the latter."

"Depends on the paycheck."

He named an amount that was twice my annual salary, with the caveat ". . . once you convince me you're the right person for the job."

"What will the translations be used for?"

"Classified."

I tried to think of reasons not to pursue this lucrative diversion. "Could they somehow be justification for unethical actions, or physical violence, on the part of your shadowy government entity?"

"Classified."

"That's a yes, then," I said. "Or at least a possibly. You'd have just said no otherwise."

"That amount I just mentioned? It's for a *six-month* contract. Renewable by mutual agreement. Benefits negotiable. Are we having coffee together or not?" We were nearing the turn to the Apostolic Café.

"No harm in coffee," I said. Stalling for time, trying to wrap my head around the math: four times my current take-home pay, which would never include benefits. Not to mention that I'd be trading up in the supervisor department.

We entered the café, a beautiful old desanctified brick church with high vaulted ceilings, stained glass windows, and incongruously modern wood tables and chairs sprinkled across the marble floor. There was a state-of-the-art espresso station to one side and— most disconcertingly, as much as I'd overcome my upbringing—a counter set just about where the altar would once have been, and a complete wet bar curving around the inner wall of the apse. The place had only recently opened but was already very popular with the techno-geek crowd from both Harvard and MIT. It was my first time in. I felt a brief pang of envy that there weren't enough linguists in Cambridge to warrant a designated polyglot-hangout as lovely as this.

"What's your pleasure?" asked the barista, a young Asian-American woman with interesting piercings, tattoos in place of eyebrows, and a demeanor that blended *I'm sooo interesting and this job sucks* with *I have a really cool secret life and this job is an awesome front.* Her nametag read "Julie Lee: Professional 聪明的驴子·双簧管" (which I understood, roughly, as "Smart-ass Oboist").

We ordered drinks—Tristan, black coffee; myself, something I would never normally have, a complicated something-latte-something with lots of buzzwords I picked out at random from the menu over the bar, and which prompted a brief smirk from our barista. The agents of shadowy government entities, I reasoned, were likely to be trained in psychological evaluation of potential recruits, and I did not want him getting an accurate read on me until I decided whether or not I wished to pursue his offer. (Also he was rather handsome, which made me jittery a bit, so I decided to hide behind an affected eccentricity.) The result being that he sat down with a lovely-smelling cup of dark roast and I sat down with something almost undrinkable.

"You ordered that to try to throw me off the scent, in case I was doing some sort of ninja psych-eval of you," he said casually, as if just trying the idea on for size. "Ironically, that tells me more about you than if you'd just ordered your usual."

I must have looked shocked, because he grinned with almost savage self-satisfaction. There was something disturbingly thrilling about being *seen* so thoroughly, so quickly, and so stealthily. I felt myself flush.

"How?" I demanded. "How did you do that?"

He leaned in toward me, large, strong hands clasped before him on the café table. "Melisande Stokes—may I call you Mel?" I nodded. "Mel." He cleared his throat in a very official-sounding, preparatory manner. "If we're going to pursue this," he said, "there are three parts to it. First, before anything else, you have to sign the nondisclosure form. Then I need you to do some sample translations so we can get a sense of your work, and then we have to run a background check on you."

"How long will all that take?" I asked.

Four times my salary. With possible dental.

And no Blevins.

He had set his backpack on a chair beside him. Now he patted it. "Nondisclosure form is right here. If you sign it now, I can text your name and social to DC." He paused then, and reconsidered. "Never mind. They already know your social. Point is, they'll have finished the background check before you're done choking down whatever the hell it is you ordered. So it's just how long it takes you to translate the test samples and have our guys look over your translations. But"—he waved a warning finger at me—"no fooling around here. Once you sign the form, you're *committing* to do this. Unless we reject you. You can't reject us. You're stuck with me, for six months minimum, as soon as you sign the form. Got it? No half-assedness on your part. So maybe we just talk tonight and then you take the form with you and give it to me tomorrow when you've had a chance to sleep on it."

"Where would I find you tomorrow?" I asked.

"Classified," he said. "I'd find you."

"I don't like being stalked. I'd better sign it now," I said.

He stared at me a moment. It wasn't quite like that first moment, when we had stared and it had felt so strangely normal. This felt *charged*. But I wasn't exactly sure why. I would like to think I was simply delighted to be ridding myself of Blevins and quadrupling my income all in one go. But if I am honest with myself I confess there was a definite pleasure in being Chosen by someone with such agreeable features.

"Right," he said, after we had been staring for a couple of heartbeats. "Here." He reached for his bag.

I read the form, which said precisely what Tristan had described, making it at once boilerplate and singular. I held out my hand, and Tristan offered me a government-issue ballpoint pen. A far cry from the slightly blood-smeared Hughes & Sons Ltd. model number 137B, Extra Fine, with which I am writing this.

As I signed the form, he leaned in closer to me and said quietly, sounding delighted with himself, "I have some of the cuneiform in my bag if you want to take a look at it."

I believe I gaped at that. "You're carrying a cuneiform artifact around in your backpack!?"

He shrugged. "If it could survive the fall of Ugarit . . ." There was a boyish gleam in his eye. He was showing off now. "Want to see it?"

I nodded mutely. He opened his bag and drew out a lump of clay, roughly the size and shape of a Big Mac. So *that's* what had banged against the doorjamb of Blevins's office. Marked into it in tiny, neat rows . . . *was cuneiform text*. Tristan handled it as if it were a football. I stared at it for a moment, disoriented by seeing something I had only encountered while wearing gloves in the workroom of a museum, now casually sitting on the table next to my coffee-like beverage. I was almost afraid to touch it; that seemed disrespectful. But within moments I had tossed such a delicate thought aside, and my fingers were caressing it. I studied the script.

"This isn't Ugaritic," I said. "It's Hittite. There are some Akkadian-style markings."

He looked pleased. "Nice," he said. "Can you read it?"

"Not *offhand*," I said patiently. Some people have a very romanticized notion of what it means to be a polyglot. But not wanting to appear lacking, I added quickly, "The light in here is too low, it will be hard to make out the forms."

"Soon enough," he said, and pushed it back into his bag with the same casual roughness. Once it was out of sight I began to wonder if I'd really seen it.

Tristan reached back into the bag and pulled out something else now: a sheaf of papers. He pushed them across the table to me. "You still have the pen," he said. "Want to get started on these?"

I looked at the papers. There were seven blocks of writing, almost none of them in the Roman alphabet—even the Old Latin passage used Etruscan. At a glance I also recognized biblical Hebrew and classical Greek. The Hebrew I knew best, so I looked more closely at this one.

And blinked several times to make sure I was not imagining what I was seeing. I took a look at the Greek and then the Latin to make sure. Then I looked up at Tristan. "I already know what all of these say."

"You've taken this test before?" he asked, surprised.

"No," I said tartly. "I *created* it." At his confused look, I explained: "I chose these specific samples and I wrote the translation key against which to check the students' work." I felt my cheeks grow hot. "I did it as a project under Blevins when I was a graduate student."

"He sold it to us," Tristan said simply. "For a lot of money."

"It was for a graduate seminar on syntax patterns," I said.

"Mel," he said, "*he sold it to us*. There was never a graduate seminar on syntax patterns. We—that is, people high up in my shadowy government entity—have been working with him for a long time. We have *contracts* with him."

"I would happily sign that nondisclosure form seventeen times over," I said, "to express the depth of my sentiments toward Roger Blevins at this moment."

Julie Lee, Professional Smart-ass Oboist, swept by us, bussing our cups without asking, as Tristan's phone made a noise and he glanced down at the screen.

He typed something into the phone and then pocketed it. "I just told them you passed with flying colors," he said, "and they just told me you passed the background check."

"Of course I passed the background check," I said. "What do you take me for?"

"You're hired."

"Thank you," I said, "but whoever *they* are, please let them know I'm the *creator* of the test I just passed."

He shook his head no. "Then we get into an IP inquiry with the university and things get messy and public, and shadowy government entities can't go there. Sorry. If this project falls apart, though, feel free to take it up with Blevins." His phone beeped again and he checked the new incoming message. "Meanwhile, let's get to work." He pocketed the phone and held out his hand for me to shake. "You have an agreeably uninteresting existence. Let's see if we can change that."

Diachronicle
DAYS 34-56 (SEPTEMBER, YEAR 0)

In which magic is brought to my attention

TRISTAN DETERMINED TO BEGIN THE translations immediately—
that very evening—and so he ordered carry-out Chinese, asked
for my address, and said that he would show up in an hour with
the first of several documents. I was, please know, outraged that
he was driving around with ancient artifacts in the backseat of
his beat-up Jeep.

At that time, I dwelt alone in a one-bedroom walk-up flat in
North Cambridge (without being considered a spinster or a loose
woman, as would be the case in my current environment). It was
walking distance from the Porter Square T stop and an easy bicycle ride down Massachusetts Avenue, cutting through Harvard
Yard, to the department (although I would no longer be making that ride). Tristan appeared punctually with bags of Chinese
and a six-pack of Old Tearsheet Best Bitter, which as I was to
learn was the only beer he would consider drinking. He casually
commandeered the living/dining/cooking area, placing the food
on the counter, far from the coffee table, where he laid out four
documents and the cuneiform tablet, a notepad, and several pens.
He looked around the space, zeroed in on my personal reference
library, pulled out four dictionaries, and set them on the table.

"Let's eat first," he said. "I'm starving."

For the first time, we made small talk. It was only brief, for
he eats too fast, although I did not comment on it that first time.
Tristan had studied physics at West Point but ended up assigned to
the Military Intelligence branch of the Army, which—in round-

about ways he constantly deflected with the term "classified"—led to his recruitment by his "shadowy government entity."

For my part, since nothing was classified, I divulged the source of my polyglot tendencies, that being: my agnostic parents having been raised Catholic and Jewish, my two sets of grandparents competed for my faith from my earliest years. At the age of seven I proposed to my Catholic grandparents that I learn to read the New Testament in Latin, in lieu of attending Sunday school. Thinking I would never attain this, they agreed—and I was functionally fluent in classical Latin within six months. Emboldened by this, shortly before my thirteenth birthday I similarly evaded being bat mitzvahed by testing out at college level for classical Hebrew. My Jewish grandparents offered to fund one semester of university education per each ancient language I mastered at college level. That was how I afforded my first three years of school.

Tristan was very pleased with this story—almost as pleased with himself as with me, as if patting himself on the back for having chosen such a prodigy. When we finished our meal, he collected the disposable containers, rinsed them, and packed them neatly back in their bag. "All right, let's start!" he said, and we moved to the couch so I might examine the documents.

In addition to the cuneiform tablet there was something in Guānhuà (Middle Mandarin) on rice paper, about five hundred years old—Tristan to his credit at least knew to handle this with gloves on. There was also, on vellum, a piece written in a mixture of medieval French and Latin, I would say at least eight hundred years old. (It was ~~fucking~~ *insane* to see these things sitting casually on my coffee table.) Finally there was a fragment of a journal, this written in Russian on paper that looked positively brand-new in comparison, and was dated 1847. The librarian in me noticed that all of them had been marked with the same stamp—a somewhat ill-defined family crest, surrounded by blurry words in a blend of Latin and Italian. They had, in other words, been acquired by a library or a private collection, and been duly stamped and cataloged at some point.

As he had warned, Tristan would not tell me where he had obtained these artifacts, nor why it was such a (seemingly) random collection. After several hours with them, however, I saw the common theme . . . although it was hard to believe what I was reading.

In short, each of these documents referred to magic—yes, magic—as casually as a court document refers to the law, or a doctor's report refers to medical tests. Not magician-trick magic, but magic as we know it from myths and fairy tales: an inexplicable and supernatural force employed by witches—for they were, per these documents, all women. I don't mean the *belief* in magic, or a mere weakness for magical thinking. I mean the writer of each document was discussing a situation in which magic was a fact of life.

For example, the cuneiform tablet was a declaration laying down what a witch at the royal court of Kahta was due in recompense for her services, and regulated the uses of magic that courtiers were allowed to ask of her. The Latin/French one was written by the Abbess of Chaalis regarding the struggles that one of her nuns faced, trying but failing to renounce her magic powers, and the abbess wondered if she herself was to blame, as she was not truly wholehearted in her own prayers for the sister to be relieved of her powers, since those powers often made life easier at the abbey. The Guānhuà took a little more work—I had but a cursory relationship to Asian language groups by then. It was itself a recipe from the provinces for a dish involving various hard-to-find aromatic herbs, as described to the writer (a circuit-riding Mandarin magistrate) by self-reported witches (whose activities were referred to as a footnote on the side of the recipe). Finally, the nineteenth-century Russian was written by a self-identified (aging) witch and lamented the fading powers of her sister witches and herself. This one also made a passing reference to the desirability of finding certain herbs.

These were rough, almost off-the-cuff translations. When I had finished the fourth one, there was a silence between us for a moment. Then Tristan gave me a disarmingly sly grin, and spoke:

"What if I told you we had more than a thousand such documents. All eras, from six continents."

"All bearing this family crest?" I asked, pointing to the blurry stamp.

"That is the core of the collection. Others we collected on our own."

"Well, that would challenge certain assumptions about the nature of reality that I did not even know I had."

"We want you to translate all of them and extract the common core of data," said Tristan.

I looked at him. "I assume there's a military purpose."

"Classified," he said.

"If I have a context for translating, I can do a better job of it," I protested.

"My shadowy government entity has been collecting documents of this nature for many years."

"By what means?" I sputtered, both fascinated and dismayed to learn that a well-funded black ops organization was competing against academic researchers in such a manner. That sure explained a few things.

"The core of the collection, as you've been noticing, is from a private library in Italy."

"The WIMF."

"Beg pardon?"

"The Weird Italian Mother Fucker," I said.

"Yeah. We acquired it some time ago." His face twitched and he broke eye contact. "That's not true. I was just being polite. We stole it. Before other people could steal it. Long story. Anyway, it gave us plenty of leads that we could follow to acquire more in the same vein. By all means fair and foul. We now feel we have a critical mass that, upon translation, might yield a sense of what precisely 'magic' was, how it worked, and why there are no references to it anywhere after the mid-1800s."

"And you wish to have this information for some kind of military purpose," I pressed.

"We wish to have one person do all the translations," Tristan said, firmly not answering my query. "For three reasons. First, budget. Second, the fewer eyes, the safer. Third and most important, if the same person processes all the material, there is a greater chance of gleaning subtle consistencies or patterns."

"And you are interested in those consistencies or patterns why, exactly?"

"The current hypothesis," Tristan continued as before—that is, without actually answering me—"is that perhaps there was a worldwide epidemic of a virus that affected only witches, and magic was literally killed off. I don't think that's it, but I need to know more before I offer an alternate hypothesis. I have my suspicions, though."

"Which are classified, right?"

"Whether or not they are classified is classified."

The documents were many, but brief; most were fragmentary. Within three weeks, working alone at my coffee table, I had produced at least rough translations of the first batch of material. During that time I also gave notice, apologized to my students for abandoning them before they'd even gotten to know me, moved out of my Harvard office, and managed to reassure my parents that I was still working, without telling them exactly what it was I was doing. Meanwhile, Tristan was in communication with me at least twice a day, usually appearing in person, occasionally calling and talking to me in the most oblique terms. Never did we email or text; he did not want anything said between us to be on record. There was something rather swashbuckling, if unsettling, about the need for such secrecy. I had no idea what he did with the rest of his time. (Naturally, I asked. You can guess what his answer was.)

Our dynamic was singular, unprecedented in my life certainly. It was as if we had always been working together, and yet there was an undercurrent of something else, a kind of charge that only comes at the beginning of things. Neither of us ever acted on it—and while I am the sort who rarely acts on such things, he is (while extremely disciplined and upright) the sort who *immediately* acts on such things. So I attributed the buzz to the excitement of a shared endeavor. The intellectual intimacy of it was far more satisfying than any date I'd ever been on. If Tristan had a lover, she wasn't getting the real goods. I was.

At the end of the three weeks, when he came to my apartment to receive the last (or so I innocently thought) of my translations, Tristan glanced around until he saw my coatrack. He studied it a moment, then took my raincoat off of its peg. It was late September by this point and the weather was starting to turn.

"Come on, we're going to talk at the office," he said. "I'll buy you dinner."

"There's an *office*?" I said. "I assumed your shadowy government entity had you working out of your car."

"It's near Central Square. Carlton Street, about fifteen minutes' walk from the Apostolic Café. How's Chinese sound?"

"Depends on the dialect."

"Ha," he said without smiling. "Linguist humor. Pretty lame, Stokes." He held my coat out. I reached for it. He shook his head and glanced down at it. Giving me to understand that he was not handing it to me, but offering to help me put it on—a gesture much more common in 1851 London than it was in that time and place. Some low-grade physical comedy ensued as I turned my back on him and tried to find the armholes with my hands. What a weirdo.

Carlton Street was the poor stepchild in an extended family of alleys and byways near MIT, where scores of biotech companies fledged. Most of the neighborhood had been rebranded into slick office complexes, with landscaped parks, mini-campuses, double-helix-themed architectural flourishes, and abstract steel sculptures abounding. Tristan's building, however, had not yet been reclaimed. It was utterly without character: a block-long two-story mid-twentieth-century building thrown together of tilt-up concrete slabs painted a dingy grey that somehow managed to clash with the sidewalk. There were a few graffiti tags. The windows were without adornment, all of them outfitted with vertical vinyl blinds, all dusty and askew. There was no roster of tenants, no signs or logos, no indication at all of what was within.

Laden with bags of Chinese food and beer, we approached the glass entrance door at dusk. This building was one of the few places on earth that not even twilight could improve upon. Tristan slapped his wallet against a black plate set into the wall, and the door lock clicked, releasing. Inside, we moved between buzzing fluorescent lights and matted industrial carpeting, down a corridor past several windowless doors—slabs of wood, dirty around the knobs, blazoned with signs bearing names of what I assumed were tech start-ups. Some of these had actual logos, some just cutesy names printed in block letters, and one was just a domain name scrawled on a sticky note. We walked the entire length of the building and came to a door next to a stairwell. Its only distinguishing feature was a crude Magic Marker drawing of a bird, seen in profile, drawn on the back of a Chinese menu blue-taped to the wood. The bird was somewhat comical, with a prominent beak and big feet.

"Dodo?" I guessed.

Tristan made no answer. He was unlocking the door.

"I'll take that as a yes—you'd have jumped all over me if I'd guessed the wrong species."

He gave me an inscrutable raised-eyebrow look over his shoulder as he pushed the door open and reached for the light switch. "You have a gift for caricature," I told him as I followed him in.

"DODO welcomes you," he said.

"Department of . . . something?"

"Of something classified."

The room was at most ten feet by fifteen feet. Two desks were shoved into opposite corners, each with a flat-panel monitor and keyboard. The walls were lined with an assortment of used IKEA bookshelves that I suspected he'd pulled out of Dumpsters a few weeks ago, and a couple of tall skinny safes of the type used to store rifles and shotguns. Perched on top of these were military-looking souvenirs that I assumed dated from some earlier phase of Tristan's career. The shelves were filled with ancient books and artifacts I recognized very well. In the middle of the room was a long table. Beneath it was a bedroll: just a yoga mat wrapped around a pillow and secured with a bungee cord.

I pointed at the bedroll. "How long have you—"

"I shower at the gym if that's your worry." He pointed to the closer of the two desks, by the door. "This one will be yours."

"Oh," I said, not sure what else to say. "Do you have . . . guns in here?"

"Would that be a problem for you?" he inquired, setting the Chinese food on the table in the middle. "If so, I need to know sooner rather than later because—"

"How much firepower were you expecting to need?"

"Oh, you noticed the gun safes?" he asked, tracking my gaze. "No." he turned to one of them and punched a series of digits onto the keypad on its front. It beeped, and he swung the door open to reveal that it was stuffed from top to bottom with documents. "I keep the most sensitive material in these."

My gaze had wandered to my desk. I was looking at the flat-panel display, which was showing a few lines of green text on a black background, and a blinking cursor where it was apparently expecting me to type something in. "Where did you get these computers? A garage sale from 1975?"

"They are running a secure operating system you've never heard of," he explained. "It's called Shiny Hat."

"Shiny Hat."

"Yes. The most clinically paranoid operating system in the world. Since you have an overdeveloped sense of irony, Stokes, you might like to know that we acquired it from hackers who were specifically worried about being eavesdropped on by shadowy government entities. Now they work for us."

"Have they got the memo about the invention of the computer mouse? Because I don't see one on my desk."

"Graphical user interfaces introduce security holes that can be exploited by black hat hackers. Shiny Hat is safe against that kind of malware, but the user interface is . . . spartan. I'll bring you up to speed."

His desk was crowded with copies of everything I had been translating for him over the past weeks. My notes were marked up with colored-pencil notes of his own. He transferred some of those to the central table while I set up the Chinese food. He read over my day's work as we ate.

Then we reviewed all the material to date. It took us until sunrise.

In all the documents I'd deciphered, there was almost no useful information to be gleaned regarding the "how" of magic, which is what I assumed Tristan's bosses had been hoping for. We discovered some *examples* of magic, in that we learned what was valued by both the witches themselves and those who employed them. Of highest value was what Tristan called psy-ops (psychological operations—mind control, essentially) and shape-shifting (themselves or others). This was considered a weapon of considerable significance, whether it meant turning oneself into a lion or turning an enemy into a lower form of life. In homage to Monty Python, we employed "newt" as shorthand. Of middling value was the transubstantiation of materials and the animating of inanimate objects. Of low value was space/time-shifting, such as teleportation, which was viewed as a laborious leisure-time diversion across all witch populations. Much of what I had associated with "magic" in my bookish youth was disappointingly absent—there were few references to the mastering of natural forces, for instance. And there was absolutely nothing about the mechanics of making any of it happen.

We did, however, glean something significant about magic's decline, and this is what led to our next stage of inquiry.

Diachronicle

DAYS 57–221 (WINTER, YEAR 0)

In which Tristan determines to fix magic

AT DAWN, TRISTAN DROVE ME home to collect my library, which had been taking up a significant section of my living room since I'd moved out of my faculty office. He plied me with coffee and croissants until I felt able to start a new day without having completed the previous one. Back at the office, he smiled broadly and presented me with the combination to one of the gun safes. It was full of photocopies of manuscripts, documents, and artifacts I had not yet seen. "At the rate you've been working, this box will probably take you about a month."

"I had no idea there was this much still to do," I said.

He was pulling documents out of the safe, arranging them on the table. "Why would I hire you for a six-month contract if I only had one month's work for you? There's a lot more where this came from. But it should be easier now that we've sketched out the general picture. You know what you're looking for now."

"I still don't know why I'm looking for it," I said.

"You know that's classified," he said, almost paternal. "Have a seat. Want some more coffee? Working on a shoestring budget here, but I can spring for Dunkin' Donuts."

"DODO," I said. "Department of . . . Donuts?"

"Do you like sprinkles?" he asked.

While he got donuts, I unpacked my dictionaries and lexica and got to work.

IF MY TRANSLATIONS were to be believed, at the start of the Scientific Revolution (Copernicus in the 1540s, etc.), magic was a ubiquitous and powerful force in human affairs, and witches were both revered and feared members of most societies every bit as much as military leaders or priest-mystics (although they were rarely written about, their work being so often the equivalent of "classified"). However, once the Renaissance gave way to the Enlightenment, magic became less omnipresent and less powerful, especially in institutions of learning and government. Judging by the hundreds of references in the texts, it paled increasingly through the Industrial Revolution—remaining most potent in artistic circles and least potent in philosophical ones (these two populations diverging after many generations of entwining), more potent in societies not blessed with booming industrialization, and slightly more potent too in Islamic cultures—and then it vanished altogether in the nineteenth century. The latest text was dated from July 1851. DODO had not been able to find any references to magic after that, except as something that "once was but is no more."

I translated the box of photocopied documents in less time than Tristan had anticipated, but there was no letup. I began to dream in dead languages as ancient books, scrolls, and tablets kept coming, delivered to the drab office building almost every morning by unidentified couriers in unmarked vehicles. Department of—Dusty Objects? There were plenty of documents in English or modern Western languages—mostly these were transcripts of early anthropologists interviewing the elders of indigenous peoples. I translated the ones that Tristan couldn't read for himself, and he built a database. Reader, if you don't know what a database is, rest assured that an explanation of the concept would in no way increase your enjoyment in reading this account. If you do know, you will thank me for sparing you the details. A dreary enough task even with modern user interfaces, it was a mind-numbing death march when implemented on Shiny Hat. Tristan had to write little computer programs to automate some of the data entry tasks.

One of the things we kept track of was the provenance of each document: Had it come from the Library of Congress? Was it simply downloaded from the Internet? Or was it a rare, perhaps unique original? Did it bear any stamps or markings from library collections? In that vein, a disproportionate number had that mysterious stamp on the title page, an image I'd come to know well: the coat of arms of some aristocratic family, with extra bits of decorative gingerbread all around it. Lacking any other information, I just entered this into the database with the code WIMF. Quite a few of the WIMF documents bore older stamps from no less than the Vatican Library, raising the question of whether the WIMF had stolen them? Or borrowed them and never brought them back? Tristan wasn't talking.

Almost as fast as they could be translated, more books showed up. We would empty out a new crate and then fill it right up again with books that had already been translated, and the bland couriers would haul them away. To where? Many of the boxes were stenciled with a logo I did not recognize at the time, but which I now know to be a modernized, streamlined version of the brand used since time immemorial by the banking family known as the Fuggers.

This phase ate up most of my six-month contract, as a fierce New England winter yielded muddily to spring. Other tenants in the building—scruffy start-up companies, mostly—failed or got funded and moved out. Whenever they did, Tristan made a couple of phone calls and ended up with a key to the space they'd just vacated. In this way, DODO's footprint in the building expanded. We inherited cheap plastic chairs, duffed-up coffeemakers, and crumpled filing cabinets from the former neighbors. Clean-cut technicians showed up in unmarked cars and put card readers on all the doors, expanding and sealing what Tristan called "the perimeter." The database grew like a dust bunny under the bed. Tristan thought of ways to query it, to search for patterns. We printed things out, stuck them to the walls, tore them down and did it again, stretched colored yarn between pushpins. We went down blind alleys, then backed out of them; we constructed huge Jenga towers of speculation and then, almost gleefully, knocked them over.

But there was never any doubt as to the gist: some manner of cause-and-effect relationship existed between the rise of scientific knowledge and the decline of magic. The two could not comfortably coexist. To the extent that the database could be cajoled into spitting out actual numbers, it was clear that magic had declined gradually but steadily starting in the middle of the 1600s. It was still holding its own in the opening decades of the 1800s, but plunged into a nosedive during the 1830s. From then through the 1840s, magic declined precipitously. As our store of documents—many written by witches themselves—grew to fill a phalanx of used filing cabinets and gun safes that Tristan scored on Craigslist, we were able to track the decline from year to year, and then from month to month. These poor women expressed shock at the dwindling of their powers, in some cases mentioning specific spells that had worked a few weeks ago but no longer had effect.

As it turns out, in 1851—the year in which I find myself as I scribble these words—all of the world's technologies were brought together for the Great Exhibition at the newly constructed, magnificent Crystal Palace in Hyde Park, London. Tristan's hypothesis therefore held that this coming together, this conscious concentration of technological advancement all in one point of space-time, had dampened magic to the point where it fizzled out for good. Like a doused fire, it had no power to re-kindle itself once extinguished.

The causal relationship between the two eluded us for a time. I suggested that magic's flourishing required people to believe in it, but Tristan dismissed this mentality as belonging more to children's literature than to reality. He was certain there was a mechanical or physical causality, that there was something about the technological worldview, or technology itself, that somehow "jammed the frequencies" magic used. We both began to read whatever we could about the Great Exhibition in the hopes that it might illuminate something.

(You may notice that I was exceeding by far my responsibilities as a translator. Translating, especially of obscure texts written in extinct tongues, often resembles the solving of a riddle. Here was a riddle to put all others to shame! Tristan's enthusiasm was infectious and I could not divest myself from it. Having no other responsibilities, I became as preoccupied with his project as he was himself.)

Per Tristan's suggestions, I took out stacks of books from Widener Library (Harvard had not figured out yet that I'd quit—I suppose Blevins wanted to hide the fact lest it reflect poorly on him). These included tomes on everything from heliography to Queen Victoria's private life to Baruch Spinoza's sexual proclivities to Frederick Bakewell to the Tempest Prognosticator to Strouhal numbers. I would bring these to Tristan, and we would divide our time between perusing them and Internet searches.

We soon knew more about the Great Exhibition and its thirteen-thousand-odd exhibits than Prince Albert ever did. We knew more about its showcase, the Crystal Palace, than even Joseph Paxton, the gardener who'd designed the ~~fucking~~ blessed thing. We learned little that was helpful. However, one evening in March, as I sat on the consignment-store couch I'd insisted on bringing in to spruce up the place, and Tristan lolled on the rug (provenance ditto) beside a low table with a beer, each of us bleary-eyed from reading, I encountered a passage in an obscure booklet entitled *Arresting and Alluring Astronomical Anecdotes*, published in 1897. Here I learned that while the Great Exhibition of 1851 was in process (it lasted for several months), an event of relative interest occurred elsewhere in Europe, to be precise, in Königsberg, Prussia: for the first time in history, a solar eclipse was successfully photographed.

I read this statement aloud. It set Tristan on fire with excitement. He had already suspected that photography in particular, of all technological developments, was the likeliest to have somehow impeded magic. Now, somehow, he was certain. It took me a while to calm him down to the point where he could explain himself.

"I'll be honest with you: as a physicist, I am a hack," he admitted. "I majored in it, yes, but I was never employed in that capacity. But if you cut me I still bleed physicist blood. I'll go to my grave believing that, if magic existed, there's a scientific explanation for it."

"That sounds like a contradiction to me," I said, "since our whole working hypothesis is that science broke it somehow."

He held up a hand. "Work with me here. Have you ever heard of the many-worlds interpretation of quantum mechanics?"

"Only in cocktail party discourse that would make you roll your eyes and heave deep sighs."

"Well, there are certain experiments where the results only make sense if the system that's being observed *actually exists in more than one state* until the moment when the scientist makes the observation."

"Is this Schrödinger's cat? Because even I have heard of that."

"That's the classic example. It's just a thought experiment, by the way. No one ever actually did it."

"That's good. PETA would be all over them."

"Do you know what it is?" Without waiting for me to answer, Tristan went on: "You put a cat in a sealed box. There's a device inside of the box that is capable of killing the cat, by breaking open a vial of poison gas or something. That device is triggered by some random event generator, like a sample of some radioactive material that either decays—producing a bit of radiation—or doesn't. You close the lid. The cat and the poison gas and the radioactive sample become a sealed system—you cannot predict or know what has happened."

"You don't know if the cat is alive or dead," I said.

"It's not just that you *don't*. You *can't*. There is literally no way of knowing," Tristan said. "Now, in a classical physics way of thinking, it's either one or the other. The cat is either alive or dead for real. You just don't happen to know which. But in a quantum physics way of thinking, the cat *really is both alive and dead*. It exists in two mutually incompatible states at the same time. Not until you open the lid and look inside does the wave function collapse."

"Whoa, whoa, you had me until the very end!" I protested. "When did we start talking about—what did you call it? A wave function? And how does that—whatever it is—collapse?"

"My bad," he said. "It's just physicist lingo for what I was saying. If you were to express the Schrödinger's cat experiment mathematically, you'd write down an equation that is called a wave function. That function has multiple terms that are superimposed—it's not just one thing."

"Multiple terms," I repeated bleakly.

"Yeah. A term here means a fragment of math—it is to an equation what a phrase is to a sentence."

"So you're saying there is one term for 'cat is alive' and another for 'cat is dead'? Is that what you mean in this usage?"

"Yes, O linguist."

"And when you say they are superimposed—"

"Mathematically it just means that they are sort of added to each other to make a combined picture of the system."

"Until it 'collapses' or whatever."

He nodded. "Multiple terms superimposed is a quantum thing. It is the essence of quantum mechanics. But there is this interesting fact, which is that that kind of math only works—it only provides an accurate description of the system—until you open the lid and look inside. At that point, you see a live cat or a dead cat. Period. It has become a classical system."

"Department of . . . Deadly Observations?" I asked.

He rolled his eyes.

"Anyway, that's what you mean by the collapse of the wave function."

"Yes, it's just physicist-speak for the thing that happens when all of the superimposed terms—the descriptions of different possible realities—resolve into a single, classical outcome that our brains can understand."

"Our scientific, rational brains, you mean," I corrected him.

A look of mild satisfaction came onto his face. "Exactly."

"But now we've circled back to my theory!" I complained.

He looked mildly confused. "Which theory is that?"

"The one that belongs more to children's literature than to reality—remember?"

"Oh, yeah. People have to believe in magic."

"Yes!"

"That's not exactly what I'm saying," he said. "Yes, human consciousness is in the loop. But hear me out. If you buy the many-worlds interpretation of quantum mechanics, it means that all possible outcomes are really happening *somewhere*."

"There's one world with a live cat and another with a dead cat."

"Exactly. No kidding. Complete, fully independent realities that are the same except that in one of them, the cat's dead, and in the other, it's alive. And the quantum superposition? That just means that the scientist standing there with his hand on the lid of the box is at a fork in the road. Both paths—both worlds—are open to him. He could shunt into one, or the other. And when he hauls the lid open, the decision gets made. He is now in one world or the other and there's no going back."

"Okay," I said. Not in the sense of *I agree with you* but of *I am paying attention*.

"The scientist can't control which path he or she takes," Tristan continued.

I saw that he was trolling me—waiting for me to pick up the bait.

No, it was more than that. He wanted me to mention a possibility that he could think about, but never say out loud—because he was all Mr. Science.

So I did. "Let's switch it up a little, then," I said. "And swap out the white lab coat and the clipboard for, I don't know, a pointy black hat and a broom. And lose a pronoun. If she *did* somehow have the ability to choose which world she was going to be shunted to when she opened the lid—if she could control the outcome—"

"It would look like magic."

"What do you mean 'look like'? It would *be* magic."

"Just saying," Tristan said, "that it's about choosing possible outcomes that already exist—slipstreaming between closely related alternate realities—as opposed to bringing those realities into existence."

"But that's a distinction without a difference."

"As far as normal observers are concerned? People who haven't studied quantum physics? Sure," he agreed.

"Put it however you like," I said. "A witch may summon the desired effect from a parallel-slash-simultaneous reality. Thus the historical references of witches' magic as 'summoning'—that is quite literally what they were doing."

"My hypothesis," Tristan said—pronouncing the word with exaggerated care, since he had a few Old Tearsheet Best Bitters in him—"is that photography disables this summoning, as you called it. Photography breaks magic by embalming a specific moment—one version of reality—into a recorded image. Once that moment is so recorded, then all other possible versions of that moment are excluded from the world that contains that photograph."

"I get it," I said. "There is no wiggle room left in which to function magically."

He nodded. He seemed relieved to have got all of this off his chest. And that I hadn't laughed him out of the room.

"You've been thinking about this for a while," I said.

He nodded.

"But it wasn't until we saw the daguerreotype of the solar eclipse that the penny dropped."

"That's right."

"That was only about the bazillionth daguerreotype ever made," I pointed out. "People had been taking photographs for sixteen years by that point. What's so special about that one?"

"The scope of it, I think," Tristan said. "The number of minds, and worlds, affected. If I'm Louis Daguerre screwing around in my lab in Paris, taking pictures of whatever is handy, then I've collapsed the waveform, yes. But only inasmuch as it encompasses my brain and a few little objects in my lab. If I show the daguerre-otype to my wife or my friend, then the effect—the collapsing of the waveform—spreads to them as well. And we can guess that witches who live in the neighborhood might sense a dampening of their magical abilities, without understanding why. But the total eclipse of the sun on July 28, 1851, was probably witnessed by more human beings than any other event in the history of the world up to that point."

"Of course," I said. "Everyone in Europe could see it—"

"Just by looking up into the sky. Hundreds of millions of peo-ple, Mel. That event captured more eyeballs, at the same moment, than any Beyoncé video on YouTube. And to the extent that it was frozen, embalmed, on a daguerreotype, well—"

I was nodding. "If previous uses of photography had dampened magic, then this was like dumping the Atlantic Ocean on it."

He nodded. "When the shutter opened to capture that first per-fect image of the eclipse, magic ceased to function across all hu-man societies."

We back-checked the dates of all documents from 1851. Indeed: there were three from the first half of the year (two English, one Italian). There was a fragment of one in late July (Hungarian). There were none after July 28, the date of the eclipse. None.

"That's it," muttered Tristan, preoccupied, getting to his feet. He rested his hands on his desk and stared absently at the wall.

"Yes," I said. I felt deflated. Although he'd never told me *why* DODO was so interested in understanding magic, common sense screamed it was because they wanted to be able to *do* it. Department of Doing the Occult? Which clearly could never happen: "There's no getting rid of photography, so there's no bringing magic back."

Tristan froze and, after a beat, jerked his head in my direction. "You're right," he said, staring. "That's it. Where there is no photography, there could still be magic."

"That's not quite what I said."

He began to pace the office. We had made it somewhat larger by knocking out walls that separated it from adjoining spaces, but this still required following a figure-eightish path between piles of books, artifacts, freestanding gun safes, to-be-recycled beer bottles, and still-unexplained high-tech military gear. "How do we get rid of photography," he murmured, more to himself than to me.

"We cannot 'get rid of photography.'"

"No, it's definitely possible," he insisted, eyes unfocused as he paced. "I just have to figure out how it's done."

"What do you mean, *how it's done?*"

He shook his head, grimacing, dismissing me. "I'm not seeing something," he said. "What am I missing?"

"You're missing the part where photography became ubiquitous and all magic went away forever."

He turned to look at me, his eyes focused now, and bright. "No," he said, almost scolding me. "*It's not a lost cause.*"

That was not the tone of hypothesis or theory; that was the tone of either faith or knowledge. I felt a shiver run down my spine.

"I realize there are a lot of things you can't tell me," I said, "but whatever it specifically is you're not telling me at this precise moment . . . *fucking tell me.* Otherwise I'm useless."

His gaze went fuzzy again as he engaged in some brief mental soliloquy. Then he nodded. "I can't tell you much," he said. "But I can tell you that we know it's possible."

". . . we?"

"DODO," he confirmed. "There's evidence. That's all I can say."

"Wow," I said, feeling pathetically inarticulate for a linguist. "Good God."

"Yes. It's a *thing*," he said. "It's real. There's just"—he made a frustrated reaching gesture—"there's a missing piece. And I'm so close. It's got to be photography, that makes sense, it aligns chronologically, it aligns with magic failing slightly earlier in societies that valued and used the photographic image, and lingering just a little in cultures that didn't, like Islam and aboriginal tribes. That's got to be it. There has to be some way to make photography not happen."

"But the existence of cloud technology, cell phones, video surveillance, means photography is literally everywhere."

"I don't need to get rid of it *everywhere*," Tristan said impatiently. "Just within one manageable space." He stopped short, in the middle of the room, and looked around through narrowed, thoughtful eyes as if at invisible colleagues. "Okay, that's part of it. A controlled environment. If we can create an environment in which photography not only does not happen, but *could* not happen, then perhaps magic could exist *within* that space."

"And you guys, you DODOs, think someone's already doing that?"

He nodded slowly. "If they can do it, we can do it. We just have to figure out how." For a moment he was gone, lost completely in thought, even the alertness of the trained soldier distracted by the intense introspection of the thinker. "Let's break it down," he said. "First: photography collapses the wave function of light."

"Yes. Or so you told me. So I'm just going to sit here and say yes."

"So," he continued, "if we can interfere with that collapse—" And then seeing the stupid look on my face, tried, "If we can keep the quantum balls in the air—"

"Like, by not opening the lid of the box?"

"What box?"

"The box with the cat in it. Schrödinger's cat."

He gave a little shake of the head. "That's just a thought experiment. But you're onto something," he said.

I knew perfectly well that it was a thought experiment. But that could wait. It felt like we were on the trail of something. And I was fascinated—and a little alarmed—by the subtext, which seemed to be that this wasn't all just a dry academic research project, but something akin to an active military campaign. Someone, somewhere in the world was doing magic. The government of the United States didn't know how—or perhaps even *who*. It was a Sputnik moment: someone else had stolen a march on us. Tristan's shadowy government entity had obviously been thrown together in a panicky effort to catch up.

Tristan settled back down, and muttered buzzwords ("collapse of wave function," "quantum entanglement"). I typed them into Google, while Tristan, hunched over his Shiny Hat terminal, used other search engines only available to people working for shadowy government entities. An initial search for "quantum wave function" yielded four hundred thousand responses (it went up to three million without the quotes) and advanced searches—adding "collapse," etc.—had brought it down to about thirty-five thousand. Mostly what came up were YouTube videos of geeky-looking high school kids attempting experiments in their parents' cellars, often with refrigerators or the remnants of darkroom chemicals, frequently resulting in small but interesting explosions. There were also a kajillion academic papers that Tristan, the undergraduate physicist, dismissed by their titles alone. We added more and more modifying terms to focus the search. In this way, several hours passed. No dice.

We stopped for dinner (take-out Indian—actual Indian food, not the insipid so-called 'curry' now coming into fashion here in Victorian London thanks to the East India Company's running riot over the Punjab). We then continued the search all evening; I biked home, slept, and biked back, and we kept searching. Late morning, we paused long enough to take a walk along the Charles, as being cramped in that small dingy office so long was crazy-making. For most of the walk, Tristan continued to brainstorm in a soliloquy that further convinced me he was both brilliant and a pretty bad listener.

Back at his office after the walk, he ransacked the fridge for some leftovers that hadn't gone bad, while I returned to my desk to scroll through the results of yet another highly modified Google search. As long as Tristan wasn't looking over my shoulder, I tried something: I searched on "Schrödinger's cat experiment" and then began adding in other terms to narrow it down. I excluded "thought experiment" and its German equivalent, *Gedankenexperiment*. I threw out anything that included such phrases as "will shock you!" and "you won't believe what happened next!" I skewed the search in favor of words like "actual," "practical," and "real-world."

Reader, you won't believe what happened next. A single response came up.

"Rejected patent application," I read aloud to Tristan. "Someone from MIT applied for a patent for . . . hang on . . ." My eyes skimmed over the legalese and bureaucratese (two languages I had never mastered), until I found something descriptive to read. "Something he calls a cavity, intended to quote 'jam enemy nations' surveillance systems by maintaining a feline test subject in an indeterminate state of existence.' Unquote."

I heard the microwave shut down. "I can't hear a thing when

this is running," Tristan said. He turned to look at me. "I could have sworn you just said something about a feline test subject."

I looked him in the eye and nodded. "It's called the Ontic Decoherence Cavity. ODEC. Proposed by Professor Frank Oda. Kind of a narcissist, I guess."

"How do you figure?"

"He named it after himself. Oda—ODEC."

"I'm not so sure. 'Ontic' means—"

"I know what it means."

"Something to do with knowledge. Decoherence, as I am sure you are well aware, means its negation. Something about this cavity prevents the formation of definite knowledge. So, it lines up pretty well with what we are looking for."

"Cool!" I exclaimed, and began Googling Frank Oda. "Let's figure out where he lives and—"

"But it's a joke," Tristan said flatly. "The guy is a troll. Oh, a scientifically sophisticated troll. Making a very clever in-joke. But a troll nonetheless."

"What makes you so sure?"

"The part about the feline test subject. Mel, this is just a prank. A fake patent application that this guy put on the Internet for the lulz. He slipped it past some dipshit patent examiner who didn't know physics, had never heard of Schrödinger's cat. Any physicist who stumbles across it will get a belly laugh out of it and move on. But we need to confine ourselves to serious—"

He stopped to read the screen of my laptop, which I had swiveled around to aim in his direction.

It was a thirty-year-old article I had dredged up from the archives of *The Howler*, an alternative weekly newspaper, now defunct, but once a common sight on the streets of Boston and Cambridge. Known for its leftist politics and muckraking fervor.

The article featured two photographs. On the left, a middle-aged Asian-American man, captured by a sidewalk paparazzo as he took out the garbage. On the right, a stock photograph of a wire mesh enclosure in some animal shelter, housing a menagerie of stray cats.

CAT'S OUT OF THE BAG, PROFESSOR ODA!
MIT professor denies cruelty to animals, but accepts early retirement.

Tristan licked curry from his fingers, reached for the trackpad, and zoomed the image on the left. "Empty boxes, old newspapers, a milk jug, and a wine bottle."

"You're identifying the contents of the garbage bag?"

"No dead cats. Or live ones."

"Maybe it's a Schrödinger's Hefty bag." I spun the computer back around to face me, and Tristan scampered around the table so that he could read it over my shoulder. Parsing the story wasn't easy given the amount of tabloid-style innuendo and leaps of inference, combined with the heavy presumption that Frank Oda was guilty of something. But the bottom line seemed to be this: Professor Frank Oda, a theoretical physicist at MIT, had, three decades ago, gone off the reservation and started attempting to do *experimental* physics.

It had started with what seemed like a gag: a prop, for use in undergraduate physics lectures, consisting of a box with an actual cat in it, and a mockup of the apparatus envisioned in the Schrödinger's cat *Gedankenexperiment*. So far, so good. A fine way to liven up an otherwise dry lecture. No cats were harmed; the cat-killing mechanism was obviously fake, just a glass bottle with a skull and crossbones painted on it and a Rube Goldberg contraption involving a rat trap and a Geiger counter. But if the story was to be believed, the construction of this device had caused Oda to become obsessed with the underlying concept. Which was very real—foundational to quantum mechanics, and not disputed by anyone.

"Holy fuck," Tristan exclaimed. Which for him, clean-cut West Pointer that he was, was a mickle oath. We were on page three now. "He actually did it."

"No way, they must have got something wrong."

Tristan pointed to a phrase in the middle of the screen.

Records obtained by *The Howler* from the Somerville Animal Shelter indicate that Dr. Oda "adopted" no fewer than six cats from the facility over a span of three months in spring of last year. This coincides with a formal request made by MIT authorities that Oda remove "all apparatus involving living test subjects" from his on-campus laboratory. According to a former graduate student interviewed by *The Howler*, who requested anonymity for fear of possible professional repercussions, Dr. Oda complied with the request by relocating the ODEC project to the basement of the Cambridge home that he shares with his wife, Rebecca East.

"Maybe Rebecca's a cat lover," I said.

"Then why were the cats being kept in his lab at MIT until they kicked him out?"

"There's gotta be an explanation."

"Keep scrolling."

Contacted at his home by a reporter from *The Howler*, the disgraced mad scientist denied all wrongdoing. "This was never about the cat being alive or dead," he insisted, repeating a claim he had also made in internal MIT documents obtained by *The Howler*. "Killing the cat isn't of the essence. The point is that the cat is in either one state, or another. I was experimenting with other states—non-fatal, non-painful." Pressed by the reporter to provide specific examples, Oda seemed flustered and became inarticulate—which is consistent with the claim made by anonymous sources in his neighborhood that he has, in recent years, exhibited signs of mental impairment consistent with senile dementia. "I don't know, how many states is it possible for a cat to be in? Asleep or awake. Sitting down or standing up. Purring or meowing. Any of them is as good as alive or dead for purposes of the experiment." Asked why an equivalent experiment couldn't have been performed on a non-living subject, Oda shook his head condescendingly. "The test subject must contain living, active brain tissue," he said. "That's how the apparatus works." The interview was cut short at that point by Oda's wife, Rebecca East, who emerged from their house—a colonial-era dwelling on a tree-lined street near the Harvard campus—brandishing a broom at the reporter. Ms. East, who appeared upset, insisted that none of the cats had been mistreated, adding that the shelter from which they had been adopted was a so-called "kill shelter," meaning that all of the animals had been earmarked for euthanasia anyway. *The Howler*'s reporter, fearing for her personal safety, fled from the premises and later filed a report with the Cambridge Police Department. The subsequent criminal investigation was terminated when Ms. East claimed to the investigating officer that she had been using the broom to sweep vegetable debris from her front walk.

"Off with their heads!" I exclaimed. Tristan had already tired of reading the article and begun searching Oda's background using his top-secret equivalent of Google. "That's pretty old history, Stokes," he said, without looking up. "And not even accurate. Let it go." He kept reading. "Check it out—this guy also worked for DARPA, and what he did there was—"

"What's DARPA?" I asked.

Tristan looked appalled. "Wow," he said, almost thoughtfully. "Wow. You really aren't up to speed, are you?"

"I study dead languages for a living," I said. "That's why you *hired* me. Why should I be up to speed on your line of work? How's your Serbo-Croatian? What's your position on the relationship between Oscan and Marrucinian?"

He gave me an amused look. "Wouldn't have pegged you as pissy, Stokes," he said. "Okay. DARPA. Defense Advanced Research Projects Agency."

"Ah. The stealth bomber guys. The ones who develop clever ways to kill people."

"They've developed all kinds of things," said Tristan breezily. "Not just weapons. Night-vision technology, GPS satellites. Surely somebody living in Boston can appreciate GPS."

"I bike everywhere," I said in a superior tone. "I read *maps*. I don't rely on Big Brother to tell me where to go."

Abruptly, he sobered. "If you're going to get anti-establishment on me, this won't work. The first thing you learned about me was that I work for the government, and the second thing you learned was that I went to West Point. Eighty-six the attitude."

Taken aback by this sudden intensity, I held my hands up briefly. "Fine," I said in a conciliatory tone. "DARPA."

"And even after his forced retirement from MIT, he kept on doing work—serious work—for them."

"Did it involve cats?"

"Classified. But my point is that the accusation of senile dementia is reckless, unfounded. He turned in good work as recently as"—he paged to the bottom of a screen—"four years ago."

"The patent application said something about jamming foreign surveillance devices."

"When DARPA signs your paychecks," he said, "everything you do relates to national defense. Frank Oda was trying to create a defensive technology involving the sort of science we're interested in. But . . . the patent application was rejected."

"What do you think he meant by this line . . ." I scrolled back in the *Howler* article. "The test subject must contain living, active brain tissue?"

"Something to do with how the ODEC works, I guess."

"I find it mildly unsettling."

"Maybe we should just ask him." Tristan typed something into the computer. As he read the result, his eyes went wide, as they usually did when he was pleasantly surprised by something.

"Stokes," he said. "He's still around. Right here in Cambridge."

"That's convenient," I said. "What address?"

By way of an answer, he swiveled his screen around so I could see the map he'd Googled up.

I almost choked on my saag paneer. "It's right down Mass Ave from where I live!" I said. "We could *walk* there from here in less than half an hour."

Tristan grinned and reached for his pocket. "We can *call* even faster than that." He punched a number into his phone, reading off the computer screen. As it connected and began to ring on the other end, he gave me a sideways grin, like a child about to be awarded a prize for solving a riddle. I smiled back.

But the moment wore on and his smile faded until finally he

hung up. "Huh. No answer." He looked at his phone as if it had insulted him. "Not even an answering machine. That's weird. Nobody does that these days."

"Maybe he's a Luddite," I said.

"An MIT physics professor who tried to patent groundbreaking technological inventions is a Luddite?"

"He was rebuffed," I pointed out. "He overreacted and now he's a Luddite."

"Lunchtime's over," said Tristan, standing and reaching for his Yankees sweatshirt. "We're going for a visit."

THE ODAS LIVED on a street of grand houses, most of which, judging by appearance, had been built in the late 1800s. But theirs stuck out like a pilgrim at a White House dinner. A plain, gable-roofed three-story, it was older than the others by well over a hundred years. Its garden outshone every other yard on the street. It was full of flowers and herbs and ornamental shrubbery, with the efficient use of space associated with Japanese gardening.

We rang the bell. The door was answered by an older woman. Caucasian, not Japanese. In fact, downright WASPy, including her reception of us.

"Rebecca East, I presume," Tristan said, holding out his hand.

"Rebecca East-*Oda*," she corrected him. She was in her seventies, with a salt-and-pepper bob and Laura Ashley sweater, and she was the epitome of a particular New England Congregationalist bloodline that manages to simultaneously suggest cool, contained patrician and indefatigable peasant stock. The kind of woman who could pleasantly instruct you to fuck off, dear, and you immediately would because you'd just hate to disappoint her.

Luckily she did not explicitly request us to do so. Tristan explained that we were here to talk to the professor about an old project of his from his MIT days. She pursed her lips uncertainly. "It's important," said Tristan.

"Frank does not like to talk shop much in his retirement," she said.

"We won't take long, and he'll be glad we came," said Tristan.

She gave him a wary look. "He's napping at present, why don't you come back tomorrow."

Tristan opened his mouth again, but I clutched his arm, dug my fingernails into his wrist, and spoke over him:

"Please pardon our rudeness, but we would be deeply indebted to you if Oda-sensei would consider giving us a moment of his time."

She studied me with guarded amusement. Then her eyes flicked meaningfully at Tristan—as if making sure he noticed that *I* was the one she was responding to—before looking at me again to say, "I will see if he's awake."

When she was gone I glanced up at Tristan. "When speaking Japanese," I said, "it is impossible to grovel too much or too often."

"She's not Japanese," he grunted dismissively.

"I just demonstrated to her that I understand her husband's culture," I said. Goodness how I appreciated being the more informed one, for a change. "Which suggests we will be respectful, which is obviously important to her or she wouldn't have deflected you to start with."

"Women make everything so complicated," Tristan said in mock dismay.

"If you're going to get sexist on me, this won't work," I said. "The first thing you learned about me is that I am a woman. Eighty-six that attitude."

"You're all right, Stokes," he said, and roughed up my hair as if

I were his kid sister. I smacked his hand away. Before the rough-housing could progress any further, we heard Rebecca East-Oda's clogs clunking back down the stairway.

Diachronicle
DAY 221 (EARLY MARCH, YEAR 1)

In which we meet Dr. Oda. And his wife.

SHE LET US INTO THE house, which had the subtle smell of old wood and old wool—as I used to imagine Victorian homes smelled in Victorian times, before I was recently alerted to the painful truth that actually, at least here in London, they stink of whale oil, patchouli (woven into shawls to keep worms from eating the fabric in transit), and backed-up sewers. I am now convinced everyone here goes to church for the incense.

But to our story: Rebecca diverted us immediately to the front room on the right, which had been a formal dining room back in the day but was now her husband's study. The double-hung windows let in plenty of light; the two inner walls were lined with bookshelves (except where the fireplace was), most of them packed with piles of papers, journals, and folders in no discernible order. Dr. Frank Oda, seated at a desk that faced toward the street, was a slender, cheerful, absentminded-looking Japanese-American gentleman. Rebecca introduced us and offered to serve us tea, in a tone suggesting she'd be perfectly happy if we weren't staying long enough to drink it. Tristan, socially tone-deaf, accepted her offer.

The professor, smiling, invited us to sit on a couple of Harvard chairs that faced his desk, hastening to remove tattered copies of *Anna Karenina* and *Geometric Perspectives on Gauge Theories (Dr. Frank Oda, ed.)* from one of them. We sat, and Tristan immediately launched into an explanation of what we were trying to do (although not why we were trying to do it) and how we had encountered his rejected patent application online. Professor Oda's expression settled into thoughtfulness.

"Rather than inventing the wheel, we thought we'd ask you if you could explain your work to us, and why it did or didn't work," said Tristan.

Oda gave him a considering look. "You're not with DARPA, are you?"

"No," I said quickly, reassuringly. "This is a different kind of project altogether. I'm a linguist," I offered, as proof of how benign we were.

He shook his head, frowning. "I do not understand the point of your research, then," he said.

Tristan smiled that Boy Scout smile of his. "I'd need you to sign a nondisclosure agreement before I can tell you any more about what we're doing. I was hoping this could just be a casual conversation about what *you* were doing."

Oda smiled back. "I should share information with somebody who won't share information with me?"

Tristan upped his smile to Eagle Scout. "You're not willing to talk physics with a fellow physicist in the name of science?"

"If it is *applied* physics, he would like to know what it's being applied to," said Rebecca East-Oda from the study door.

The professor smiled at her. It was such a sweet smile. "It's all right, Rebecca," he said. "They're kids. They're curious. I like curious. And if you're here to ask, let's make it Darjeeling." She nodded and left; he returned his gaze to Tristan. "As you must have read in the patent application, I was trying to interrupt the collapse of the wave function—specifically in living neurological tissue."

"Brains," Tristan translated.

"Cat brains," I added.

Oda got a *here we go again* look, and drew breath.

"We're not from PETA," I assured him.

Tristan threw me a look.

"We totally get it that you weren't killing the cats," I went on.

"The cats that you saved from the kill shelter," Tristan concluded.

Right on cue, a black cat jumped up into Oda's lap and settled in for a long purr.

"I was wondering," I ventured, "why cats? Could you have done the experiment on worm brains, for example?"

"Yes," Oda said, "but it would have been difficult to gauge the outcome, because it's hard to know what a worm is thinking. With a cat, you are rarely in doubt."

"Ah. Well, in that case, why not just use a human subject?"

"Because of the Helsinki Declaration!" Tristan scoffed.

Oda nodded. "Partly that. But even if there were no regulations on use of human subjects, I would have been stymied by physical limitations."

For the first time since Tristan had become energized about the solar eclipse photographs, he looked a little deflated. "The ODEC won't work on a human?" he asked almost plaintively.

"Oh, it would work," Oda said, "if you could fit a human into it."

The relief in Tristan's voice was obvious. "So you would just need to make a bigger one."

Oda held back before answering, giving Tristan's face a careful study, with occasional glances at me. "*If you wanted to use it on a human,*" he said, "then yes. But this was impossible at the time."

"Your lab space wasn't big enough?" I asked.

"It was plenty big," Oda returned, "but that wasn't the problem."

My colleague was back to being Sad Tristan. "What *was* the problem, Dr. Oda?"

"Maybe it's easy if I just show you," Oda said, standing up abruptly and spilling the cat onto the rug. He was a slight man, hardly taller than I. "I have it in the basement."

"You have *what* in the basement?" I asked.

"The ODEC. Rebecca wanted me to throw it out, but I have a . . . bittersweet sentimental attachment to it, and it doesn't take up much space."

He began leading us toward a narrow door beneath the stairway. "Rebecca," he called out. "I'm taking them down to see the ODEC."

No answer, just some indistinct clacking of dishware. He gave us a rueful smile. "She doesn't approve," he said in a conspiratorial voice. "But she's making us tea all the same."

The cramped wooden steps down to the basement were nestled underneath the hall stairs to the second floor. He switched on a light, and the three of us slowly descended.

The basement was wonderful: low ceiling, thick stone walls with small transom windows, and a pounded-earth floor, very musty in a way that said *this is an authentic old house* (although of course I now know most houses smell that way almost as soon as they're built, in any time period but the modern). Near the hatch stairs to the yard lay a tangle of wood and wicker lawn furniture, with satellite baskets of sandbox toys, suggesting grandchildren. To the other side of the steps was the furnace, and other systems-

viscera of the house. Along almost every wall were shelving units on which were neatly stacked old apple crates, labeled and color-coded. Tristan at once began to read these, muttering his findings aloud. There was a very orderly garden worktable and grow lights in the corner nearest to the hatch. "Rebecca's the gardener," the professor said in an affectionate voice. He gestured around. "This house is architecturally interesting because it has an unusually deep cellar for its time."

"Is that so?" I asked politely, while Tristan kept scanning the crates for the ODEC.

Oda nodded, looking almost tickled. "Becca is the one officially qualified to give the tour, but after fifty years I guess I know the spiel. The whole area, for blocks around, was a farm back in the colonial era. The farmhouse was torn down a few decades ago, there's a gas station in its place now down at the corner of Mass Ave. This house we're in was built for the farm manager's family, when the estate was large and prosperous, and we think he dug the cellar so deep to hide extra food, all the end-of-year gleanings from the field. It was a stop on the Underground Railroad. Rebecca's family were abolitionists—but the farm owner, in the big house, was not."

"Her family's been in the house since before the Civil War?" I asked, surprised. Tristan continued to eye the neat storage stacks, looking for the ODEC.

Oda nodded. "It was built for her ancestor, Jeremiah East, that very farm manager. And Jeremiah's great-something-grandmother was—"

"Is that it?" asked Tristan, pointing to the far corner beyond the furnace. God he could be rude.

"Yes," said Oda, not minding, and led us toward it.

In the corner, under a heavy canvas tarp peppered with mouse droppings, was a large rectangular object. Oda dragged the tarp aside and it folded stiffly onto itself as it fell to the floor.

The ODEC was a little larger than I'd expected; as advertised, the interior volume could just accommodate a cat, but the apparatus constructed around it made it as big as a clothes washer. The cat box itself—plywood, and covered with slabs of pink insulation foam from the home improvement store—was suspended by a web of thin, taut cords inside of a somewhat larger fiberglass tub. This was in turn surrounded by more pink foam insulation. All of it was hung from, and supported by, a sort of exoskeleton of slotted angle irons. Wires were coming out of it all over the place: thick, round black cables like the ones that the cable guy staples to your house, hair-thin copper wires coiled millions of times around hidden cores to make what I guessed were electromagnets, medium-sized wires with colored insulation, flat rainbow ribbons, tubular braids, bare copper that had gone greenish-brown with age, and power cords with two-prong plugs at the end, their plastic insulation now stiff and cracked.

On a shelf beneath the cat enclosure rested a plastic box that looked like the CPU of an old desktop computer, except that instead of beige it was an intense purple color.

"Silicon Graphics Indigo," Tristan said, reading the logos on its front.

"An awesome machine," Oda said, "before you were born. Fastest thing I could get at the time."

The entire thing was mounted on rubber-wheeled casters. When Oda tried to pull it away from the wall, these made noises suggesting they hadn't moved in a long time. "May I, sir?" Tristan offered, and then put his considerably broader back into it. The ODEC creaked and squeaked its way out into the middle of the room, leaving a trail of mouse turds, dust bunnies, and dead spiders across the floor. I was now looking at the back of it. From here it was obvious that Oda had opened up the back of the Silicon Graphics workstation and routed a number of cables into it.

A miniature Manhattan of electrical stuff covered the top. Oda pushed, and this chittered out of the way on ball-bearing drawer slides, revealing the foam-clad lid of the fiberglass tub. Oda picked this up and handed it to Tristan, who found a patch of bare stone wall to lean it against. Exposed in the middle was the lid of the inner plywood box. Oda reverentially unhooked the simple clasp holding it down. He paused a moment, smiling to himself. I wondered how long it had been since he'd last opened it.

Then he lifted the lid, hinged on the far side. A pair of little chains kept it from flopping back. I don't know what I had been anticipating, but it was no clumsy contraption. The box itself was plywood, but it was lined on the inside with thin sheets of green plastic, scribed all over with fine copper traces that I recognized as circuit boards. In some places, little electronic components had been soldered to these, projecting out into the airspace within the box, but in others, the copper tracery itself seemed to be what mattered. The linguist in me couldn't help fancying a connection between these fine whorls of metal and the interlaced figures in old Irish manuscripts. Neat holes had been drilled through the plywood in many places to allow wires to pass through and make connections with these circuit boards. In many cases, these coincided with the massive coils of copper wire mounted outside the box. I now began to see these as being aimed inward, like science-fiction weapons.

Aimed, that is, at the cat inside the box. For resting on the box's floor was a flat circular pillow upholstered in red velvet that had become permeated with cat hair down to the molecular level. A tiny saucer of spun stainless steel sat next to it, a thin disk of brown residue congealed in its bottom. I needed no forensic analysis to know that it had once contained cream.

Tristan had a look on his face as if all this was exactly what he'd been expecting. I confess, it mystified me.

"Call me stupid," I said, "but I don't understand the connection to photography."

"Photography?" Oda asked, puzzled. As if I had just wandered into the wrong eccentric professor's basement.

"There's a connection," Tristan reassured him. "I give you my word I'll explain it—once you have completed certain paperwork that, I regret to say, is mandatory. In the meantime, I wonder if you could explain the ODEC to us."

Oda-sensei shrugged. "In a nutshell," he said, now entirely immersed in the science of the moment, "here is the premise. You insert living nerve tissue. You close the lid, creating a sealed environment. You pump in the liquid helium . . ."

"Wait, wait!" Tristan protested. "This is the first you've mentioned cryogenics."

"You freeze the cat?" I exclaimed, aghast.

"No, no," Oda scolded us. "That would just be mean. See for yourself, the box itself is super-insulated! And it has its own air supply, enough to keep a cat alive for an hour." He was directing my attention to the thick foam mounted to the outer surface of the plywood. Then he moved his hand a couple of inches outward and patted the inner surface of the enclosing fiberglass tub. "The inner box is completely surrounded by a bath of liquid helium, chilled to a few Kelvins above absolute zero."

"Cold enough," Tristan hazarded, "to form a Bose-Einstein condensate?"

"I love it when you talk dirty," Oda said, so perfectly deadpan that I did a double take. "Yes, we begin by isolating the subject—"

"Within a jacket of matter that all exists in the same quantum state," Tristan said.

"You're completing each other's sentences. Great," I said.

"I'll explain later," Tristan returned.

"Conveniently, the low temperature also brings some of the coils down to the point where they become superconductors," Oda added, tapping a fingertip against some of the things that I had identified as big magnets. "A continuously recirculating and self-reinforcing current pattern establishes itself in these. Its state can be read continuously by analog-to-digital converters at a sampling rate of about a megahertz. Which we used to think was fast."

"So you're reading the cat's mind?"

"Not so much that," Oda said, "as looking for the signatures of nascent wave collapse events."

Tristan stood frozen for a few moments, then shaped his hand into a blade and whooshed it past his head. *Good*, I thought. *Have a taste of what I'm experiencing.*

"I lost you?" Oda inquired.

"Yes, sir."

"I'm messing around with renormalization."

"Oh."

"That's what determines what the wave function is most likely to collapse into. By messing around with it, I can alter the probabilities."

"You can do magic," I blurted.

"Sort of," Oda said. Then, in a curious, polite tone, he asked, "Is that what you're here to talk about? Magic?"

"Classified," Tristan said, and gave me the stink-eye. Then he turned to Oda. "Under normal circumstances we can make educated guesses about what is likely to happen when the wave function collapses. You're screwing around with that."

Oda nodded ruefully. "But only sometimes. And I can't account for the variations. That's why the patent was rejected. Why DARPA didn't renew my grant."

"What's the computer doing?" Tristan asked.

Oda sighed. "Not enough, unfortunately. As I said, it was a fine machine for its time. Even so—despite a lot of code optimization—it wasn't up to the job, even when it was running flat-out."

"So it's of the essence. It's not just a data logger."

"It is very much in the control loop," Oda said. Glancing at me, he explained: "For the ODEC to work, it has to take in sensor data, perform certain calculations that are highly nontrivial, and make decisions about how to alter the current flowing through the coils. It has to do so quickly, or else the whole project fails. And it wasn't quick enough."

"What are the specs on that Indigo?" Tristan asked.

Oda sighed. "I don't even want to tell you."

"Why not?"

"Because you're going to laugh."

"I won't laugh."

"One processor; 175 megahertz; 512 megabytes of RAM."

Tristan laughed.

"I told you," Oda said.

Tristan stood there a moment, eyeing the contraption. "With modern computers . . . or a cluster of them . . . some GPUs cranking the numbers . . . faster clocks . . . all of your problems on that front would be solved."

"Possibly," said Oda with a nod. "But I had neither the funds nor the space for that, and the *Howler* article pretty much made me a laughingstock in the academic community, so I'll never get funding again."

"Sorry to hear that," I said, "especially if the theory is sound."

"No one funds theories. They fund results," said Oda. "The results were not reliably reproducible. Using cats was a mistake; the premise was very easy to mock among lay people."

"What if you were given the funding to rebuild this the way I just described it, room-sized?" Tristan said.

Oda gave him a cautious, wise-old-man smile. "Scaling issues would become huge. The amount of computational power required goes up as the square of the cavity's *volume*."

Tristan made a quick mental calculation. "So, as the sixth power of the box's size. That's okay. We'll make it a *small* room. Moore's law will take care of the rest."

"Don't even suggest this in Rebecca's hearing or she will chase you out of the house with her gardening shears. It was a very draining and humiliating period. She would never endure it being brought back to life."

"This would all happen under a cloak of secrecy. *The Howler* would never hear about it. Nobody would."

Oda pondered it.

"If Rebecca said yes?" I asked.

Oda shrugged. "It was my pet project, of course I would love to see it work. And I tend to say yes to things. But I would want to know *why* you were pursuing this."

"I can tell you all about it as soon as you sign a nondisclosure form," Tristan said.

Oda smiled to himself a moment, then returned his attention to Tristan. "Well, then you must ask Becca to sign the form as well," he said. "I could not keep this from her."

"Go on upstairs and work on that, Stokes," said Tristan, without even looking at me. "I want to talk shop with the professor for a few minutes."

Journal Entry of
Rebecca East-Oda
MARCH 6

Temperature today about 43F, fair and dry, with slight breeze from the west. Barometer steady.

Snowdrops blooming. Crocuses will bud soon, Buddleia just cut back, Hellebore has just come up. Witchhazel blooming and lilacs have tight buds. Planted the first of the basil, peppers, and tomatoes inside (under the grow lights) and harvested the last of the kale. Harvested the parsnips, sweeter for enduring the hard winter.

Strange event today. Frank received visitors, a couple named Tristan and Melisande who somehow happened upon his old ODEC patent application from DARPA, something I would just as soon forget ever existed. They appeared at the door without warning this afternoon. He is clearly military, has the energy of a Labrador retriever (thinking in particular of the one Uncle Victor trained for duck hunting). She milder, more reserved, better-spoken than he.

Frank received them in his current study, the dining room. (Melisande was charmed that although that chandelier was wired for electric lights about a century ago, and outfitted for gas light before that, it can still be lowered by a pulley system from the days of candle-lighting. Tristan was not as charmed, because the chandelier wasn't the duck he was here to hunt.)

They told Frank they believe that they know why the patent application failed and that furthermore, they know how to rectify this—that, with his assistance, they can actually create an ODEC that will successfully suppress the collapse of the wave function. I was not sure how I felt about hearing this, remembering the stress and bother that went into our last go-round with this enterprise.

Frank said they would have to convince *me*. Melisande was tasked with doing this. I could tell from the way she approached me in the kitchen that she did not expect to succeed. She was surprised.

I will support Frank in anything he does and any decision he makes. Since he did not immediately say no to them, it means he is excited by the prospect of being vindicated all these years later. I truly wish he wasn't. But he is. And I understand that. To make a short story shorter, we both signed a nondisclosure agreement, and they joined us for tea.

Then things got quite strange.

They shared something preposterous, which is hard for me to write down without shaking my head. They claim to be interested in the ODEC not for its defensive capabilities, but because they believe it can be used to perform acts of—I cannot write this steadily—*magic*. Not sleight-of-hand; not wishful thinking. Sorcery. They are sincere about this. She attempted to validate the claim by citing ancient documents she has been translating. He gave a passing technical explanation, which I admit sounded as plausible as anything else re: quantum theory, but that's not saying much, is it?

But Tristan played the winning card re: Frank's mental constitution: he said that ultimately it should not matter if we believed about the magic or not, we should sign on to this for the sake of the science itself. That is like offering catnip to a cat. Of course Frank said he would assist however he could.

They'd explained why magic is no longer possible today, and further, why, even were magic to become possible (within the ODEC), it would require the application of specific people ("witches") who could "perform magic." So naturally, I asked them *who* they were expecting to "perform" it. It was the only time I saw them at a loss: this most obvious and basic of concerns had never crossed their minds.

I don't know who they are, or where their funding comes from—it definitely isn't MIT this time. God forbid MIT even suspect he's tinkering with this nonsense.

Diachronicle
DAY 221 (CONTD.; EARLY MARCH, YEAR 1)

In which we divide to conquer

REBECCA EAST-ODA SERVED TEA LIKE a proper New England matriarch—not mugs with teabags, but loose-leaf tea steeped in and poured from a china teapot into teacups resting on saucers, with rock sugar on sticks and a little porcelain pitcher of milk, all set out on a wicker tray. She also presented a plate of biscuits both ginger and savory, which of course at the time I'd have called cookies and crackers. I spirited these to my side of the tea table so that Tristan would not swallow them whole.

For early March in New England, it was uncharacteristically gorgeous, and crisp afternoon sunlight streamed at a low angle through the bay transom windows, hitting the dangling crystals of the fancy old chandelier that hung incongruously above us all, throwing dozens of little rainbows around the walls.

"So we have this space. Not far away from here actually," Tristan was saying, and on reflex glanced around for sweets.

"Have some more tea," Rebecca offered Tristan, who of course had downed his almost instantly. She held out her hand for his teacup and saucer.

He gave it to her with a nod of thanks, but then his attention re-turned to Frank Oda, talking amps and circuitry requirements—

"How does he take it?" Rebecca asked me.

How odd that she assumed I'd know this. "Based on his dietary habits, probably milk and sugar," I said.

"All right then," said Tristan, staring fixedly at a blank place on the wall. "The human-rated ODEC has to be built . . . this becomes a four-part strategy." (I had not realized he'd fashioned even a three-part strategy.) He held up a fist and stuck out his thumb: "One, extensive modifications to our building."

"Hang on," I said, "it's not DODO's building!"

"What is DODO?" Rebecca asked.

"Department of Diabolical Obscurantism," I guessed.

Tristan was still frozen in midsentence, like a video when you hit the "pause" button, thumb in the air, gazing at me patiently while he chewed a biscuit he had somehow snagged from my side of the table. "Anyway," I continued, "you can't just modify some-one else's building . . . can you?"

"We will acquire the building," he announced. Then he ex-tended his index finger. "Two, design of the human-rated ODEC. Three, its construction. Four, find somebody who can do magic." He looked around at us. "Conveniently, there's four of us. Pro-fessor, you work up a design, then oversee the construction. My bosses can fly up some fellows from DC to work with us, Stokes and I will help—you can manage a screw gun, can't you, Stokes?" This was a throwaway, almost rhetorical, question; he did not even glance at me.

Oda nodded, his face still but radiant. I could see him restraining himself from glancing at his wife. Her face was also still, but not so radiant. "We'll need people with expertise in bulk cryogenics."

"NASA," Tristan said dismissively. "Those guys don't have

enough to do. Then there's procuring and installing all the hardware. We can get as much computational muscle as we need from cheap off-the-shelf hardware. Weird fabrication can be sourced from Los Alamos. Witches is you, Stokes. Ask around at New Agey places. Yoga studios or whatever. That should be easy enough, and you look the part."

"What does *that* mean?" I demanded.

"Grad student. Primary demographic for magical thinking."

"Tristan. It's the twenty-first century. Get a clue. I will look for witches online."

He was already shaking his head. "No. You can't leave a paper or electronic trail. You have to show up somewhere witchy in person and ask questions, without giving them any information about yourself." Before I could respond he turned to Rebecca. "Wanna help Stokes find a witch?"

Rebecca said, "No." She said it politely, calmly stroking a calico cat that was curled placidly on her lap. It was clear that she would not be changing her mind about it.

"You're the one who gets credit for thinking of it," he said, almost (by Tristan standards) cajoling.

"I am here for Frank," she said. "I'm not a soldier in your army, Mr. Lyons."

"All right then," Tristan said, after a pause. He suddenly brightened, grinned at me. "Stokes, you own witches."

"What the hell, Tristan. How does one find a witch, anyhow? Not in a yoga studio, that's for sure. Nobody's been able to do magic for about a hundred and seventy-five years, so what does that even *mean*, for somebody to 'be a witch'?"

"In Japan, still today, there are *tsukimono-suji*," said Oda, as casually as if he were discussing lunch. "Witch families. Witchcraft is considered hereditary—matrilineal—and I don't know what

kind of magic they claim to do, but the witch identity remains."
He grinned slightly. "Maybe if you find the *descendant* of a witch,
you've found a witch waiting for her broomstick."

"Very funny," said Rebecca. When Tristan and I turned curious eyes upon her, she explained in a desultory tone, "An ancestress of mine was hanged in the Salem witch trials. Frank finds
that exotic."

"Salem doesn't count," I said. "That was mass hysteria induced
by ergot-tainted rye."

"Correct," said Rebecca in a *so-there* tone, her eyes darting toward her husband.

"But Salem *is* the epicenter of modern American witchiness,"
said Tristan.

"That's a bunch of commercial tourist-trap nonsense, and anyhow, what would I be *looking* for?" I asked again.

"If there really *were* witches," Oda-sensei suggested, "maybe
there are people today who know they were descended from them,
and who continue some of the ritual elements even if the magic
isn't active. That is probably the case with the tsukimono-suji."

"We can work with that," said Tristan. "Stokes, get on it."

"Salem won't *have* any witch-descendants because—as I just
said—Salem never had witches to *start* with," I insisted. "If we're
looking for witch-spawn, we should check out someplace like
New Orleans."

Tristan considered this. "Go poke around Salem first. If you
don't find anything, maybe I'll send you to New Orleans."

Crikey, that was easy. And a perk I'd never get under Blevins!
"Is this taxpayer-funded?" I asked. "No judgment. Just curious."

"Classified," he said, and gave me a wink.

Diachronicle

DAYS 222-244 (MARCH, YEAR 1)

In which there are constructive developments

TRISTAN LATER MODIFIED HIS PLAN, deciding not to send me witch-hunting until we had a feasible chamber in which to put our witch. As there was nothing to occupy me, and I'd let slip that I had taken (one semester-long) shop class in high school, he declared me his aide-de-camp for the campaign of Office Reform that was to come.

During the next few weeks the office, as I had known it, rapidly ceased to exist. Even before taking ownership of the building, Tristan had, with sledgehammer and Sawzall, wrought changes on it that, at the time, had struck me as quite material. He had perfected the art of gazing thoughtfully at a wall between office suites, casting his gaze hither and yon, and blithely announcing that it was not load-bearing and hence a candidate for being knocked out. In this manner the original DODO office had tripled its square footage during the time I had been working there, with several of its walls already marked for death whenever the neighboring start-ups went "Tango Uniform."

"Department of Demolishing Offices" was all I could say the next time I went to the building after our teatime strategy session at the Odas' house. Less than twenty-four hours had passed, but Tristan appeared to have spent most of them walking freely through the building with a can of fluorescent green spray paint marking doors, walls, and other impedimenta with the word DEMO or, when he ran low on spray paint, with a simple X. In the center of the building was a large conference room, meant to be shared by all of the tenants. Tristan had hurled the conference table against the wall, Xed it, and then spray-painted a huge rectangle directly onto the industrial-carpeted floor and filled it in with the inevitable X. Young, lavishly bearded tech entrepreneurs were trudging forlornly down the hallways, laden with computers, printers, high-end coffeemakers, and foosball tables. Like digital Okies they loaded their stuff into their Scions or Ryder trucks and rumbled off into the unforgiving Boston commercial real estate market.

"So you're going to, uh, remove basically the entire floor of the conference room?" I inquired.

"The conference room will cease to exist," he said. "DODO is not about meetings. Not about PowerPoints."

"I never imagined otherwise," I said.

He had lost focus on me and was now looking over my shoulder at a wall, which currently supported a large flat-screen monitor. Something about the look on his face told me where this was going. "Not load-bearing?" I guessed, glancing back over my shoulder. He sidestepped by me, raised his can of acid green paint like the Statue of Liberty's torch, stood up on tiptoe, and sprayed a dripping, diagonal slash across the entirety of the wall, passing directly across the monitor screen en route. As he completed the other leg of the X he explained, "Between the loading dock and here we need to clear a path for the tanks."

"You seem a little preoccupied," I said, "and I don't want to elbow in on your painting. I'll just take all the translation notes back to my apartment before you paint them green."

"Remember to maintain—" he began.

"—operational security," I ended. "Not to worry." I found my way to the part of the building where it had all started. Oda was there, perched on a large blue yoga ball before the largest computer monitor I had ever seen, peering intently at some tiny widget in the user interface of what I guessed was a computer-aided design program. Next to him was the cell phone Tristan had bought for him (his first) and a bowl of foamy green Japanese tea. Matcha. Still steaming and filling the room with a fresh but bitter fragrance. It had to have been made only seconds ago. A faucet gushed briefly down the hall, in the ladies' room, and I guess Rebecca was here washing up. I snapped a couple of file folders marked UNCLASSIFIED: TRANSLATIONS out of a cabinet and went to find her. She had spread all of her matcha-making whisks and paraphernalia out on the counter.

"Herbs," I said.

She looked up and gazed at me in the mirror.

"Just a thought," I added.

"What about them?"

"Witches were obsessed with them."

"It is a familiar stereotype," she pointed out, and returned her attention to drying her matcha gear.

"One based on reality. All of our research points to it." I rattled the folders in the air, as if this would lend authority to my words. "I thought of it when the fragrance of that tea filled my nostrils. Powerful stuff, fragrances."

"Yes," she said drily, "so perhaps you should be recruiting the descendants of famous perfumers, or incense-makers, rather than those of famous non-witches hanged in Salem."

Taking the hint, I used the facilities and moved on. As I was walking back to my apartment, folders tucked under my arm, I had time to ponder Tristan's statement *we need to clear a path for the tanks*. Given his military background, my mind had immediately flashed up an image of a column of huge armored military vehicles thundering through the building. But of course he didn't mean that kind of tank. He meant a large vessel for holding fluids. To be specific, for holding liquid helium.

When I returned to the building the next day, my keycard didn't work. This was due to the disappearance of the entire keycard-reading machine. In its stead was a contraption, apparently some kind of eyeball scanner. I went around back and pounded on the loading dock door until Tristan let me in. "New perimeter security," he explained. "Max will get you squared away."

"Who's Max?"

Tristan was leading me down a broad open corridor that had been sledgehammered through the building overnight. It terminated in the ruins of the conference room. A huge square hole, perhaps fifteen feet on a side, had been cut through the floor, and yellow caution tape strung up around it to prevent people from falling through into the cellar. Hard at work down there were what appeared to be the offspring of a Benetton ad and a UPS commercial: four attractive, buff young men in nondescript brown uniforms, one African-American, one Asian (Korean?), one Hispanic, one with a Persian aspect, all impeccably kitted out with eye and ear protection. Two of them were framing in a wall with steel studs, and the other two were wrestling with cables. Tristan hailed them and they paused in their labors to greet me briefly. To a man, each identified himself as Max.

"What, do they row for the DODO crew team?" I asked, when they had returned to their work.

"Classified," Tristan said. When I made a face, he added quietly, "Don't talk shop in front of them. They know it's a physics experiment but they don't know about the magic." Then he nodded at a work party of Hispanic men busy heaving shattered drywall and rolls of nasty old carpet into huge rolling bins for disposal. "And those guys are from the sidewalk in front of Home Depot. If my higher-ups knew . . ." He shook his head.

I was busy gazing at my colleague in a somewhat new light. Until I saw him in command of people and a place, there had been, truth be told, no evidence that Tristan Lyons wasn't merely a convincing psychopath renting a tawdry room in an obsolete office building for unsavory purposes that could have endangered my life. The possibility had never entered my mind, but in retrospect, it really should have. I'd been a sucker for both the smile and the paycheck. I still consider it pure dumb luck that my trust had been well placed.

Journal Entry of
Rebecca East-Oda
MARCH 29

Temperature 49F, sunny, mild, very still. Barometer steady.

Lettuce coming along nicely; yesterday, planted peppers, Swiss chard, radishes. Weathervane needs fixing.

Working on the native-herb garden in the front corner of the yard. Already thriving: thyme, hyssop, spearmint, lemon balm, fennel, chamomile, marjoram. Must add: lavender, ambrosia, valerian, mugwort, pennyroyal, gillyflower, and (when it's warmer) sweet basil. Might take out the Japanese moss to make room, and bring Mei's bonsai indoors, now that Frank has lost interest.

They are continuing with the ODEC, on a magnitude I can barely fathom. Frank is happily preoccupied with something I cannot believe will actually ever come to anything, but it is good to see him absorbed in work.

In which constructive developments continue

I BEGAN TO HELP THE Maxes and Tristan complete construction of the ODEC under Oda-sensei's guidance. The memory, now, of such tomboyishness, freedom of movement, the liberty of a day innocently alone with unmarried young men, and above all, the virtue of labor—these things make me almost pant with longing today, as I sit here breathing the fumes from this stinking whale oil lamp in my whale-bone corset (*very* difficult to believe Victoria Regina is about to rule over half the planet dressed like this. Just saying.).

As I had guessed, the "tanks" Tristan had referred to were industrial vessels made to contain thousands of gallons within their fiberglass walls. There were two of them, an inner nested within an outer, with a few inches' separation between them. We had to cover both of them with insulation to keep the liquid helium from boiling away. This was a combination of four-by-eight-foot slabs of pink foam from Home Depot, and some kind of weird brew that you would mix up in a bucket by stirring two different chemicals together. Then it would expand enormously as it foamed up and stick to everything like Krazy Glue before it hardened.

After it had been clad in its insulating jacket, the outer tank just fit through the hole cut through the floor of the former conference room, and rested on the cellar floor below, its upper part projecting up into the ground floor. Here the Maxes cut a rectangular hatch through it, and a matching one through the inner tank several inches away. They fiberglassed the two rectangles together to form a hollow door capable of being filled with liquid helium, and likewise sealed the jambs. Meanwhile, expensive-looking stuff kept showing up at the loading dock. I didn't need a West Point physics degree to understand that this was cryogenics equipment.

Though the new ODEC (the Mark II) was much bigger than Professor Oda's cat-sized Mark I, it was recognizably the same machine. Instead of an inner plywood box with a cat bed and a cream saucer, this one had that inner tank, which was just large enough for one person to sit in a chair, or two to stand upright. Much of its volume was spoken for by what Tristan referred to, somewhat unnervingly, as "life support stuff." I made a mental note to ask him about that later. Its walls, for the time being, were just bare fiberglass, as it had come from the factory. If the Mark I was any guide, however, those walls would soon be lined with circuit boards. I had overheard enough snatches of conversation between Oda and Tristan to know that these were being produced offsite and that some were already inbound, plastered with tracking numbers that Rebecca was checking several times a day. When they showed up, and when the Maxes installed them, they would be connected to the inevitable web of cables, which would be routed under the floor and then up into the server room. This was being bolted together and brought online by a trio of bearded men who all politely introduced themselves as Vladimir.

Once the Vladimirs had bolted the vertical racks into the floor, they devoted whole days to opening cardboard boxes, which had been piling up in ziggurats on the loading docks, and extricating black slabs, approximately the size and shape of pizza boxes, and slamming them into rails on those racks. Each of them, I was assured, contained sixteen computers, each of which was a bazillion times more powerful than the single, forlorn Indigo that had served as the brains of the Mark I. The Vladimirs were nothing if not friendly. I got the sense that this would be my last opportunity to have anything like a normal conversation with them. Once all of these pizza box servers were up and running, they would revert to their natural behavior patterns. For now, working on their knees with screwdrivers, performing tasks well below their pay grade, they were just happy to have someone to talk to. And talk they did, with a kind of messianic zeal, about the awesomeness of the cluster they were assembling. One of them, whom I'd mentally renamed Longbeard, actually did have an Eastern European accent. I got the impression from stray remarks dropped here and there that he'd had a hand in the creation of the uber-paranoid Shiny Hat operating system that had been the bane of my existence these six months. Perhaps he was the ur-Vlad.

I was drawn into the mindless but satisfying activity of flattening boxes and stuffing plastic packing material into garbage bags. On a trip to the Dumpsters, I noted that it was dark. Perhaps we would knock off soon. But the Vladimirs had just ordered another round of quadruple-shot espresso drinks from the Apostolic Café, and Tristan announced that he and the Maxes were going to pull an all-nighter and leak-check the entire chamber so that it could be test-filled in the morning. Frank Oda kindly gave me a lift home. I wondered what Rebecca made of all this, but suspected this was perhaps a delicate subject, so refrained from asking.

It was strange spending an evening in my own apartment. I'd anticipated a sense of relief, but the solitude was almost disorienting. I heated up some leftovers, settled down with my laptop, and checked my email for the first time in days. I had three notifications from Facebook.

I usually forgot about Facebook; I checked in about once a month. I logged in now, to see that my account had three "friend requests." One was from my mother, one was a nearly pornographic image of an attractive young Chinese man whose name translated to "Jade Dagger," and one was a woman named Erszebet Karpathy whose picture appeared to be a state-issued ID of an octogenarian drag queen. I accepted my mother's request, disregarded the other two as spam, sent my mother a perfunctory "Welcome to the Twenty-First Century" post, and checked my wall.

There was a message posted on it from Erszebet Karpathy, dated three days earlier. "I am still waiting! Let me know when you are ready to begin."

Odd.

I scrolled down. The next most recent post on my page was also from this Erszebet Karpathy, ten days earlier: "I am waiting for all to be placed in readiness."

Next was a request from one of my former students to play some kind of dumb social media game.

Then another post from Erszebet Karpathy, this one from nearly a month earlier: "Melisande, is it time yet? You said April or May of this year."

That was unnerving. Who was Erszebet Karpathy? I went to her "About" page, to find it blank. Occasionally I accepted private students, usually interested in Bible studies, who wished to parse something in Aramaic. But it had been at least a year since I'd fielded any requests. Tired from a long day, I closed the laptop and went to sleep without even finishing dinner.

The next morning, when I opened my laptop again to check the *New York Times* headlines, I was still logged in to Facebook, and there was a new message from the Karpathy chick: "Melisande. I see that you have been active on Facebook within the past 12 hours, so I KNOW you are receiving these messages. Contact me and I will tell you where to collect me." She had changed her profile picture: now it was a "vintage"-looking, sepia-toned portrait of a matron in Edwardian costume, the kind of photo you dress for at Ye Olde County Faire.

If life had not become so exceptionally peculiar over the past month, I would simply have blocked her. Instead, chewing on my lower lip, I sent her a private message: "Who are you and what do you want?"

Before I could even log out, I received a response: "Come and get me. Elm House, 420 Common Street, Belmont. Do not make me wait any longer. Do you have any idea how much I have suffered?"

I stared at this statement, flummoxed.

"I know you are online," came a new message. "There is a little green light next to your name. Come at once. I shall be waiting near the front desk with my luggage."

After an unsettled moment, I typed back, "What are you expecting of me?"

"That you will help me to do magic once again. As you promised."

Thirty seconds later, laptop under my arm, I was dashing out the door to get to Tristan.

Diachronicle
DAY 290

In which adjustments are made

I SPRINTED INTO THE BASEMENT office ready to thrust my Facebook page at Tristan. But he and the assembled Maxes, all bleary-eyed yet full of pep, were cheering the results of the overnight test, which had apparently found no leaks. Frank Oda (radiant) and his wife, Rebecca (stoic), were also present, creating yet another mound of empty boxes and packing material as they uncrated the newly arrived circuit boards.

"Tristan, I found—!" I began, but he was moving so quickly as to resemble an animated character, without the least interest in anything I had to say. He seemed to be headed for the server room, so I darted past him, executed a 180, and blocked his path. "I found a woman who says she can do magic. That is, she found me," I clarified, seeing his eyes go wide with wonder. "On Facebook. We haven't met in person."

Tristan frowned. "Oh God, not some social media thing, Stokes. *Please* tell me you didn't put out a call for witches."

"Of course not," I snapped. "I signed a nondisclosure form, I know what that means. Give me some credit, *Lyons*. She sent me a message out of the blue, saying she was waiting for me so she could do magic."

He blinked. "Strange."

I reached for my messenger bag. "I've got it right—"

He held up a hand, shook his head. "Stokes. I forbid you to communicate with this person, whoever she is, over social media channels. It is totally insecure. You have got to go about this systematically—not by sitting around your apartment waiting to get friended by supernatural trolls."

"Well, now that we've ruled out the use of the Internet and all other modern communications devices," I said, "what systematic approach do you recommend for responding to the only lead we have?"

"Don't do anything till we have a chance to hack into Facebook and get this person's real identity for a background check. Leave your laptop with the Vladimirs."

"And what do I systematically do in the meanwhile?"

"Go to Salem."

"We've been over this. There never were any actual witches in Salem. Even the Puritans ended up admitting as much."

"Back in the day, yes. That's true," Tristan said agreeably. "But now, because of its reputation as a witchy place, it is a magnet for people like that."

"And you know this how?"

"I drove through it once. There was witch shit all over the place."

"Good. Now I understand what you mean by systematic."

"Try to see it through the eyes of my higher-ups," he suggested. "Salem. Witches. Go. Get on it. See if you can find a witch, or a witch's descendant, or a witch's DNA or something, just so I can tell them it's being worked on. I've got to work my contacts at Lawrence Livermore, they're hoarding helium."

"Of course," I said, and wished for a brief, exhausted moment that he had asked me to translate Tartessian, or something simple like that.

Feeling like a dolt before I'd even departed, I borrowed Tristan's Jeep and drove up Route 1 to Salem, about an hour away. In that vehicle, on that road, this was like being beaten with sacks of gravel.

Like many New England towns with something of historical note to recommend it, Salem was a bizarre combination of well-preserved, beautiful old buildings and ugly commercial developments. The commercial developments were winning, however. Ignoring the various signs for the Salem Witch Museum, the Salem Witch House, the Salem Witch Village, the Salem Witch Day Spa, and so on, I found a parking spot on a broad street, marveled at how cheap the parking was, and walked into the older part of town. I have no words to describe how unenthusiastic I felt about this assignment. Three and a quarter centuries after nineteen innocent people were hanged for no reason, a bunch of New Age types whose concept of witchcraft had zero in common with the seventeenth-century concept of witchcraft decided to set up shop right by the graves of the victims. ~~What the fuck.~~ I have no tolerance for sloppy logic like that.

Just so I could tell Tristan I'd done it, I walked into a couple of occult shops that I found along a pedestrian stretch of Essex Street, then fled before the incense overwhelmed me.

There's another context-is-everything moment, because now I *live* for incense—if I really am to be stuck permanently in 1850s London, I might have to become an Anglican nun. God, I hope it doesn't come to that.

In the end, though, the scholar in me won out, and I ended up visiting a few of the legitimate historical sites in the Salem area. The name of Mary Estey—one of the victims of the witch hysteria—kept jumping out at me. Rebecca East, Frank's wife, had mentioned that she was a descendant of this family, the spelling having changed and the final syllable having been dropped from the surname at some point in the intervening three centuries. In typical WASP style, Rebecca underplayed its significance, pointing out that the families of that era had been enormous and that, if you did the math, every second or third white person you encountered on the streets of America was probably descended from someone who had lived in Salem. But I felt that the least I could do was pay my respects.

Then, suddenly feeling as though it was late in the day and that I must be missing important developments, I got back in the Jeep and fought my way back through late afternoon traffic to the office. I can't say I mourned my failure overmuch, as it meant I'd get a free trip to New Orleans out of it, and that would ~~rock~~ be most excellent.

I DROVE BACK to the office late in the day to find Tristan collapsed on the couch from exhaustion. I began to make coffee in one of the high-tech machines we had pillaged from a departing tech start-up. While it gurgled and hissed, I idly and out of habit took my phone out and glanced at it. There was a banner notification from Facebook Messenger.

"I will wait in the lobby," said a private message from the Hungarian woman, with a 9:04 a.m. time stamp on it.

"Oh God," I said out loud. How could I have gone the whole day with hardly a thought of her?

A mechanical chime sounded as an instant message sprang up. "I waited the ENTIRE DAY. Where were you?" She had changed her profile picture again, this time to an artsy-looking purple blur.

I went to the couch and nudged Tristan. Deep asleep, he almost instantly awoke and leapt to his feet, shoving me sideways without registering my identity, glancing around for an assailant.

"It's just me," I said with irritation. "Calm down."

"You startled me," he said, as if I should have known better.

I gestured to my phone. "Take a look at this."

Even as I showed him her comments, our exchange, and her blank "About" page, several more prompts popped up on the bottom of the screen with mechanical chimes, as Miss Karpathy informed me she could see I was online and why was I not answering?

Tristan considered the screen a moment. "The Vladimirs have been all over this. Intriguing-slash-disturbing-in-the-extreme.

Tell her you'll speak to her tomorrow. Today's got to be about the dry run."

I tapped in, "Sorry. Will be with you tomorrow evening."

Immediately the response: "Why the delay?"

"Technical difficulties," I typed.

"With the ODEC?" she typed back instantly.

I looked at Tristan. "Jesus," he said under his breath. "Who *is* she?" He moved closer to the screen and nudged my shoulder with his. "Tell her you can't discuss it online," he whispered, as if worried of being overheard by somebody. I typed this in, and a response came back:

"Will you come with your Mr. Tristan Lyons?" she typed back. "I wish to meet him."

I looked up over my shoulder at my Mr. Tristan Lyons. He nodded, staring at the screen.

"We could go now," I suggested.

He shook his head. "We don't know what we're getting into. Tell her yes, I'll come with you. But tomorrow."

"With Mr. Tristan Lyons," I typed. "Tomorrow evening."

"Come before 6 p.m. or it will be harder to leave because of the Night Guard."

We both continued to stare at the screen for a moment in silence. Then Tristan reached out and gently took the phone from my hand, tossed it on to the couch.

"Can't wait to hear the explanation," he said, sounding weary. Then, with a tired grin down at me: "Funny how she called me *your* Mr. Tristan Lyons."

I felt my face flush. "Maybe she's dealt with another Tristan Lyons," I said. "Surely the multiverse contains more than one. The coffee's ready."

"Good," he said, "because so is the ODEC."

During my sojourn to Salem, the crew had mounted all of the circuit boards to the walls of the inner cavity and also bolted in the electromagnets; these were mounted to a sturdy framework of steel angle irons that had been welded together around the external tank. Black melted areas on the floor suggested that welding sparks had set the occasional odd fire to the carpet; larger burns were surrounded by penumbras of powder that had apparently been shot out of the various fire extinguishers, which now lay scattered around the floor like empty beer bottles after a frat party. As Tristan led me in, he absentmindedly nudged these out of the way with his foot, cautioning me to watch my step.

"Did your friends come through with the liquid helium?" I asked. Certainly the first time in my life I had uttered that sentence.

"They will."

"That's a no?"

"We're testing it with liquid nitrogen. Much cheaper."

As if on cue, the persistent, infuriating *beep-beep-beep* of a truck's backup alarm sounded from the street; we could hear it through the roll-up door at the loading dock.

"Woo hoo hoo!" Tristan shouted. "LN2! Up and at 'em, folks!" He strode down the tank right-of-way to the loading dock and hit the button that opened the dock door. A semi-trailer rig consisting largely of a large white sausage-shaped tank was backing down the ramp from the street, scattering nests of rats and pissing off seagulls. Suddenly there were weary-looking Maxes and Vladimirs all over the place. In block letters that could be seen from space, the truck was labeled LIQUID NITROGEN. Ah, of course: liquid nitrogen, aka LN2. After Tristan's brief, disgustingly cheerful exchange with the driver, hoses were connected between his truck and some storage tanks that, in my absence, had been crudely bolted into the concrete walls of the building. Impressive whining noises came from a thing that, I was informed, was a cryogenic pump. When the LN2 first hit the warm innards of the storage tanks, there was an amount of hissing that defied description, unless you have ever heard all of the bacon in Iowa being dropped onto a red-hot griddle the size of Delaware. With that was a concomitant amount of milky, chilly fog. Tristan grabbed me by the arm and dragged me out of the building. "Non-toxic," he assured me, "but—"

"But I need oxygen."

"Yeah. I knew I liked you, Stokes."

"Is this why the ODEC contains life support equipment?"

He shrugged modestly. "There are certain failure modes," he said, "such as freezing to death and asphyxiating, that come naturally to mind when we are getting ready to lock human subjects in a sealed chamber completely surrounded by cryogenic fluids chilled to within four degrees of absolute zero."

That initial spasm of hissing and fog production was because the walls of the tank were at room temperature. Once they had been chilled down, the pumping of the LN2 continued with no more drama than if it had been tap water. The fog dissipated and Tristan made a decision, which I assumed was science-based, that it was safe to go back inside. I followed him through the loading dock doors, past the tanks, and all the way to the door of the ODEC, which now stood ajar. I took a small step up to stand on its threshold, and had a look around.

Every square inch of the cavity's interior surfaces, including its floor and ceiling, had now been tiled with circuit boards: plates of green plastic covered with fine traceries of orange-red copper and studded with electronic components. Most of these were the tiny black rectangles of integrated circuits, but there were also LEDs blinking in a range of colors. Dangling from the ceiling by their hoses was a pair of oxygen masks—part of the life support equipment, clearly: should helium leak into the cavity and displace the breathable air, its occupants could pull these down and strap them over their faces. (I was never a hard-science chick, but my high school chemistry teacher near enough resembled Orlando Bloom that I had diligently aced the class.)

Still balanced on the raised threshold, I turned around to look out the ODEC door into the space surrounding the chamber. Where the head of the conference table had formerly stood was a control console, attached to the ODEC by a large plastic pipe, channeling gouts of cables. Above it, a cable ladder from the server room disgorged a waterfall of Ethernet cables and fiber-optic lines. Seated at the console, running through some kind of checklist on an iPad, was the probably-Korean Max. Oda-sensei and his wife, Rebecca, were watching over his shoulder.

"Wow," I said from the threshold.

"Right?" chirped Tristan happily. Somewhat unnecessarily, he extended a hand to assist me back down to the floor. "The professor is *giddy*. Tell him he should throw the switch."

"It is your project," Oda-sensei said peaceably, sipping coffee from a blue thermos. "The honor should be yours."

"It was your project first! We've been arguing about this all week," said Tristan to me with a grin. "You call it, Stokes."

I called it in favor of Oda, and Tristan saluted him with a flourish more Renaissance than military. Tristan then closed the ODEC door and engaged several massive mechanical latches.

With a childish, nervous smile, Oda-sensei handed off the thermos to Rebecca, then responded to Tristan with a gesture something between a nod and a bow. Console Max stood up, stepped back from the console, and made a similar gesture, inviting him to sit down. Oda, with a little *don't mind if I do* smile, took the Seat of Authority behind the console and pulled on a communications headset.

There was one moment of potent, expectant stillness. *What a thrill this must be for him*, I remember thinking. I was desperately curious. The enormousness of it far exceeded my urgency to discuss Erszebet Karpathy.

"Exterior vent ports open," Oda intoned.

I had no idea what he was talking about until I heard the familiar rumble and groan of the loading dock door being hauled up. "Check," shouted a Max. He was echoed by another Max who had just opened the door that fronted the street.

"Atmospheric exchange augmentation systems to full power," Oda said.

Tristan darted over to a white plastic window fan—one of a pallet load of such that we had acquired from Home Depot—and turned it on full blast. I saw now that several more were scattered around the room. Feeling a desire to be part of this momentous occasion, I turned on all that were in reach.

"Check!" Tristan called, when all of them were spinning. I could hear a much larger, industrial-sized fan humming out by the loading dock, and another "Check!" from that quarter.

"Burst disks and pressure relief valves are all green," said Oda, glancing at his display. "Initiating cryogenic chill-down sequence in three . . . two . . . one . . ."

Cryogenic pumps began to hum, and a few seconds later we heard the sizzle and hiss of liquid nitrogen coming into contact with room-temperature plumbing. The idea was simple enough, now that I understood what was happening: we needed to pump the LN2 from the big storage tanks by the loading dock, through piping that the Maxes had installed, to the gap between the ODEC's inner and outer vessels. But since the plumbing and the vessels alike were currently warmer than the boiling point of LN2, the liquid was going to boil off at first, until everything got chilled down. As before, clouds of milky, chilly fog spilled out of valves all over the facility. But the "atmospheric exchange augmentation systems" did a good job of pushing it out the "exterior vent ports." Outside of these—as we could all tell by checking surveillance monitors that had been racked up on the half-shattered remnant of a nearby wall—several Lukes were standing guard to make sure that random people didn't just wander in off the street. The Lukes had begun showing up a couple of days ago; they were big, beefy, taciturn, and dressed in rent-a-cop uniforms devoid of insignia. They seemed to think Tristan was cool.

The cryogenic drama lessened as (one inferred) the plumbing and vessels became super-cold, and then we could hear the fluid level rising between the ODEC's inner and outer walls. Oda had purchased a large number of cheap digital thermometers from Home Depot and duct-taped them all over the place, and it was fun, for a while, to see their readings plummet into triple-digit negative numbers.

"How much farther?" I asked Tristan, during a lull.

"To what?" he inquired.

"To absolute zero."

He shook his head. "Not going there today."

"I thought that was the whole point."

"Don't pout. This is a dry run. With LN2. Which costs less than milk. If it works we'll source the liquid helium and do it for real."

"Vessel is full. Hatch is full. Both holding steady," Oda announced. "Confirming criticality in lower magnet ring."

"Criticality? Sounds very MLA," I said.

"MLA?"

"Modern Language Association."

Tristan sighed. "He just means that the magnets in the bottom-most ring have now been cold enough, long enough, that they have dropped through their TC—their critical temperature—and become superconducting." He seemed mildly offended by my quip.

"Ah, so that's the purpose of the dry run," I said.

"Yeah. Until all of the magnet rings go superconducting, we can't even turn the ODEC on in any meaningful sense of the word."

This at least gave me something to watch. The vessels, of course, had filled from the bottom up, and so the magnets on the bottom had spent a longer time exposed to cryogenic tempera-tures. From bottom to top, there were thirty-two distinct rings of little magnets, each of which completely encircled the cavity—the ODEC's inner vessel. The rings were stacked one above the next, spanning the full height of the cavity. The Maxes had mounted an LED on each ring. It was red when the magnets were warm, but turned blue when they had gone superconducting. Over the course of a couple of minutes we enjoyed the simple but weirdly exciting spectacle of watching that column of LEDs turn from red to blue, from the bottom to the top.

"We have full criticality," Oda announced when the upper-most one turned blue.

I had found myself standing next to Rebecca. On an impulse, I turned toward her and raised my hand, palm facing out. Startled by the movement, she swiveled her head to place me under her blue-eyed gaze. It was like staring into a couple of those LEDs.

It occurred to me that she might not recognize the gesture. "High five?" I said weakly. She looked away as if hoping that the whole regrettable incident could be forgotten.

Meanwhile her husband was busy. "Internal sensor calibration matrix has been computed and flashed to embedded firmware. Ready to boot the renormalization feedback loop, Vladimirs?"

"Check!" shouted a Vladimir from the server room.

"Booting it," Oda said, and reached out toward one of the very few mechanical switches on the console. It was military hardware, eBayed (Tristan boasted) from some collector of Cold War electrical components. It had a protective cover that had to be flipped up out of the way to provide access to the switch itself, imbuing it with more ceremony.

I nearly suffered a heart attack after Oda snapped the switch to "on": an alarm Klaxon began to sound and it happened to be mounted directly above my head. I jammed my hands over my ears and pivoted away from it; Rebecca was doing the same, in mirror image. At the same time the room lights dimmed, flickered, and went out, prompting battery-powered red emergency lights to switch on. I tripped over a discarded fire extinguisher and staggered a couple of paces, finally breaking my fall by colliding with a rolling coatrack that had been set up to one side of the console. This had been stocked, for some reason, with a row of snowmobile suits in various sizes and colors. They were soft, and cushioned my fall as I knocked the whole thing over and went down onto the floor. It must have made a loud noise. No one noticed because of the Klaxon.

Tristan was either a perfect gentleman or no gentleman at all. At the moment he was too fascinated by goings-on surrounding the ODEC to know that I had taken a pratfall. Probably just as well. I clambered to my feet and reached into my pocket, where I'd got in the habit of stowing a pair of foam earplugs. Recently I had been using them when operating power saws, but they were just what I needed now.

Tristan signaled Oda to switch the power off. The Klaxon went silent. The room lights flickered back—this took a few moments, since one of the Vladimirs had to run to the electrical panel and flip a number of circuit breakers back on. The collective excitement of the room palpably dissipated. So much drama, so many sound and visual effects, for—what?

"Anything?" Tristan inquired.

"The data loggers inside the cavity all went dead. Completely zorched, as far as I can tell," Oda said. The words sounded like bad news but his tone of voice implied fascination.

"So we don't even know if anything happened in there."

"Something friggin' happened," insisted the most long-bearded of the Vladimirs, who had just stormed in from the server room. "While that thing was on, we ran a ridiculous amount of data through our servers."

"How much?" I asked.

He looked exasperated. "Enough that I could make up some kind of strained analogy involving the contents of the Library of Congress and the number of pixels in all of the *Lord of the Rings* movies put together and how many phone calls the NSA intercepts in a single day and you would be like, 'Holy shit, that's a lot.'"

"Holy shit, that's a lot!" I exclaimed dutifully.

"And as to the amount of computational processing performed on that data, using Professor Oda's algorithms—well—same basic story."

"Fantastic," I purred.

"I believe you," Tristan said, "it's just that we don't appear to have any data on what actually happened in there."

"Confirmed," Oda said. "The renormalization loop appears to interfere with normal functioning of the sensor package we left inside."

"That's exactly as it should be—right?" I said.

"Could be," Tristan said, "or could be it just went on the fritz. We are blind in there. No real way to know if it's working."

"Maybe if we had a cat," the professor said.

"Maybe if we *go inside*," said Tristan. Rebecca made a disapproving sound under her breath as the Maxes and Vladimirs made anticipatory sounds under theirs.

Oda shook his head. "A cat is one thing. But I'm not going in there."

"I'll go," said Tristan.

"It's your funeral," muttered Rebecca, as if to herself, and paced away from the console table.

Tristan turned to look at her, and then at Oda. "Does she mean that literally?" And to Rebecca: "Do you mean that literally?"

Oda answered before she could. "It won't kill you. But . . . you will not enjoy it. The cat certainly didn't."

Tristan waved this away dismissively. "As long as it's not lethal, I'm going in." And then with an inviting grin: "Want to come with me, Stokes?"

Flattered as I was that he considered me a peer in this undertaking, and eager as I was to know what would come of it, I thought of the cat. "Next time," I said.

"Internal temp of the cavity?" Tristan asked.

"Twenty-three below zero, Celsius, and holding," reported Console Max.

"Gotta get better insulation," Tristan muttered. He pivoted and made for the rolling coatrack, which was still all kinds of messy on the floor. I stiffened, awaiting a reprimand, but he didn't even seem to notice that it had been knocked over. He found the end of the pile where the larger snowmobile suits had ended up, pulled one out, and stepped into it. "We still go? Everything nominal?"

Half a dozen different Maxes and Vladimirs hollered out "Check!" from various parts of the building.

Tristan zipped up the suit. In a side pocket he found a balaclava, which he pulled on over his head. I helped him yank it around until his eyes were shining out from the oval hole. He gave me a wink and then pulled on a pair of bulky mittens while striding toward the ODEC door. Oda hauled it open for him, then appeared to regret this gesture as the cold burned his hand.

Tristan stepped over the threshold, displacing a column of air that turned cloudy as it spilled out into the room.

A torso flew out and did an end-over-end bounce across the floor, shedding batteries and thumb drives. It was the upper half of a store mannequin that we had instrumented with sensors. Tristan had tossed it out.

Having thus made room for himself, Tristan sat down on the wooden stool we'd put in there to support the mannequin. Providing a bit of padding under his bum was the cat-hair-saturated cushion from the Mark I; Rebecca had moved it to the Mark II to supply a feeling of continuity. He reached out, pawed at the door, and closed it behind him. The Maxes exchanged expectant glances. Rebecca rubbed the space between her eyebrows and paced silently. Oda-sensei resumed his position at the control panel. He reached out and flipped up the protective cover on the switch. Rebecca stuck her fingers in her ears.

For a few moments we all stood at rigid attention, our eyes on Oda's finger. Then he flicked the switch. Again the lights went out and the Klaxon came on. He checked his wristwatch and let the machine run for fifteen long seconds. Then he flicked the switch back off and gently replaced the cover.

Tristan walked out of the ODEC, pulling off the balaclava and shaking his head as if he had swimmer's ear. He saw all of our party staring at him, and he stared back a moment, frowning.

"That was unpleasant," he reported gruffly. "Like being in a Russian disco. But that's all."

"I'm glad you're all right," I said. "But . . ." And I thought better of saying more.

"But it would have been cooler if you had to carry me out strapped to a back board. I know," Tristan said ruefully. "Vladimir? Got anything for me?"

The Vladimir with red hair was strolling carefully into the space, kicking fire extinguishers and empty Red Bull cans out of his way while studying an iPad. "Preliminary diagnostics suggest a large number of wedged processes. Probably a bug we can fix overnight."

"What does that mean?"

"The ODEC was running at maybe one percent efficiency."

"Sounds like you have a long night ahead of you, then," Tristan said.

Diachronicle
DAY 291

In which we become decoherent

WHEN I ARRIVED THE NEXT morning, Frank Oda was already there, and with him—arms crossed, slightly pacing—Rebecca. Two of the Vladimirs were lying on the server room floor asleep. Longbeard was in our little kitchen, supporting himself on his elbows and gazing fixedly into a cup of coffee.

On Tristan's cue we all resumed the places we had occupied for the previous day's failed experiment. The vessels had remained filled with liquid nitrogen overnight, so there was no need to repeat the chill-down process. Tristan donned his snowmobile suit—it would be just about freezing in the chamber itself—and gave us all a grin and a thumbs-up signal, before walking into the ODEC and closing the door behind himself.

Oda-sensei seated himself at the console and ran through the checks, then flipped the switch. Someone had zip-tied a blanket over the Klaxon to dampen the volume. The surge of electricity sent shivers down my spine. *Something* was about to happen now. I'd no idea what, but I knew that it was history in the making, and I was present for it and not grading papers, and that was *extremely* satisfying.

For fifteen seconds, Oda watched, frozen, and we all watched him. Then he shut it down. In the silence that followed we could hear the Vladimirs celebrating.

Tristan exited the ODEC clutching the sides of his head and staggering drunkenly in his snowsuit. On instinct I moved toward him to steady him, but he veered away from me and collapsed, kneeling, to the floor, looking dazed.

"Yeah, we're, um, we're getting, eh, closer," he said in a distracted voice, peeling off the balaclava, and then yawned. He looked up at Oda-sensei. "Did I fall asleep? How long was I there for?"

"Fifteen seconds," said the professor, surprised.

Tristan shook his head and slapped his cheek a few times. "Well, we're onto *something*, then—whatever happened to me the first time, *lots* more of it happened this time." He grimaced and tried to shake it off.

Journal Entry of
Rebecca East-Oda
MAY 15

Temperature 66F, bright sun. Barometer falling.

Peppers and chard germinated. Lilies of the valley in full bloom. Lilacs at peak. Swapped out storm windows for screens (finally).

Work on the new ODEC continues, and has become the sole topic of discourse in the house. Frank is just as obsessed as he was the first time. I read over my diary from back then, and must remind myself that this time at least he is working with a willing and supportive cohort (besides me, I mean). Jury still out for me re: Tristan. Prefer Melisande but she's not in charge. (Not clear if their relationship is personal or just professional. Not sure they're clear either.)

The schedule has been extended by two days to accommodate upgrades to the software, and improvements to the building's electrical service. Whomever Tristan works for takes him seriously; Frank faced endless red tape whenever he requisitioned *extension cords*, for heaven's sake.

Two concerns regarding this project, besides the obvious reservations.

First: Tristan insists on being inside the ODEC while it is in operation. He can't understand how that makes him the observed, not the observer. Uncle Victor's Labrador retriever is in charge.

Second: Frank—satisfied to be working on the physics—turns a blind eye to the supposed application. Magic. There are Powers That Be who take the Magic premise seriously enough to buy Tristan a building and send him tanker trucks of liquid helium without any paperwork. Hard to reconcile this with common sense. Frank heedless.

Also, Mel is concerned about a woman who contacted her claiming she can do magic. T&M's rendezvous with this woman has been delayed several times, and the woman is becoming verbally abusive. This does not stop them from intending to meet her, which will possibly happen tomorrow after the next ODEC go-round.

Diachronicle
DAY 294

In which we become even more decoherent

TWO DAYS LATER, WHEN THE liquid helium showed up in the unmarked stainless steel tanker truck, Tristan velcroed and zipped himself into a snowmobile suit, gave us the thumbs-up, and stepped up into the ODEC, where, just for safety's sake, he pulled on an oxygen mask. Apparently liquid helium was adept at finding and seeping through the tiniest leaks, so the cavity might fill up with helium and asphyxiate him before he knew it was happening. Once again, Oda walked around the building going through his checklist, and took his place before the console. By now, our expectancy was tempered by experience.

Liquid helium, as I now knew, was fifty times as expensive as the liquid nitrogen we had been using, and a lot colder. Nitrogen became a liquid at 77 degrees above absolute zero (the point at which atoms would stop moving, if such a state could be reached), but to do the same trick with helium you had to chill it all the way down to a mere 4 degrees. By the standards of the normal human world, it was a distinction without a difference—both were very, very cold. But to scientists like Oda, there was a world of difference between 4 degrees and 77. The liquid helium jacketing the ODEC would have radically different properties from LN2—properties explainable in terms of Bose-Einstein statistics, an advanced concept in quantum mechanics that Tristan barely understood and I couldn't make sense of at all. The gist of it seemed to be that the liquid helium would cloak the inner cavity of the ODEC inside a seamless jacket of matter, all of which was in the same quantum state. This was supposed to have some effect of isolating the cavity from the rest of the universe quantum-mechanically, and greatly intensifying its effects.

Cold as they were, the plumbing and the vessels were still boiling hot by liquid helium standards, and so after the LN2 had been pumped out we had to go through another cycle of "atmospheric exchange augmentation" out the "exterior vent ports" before the system settled down. The digital thermometers began to read dramatically lower temperatures.

Once the system had stabilized at 4 degrees above absolute zero—negative 269 degrees Celsius—Oda flipped the switch. This time he let the system run for only five seconds before turning it back off.

Tristan stumbled out of the ODEC, tugging convulsively at the oxygen mask. The balaclava came off with it. He was ashen-faced, and looked as if he might be sick. He stumbled dizzily and then collapsed to his knees barely beyond the threshold of the chamber.

"Tristan!" I cried, as Oda knelt down to help him, but Tristan pushed him away and looked around at us all, dazed and yet wild-eyed.

"Where am I?" he asked. "Is this a dream or are we really here?"

"We're really here," said Oda gently.

"Are we in Boston?" asked Tristan, and groaned. "God, what a terrible headache. Where's Mom?"

I looked at Oda in alarm. "Give him a moment," he said reassuringly.

"What just happened to him?" I demanded, not reassured.

"I think he's just very disoriented."

"Isn't it five minutes ago?" said Tristan. "Don't I have to go into the ODEC before we can have this conversation?"

"Somebody get him a glass of water," said Oda to the room in general. And then gently: "Tristan, close your eyes for a few moments, you'll be fine."

Oda gestured me to step away, and I followed him, but my concern and attention remained on Tristan. He was now very still, glancing around at his surroundings with eyes only, as if trying to avoid vertigo. It seemed horribly wrong for Tristan Lyons to be so vulnerable.

"Is this what happened to the cat?" I demanded of Oda.

"Well, you can't have a conversation with a cat. When I'd open the cavity, he would leap out in full Halloween mode. But I'd leave him, come back down an hour later, and he'd be fast asleep. When he woke up, you'd think nothing had happened. I repeated the experiment a few times, and the cat never seemed to remember what he was about to be subjected to. But then Rebecca saw and made me stop."

Journal Entry of

Rebecca East-Oda

MAY 18

Temperature about 64F, moist, no breeze. Barometer rising. Flowers and vegetables fending for themselves due to ODEC activity.

To begin, this morning the new ODEC was "successful," insofar as Tristan came out of it in the same state the cat once used to come out of the old ODEC. Melisande kept her head better than I did when I first saw the cat, but was clearly concerned. The following conversation, more or less:

FRANK: I predict Tristan will be fine shortly. But I don't think we should allow anyone to go into the ODEC until we have figured out how to protect them from that effect.

MEL: What is the effect? Why is it happening?

FRANK: He is teetering on the edge of becoming non-local.

MEL: Non-*what*?

FRANK: His brain was suddenly not sure which precise reality it was operating in—and perhaps his body too. So much to discover still! (*NB: sounding like an eager child. Sounding as if none of it happened thirty years ago.*)

Five minutes pass

TRISTAN (*fully recovered*): Why didn't you take notes of what I said when I first came out?

MEL: Trust me, you said absolutely nothing noteworthy.

TRISTAN: That just sounds like your usual lip. I need corroboration.

FRANK: We were all here. She's right.

TRISTAN: You do it, Stokes, so I can see what happens when you come out.

MEL: I don't think so. Seriously, it was as if you'd gotten plastered at a frat party.

TRISTAN: Sounds like fun. Give it a go.

FRANK: I really don't think that you should push her—
  (interrupted by)

TRISTAN: She could use a little loosening up. Come on, Stokes, it's a hazard of the job.

MEL: I fail to see how "becoming non-local" falls within the parameters of my contractual obligations as a translator of dead languages.

TRISTAN: It falls within the parameters of your wanting to know what it's like.

MEL: Apparently it's like being drunk. Been there, done that.

TRISTAN: Y'know, you could be stuck in your tiny little office right now, grading papers about Aramaic declensions. Get your butt in there. Somebody get her a snowsuit. With a balaclava. And an oxygen mask.

I wish that had been the end of the nonsense. It was barely the beginning.

Diachronicle
DAY 294 (CONTD.)

NINETY MINUTES LATER, DESPITE MY own best judgment, I was geared up and ready to begin the most ill-considered experiment of my life (to that point, I mean. *Clearly* I have engaged in more boneheaded enterprises since then, else I would not currently be sitting here trying not to spill ink on my borrowed day dress.).

I hope it does not reflect badly on me to admit that I would have refused obstinately were I not so keen to please Tristan. A ridiculous impulse, given that he seemed to treat me as if I were his personal R2-D2 (which was still preferable to Blevins's modus operandi). But there was something about his relentless, focused clarity of purpose that made all things else fade in significance—including my own mental balance. I submit that I was not falling in love with him, but there was inarguably an intellectual seduction at work. He operated on my psyche the way a lively Mozart sonata might.

And so, suited up to look like a cartoon character, I toddled into the ODEC. It was frigid inside, and my breath came out in clouds until I put the oxygen mask on. The cavity had a cool, clinical feel with all those LEDs staring at me. I felt as if I were on the set of a half-assed low-budget sci-fi flick. "All right," I said with a purposeful nod, and the door closed. I could feel my pulse at my temples, hear my breath amplified within the mask. It was frightening and exhilarating and I had never felt so alive! Blevins could eat my shorts.

I cannot describe what happened next, because I do not remember. Immediately, it seemed, I found myself in a very bland, undecorated office, in a hard plastic chair near a Formica table under ugly fluorescent lights, shaking uncontrollably for no good reason. I was not cold or scared, simply . . . confused. And exhausted.

"Fascinating," said a very handsome fellow about my age, with dazzling green eyes and neat, close-cropped hair, who was standing over me and contemplating me with a grin. "If that's what you were like when *you* got drunk in college, no wonder you don't have a boyfriend."

"Give her a few moments," I heard an older, softer male voice say. I knew that voice had a name attached to it—Yoda? No, Yoda was from *Star Wars*. *Star Wars* was on my mind because of R2-D2. And the fellow in front of me, I had seen him brushing his teeth before, so if he wasn't my boyfriend maybe he was a brother I'd forgotten about.

He began to laugh. "Stokes," he said, "you're saying all of that out loud. I wouldn't speak until you feel like yourself. But hurry up with it!" He leaned closer and whispered into my ear, "We've got our witch vault. Let's go get our witch."

Diachronicle

DAY 294 (CONTD.)

In which we meet Erszebet. And then we meet Erszebet.

FIRST TRISTAN HAD TO BREAK the news to the Maxes and the Vladimirs that they had been working all this time on a project whose end goal was magic. He did this in the one remaining non-demolished office, so I didn't have the satisfaction of seeing it happen. They seemed to me to be biting back amusement when they filed out of the briefing: to a man, they all avoided direct eye contact and the corners of their pursed lips occasionally wiggled.

Tristan and I arrived at 420 Common Street in Belmont in earliest afternoon, to find—to our dismay—a desanctified church converted into some kind of institutional group housing. WELCOME TO ELM HOUSE read a non-elucidating pastel-blue plastic sign planted in the forecourt.

"Hmm," I said.

"Could be interesting," said Tristan. "Could mean someone's messing with us."

We parked on the street and followed the walkway around the side of the old church and across a modest lawn dotted with generic, dutiful landscaping. The old church had been built on a very large lot, much of which was now occupied by three- and four-story buildings with a decidedly mid-twentieth-century institutional vibe. The main entrance was in one of those. The inside was bland and sterile, like a hospital admitting room. There was a linoleum lobby floor and laminate receiving desk, where two bored thirty-something women chatted quietly and ignored the handful of elders beyond them, in a carpeted room full of primary-color bingo charts and large posters of MGM movie stars.

"At least it's not a loony bin," Tristan muttered, relieved.

All of the residents were either asleep, or muttering to themselves despondently, or staring up at a very loud screening of *The African Queen*. It smelled of old furniture in here, and disinfectants.

As we stepped into the lobby, a twig of an ancient woman, keen-featured and remarkably upright, immediately approached us. She was wearing a 1950s-style cocktail dress, which might have flattered her in the 1950s, but looked absurd on her now. She was clutching a large Versace knockoff bag under one arm.

Before I even had the presence of mind to greet her, she spoke in a hushed but furious tone, with a well-educated Eastern European accent: "I cannot *believe* how long you have kept me waiting, Melisande! It is *very* rude and after all this time I deserve better. I see you cut your hair. It looked better long. With those bangs you resemble a rodent."

I stopped so abruptly that Tristan bumped into me. He began to say something, but she pushed ahead before he could: "You must be Mr. Tristan Lyons. Are you her lover?"

"Did she say I was?" Tristan asked immediately, which was a pretty good recovery.

The old woman made a dismissive *tch*. "No. Only she is a woman of unreliable morals, and you have a powerful secret government position, so I presumed."

"Ma'am, how about we talk in private," Tristan said. "You've cited a few things that raise security questions."

"Of *course* we talk in private. You're taking me to the ODEC—this instant."

Tristan took her skinny arm in his large hand and stood over her, his chin a hand-span above the top of her head. "Ma'am," he asked very softly, "where did you hear that term?"

"From *her*," she said impatiently, poking me in the shoulder.

"I have never met this woman," I said to Tristan, recoiling from her, and then to her: "I have never met you."

"Not yet, but you will," she retorted impatiently. "I am Erszebet Karpathy. It is absolutely time to get out of here and go to the ODEC. I dressed specially." She gestured to her cocktail dress. "Do you know *how long* I have been waiting for this day?"

"Ma'am," said Tristan. It seemed he was stalling for time until he could form a complete sentence. "How long have you been waiting?"

"*Far* too long," she said.

"Her first post to me on Facebook was a month ago," I offered.

"You've been waiting a month?" asked Tristan.

"*Pft*," she said. "That's because I got tired of waiting for you to find me. I joined Facebook as soon as it was available to the public, as you told me to."

A pause as Tristan considered this. "You're saying you've been waiting more than a decade for us to come and find you?"

"Ha!" It was a dry, humorless sound. "I have been waiting for more than one century and a half. And this woman"—she pressed on, before we could interrupt incredulously—"gives me the words *Facebook* and *Tristan Lyons* and *ODEC* and tells me this, now, *this* is the exact month to use those words to find you after so much time. So. We have found each other. Take me to the ODEC."

Tristan nudged his shoulder against my back, encouraging me to speak. Was it possible he was speechless? And did he expect me to be less so than himself? "Why are you so eager to get to the ODEC?" I asked.

"Because I can do magic again in the ODEC," she said impatiently. "*Obviously*."

Tristan frowned at her. "Ma'am, I need you to know that if this is your idea of a joke, you're making trouble for yourself. If somebody has put you up to saying these words, I need to know who it is, and why—"

"Her! It's her!" she said irritably, jabbing her bony little finger into my shoulder again. "I would be dead right now except for her. I have stayed alive all these years because she commanded it."

"Ma'am, I've never *met* you—" I protested again.

"Don't you call me ma'am, you hussy! You're older than I am."

She checked herself, with obvious effort. "That is, you *were*. When we met. I have now been old for longer than most people have been alive. Do you know how boring that is?"

Tristan had collected himself enough to play the polite West Point cadet card. "We'd love to relieve your boredom, ma'am. Let's step outside and you can tell us the whole story, how about that?" he said. "Do we have to sign you out or something?"

"*Pft*," she harrumphed, with a dismissive gesture toward the reception desk. "Nurse Ratched has given up trying to control me."

"Which one is she?" Tristan glanced toward the desk.

"Tristan!" I said. "Come on. My not knowing DARPA *pales* compared to your not knowing Nurse Ratched."

"I call all of them Nurse Ratched since the movie came out," Erszebet was meanwhile saying. "It amuses me."

"You've been here since *One Flew Over the Cuckoo's Nest* came out?" I asked.

"Yes. Do you see why I want to leave? Boring."

"Let's get her outside," muttered Tristan.

It was cool outside, and nobody else was out there. The uninspired landscaped path wended its way around groupings of wrought iron benches, at which the residents might have a modicum of privacy with guests. Erszebet, with a remarkable grace of movement, seated herself in the center of one bench, leaving me and Tristan to share the one across from her, squinting into the bright spring sunlight.

"This is where people argue with their children about their inheritance," she informed us. "I have no children, so I do not have this problem."

"If you will, ma'am, let's start from the top," suggested Tristan. "Name, date of birth, place of birth, basic background."

She sat pertly upright and gave him a self-important look. "You will take notes?"

He tapped his head. "Mental notes, for now. Begin, please."

"I am Erszebet Karpathy," she said. "I was born in Budapest in 1832."

"No," said Tristan. "No you weren't, ma'am. That's absurd."

She glared at him, and seemed to relish doing so. "Do not disrespect me. I am a witch. When magic was fading from the world, Melisande warned me that it would end soon, and the last magic I ever knew was a spell to slow my aging by as much as possible so that I would still be here, now, when we could be useful to each other. I did not want to do that, you know," she went on, directly to me. "I could have just grown old and died. Death would have been less boring than surviving this last century. This is a *terrible* country for old people. You put them away in horrible buildings that are completely shut off from life, and then do everything possible to keep them alive. It is a *very* stupid system. You should all be shot. Nevertheless," she pressed on, when we failed to agree or even respond, "here I am. And here you are. So put me in your automobile and take me to the ODEC. I am very eager to do magic again."

Tristan rubbed his face with both hands as if he were suddenly very tired. "Give me a moment, ma'am," he said. He pulled out his phone. "How do you spell your name?"

"If you Google me, you will be disappointed," she said. "I know how to keep my profile low, as you say."

"I use a different search engine," he said. "You'll be on it. Just spell your name, please."

The only Erszebet Karpathy in Tristan's secret search engine was a thirty-seven-year-old aerialist turned legal clerk, currently living in Montreal. There was an Erszebet Karpaty living in Rome, but she was a madam, and anyhow our interlocutor sneered that the name without an *h* was Ukrainian, which she *most certainly* wasn't.

"Then maybe Erszebet Karpathy is not your real name," said Tristan. "Ma'am."

"Can we go now?" she said, standing up. "I have been thinking about my first spell for decades, and I am very eager to perform it. And then I want to go roller-skating. They won't allow that here, those toads."

Tristan remained seated, and leaned against me to signal me to do likewise. "And what spell might that be?"

She grinned at him. "You'll just have to see. It's *entirely* beneficent, if that's what you're worried about. We go."

"The ODEC doesn't work yet," he said, studying her face carefully. "Since you claim to know about it, maybe you can help with that."

"You need to up the sampling rate on the internal sensors," recited Erszebet smugly, in a triumphant tone, as if she'd just won a spelling bee.

Wow, I thought.

Testing her, Tristan replied, "It's going to be hard pushing that much data down the leads."

"Swap the twisted pair out for fiber," she rejoined promptly. It was a recitation; something she had memorized the way a child memorizes "indivisible" in the Pledge of Allegiance.

"All right, let's go," said Tristan, standing up and again putting his large hand around her tiny arm. "The car's right there, and you are not leaving my sight until I understand what you're up to."

"*Thank* you," she said. "*Finally.*"

She did not say a word on the twenty-minute drive from Belmont to Central Square, merely stared out the window with the bored rapture of a dog or a baby. I used the silence to recollect myself. Everything this woman claimed seemed insane, and yet . . . she knew me by sight, she knew Tristan by name, she knew about the ODEC . . .

To accept her claims meant . . . it meant we were about to witness genuine magic performed for the first time in at least one hundred and seventy years. *That rocks!* I thought. That was *much* more exciting than going to New Orleans. I glanced at Tristan as he drove, but he was lost in his own thoughts, which seemed grumpier than mine.

When we pulled up in front of the building, Erszebet sighed heavily. "This is it? *Pah*, I thought it might be a *nice* place," she said from the backseat. "This is worse than where I have been living."

"It won't be as boring," I promised.

"That's true," she said with a sudden grin, and leaned forward to tap my shoulder. "I am *very* much looking forward to this." Then to Tristan: "I think you will be pleased with the results, Mr. Tristan Lyons."

"I'm certainly looking forward to seeing what happens, ma'am," he said tersely.

I realized he was nervous. For what would happen if after all this, we found the world's only surviving witch and she was a dud? He still wouldn't tell me who he was answering to, but his derrière was on the line in a way mine wasn't.

When we entered the building, I walked toward the professor and his wife, gesturing for Erszebet to join me, but she spared them only a brief glance, then waved dismissively in their direction and gazed at the large contraption taking up most of the space.

"Is this it?" she asked Tristan, sounding offended. "But it's so *ugly*."

"She's a little preoccupied," I said apologetically to Oda-sensei and Rebecca. They, in turn, were so fascinated by her appearance that they hardly noticed my speaking to them. Likewise, the Maxes stopped their sundry duties and paused to look at her sideways, nudging each other's shoulders and murmuring between themselves. She took no interest in any of that.

"This?" she demanded again. "I go in here and I can do magic? Just like that?"

"Hang on a moment," said Tristan, pulling out his phone. "I need to document you, since there's no record of your existence. I need your signature and a photo." Before she could object or even notice, he snapped a photo of her on his phone.

"You don't need my signature," she said. She stared at the ODEC with a rapture greater even than Oda-sensei's, face aglow with anticipation. "I forgive its ugliness if it does its job well. I just go in and start doing spells again?"

"That's what we're hoping," said Tristan.

She looked at me, her eyes dewy and bright. "Thank you, Melisande, *thank you* for bringing me here." And back her attention went to the ODEC door.

"Hang on," said Tristan as she approached it. "Let me explain what happens when it's activated." He opened the door with an oven mitt and gestured inside—we could all hear her expressions of surprise—and then he leaned in close to her, voice calm and businesslike, detailing what was to come.

The Odas, the Maxes, and I looked round at each other with various facial expressions, all of which were a way of saying, in silence, *Holy shit.* "This is really happening," I said, my pulse dancing. Seeing Tristan and a witch standing at the ODEC door suddenly made my heart thrill. But for him, I at this moment would be grading worksheets on syntax.

I sashayed over to them. "Should we put her in the ski suit?" I asked Tristan.

"I need no protection from the forces that restore my magic to me," Erszebet scoffed.

"But it will be cold in there, like Siberia—"

"*Pft*," she said. "It will be invigorating."

"It might invigorate you to death," warned Tristan.

She made a face that had already, in the last forty minutes, become her signature look: a dismissive pout with contemptuously knitted brows, head tilted slightly to one side, and a brief subtle eye roll. I suppose on another sort of face—a sexy villainess from a silent movie, perhaps—it would have had a sultry quality, but on a centenarian it just looked silly.

"I am strong in ways you do not know," she assured him.

Tristan and I exchanged looks. I felt myself increasingly thrilled that this was happening, and impressed with Tristan's unflappable calm (although it is true his face was proverbially shining with excitement). "Stokes, suit up and be in here with her, will you?"

"Do not call her Stokes, that is disrespectful." Erszebet scowled. "You are a disrespectful man. You called me a liar before. Do not get on my bad side. You will regret it. But"—and here she turned to me with a smile no less fierce than her scowl—"I agree for Melisande to be with me for the first spell. It is fitting. She was the cause of the last spell."

Tristan and I exchanged confused looks, without commentary.

"Tell us about this first spell of yours," Tristan requested.

She shrugged offhandedly as she set her bag on the console and riffled through it. "It is nothing, it is very simple. I must simply undo an earlier spell, that's all. Then I can begin doing what you ask of me. Hurry, Melisande."

I left the chamber to find the snowsuit, donned it, and re-entered the ODEC pulling on the oxygen mask. Erszebet regarded me, appalled. She was fidgeting with something I could not see well—

through the shield of the mask it looked like she was massaging a mop head. Before I had a chance to ask her about it, she was onto Tristan again:

"You make her dress like that?" she said to him. "I don't like you at all."

"It's for her own protection," he said tersely. He had stopped calling her "ma'am."

Erszebet (in her outsized vintage cocktail dress) and I (in my snowsuit, balaclava, and oxygen mask) stood beside each other as Tristan, just outside the ODEC, raised his thumb and closed the door on us. There was a brief wait as Oda and the Maxes and Vladimirs went through their checklists. I glanced at the old lady across from me and felt an extraordinary combination of sentiments all at once—excitement, disbelief, anticipation, confusion, fear, hope. Had anyone told me this would be how my spring were to unfold, I'd have ~~laughed my ass off at them~~ scoffed. Seriously.

I remember what happened for about the next quarter second: the dim sound of the Klaxon outside, the hair standing up on the back of my neck, the lights going out. In that precise moment, a lovely aroma both floral and musky overwhelmed me, and then—as before—I lost all clarity, and the next thing I was aware of was somebody peeling a balaclava off my head. I was lying supine in a vaguely familiar office, my back propped up against that somebody's knees.

"Stokes? You okay?"

I took a moment to think about this. Only the fellow from the shadowy government entity called me Stokes, so this must be him. His name was something from a medieval romance. Percival? Lancelot?

"Tristan," he corrected, grinning down at me. "But I get the

Lancelot thing a lot." He roughed up my hair. "Come on, sit up. Meet our new witch."

Memory came flooding back. "Yes," I said unsteadily. "Erszebet. I've met her."

"No." He chuckled. "You haven't. Take a look." He propped me farther up so I could look across the room.

About twenty feet away from me, near the control console, stood a stunningly beautiful young woman, hardly more than a girl, wearing Erszebet's dress. The garment now curved and clung to an exaggeratedly shapely physique, almost perfectly hourglass. Her hair was shoulder-length, thick and full and dark, her eyes a deep green. She mesmerized us all by simply standing there, with a gleeful, impertinent smirk tugging the perfect curve of her mouth to one side.

With Tristan's assistance, I rose to my feet terribly awkwardly, the snowsuit making synthetic slithery noises as I moved. I felt like a yeti in the presence of a gazelle.

"Meet Erszebet Karpathy," said Tristan, beaming. "She's our witch."

Diachronicle

DAY 294 (CONTD.)

In which every little thing she does is magic

EVERYONE IN THE ROOM WAS staring at her—Oda-sensei, Rebecca, the Maxes. The gleeful impertinent smirk fixed on Tristan.

Tristan started to laugh in a breathy way, trying but failing to suppress glee. "Wow," he said. Against my upper back, his torso shifted slightly. "We did it." He sounded giddy. Everyone applauded, looking rapt.

"*I* did it," she corrected him. The accent, which had made her sound crabby when she was nearly two hundred years old, now made her exotic, adding to the glimmer of her beauty. "I warned you do not want to get on my bad side."

"Doesn't look like you have a bad side," I said, so that Tristan wouldn't.

Her attention turned to me, and she grew more serious. "Do I look more familiar now?" she asked. "This is how I appeared when we first met. I was only nineteen, but I was a prodigy. You were lucky that I was the one you found."

"I'm sorry, but we really have never met before," I said. And then to Tristan, almost under my breath: "I . . . I'd like to get out of this thing, please." It was foolish to feel so self-consciously lumbering just because there was another young female in the room who happened to be crazy-gorgeous. I was not used to being fawned on by anyone—Tristan treated me like an extension of himself—but suddenly I felt somewhat gruesome.

Tristan, eyes glued to Erszebet's face (and curves, I am sure), released me so I could unzip myself from the snowsuit. But even wearing civvies, I felt doltish while this elegant creature held us all entranced. Entranced is not the right word, though—that conjures a sense of a doe-eyed fairy-tale princess, and Erszebet was not that. She was fierce. Not deliberately, not like the Alpha Girl in a high school clique . . . it was effortless on her part, elemental. And she seemed amused by how her transformation distracted the rest of us.

"The experience was very pleasant," she continued to Tristan, in a *so-there* tone. "Do not presume to tell me what is good for me or not. Ever again."

"Got it," he said almost meekly. His eyes kept sinking toward her ~~boobs breasts~~ bosom, as if lead weights were attached to them; then, with visible effort, he would wrench them back to her face.

There was a long pause as we all continued to register what we were witnessing, and she continued to bask in our collective gaze. Various low voices said "Wow" or something equally articulate. We were more dumbfounded by the fact of the transformation than by its result (although I cannot stress enough how impressive the result was)—but we were definitely dumbfounded. And she was definitely preening.

Then Tristan collected himself. "So." He coughed slightly. "All right then. How did you just do that?"

"It was a big spell. Not easy," she said offhandedly. "But I have been thinking about it, rehearsing it in my head, for a hundred and sixty years—since the groundwork for it was laid in Budapest. I did it to see if your ODEC works to my satisfaction." She smiled, and shifted her hips a few times so that the hem of the cocktail dress swirled around her knees. "It does. In fact it was never so effortless to do a spell as in this ODEC, which I like *very* much. What shall I do next?"

"What kind of magic were you in the habit of doing before?" Tristan asked. Without taking his eyes from her, he pointed toward the small table on which sat a MacBook Air. "Stokes."

I collected the laptop and dutifully seated myself, opened the audio recording software, and pressed "record"; for backup I decided to take dictation and remained there, fingers poised over the keyboard.

Erszebet sobered abruptly. Even grave, she was mesmerizingly beautiful. "I was young, and magic was waning, and it was a very turbulent time. My mother was in the service of Lajos Kossuth, and if you know anything about our history, you will realize her magic was often ineffective. I assisted her when she required it."

Eyes still on Erszebet, Tristan signaled to me. "Lajos Kossuth," I said, typing.

"With a *j*—" she said to me; I overlapped: "A *j*, I know."

Her beautiful dark eyes flitted back to Tristan. "I like that she is educated," she said, as if approving of *him* for this, then continued her narrative: "After the revolution failed, after Kossuth fled in late '49, the aristocracy would call upon my mother or myself to perform stupid parlor tricks. We would change the color of some-body's hair, or force somebody to speak a childhood secret out loud. It was deliberately degrading to us, and I resented it, but my mother was so alarmed at our weakening powers that she grew fearful of displeasing those horrid people. She became sycophan-tic, which disgusted me, and so I went abroad."

"Where to?" asked Tristan.

"I wanted to follow Kossuth, but his wife did not want me in his sight. Instead I went to Switzerland awhile, to train with a pow-erful witch who was making sure younger witches still learned certain spells and charms that had fallen out of use as the world perceived we were losing our power and relied on us for fewer things. Her efforts were, in retrospect, somewhat romantic, as if somebody in today's world were teaching how to measure longi-tude with a timepiece. I learned much that I had little occasion to use, but I was still glad for the learning, although eventually I rejoined my parents in Budapest."

"So can you change somebody into a newt?" Tristan asked, getting to the point.

"Of course I can," she said. "What a stupid question."

"Can you change them back?" I asked quickly.

"If I feel like it," said Erszebet complacently. She gave Tristan a slightly defiant look. "Do you wish to test me?"

He pondered a moment, assessing her on so many levels. "Let's start with an inanimate object," he said. "I assume that's possible? I mean, can you . . . transubstantiate inanimate objects?"

"Tell me what you need," she said with a suddenly inviting smile. Truly, it was almost a grin. For the first time, she and Tristan were in the same groove, and they smiled at each other. He bit his lower lip excitedly, which made him look charmingly like a goof.

Then he clapped his hands together in front of him, actually squatted slightly like a coach laying out a game plan. It was the first time I noticed—fleetingly—that he had a cute butt. "Just going to put you through some paces on the most basic level today. Stokes will take notes. *Ms.* Stokes will take notes," he corrected himself quickly, staving off her irritation.

"I wish those stupid aristocrats who made us do parlor tricks were still alive," Erszebet said eagerly. "The pains I would bring upon them now."

"Never mind about them," said Tristan. "You'll have plenty to occupy you right here."

For the rest of the afternoon, Tristan tasked Erszebet with simple assignments, for which we were all the amazed witnesses. I can hardly describe the electricity in that dull warehouse that day, our breathless wonder at the impossible-turned-evident. Even though she began with the humblest of efforts, the whole thing was totally ~~fucking~~ mind-blowing. Here follows a sampling, and then I must move on to what happened afterward, as I still have not accustomed myself to writing with a dip pen and this is far more painstaking than I had realized when I began this project—and *I am running out of time.*

To begin, Tristan put a gallon of white paint into the ODEC with Erszebet, and asked her to turn it black; she did so, and after the Maxes took a sample to have analyzed, she returned it to white, which was also sampled. She could turn it any color, we learned; she could match it perfectly to colored objects Tristan gave her to take into the ODEC with her. (She could not reproduce this effect when the paint or objects sat outside the ODEC, to the frustration of both herself and Tristan.) He then had her bend metal rods into perfect circles; splinter stones; break glass and then restore it.

It was clear now that anybody actually inside the ODEC with her could not (by definition, really) remain mentally coherent, and so each time she set about to work her magic, she did so alone. Sealed up within the ODEC, her workings remained a perfect mystery.

These acts of magic each took between five and thirty minutes to achieve. While happily invigorated after the first dozen or so, she presently showed signs of tiring. Tristan chose not to notice this, and tried to step things up a notch: he asked her to material- ize something out of nothing.

"There is no such thing as *nothing*. Not even in what you call a vacuum. But I am tired now," she said, lolling against the con- trol console. "Materialization is a complicated summoning and requires many calculations. And I am tired of taking orders from you, Tristan Lyons. Perhaps tomorrow."

It was clear from her tone that Tristan should not bother asking more of her. He looked both contented and resigned. "That's a wrap, then," he announced to all of us. "Back here at 0900 to- morrow. And Miss Karpathy, thank you for your efforts today. You have begun to change the future of magic. Thank you."

She made her now-usual dismissive face, and otherwise did not respond.

As the Maxes—who had scarcely left off staring at the beauti- ful witch when she wasn't in the ODEC—began to collect their jackets and such like, I had the sudden thought: *Where are we going to put her?* Clearly we could not return her to the nursing home.

I was startled by Rebecca's soft voice behind me: "How large is your apartment?"

I turned to her. "Not large enough," I said.

Rebecca sighed rather pointedly to get Tristan and Oda's attention. "*Well* then," she said in a slightly raised voice. "I suppose we must. But only for the one night."

Erszebet heard this, and smiled. She straightened up and strolled toward us. And then—in a moment of unguarded bliss—she threw her hands up and cried triumphantly, "How *wonderful* not to be in prison anymore!"

"How many guest rooms do you have?" Tristan asked Rebecca quietly. "I'm responsible for her, I have—"

"You are not *responsible* for me," said Erszebet, immediately exchanging glee for contempt. "And you have no authority over me at all."

"Excuse me, miss, but if it wasn't for me, you'd still be a crone living in a retirement community."

"You had nothing to do with that," she said dismissively. "It was Melisande who found me. Not that she has authority over me either, but I owe her at least a debt of gratitude."

Journal Entry of
Rebecca East-Oda
MAY 19

We've brought all three home for the night. I made it clear they must respect this as *our home*, not merely a dormitory for experimental physicists and their sideshow curiosities. (Obviously didn't say that. Still in shock about Erszebet.)

Immediate disagreements about sleeping arrangements. We have the guest room (double bed) and Mei's room (twin). Tristan said he would take Mei's room, but Erszebet demanded to sleep alone. Then:

ERSZEBET: It is ridiculous that you (*Tristan/Mel*) refuse to share a bed.

MEL: We don't *refuse* to—

ERSZEBET: Good, then, do it.

MEL: It's just that we *don't*.

ERSZEBET: Why not?

MEL: We're not romantically involved.

ERSZEBET: Why not?

MEL: Because we're just not.

ERSZEBET: That answer is too stupid to justify depriving me of my own room. Even in that *prison*, I had my own room to sleep in at night.

MEL: He snores very loudly and I won't be able to sleep.

TRISTAN: Yeah, it's terrible, women leave me all the time because of it.

ERSZEBET: They leave you for other reasons.

MEL: So please, let's you and I share the double, and Tristan has his own room.

ERSZEBET: I cannot believe the indignities I am already having to suffer under your regime. Sharing not just a room but a *bed*. I haven't had to do that since the *1930s*.

TRISTAN: You want to go back to Elm House, I'll drive you.

MEL: Let's everyone just calm the f**k down.

Tristan took Mel aside to discuss surveillance of Erszebet. Assuming my role as hostess and lady of the house, I stepped in to see how she was settling in. She had left the elder-hostel with only one large bag of faux leather that looked stolen from a fashion shoot. She was removing her possessions from this bag and laying them out neatly on the painted wooden dresser: ancient boar-bristle hairbrush, couple of camisoles and dresses, small satin bag for toiletries and makeup, nylon stockings. Plus one object made of yarn or string, a kind of fiber-sculpture. The calico had leapt up onto the dresser to examine this, but seemed to know better than to swat at it.

I looked closer at it. It was very old and frayed in places. Its central artery was a length of spun wool perhaps as long as my forearm, and tied to it were several hundred more slender strings, of varying lengths. All bore multiple knots along their lengths—knots of varying shapes, sizes, complexities, and densities. A number of strands were deliberately entangled to each other, and some of the strands were tied together into bundles thick as my thumb, creating an effect like dreadlocks. It resembled a design I remembered from my favorite college class, on South American anthropology, so I assumed that what appeared to be the ruins of a mop was in fact a calculation-and-record-keeping device.

"Looks like an Andean *quipu*," I said.

"Mm," said Erszebet absently, removing her shoes and wiggling her toes. "Mine is better." She shooed the cat off the dresser. "What do you use?"

"Sorry?" I said.

"What do *you*—" She stopped herself, blinked, looked lost. "Never mind," she said, sounding cross but looking confused. "I forget there is no magic now except in this ODEC." She gave me a searching look. "So you can't do magic? Ever?"

"That's right," I said. Neutral voice, neutral expression.

"Well, you can now, with this ODEC-room," she said.

"I don't do magic," I clarified, hoping Mel would return and interrupt this conversation. "I have no idea how to do it."

"Ah," she said, still distracted, and began to brush her hair. "Of course, if it cannot be done, then it cannot be practiced or remembered. I wonder will Tristan Lyons require me to show witches how to do magic. Probably."

"I don't see myself volunteering to become a witch," I said.

She paused in her brushing to give me a curious look. "You are already a witch."

"Excuse me?" I said. "I don't know where you would get that impression from. Do you think that just because I knew what a quipu is? That's nothing to do with magic, it's because—"

She resumed brushing her hair. "Of course you are a witch," she said with offhand impatience. "You smell like a witch."

"*What?*" I demanded. "What do you mean by that?"

She shrugged. "What is the scent of a baby or an old person or a man in love? There are different human scents. You have the scent of a witch. How *wonderful* it feels to have a full head of hair to brush again! You take these things for granted when you're young."

"Excuse me, I'm not a witch," I said. "That would be ridiculous."

"Then your mother's mothers were," she said very matter-of-factly, setting the brush on the dresser. "Some ancestress. You carry the blood."

Suddenly I was irrationally angry at Frank. "Did my husband tell you to say that to me?"

"I would not say something because your husband told me to. Ha! What an idea."

"I have an ancestor who was hanged in Salem, but she was not a witch—"

"Well, *somebody* was," she said, and peered into her toiletries bag for something.

"This is nonsense," I said, ruffled. "I don't have one of *those*"—

pointing to the quipu-like object—"and I don't do magic, and I'm not a witch, and I shall go put on deodorant right now if you think I smell like one."

"You act as if I have insulted you," she said, sounding amused. She took a bottle of witch hazel and a cotton pad from the little silk bag. "I have given you the greatest compliment."

"Not by my lights," I said.

As soon as I left her, I confronted Frank, who never understands that the Salem witch hysteria is inappropriate for jokes. He claimed innocence, pointed out that he had never been alone with Erszebet, but then—since the matter had been raised, I suppose—repeated his perennial joke-theory that Mary Estey really was a witch. "Now that we know there *really are* witches, don't you want to know?" he said with his eager little knowing grin. "Wouldn't that be something?"

How could I ever fault him his curiosity? So. Made sure the guests were settled in with bath towels and water glasses, and then went up into the attic to Nana's trunk, which I have managed to avoid opening for a quarter century, despite Frank's nudging. God knows why I felt compelled tonight. I already know the family tree; I don't require seeing it in writing. But something pushed me to go up.

I pulled the string on the bare bulb that hangs from the attic ceiling, knelt down by the heavy cedar chest that lives equidistant from the central chimneys, windows, and attic door. Blew the worst of the dust off the top. Grasped the two near corners and lifted carefully as the wood creaked in protest; the clasp broke at least a century ago.

Inside, I saw the sheaf of family papers I knew would be there—but then I saw something I had never noticed before. I thought it was a cowl or scarf, maybe a battered swaddling cloth. Then I realized. Froze. Felt dizzy. Its similarity to Erszebet's was unmistakable. *I should look at that more closely*, I thought. *I should reach for it. Yes, I'll reach for it.*

My limbs would not obey me. I watched my own hands carefully close the lid of the chest. I stood up and left the room very quickly as if propelled by an external force, shutting the light behind me. I sat on the top stair, staring into the darkness until I was sure even Frank had gone to sleep.

Diachronicle
DAYS 295–304 (LATE MAY, YEAR 1)

In which there isn't enough magic to go around

THE NEXT DAY WE RETURNED to the ODEC to begin a more sophisticated series of experimentations. Rebecca East-Oda made it clear that she felt Oda-sensei's involvement in the project had reached the end of its natural course, and so neither of them returned with us.

We were to essentially sequester ourselves for a fortnight as Erszebet eased back into the habit of performing magic and displayed her skills for us. Although we were free to leave the building to eat, exercise, take the air—even to return to my apartment occasionally to shower—Erszebet and I would sleep in the ODEC room; Tristan was already happily ensconced in his bachelor pad of an office. By the time we arrived that first morning, the Maxes had brought in camp cots, towels and linens, a couple of well-fed lab rats and lab-rat grub, a case of Old Tearsheet Best Bitter for

Tristan, toothbrushes and toothpaste (oh God, I'd barter my body for a tube of Crest now! Cleaning my teeth with a paste of borax and ground cuttlefish bones, with anise to "sweeten" it. *Ych.*) . . . and as many breakfast groceries and snacks as the college-dorm-style refrigerator in the upstairs office could hold. There were also several boxes of seemingly random props from a list that Tristan had texted the Maxes the night before. As soon as they'd set up our bunker, the Maxes packed up and moved on, presumably to their next shadowy government assignment. They took all but one of the Vladimirs with them. We still had a full complement of Lukes to guard the building and assure our security, but they were otherwise useless.

The days that followed were long ones, the take-out food we lived on relatively tasteless (by twenty-first-century standards . . . context really is everything!), and by night we were each too tired even for conversation. Tristan in particular was worn down and preoccupied. My memories of that time are drab and bleary, despite the remarkable nature of our undertakings.

The first week's experiments, dictated by Tristan, included: manifesting inanimate objects, both those occurring in nature (e.g., sticks and stones) and those man-made (e.g., a cap gun . . . or at least something resembling one); changing the chemical composition of liquids (e.g., water to salt water); moving small things (e.g., the manifested cap gun) from one spot in the ODEC to another. The array of requests evolved over the days from the mundane ("turn this sweater inside out") to the fanciful ("turn this vanilla ice cream into Rocky Road") to the creepy ("animate the stuffed cat") to the startling ("turn this lab rat into a newt").

Erszebet was willing to show off her powers, although after a day or two of adjusting to having them back, she made it very clear that she found the assignments themselves tiresome and stupid. She would, she informed us, perform magic because it pleased her to do so after so many years deprived of it; she would *not* perform it simply because Mr. Tristan Lyons required it of her. She was flexing a muscle she'd longed to flex for many scores of years, and to a certain degree she was preening. Once the buzz of that wore thin, we knew she would feel no obligation to continue the dog-and-pony show.

Tristan did not waste breath explaining to either of us what his higher-ups were expecting from this sequestration; I just took his lead, trying to learn as much as we could about Erszebet's powers, although it was a trying undertaking. Erszebet herself had cast us as good cop/bad cop, and it was natural enough to play those roles. Tristan pushed her; I cajoled. He made her feel significant; I made her feel appreciated. Truth be told, after three days of it, his job proved far easier than mine, for she was, to use a post-Victorian turn of phrase, high-maintenance.

Other than her attitude, our biggest headache was that obviously we could not tape or photograph what she was doing in the ODEC; we could not be in there with her without blacking out. She had to thump on the door just to let us know she was finished with each spell.

Our only recourse for research, therefore, was for me to interview her after each exercise. Since she would not answer Tristan's questions (or rather, answered them, but only with gratuitous derision), he divided his time between measuring and studying whatever object she'd worked her magic on, and hourly emailing his bosses at the shadowy government entity regarding our progress. Apparently the Maxes had delivered glowing reports on the results of Erszebet's first spell and it seemed the bosses wanted everything she did to be as attention-grabbing as she herself now was.

Erszebet, in these interviews with me, was not illuminating. Here follows almost verbatim, as I can remember it, the gist of an early attempt:

(Upon the occasion of Erszebet taking my sweater into the ODEC with her and changing it from green wool to lavender polyester, which took much longer than we expected—an entire afternoon—and left her strangely exhausted. NB: Yes, Tristan had specific reasons for such peculiar and frivolous-seeming instructions.)

MEL: Can you explain to me how you did this?

ERSZEBET: *Pah.* I found where you were wearing lavender polyester and brought that here. It was hard to find. There are not many opportunities to find you owning polyester.

MEL: The physicists would say that in some parallel reality to this one in the multiverse, there is a Mel wearing a lavender polyester sweater.

Erszebet makes her dismissive face, and shrugs to make it clear she doesn't ~~give a fuck~~ *care what physicists would say.*

MEL: What we want to understand is, how does it end up here, in this reality, and what happens to the original sweater?

ERSZEBET: I summon it here and get rid of the other one.

MEL: *How*, though? By what *mechanism*?

ERSZEBET: The same way you do anything. You do what causes the desired result. If you want something to burn, you set it on fire, if you want something to be wet, you pour liquid on it. If you want something that is upstairs to be downstairs, you send someone to collect it. It is exactly the same. Except it is more complicated to calculate what to do—for example, in that metaphor, what route to tell the servant to take upstairs, how fast to move, and so on.

MEL: But can you explain technically, mechanically—not metaphorically—*what* you are doing and *how* you do it?

ERSZEBET: *Pah*, if you don't understand a perfectly simple explanation, then you are too stupid to understand a more technical one.

MEL: Fine. Can you at least explain to me why some people can perform magic and others can't?

ERSZEBET: This is like asking why doesn't a blind person know what blue smells like.

. . . and thus went all interviews. There are transcripts of two dozen such on that original laptop. They are probably now either archived or expunged. If I don't escape from 1851 within the next three weeks, I will never know which.

FURTHER, ERSZEBET WAS capricious, and she knew she held all the power. We were demanding something of her (quite a lot of something, to be fair), while there was nothing we could offer her in recompense. Her greatest desire was fulfilled by circumstance: as a nineteen-year-old bombshell, she would never be re-incarcerated in the retirement home. She had other desires, but expressed them only erratically at first. Most significantly, on our twelfth day in seclusion, when we had stopped for lunch, she announced she wished to go to Hungary "to spit upon the graves of my enemies."

"We don't have the budget," said Tristan, and took a bite of his tuna sandwich. He had said nothing about it, but his mysterious revenue stream seemed to be drying up. Deliveries of liquid helium were fewer and further between, and seemed to involve his spending a lot of time in exhausting phone conversations. He kept having to call Frank Oda in to help debug the ODEC, which I could see he felt bad about, since Frank wasn't getting paid. And he kept pressing our Lukes and our Vladimir into service doing things that, to judge from the looks on their faces, weren't in their job descriptions. Tristan had always suffered from a certain ADHD-ness, which was alternately charming and exasperating. His phone had lately been going off every few minutes, which made this even worse. He'd programmed it to produce different ringtones and vibrate-patterns for different incoming callers, so he could tell without even looking at it who was bothering him. One of those was a snatch of John Philip Sousa's "Liberty Bell March." It was typical American patriotic bombast, military parade stuff. Overlaid on that was a whole different set of associations based on the fact that it was the theme song for *Monty Python's Flying Circus*. Every so often I would hear it coming out of Tristan's phone. When it did, he would drop what he was doing and visibly snap to attention and take that call without delay, hurrying off to a quiet part of the building and saying "Sir!" and "Yes, sir!" a lot. Obviously, this was the ringtone he'd assigned to his boss. What I didn't know, and what I was dying to ask, was its meaning. Was "Liberty Bell March" just a snatch of patriotic music to him, or a wry allusion to an absurdist British comedy show that had been canceled before he had been born?

We were in the office just outside the ODEC, at the small table where I usually interviewed Erszebet. I had been about to suggest we repair outside to stroll down to the Charles, perhaps even drive to Walden Pond for some fresh air and sunshine (it was Memorial Day weekend in New England and we were living, working, and sleeping in a basement under fluorescent lights. I mean really, WTF.). Often I still wonder how things would be different now if I had pressed for such a constitutional. Surely in some other—better—universe, Mel made that suggestion, and so the trio left the building and was not there when General Schneider arrived.

But in our universe, the trio stayed in the basement, having this conversation:

"If you cooperate with us," Tristan continued, swallowing his bite of tuna salad, "we can probably *get* funding, and then if you really want to go spit on the graves of your enemies, we can discuss it." And then, putting down his sandwich, eyes lighting up: "Wait a minute! We *can* get our own funding. If you can change water to salt water . . . why not change—"

"—lead to gold," she said with him, with an adolescent groan of disapproval. "Or anything to gold. That is the most unoriginal suggestion in the *world*. From the dawn of magic this is the first thing people ask of witches."

"And?" prompted Tristan.

"We don't do it," she said. "*Obviously*."

"Why not?"

"Ask the Fuckers."

"*What!?*" Tristan and I exclaimed in unison. Erszebet had many disagreeable traits, but use of vulgar language was most certainly not one of them.

She was taken aback by our reaction. "The Fuckers," she said. "You know. *The Fuckers*."

Tristan and I looked at each other as if to verify we'd both heard it.

Erszebet laughed in a way that suggested she wasn't really all that amused. "You people have such dirty minds. It is a perfectly normal German name. Maybe you spell it F-U-G-G-E-R just to be polite."

"Oh," I said, "Fugger, as in the old German banking family."

"As in them, yes."

"So, back to where we were," Tristan said, shaking his head. "You're saying we should ask some old dead German bankers why you don't change lead into gold."

"They are not all dead," Erszebet corrected him. "If you go down to the financial district, you can probably find one right now, sitting in a nice discreet office."

"Well," I said, "obviously bankers would have something to say about changing lead into gold."

"They would not like it," Erszebet said. And this was the first time I ever got the sense from her that she actually *cared* whether someone else would or wouldn't like a thing. She considered Fuggers—or Fuckers, as she pronounced the name—people to be reckoned with.

"Let's try a different example, if you don't like gold," Tristan said. "I'm going to show my cards a little bit more than I usually do." And he pocketed his phone, which he'd been looking at under the table, and laid both hands on the table's upper surface—as if literally showing his cards. "To hell with gold. Could you produce enriched uranium?"

She considered it. "The stuff they use in bombs?"

"The stuff they use in bombs."

She shook her head. "Certainly not. This would cause too much change too quickly, and bad things happen when magic is used that way."

"What bad things?"

"Bad things," she said with finality. "Worse than your 'nukes.' We don't even have words to describe them. So we don't do that."

"Then there are rules," I said, opening the laptop to take notes. "Not changing things too quickly is a rule. What are some other rules?"

"There is no *rule*," she said. "We just don't do it. Is there a rule telling you not to jump off a cliff? No. But you don't do it."

"What else don't you do?" asked Tristan.

"What a ridiculous question," she said. To me: "He only asks ridiculous questions. I hope he is not your lover, because he is not worthy."

"Why is it a ridiculous question?" pressed Tristan.

"Can you tell me all the things you would not do? No. You only know what not to do when you're faced with the prospect of doing it. It's like that with everything, including magic."

"Can you give me some *examples*?" he asked with exaggerated patience.

She looked thoughtful, and for a happily deluded moment, we both thought she was going to be cooperative. "I am tired of doing all the giving," she said. "So. Your turn to give me something. You will give me a cat."

After a confused pause, I asked, "As a pet?"

"No, as a *cat*," she said.

"A live cat?" asked Tristan.

"Of course a live cat! What would I do with a dead cat?"

"Okay, you can have a cat," said Tristan indulgently. "We'll get you a cat next week, as soon as you've done something we can show the brass."

"I will show the brass something after you give me a cat," she corrected triumphantly.

"Erszebet," I said in a friendly, intimate tone. "We have no time to go fetch you a cat, or a litterbox, or any of the other stuff a cat needs. But if you would like to be employed again by powerful people, who can give you as many cats as you like, then please cooperate with us for the next few days."

She pursed her lips and glanced between the two of us. "Put me with those people you speak of. Why am I wasting my time doing stupid tricks for minions?"

"Because these minions have an ODEC," said Tristan abruptly and openly irritated. "Without this ODEC, you are *nothing*. And this ODEC is *ours*. So play nice."

She gave him a furious, disgusted look. "I want to be very clear with you about something," she said in a warning tone. "There are many novels in which there is a handsome man and a beautiful woman and they argue all the time and are at odds and constantly clash and it is because secretly they want to make passionate love to each other. That is *not* the case here."

At this, Tristan let out a huge guffaw, a rumbling, raucous belly laugh, head thrown back.

"I am serious," she protested hotly.

"I'm so glad you clarified that," he said, huffing with laughter. "Because I gotta tell you, with General Schneider breathing down my neck to learn what your magic is good for, with my spending every free waking moment trying to convince him and his bosses that this is useful even if you haven't already materialized enriched uranium for them, I gotta tell you, when I am so *totally preoccupied* with your being seen as a valued commodity that the time it takes me to *shave* feels like a personal overindulgence, I love knowing that your number one priority is devaluing me even more than my bosses want to devalue you. That's *awesome*. You're the best. I'll be *so fucking devastated* when they pull the plug on this and you end up in the street without even a nursing home to take care of you." He stood up and stormed to the far side of the room, his hands at his temples. "*Jesus*."

Then he turned back toward us and said, from a distance, "I apologize. That was totally uncalled for and I should have more control over myself. It's been a tough week."

"They want to pull the plug?" said Erszebet, scandalized.

"How long has that been true?" I asked, shocked.

He ran his hands through his short hair a few times roughly, and then returned to sit by us again. "Almost from the word go," he confessed, pained. "General Schneider was excited for about thirty minutes and then he and Dr. Rudge wanted immediate gratification. They wanted her to start manifesting stealth bombers, or teleport invisibly to Syria, that sort of thing."

This was the first time he had mentioned names. Until then, Tristan had maintained impeccable secrecy concerning his chain of command. Either he really was at the end of his rope, or else he thought he could gain Erszebet's trust by personalizing the discussion.

If so, it wasn't working. "And instead you had me turning sweaters inside out?" demanded Erszebet in disgust. "And you wonder why they do not value me? You are more of an idiot even than I thought."

"Every task I gave you was a beta test for something else that would have obvious military use. They want you to turn a *person* inside out. *Obviously* I have to test that on a sweater and not a person, or even on a lab rat. And of course I'll fulfill their agenda, but ideally I'd like to *exceed* it. I've got more scruples than they do, so I'd like to present you to them—brand you, so to speak—as being useful for something *other than* turning a person inside out."

"Such as?"

"Turning lead into gold would be pretty awesome," he said, sounding wistful.

She shook her head.

"Why don't you suggest something, then," he said to her. "Given that you can only work your magic inside the ODEC, you're a little limited, you realize that?"

"She can turn rats into newts," I reminded him.

"So can your average kids'-birthday-party magician."

"Not for *real*. Anyhow, what about a person?" I said. "What if I let her turn *me* into a newt?"

"I would not turn a person inside out, probably," Erszebet informed Tristan. "That would be tasteless. You Americans are so tasteless."

"Turn me into a newt," I insisted. "The bosses will like that."

And that, as I recall, was the moment when Tristan's phone began playing the "Liberty Bell March."

He pulled it out of his pocket and double-taked, then used his finger to scroll down. "Snap inspection!" he announced, looking up to make eye contact with me and Erszebet. "Shine your shoes and polish your belt buckles!"

Diachronicle

DAY 304

In which General Schneider is impressed

NO MORE THAN FIVE MINUTES later we were joined by a broad-chested gentleman in uniform, trailed by a younger man, similarly attired, whose sole purpose in life seemed to be to open doors for, and to hold the hat of, the boss.

At the time, I knew nothing of uniforms, rank, or insignia. A few years later, having spent a lot of time around active-duty military, I'd have been able to recognize this man as a brigadier general

(one star) and his aide as a lieutenant colonel. Both were wearing dress uniforms—the military-world equivalent of business suits.
Conveniently, they were wearing name plates on their right breast
pockets, and so I knew that their last names were Schneider and
Ramirez even before Tristan made introductions, which he did
with even more than his accustomed level of military crispness.

General Schneider moved about the room in an asymmetrical
gait, shaking first my hand, then Erszebet's. His manner was extraordinarily grim and formal. He paid only cursory attention
to me. Then his gaze settled on Erszebet, taking her in head to
foot, and for a fleeting moment he looked impressed. But then he
frowned and turned his attention to Tristan.

"I assume that's the Asset," he said, pointing.

"Pointing is *very* rude," said Erszebet.

Tristan hastily said, "General Schneider, yes. Miss Karpathy is
the one I told you about."

"This must be the one who wishes me to turn people inside
out," said Erszebet, looking away with wounded dignity. "Very
tasteless."

Schneider gave her a strange look, but then returned his attention to Tristan, who said quickly, "You came at a great time, sir.
We were just in the middle of a very productive conversation."

"You said a couple of weeks, Major Lyons. In my dictionary, 'a
couple' means 'two.' It has been two."

"General Schneider—"

"You're not doing what we discussed, Major Lyons. You're going off script. You're giving us a science project."

"Sir, I explained in my report—" Tristan began, but Erszebet
talked over him:

"My powers are so little to a man who requires an assistant just
to walk into a room?"

"She was just about to turn me into a newt," I offered urgently.

General Schneider gave me a look and then turned condescendingly to her. "Yeah, I've been hearing about the newt thing all week. That might have been impressive a thousand years ago—"

"I was born in 1832, I was not alive a thousand years ago," she retorted. "If you cannot grasp simple arithmetic, then you will never have any idea what Mr. Tristan Lyons is trying to accomplish here."

Schneider continued speaking over her: "Those kinds of tricks are *nothing* in a world with drones, cruise missiles, and assault rifles. And according to *Major* Lyons's reports, it takes you all day to pull it off. By the time you get that spell half out of your mouth, I can rack a round into my sidearm and put it between your eyes."

"Do you need your minion to help you with that too?" she asked.

He looked back over his shoulder at Lieutenant Colonel Ramirez. "Have a look around the facility," he said. Ramirez departed wordlessly.

"I liked the Maxes better," Erszebet announced.

"Do you get my point?" General Schneider demanded. "If you want the taxpayers of the United States to go on subsidizing your beauty treatments, you had better impress me. Now. Today. *Right now.*"

"Very well, then," purred Erszebet, so immediately cheerful that my skin prickled. I glanced at Tristan; he was looking at her keenly, and not in the usual slack-jawed way that men would look at such a woman.

Erszebet stood and gestured to the open door of the ODEC, smiling like a 1950s housewife on a television advertisement. "If you would like to step inside, General, I will demonstrate the kind of magic you desire. In fact I would be delighted to give you what you're asking for."

"General—" said Tristan tentatively.

"Good," said General Schneider, all too obviously charmed by Erszebet's physical endowments. I got the clear sense that in his world he dealt with a lot of submissive women who thought of nothing but pleasing him. "*That's* what I was after, Major Lyons. Why did it take *me* coming all the way up here to get that kind of compliance? Where's the whatever-it-is I have to wear?"

"In that corner," I said, gesturing toward the rack of snowmobile suits.

Tristan respectfully asked to speak in private with Schneider. They stepped into the server room for a moment, and I could hear Tristan's voice trying to explain something and the general's interrupting him. The door opened suddenly and Schneider limped back in, rolling his eyes. I handed him the snowsuit, and then gestured with my head for Erszebet to step aside with me. She joined me by the console panel and—an occasional habit of hers, like a nervous tic—reached into her bag and riffled through it without looking at what she was doing.

"Don't turn him inside out," I said.

She looked insulted. "Of course not. Blood—body fluids—all over my dress."

"You know what I mean. Don't hurt him. You said you owed me a debt of gratitude—I'll consider it fulfilled if you promise me that."

She smiled innocently, which filled me with a sense of dread. "I promise, *I* am not going to hurt him." And then, grinning as broadly as she had her first day with us, she stopped fidgeting with the things in her bag, marched into the ODEC with her dress flouncing about her, and waited for Schneider.

Meanwhile Schneider zipped and velcroed himself into the largest of our snowmobile suits. Schneider was hefty and the suit was tight. I noticed something that explained his rolling, asymmetrical style of walking: he had one artificial leg.

"Give us fifteen minutes, please," Erszebet called out to Tristan as Schneider squeezed into the ODEC with her. "To impress the general will require some effort."

We closed the door, and Tristan walked to the control console to turn on the ODEC.

There was, of course, no way we could know what was going on inside the ODEC—that was an unavoidable part of the whole Schrödinger's cat thing. But after eleven minutes we heard the thump on the door that told us Erszebet was finished.

Tristan went to the console and powered down the ODEC. I slipped on the oven mitts that we used whenever we wanted to touch the dangerously cold door latches, and opened the door.

"And so," said Erszebet, radiant and fresh-faced, her tone sparkling, "I have shown your master a magic trick." She walked out into the room, leaving the coast clear for us to see inside. And what we saw—or thought we saw—was the motionless body of General Schneider, crumpled on the floor.

"General Schneider!" Tristan exclaimed, and stepped in through the door. There wasn't enough room in there for me to join him, so I contented myself with sticking my head in for a look.

Schneider wasn't actually there. Collapsed on the floor, apparently empty, was the snowmobile suit. An empty oxygen mask was still lodged in its hood. "Where is he?" Tristan demanded, horrified.

"Did you turn him into a newt?" I asked.

She examined her fingernails. "Oh, no! It takes me all day to pull that off."

Tristan picked up the suit and held it upright; one of the legs fell straight down as if weighted with something, and clanked onto the floor of the ODEC.

"Give it to me," I suggested, and reached through the doorway. He thrust the shoulders of the suit at me. I grabbed them and pulled the whole thing out through the door and into the room, where I laid it out flat on the floor. Left behind in the ODEC was an articulated contraption consisting of a stump cup, some straps, and a carbon-fiber strut terminating in a man's dress shoe. Schneider's artificial leg.

I unzipped the front of the snowmobile suit with some care. I had an idea as to what had happened. Somewhere inside of this bulky garment was a living, breathing newt. I needed to find it, catch it, and return it safely to the ODEC where Erszebet could reverse the spell. No harm done. Point made.

Inside the suit was an empty suit of clothes—shirt buttoned, tie knotted, sleeves of the shirt fitted into the sleeves of the jacket. But no person. Tristan had emerged from the ODEC, carrying the artificial leg in one hand and Schneider's remaining shoe—sock dangling from it—in the other.

I grabbed the oxygen mask and pulled it carefully away from the snowsuit's hood. A little gleaming cascade of glinting objects fell out of it, followed by a pair of fake teeth held together by a bridge of pink plastic. That gave me a clue as to the little gleaming things. They were tiny bits of curiously shaped metal.

They were fillings from Schneider's teeth.

Groping carefully through Schneider's jacket and shirt, Tristan's hand found something. He unbuttoned the garments and spread them apart. Exposed in the middle, resting neatly on the back of the white shirt, was a small smooth object with a couple of wires coming out of it.

"That," Tristan said, "is a pacemaker."

I couldn't even speak properly, so I held out my hand with the fillings and the false teeth for Tristan to look at.

Tristan was squatting on his haunches. He looked at these exhibits for a while, thoughtfully. Acting on some kind of military-guy autopilot, he rummaged in Schneider's clothes until he came out with a small pistol, which Schneider had evidently been packing in a holster on the back of his belt. Tristan ejected its magazine and then worked the slide once to eject a round. Having rendered the weapon safe, he set it back down again, then climbed to his feet and turned to face Erszebet.

"What have you done to him?" Tristan demanded, very calm.

"Google it," said Erszebet breezily.

"Google *what*?"

She put her index finger to her chin and looked up at the ceiling. "Mmm, Hungary, Nagybörzsöny, 1564, one-legged man, naked. Perhaps *taltos*. You might discover something interesting."

"Stokes!" said Tristan irritably. I grabbed my laptop, brought up Google, and typed in the words. Nothing useful came up.

"Well?" demanded Tristan. I shook my head.

"Try refreshing," said Erszebet. "Perhaps it takes a moment for it to catch up."

"Catch up with what?" Tristan demanded.

"With *me*," she said, and began humming Liszt to herself.

I opened another window and tried Googling the Hungarian words she'd used. Nagybörzsöny turned out to be the name of a village. Taltos I already knew, it meant something like "warlock."

I went back to the first window and clicked the refresh button. Tristan came around to my side of the table and stared over my shoulder. Erszebet preened. I refreshed the page a second time.

"Nothing," I said.

"Try variations," she suggested, turning away as if in a reverie. "Amputee. Gibberish."

"*Where is he?*" Tristan demanded again.

I refreshed the page again. One search result came up.

"There's a Wikipedia entry," I said.

"What the—" Tristan muttered, as I clicked on the link.

"I made it into Wikipedia," sang Erszebet. "I'll bet none of my enemies ever made it into Wikipedia."

The page came up, entitled "Nagybörzsöny 'Warlock' incident," containing a short paragraph, with one notification saying the entry was a stub and encouraging us to help them supplement it, and a second saying the article needed additional citations for verification. The paragraph itself read:

In 1564, in the small village of Nagybörzsöny, a naked one-legged man is recorded as having materialized in the middle of a small lane, babbling in an unknown tongue. The townspeople were weary from a recent outbreak of typhus and on edge from years caught between the warring armies of the Ottoman Empire and Holy Roman Emperor Maximilian II. Once they recovered from their astonishment, the villagers bound the man and dragged him to the town square with the intent of burning him at the stake. This was prevented by the local priest of Szent István, who instead caused him to be taken to the dungeon of the Inquisition. The priest examined and interrogated him for several hours, but was unable to make sense of a word of the man's foreign gibberish. The local mob, by now in a frenzy, finally broke in, dragged the man out, and burned him to death.

I leapt to my feet. We stared in horror at the entry.

"*What have you done?*" Tristan cried, practically leaping toward her. He grabbed her by the shoulders and shook her. "You *killed* him!"

She struggled against him. "Unhand me. I did not kill him, the mob did. It says so right in Wikipedia. I'll bite you if you don't let me go."

"What *did* you do?" he demanded, his voice sounding strangled, but then released her.

She shrugged, adjusting her dress. "I Sent him back to 1564. This is all I did. What happens once I Send him is his responsibility."

"Time travel," I said hesitantly. "You can send people back in time."

"People can be moved to other Strands," she corrected me. "It is usually just a parlor trick, but sometimes it is useful to get somebody's attention."

"How much control do you have over it?" Tristan demanded, thinking fast. "Can you bring him back here before the crowd gets to him?"

She shook her head. "No, because I am not there with him. If he had asked a witch in Nagybörzsöny, politely, then she could have Sent him back here."

"Why didn't you mention you could do this?" I asked, trying pathetically to reap some useful research out of the situation. In truth, we should have known—it was in a couple of the translated documents, but always dismissed as being of minor significance.

She shrugged her dismissive shrug. "It is not a practical skill, there are so many . . . *variables* to contend with that it is of no practical use. It is seldom worth the bother."

"You just *murdered* someone," Tristan said.

"I just Sent him away," she protested. "He was very rude to me."

"That's bullshit. You sent him there knowing he could die. You had control over a situation that resulted in a man's death, how is that not murder?"

"There is never control when magic is involved," she replied philosophically.

Tristan was nearly hyperventilating. "Moments ago he was in this room and now he's dead. How is that not at least manslaughter?"

"He was going to shut the ODEC down," she said. "I had to stop him."

"You could have just turned him into a newt or something," I said.

"You already know I can do that," said Erszebet, preening again. "I wanted to show you something new." To Tristan: "Isn't that what you asked for? Something unexpected? To, what was your phrase? To 'brand' me?"

"This is a fucking catastrophe," Tristan shouted, and kicked a chair. It tumbled across the room to the far wall, where the seat busted apart from the legs. "*Fuck!*"

"He was so *disagreeable*," said Erszebet.

Tristan put his hands on his face and shuddered. "How the fuck am I ever going to explain this to . . . oh, Jesus Christ, you've ruined everything. Your own life. Do you understand that? That's it, it's over. You're done. We're done here." He was pacing wildly and kept making the same anxious gesture of throwing his hands to either side as if he'd just walked into a spiderweb and were trying to free himself of the gossamer.

"I mean it," he said, after a moment of silence. "Leave. Stokes, get out of here before you get embroiled in all of this. Leave her here."

"I am no coward, I would not flee," said Erszebet haughtily.

"That's right. You're going to prison," he said flatly.

"That will be more interesting than the nursing home," she replied, unfazed.

"Or I might just shoot you myself," he said, suddenly weary. He uprighted the chair he'd destroyed, discovered it was broken, sat down on the floor.

Erszebet, perversely, looked delighted with this declaration. "*Now* you are speaking like a man of *action*. I have not seen such a side of you before. I approve of it."

"I mean it, Stokes," he said. His voice was husky. "Just get out of here. I've got to tell them what happened." He put his hands over his face and began to mutter the phrases he would soon be typing into a report. "Diachronic effects confirmed . . . results unpredictable . . . Casualties . . . one KIA."

Diachronic. Meaning "through time."

Department of Diachronic . . . something?

"Go ahead and fetch his minion. I will Send him somewhere nicer," Erszebet offered. "And then we can all pretend they never arrived and just go back to what we were doing. Only now we will do more interesting things, yes?"

Tristan pressed the heels of his hands hard against his closed eyes and groaned. "Shut up," he said. "Stokes. Go. Really."

"Go where?" I asked.

He moved his hands away from his eyes. "Just get out of town, let me deal with this. Somehow. I'll let you know when it's safe to come home. Let Professor Oda know what happened so he doesn't show up in the middle of a shitstorm offering to help with something." He sighed heavily. "On your way out, tell Ramirez to come down here. I guess I start by breaking the news to him."

I hesitated. I had an instinct to go to him, but as if he sensed this, he made a waving-away motion, like he was flicking something from his hand. "Go," he repeated. "I'm sorry I dragged you into this. I'll be in touch when I can. Thanks for everything. Leave. *Now.*" He turned away from me.

Diachronicle
DAYS 305–309 (EARLY JUNE, YEAR 1)

*In which not all is lost, although in retrospect
perhaps it should have been*

I SHALL SKIP OVER THE miserable, dreadful limbo of the next few days. Suffice it to say: after alerting the professor and his wife of the tragic developments, I retreated to my third-floor walk-up and never went out except to buy groceries.

I checked Facebook obsessively on the chance Erszebet would reach out to me that way. Nothing. I read the papers, actual and virtual; I ran Google searches (so what if they could trace me, they already knew who I was and where I lived). The dead taltos in Hungary remained an established historical fact. Erszebet Karpathy—the Asset, Schneider had called her—remained non-existent.

I sniffed out possible job openings at universities so far below my pay grade that no prospective boss would bother contacting Blevins for a reference.

And—although this sounds dramatic—I suppose I grieved. I had thrown myself (uncharacteristically) with such abandon into the most remarkable adventure of my regimented little life, had reshaped myself as a trailblazer alongside a man I realized was the most vital human being I'd ever known . . . and now it was all gone. The life, the trail, the trailblazing, the man. I was an unemployed academic with a disastrous employment history and nothing to offer the world but an uncanny facility with (mostly dead and dying) languages. Nothing I might ever do would come close to seizing my attention the same way.

After what was easily the longest, most uncomfortable four or five days of my life, on an afternoon when I was so close to going mad that I began to re-alphabetize my vintage cookbook collection according to the Japanese syllabary, just to shut my brain up . . . the buzzer to my apartment blared. I almost jumped out of my skin.

I went to the door. "Who is it?" I shouted into the intercom.

"Stokes!" came a blessedly familiar voice through the crackle of crappy wiring.

I shouted with relief as I buzzed him in; he bounded up the stairs, and as he neared me, I can't believe I did this, but I threw my arms around his neck and gave him an enormous hug. "Tristan!" I cried, and even ~~planted a wet one on~~ kissed his cheek. "You're in one piece!"

Almost equally surprising, he was hugging me back, and he being so much taller than I, by the time he reached the landing, he had hoisted me off the ground. He squeezed me hard and then released me. "Better than one piece, even. Good to see you, Stokes."

"Where's Erszebet? What's happened?"

"She's fine, I'll explain. What do you have for beer? Those pencil-pushers in DC all drink Bud Light." He strode into the apartment. "Missed you, Stokes." He gestured grandly around the small room. "This is where it all began. Someday there'll be a plaque down front saying that."

"What's going *on*?" I demanded, opening the fridge. From the door I took the last Old Tearsheet Best Bitter from the six-pack he'd brought up the first day we met. He took it from me, found the opener, and a moment later was seated happily on my couch. He patted the spot next to himself and I sat.

"They were batshit-insane-happy about the diachronic effects," he said. "They're *all about* the time travel."

"But she *killed* someone!" I said.

"That's *why* they're all about the time travel. It got *results.* General Schneider gets a star on the wall."

"Huh?"

"He has been declared a martyr for his country."

"How is that helpful? Are they going to trick our enemies into standing in an ODEC so Erszebet can Send them to the moon?"

"See, what you and I were too freaked out to think about is that it's possible to get sent back in time and *not* end up dead," said Tristan. "It's actually possible to go back in time and *do* stuff. In fact, it may have happened already."

"What?"

He sat up and took a big swig of his beer. "The intel community has been noticing some inexplicable shit going on, but it's a little less inexplicable *if* it is the case that foreign powers are engaging in diachronic operations."

He gave me a moment to digest this. "DODO," I said. "Department of Diachronic Operations. You've known all along, haven't you?"

"We have suspected. Now we know."

"Are you serious?"

He nodded.

"You mean there's another Erszebet out there?"

He shrugged.

"What exactly are you saying, Tristan?"

"Well . . ." He sat up straighter, put the beer on the coffee table, rested his forearms on his knees, and looked at me. "IARPA—the Intelligence Advanced Research Projects Agency, which has been running this thing until now—thinks other countries might have, or might soon have, access to . . . others like Erszebet. Somehow. Purely theoretical at this stage, but the time travel was new information, and all of a sudden, pieces started to fit together. So *in case* certain other countries have found their own Erszebets and are sending people back in time to fiddle with things, the DNI doesn't want to see a Magic Gap opening up."

"DNI?"

"Director of National Intelligence. General Octavian Frink. Reports directly to POTUS. The Director of IARPA reports to Frink. General Schneider, God rest his soul, worked for a black-budget arm of IARPA. And what has happened now—less than twenty-four hours ago, Stokes—is that DODO has been bumped up the org chart. Now it's directly under General Frink, with a dotted line to Dr. Rudge at IARPA."

"Dotted line?"

"It just means Rudge is an advisor. We keep him in the loop."

"Who's 'we'?"

"Well . . . I have been promoted to lieutenant colonel and made the acting head of the Department of Diachronic Operations. I've been tasked with taking the ODEC and Erszebet to the next level, focusing entirely on time travel."

For a moment I was so amazed by this reversal of fortune I couldn't respond. Then: "Great! So . . . you're not in trouble."

"I'm not in trouble," he said with a small, contented smile.

"Wow, Tristan!" I hooked one arm around his neck and gave him a side-hug. He grinned but took it a little stiffly. "That's *amazing*. Erszebet's willing to cooperate?"

He rolled his eyes, but did not look too worried. "We're working on that. The Asset likes to be pandered to by powerful men in suits. She likes Constantine Rudge because he wears cuff links and went to Oxford. So I think I can chart a course."

"Well then, congratulations. When do you start?"

"As soon as we can get ourselves to DC for the swearing-in."

"You and Erszebet."

He gave me a funny look. "Stokes. We're going to be sending people *back in time*." He jerked his left thumb over his shoulder as if that's where back-in-time was.

"Right, I got that."

"So?"

"So, what?"

"So who do you think is qualified to go back in time?"

I shrugged. "Athletes? Assassins?" He was shaking his head. "Historians?"

"Stokes!" He laughed. "Whoever goes has to be able to function in a setting where nobody speaks modern American English. We need polyglots and linguists. We need"—he pointed—"*you*."

I stared at him, eyes wide. I bet my mouth dropped open too.

"*I* need you," he added, realizing I was incapable of speech at that moment. "And I'm pretty sure you're otherwise unemployed."

Although safely seated, I suddenly felt so lightheaded I put a hand on the coffee table to steady myself.

"So what do you say?" he asked, with a comradely grin. "I can't promise you'll get to practice your conversational Sumerian, but you never know."

I felt like I was on the crest of a roller coaster, just about to plunge down a steep, joyfully terrifying thrill ride. I would have to be mad to agree to such a thing. "You want to send me back in time?" I heard myself say, not really sounding like myself.

"Well, not *permanently*," he said. "I'd miss you too much, Stokes." God damn that grin of his. And he even roughed up my hair, the bastard.

"When do we leave?" I asked.

PART
TWO

MATERIALIZING WAS FAR more startling than any practice session we'd attempted in the ODEC, chiefly because not only was I (as usual) extremely disoriented and confused, but I landed completely naked. Outside.

My balance wobbly, I felt warm grass and earth under my feet, and then collapsed at once sideways so that the smell of moist, sun-warmed soil filled my nostrils. I spent a few moments just breathing. Consciousness—the here-and-now of the human mind—is linked to the body's surroundings by a thousand strands, most of which we're never aware of until all of them are severed. The modern analogy would be to what happens when an errant backhoe slices through a fat underground cable, in an instant cutting off countless phone calls and Internet connections. One's senses are always tracking sights, sounds, smells, and sensations. When a witch Sends you, all of those are interrupted, and your mind doesn't know what to do with itself until it has knit itself into its new surroundings. It takes a minute.

Sun, dappled by the branches of a tree, warmed my left side, as my right side felt the bumps of grass and earth, scattered twigs, knotty roots. As my consciousness adjusted to the new environment, I noticed an absence of the constant ambient noise of modern civilization. In its place was tremendous birdsong and the buzz of insects.

A whizzing noise droned over me, barely overhead, like a huge insect, and terminated in a *thunk*. I looked over to see an arrow that had just embedded itself in the protruding root of a huge tree. Its fletchings of grey feathers were just a vibrating blur. It would have hit me if I hadn't toppled over.

Immediately the hazy sun was blocked by a tall figure looming over me. Naked, dizzy, and unarmed, I could not protect myself from him. Erszebet had just sent me to my death as surely as she'd sent General Schneider. What fools we'd been to think otherwise! He stepped directly over me, standing astride me, as if I were not there, his long robes covering my naked middle. A minister? A chieftain?

But the figure shouted in a woman's voice, deep and stern: "Samuel! Hunting is not for rabbits, you must *trap* them. We have told you so already. Save your arrows for the deer and do not shoot them so close to my house." A native English speaker, with a lilt almost Appalachian or Irish. A distant voice, a boy's, plaintive, giving her some back-sass.

"Samuel, you saw no such thing, it is your devilish fancy getting the better of you again. You are disobedient. Go in to your mother." A pause. "Go in to your mother, I say. You may fetch your arrow back later. It is easy to find—in the root of the tree." And then, a whisper in my direction: "Do not move until I tell you to." And back up: "Samuel! *Now!*"

A long pause, as I began to collect my wits. Massachusetts Bay Colony. August 1640. The village of Muddy River, someday to be more attractively renamed Brookline. Yes, it was coming into focus now.

Finally, the woman stepped back from me, and I could see her clearly. She was a Puritan, in a fitted dark blue top and long skirt, and a simple white cap. A large white collar covered her throat and shoulders. I had expected her to look like this, and yet seeing it was dizzying. She was not wearing a costume, she was simply wearing her clothes. I was *here*. It was *happening*.

I would judge her to be about forty years of age, but I knew her from our research to be closer to thirty. She gave me a critical look. "Why have you come?" she demanded. "This is no place for us. How thoughtless of you, to appear where anyone may see you or harm you. That arrow would hit you another time. And the boy saw you. You have made me a liar to say he didn't. If he calls us out, we'll both be hanged."

"I . . . I'm sorry, Goody Fitch, I . . ."

"Stay down," she said, completely unsurprised that I called her by name. "I will get something to cover you." She turned and walked out of my view.

I raised my head a little. The silence and birdsong continued their counterpoint, and in the distance now I could hear, and smell, a river. The still air had the clinging, heavy humidity of high summer. I was a stone's throw from a small wattle-and-daub house with a thatched roof, a small door, but no windows on the back wall. A hundred paces away in either direction, barely in view, were similar dwellings. The land had mostly been cleared, with big axe-scarred tree stumps still protruding from tilled ground here and there, but a few huge old trees, too much effort to chop down, remained scattered about. I was beneath one such, a sugar maple.

Behind the house was a fine, verdant kitchen garden, and beyond that, a forest, densely leafed, mostly oak, some pine. The boy whom Goody Fitch had scolded had been to the right of me—to the south, I realized, superimposing the map of Muddy River over what I could see. That meant it was the Griggs family. Samuel Griggs . . . the name was not familiar, but I hadn't memorized the whole village, just enough that I could passably seem to be familiar with it. Perhaps he would die before he reached maturity.

It was a settlement of fewer than two hundred souls, so of course I could not convince anyone that I belonged here. But these lots were large—a dozen acres or more—and so it should have been easy to arrive unnoticed. That had been the intention: I was to arrive on the property of someone we believed to be a witch, out of sight of prying eyes. A fine scheme if there were no complications.

Dear reader: there are always complications. Every ~~fucking~~ time.

Goody Fitch returned with a thin dun-colored woolen blanket and offered it down to me. "Come inside quickly," she said. "We are about the same size, I will clothe you. And then you must leave quickly in case Goody Griggs comes here, set on by her son." A pause, as I gathered the blanket around my shoulders and carefully got to my feet. She did not offer a hand to assist, just stood watching me, evaluating. "But before you go, you will tell me why you are here."

"I'm here on an—"

Her eyes flicked sideways, noticing some distant movement. "Inside."

Her caution seemed extreme; we were in the middle of the wilderness. But I pursed my lips closed to reassure her and followed her around the house, past an axe resting on a pile of recently split firewood. Rosemary bushes grew to either side of the door, flanked by chamomile plants. A remarkable coincidence: Rebecca East-Oda's cellar hatchway was framed by the same set of plants.

The atmosphere in the house was far more pleasant than I'd expected. The floor was pounded dirt, and therefore both cool and cooling. There were glowing coals on the hearth but the room was not hot, as the southward-facing door stood open. Two windows—one east, one west—were unglazed, so a very feeble breeze could move through the space. Beside the hearth was an open doorway into a back room, where I saw beds.

This main room was uncluttered and unadorned, every item in it neat and practical and made of wood: two small benches, a stool, one central table and another along the wall; two chests.

"Sit," said Goody Fitch, gesturing toward the stool. She disappeared into the back room and returned a brief moment later with clothes draped over one arm: a sleeveless white linen smock, a reddish skirt and matching waistcoat, a simple decorative collar, and a long apron (somewhat stained). In her other hand, she held a linen cap, a small drawstring bag, and a belt.

"Of course I have no extra stays," she said. This I knew to be the equivalent of a corset. "This is the best I can manage for you. My extra petticoats are wrapped away, so you must do without them, or stockings. I have an extra set of boots, tattered but useable. They are by the door."

"Thank you," I said, taking the clothes she offered. I began to put on the smock. "So you know, I am not a witch. I was sent here by a witch to fulfill a task. Would you consider helping me?"

She *tch*'d without responding directly, making it clear this was an imposition. "Are you hungry?" she asked, as if to avoid the topic of magic. "Thirsty? I have ale, and there is also some meal I can cook. I cannot give you any wheat as my husband will notice the absence, but he does not pay as much attention to the maize."

"The maize is more plentiful and therefore less dear," I said deliberately, fastening the smock closed at the neck.

"Yes." She crossed her arms and stared at me. "Are you from elsewhere in the colony, that you know that?"

"No. You are . . . historical to me," I said. She nodded, understanding. "Let me tell you my errand?"

"I'll not stop you from speaking," she said, going to a barrel in the corner and taking off the wooden lid, then scooping out cornmeal and putting it into an iron pot. "But do not assume I'll help you. 'Tis impossible to do magic safely here. These halfwits are all obsessed with Satan." She poured a frothy liquid into the pot from a pewter pitcher, and then attached the pot to an iron arm that hung over the hearth coals. She raked the coals and blew on them a little. "This will take some time," she said. "Give you a chance to explain yourself."

It would have been extremely rude for me to say so, but I was in no hurry to be fed. My digestion was a mess. Our research into the fate of the late General Schneider had uncovered evidence of an epidemic that had started in the village of Nagybörzsöny at the same time as his brief stay there. It was some sort of bowel complaint that had taken a number of lives before burning itself out. The village's isolation had prevented it from spreading farther, and the surviving locals had, of course, attributed it to witchcraft. But the lesson to us was obvious: time travelers could infect historical communities with diseases to which they had no immunity, and vice versa. So I'd been given every vaccination and antiviral drug known to modern science before stepping into the ODEC, to protect myself. And to protect the people of Muddy River, I'd taken a course of antibiotics that had killed everything in my gut, and scrubbed with disinfectant immediately before the mission. I wasn't sure what would happen if I ate Goody Fitch's gruel.

I began to tie the skirt at my waist, and opened my mouth to speak, but before I could say anything she spoke again, and as she did so, also came to fuss over my skirt.

"They've been mad with witch-hunt zeal because '38 nearly killed us all," she said. "Muddy River had just been chartered, we had all barely begun to build our homes and clear our gardens, and we were almost destroyed before we could take root. We had to plant the corn twice because it rotted in the frozen ground, then the spring was too wet, the summer too hot, and full of tempests, then it rained all autumn until October, when the snow came and never left. Many other settlements along the Charles did not survive the year. They attributed Mother Nature's handiwork to witchcraft, and the survival of the village to the Lord's Grace. *I* saved the village, but they do not know it, and they may never know it. If they even suspected, they would not thank me, they would kill me for witchcraft because they believe witchcraft is the work of the devil. Stupid folk." She tied the drawstring sharply tight around my waist. "That was the very year they excommunicated Anne Hutchinson, one of the best among them. And then brought in a slave-ship. And they call themselves Christians. Thick-waisted you are, for your size," she said.

"I did not grow up wearing stays. No women of my time did."

She made a bemused sound, and then continued her monologue as she helped me into the waistcoat. "Stab themselves in the foot. I cannot imagine this place will ever amount to anything."

"Why did you come, then?" I asked.

"I wanted to meet new witches," she said. "I am from a family of chroniclers and sages, I have always been encouraged to learn as much as possible. I was curious to compare information with the witches here—I assumed there must be some. My husband was never a Puritan but he favored their thinking and was anxious to be gone from England for his own reasons. So we sailed to Boston. Later we took the first chance to settle away from the peninsula. I had great hopes. But the settlers are all such sanctimonious asses that none of the native witches will speak to me about witchcraft, or anything else. They fear I will try to lead them away from their own gods and beliefs, that is how relentless and irritating these Puritans are. There are so many plants here we don't have back home, and I fain would learn them, but I find nobody who can teach me."

That was my in. "Like partridge-berry?" I said as casually as possible. "Or perhaps you still call it squaw-vine?"

She stopped suddenly as she was buttoning the waistcoat, and then resumed. "How do you know about that?" she asked. "That is the very plant I am most keen to understand. It seems to me it requires magic to find out all its possibilities."

"And cranberries," I added, "but maybe those are easier to understand."

"Cranberries are magnificent," she agreed. "And the elder-flower, which I know from its cousin in England. But the squaw-vine is something else again."

"It grows near pine trees," I said. "Do you know that much as yet?" She nodded cautiously, looking at me with new interest. *Thank you, Rebecca*, I thought. *Well done.*

"I know a lot about it," I continued, in an offering tone. "How and when best to harvest it, what parts of the plant are most useful—I know a great deal, although not of course what can only be known through magic, since I'm not a witch. But I can help you. If you'll help me."

She was tempted by this offer, I could tell, but remained uncertain. "Do you understand the danger you are putting both of us in?" she asked.

"I also know some interesting things about skullcap," I added. "And bee-balm."

She shook her head. "I know them already. They haven't the scent of the squaw-vine. They're just medicinal, not magic. The squaw-vine *calls* to me. But in a language I do not speak."

"We'll fix that," I said. "Help me with my errand, and when I return, I'll tell you everything I know. And then you'll send me back to where I came from."

A pause. "I will," said Goody Fitch. "What are you called?"

"Melisande," I said. "I am unmarried."

"I am Goody Fitch," she said. "My Christian name is Mary."

"I know," I said, then briefly told her my errand: that I must obtain a copy of the newly published Bay Psalm Book, coop it safely into a barrel to protect it from the elements, and then bury it in a very precise spot in a field to the northwest of the palisaded village of Cambridge.

Instead of questioning why I needed to have the book, or to bury it, she simply asked, "Why there, particularly?"

I considered how fully to answer. "That is where a descendant of yours will eventually live," I said. "Someone I know in my time. They need a copy of the book. If I do not . . . *reserve* one for them now, they will never be able to get one."

To my surprise, she responded to this news with an outburst of laughter. "How preposterous to imagine civilization ever flourishing in such a backwater!" she said. "And how disappointing to think my own begotten will not have the sense to get out of such a place!"

I bristled on behalf of my adopted city. "Cambridge becomes one of the greatest places of learning in the world," I said—rashly, for it is always ill-advised to speak of future times. "It easily rivals, arguably outshines, its British namesake."

"Bollocks," she said, amused. "A terrified village with the greatest invention in the world—a printing press!—and all they do with it is publish religious nothings. The only school in the New World and what do they teach? Only religion. And only *their* religion."

"Well, in fairness," I said, "if it weren't for their religion, none of this would exist right now. You wouldn't be here."

"I'd be in Virginia," she agreed briskly. "Where the religion is mercantilism. It is a marginally preferable religion, although the Americans suffer more under it than they do under Christianity. Anyhow . . . we've finished dressing you, so let's not tarry. Tell me directly what you need from me."

"Most of all, I need you to send me back to where I came from when I return here," I said. "And if you can point me the way to Cambridge, I'd be grateful."

"Easily done. You'll need toll for the ferry," she said, and went to one of the chests against the wall. There was a small locked box sitting atop it, about the size of a breadbox; she opened this with a key that she wore around her neck on a thin leather strap. From the box, she removed two tiny spheres, one a lead musket ball, the other larger, much lighter in color and weight, and highly polished. "Each of these will suffice for the ferry toll in one direction. I would give you some commodity money, but my husband keeps track of that and he would notice the absence of a cabbage head."

"Have you a shovel I might borrow?"

She thought a moment. "Yes. But 'tis a strange thing to meet a young woman roving the land by herself, stranger yet if she is brandishing a shovel. Say you are my cousin newly arrived from Shropshire and you are returning it to Goodman Porter in Watertown, you will need to take that road anyhow. There is none in Cambridge know me enough to ask questions that would get you into trouble. I think there be a cooper there, very near the bookseller's shop. I can give you nothing to buy his services, though, nor any way to get the book."

"I don't suppose I could ask you to assist me magically?"

"You can ask whatever you wish, but I will not risk it. I would have in England, if I felt your cause was just. Not here. Still, I wish you luck. You must be desperate in your cause if it forces you to come here. Fortify yourself with the maize-meal and then be off."

AS I ATE the tasteless, dry, crappy meal, which would make Cream of Wheat seem like a gourmet dessert, I reviewed what was to happen next. Which meant reviewing what had happened previously—in the distant future, I mean.

The day after I'd accepted Tristan's offer, just after sunrise, the whole crew had come back together at Hanscom Field, an Air Force base–cum–executive jet terminal northwest of Boston. For me, air travel had always meant Logan Airport. But it turns out that the kind of people who fly around in private jets fly through Hanscom Field—as do air travelers from the parallel universe of the military. I, Tristan, Erszebet, Oda-sensei, and even, to my amazement, Rebecca piled onto a plane that fit somewhere in the Venn diagram crossover between those two worlds, being a small eight-seater jet with military markings. Before we'd even had time to explore the plane's comforts, we were landing at Reagan National Airport across the river from Washington, DC. En route Tristan had monopolized the plane's washroom for a little while and changed into his Army uniform—the first time I had seen him so attired. It was the dress uniform with necktie and all kinds of little badges and insignia that might as well have been a secret code to me. He looked, if I may say it, swashbuckling, in a repressed sort of way.

I had been assuming a government van would pick us up at the airport, but instead Tristan led us across the skybridge to the Metro station and dealt out keycards. "Faster than fighting traffic—it's only three stops up the line!" he explained. We got on the next northbound train, passed through Crystal City a few minutes later, and shortly pulled into the Trapezoid City stop. I picked up my bag and got ready to detrain, but Tristan caught my eye and shook his head. "Trapezoid City is a shopping mall, Stokes—not the real deal. If we have time, we can go there when we're done!"

Erszebet was bemused by the Metro, and the Metro was fascinated by her. To date, we hadn't been out together much in public. So I'd had few opportunities to see how random strangers reacted to her looks. Reader, I don't think it would be boastful for me to say that I am not a bad-looking woman. I get my share of looks and compliments. But sitting near Erszebet on a subway train was enough to make me believe that invisibility potions were a real thing and that she had slipped one into my coffee.

The next station was called simply TRAPEZOID, but I could have guessed as much from the fact that more than half the people getting on and off the train were dressed in military uniforms of one service or another. We all followed Tristan up the escalators to a bus terminal complex aboveground, and from there to a huge, modern security checkpoint—a separate facility in its own right, built far enough from the subdued limestone façade of the Trapezoid proper to provide a security buffer. We'd arrived during the morning rush, and so ended up standing in line for a few minutes—long enough for me to stare across the parking lots at the front of the famous building, and to develop a sense of this-can't-be-happening unreality every bit as strong as anything associated with the ODEC. As the headquarters of the American military and presumed ground zero for any hostile military strike, the Trapezoid had, for me, always been more mythic than real. Like Mount Olympus or the River Styx, it was a thing alluded to in books and movies, or used in synecdoche to mean the American military as a whole. The terrorists had targeted it on 9/11, and I could see part of the memorial that had been built on the side where the plane had crashed into it. In a weird way, it was almost a letdown to see that it really existed and that it was, at the end of the day, just another wartime office building with windows and doors like any other.

Lacking normal credentials such as a birth certificate, Erszebet had to be whisked through a special lane by aides who had come down to meet us. Tristan stayed with her. The rest of us presented our Massachusetts driver's licenses and got scanned for concealed weapons. Erszebet's idiosyncratic 1950s-era wardrobe left very few places where she could have hid anything. I suppose they x-rayed her clutch. A lot of walking ensued. Erszebet in her heels and Frank Oda with the weight of his years were not particularly fast walkers, so we dawdled and shuffled down endless corridors in the bowels of the Trapezoid until we came to an elevator that took us up to a nicer-than-normal office zone. "The Acute Angle," Tristan explained, "the nice one, with the view over the river."

Anywhere else they'd have called it what it was: a corner office suite on the top floor. It was nice, old-school, paneled in wood, hung with pictures of battleships from the Age of Sail, Washington at Valley Forge, and the like. After passing through a couple of layers of receptionists and aides, and surrendering our electronic devices, we were ushered into a conference room, invited to take seats, and plied with ice water. Erszebet insisted on water with no ice and gave us all a piece of her mind about the American obsession with putting ice cubes into everything.

We waited there for twenty minutes or so, which Tristan seemed to think was only mildly remarkable. Then another door—not the one we'd come through—was opened by an aide, and in walked a man in a civilian business suit. Even I, with very little taste in clothes, could tell that this was a fine suit indeed. "Dr. Rudge!" Tristan said. "Good to see you again!"

Rudge was trailed by a couple of younger civilian aides who quietly took seats along the wall of the room and opened up their laptops as the rest of us did introductions. "Oh, please, don't get up," he told us in the sort of mid-Atlantic accent that I associated with Franklin Delano Roosevelt and midcentury newsreel announcers. "I'm so sorry to be late, we were detained in the West Wing—everything's running late there today. Dr. Stokes! Charmed! I've heard so much about you and I'm looking forward to talking about the Breton language at some point if we ever have time. Old family connection—long story. And you must be Mrs. East-Oda."

And so on. Dr. Constantine Rudge was as immaculate in his manners and breeding as he was in his attire. In his early forties, he had the gravitas of an older man, but was styled younger, with somewhat longer hair than most men in the Trapezoid, and heavy, stylish eyeglasses that I thought of as European. His jovial confidence made me feel somehow as if I were missing something—was this guy really famous? Powerful? Important? Later I Googled him, to discover that he was classic Yale, Rhodes Scholar, Fulbright, City of London, and all that, but kept a low public profile. Rudge was the head of IARPA, the Intelligence Advanced Research Projects Agency, which like a lot of the intelligence world was a blend of civilian and military personnel. He'd been the boss of the late General Schneider. As Tristan had already explained, he would be an advisor—a "dotted line" on the org chart—to the newly re-founded and upgraded DODO.

Anyway, he got off on the right foot with Erszebet by kissing her hand—incidentally giving her a chance to admire his cuff links—and greeting her in what sounded like passable Hungarian. To my astonishment they actually conducted a short exchange in that most difficult of tongues before Rudge begged off, apologized for his butchering the beautiful Magyar language, and switched to High German. Catching my eye at one point, Rudge remarked, "Dr. Stokes will have noticed an Austrian accent. I lived in Vienna for some years in my twenties, working on a dissertation about interwar banking. It took me to Budapest frequently." And yet somehow Rudge managed to say all of this with little eye rolls and shrugs that actually made it seem self-deprecating.

I didn't much care, all I knew was that Erszebet clearly thought Rudge was the only person of any sophistication in the room, which meant that the rest of us didn't have to expend energy trying to keep her happy. Tristan checked his watch a couple of times, once raising his eyebrows and saying to me, "Looks like we won't have time to go shopping after all, Stokes!"

Finally General Frink showed up, preceded and followed by more aides, some civilians, others in uniforms of various services. He had a row of three stars on each lapel, which even I knew made him a very big deal. I wouldn't need to Google this fellow. He was the Director of National Intelligence, reporting directly to the President. He was Rudge's boss, and now Tristan's. As he blew in, he was in full conversation with two members of his entourage, and scarcely seemed to notice that he had entered another room with a different set of humans in it. His crew formed a sort of football huddle around him for a minute and they held an acronym-studded conference that didn't concern us. Then half of them speed-walked out of the room. Of those who remained, some took up seats along the wall. General Frink slammed his formidable arse down into a chair that had been pulled out for him by a junior officer. That seemed to be Tristan's signal to sit back down—for he had exploded out of his chair when Frink had entered the room, and stood at attention waiting to be noticed.

A civilian aide skimmed a sheet of paper onto the table directly in front of General Frink. Frink reached into the breast pocket of his uniform, which was stiff with ribbons and decorations, and drew out a pair of reading glasses, put them on, and scanned the page for a minute before finally looking up and acknowledging our presence. "Yes," he said, "Department of Diachronic Operations." His eyes scanned the row of faces on our side of the table, and I suppose it was a credit to his powers of discipline that he lingered only briefly on Erszebet. The civilian whispered something in his ear, and I was pretty sure I heard the sibilant word "Asset," which was the term that the late General Schneider had used to refer to Erszebet. Frink's eyes went back to her for a moment and he nodded. He then thought silently for a while, and heaved a sigh.

"I am going so far out on a limb for you people," he said, "that if I hadn't seen even stranger things during my career in Intelligence I would shitcan this project in a heartbeat. But all the evidence points to this being real. Roger Blevins has vouched for it, and that means a lot to me."

"Roger *Blevins*?" I blurted out.

A few moments of silence ensued. Everyone was startled—most of all me. I'm not a blurter in general. But hearing that name in this context could not have been more astonishing. Tristan kicked me under the table.

More whispering from the civilian aide: a buff-looking bro in his early thirties, with heavily gelled hair. "You're Stokes," Frink said. "Roger's your mentor. At Harvard."

This really did render me speechless, but Tristan kicked me again just to be sure. "General Frink, if I may, Dr. Stokes here is just a little surprised to hear Dr. Blevins's name brought up, because she doesn't know of his connection to the program. Operational security."

"Ah, I see. Very good, Lyons. Ms. Stokes, the connection goes way back—Roger and I went to school together," General Frink explained. "When we first began observing these historical anomalies, he—along with Dr. Rudge here—were part of the brain trust we brought together to seek explanations."

I was thoroughly tongue-tied now, but the ice was broken as far as Frink was concerned. He pulled off his reading glasses and fidgeted with them as he went into a long mansplanation of what magic was and why the United States needed to avoid a "Magic Gap" with other nations.

"Excuse me," Erszebet said sharply, as Frink began wandering into an explanation of the many-worlds interpretation of quantum theory that even I could sense was painfully cack-handed. "Have you taken up a day of my life and *quite* a lot of taxpayer money to bring me in your foul-smelling airplane, all the way here, to this room, where you do not have the courtesy of introducing yourself to me . . . just so *you* can inform *me* who I am, and why that is important to you? Is this what you have done here?"

It was the first time I'd ever been grateful for Erszebet's . . . Erszebetness. Frink gave her a slightly offended look and tried to carry on his monologue, now aiming it exclusively at me, but she was having none of that.

"This is a yes-or-no question I've asked you," she said, standing up and placing herself in front of me to intercept his gaze. "Are you incapable of answering yes or no?" She looked at Tristan, appalled. "Do not work for this man. This man is an *imbecile.*"

Within three minutes, she had berated Frink into a huffy submission, enough that he rose to his feet and gruffly shook hands with each of us. During this little outbreak of sociability, I also learned the name of the civilian aide-bro: Les Holgate, who went around and shook hands with the perky vigor of a man who had sat through one too many free webinars about the importance of networking.

Erszebet was unconvinced: Frink's effort at politeness lacked the requisite enthusiasm, and Les Holgate overdid it. We all resumed our seats. Frink took the floor again, and explained to us about

How Things Are Done In This Town, including brief introductions to the concepts of Belt Tightening and Fiscal Responsibility. This led to another brief vituperative interjection from Erszebet regarding taxpayer money being used to bring four people to him when wouldn't it be cheaper for him to just hop aboard a civilian flight and take the T to Central Square, thus saving money that was better used for the collective good? I had not credited her with such socialist sensibilities before. Nor have I seen her express such sentiments since then, so perhaps she was merely being disagreeable for effect.

It was the kind of sermon that would only be delivered before bad news, and indeed Frink went on to explain that we would be given just enough seed money to figure out how to use magic to self-fund.

Erszebet, alarmed, put aside her 'tude to explain very plainly that there could be no changing water to wine or lead to gold—to say nothing of plutonium. She wanted it understood that magic could not be used that way in any era, or it would long ago have led to the self-destruction of the human race.

"I say, to heck with gold!" announced Les Holgate. "There's something a lot more valuable than that: Microsoft stock. Why not go back in time to the 1980s and buy up some of that?"

Erszebet drew breath to burn Holgate to the ground, but was cut off by a few words in Hungarian from Dr. Rudge. "Miss Karpathy, if I may." He turned his attention to Holgate. "Les, this is covered in the briefing documents. Maybe you didn't get a chance to scan them. I know you're more of a PowerPoint guy." This was delivered in such a light tone that Holgate's face didn't start turning red until a few seconds later. "The Sending—the movement of the subject to a DTAP, or Destination Time and Place—is a magic-based process. As such, a DOer—a Diachronic

Operative—can only be Sent to a place and time where magic works. Between 1851 and now, magic hasn't worked anywhere. So the most recent DTAP we can Send people to is late July of 1851. The Microsoft gambit can't work. And we can't go back in time and kill Hitler either."

Holgate hadn't fully caught on to how deeply Dr. Rudge had just buried him, so he came back for another round. "Okay, well then, go back and invest in whale oil futures or something."

"That is in essence what we propose to do, Les," Tristan said. And he went on to explain the Bay Psalm Book gambit.

Some years earlier, a copy of this 1640 volume—the first book ever printed in North America—had been unearthed in a church basement, and sold for millions of dollars at auction. Tristan suggested we go back in time, find another copy, conceal it someplace where we could retrieve it in the present day, and put it up for sale. The operation would be relatively simple. It wouldn't involve killing anyone, or any other heavy-handed intervention in history. It would be confined to the Boston area. And it would generate enough revenue to keep DODO afloat for the better part of a year.

General Frink liked this idea immensely. Dr. Rudge, acting in his advisory capacity, asked a couple of good questions about the money end of things, then nodded approval. Frink wound up the meeting briskly, and sent us all back to Cambridge to begin the research required for this escapade.

A few minutes later, having been reunited with our electronic devices, we were out-processing through the security checkpoint, and headed back down the escalators to the Metro stop. We even had time for a quick turn around the Trapezoid City shopping mall, where a young man in the food court approached Erszebet—fresh from raiding a high-end cosmetics boite—and asked her for her autograph. He had no idea who she was. He simply assumed that she was a movie star.

The Bay Psalm Book gambit had been news to the rest of us. But on the flight home, Rebecca became unexpectedly useful. I had considered her a reluctant soldier, signing on only because Frank wouldn't do anything without her and she was too indulgent to deny him. But as we flew back, she volunteered a new-found suspicion that her accused ancestress from the Salem witch trials had, in fact, *been a witch*.

When we got back to Boston where she could get access to genealogical records, Rebecca then traced this unfortunate woman's lineage back another half-century, to Muddy River, a settlement just inland from Boston. We could not, of course, know if Goody Fitch was a witch, even if we could be sure that her granddaughter Mary Estey had been. Erszebet was cavalier and vague about the hereditary nature of magic, but when pressed by Tristan to give it serious thought, said she *supposed* it was a matrilineal affair, although she knew plenty of instances of a woman receiving the ability through a paternal ancestress. Goody Fitch being Goody Estey's maternal grandmother, we had a good chance—but no certainty—of success.

And for the burying site of the book, that too had been Rebecca's call. As steward of the oldest house in the area, she was well versed in local history going back to the founding of Cambridge, when it was still the small, wooden-walled village that Goody Fitch had just mocked. Rebecca's present-day backyard included a large boulder, the only unadulterated topographic detail for blocks in all directions. In the colonial era there was a creek running near the eastern side of it, but that bed would dry up in a year or two, when a mill was built on the Watertown Road and the creek was diverted to power it. We determined I would bury the book, in 1640, against the western side of this boulder, at a distance of my arm's length and to the depth of my arm's reach.

Rebecca and I then researched what I would need to do to "pass" as chronologically local—the manner of dress, of speech, of courtesy—while Tristan established how to best protect the book from the elements during its long rest. He determined that of the resources available at the time, a small watertight barrel filled with flour or dry sand for "packaging" was our best bet.

I consigned all we had learned to memory, and then prepared to be the first DOer (Diachronic Operative) going back to do the first Deed (or as we spelled it, DEDE—"Direct Engagement for Diachronic Effect") under the banner of the Department of Diachronic Operations.

HAVING FINISHED THE maize (which sat like a cannonball in my sterilized belly), I rose, and Goody Fitch beckoned me to follow her to the small barn that was a moment's walk downwind from the house. As a few sheep and one sullen cow stared at us incuriously from the pen, she examined the row of neat farm tools and handed me a long-handled shovel with a pointy tip.

"My husband and son are out with the oxcart to check the fields, but Goodman Griggs is on his way to the ferry landing this hour," she said. "I'll ask him to convey you on the cart. It will save you an hour of walking."

Goodman Griggs was dressed like he was right out of Central Casting, in dark doublet and breeches with a wide-brimmed felt hat and a barber's bib of a collar. He was a farmer, as anyone in this settlement must be, and a bit grizzled. He seemed to do a double take when he saw me, before turning his head sharply away. For a moment I feared I had been detected as a poser, but he said nothing. He radiated the sort of pompous complacency that suggested fundamentalism, so I ran through all my memorized scriptural passages in case I needed to demonstrate my affected faith. But he was not one to speak. He nodded gruffly when I was presented to him, as if he did not approve of me but could not say no; he made no gesture to help me up into the cart, which was filled with barrels of corn and squash.

A seventeenth-century rustic cart is no BMW convertible. It is not even a carriage, for it has no springs, is purely utilitarian, and bumps one fiendishly with no regard for dignity or comfort. The ox that drew it was flatulent. Being grass-fed (not because it was environmentally correct but because grass was then the cheapest and easiest way to feed an ox in summer), its gas was less odorous than I'd expected, but still was nothing pleasant, and with the fine film of sweat that covered me, I was to feel the putrid scent molecules clinging to my skin all the rest of the day.

Shortly, we had come through the woods and arrived at the Charles. No clean-cut banks as I knew it, however: across the river was an enormous marsh, broader by half than the river itself. A narrow channel had been hacked and dredged through it so that the ferry could reach the landing. Beyond that, shimmering in the heat, I could see a palisade of vertical logs. This barrier, I assumed, was to protect the town's most valuable commodity—four-year-old Harvard College—from marauding Indians. There had recently been a war between the Pequot and Mohegan tribes, won by the latter with help from the settlers. But now the Mohegans were quarreling with the Narragansetts. I had not educated myself as to where that feud would lead, lest I inadvertently say something too prescient for 1640. (I was pretty sure it didn't turn out well for anyone, though.)

The ferry service was very new, and at present comprised just a dock on either bank plus a flat-bottomed boat, a raft with skeletal bulkheads, really. Standing beside it were two young rowers who looked like brothers. Despite the unflattering Puritan uniform, they had the agreeable build of a crew team, but I knew better than to stare, and averted my eyes.

"I do not know her, she came from Goody Fitch," Goodman Griggs said to them in a grumpy tone as he pulled up the ox. The two younger ones gave me a quizzical look, then turned their attention to their work: the three men, forming a line, began to unload the barrels of vegetables into the ferry. I waited until they had finished, then took from the drawstring bag at my belt the little musket shot. I presented it to the nearer ferryman (the younger one) as casually as I could, as if I was accustomed to such barter. The fellow looked at me oddly, and again I feared I was about to be unmasked. He examined the musket shot to make sure it wasn't scant—lead is such an easy metal to carve off bits of. He put it in his own satchel, wiped his brow with the back of his arm, and paid me no further heed. I took that as allowance to board the ferry.

The older brother, stabilizing the last of Griggs's open barrels, glanced at me and . . . smiled. His teeth were grey but well-shaped.

He caught himself smiling, blushed, and looked away.

They were strong and fast, those two rowers, for such an unwieldy boat cutting across the current. The older brother was nearer to me, avoiding my gaze; I found my eyes straying from the water to him, and enjoyed watching his movements, sure and confident and smooth despite the oppressive heat and his heavy clothes. He must have felt my stare, for at one moment, between strokes, he turned slightly to look at me, and—as if despite himself—he smiled shyly. I smiled back. He blushed again and looked away. I had not expected Puritan flirtation!

When we got to the north bank of the Charles, there was another dock at which the boat was roped, and two boys there waiting. I'd watched them splashing water at each other as we approached, and laughing merrily, but now they were all business. I envied them the freedom to frolic in the river—it looked wonderfully cooling. The palisades came down to the river's edge a stone's throw to either side of the landing, creating a sense of urgency and purpose, the pretense of a city without any sign of one from here. I'd have to walk several hundred yards up the slope, nearly to the future Harvard Square, before I'd reach actual civilization.

One of the boys quickly counted the barrels of corn and squash, and nodded, looking satisfied. He turned and ran up toward the town. The other lad helped the two ferrymen to unload the cargo. I disembarked, glancing one last time at the older rower. He was already staring at me, and our eyes met again. Again he smiled; again I smiled; again he blushed, and turned away. I am not one to make eyes even in my own era. Only an hour in this strange new world and already I was contemplating pulling a Hester Prynne! How very disorienting it all was.

I began to walk up the wide dirt path to the village, using the shovel as a walking stick.

Of all the skills I'd had to learn for success in this DTAP (Destination Time and Place), the hardest of all was thievery. Language was no issue, nor was my accent: settlers were coming through Boston from all over England, and the English regional accents of the time were even more diverse than today's. Learning to dress myself had been simple enough. I'd found a stable at which to practice riding horses for the first time since I was ten, although I was quite certain I'd have no chance of it here. A trip to Plimoth Plantation had felt almost like a cheat sheet, supplemented by a visit to the Americas wing of the Museum of Fine Art. A costume shop that kitted out Boston theatres rented us a colonial outfit—smock, stays, petticoat, skirt, waistcoat, stockings, garter, collar, coif—which I'd practiced lacing and buttoning myself into and out of until I could do it fluidly. I'd memorized and practiced quoting certain passages from the Geneva Bible (very popular among the Pilgrims), and taken a crash course in celestial navigation from an MIT grad student, whom Tristan signed to secrecy and paid well not to ask any questions. This was only the first of many whom we would later call HOSMAs—Historical Operations Subject Matter Authorities—and whom we would end up hiring to teach DOers things they would need to know.

All of that had been a cinch. Harder by far was to work out how to steal a book from under its owner's nose. First, there was my own moral and ethical conditioning to overcome. Then there was the matter of simply how to *do* it. Having so little recon to rely on, Tristan had proposed five possible schemes, and I'd memorized all of them step by step. They all seemed preposterous. Especially now that I was here.

I reached the village—a loose collection of small thatched-hut buildings, some wattle-and-daub, but many full-timbered, and many with second floors. A subtle but pervasive odor of waste wafted about the hot, dusty streets, and I felt the porridge curdling in my stomach. There were no street signs, but having memorized the map of Cambridge for this era, I knew the bookseller would be on the right at the first intersection I came to, at Water and Long Streets (or as I knew them, Dunster and Winthrop). A block farther up Water would be the Meeting House, which was also the church. We had considered my taking a copy of the psalter from the pews there, but decided that in such a small community a newcomer would be eyed ceaselessly, and perhaps suspiciously, at church. I would have to pinch it from its secular source.

There was the bookseller's, just ahead. It was a two-story building with planks lying on the ground in front of the threshold to approximate a front stoop. The door was open, and two front-facing windows were unshuttered. I saw a wooden floor within, and a long table, and many barrels and crates: it was not specifi-cally a bookshop, but a shop that happened to sell books. I leaned the shovel against the building and went to the doorway. I wiped away a layer of grime and dust from my face, using the sleeve of the waistcoat, and looked in.

Behind the long table (his position suggesting he was the propri-etor of the place) was a round-faced, proper-looking gentleman of perhaps five and twenty, frowning up at a taller fellow on my side of the table. The taller fellow was frowning back down at him. The proprietor looked unaccustomed to frowning. The tall fellow looked quite used to it. They were both in grey doublet and breeches. The shorter man also sported a canvas merchant's apron. Between them, on the table, was an impressive stack of leather-bound books.

"It will destroy my profit to reprint them," the tall fellow was complaining. "Let alone rebind all the reprints. I have created an errata to go with it, that suffices. 'Tis selling well enough for you, isn't it?"

"'Tis selling very well, but the errata misses half the errors and I am forever deflecting comments about it from the people who have given me their money for it," said the merchant, in the tone of a parent issuing a firm but gentle rebuke. He had a benign energy to him. Instinctively I liked him more than the other fellow. "It makes them disinclined to give me their money for other purchases."

"It's the only book you're selling," protested the printer.

"I've got Bibles coming over from England, due next week," said the merchant. "And there is plenty I sell here beside books."

The printer looked taken aback. "Why be you importing Bibles from England when you have finally got a printer in your own backyard?"

"Maybe he is not a very good printer," said the merchant, as kindly as possible. "Also there is a new book written by a doctor, about the circulation of blood. 'Twill be here on the next ship."

"Yes, I've heard about the blood, 'tis a ridiculous rumor," said the printer, quite put out. "And nobody decent will ever want to read about such unsavory subjects. Especially in this town, where we have a *college*!"

I decided this was a fortuitous accident, and that I could use it better than any of the scenarios Tristan had proposed for the theft. So I stepped into the shop.

The merchant gestured to the pile of books. "They are no good to me, Stephen. Reprint them. I'll buy them from you at a higher price if that will help keep you from ruin." At that moment, they both saw me, and paused from their discourse to examine me. The merchant nodded and then returned his attention to the books, while Stephen the Printer ogled me a moment longer, before saying hurriedly to the merchant, "You've a wife and babe to feed and another due this leaf-fall, Hezekiah. 'Twould be wrong of me to take money from your children's mouths." He said it not as if he really meant it, but as if he knew he must because there was a witness present.

"'Twould be wrong of me to sell any more of this printing," said Hezekiah matter-of-factly.

"Is that the new psalter?" I asked.

"'Tis," said the merchant, looking at me with some skepticism. "You're not here to purchase one, are you?"

"No, sir, I am here to purchase three. My master sent me to fetch them up," I added, since nobody dressed as I was dressed would be in a position to buy one for personal use.

"Who's your master, then?" asked the printer, in an almost lecherous voice.

"A squire of Boston," I said with a little attitude. "He wants one for himself and two for family gifts."

Stephen gestured to the pile. "I'm Stephen Day, I'm the printer, have a look."

"I'm Hezekiah Usher, the bookseller, and I'm not selling these books," said the merchant, still very matter-of-fact. "You'd best come back in a sennight."

I made sure to look crushed. "Oh, but Goodman Usher, it is a long way from Boston, and I've the harvest to help with when I return. I've not the time to return. Might you sell some of these to me, even if they be not perfect?"

"Yes. Look," commanded Stephen Day. The merchant was about to protest, but instead smirked and raised his eyes to God with a shrug of resignation. I walked to the table, ignoring the intense stare of the printer, and picked up a book. The leather was supple. When I opened it, the binding was stiff and fresh, a faint smell of glue still on it, as well as the clean smell of paper, and another smell, almost metallic, which might have been the ink. They were elegant, the shape a little narrower than modern books, with a bold exquisite font on the first page: "The WHOLE booke of psalmes faithfully translated into ENGLISH *metre*." By modern standards, yes, okay, the typesetting was an embarrassment, but the book itself was handsome. I thumbed through a few pages, pretended to study a leaf, set the volume aside, thumbed through another with a studious expression. Then another. Then a fourth. The two men watched me.

"What do you look for?" asked the printer.

I was about to give him a polite smile and then remembered

that this population never seems to do that. "You said these had faults and I am looking to find the least faulty of them."

"They are all from the same plates," said the printer impatiently. "I don't know if you can read but they're all exactly the same."

"Not so," I said, and presented the book I held. "Do you see how the printed area is slightly askew on this page? The others I looked at also had uneven pages. I am trying to find one where the paper was set just right on the press. I do not know the term for it, but I know what I am looking for."

The printer huffed a bit at that. The merchant chuckled and reached for a book. "Let us see if we can find any perfectly set books. If we can, Goodman Day, then I'll buy them off you and sell them to my customer."

I expected Stephen Day to instantly declare he'd sell the books to me directly, as his profit would be greater and Goodman Usher had already refused to carry them. That is what any enterprising person of my era would do. But this notion did not seem to enter Stephen Day's head. How very particular this society was: everyone kept to their place.

Or perhaps Stephen Day was simply dull-witted.

In any case, he agreed to this readily, and the two of them began to help me search for a book with every leaf of every octave perfect. As the three of us perused them, the men resumed arguing over the fate of the remaining books. Now their eyes were busy and their attention distracted. Good. I placed one book down to my right rather than back onto the pile (which was to my left). Each time I returned a book to the pile and reached for a new one with my left hand, I would push this hijacked volume an inch or so farther to the right, so that eventually I had inched it all the way around a small barrel on the table, where neither man could see it without searching for it. Their argument had continued to grow until they were truly bickering, so that when we finished reviewing all fifty-odd copies on the table, they looked not to me but to each other, teetering on the edge of vitriol.

"I shall have to disappoint my master," I said decisively. "None of these would be to his standards. Good day."

"Do you hear that?" said Hezekiah Usher to Stephen Day, as I turned to leave.

"This *strumpet* is failing to obey her master," said Stephen Day to Hezekiah Usher. "He told her to bring back three copies of the psalter, and she leaves here without even one. He did not tell her to check the *quality* of the *work*—"

But I was already out the door. I grabbed the shovel with my right hand and continued up Water Street.

My left hand clutched the hijacked copy of the Bay Psalm Book.

Reader, I had walked out the door right in front of them, holding it in plain sight, but they did not see it. Not only had they ceased to regard me, but even to the degree I was in their peripheral vision, they *did not see theft*. What I had just done was unthinkable to them. They could not see what they could not imagine. Still, it had been a shuddery moment, and I barely suppressed the urge to run, or at least look nervously over my shoulder. But I had it, and had gotten cleanly away.

Shovel—check. Psalter—check. That was the hardest part. Now to the cooper's, and then to the boulder, and then the return trip. I could do this! Feeling more confident, I held myself more upright and walked more briskly. I turned right at the next intersection, passed a leather-worker and an apothecary, and then on the left, as I knew from the old maps, there was a cooperage.

The cooperage had a yard that fronted the street. It was crowded with buckets, barrels, and casks, and on a huge tree stump in the center was a stash of metal hoops of different sizes. Various axes, knives, and adzes rested on a long, low bench beside this. The lovely smell of wood shavings neutralized the general stench of filth. The cooper, a man of Tristan's build, dressed in Puritan garb of faded maroon with a leather work-apron, hatless and collarless, was bent over a large half-finished barrel, using a hammer and what looked like an adze to pound a hoop into place around the staves.

"Are you a dry-tight cooper?" I asked.

"Can be," he said without looking up. "What is your need?"

"I have a thing in need of storage," I said, and held out the book.

He looked up. He was handsome, and held himself like somebody extremely comfortable in his own body—very different from the other men I'd encountered today. His eyes glanced briefly at the book but then strayed to me, and considered me a moment—the whole of me, not my face. His look gave me shivers. Then he suddenly shook his head, made eye contact, and said, "What, then?"

"I need this bound into a dry-tight vessel," I said. "'Tis an errand for my master in Boston."

"Your master in Boston. Is that the book everyone has been speaking of?" he asked, without much interest.

"The first book printed in America," I said, and I confess I was (and to this day, remain) awed by the thought.

He shrugged. "That's fine for those who read," he said. "It does less for our common good than did the first grist mill or the first forge."

". . . True," I said.

He set down the adze, held out his hand. "Let me see the little treasure," he said. I stepped off the street into the yard (in truth, there was hardly any difference between the two) and offered it to him. He took it in his large callused paw of a hand and regarded it. "Too small for a firkin," he murmured to himself.

He looked up at me. There was something slightly charged in his look—this had been true of Goodman Griggs, of the ferryman, and of the printer. Perhaps it was simply how Puritan men always looked at women. Perhaps my fear that they would find me suspicious was causing me to imagine things. "I have no barrel of the right size, but there is a lidded bucket I could alter to suit your need."

"I thank you," I said. "If you are sure it will be watertight."

"You could throw it in the ocean and a hundred years from now there will be no moisture in it," he said with casual confidence.

"I must probably still pack the book in something to keep it from getting bumped around on the journey," I said.

"I've some felt in the shop for oiling staves. Wrap it in some of that, 'twill suffice."

"Again, I thank you," I said, starting to feel slightly unnerved by the intensity of his eyes. He looked at the barrel he'd been working on, considered it, and then seemed to decide it could be left alone for a bit, for he then glanced around the yard until he found a small lidded bucket. He tossed the book into the bucket, with no reverence for either its physical or spiritual worth.

After snatching some felt from the back of his shop, he hunted through the hoops for a small one, and used his cooperish tricks to seal the top as tightly as any cask. I stood waiting, confused by how handsome I found him and wondering how best to negotiate the payment. All I had was the white wampum bead from Goody Fitch. I knew that white wampum was less valuable than purple, but beyond that had no idea how this would rank against, say, the musket shot.

When he finished, he held out the sealed bucket. I smiled gratefully and reached for it, but just before my hand touched it, he raised it out of reach. "Now for the issue of payment," he said. "What have you for money?"

"Just this, from my master," I said, pulling the wampum out of my drawstring bag. I offered it to him.

"'Tis a pretty bead," he said, "and a good start, but it will not cover this."

"I have nothing else," I said.

"Of course you do," he said in a low, meaningful voice. I felt a prickling down my spine.

"I do not know what you mean," I said.

"I think you do," he said, staring at me. Before I could move away, he reached toward me with his free hand and clapped it around my rib cage. I reflexively pulled away, but he had me fast. "That's a body not wearing a corset. I could tell just from how you hold yourself." I shuddered and tried to pull away; he held on tighter. "Your master sends you out to do his bidding, with insufficient currency, unlaced. Do you think I don't know what that means?"

"My . . . corset is damaged," I said, trying to keep my composure. I could not hit him with the shovel, as I wanted to—he had the book! I had to keep him close enough to get the book back!

He laughed at my claim. "And how does a maid's corset get damaged? Did your master damage it? I trust there was enjoyment in the damaging."

"You have completely misconstrued—"

"Don't worry," he said easily. "I will not report you to Reverend Shepard. But your master has set you up to be generous to me in exchange for my generosity. Luckily, it is an exchange I am happy to indulge in." He pulled me closer to him and then wrapped his arm around my waist.

I put a hand on his chest to repel him, but he mistook it as a sign of intimacy, and looked pleased. I could not avoid this problem, so instead I would have to use it: "You have hit upon the truth," I said resignedly. His smile grew much broader.

"Good," he said.

"However," I pushed on, trying to keep my voice calm (I knew it would be best to sound suggestive, but I could not quite push myself to that extreme), "I have urgent errands to attend to, and you've a barrel not yet finished. Give me the bucket now and I will return here in an hour with the freedom to . . . be generous."

He looked even more pleased. "After you are generous, I will give you the bucket," he declared triumphantly.

"My errand requires the bucket," I said. "But I will leave you with the wampum bead, plus a little taste of what's to come." I glanced up and down the street, but nobody was about. Knowing this was foolish—and yet necessary—I reached down and lifted my skirt halfway up my leg. I did not need to point out to him what was missing—no petticoats, no stockings, nothing but a skirt. I doubt he often saw a woman's ankle, let alone her shin, and I was flashing him up to the *knee*. Immediately he pulled me against him and I could feel him growing hard. I made myself smile. He no longer looked at all handsome to me. "I shall enjoy being generous with you," I whispered, and kissed him on the cheek. *Blech.*

At this he looked so radiant I feared he might fancy himself in love with me. He kissed me back, and released me. "You will return," he said sternly.

"Upon my soul, I will," I answered.

He gave me the bucket. I thanked him with a smile, and then hurried down the lane, my heart beating so hard that I could feel it pulsing in my neck.

Reader, I am relieved to inform you that the next leg of my

undertaking was without incident, although it was ~~fucking~~ hot and dusty work. I knew I had to take the Watertown Road (the Massachusetts Avenue of later centuries) to a certain bend, where it would intercept the creek that I could follow to the boulder. Easily done. It was peculiar recognizing the boulder in a world that was otherwise so unfamiliar.

The shaft of the shovel gave me a nasty splinter in the web between my thumb and forefinger, and digging the hole took longer than I'd anticipated, perhaps because my body was fatigued by the stress of the day. As I worked, I unearthed a midden—a deposit of oyster and clam shells that had apparently been left there by the natives. I buried the bucket, reburied the shells, and stomped the earth down as firmly as possible. Then, shovel in hand, slightly begrimed on face, hands, boots, and skirts, I returned to the village. Sticking to the western wall (as far from the cooperage as possible), I hurried down to the ferry landing.

Luck was with me again, for the ferry was on this shore. But of course I had nothing to pay for passage with.

Except an offer of *generosity*. Clearly all the men who had been eyeing me today could tell from my posture that I was unfettered beneath my waistcoat. That accounted for their unsettling looks. Now that I understood this, perhaps I could use it to my advantage with the ferryman.

Although there was his younger brother to consider. The younger brother had *not* eyed me—perhaps he didn't go for girls, or was nearsighted, or was a fierce Puritan. In any case, he was in the way.

I went directly to the older brother. "I'm here for my return trip," I said with a smile.

He flushed slightly, so I knew I had him in the palm of my hand. "Good day," he said, and held out his hand. "Your fare."

"I thought the earlier fare I rendered was for a two-way trip," I said.

He shook his head slightly. "Who told you such a falsehood?"

"'Tis how the service worked in my town back in England. I'm new to America and I made a rash assumption," I said. "If I had known to ask it, sure my master would have given me more for the fare."

"Your master should have known the toll without you asking," said the young man. His eyes strayed very briefly to my clothed but uncorseted torso, and then back up to meet mine. "I do not like how your master treats you," he said quietly.

I made myself blush. (I did not know I could do that until that moment.) "It is my lot, for now," I said. "I erred grievously in not establishing what I would need for the ferry toll, but I pray you let me across this one time. Next time I shall be prepared." I gave him what I hoped was a doe-eyed, damsel-in-distress look, feeling ridiculous and very glad Tristan was not there to tease me for it.

The ferryman considered me a moment and then moved his oar away, so that I could enter the boat. "Go on, then," he said, both kind and grudging. "I'll make excuses to my brother. But see that your master does not see fit to try to cozen us again."

"Cozen you?"

"He knows what he is doing, sending out an underdressed female servant as a . . . commodity."

I blushed even more deeply, this time sincerely. "I am astounded to hear you say it. I will speak to the minister about him."

He nodded approvingly . . . and then gave me the same shy smile I'd enjoyed earlier in the day. How very charming: he could only allow himself to ogle me if he was certain to receive no satisfaction for it.

The trip back across the Charles was uneventful, and so too was the long, hot walk back along the road I'd taken the cart ride on this morning. I met not a soul. The sun was starting to lengthen the shadows when I wearily returned to Goody Fitch's home.

The witch was in the front room of the house, settling an iron pot over some covered coals in the hearth. It smelled mostly of vegetables and slightly of mutton, and not at all of seasonings. There was a girl, perhaps eight years old, sitting by an open window, spinning yarn with a drop-spindle and looking bored. Her eyes lit up when she saw me.

"Mama, is this the woman?" she said.

Goody Fitch looked over her shoulder. "Yes." And to me: "My daughter is as I am. I told her about you."

The girl, dressed almost identically to her mother—or rather, identically to me, since she was not yet corseted—put her spinning down and came to me with a wide-eyed unsmiling look of reverence. "Where have you come from?" she asked.

"Somewhere else," said her mother almost tartly. "Children listen, Elizabeth, they do not speak."

"Perhaps she would like to listen to me tell you about squawvine," I said, eager to fulfill my part of the bargain so that she might fulfill hers by sending me home.

"Yes. But more than that. If you be willing to tell us more about what you are doing, we want to help you in a greater way than just this day's work."

"Really?" I asked, pleased but astonished.

She gestured to the stool, now situated in the center of the room to catch the faint cross-breeze. Gratefully, I sat on it. "I have been meditating on this matter all day," she said. "I am a settler, a pioneer: I know the importance of planning with a mind to future generations. My daughter is gifted, far more subtle with her skills than I was so young, but she will never be allowed, in this place, to show herself as she is. If you can use her, and the ones that come after her, then our coming here will perhaps have served some purpose, even if not the one I intended."

The girl plunked herself at my knees and looked up at me with an almost imploring look. "Hello, Elizabeth," I said. "I am Melisande."

"I know," said the girl. "You already told me." I grimaced in confusion, having no memory of such a thing, and her mother frowned at her. "I did not mean that," said the girl, but she sounded uncertain, as if she were following a prompt that did not make sense to her. I was very fatigued and could not think about this peculiar moment with any depth.

Given this remarkably happy development, I stayed with them for the next two hours, explaining (in terms that would not bewilder them) the fundamental essence of DODO. Goody Fitch, once again, fell into gales of laughter at the claim that this small-minded enclave of religious extremists could ever blossom into a force that influenced the whole globe—but all the same, she insisted her daughter listen to me. Somewhere inside, she took my descriptions to heart. We pledged mutual benevolence and peace, and as the sun came in at a blinding angle through the southern window, I prepared myself to be Sent home.

Diachronicle
DAY 323

In which we learn quite rudely that nothing is ever simple

I WAS IN THE ODEC. As before, the sudden severing of my connections to the world of 1640 Boston left me disoriented, and obliged me to sit down. As I got my wits about me I had the presence of mind to grab for the oxygen mask, just in case the chamber was full of helium. But I was naked, and soon shivering with cold. Glancing down at myself, I was delighted to see that I had brought back with me none of the dirt and dust and grime of 1640. Even the splinter from the rough-hewn shovel handle had stayed behind, although my skin was still angry-looking. My clothes— T-shirt and jeans—were nowhere in sight.

I slammed a big red button that cycled the door. During the weeks of preparation for this day, the Maxes had come back in force and made a number of improvements. No longer did test subjects have to be released from the ODEC by outside helpers wearing oven mitts. Now the door opened automatically. For a moment my nakedness must have been hidden from view by a cloud of vapor— long enough for me to snatch a blanket from a hook by the door and wrap it around me.

The big room that had formerly contained the ODEC, the control panel, and everything else had been rearranged, tidied up, and cut in half by a wall of glass. The control panel was on the other side of it. Through it I could see Tristan, Erszebet, Rebecca, and Oda applauding and giving me the thumbs-up.

The Maxes had also installed a shower stall in the corner of the ODEC chamber, and plumbed it with a system that would inject a sterilant into the hot water. I went in there and warmed up with a long shower, scrubbing myself all over with some manner of liquid soap that was supposed to kill all bacteria and viruses. I emerged from that to find more pills awaiting me on a stainless steel tray, and swallowed those. Meanwhile the ODEC and the chamber surrounding it had been sprayed down with more disinfectant and irradiated with germ-killing purple light.

I stepped out into a small dressing room where my clothes were awaiting me, and put them on. Then out through another door into the control room, where I was received as a conquering hero.

"So you have survived," said Erszebet proudly. "I knew you would. You are not like General Schneider."

Rebecca looked at me with wide eyes, shaking her head. "I . . . I don't even know what to ask you."

"That's good," I said, "because I don't even know what to say. Let's go check the site and see if it's there. I can describe the rest later."

But: "Stokes!" came an exuberant voice from the hallway, and of course when I exited I was briefly embraced by Tristan—who'd been on the phone to his higher-ups in DC, giving them the good news. It was almost exactly like being grabbed by the cooper, but without the erection or the general sense of ickiness. I realized how tense I had truly been. There was nothing more I needed in that moment than to feel that comforting clutch.

I did not say such a thing, of course; I just nodded, clapped his shoulder, and waited for him to release me. "Tell us," he said. "Tell us *all* of it."

"On our way to the boulder," I said.

His face lit up. "You did it! You buried it!"

I tried not to preen. "Sure. But I want to go there while I still have a very clear sense of *exactly* where I buried it."

"She did it!" he shouted to the world at large. "Good work ethic, Stokes. The professor's car is behind the building."

I could not believe how immediately overwhelmed I was, by the air pollution and ambient city noises, by the seams in my blue jeans, by the *squishiness* of the car seat. I felt strangely bereft of something. As we drove through Central Square and up Mass Ave, I gave the four of them—Oda was driving—the clearest depiction I could of my day. Erszebet was gleeful to hear that she lived in a better time period than the poor miserable Puritan witches. "It heartens me to hear somebody else suffered even more than I did for being in the wrong place at the wrong time," she informed us.

We were learning to ignore her when she got like this.

Finally we arrived at the Odas' house and the professor pulled into his driveway. An eager cluster of five, we all went through the gate into the garden and straight through to the back of the property.

There was the boulder, looking more worn and slightly shorter than it had four hundred years ago, but not by much, and mostly because it was now surrounded by landscaped gardens. It was almost impossible to imagine where the stream had been, but it was this near side of the rock I wanted anyhow. I recognized a particular bulge in the stone and oriented myself around it, lay on the ground, and reached toward the stone, then tapped the earth below my shoulder.

"It is right under here," I said. "In a sealed wooden bucket."

They already had the tools for digging handy. We all dug. Even Erszebet took a mostly symbolic turn at it.

An hour later, there was a hole five feet deep and twice that wide, obliterating Rebecca's vegetable garden. The back of the property resembled an archaeological excavation. And indeed it was: we found a rusty toy truck that looked to be from the 1950s and some bones that looked to have been buried by a dog. Below that, the rust-skeletal remains of a nineteenth-century lantern. Below that—as my heart beat more quickly—the broken-up oyster and clam shells I'd held in my hands four hundred years ago, a few hours earlier . . .

And that was all.

There was no bucket.

Journal Entry of
Rebecca East-Oda
JUNE 16

Temperature today about 75F, bright and sunny, no breeze. Barometer steady.

All vegetables: deceased. Flowers: largely trampled. South-side peonies (blooming), flame azalea (blooming), and most rose bushes still in good form. South-facing herb bed generally doing well.

The garden has been completely destroyed in the interest of digging up the book Melisande says she buried four hundred years ago. No sign of it. I have never seen her so distraught or confused. We stood about a large hole that had been my vegetable bed. Tristan offering condolence that "at least the soil is getting aerated." Mel circling the hole, shaking her head, climbing into it, searching on her hands and knees, trying to dig even deeper with her fingers.

Erszebet, retro-chic handbag clutched to her side as usual, watching all of us with superior amusement. "Obviously not here," she said. "We have to try again on another Strand. This is quite normal."

Mel looked up from the hole, gave Tristan a questioning look. Tristan and Frank also swapped glances. "What do you mean by 'another Strand'?" asked Frank.

She shrugged. "I mean another *Strand*. Of *time*," she clarified, seeing their confusion. "You have your fancy technical language to explain it. I have only what it really is. There are many possibilities and you cannot completely control which Strand you are on when you are summoning. It is not up to you. Magic does not make you omnipotent. So Melisande went back on just one Strand, and that one Strand did not change things to your liking. Maybe she will go back on another Strand, and then another, and when enough Strands have been shifted a little by this, then maybe it will help here and now."

"That makes my brain hurt," Mel said, sounding tired. "Do you mean I have to go back and redo everything I just did? Relive the entire day?"

"Of course," said Erszebet. "Several times, most likely."

Melisande groaned and threw herself onto the earth at the bottom of the hole, a dry-dock Ophelia. "I'd almost rather go back to working for Blevins."

Erszebet (*scolding*): "You have a simplistic notion of how complicated things work. It is like when the euro came into being." (*Uncomprehending looks from all of us.*) "If somebody had made up a new coin and called it the euro and walked in someplace to use it, it is not suddenly money. But because many people all agreed to make up a new coin, and then use these new coins over and over, now the euro is used and the old coins are not."

Tristan (*irritated*): "Bad metaphor. That was an economic policy move on the part of governmental bodies, it wasn't—"

"It may have been *decided* by governmental bodies, but it did not *happen*, it was not *real*, until many people stopped doing things one way and started doing them another, consciously and deliberately. Now, of *course* one uses the euro. One does not *think* about it."

Mel stood up and brushed the moist dark soil from her jeans. Erszebet is appalled that Mel "dresses like a man," and not even a proper gentleman but a farmhand. She keeps trying to get Mel to wear dresses and lipstick. Some of her advice is not without merit, for she has tastes that are highly refined, albeit stuck in the 1950s. But today jeans were the right attire.

"How many times must I redo it before it *takes*?" Mel asked, sounding exhausted.

"I cannot say for certain, but I will try to determine, because I like you," said Erszebet. Reached into her bag, pulled out the frazzled-mop-looking thing.

"What is that?" Tristan demanded, in such a tone I realized he hadn't seen it before.

"My *számológép*," she said, haughty. She began to pick through the strings—the *strands*—of it. Tristan turned to Melisande with a questioning expression.

"Calculator," Mel translated. "Not like a desk calculator, more like an accounting device."

We all watched Erszebet as she selected a strand, examined it, muttered to herself, pulled it away from the mass. It was entangled with another strand near the bottom. "Yes," she said, shoving the whole thing back into her bag. "You have to go back. We will see a difference next time."

"You mean the book will be here next time?"

"Almost certainly not!" Erszebet scoffed. "But we will be closer to the book being here next time."

"Excuse me," said Frank with his gentle smile, "would you show me how that object works?"

Erszebet looked almost shocked, and squeezed her arm tighter over the bag. "I cannot give you my számológép," she said. "I made it myself with my mother. It took years. I would sooner cut my hair off and give it to you."

"I don't want to keep it, I just want to look at it."

"It will mean nothing to you. And if you start to fiddle with it you might change it. So, no."

"May I *ask*, at least, what you use it for?" he said. Mel, with a hand up from Tristan, climbed out of the hole and reached for the sweatshirt I handed her. It was early evening and the air was beginning to cool.

Erszebet looked at the object in her hand as if Frank's question put it into an entirely new light. "What do I use it for? It is . . . a kind of cheating." She laughed a short, harsh, *scold-me-if-you-dare* laugh.

"Cheating?"

"Every action has reactions which have reactions. So, many consequences. You must keep track of all the possible consequences or bad things maybe happen. Nobody has the capacity to hold that much information in her mind at once. The számológép helps me to track the possible consequences."

"And how does it work, exactly?" asked Frank, his face now glowing with anticipation at getting his Physics Itch scratched.

"It will be easier to show you after Melisande has done it a few times."

"A few times," said Mel under her breath, sounding like she had the flu. "All right. But I need a decent meal first."

"I'll get you home," said Tristan, tossing her one of my clean gardening rags to wipe the dirt off her face. "Good work, soldier, we'll try again tomorrow. Erszebet, let's go. Eh . . ." He looked at the hole, then at me. "Sorry about the garden, ma'am. I'll call some men to come in tomorrow morning and tamp all the soil back down in there."

"Won't save the tomatoes," I said.

"Well, we need it intact so we can dig it up again," he said, almost sheepish.

When they were gone (Erszebet now bunking with Mel, who has moved to a larger apartment), Frank and I gazed at each other through the deepening twilight, over what had been the best of my cucumber patch. "Such an interesting thing, that . . . számológép," he said, pronouncing it wrong. "I wonder if I could figure out how it works, what she's doing with it." (I should have known that would be his takeaway from the entire day: not the failure, not the future, not the ruined garden, but the interesting gadget.)

I thought about what was in the attic. I wished it were not in the attic, and that being unavoidable, I wished I did not know that it was in the attic. But that glowing, boyish eagerness on his face . . . for more than fifty years now I have been charmed by it.

"I know where to find one," I said. "Stay here. I'll be right back."

Diachronicle
DAY 324 (COLONIAL BOSTON DTAP, 1640)

In which, having not succeeded, I try, try again

THE SECOND TIME, THE ARROW struck me before I fell out of its way.

I cried out, too dizzy and disoriented to keep quiet, and found myself remembering what Goody Fitch had said the first time: "It would hit you another time." What she'd meant was, it *does* hit me another time. She knew. She knew I arrived here more than once. What else did she know?

In a dreamlike state, I heard her shouting out to Samuel, heard her tell me not to move, waited until she came back with the blanket—and this time, a small roll of linen that she used to bandage my calf. The wound was only a superficial graze, really, enough to require tending but not enough to lame me. Enough, however, that it would make the slog of the day even more of a slog.

What followed was a six-hour stretch of déjà vu, ameliorated by the benefit of hindsight-as-foresight. The witch and I had almost the same conversation we'd had before. I declined the maize, knowing what it would do to my innards. When she offered me the musket ball and piece of wampum, I begged her for a second wampum bead, and she gave it to me. I asked her if I might wear her corset, since I was going out into the world and she was not, but she declined, as she expected Goody Griggs to be by to quilt midday and did not want to appear slovenly to a neighbor.

"Always feel free to ask me, though," she added. "Sometime it might be available."

That was the closest she came to telling me she knew that I was visiting her multiple times. Now the daughter's comment when I'd given her my name—"You already told me"—made sense too. Once I'd returned from my tasks in Cambridge, I was determined to interview Goody Fitch, to ask her to explain her understanding of the Strands, as Erszebet called them. Perhaps if various witches described it, we could, between all their descriptions, come to grasp it.

The déjà vu returned as Goodman Griggs gave me his furtive, grumbling look and drove me to the ferry. The ferryman once again ogled me and the boys once again splashed water at each other across the Charles. With a slight limp, trudging, shovel in hand, I again strode up Water Street, into the shop where Usher and Day were arguing about the quality of the printing. The same trick worked to steal the book again—remarkable, how at ease I felt, now that I knew I would accomplish it—and finally I approached the cooperage. I felt my pace slow. Even if I offered this unsettling fellow both of the wampum beads (one was intended for the ferry back to Muddy River), I suspected he would claim that it did not cover the fee. My real trouble was my want of a corset.

But at least I knew what I was in for, and that was oddly comforting. I presented myself to him with a slight brazenness, so that at least I avoided the unpleasantness of being groped—I came near to actually teasing him, promising future "generosity" before he even asked for it. I had his full attention and cooperation, and I was out of there sooner, and less grossed out, than last time.

So: déjà vu continued up the road to Watertown, and into the copse of trees where the creek was, and the boulder. I took off my apron, wrapped it around my hand while I was shoveling, and thereby saved myself the splinter of the last visit. My muscles were sore from all the digging yesterday—for my body knew that to have happened yesterday, even if I was now situated long, long before yesterday. Also, I was terribly hungry. And my leg was now throbbing ~~like a motherfucker~~ badly. So I was not in good humor.

I found the same Native American midden, and this time, when the hole was deep enough, tossed the shells in first and then put the bucket in atop them. I buried it, and then in a state of filthy exhaustion limped back to the ferry, where I paid my way and therefore had no need to even talk to the ferryman; miserably, I dragged my fatigued butt back to Goody Fitch's, and barely had the energy to thank her or speak to her daughter. I had no energy at all to follow through on my earlier intention of interviewing her regarding the Strands of time. Still, she made the same offer she had the first time, which was heartening.

This time, her daughter did not say, "You already told me." I took that as a good sign: this must be the visit she'd been referring to the other time. There need be no more. Two visits should suffice. Please, God, let two suffice.

Goody Fitch sent me forward to the ODEC, where I arrived shivering and naked, the superficial gash on my calf crusted and angry. I went through the decontamination procedure as before. Tristan, without the excited fanfare of the previous day, drove us back to the East-Oda homestead, where Rebecca tended my wound with a salve she had whipped up herself—a combination of modern antibiotics from the pharmacy and herbs from her garden. The menfolk once again dug up the backyard. Or rather, Tristan dug, while Frank Oda watched with the interest of a schoolboy who was illicitly attending a ballgame.

Early that morning, Tristan had "sent some men around" to fill in the hole. This had further torn up the yard and made a terrible noise, as it involved the kind of pounder that is used to smooth out new asphalt laid down over potholes. The neighbors were up in arms, Rebecca told us with a sigh, although mostly she was upset about her garden. Tristan of course was indifferent to the controversy.

Once I was sufficiently bandaged and plied with painkillers, we went downstairs and out the back to see how the digging was coming, ignoring the black and calico cats who were trying to trip us. Frank Oda was leaning against the boulder with a cup of tea; we three women stood on the small back deck of the house, staring over the railing. The midden of oyster and clam shells— which I had deliberately placed *under* the bucket this time—had been unearthed . . . yet still no bucket.

As I watched, it seemed to me that my exhaustion, or perhaps a side effect of the painkillers, was affecting my eyesight, for Tristan suddenly looked slightly blurred, as if I were looking at him across a lit BBQ grill.

"You see?" said Erszebet, sounding satisfied. She gestured casually toward Tristan. "It's coming along."

"Is he . . . *wavy*?" I asked.

"*He's* not wavy," she said in her usual being-derisive-about-Tristan voice.

"*Something* is wavy," said Rebecca decisively.

Tristan stopped digging and leaned on the shovel, breathing harder than he had yesterday although the soil was looser and the hole was smaller (but then, this time, he was the only one digging it). "Ma'am, could I trouble you for some saline drops?" he asked Rebecca. "I've got something in my eyes."

"No you don't," Erszebet informed him. "That's just the glimmer."

A childlike surge of excitement overrode my exhaustion, briefly: "Like in . . . like in old stories about witchcraft? You mean 'glamour'?" I asked. For with her accent it was difficult to tell.

She shrugged. "I don't know what it is called in old stories. We called it *pislákoló*, this is 'glimmer' or 'glamour' or something in English. I never knew the English term for it, magic was nearly gone by the time I was fluent in your language so there was no occasion to describe it. And now the word 'glamour' is ruined by that magazine."

"What is it, exactly?" said Tristan. "What's going on?"

"It happens because it is the spot . . ." Erszebet paused, then sighed noisily, as if put upon. "When magic existed, this was common knowledge and nobody ever had to explain it any more than you would have to explain why you sweat when you are hot or need air to breathe. But I will try." She pressed her elbow upon the deck rail and leaned her chin into the back of one lithe hand, lips pursed—Lauren Bacall imitating Rodin's *Thinker*. "This spot is where we are trying to make change. When there is no magic happening, things look normal. But when magic *is* happening, then what-*could*-be becomes . . . *louder*, or *bigger*, than whatever-currently-is. That causes the glimmer. So glimmer is a good sign." She reached into her bag, pulled out the számológép, and began to finger certain strands with seemingly random dexterity. Then she put it away, looked directly at me, and declared, "I think seven more times back to this DTAP without complications, and we will find the bucket when we dig for it here."

I heard myself groan before I could contain it. Seven more days of being ogled by the cooper. Of digging a deep hole in virgin soil with an unwieldy shovel. Of that long, swampy trudge back to Muddy River. "And it has to be me, correct?" I said. "We cannot swap me out for Tristan. That would be like resetting the counter to zero?"

She nodded.

"I'll take the next DTAP," said Tristan. "Scout's honor."

"What if the next one requires conversational Sumerian?" I asked.

WE WAITED A couple of days for my leg to heal, and then Erszebet sent me back again.

And then she sent me back again. And then again and again and again.

It was as if I inhabited a perverse universe at the intersection of *Groundhog Day* and a computer game. I knew what I had to do to get to the next level, so to speak . . . and I could do it, increasingly well, but dammit, that did not release me from the requirement of repeating it.

There were always slight variations, of course. For that was, in a way, the whole point of what Erszebet called the Strands. They were never exact clones. They were more like a family of similar pasts that all got to vote on what their shared future was going to look like. My next visitation, the witch's house was sited slightly closer to the river; otherwise, all was the same. But the time after that, Goodman Griggs was blind, and his son drove the cart for him—and thus, being a young man responsible for the well-being of a household, he had not been out illicitly shooting rabbits as I arrived. The time after that, it was the younger ferryman who looked at me, not the older. In that Strand, the witch had only a son, but said she would pass the word on to any other witches she met, not that there were likely to be many in such a society. The next time around, the printer Stephen Day was drunk, and as I left the shop, I heard him slur to Hezekiah Usher, "There is something about that woman, she seems so *familiar* . . ."

Journal Entry of
Rebecca East‑Oda
JUNE 22

Temperature about 75F, pleasantly humid. Slight SW breeze. Barometer falling.

Seedlings planted in container garden on front steps: kale, lettuce, seed onions. Tea roses transplanted to south side of house to avoid further damage to root system; hate to do that this time of year, but no choice, really.

The digging continues. Tristan has ceased claiming the aeration is good for the soil. Has offered to have fertilizer mixed in after the final dig. Neighbors registering complaints about the early morning noise. Cats stressed even though they are strictly inside.

Today was the fifth dig. Each time we collect to watch Tristan at work, the glamour is stronger. It feels almost as if, when I attempt to look directly into the hole, some force shunts my vision aside. A very strange sensation, but Erszebet says it is a good sign. Frank is pleased with himself for coming up with an acronym: GLAAMR, for Galvanic Liminal Aura Antecedent to Manifold Rift. I hope he is not just being optimistic.

It is clearly exhausting for Mel to make these excursions day after day, but she keeps her chin up. Tristan getting increasingly agitated (in a contained but obvious way). "Can you make it happen any faster?" he asked Erszebet today.

Erszebet's answer: "No." And then continued, as if the same conversation, "I am ready to go to Hungary now to spit on the graves of my enemies."

Tristan: "We've already had this conversation. We need money. What we're doing now, that's how we get money."

"I know, I was present at the rude idiot's office in Washington, DC, when you volunteered me for this indentured servitude."

A pause as he reclaimed his cool. "The sooner we're successful, the sooner we fly you to Hungary to spit on the graves of your enemies."

"I cannot alter the laws of the universe, even if you tell the idiot I can. But when I Send back Melisande this time, I will try very hard to summon her toward a Strand that is especially conducive to change. That is the most I can do."

Diachronicle

DAY 335 (COLONIAL BOSTON DTAP, 1640)

In which I am foundationally challenged

FOR WHAT I HOPED MIGHT be the final repetition, I just wanted to hurry through the motions and be done with it. I realized the witch was aware of all my other visitations, but referred to them only occasionally and only very obliquely—they were, in a sense, all happening at the same moment in time to different versions of her. And to all of her non-witch neighbors, of course. But part of what it was to be a witch, I was beginning to realize, was that all of those different versions were somehow in closer touch with one another than was the case for non-witches. So on this visit I was less conversational, got out the door faster—finally (to my great relief, uncomfortable though it was) borrowing the witch's corset. Happily, Goodman Griggs was also leaving earlier, and his ox had more oomph to his step as the sun had not gotten to its hottest point yet. I was over the river in record time, walked out of the shop holding the Bay Psalm Book scant minutes later, and even the cooper was prompt and respectful (perhaps because I was finally dressed like a goody rather than a hussy). The day felt like the last fortnight of high school, senior year: I had to show up, but no Powers On High expected me to do anything but phone it in.

I was in such a good mood, and now so familiar with the way, that truly I was operating on autopilot as I approached the creek that would lead me to the boulder. This may account for why I did not quite register that something was suddenly *extremely* different: the creek, which had heretofore dwindled in size and force as I approached the boulder, was now running rapidly and loudly. I looked at it . . . and stopped in my tracks. It had been recently dredged and the banks cut back to allow for a faster flow. I was moving upriver, so looked ahead to see how far this man-made alteration went.

I saw the foundation to a building. My jaw dropped open in shock. The earth and vegetation all around the boulder had been cleared for many yards, and the boulder itself incorporated into the half-built foundation, although it was of course much higher than the other foundation stones, high enough to be a section of wall for the ground floor. The site was unmanned at present, but there were stacks of lumber and shaped rock; instruments and tools rested on canvas tarps, and beyond the boulder, near the stream, was an enormous mixing vessel with bags of sand around it. The stone foundation must have cost a fortune; hewing and bringing in the stones alone would have been an ambitious undertaking.

What was this thing? How could it have come out of absolutely nowhere, and what was I to do about it? Clearly I could not bury the book here. With a sigh of resignation, I collected myself and began to slog back toward the Cambridge palisades. The tall gates being unmanned by daylight, I let myself through and headed back to the bookseller's.

Merchant Usher and Printer Day had just finished arguing, with Usher apparently the victor, for Day was gloomily boxing up his stacks of books. I begged pardon and placed the bucket down so they would not think to ask about it.

"What might be the building under construction up the creek, off the Watertown Road?" I asked.

The merchant laughed without malice—or humor. "That is the most ambitious undertaking the devil ever spurred anyone to. It is to be a maple sugaring factory. A very enterprising company from back home has decided to stake a claim in the future fortune of the colony, and has determined that sugar maples are what Providence has provided to enrich us."

"The name of the company?"

"The Boston Council for Boston," he said.

"Have you a share in it?" I asked.

He shook his head. "I was invited to invest, and I confess I was tempted, to engage in something so forward-thinking. But I fear it is a bit *too* forward-thinking. Every joint-stock company of the New World so far has failed, or been taken over by the crown, and I see no sign this one should fare any better. When the town requires palisades for safety because all the American tribes are at each other's throats, and the factory is half a mile's walk outside the palisades . . . I fear they are doomed."

"'Tis a wondrous thing," the printer said to me, dismissing Usher's concern. "Any bettering in our circumstances is to be applauded."

"Only when it is done well, Stephen," said Hezekiah gently, as if in regretful rebuke.

Thanking them, but rather flummoxed, I left the keg on the step of the booksellers, as it was not worth it to cart it back to Goody Fitch's, who would then be left with what to do with it. I took the ferry back across and walked in great agitation the now-familiar route to the witch's home.

Journal Entry of

Rebecca East-Oda

JUNE 28

Temperature 70F, raining steadily.

Seedlings: no sign of germination, but it is too soon. Flame azaleas and peonies a smidge beyond peak. Herb garden thriving. Roses seem adjusted to new spot. The rain helps.

A complication has arisen in the project, that being the foundation of a factory having sprung up where this house now stands. Tristan phoned, asked us to come in to brainstorm. Frank was distracted poking about with the quipu-like object I had brought down from the attic, and I did not want to interrupt him, so I told them to come to us. We settled in Frank's office and I made a fire, for ambience. A summer thunderstorm was passing through, and rain was lashing the windows.

Melisande was exasperated, Tristan grim. Frank curious, when brought up to speed, and questioning Erszebet, who demonstrated boredom.

"Does that mean there is a parallel universe in which our house does not exist?" Frank asked Erszebet.

"I do not know if it is parallel, I have never measured it," she said. "But clearly, something like that. If I were you, I would not try to return to that world."

"Why did you send me there in the first place?" Mel demanded, cross. She sat closest to the fire and held her hands right above the flames, still chilled from her return. Calico trying and failing to convince her to scratch his head.

"You think I have control over the universe?" said Erszebet. "If I had such control, I would not have allowed magic to be ruined in the first place. There is no certainty. There is never certainty."

"How do we get rid of the factory? What are our options?" Tristan asked.

Erszebet said, "You cannot get rid of it, you can only uncreate it." Then explained that the usual means of resolving such problems is to go back to an even earlier time and prevent the conflict, by slightly (and multiple times) altering something prior to the event in question. All shoulders in the room sagged at this notion.

"Could we not simply go back to 1640 and try again?" I suggested. "There has only been one reality in which there was a maple syrup factory, and many more in which it didn't exist, so perhaps we can simply continue the effort in another Strand without the factory—sidestep the problem, so to speak."

"You can try that, but clearly things are tending toward the factory being there, so I recommend that you address the factory." She yawned expressively to make sure we'd noticed how dull this sort of talk was.

"Why?" asked Frank, who was as usual the least exasperated person in the room. "*Why* are things tending toward the factory being built?"

"Yes, what are the mechanics here?" demanded Tristan, almost interrupting him.

"There are no *mechanics*," said Erszebet disdainfully. "It is *magic*. Magic does not speak your language, Mr. Military-Physicist. Study it as hard as you wish, some part of it will always elude you. I am giving you the best advice there is."

"You are saying," said Tristan (*patience exaggerated*), "that we must go back to a time before the factory was built, and prevent the factory from being built."

"Several times."

Tristan swore under his breath.

"All of this effort for an unreliable result is why time travel has never been a smart use of magic," she added in a superior tone. "I knew it would be a terrible way to try to influence anything."

"Why didn't you say that when I first suggested it to Frink?" Tristan demanded.

"Agreeing to try it was the quickest way to earn a salary, which gives me a chance to go to Hungary and spit on the graves of my enemies." She added darkly, "Not all my enemies are in Hungary, you know," and with that glanced briefly toward Mel, who was staring at her hands poised just above the flames and did not notice.

I requested Erszebet to help me with the tea, and, once alone in the kitchen with her, asked why she had shot that look at Mel.

She tossed her dark hair back over one shoulder. "I am only still alive because of Melisande." She is so beautiful, and so very *present* in her young body, that it is continually difficult to remember how old she really is.

"Is that such a bad thing?"

"There is no benefit to my staying so long," she said. "Now I am treated like Tristan Lyons's trained dog. His *Asset*. If I had died in natural time, I would be at peace now. *This*"—gesturing out the window toward my ruined garden plot—"is *not* what I ever believed it would be like when I finally could perform magic again, and in the meantime I have survived one century and a half of unnatural alienation and boredom and loss."

I did not know what to say. I could not blame her the bitterness.

"So," she continued briskly, gesturing now toward her own splendid figure, in tight-waisted sundress and heeled sandals. "I am going to have some enjoyment now, to make up for all those years. But even so"—and here she darkened—"I am only making the best of a bad situation. And I am in that situation because of Melisande Stokes."

"Whatever it was that happened, I'm sure she meant you no harm," I said quickly.

"Neither did the first photographer," said Erszebet, and walked briskly back toward the study.

I feel for her, deeply, but I wonder if she is a reliable participant in this undertaking. Which is worrisome, as she is the only one involved who is irreplaceable.

Diachronicle

DAYS 335–352 (EARLY JULY, YEAR 1)

In which we are London-bound

I DO NOT KNOW IF the Boston Council for Boston was a going concern before I stumbled across that stone foundation on the Watertown Road. But since I'd discovered it, it existed historically. An upstart private company of enterprising Calvinists in the original Boston (in Lincolnshire, England), it was created twenty-five years before the founding of the New World's Boston and actually had nothing to do with it; its purpose was to bring money back to its founders' local economy. An odd mixture of socialism, isolationism, and snark, the Boston Council for Boston's name really meant: "Our Council for Us."

Research into the Boston Council for Boston quickly revealed that in late September 1601, the company (which was otherwise about to fall apart before it had so much agreed upon an initial investment) got backing from one of its native sons, Edward Greylock, whose father had adroitly married into a family of Continental bankers, and as a result, risen in prominence in Queen Elizabeth's court—albeit on the outskirts. As of 1601 the son—Sir Edward Greylock—lived primarily in London. Further research into Sir Edward showed him (and his fortune) to have cavorted a good bit with the adventurer George Clifford, Earl of Cumberland, founding member of the East India Company, which had been founded only at the end of the previous year.

If Sir Edward could be persuaded to give the East India Company his coin, and not merely his society, then the Boston Council for Boston would never get the funds required to go to America, and thus never build their inconvenient syrup boiler on the road to Watertown. The next DTAP would have to be the city of London, 1601.

This is how we met Gráinne.

Temperature 81F, slight breeze from southwest. Barometer steady.

Container garden on front steps: kale, lettuce have germinated. Tea roses doing well in their new setting. Flame azalea almost passed.

It is decided: Tristan will go to Renaissance London. I find myself relieved to be off the hook now as I can be of no practical help. There have been long days of discussion and theorizing and research to establish a possible witch in that DTAP, but there is no way to know.

In the absence of an individual witch to target, Tristan has proposed he be Sent to a setting that is likely to attract witches. Erszebet followed the development of this plan with some private amusement, it seemed to me. I am not at all certain that she cares whether or not we succeed.

To determine the sort of place witches might be drawn to, it becomes necessary to psychologically profile the average witch. Having only Erszebet and a cursory experience of Goody Fitch as a sample population is hardly sufficient, but the only other source is secondary: Erszebet's memories of other witches. These memories may say more about Erszebet herself, or her circumstances, than they do about her mother, her mentor, etc. But the general type we arrived at was this:

A witch generally speaks her mind when she can get away with it, doesn't care much about what men think, and is determined to have agency over her fate, even in a time and place when such a thing was hard to come by (which, Erszebet added, was most of human history). Based on Erszebet herself, and her claims of her mother's behavior, it is also possible witches enjoyed the influence they had over men by their attractiveness, but this does not seem to be tempered by any fondness for the men whose heads they enjoyed turning.

Sitting in Frank's study—where I preferred we congregate when the ODEC or office equipment was not specifically required—the four of us, with Erszebet watching, sat musing upon this collection of traits, as the two household cats wound their way around Frank's legs.

"This isn't flattering," said Tristan, "but this also fits the psychological profile of a lot of prostitutes."

Erszebet laughed.

"No disrespect," Tristan said.

"It is amusing that it has taken you so many hours to come to this conclusion."

"You mean you already knew? You could have told us this and saved us a lot of time."

"Yes," said Erszebet, pleased.

"Why didn't you?"

"You put me through my paces to see what I could do, I wanted to see what it was like to be in your position. I have enjoyed it."

A moment of Tristan silently grinding his teeth. "So you are confirming that we need to look for prostitutes."

"Not *any* prostitutes. But it makes sense, yes?" she said. "It is one way to have children without the bother of husbands."

"I don't buy that," said Melisande. "That's a totally romanticized image of sex workers. They're generally poor and disenfranchised, and a witch with any savvy at all would never choose such a life, for herself or her children. In the documents I translated, witches were considered powerful and valuable by whoever was in charge. Even if they were seen as dangerous, they were *valued*."

"That doesn't mean they were *married*," said Erszebet. "We didn't need to be married to have power."

Mel looked doubtful. "So was that the norm for witches? Being, what, a courtesan, or at least someone's 'kept woman'?"

Erszebet gave Mel a look. "I am only one witch and have lived in only one society of witches, at one moment in history. You with your translations have a broader knowledge than I do. But such a thing was referred to casually by my mother's friends. If a witch wanted children, there were always the wealthy men around who can treat you well and support a bastard without wanting to have to publicly acknowledge it."

A heavy thought came over me. "Did you do that?" I asked. "I mean . . . did you have children?"

Erszebet gave me a look that scorched my liver. "Of course not," she said after a moment. "I could not bear the thought that I would live to watch them age and wither and die and I would still be here and have to bury them."

There was a long and uncomfortable pause. Mel looked down, seemed almost to huddle over herself.

Tristan coughed. "So we need to look for . . . courtesans? High-ranking mistresses, that sort of thing."

"I would say so," said Erszebet loftily.

"Hang on," said Mel, looking up. "This DTAP was near the end of Queen Elizabeth's reign, right? I don't know how much autonomy attractive, powerful women would be allowed in courtly circles, I think Elizabeth was increasingly paranoid and jealous as she aged. So maybe common prostitutes after all."

"No," said Erszebet. "We would not tolerate being common."

"Maybe an *uncommon* prostitute, then, who had her own reasons for staying away from the court," Mel suggested.

"There were a lot of brothels in Southwark, where the theatres were," I offered. "I read that in the program notes for *Henry IV* when Boston Shakespeare did it."

"What do you think?" Tristan asked Erszebet. "Does Southwark sound right to you?"

She sniffed. "I have never heard of this place. But if it is full of troublesome women then you might be in luck."

Diachronicle
DAYS 335–352 (CONTD.; EARLY JULY, YEAR 1)

In which Tristan learns a euphemism

THIS PEN WRITES NO FASTER, the eclipse is now just twenty-three days away, and I continue to entertain foolish fond thoughts that somehow I may yet escape 1851 London. I am sure I have already complained in these leaves about the stench, but as summer ripens, so too do its smells. No pension plan is worth this shit, in quite the most literal sense. I must tell this story more quickly and elide some details to get it all down.

I pled travel fatigue, and Tristan honored his word to take the next DTAP. He required a specific place to land in London, September 1601, during the week before the investor, Sir Edward Greylock, agreed to put his money into the Boston Council for Boston. This was an event we were able to date with precision from legal records. Finding a suitable landing place in that DTAP was more of a project.

During the course of our research, we obtained scans of city maps that had been drawn up circa 1600 and printed them out on huge sheets of paper that we taped up all over the walls. There, they accumulated sticky notes, pushpins, and written annotations. It was while studying one of those that Tristan let out an oath much more explicit than we usually heard from him, and jammed his finger into a smudge on a map so hard that it must have hurt. The smudge, magnified and examined, turned out to be the words YE TEAR-SHEETE BREWERY.

As mentioned previously, Tristan had a sentimental regard for Old Tearsheet Best Bitter, the flagship product of Tearsheet Beverage Group Ltd., which claimed to be one of the oldest continuously operating breweries in London. He'd spent a semester abroad in the city, and thought himself sporty for having acquired a taste for something so obscure—not quite a microbrew but neither a household name anywhere. Bottled, it was available at a select few package stores in New England. On tap, it could be had in some pubs that catered to Anglophiles and expats.

Improbable as it might sound, further research bore out that Tearsheet Beverage Group Ltd. really was the survival into modern times of the enterprise labeled on that old map. To Tristan's delight, TBG Ltd. were proud enough of their heritage, and savvy enough with their marketing, that a section of their website was devoted to the history of their plant in London. In the early seventeenth century, the brewhouse proper had boasted an adjacent public house. It was at most two hundred yards from the Globe Theatre. Though the site did not mention it, the area had famously teemed with brothels.

I went back into the Widener Library stacks. Where I discovered—to no great surprise—that the adjacent pub was too large, with too many upstairs nooks, to have been merely a pub. Given the neighborhood, it probably wasn't merely an inn either.

"So there it is," said Tristan, pleased, when I showed him a map I'd scanned at Widener. "That's my ground zero. What else do we know about it?"

"The very word 'Tearsheet' was a slang term for a prostitute," I said.

He pulled a face. "I had no idea."

"The place was famous for always having 'six comely maidens' working there," I said, with air quotes, "'serving the customers ale and aught.'"

"What's aught?" asked Tristan.

"Whatever you want it to be," I said. "Their names are not recorded, but as of 1600 we know that one was Irish and two were Scottish. If we're looking for loose women who would never fit in at Elizabeth's court, those three fit the bill. Especially the Irish one, she had to travel by sea to get there, and the seas between Ireland and England were full of pirates. And she would have almost certainly been Catholic—so why would she go there unless she had a very good reason?"

Tristan sat at his desk examining the papers. The Tearsheet website had airbrushed the map a bit. In reality, not only was the "pub" next door bigger than the brewery claimed, but it was connected, by an underground tunnel and secret passages on every floor, directly to the brewery itself—thus allowing johns who needed to remain anonymous a way to escape if the brothel were raided by the constables. Too bad none of that was on the website. I think their sales might have improved if they'd shared all the dirt.

Over the next two weeks, Tristan was on a crash course in

preparing to pass as a visitor to Elizabethan London. We knew he would never get the accent right, but as with myself in Boston forty years later, this was not an urgent issue: London's population was exploding, and the city was babbling away in different accents and dialects from all over.

A benefit to choosing this DTAP was that it corresponded with the height of William Shakespeare's career, and American theatres are simply obsessed with Shakespeare. Therefore Boston, despite its small size, was crawling with fight choreographers who specialized in the swordplay and knife skills common in Shakespeare's time—or at least in his playhouse. Tristan learned drills he could do on his own and then honed his skills for hours each day in the one still-separate office space in the DODO building. He also practiced bowing, cap-doffing, eating without a fork, and sundry other small niceties, whilst I drilled him on Elizabethan turns of phrase. Our costumer friend helped again with clothing, renting us a variety of different men's outfits so that Tristan could practice putting them on and off, as we had no way of knowing what clothes he might eventually find himself in. He would be enormous by the standards of the time; the chances of his actually blending in were slim to none.

I enjoyed watching him at his drills even more than I'd enjoyed watching the ferryman row me across the Charles. I truly did not *want* to enjoy watching him. It seemed incestuous. I thought Tristan was a looker from the moment I'd laid eyes on him, but all of that had been swept to the back of my mind immediately because of the peculiarity of our meeting and then our unceasing work. Except for the small talk of our first meal together, we had barely ever "chatted." Tristan, as a general rule, does not chat. I knew him so well and trusted him quite literally with my life, and yet I hardly knew him at all.

When he had been the brains of the operation, the guiding hand, the commanding officer, I somehow hadn't noticed that . . . but now as he was in training, I became the guide, and the dynamic shifted. I became his equal, in some ways his superior, and this in turn made me proprietary. I felt secret jealousy toward the rest of his life—how absurd, as he had no "rest of his life," and in fairness neither did I anymore. He seemed to have no friends locally, never mentioned his family, and I can't remember him referring to any memories or relationships. He was an unformed block, from which he was now laboring, literally, to sculpt a Renaissance Man.

Reader, that was an attractive thing to watch.

It felt like failure and betrayal to admit this to myself.

But the truth is, I ~~had a fucking crush on~~ somewhat fancied him. Always had. How ridiculous. Anyone could fancy Tristan Lyons; it took no special qualities. I wished to demonstrate, at least to myself, that I was made of special qualities. So I chose to disregard my sentimentality.

This was hard because: first, he looked pretty hot when he was thrusting that rapier, and second, I was aware he was about to go away to a place far more dangerous than my DTAP had been, and while it was possible he would return immediately, it was also possible he would not return at all. That he would be really, truly, not just Schrödinger's-cat-like, dead.

Nothing like the possibility of eternal separation to bring out the romantic in a girl.

But I squelched it. Before he went into the ODEC on July 19 with Erszebet, I just clapped him on his shoulder. (Said shoulder was clad only in a T-shirt; recent improvements to the ODEC had included a heating system that made it into a shirtsleeves environment, and we had taken our rack of snowsuits to Goodwill.) I squeezed said shoulder but did not speak any of the words that my mouth suddenly wanted to form. I gave him a peck on the cheek, and watched as he passed through the airlock into the decontamination chamber. He'd already taken the medicines to sterilize his gut, but now scrubbed himself in the disinfectant shower and emerged in a pair of surgical scrubs, the ungainliness of which helped to dampen my romantic stirrings. Through the glass I waved like a younger sister as her brother goes off to summer camp. He nodded while backing into the ODEC, where Erszebet was waiting. He closed the door behind him. Oda-sensei, at the control console, flipped up the cover over the toggle switch, switched it on. The Klaxon clacked, however muffled. We waited.

It felt like years passed.

Finally, Erszebet opened the ODEC door. Oda-sensei powered down the ODEC. I had been hovering anxiously at the door. When he signaled me it was safe, I went inside.

Lying on the floor were Tristan's scrubs and two white ceramic fillings I hadn't known about. How ridiculous to confess this, but it saddened me that I had not known about his fillings. The gulf of my ignorance regarding his dental work left me feeling irrationally bereft.

Erszebet grabbed my arm and tugged it to get my attention. I forced my eyes away from the artifacts of Tristan to look at her.

She reached gently for my face and with her thumb and finger caressed the very pursed space between my brows. I hadn't realized I'd been frowning. "If he doesn't make it back, you will easily find a better lover," she said consolingly.

I blushed so intensely it almost made my eyes water. "He's not my lover," I said irritably.

Erszebet gave me a knowing grin. "He's not your lover *yet*," she said.

LETTER FROM
GRÁINNE *to* GRACE O'MALLEY
A Monday of Mid-Harvest, 1601

Auspiciousness and prosperity to you, milady!

Gráinne it is who's writing this, and 'tis the most astounding news I have to share with Your Grace. I'm after meeting a gentleman by the name of Tristan Lyons. You'll want to add him to your stable of faithful vassals, and I think he can find his way there with the proper inducements. I'll be working on him to that end, anyhow.

I was putting in my time at the bawdy-house beside the brewery. I know Your Grace would rather I not, but truly it's the best way to hide in plain sight, and sometimes it's great crack. I was servicing—or, to put it another way, being serviced by—a gentleman of Bess's court, a lumbering heap of a knight and not the brightest candle in the chandelier. He thinks he's never revealing any secrets, but sure it's as easy to read him as it is to read the signs on the High Street, so it's a mutually beneficial arrangement. Himself it was who let slip the rumour about the Earl of Essex some months back. As you might recall this allowed Your Grace's agent to adopt some of His Lordship's silver that was left tragically unattended during His Lordship's arrest.

So there we were getting along with business, and I look over his shoulder and what I see there in the corner is a bit of glamour. So I know there's some magic afoot but it's not me performing it, and there's nobody else in the room. And just as it's occurring to me that another witch must be Sending me something, what is there in the corner suddenly but a large handsome man, buck naked, looking dazed as a newborn, and doesn't he fall right to his knees and clutch at his head in utter confusion. And then he moans a bit, louder than my dim fella, and my dim fella hears him, stops abruptly in his exertions, and looks over his shoulder.

You don't want to have to go explaining to a man in the heat of passion why there's suddenly another naked man in the room. Especially one who's a better specimen. This new naked fella, he was tall and broad and the healthiest looking lad I've seen in ages, even finer than the lads back home. I guessed right off he was probably from the Continent or maybe the Golden Age, you know how them idiot pagans like to mess around—not from around here, anyway, which means he would be needing clothing and some dosh, like they do.

So I thought fast and said to your man who was on top of me, "Hey now, look I've got you the voyeur you were importuning me for last week, but it's going to cost you extra for the privilege, so let's finish up here and give me the silver for it." He was too astonished to speak and that gave me a moment to consider the situation.

I had to reckon what the new fellow would be doing here, given he clearly was not Irish. He looked more Saxon, but what did that mean now the Vikings are no more? Was he an enemy or a friend? Did he come here deliberately to me, or maybe a blunder it was? He looked familiar, yet I knew of a certainty I'd never clapped eyes on him before—and as I needn't belabor to you of all people, milady, this told me that what was occurring here and now was sure to be repeating itself on other Strands. Something was afoot. Some shite-for-brains was actually trying to *accomplish* something by sending this poor young buck to other times and places. He was still looking bolloxed so I couldn't ask him yet.

Meanwhile my dim fella had collected his meagre wits enough

to protest that he'd never wanted a voyeur. I said, "Oh, come now, I know you too well for you to hide anything from me, you're falling all over yourself for the opportunity. Finish off and be giving me the money, so."

He's out of the humour now, which I don't mind. Very grudgingly, in a foul mood, he reaches for his belt on the floor and yanks out some extra coin and tosses them to me in a huff. The fellow on the floor has pulled himself together a bit, looks around the wee room and his eyes widen.

"It's all right, lad," says I to him. "You've played your part well so far."

"You'd be Gráinne?" he asks, pronouncing it almost right, like he's been practicing. Which was awkward since I'm never going by that name at the Tearsheet.

"No," says I, giving him a wink to put him at his ease, and making a glance at the other fella.

Which is where it all went sideways. This new fella is one of those literal-minded sorts so tediously common in this nation, who actually believes what he hears. He's not looking at me, supposing it were indelicate to gaze upon a naked lady, so he doesn't collect the wink. "I beg your pardon," he says, ever so polite, and clambers to his feet, moving well, with an eye on the door.

Increasingly displeased, is my dim fella about this turn of events, the more he thinks about it. He has no scruples about looking at a naked lady he's bought and paid for, so he takes in the wink and the glance, and even more displeased they make him. He pushes off of me and turns around just in time to see the new fella thoughtlessly getting between him and his baldric, which he's slung over the peg beside the doorway. Suspended in that, of course, are the scabbards containing his rapier and his dagger. The new fella's still looking about himself in that way people do after they've been

Sent somewhere for the first time, it's all new to him, he doesn't appreciate that it's bad practice to come between a knight and his arms—doubly so when the knight's buck naked and just had a perfectly good fuck interrupted by a nasty surprise. My customer moves, fast, dropping one shoulder and barreling into the new man from behind, catching him in the ribs and giving him a good bash. It wouldn't have been an equal contest had the new lad been looking him in the face, and on his toes, but as it was the blow staggered him out of the way. While he was pivoting about and getting his balance, my customer made straight for the door and pulled his dagger out of its sheath—the chamber being far too small, you'll understand, for the rapier to be of any use.

Well, to that point in the proceedings, the new arrival might've been in a bit of a daze, but the sight of bare steel in another fella's hand snapped him out of it in a trice, and suddenly wasn't he moving with marvelous speed and sureness, as if he engaged in naked dagger fighting several times a day. Rather than stepping back, as an ordinary person might've, he moved toward the knight and got in close, stifling his movement even as he was drawing back to stab. Then something happened too quickly for me to follow it, and next thing I know the dagger's clattering on the floorboards and the Saxon has the knight's arm all twisted about in some manner of wrestling hold, I reckon. The knight tries to squirm out but the visitor pushes a bit harder, and I can hear something threatening to give way in the shoulder joint. "I yield," says he who's clearly got the worst of it. The new lad lets him go, but not before kicking the dagger across the floor, out of reach. I snatched it up so there'd be no more such foolishness, and clasped it to my breast. Rarely have I enjoyed such spectation at the Tearsheet. The new lad was so fine to look at and the other fella was so dull, and I haven't got out to a bear-baiting or even a play in the longest time. To watch naked men have a go at each other with weapons is better than either. Makes me homesick, so it does.

"I humbly apologize for this misunderstanding," says the Saxon. I couldn't recognize the accent. His teeth were gorgeous. "And for my unmannerly arrival." He said *unmannerly* as if it weren't a word used to coming out of his mouth. So I figured he were from a place where manners aren't important but he's trying to respect the occasion, and I liked that well enough. Enough to want to keep seeing him naked, anyhow.

So I take the dim fella's purse, help myself to my newly augmented fee, toss him his clothes, and give him a wink. "Be changing outside now," I say, and send him off.

That makes it easier to stare at your naked Saxon.

"Gráinne," he said. "But you don't go by that name. I understand."

"You're not one of them locals," I observe.

"What gave it away?" he asked. I like a bit of dry humour. I laughed.

"So tell me, then, who are you and what is it brings you here? Who Sent you?"

"Classified," he said.

"Never heard of him. Perhaps a Cornish name, is it? Protestant or Catholic?"

"'Tisn't a name," he said. "It means I cannot tell you. I am under orders not to tell you."

"Are you? How's your master expect you to get anything done, then? Once you've answered my questions to my satisfaction I'll give you this extra money the fella left, and get you some clothes, both of which you'll be needing. We've some extra shirts and drawers around for our favorite customers, since things do tend to get nicked here. But you'll get no help from me until you answer my questions. Right idiot your master is if he thinks it works any other way."

Clearly the fellow's never been Sent before; he got a caged bear look on his face, and I felt for him, but obviously it's not safe to do anything until I know more. I'm passing as Protestant Irish, it's my excuse for being in London instead of back home, but Protestant Irish is a hard act to play without giving it the full Puritan extreme and that's not safe either. I have to watch my back all the time. I needed to know where his sympathies were.

And then he uttered such an idiot claim: "I'm here for a purely economic concern," he says. "It's just financial, I've got no political or religious affiliation."

"Is it Protestant money or Catholic money you're after?" I ask.

"It does not matter," he says. "Not where I come from."

"Where in God's name do you come from?" I ask again. "May I go there with you? Because in the name of Our Lord's mammy, if I could be someplace where money's got no religion and religion's got no money, I'd be a happier woman."

He sits on the bed beside me, turned a little away so I can't see his front so well (I did try to peek though). He said he would tell me as much as he could—anything that wasn't "classified." And here's what he told me. I'll make it as brief as I can, but it was quite the long chat we had about it:

He is from the future, from a land that will become an English-speaking nation some day—but not a part of England! So their accursed language triumphs, but they themselves do not. The fuckers lose most of Ireland as well, turns out. I don't know how long it will take this to happen, maybe ten years, maybe a hundred. I pressed him for details, especially about Your Grace's legacy of course, but he said he couldn't give me any unless I let him get dressed, which I wouldn't. It was great crack to see how uncomfortable he was being naked.

"Guess you don't do that much in the future," I teased him.

"Thought that would be a constant across the ages—how bawdy-houses work."

"I have never been to a bawdy-house before," he said.

Of course I didn't believe him, but it wasn't important, so I pressed on, trying to learn more about this Future where the best-looking fellas speak English but are not, in fact, English. We spent no small sum of time discussing why wearing clothes would make it easier for him to speak. Otherwise, all I could get out of him was that the land that the English are now preparing to settle in the New World breaks away from England to become its own nation, and keeps speaking English but becomes notable for its deep regard of Ireland. This is especially true of the area where he himself had come from directly, which is a province with the queer enough name of Massive Shoe Hits (code, I expect). Anyhow, seems in the future there will be lots of Irish running around over there, but they'll be speaking English.

"So where's their loyalty?" I demanded, and he said it's with themselves. "They get distracted with their new world, they don't have the energy to stay preoccupied with old grudges. Eventually, I mean. It takes awhile."

Beyond that the most I could get out of him was that he had come back in time to *me*, specifically, to seek my assistance. Wasn't I flattered at that, I confess. "How did you know to find me?" I asked.

"Classified," he said quickly, and then grimaced and corrected himself: "I can't tell you. But I know you're the right one for me to ask for help."

"All right then. What be in it for me?" I asked. "Given you've no money to offer me, and refusing you are to tell me about the future, which is the only reason I'd be interested in you. Except maybe for playing around because you are a *beautiful* specimen of a man. I'll wager all your children are beauties."

"Might we continue this conversation once I'm clothed?" him-self asks again, with a bit more urgency now as my words are hav-ing their effect and he's beginning to get big and firm down below.

"Lordy, no," I say. "I am enjoying this too much. Do you know how rare it is to sit next to a fellow who's clean and nice-looking and isn't asking anything of me? It's enough to make me want to offer myself."

"That's not why I'm here," he says, crossing his legs more than a bit awkwardly.

"Well then tell me why you are here," I ordered.

"I need to convince a man named Sir Edward Greylock that he should invest his money in the East India Company."

"Sure, I've heard of Sir Edward, we've some friends in common, if you take my meaning."

"Oh, do you know how to find him?"

"I might," I say, and it's pretty confident I am about it. Your Grace might remember the wee peccadillo of last year with that Ger-man banker fellow and the silk merchant? Sir Edward is the German's grand-nephew on his ma's side, and I met him in passing at the funeral, but he was quite drunk so he wouldn't remember me. However, knowing the family to be Protestant bankers I've kept a careful eye on all their spawn. And as Your Grace knows well, I've made it my business to win the confidences of some of the wenches working the taverns near Whitehall Palace, and I keep an inventory in my head of their regulars' habits, same as they themselves do. So I happen to know that Sir Edward Greylock is a regular for late dinner at the Bell, on King Street, right by the stairs. I didn't tell my Saxon all this, of course. First I had to know more from him. "Is it that you want to ruin Sir Edward, and the East India Company is going to fail?" I asked. "Or is it that you want him to succeed and it's going to thrive? Answer if you want my help."

"Neither, really. I just want to distract him from putting his money into another company. I'm trying to *avoid* something."

"So it's another enterprise that you want to see fail," I said. He nodded once. "Is it Protestant or Catholic, this other one?"

"That's truly got nothing to do with anything," he insisted.

"If you know what comes of the East India Company, tell me, since that will be useful to somebody I know, and you'd better make yourself useful if you expect me to give a shite about you."

"I can't tell you what happens with the East India Company."

"Classified, is it?"

"Yes. Classified."

"Goodo. God ye good day, then," I said cheerily, stood up from the mattress and headed for the little curtained doorway.

"Where are you going?" he demands, paling a little.

"I'm leaving you with your classifieds," I said. "I'll keep my own classifieds until you're willing to have a fair exchange."

And I left the room, went down the wee corridor and climbed down the steps to the ground level where the tavern is. I went out back, used the privy, then stepped back into the tavern to see if anyone was in need of me. But it was that time of day when the few men there are mostly there for the drink.

So having left the Saxon alone for about as long as it would take to walk a half mile, I returned to the wee chamber, and as I anticipated he was more willing to negotiate.

He allowed that the East India Company is a good investment for those who can risk it—it takes awhile to come to much, but then it will be around a long while and 'tis a private company with good returns on the investment in time. So, Your Grace, let me know if you're interested in channeling some funds that way, and I'll alert your agent here. If it's good enough for a Fugger, it's good enough for a Fucker.

Meanwhile, since I wanted him to see he'd get rewarded, and since sadly it seemed we weren't going to have any kind of adventure while he was naked, I pulled out the extra set of drawers and shirt that were hiding under that very mattress the whole time and tossed them to him.

"I'll help you find your Sir Edward," I said, "but first we need to kit you out in more than underwear. Lucky for you it's me you sought out, as I'm the one best knows how to get togemans for such a large lad."

Once he had donned the threads I had for him, he relaxed a bit and even introduced himself properly: Tristan Lyons, he claims to be. Can't make out where he's really from by the name, any more than by the looks. (French, maybe? In which case likely Catholic, but not likely an ally even so. The French are slippery that way.)

I decided to take him to the Globe, on account of Dick Burbage has a closet full of costumes he did steal from Ned Alleyn. He played a heap of roles in his day, did Ned, so I was hoping we could make Tristan over into whatever would be most expedient for his undertaking.

'Tis a short walk from the Tearsheet to the Globe, mostly along the river, and one I never thought of as remarkable, but you'd think I was asking Tristan to eat a sewer. Practically retching the whole way he was, despite my taking him along the broader lane where gravel is laid down over the clay, and all the sewage lies neatly in the drainage ditches to the side of the streets, not like some alley where the offal sits right in the street once it's dumped from above. 'Twas only a turd or two we had to sidestep, not counting the horse manure, which isn't at all offensive, in fact it has a barnyard smell that reminds me of home.

Tristan Lyons had only his underclothes on, of course, but in this part of town that hardly draws attention, no matter he was such a large fella. Crowds were streaming into the Globe's gates. Trumpets did sound from within, and then I recognized Hal Condell's voice like an oratorio, which meant they were beginning some fool play. Tristan's attention turned toward the gate as if he were curious to go in.

"'Tisn't that way we're going," I said.

"That phrase," he said, looking surprised. "Even *I* know that phrase. 'Star-crossed lovers.' They're doing *Romeo and Juliet* in there. The *original Romeo and Juliet.*"

"No, the original had Saunder Cooke as Juliet," I said. "That was much better than whoever's doing it since Saunder grew a beard. Anyhow it's a shite play, just a stupid court-sponsored rant against the Irish." I grabbed his arm and began to pull him through the floods of people streaming back into the theatre. We must need get around to the back of the stage where the tiring-house was.

"How is it anti-Irish?" Tristan asked.

"The villain is a Catholic friar," I pointed out. "He being a meddling busy-body who traffics in poison—he's the reason it's a tragedy and not a comedy, and everyone knows *Catholic* is code for *Irish.*"

"Aren't the French Catholic?" asked Tristan. "And the Spanish?"

"The friar's name is Lawrence," I countered, as I pulled him along. "So obviously named after St. Labhrás. He was martyred by drinking a poison of his own concocting. The whole play is just a coded insult to the Irish, a demonstration of how amoral we supposedly are. It's bollocks. You be missing nothing. Especially now that Saunder's grown a beard."

"I don't want to see it, I just never heard that Shakespeare hated the Irish before," said Tristan, only it was so crowded there that he was shouting just to be heard as all the people pressed past us to get inside.

"Why would anyone in your time give a shite about Will Shakespeare's politics? But, aye, he does," I said. "I can quote reams of examples, same as anyone. Worst of all was just the other year, one of them plays about some English king, and there was a terrible drunk Irish character staggering about the stage wailing about how all the Irish are villains and bastards and knaves. And awhile before that he had a play about some other English king who went to conquer Ireland, and he said the Irish live like venom. Venom. That's poison, so it is. He's obsessed with the Irish and poison. Trying to convince the masses that one of us is planning to poison the Queen."

"Are you?" asked Tristan.

"Course not. Not worth the risk. She'll be dying soon anyhow and 'tisn't as if she could suddenly produce an heir at her age. There'll be chaos soon without us meddling."

"Fair enough," he said.

"It is *not* fair enough. It would be fair if she'd died *years* ago. 'Tis always the wrong ones living too long and the wrong ones dying too young." And then because this touches a subject near to my sensitive heart, of course I pressed on: "Like my Kit Marlowe."

"Who's Kit Marlowe?"

I stopped walking, and let the crowd bump past me as I turned to him. "Christopher Marlowe? Are you telling me you've never heard of *Christopher Marlowe?*"

"*Christopher* Marlowe. Of course I know the name." He thought a moment. "He was a spy and a writer, but I was not briefed about him in depth because he died years before I needed to arrive here."

"Briefed? There's nothing *brief* about him, except his life, he is only the greatest playwright that ever was, who only wrote the greatest play that ever was." And because no light of recognition went on in his pretty eyes, I prompted, "It's *Tamburlaine* I mean."

He shrugged. "I do not know it." I was incredulous and I expressed my incredulity with colorful language. "More famous than *Hamlet?*" he asked.

I figured he was codding me and almost fell over with the laughter. "Are you taking the piss, Tristan Lyons?" I asked. "*Hamlet*'s a dull fuck of a story where a fellow stands around lamenting how useless he is even to his own self, and then there's one pansy swordfight and it's over. The only good part of that is what he nicked from Kit's *Dido.*"

Tristan shrugged again. "I'm not much of a theatre-goer."

"No theatre, no whoring . . . pray what *is* it you do for recreation, then?"

But before he could answer, we'd reached the back of the Globe, and they know me in the tiring-house, so I grabbed him by the hand and in we marched.

The tiring-house is a fair way to madness, and it was a big masquerade-ball scene they were gearing up for, with all the supernumeraries donning gorgeous gowns and robes and masks the like of which could have afforded us half Your Grace's navy for a season. The Prop Man (I never have learned that fella's name) and his lads were flying around, handing out masks and candles and chalices and bated rapiers and kerchiefs, and I could hear the musicians in the gallery above tuning quietly, while Dick Burbage was bellowing on the boards, pretending to be a horny young man, which he is, except for the young part.

"Here to see Dicky," I say to the Prop Man. He looks disgruntled, which is his usual state, and he says, "Come back after the show is down." Then he sees Tristan and his eyes fix on him, because Tristan is big and I realize Prop Man is worried about costuming him—he's there in nothing but undergarments, so he looks as if he must be expecting a costume (which is true in a way).

"He's with me," I say. "Only I need to speak to Dicky about some clothes for him."

Prop Man frowns, cocks his ear toward the upstage center curtain. "He's almost off," he whispers. "And he's not in scene three."

Tristan and I try to stay out of the way of all the foot traffic by pushing ourselves against the wall. It smells foul in there—there's some silks being worn by boy actors that stink like they came right from a brothel, and I don't mean that in a nice way. But we're only there a few moments when in through the curtain, right from the stage, comes Dick, trussed up like a boy although it's a bit long in the tooth he is now for the likes of Romeo.

He sees me through the crowd of milling minions and the smile he gives me could light the heavens, he's that fond of me, and sure why wouldn't he be? "Gracie," he calls out to me, for that's how they say my name here (and yours as well, Your Majesty—in England they do say Grace O'Malley). The Prop Man hushes Dick with irritation, but like always, Dick ignores the Prop Man. "What do you mean finding a bigger man than I?" Burbage says. He pushes his way through the crew of underlings, all of whom disregard him as if he were one of them and not the richest and most renowned actor in all Creation.

He comes to us, looking Tristan Lyons up and down. Tristan Lyons says nothing, just gazes levelly back at him. "You a comedian, fellow?" he asks Tristan, and claps him hard on the shoulder. Then he looks surprised, as if he had just struck a boulder while thinking he'd be striking wool.

"No," says Tristan. "Soldier."

And Dick, he backs up a bit, looks respectful. "Who do you fight for, then, lad?" he asks.

"Classified," I say.

Dick looks impressed.

"If you be Gracie's friend, then you're a friend of mine," he says, without introducing himself (assuming he would not need to, as-suming everyone knows him already, sure). "And I'll help you out howe'er you need it."

"It's costumery he's needing," I say. "Nothing outlandish, mind you. Needs to blend in with some fellas down by Whitehall. I was thinking you had Ned Alleyn's—"

"I do indeed," says Dick. And to Tristan, "Honored to be of ser-vice to you, sir. I'm back on in a moment so we must be quick, but follow me." He gestures us to follow him through the whispering mob, to a tiny closet along the inner wall—he being a principal shareholder, he has the privilege of some small privacy. In this closet are some pegs and on them hang clothes custom-made for a man of easily Tristan Lyons's height. These were some of the cos-tumes of Edward Alleyn, tallest actor of our age and the leading man of the rival company the Admiral's Men. So tall he is, nobody can fit into his clothes, not even Burbage, who stole them as a prank when Ned retired a few year back.

"Make him a gentleman or a knight or a wealthy merchant," I suggested, as Dick glanced between the pegs and Tristan.

"All right, I've an idea," he said. He chucks aside some galli-gaskins and then a pair of French hosen filled with bombast, and Tristan's looking relieved he won't be wearing anything so ponce-like. Finally Dick pulls out some longer Venetians, that tie below the knee. They're made of damask, pluderhosen-style, a dark blue with red showing through at the slashes. He also pulls out some black silk netherstockings to go under them. And then a blue vel-vet vest. Also a blue worsted doublet with a codpiece attached, but I protest that, on account of the heat of the day. "Haven't you a mere jerkin?" I ask, and sure enough he has, a red velvet one with gold and ivory buttons, and stiff shoulders sticking out like the stubs of angel wings. "No codpiece with it though," says Burbage.

"Sorry, fellow." Then a crowned felt hat and a ruff for the neck, and cordwain boots, which are nicer than the workman's galoshes I'd found for him back at Tearsheet. "You'll have to dress yourself, I'm back on stage in fifteen lines," he says when he's hauled it out and then reclosed the closet. I thanked him and promised him to return the costumes quickly. He kissed my cheek, saluted Tristan, and dashed back out onto the stage, groaning like a man suffering unrequited love, followed by a handful of merry lads with masks and torches and one godawful pipe player.

Tristan had throughout this remained quiet and somewhat stiff, taking it all in. I wonder what his home-time must be like in comparison. I help him to dress, the mad hushed bustle of getting ready for the ball scene all around us. He's a wee bit shorter and a wee bit broader than Ned Alleyn, but the clothes fit him well enough.

"Who was that man?" he asked when we're safely outside the bounds of the Globe.

"Among many other fellows, Hamlet," I say, and I roll my eyes. "And Romeo." He doesn't look so very impressed and my regard for him, it rises a bit. Plus he's easy on the eyes, with the jerkin all laced up and his muscles nearly bulging through it. Ned Alleyn didn't have those lovely teeth either. So I'm enjoying our little assignment, it's a grand way to pass the day.

I say it's to Whitehall we're heading. He appears to know something of it. We walk out to the Thames, and himself sees that massive long London Bridge to the east, with all its fine buildings, and some two dozen traitors' heads decaying on the Great Stone Gate, and his eyes pop right open like a caged monkey's, so I reckon he's from a place without much architecture to speak of. I can't wait for him to see Savoy Palace and all them—he might fall right into the Thames! I budge his elbow and point to the west. "This way,"

I say. He follows, looking like I did the first time I ever stepped into St. Paul's. The tide's starting to turn and the upstream boats are starting to struggle, so I decide we'll walk to the river-bend and go across there.

I find the walk refreshing, for there's open air over the Thames which is nicer than the open sewers of Southwark, but the mild dyspeptic look he's had on his face hardly lessens as he walks along. He must be from some small village in the New World, to have such a hard time with the city air. But then, he gazes upon all the barges and ships and wherries with a keen look that makes me think he might have a nautical background. He's fascinated by all of them—the dung boats no less than the Queen's glass barge, and he asks questions that I answer best I can. I try to make some conversation about himself, but he's not at all forthcoming about himself or the reason for his mission. I don't push him for it now— that can come in time. Trustingly dependent I'll make him, then when he is particularly in need of my assistance, I'll demand cooperation. I've done it often enough.

We walk by the Paris Gardens, and you can hear the bears and the dogs and isn't the crowd loving it. It always gives me a laugh that the Queen will bring herself all the way over here to watch the bear-baiting but has never once stepped into the Globe, for all Will Shakespeare's trying to kiss her arse with his Irish-hating sentiments.

Less than halfway along our walk, where the Narrow Wall begins on our shore, all the palaces of bishops and nobility become visible on the far bank—Salisbury House, all the Inns of Court, Arundel House, and the rest. I point them out to him (of course I know them all from various dalliances I have contrived on Your Grace's behalf), but he does not goggle at them as he had at London Bridge. "A little different from my own time," is all he says.

At this point, the Thames bends to snake south, and soon as I hear a ferryman calling "Westward ho!" I hail him. "We're taking this wherry," I explain to Tristan, "for a penny, which will come out of your money that I procured so cleverly for you from the dim fella." The ferryman fetches us across, brings us to the far side without the tide causing him too much grief. Tristan pays his penny, and then it's just a street away we are from King Street, in the shadow of Whitehall Palace, and right away is the Bell Tavern. One of three taverns where the minor courtiers like to eat and drink and sometimes do other things. I'm more at home in South-wark, and less conspicuous, but as Your Grace knows, it's plenty of time I spend here.

It was quiet there for the time of day, as the last of the diners were finishing. A strange stillness after the din and bustle of the streets and the Thames. I nodded to Mary, who works there. She nodded back at me—and her eyes found Tristan, and they opened wider, then she gave me an approving look. I sauntered over to her and said low in her ear, "Sir Edward Greylock? You have said he was a dinnertime regular."

"Indeed he is, and you're in luck, he's just finishing his lamb." With a jut of the chin she gestured toward a fellow of perhaps thirty years, tall and elegant but with a willowy, pale presentation, sitting alone at a table by the door, the dregs of another diner's meal across from him. As if a strong wind would bend him over. Curly reddish-brown hair and pink cheeks made him look almost feminine. A pretty man all around, but not impressive. I recognized him from a few times when I was spending the evening with one of his acquaintances. I in turn pointed him out to Tristan.

It is now that Tristan begins to impress himself upon me in a good way. For what does he do but approach Sir Edward and with the most nuanced mixture of respect and swagger, he does bend the knee just a wee bit and lowers his head, doffs his hat and holds it down by his right leg, kisses his left hand and says, "God give you good day, m'lord," and then as if turned to stone, he awaits to be noticed by Sir Edward.

Sir Edward looks up from his lamb pie and stares at Tristan, perhaps as distracted by his manly physic as Mary was. "Well met, sir," he said, uncertain of Tristan's rank from his piecemeal attire.

"I cry you mercy, m'lord," says Tristan, not at all like a fellow who comes from a time and place without any English nobility oppressing him. "I'm a gentleman soldier from the Isle of Man and I would beg a boon of you." And when Sir Edward did not appear ready to disregard him, he pressed on, in a steady enough voice: "The world speaks of you as friends with the Earl of Cumberland, and he is a lord I fain would meet, but have no means of introduction."

"And who might you be, sir?" asked Sir Edward, without malice he said it, studying him.

"I am called Tristan Lyons, and I am a Manx adventurer, recently returned from Java."

Confusion flashed across Sir Edward's face. "An adventurer?" he said, and then seemed to choose polite caution by gesturing warmly to the seat across from him. "Pray be seated," he said. "What would you with the Earl?"

"Faith sir, in Java I befriended some agents of the Earl of Cumberland, and heard from them of some ambitious plans intended by the Earl and his aldermen and knights."

"Ay, the East India Company," says Sir Edward.

"Just so, m'lord. My connexions are all abroad and I fear I cannot write to them in time for them to send references of my character before the Earl sends Sir James Lancaster off on his next voyage. I would be deeply in your debt if you would consider brokering an introduction. I can hardly conceive of a better investment to be

made with my inheritance." At this I nearly burst out laughing for
he sounded not at all excited, but as if he had been carved from a
bit of peat and only half-animated. But *then*, Your Grace, he continued to speak, and to describe in such details the quality of the
Javanese pepper harvest that in faith my own mouth was watering,
and I have never even tried the stuff. And since I knew his motives, didn't I marvel at how well he kept his true intention from
this fella, spoke as if he hadn't one jot of interest in seeing the fella
himself invest in the Earl of Cumberland's schemes.

Sir Edward says he regrets to inform Tristan that Sir James set
sail back in April, and Tristan begs his pardon and asks him does
he think it might be possible to make an investment anyhow, toward future returns?

Then Tristan goes on a bit and begins to speak in tones of wonder and reverence, as if he were merely musing aloud to himself,
of Hither India. There is one thing in particular he goes on about,
and that's spices called turmeric and saffron, the both of which create a cheery yellow-orange dye for silks and cottons—fabrics easy
to obtain in Hither India. And now it's Sir Edward I'm watching, as
his face becomes a marvel of interest. Suddenly he says he's a mind
to speak to the Earl himself and see about such an investment, and
if Tristan will come to see him in two days' time, he will happily inform him of the possibilities. Tristan falls all over himself with appreciation and gratitude, honors Sir Edward as if Sir Edward were a
king and himself a peasant, and then with some assistance from me
(whom Sir Edward never once regarded directly), removes himself
from the building.

But not before making certain that Sir Edward knew he could
find some pleasant behind-the-door diversions at the Tearsheet
Brewery in Southwark, for which I am much obliged.

"That was nicely done," I said, as we walked back toward the riverbank. "Why did you go on about that dye color? Why did that hook him?"

"He is betrothed to a lady of Elizabeth's bedchamber," Tristan answered. "We studied portraits of her. She is very taken with that particular color, and it is a difficult color to come by with English or even European dyes. Theirs seems to be a match of affection as well as opportunity, so I guessed that he would know her preferences, and also want to know how to please her. Seems I guessed correctly."

"Is right you did," I agreed. "Although not so much affection he doesn't want the odd discreet diversion. I thank you for that as well."

"It seemed the least I could do for the time you've donated to my cause today."

We squeezed round a tight corner into a larger street. He might more easily have dropped back and let me go ahead of him. If he had, things might have come out differently. But intent as he was on the conversation, he was desirous of remaining abreast of me, his eyes upon mine. He tried to pass through a space too narrow for the both of us. In doing so he brushed—I don't say banged into, or jostled, but merely brushed—the shoulder of a tosser in fancy dress and a long face, leaning against a wall sucking on a long-stemmed pipe, and sulking. He probably hadn't managed to get an audience with old Elizabeth like his ma told him to expect he would. Tristan didn't even notice; but in the corner of my eye I saw this tosser giving my man a sharp look.

"I would be happy to strike up a working relationship with you, Tristan Lyons, so I would," I said. "I can imagine all manner of ways we might be of mutual benefit. So if you're ever in Southwark again, stop in."

He paused a moment and regarded me. And I regarded him

back, as it pleased me to do so. But at the same time I threw a glance back at the tosser in the fancy dress, who had dislodged himself from the wall, and was now giving Tristan a thorough inspection from hat to shoes and back up again.

I took Tristan's arm firmly and pulled him along.

"What's troubling you?" he asked, with a glance back over his shoulder.

After we had put a bit more distance between ourselves and that unsavory fop who seemed to have taken such an interest in my companion, I said, "Farthing for your thoughts." As you'll have collected, milady, I was after learning whether Tristan knew of Strands and the like.

"Did I seem at all familiar to you, when I first met your eye?" he asked.

So yes. He knew something of it. "Let's not bandy words," I said. "Whoever Sent you—whoever you cooked up this plan with—knows perfectly well that it'll never suffice to do this on one Strand only. Hence all of your preparations. Learning to pronounce my name. Looking at paintings and noticing the colors of dyestuffs and such."

"It would be idle to deny it," he said with a nod of his fine chin.

"It's in many another Strand that I'm even now meeting you again in like manner, walking these streets, having this conversation."

"As I understand it, yes."

"You understand it well enough, 'tis plain," I said, "and it's little trouble for me to Wend my way to those Strands—or *snáithe* as we say at home—and meet with you there and then and further enjoy the pleasure of your company."

"I would like that very much," he said. "Are there others like you I might work with as well?"

"Don't get cheeky, lad," I said. "Let's see how you can make things worth my while first, and then I'll decide if I want to cut anyone else in."

"If you make yourself my ally, it's quite possible. So think about what I might be able to offer you."

"Oh, I will," I assured him. "I already am. Now, if you've a good witch to Send you," I continued, "have her Send you to arrive yesterday."

"Why?"

"This is Monday. Had you arrived yesterday, everyone would have been at Sunday services. Not that I mind finding you naked in my closet each time you return, but it will be simpler if you arrive when things are quiet."

"Will you skip Sunday services to meet me?"

"If you want to pay the fine I'd be receiving for failure to appear." And since he seemed to be considering this, I said, "No, I cannot, lad. I cannot afford to be seen as shirking my religious duties, it's suspicious enough that I'm Irish and over here, while there's an armed uprising against the English back at home. But you're not on the rolls anywhere, so your absence won't be noted. Come on Sunday and dress yourself, now that you know where I keep the shirts and breeches, and just wait for me."

We were having this conversation as we came down King Street to the Whitehall Stairs, where I planned to find us a ferryman. There were plenty of wherries out there since the tide was heading out, and traffic's easier eastward. I slowed my pace as I surveyed the scene.

Then someone barreled into me from behind, knocking me off balance.

I stumble and my shoe gets caught in a tear in my petticoat, and I'm falling to my knees when, faster than I can think, there's Tristan catching me and helping me to right myself. But in doing so he jostles the rude bastard who's almost knocked me down. By the time I've got my balance and my wits back, that bastard has spun on his heel to confront Tristan. They're standing arm's length apart. I recognize him as the tosser who followed us.

This fop—who doesn't look like much, hardly any manlier than Sir Edward—instantly draws back to a distance, puts his right hand on his rapier and draws it out, no more than the width of two fingers, but enough to send a message. Other people coming and going on the steps give him a wider berth, but otherwise continue their business on and off the wherries.

"Stand off, villain!" says the fella with the rapier, pompous and angry. "What business have you touching me so rudely?"

Tristan catches himself. "Good morrow, my lord, pray excuse my abruptness."

"Once you have explained yourself, I might."

Tristan blinks, then says, "'Tis my sister you just knocked to her knees there. I'll let it be if you will."

The fellow looks utterly astounded, and then laughs in Tristan's face. "What, that common whore? That slattern? She's not your sister, you lying knave. 'Tis *she* owes *me* an apology, for being in my way." He turns to me and commands me: "Apologize!"

"She owes you no apology, sir," says Tristan, very calm.

"Let it be, Tristan," I say sharply, and I'm using my best London accent, which Tristan notices with surprise. He's sharp enough to understand I've a reason for it. "Pray pardon me, m'lord," I say to the fellow. "I did not hear you coming."

Tristan says nothing. But the set of his mouth shows a kind of annoyance and the tosser with the rapier notices. He draws the rapier a little farther.

"Do you take offense at my behavior toward this whore?" he demands of Tristan.

"He doesn't," I say.

"Shut up, whore," he says. "Tell me yourself, sirrah, assure me you understand this bawd is in the wrong here, and for even thinking of defending her, you are too. Say so and beg apology."

I recognize the tosser now—he's been a customer at the Tearsheet of my mate Morag, the Caledonian wench. He's a terrible mean streak and he loves his violence. It's not apologizing he wants from Tristan—it's a fight.

Tristan is still standing there. I sense he's about to vomit with the rage, although he looks calm enough. "To avoid a disruption of the Queen's Peace, I will apologize whole-heartedly," he says, but of course that just feeds the fellow's ire:

"If that's why you're apologizing, I reject it," he says. "I demand you acknowledge you're wrong for insulting and challenging a nobleman. And now you're being insolent as well." He draws the rapier fully from its sheath. "Will it take a taste of steel for you to find your manners?"

"I have no weapon," Tristan says, still quiet-like.

The nobleman laughs. "So?" he says.

"Would you strike an unarmed man?"

He laughs again. "That makes it easier to strike him, doesn't it?" Around us, folk are still hustling by, and by now we've missed a few wherries. I want to catch one while the tide is with us, and I certainly don't want to get ourselves stuck here.

Now the nobleman looks around, as if expecting an admiring crowd.

In truth, almost everyone's giving us a wide berth. There are only two exceptions. Standing off at a distance, observing matters carefully, is a gentleman with a long, sharp yellow beard, dressed in those sorts of clothes that look dark at first glance but on closer examination are splendid. Closer to hand, three paces behind and to one side of the tosser, is another courtier, old enough to be the fop's father, dressed as if he's on his way home from a Dutch funeral.

"But I'm happy to give an advantage to one who so desperately needs it," continues the tosser. "George," he says to the old git in the neck-ruff, "lend this varlet that rusty meat cleaver you have hanging from your belt. I'll take my apology in blood." Very familiar he is, and cheeky in his description of George's sidearm, which looks a perfectly respectable weapon to my eye, but George takes no offense; I reckon these two know each other well, and that George is some manner of retainer or vassal.

"You'll be fined again, Herbert," says George, who for one so long in the tooth and so weedy in his attire is, I confess, a bit fierce-looking.

"The fine's a trifle," Herbert says breezily. "Lend him your sword."

George tosses his cape back, reaches across his body, and draws the weapon, which turns out to be as old and out-of-date as his clothing: it's a heavy, single-edged backsword of the old school, such as you'll see Protestants toting about at home, the better to wave menacingly at Irish folk. He offers it hilt-first over his arm to Tristan, who declines to take it. "I pray you accept my pardon for all offenses uttered," Tristan says. "I've an ailing mother in South-wark and I would fain meet her within the hour."

"If she ails enough, you can meet her in heaven in half that time," says Herbert. "Take the sword."

Tristan remains where he is.

Herbert, without warning, slashes at Tristan's face. He'd have taken Tristan's nose off if Tristan's reflexes were not so fast. But like a dragonfly avoiding a bird, my Saxon has ducked the blow, grabbed the hilt of the offered backsword, and swung it around to face his attacker. Old George, no fool, steps back to give them room. A passing washerwoman utters a little shout of fear and scurries off, and suddenly I notice nobody else is on the steps now but the four of us, and sure I'm sweating in the hazy September sun much more than I was moments ago.

The fight was fierce but very short. Wherever Tristan comes from, they must use swords because it's confident, strong and graceful he seemed to me. But I think whatever their swords are, they can't be rapiers. He looked like he was dancing, like he'd learned steps he could perform very well, but Herbert—although far less elegant and less muscle on him—was so accustomed to the weapon that using it was like walking or eating for him.

Their fight moved them down a couple steps and then back up, and nobody watched overtly as they might back home, here in the city people mostly hurried away up on the road, or if they were on the river, they kept rowing toward the Westminster stairs or the nearest sandbank to disembark. Herbert was wielding his slender blade like an Italian fence-master, darting in from this angle and that, and it was all Tristan could do to set his thrusts aside with herky-jerky movements of the backsword. It looked ponderous even in his strong hands.

Suddenly, I didn't see how, the backsword went flying out of Tristan's hand and Herbert had him flat back against the stairs—his sword actually pinning Tristan against the stone by virtue of having pierced through the shirt, vest, and jerkin just at the side of Tristan's neck, and then Herbert stabbed it into the crevice between the rise and tread of the stone steps. Tristan was stuck. It seemed a fancy move from a fellow not likely capable of fancy moves.

"To fall for such an easy and old-fashioned technique," said Herbert, making a *tch-tch-tch*'ing sound. "A stupid error—and a fatal one."

But then a gloved hand came down, gently but firmly, upon Herbert's wrist. An extraordinarily fine glove it was, made of white kid, with intricate embroidery.

Herbert hadn't seen this coming. Nor had I. Both of us looked up into the face of the gentleman I had noticed a minute ago—the finely dressed chap with the sharp yellow beard. "Who are you, sirrah, and how dare you?" Herbert demanded, and tried to wrench free of the other's grip. But the white kid glove held firm.

"I am the gentleman's second," said the man with the sharp yellow beard. He had an accent—'twas *ze* he said instead of *the*, like a German. He glanced over at George, then returned his eyes to Herbert's face. Or perhaps I should say *eye*, for he was wearing a tall hat with a broad brim, gorgeously plumed, and in the best style of all the young blades, he'd pulled it down low to one side, concealing his left eye. "You have your second," the German continued, flicking that eye momentarily at George, "and so ze honorable tradition is zat your opponent in ze duel should have one also. Is it not so?"

"It is so," Herbert admitted, "but you do not even know this varlet."

The German shrugged, giving me cause to admire the exquisite silk lining of his cape. "Zis in no way alters ze honorable tradition. As you will know. Being a man of honor." And the German now turned his head to look about at the crowd of onlookers that had gathered during the pause in swordplay. The scarlet plume in his hat wafted first this way, then that. Herbert looked up to see that there were now many witnesses. Some of whom were gentlemen—capable of giving testimony and of being believed by a judge.

The German's intervention had worked; Herbert's humours

had cooled. He looked down at Tristan. "Go ask the wet-nurse how to escape next time. But first give me apologies. Varlet."

The German released Herbert's wrist, spun away, and walked off into the crowd.

"I apologize," said Tristan stiffly, from his awkward supine position.

"For *what* wrongs precisely, sirrah?"

Tristan took a moment as if trying to remember what his sins were. "For daring to show such insolence to one of my betters."

"Apology accepted." He withdrew his sword, stood upright, and casually sheathed his blade. "If it happens again, 'twill be your throat I pierce and not the clothes around it," he said, then gestured to George (who had retrieved his backsword and was inspecting it for damage). They walked down the steps, took the next wherry, and sailed off downstream.

Tristan got to his feet before I could move to offer him a hand. He shook his head slightly, looking spooked. "Well there's a lesson in that," muttered he to himself. "Learning from a fight choreographer has its limits." He gave me a reassuring smile. "It's been a very fruitful day."

And to make a quick end of it, Your Grace, back we went along the Thames, and back to the brewery, and then I Sent him back to where he came from, which is farther into the future than I had dreamed, hundreds of years it sounds like. I've kept Ned Alleyn's stolen costume for his next visit.

So that is the tale of Tristan Lyons, whom I'll surely see on many another snáithe as I Wend my way thence.

And in conclusion, let me tell Your Majesty that nobody in London seems at all aware that the Spanish are about to land at Kinsale; that Penelope Devereux, sister to the traitor Essex, has been divorced by her husband Lord Rich for having an affair (and bastard children) with Mountjoy, known to yourself also as Charles Blount, known to yourself also as "Lord Deputy of Ireland." They have but one son, Mountjoy Blount, and himself is four years old, but I do intend to put a curse on him that all of his children will be still-born or idiots, and so that line will end.

And now I shall close with great love and regard to Your Majesty, as I am off to enjoy my one personal indulgence: the honey-love of a full night spent in the arms of my sweetheart. My life is naught but secrets that I either keep or destroy on your behalf; sure it does my soul good to have one small nugget of mine own.

Whether I be near or far, may I hear only good things of you, My Lady Gráinne! Yours ever, Gráinne in London

Diachronicle

DAY 352

In which we fail better

I SET UP A VIGIL in the office, determining not to leave until Tristan had returned. What if our research about the witch Gráinne had been wrong? What if she was sloppy with her details, and returned him to the wrong time or place? So in a sense, it made no sense at all to wait, and yet I could focus on nothing else. I continued to collate our databases, determined not to leave the building despite the lovely summer weather—weather not unlike what is outside right now, given in both cases it is July in a temperate climate. The whole day passed. Erszebet took it upon herself to buy a used bicycle with what she called "pin money" given her by Tristan for sundry expenses, and she began to map out a bike route she would take to Walden Pond the next day if Tristan had not returned. She seemed to be hoping he'd be gone awhile. Frank and Rebecca, who had left the office shortly after Tristan had been Sent to the DTAP, called to invite us to dinner. This struck me as bizarrely normal when we were living under not-at-all-normal circumstances, so I declined, but Erszebet, overhearing the call, insisted I call them back so that she could go on her own.

A buzz from the control panel let us know that the ODEC door was opening. Erszebet's face fell slightly. "He's back," she said, as if he'd returned just to ruin her social calendar. "Now we'll have to take him to dinner as well."

"Don't you want to hear what happened?" I asked. I went to the glass wall and looked to the ODEC, then, realizing Tristan would be naked, stopped myself. There was now an intercom system that we could use to communicate through the wall. I flipped it on. "Tristan?" I called. "Are you all right?"

"Give me a moment," he called back out, in a hazy voice. "Actually give me five moments."

"Look at you, smiling like a girl," said Erszebet, grudgingly amused. "It is disappointing to me you don't raise your standards."

"Don't you want to know how it went?" I demanded.

She shrugged her trademark disdainful shrug. "It does not matter how it went, it is only the first time, he will have to go back and do it again. It will be days before there is anything interesting to hear about."

"I'm calling Oda-sensei," I said, feeling uncharacteristically peevish toward her. Quite suddenly I had a lot of energy and no clear sense of how to channel it. I sent them a text; Rebecca answered and said that they would, naturally, come at once.

We all convened in an office near the ODEC that we had converted into a briefing and debriefing room. It was equipped with gear for recording audio and video, though we had not yet got in the habit of using it. Tristan smelled of the disinfectant shower he'd just stepped out of. He'd changed back into his jeans and T-shirt and thrown his damp towel around his neck like a shawl. He looked fine, although he was slightly distracted as his tongue worked the small gap in his back teeth due to the missing fillings. I'd handed those back to him upon his return. They now sat before him on the table, giving him something to fidget with. He looked like he could use a beer, and so I got him one.

"I have good news and bad news," he began, after whetting his whistle with a swallow of Old Tearsheet. "The good news—the most important news—is that I believe Sir Edward will change his mind about his investment. I believe he will opt for the East India Company over the Boston Council."

"On one Strand," said Erszebet.

"Yes," said Tristan. "I realize I need to do it a few more times, although it might be worth Mel's time to go back to 1640 Cambridge just to see if there's a difference."

"There won't be," said Erszebet. "It does not work that way, you've already witnessed that. Why would you subject her to that unpleasant effort?"

"I think it's worth checking," Tristan repeated. "To see how much can be accomplished in a single go."

There was a loaded pause and then Erszebet said flatly, "Well then, you'll have to Send her yourself. I will not do it."

"You are refusing an order?"

"I reject the notion you can give me orders," said Erszebet. "I am simply refusing to do something foolish."

"Erszebet," said Frank Oda, ever the conciliatory force. "You signed papers agreeing to cooperate, do you remember that, in Washington?"

"I will cooperate," said Erszebet. "When it is in the interest of the mission. This is just in the interest of Tristan Lyons throwing his weight around, and I did not sign anything saying I would do that."

"He's your superior officer," I tried tentatively, realizing it was a mistake even as the words came out of my mouth, for she burst out laughing and said, "Him? He's not my superior anything." She sobered. "I will Send Tristan back to London in September of 1601, to the Tearsheet Brewery. I will do that as many times as it takes, my guess is four times at least, and only then will we send Melisande back to Cambridge to see if it has worked yet."

Tristan took a moment to look silently long-suffering, although in truth I think he did this just to humor her desire to discomfit him. "Fine," he said at last. "That brings me to the lessons learned. I had an opportunity to test my weapons skills, and I'm a little shell-shocked by how poorly prepared I was. Oh, grappling and knife disarms work as well in that age as today. Swordfighting is a different matter altogether." He delivered this news in his usual clipped and businesslike Tristan manner, but then paused, staring off into space, as if reviewing some action in his mind's eye.

Frank Oda and I exchanged a look.

"You saw a real swordfight?" Oda-sensei asked, fascinated.

Tristan seemed not to hear the question. He had slightly extended his right arm, fingers curled as if gripping the hilt of a sword, and was moving it this way and that. Meeting my eye, he pulled the towel off of his neck, revealing a long, superficial cut.

"You were *in* a real swordfight!?" I exclaimed.

This seemed to snap him out of it. He let his hand drop to the table, where he went back to fidgeting with the disembodied fillings. "They have more than one kind of sword," he announced. "It's not all just rapiers. There's an older style too. Bigger, heavier. Kind of like nowadays you might see an older person driving a big old Buick sedan while the younger generation is tooling around in little hybrids. I need to get good at fighting with a Buick. I need a combat historian who can drill me on the nuances of that era. My opponent did something very subtle that I wasn't expecting."

"Should I ask Darren to come back in?"

Darren was the fight choreographer from Boston Shakespeare. We had sworn him to secrecy and hired him to teach Tristan what he knew.

"Darren's wrong for it," Tristan said. "He's spot-on with the historical detail, I'll give him that. But the whole point of stage fighting is that it's supposed to look as flashy as possible, while being totally safe. And I am here to tell you that real swordfighting is pretty non-flashy and pretty fucking dangerous."

"I know who to ask," said Rebecca. She had turned herself into a resourceful Girl Friday, given she had never actually approved of any of this. There wasn't much we would put past her. Even so, we all turned to see if she was serious. "In the park down the street," she explained, "in the evenings, when the weather's good, there's a group of historical swordfighters who meet to practice."

"LARPers?" Tristan asked, clearly skeptical. Seeing that no one besides him knew what a LARPer was, he continued, "Guys who fight with foam weapons?"

"Not foam," Rebecca said. "It is steel on steel, I can hear the din of it from my garden. They should be meeting this evening. I'll go there and make inquiries as soon as you're done debriefing us."

"Great. If we can find one willing to sign the NDA, I want to book him all day tomorrow and the next day, maybe even three days in a row. I need to get back to the Tearsheet as quickly as possible, and I definitely have to be on my game." His eye fell on the beer bottle in front of him, with its ye olde lettering and its ye olde artist's conception of the original Tearsheet Brewery. He devoted a few moments to examining this, as if comparing it to the real one he had departed only a few minutes ago.

Then he turned to Erszebet. "Here's the other thing. When I go back, I need to go back to a different day, the day before I was last there. How will that affect the Strands?"

She shrugged, but this time thoughtfully, not disdainfully. "It depends," she said. "Nothing is ever certain. If you will not be traveling for a few days, I will spend that time with my számológép and try to determine this. The more different moments you visit, the more Strands there are to contend with, and it is an exponential increase in complications. I will tell you something: in the history of magic it is a general trend that all new rulers wish to use our time-transporting skills to their advantage, but the more seasoned they become, the more they understand the complications, and the less they wish to lean upon it."

"We're not in the history of magic," Tristan replied evenly. "We're outside of it. That's sort of the point."

"Thank you for . . . doing whatever it is you're going to be doing with your, mmm, számológép," I said.

"What exactly are you going to be doing with it?" asked Frank Oda.

"I already told you, you cannot touch it," she said shortly.

"And I won't," said Oda-sensei, ever affable. "But I would so very much like to watch as you do the work. I have been playing with an artifact of Rebecca's ancestress that reminds me of your számológép. Perhaps I could ask questions and you could explain it to me." A smile. "I would be so extremely grateful to be a beginner at the feet of such an expert."

"That's flattery," said Erszebet, looking pleased about it.

"It is the truth," said Oda-sensei. "Sometimes the truth is flattering."

She considered him a moment, and then smiled. It was rare she smiled, and it only further emphasized her beauty. "Very well," she said. "We start tomorrow."

And thus began Oda-sensei's initiation into diachronic calculations.

Journal Entry of
Rebecca East-Oda
JULY 22

Temperature 82F. High clouds, mild breeze. Barometer rising. All herbs faring nicely. Butterfly weed beginning to bloom. Anise hyssop approaching four feet, very healthy. Scarlet elder: flowers past, berries not yet ripe. Vegetables: kale and lettuce in containers coming nicely (lettuce harvestable as baby greens), but I fear I planted the onions too late in the season.

Generally less time and energy for gardening, to be honest. I am distracted by the distant clinking and clanking of blunt steel weapons in the park down the street, where Tristan has been learning the art of the backsword from one Mortimer Shore, a local historical fencing enthusiast whom I have recruited.

Have been watching Frank and Erszebet converse, as she attempts to describe to him what her számológép does for her. For all my years of editing his papers and carrying my weight at those awkward faculty parties (in which fundamentally non-social creatures—physicists—were expected to behave like social creatures), I cannot follow most of their discussion. This is not actually due to the calculus or physics, given that Erszebet has absolutely no training in either field. It is rather that I find it exhausting to try to be essentially bilingual, which Frank is so willing to be. She speaks in her eccentric lingo and he finds ways to respond to her with very simply layman's physics—"When you say XYZ, is that another way of saying ABC?" And she thinks, and sighs, and says she supposes so, if somebody is too thick to simply understand XYZ.

After several hours of discussion, Frank thanked her, brought home his notes, and sat down with my shaggy family heirloom to experiment with what he'd learned. He has not yet shared any of his discoveries with me—not because he is keeping it a secret, but because he most enjoys bringing me in to his work when he's accomplished something. I believe he means to construct a számológép/quipu/shaggy-family-artifact-like object that he can use whether or not Erszebet is of a mind to cooperate with Tristan. (Although since she is the only one who can actually make time travel happen, there is no practical benefit to having a quipu unless she is cooperating. There I go being a pragmatist, which is not how Frank is wired.)

The only other item of note—besides Tristan re-training himself for period combat, which I hope he is never foolhardy enough to use—is that our two young leaders, especially Tristan, seem to be growing tense about how long this is taking. I have spent fifty years married to a man who is delightedly preoccupied with the journey, and now suddenly we are working with those who care only for the destination.

This does not, in truth, seem to match their personalities, certainly not Mel's. It clearly originates from higher up the "food chain," the cast of characters we met around that conference table in the Trapezoid. General Frink must be ultimately responsible; but it is Lester Holgate, Frink's eager-beaver civilian toady, who seems to be on the other end of most of the phone calls and email threads.

LETTER FROM
GRÁINNE *to* GRACE O'MALLEY
A Sunday of Mid-Harvest, 1601

Auspiciousness and prosperity to you, milady!

It's mostly Tristan Lyons I'm writing of today, Your Grace, as precious few other developments there've been but plenty involving him. He must be in alliance with a proper witch, and depending on who and where she is, she could be useful for Your Grace.

In order for me to string this together into a proper tale I've had to Wend my way to all of the snáithe—the Strands—in which he has appeared to carry out the same set of deeds. As you and I understand, Your Grace, they all happened at once, as choristers in the church nave sing the same tune at the same time; but I cannot write many stories down in such a manner and so I'll relate them one after the other, like beads on a rosary.

He has been Sent to several Strands, always on the Sunday, and always with the same task: to convince Sir Edward Greylock to move his financial interests to the East India Company, and away from some queer little joint-stock company called the Boston Council.

He wants this as the cause of an effect forty years distant and all the way across the sea. He is not very forthcoming in his plans, except to assure me they have no bearing on Your Grace. I have not yet begun to pry him for important information, as I believe the longer I let him get accustomed to my cooperation, the easier will it be to twist him round my finger when it's time. So I will continue to knit myself into his affections. I've offered him the occasional chance for making the beast with two backs, but he never takes me up on it. It's a shame since he's cleaner and better smelling than any other fellow in the neighborhood (except my sweetheart).

It's the same each Strand: he arrives while we are all at mass, dons the shirt and drawers I keep extra at hand, and then waits for me to return from services, when I unlock my chest and give him a few coins and Ned Alleyn's costume pieces. To keep him in the habit of telling me things (although small things they are, for now), I pester him for information on his future world. I've learned things that are pleasing enough to my ear, assuming he's not codding me. He tells me of all the saints there ever was, it's only Padraig whose feast day is celebrated in his nation. He tells me the spirit of the Irish where he dwells is powerful, so powerful that many of our countrymen will hold a great many courtly offices, so great that it's our *luchrupán* used as a talisman by a guild of men who somehow earn their living playing a game with a pig bladder (I cannot fathom how this happens, but I will query further if Your Grace requests to know it). He spends the night in the bawdy house, and the next day we venture across the river. Tristan understands he must make the effort several times to see results. It's four times he's had the same conversation with the same Sir Edward Greylock at the same tavern near Whitehall. However, there have been two remarkable changes in the routine.

First of all, when we enter the tavern, 'tis no longer Sir Edward sitting alone we see, looking across the table at the remains of some other diner's food. In these other Strands, his dinner companion has lingered over his meal, drawing out the conversation. Finely dressed this fella is, in clothes that are dark and even a touch old-fashioned, but ever so well made. He's wearing a tall hat with a broad brim pulled rakishly down over one eye, sporting a scarlet plume, and when he turns his head to take note of Tristan, it's a yellow beard that comes into view, trimmed and groomed to a long sharp point. It is, in other words, the German with the white kid gloves who came out of nowhere in the first Strand and prevented Tristan from being murdered in the duel. He sits there quietly, listening to what Tristan has to say. From time to time he and Sir Edward glance across the table at each other in a manner that is full of significance. Anon he excuses himself and leaves the tavern.

Secondly: on these other Strands, we are chanced upon by the same tosser and the same weedy curmudgeon—Herbert and George—I wrote about before. As before they follow us, and Herbert has a go at Tristan on the Whitehall steps. As before the German's there, stepping up to act as Tristan's second. And you might think that Tristan would properly apologize and humble himself to avoid a repetition of the duel. But didn't he amaze me the first time he came back, accepting George's backsword straight-away, and disarming Herbert in a trice! His abilities, his skill, his confidence—all these more than trebled from one Strand to the next! I cannot account for the marvel of it, but it does make him even more lovely a fellow to watch now. The German watches all, but does less, as his services are no longer needed, and doesn't he disappear into the crowd before he can be thanked.

For Tristan's fifth appearance, things were different. This time, he reported to me that his acolyte, a woman named Melisande (not a witch), has been to the nearer future to check the outcome of his labors, but those efforts have been futile. So he asked if rather than repeating our circuit of Whitehall and the Bell Tavern, we might discourse of other ways to effect the necessary change.

This I knew to be my opportunity to start to work him round my finger. "I might be able to help you," says I, "if you give me more information than you have been."

"Fair enough," he says—as if being fair were what mattered. "What do you want to know?"

"Why are you needing this Boston Council scheme to fail? What gain you by that?"

"In my reality as it now stands, the Council builds something in the New World that we don't want there. A factory. But it's in the way of where a house should be, a house that *had been* there when we began our efforts. We need the house to still be there, meaning we need the factory to never have been built."

"Righto, but why were you meddling there to start with? Surely in your future world full of handsome creatures such as yourself, there is little enough you could gain by going to visit some house in the wilderness? What was there for you?"

He grimaced, for he wasn't in the humour to go into it, but eventually didn't I coax from him his story, that being: he and brethren were attempting to make a small fortune for themselves by secreting away an item—a printed book— that was easy enough to get in 1640 but near impossible to get in Tristan's age, making it of great worth.

"So you're thieves and chancers," said I approvingly.

"No," he objected. "It is a strategy. The money is not to save us from having to labor for a living, it is what we need *to be able* to labor for a living."

"Seems peculiar," I said. "You're saying once you've the money in hand—enough to live on for the rest of your days, in leisure and doing whatever you like—instead of doing that, you'd be using the money for something that requires you to toil more than you'd have to without the money. Be you daft?"

"The labor we want to do is important work. It means far more to us to do that work than to simply live a life of leisure."

I laughed at him. "So it's Protestant you be!" I said. "Or farmers. Sure none else would make that choice."

"Would you not?" he asked. "Is there nothing in the world that means so much to you that if you were given treasure, you would use it not for yourself but to support and protect the thing you love?"

And then didn't I shut my mouth and nod, for I understood him.

"That is why we need the money," he said. "That we can do our work."

"And what *be* your work?" I asked of course, and of course he answered, "Classified."

I shrugged then. "I can't help you figure out how to accomplish something if you won't be telling me what you're trying to accomplish," I said.

"All that matters is for the factory to disappear so that we still have a place to hide the book."

"So you say. But I need to know the nature of your work, so I know if it's something I want to be abetting. What if it's against the interests of Ireland, for all you say we prosper over there in your New World?"

"It's got nothing at all to do with Ireland," he insisted.

"Then tell me what it's got to do with. From where I sit, the only thing you've got to offer me—besides telling Sir Edward to spend his whoring largesse with me and my sisters—is that you've knowledge I have not. That's the cost of my assisting you: knowledge. Start with something simple. Such as what it is you're doing. In the bigger sense, I mean."

He grimaced. Sat for a bit, he did, as if chewing over the diet of truth in his mind. Then he finally presented this bit of business to me: "In the future—long after you are dead, but long before I am born—magic is completely done away with."

"That's impossible," I said.

"I gain nothing by dishonesty," he said. "I have nothing to offer you but truth."

"What destroys it? Is it the Inquisition? Those idiot priests go chasing after innocent women, as if *real* witches would *let* themselves be caught and tortured and killed! Almost by *definition*, anyone who is caught and tortured, and doesn't free themselves by magic, has no magic powers. It's simple *reason*. Is it the Inquisition? How do they ever manage it, thick as they are?"

He shook his head. "*How* magic disappears is a separate conversation for another time. What matters is that my fellows and I are trying to bring it back. But to bring it back requires many things, ingredients and props and general expenses that I cannot easily explain. There is only one witch left in my time."

"What, in the whole world?" I exclaimed in amazement.

"To the best of our knowledge. She is very old, and when she was young and learning magic, magic was almost gone. So we are at a disadvantage in my time. We are trying to learn more, that we may bring that knowledge into the future and make sure magic is restored."

Now it was my turn to sit a moment grimacing. "As hard as it is to believe this story," I said, "I believe you are sincere in telling it. Speaking on behalf of my sisters I thank you for the work you're doing."

"Will you aid me to do that work?"

"As much as I can," I said, "although many's the questions I still have about this, more now than before you told me anything at all."

"I realize it's a lot to hear all at once," said Tristan Lyons. "I hope that you will help me. In this endeavor, and perhaps others."

"For the sake of my sisters though I never meet them, I give you my hand and my heart. But we begin with this one task, aye?"

"Aye," he said. "Once we have accomplished this, I will know better how to proceed in general. And I'll have more to tell you."

"Is right you will. Well then. We must consider other means through which Sir Edward would not fund this Boston Council."

"Perhaps he squandered his inheritance," suggested Tristan. "Can you cause that to have happened?"

I shook my head. "That would be the act of a man of a different character altogether, and so 'twould require too many other changes. It needs must be a simple thing, one specific event. Perhaps he was never born, or died in childhood."

"That's a bit extreme," said Tristan, who I wouldn't have taken for the sentimental type. "Plus he has offspring down the line who are important enough to look up in the encyclopedia."

"In the what?"

"He has important descendants who are not born yet. We cannot change the future that much; we must keep him alive." He thought a moment. "He could put his money into the Boston Council but the ships could all be lost at sea."

"We do not exactly do weather magic," I said, "save in fairy tales. It does not really work that way. 'Tis more specific than just raising a storm to blow a ship off course. More *scientific* it is, if you understand that concept."

"I'm familiar with it," he said.

"But let me look into it," I offered, and from behind the chest I pulled out my *áireamhán* and held it out before me, to meditate upon it.

"You're going to look into it with a broom?" asked Tristan.

"It's not a broom," I said, although I realized I did not know the word in English as I've never the cause to utter it. His confusion was understandable. To him it would look like a bundle of branching twigs, bound fast in such-same manner as a sweep-broom. And indeed haven't I heard tell of witches who sweep the floor with their áireamhán as a way to allay the suspicions of priests and busybodies?

"It's a . . . measuring-counter-helper," I explained. "It's a strange look you have on your face there, Tristan Lyons. Why would that be?"

"What do you use it for exactly?" he asked, in a tone and with just the expression of an excited child first getting to touch a salamander. Wanted to snatch it from me, I think he did, but he restrained himself.

"It helps me to reckon the odds and the complications of all these undertakings. Without it, I could never have Wended my way to this Strand to assist you. You cannot play such games as you be playing without risk of very serious consequences; this assists me in knowing how those might come out."

Carefully controlling his breathing, he was. "Do you know what a quipu is?" he demanded. I shook my head. "How about a számológép?"

"What are you talking about?"

"We have—our witch has—something like that broom of yours, but made of different material. Flexible rather than stiff. But with the same branching, many-stranded structure. She employs it the way you have just now described employing yours. To calculate the possible consequences of her magic. How does it work?"

"What an idiot question," I said. "How does writing work? Can you tell me how it is I scratch thrice-ten marks on a piece of vellum and you can look at it and learn every piece of knowledge in the world?"

"Actually, in my time, we can explain how that happens," said Tristan.

"Well then, you tell me how my áireamhán works," I suggested. "Because I've not the faintest idea, I just know it does."

So that's the sort of talk we were having on that Strand, Your Majesty. I did some readings on the áireamhán and from them we concluded that there was no wisdom in trying to sink the ship that takes Sir Edward's silver across, as the first mate eventually has some offspring who has some other offspring ad nauseam, and one of them eventually writes a book about a fish, that Tristan says is important. And we determined likewise that there be *lomadh* danger in trying to destroy the factory, as likely the local American tribe would be blamed for it by the Puritans in the nearby village, who would then attack the American tribe, who would then burn down the whole village, and that imperils a school to be built whose existence must not be blotted out. All in all, it seemed to me, his likeliest course of action was for him to stay the course, try two or three more times to sway Sir Edward, and then go back to check again.

So, not to be putting too much emphasis upon it, we went as ever to the Bell Tavern, and he chatted up Sir Edward and the German, and back we came to the brewery (I do so love that swordfight, and on certain Strands, Tristan is a marvel! Although in fairness, he now knows Herbert's style very well; poor Herbert has no idea what he is getting into, and moreover seems increasingly distracted by the queer feeling that this has all happened to him before.). Then I Sent him direct to 1640 in America, for the economy of time, by checking for himself if the change had been made. I don't know if he'll Home to his own time or back to me, but in either case, it's here he'll return on some other Strand, and I shall keep working on him to learn something. His talk of the loss of magic is distressing to me, although it will happen long enough from now that it shall have no bearing on Your Grace's plans.

Little to report in other news as I just wrote you so recently. At the Globe they brought back Will's comedy *As You Like It*, which I went to see, although it irks me to see him nicking Your Grace's own story, for Rosalind is a thinly disguised Grace O'Malley (as they call you here) and doesn't all of London know it? A grand enough play it is, but only one line of true beauty in it: "Whoever loved who loved not at first sight?" And isn't that a line he stole from Kit Marlowe and furthermore didn't Kit write that line about meeting me! My poor dead Kit. That poxy arse Will Shakespeare. He's even the effrontery to speak obliquely of my sweetheart's demise, for when Will Kempe as the fool Touchstone refers to "a great reckoning in a little room," don't we all know he means Kit being murdered in that pub brawl?

Having finished my message to you, I'm off to dispel my melancholy with my paramour. If I told you who 'twas, you would not believe me, is how discreet I'm being.

Whether I be near or far, may I hear only good things of you, My Lady Gráinne! Yours ever, Gráinne in London

Journal Entry of

Rebecca East-Oda

AUGUST 1

Temperature 90F, extremely muggy. Barometer falling, hopefully rain to come.

Container garden on front steps: kale harvestable but bitter due to the heat, new generation of lettuce coming in fine. Onions will be ready soon, to my surprise. The rest of it makes do on its own. Have put in an irrigation system as I am growing forgetful of the water rotations. Almost a relief not to have an entire vegetable garden to weed and oversee. How did I ever have the time and energy? I would even forget to feed the cats if they did not remind me.

Frank continues to crunch numbers and create formulas to further understand the quipu, querying Erszebet about her object and then examining the "witch's mop" as we call the artifact from the attic chest. Tristan agrees this is a priority. He has determined to save time by traveling directly between 1601 to 1640 if possible, now that we have "Known Compliant Witches" (inevitably "KCWs") in both of those DTAPs, but it seems foolish to do this without calculating the risks, and Erszebet—although willing to do it—has warned that she can only calculate so fast. In the meanwhile, he has decided to travel from 1601 London to 1640 Cambridge but then return here—so far, without success. The maple syrup boiler remains. At least the yard is no longer getting dug up once a day.

The other item of note is the addition to our team of a new man. Frink, the fellow with the lapels and the desk in Washington, has sent us his protégé because, he tells us, based on Tristan's progress reports, we need to "boost our morale," "take the bull by the horns," and generally make ourselves more of an historical nuisance than Erszebet feels is a good idea. His name is Lester Holgate ("Call me Les"), and by a strange coincidence—is it a coincidence?—he is the nephew of one Roger Blevins, who was the chair of Melisande's department at Harvard.

Rather than attempt to describe Les and his effect on the team, I attach a "hard copy" of a PowerPoint presentation that he accidentally emailed to me.

SLIDE 1: —CLASSIFIED—

INTERIM SITREP

OPERATION "BOLSTER GAINS"

From: LESTER ("LES") HOLGATE

(currently embedded DODO Site Prime—Cambridge, MA)

To: FRINK—EYES ONLY

SLIDE 2: DODO PROGRESS TO DATE

- Key personnel recruited and papered
  - Prof. Blevins
  - Lieutenant Colonel Lyons
  - Dr. Stokes
- Auxiliary personnel
  - Dr. Oda
  - Rebecca East-Oda
- The Asset
  - "Elizabeth Karpathy" (real name, DOB unknown—FOREIGN NATIONAL)
- The Asset's personal computational device, "Smallogep" (spelling?)

- Functioning ODEC
- Magic
- Diachronic Transport confirmed—multiple insertions/recoveries of 2 DOers (Stokes and Lyons) to 2 DTAPs (Cambridge, MA, 1640; London 1601)

SLIDE 3: CHALLENGES/ISSUES

- General Schneider confirmed KIA—possible fratricide incident?
- Failure to achieve cash flow positivity on sustainable timetable
  - Bay Psalter gambit stalled
  - Requirement for multiple, redundant re-execution of same DEDE in different so-called "Strands" entails massive duplication of effort and prolonged delays
  - Unanticipated requirement to go farther back in time to complete secondary DEDE suggests possible recursive "forking" of tasks/spends
  - No end in sight ☹
- Unauthorized involvement of irregular/unpapered personnel
- ? Unprofessional conduct between Stokes and Lyons ?
- Insubordinate/undisciplined witch—murders colleagues, not on board with mission objectives, declines to disclose functionality of Smallogep
- Ad hoc/improvised mission plan
- Lyons: excessive personal investment in current roster & game plan—not enough professional detachment

SLIDE 4: GOALS OF OPERATION "BOLSTER GAINS"

- Overriding goal: secure the future of DODO by aggressively monetizing its unique skill set without further delay
- Strategy: stir the pot/incentivize current roster (the Lyons-led "Blue Team") via insertion of competitive "Red Team"
- Provisional "Red Team" leader: Lester ("Les") Holgate

- *Insert Red Team Leader @ DODO Site Prime* ← *ACHIEVED*
- *Observe/evaluate/report on performance dynamics of existing "Blue Team"* ← *ACHIEVED*
- *Challenge Blue Team to raise expectations/boost performance* ← *ACHIEVED*
- *Spearhead innovative operational modalities*
- *Possibly submit Asset's Smallogep to DC labs for analysis*
- *Take executive action with prejudice to get current DEDE back on track*
- *Cauterize Blue Team, replace with new personnel if indicated*

SLIDE 5: LESTER ("LES") HOLGATE BACKGROUND/QUALIFICATIONS

- *Education*
  - North Pointe Preparatory Academy, Marblehead, MA
    - Captain, chess team
    - Valedictorian
    - Letter (6") in lacrosse
  - Dartmouth College
    - Magna cum laude
    - Psychology/political science
    - Vice President, Gamma Theta Rho chapter
    - Intramural lacrosse
  - Harvard MBA
- *Woolsack McNair Dobermann*
  - As management consultant for America's preeminent business consultancy firm, exceeded expectations assisting various public and private sector clients in optimizing operations and maximizing ROI
- *Defense Intelligence Agency (classified)*
  - Worked with multiple stakeholders in the black ops ecosystem to obliterate institutional roadblocks and maximize ordnance

on target in complex operational environments characterized by ambiguous/ad hoc chains of command

SLIDE 6: OPERATION "BOLSTER GAINS" ACHIEVEMENTS TO DATE (1 OF 5), INSERTION OF RED TEAM LEADER TO DODO SITE PRIME, CAMBRIDGE, MA

Transportation from Washington, DC, area proceeded nominally via civilian transport modalities. Exploitation of a remote credentials override on site security system enabled Red Team Leader to achieve ingress to facility without incident at 6:04 a.m. Tactical objective was to arrive, set up temporary work base, and "hit the ground running" prior to the arrival on site of existing ("Blue Team") personnel, setting an example and jarring them out of complacent work habits.

SLIDE 7: OPERATION "BOLSTER GAINS" ACHIEVEMENTS TO DATE (2 OF 5), INCIDENT REPORT

Upon breaching secure perimeter and achieving site ingress at 6:04, Red Team Leader was confronted by Blue Team Leader (Lyons), who contrary to expectations was already on site and awake, having pushed all furniture to the walls, stripped to his underwear, and was performing drills with a long, one-handed sword [sic], later identified from Internet research as a "backsword." Blue Team Leader was perspiring heavily, indicating a high degree of physical activity, and executing a combination of thrusting movements with sweeping cuts at various angles. Upon becoming aware that Red Team Leader had ingressed the facility, and not knowing in advance of his insertion, Lyons placed the tip of his weapon in close proximity to Red Team Leader's chest. Upon visual inspection the tip was observed to be sharp, in contravention of common-sense safety procedures. Lyons advanced, obliging Red Team Leader to retreat until cornered behind a potted plant (deceased). Having thereby gained tactical advantage Lyons interrogated Red Team Leader as to his authorization, making a cellphone call with his free hand, until satisfied that Red Team Leader was duly authorized. The standoff then terminated without further incident (and without apology).

Action Item: Review and upgrade weapons safety procedures. Institute mandatory training webinars for all DODO personnel authorized to handle weapons.

SLIDE 8: OPERATION "BOLSTER GAINS" ACHIEVEMENTS TO DATE (3 OF 5), "BROKEN WINDOWS" POLICY PLACED IN EFFECT

Upon initial inspection, DODO Site Prime was observed to be in substandard physical condition with several plants deceased (presumably owing to lack of appropriate watering rota), dirty dishes in sink, a cold cup of coffee in the microwave, a low standard of maintenance in the men's washroom (the women's was not inspected), and whiteboards rendered unusable by virtue of being entirely covered with cryptic symbols. Red Team Leader spontaneously took initiative to effect a "broken windows" policy of proactively cleaning and tidying the space as a way of setting an example to inspire/motivate demoralized Blue Team personnel.

SLIDE 9: OPERATION "BOLSTER GAINS" ACHIEVEMENTS TO DATE (4 OF 5), INCIDENT REPORT

Remaining Blue Team personnel filtered in between 8 and 11 a.m., with no clear policy apparently in effect regarding work hours. At 9:13, Dr. Frank Oda and his wife, Rebecca East-Oda, entered the facility. Dr. Oda affected bewilderment at the dramatic upsurge in whiteboard usable space area, and inquired as to the fate of the "calculations" he had left on them the night before. Red Team Leader briefed him on the "broken windows" policy, but before its rationale and benefits could be enumerated, was interrupted by Mrs. East-Oda who went off agenda with a lengthy and impassioned monologue containing a litany of unprofessional remarks as to the qualifications and character of Red Team Leader. The tone and style of her delivery did not meet reasonable expectations as to social skills and concern for feelings of co-workers. Admittedly this may be a high bar for Mrs. East-Oda who according to background checks has no work experience in high-performance collaborative organizations and a history of lashing out in defense of Dr. Oda. Oda himself was entirely silent during this event, staring off into space in a distracted manner possibly indicative of neurological impairment (presumably age-related). The situation was defused when Blue Team Leader (Lyons) emerged from an adjoining room and announced that he was in the habit of photographing Dr. Oda's whiteboards and archiving the images as a hedge against mishaps of this type.

Action items: Mrs. East-Oda should be placed on a Performance Enhancement Plan with the clear expectation that she will be terminated with prejudice if her attitude does not show clear improvement. Dr. Oda should be closely observed for further signs of senile dementia and placed on medical leave as indicated.

SLIDE 10: OPERATION "BOLSTER GAINS" ACHIEVEMENTS TO DATE (5 OF 5), THINKING OUTSIDE THE BOX

Red Team Leader took advantage of a clean, available whiteboard to bullet-point a number of gambits, ranging from persuasive to kinetic, that might be employed in order to break through Sir Edward Greylock's reluctance to pivot his 1601 investment strategy toward the East India Company. Noticing a strong, intoxicating fragrance he turned about to discover that he was under observation by an ostensibly young woman matching the description of the Asset. Other Blue Team members had drifted away one by one, claiming that they had other duties to attend to, but the Asset had arrived quite late and seemed to have been observing me for a little while. She was dressed

and groomed in a manner likely (and presumably calculated) to pose
a distraction to co-workers. Speaking in a strong foreign accent, she
demanded an explanation of what I was doing. She found my response
strangely amusing. I inquired as to what was so funny. Offering her
a whiteboard marker in a contrasting color (which she refused), I requested that she supply point-by-point rebuttals (anticipating a lively
exchange of views, I had left ample whitespace for same between my
bullet points). She refused to accept the proffered writing instrument
or even to supply itemized refutations in a verbal format, instead issuing what, if I understood it correctly, was a blanket dismissal of the
entire way of thinking underlying my program of suggested Greylock
inducement modalities. During this time I witnessed her fidgeting with
the previously mentioned Smallogep, which resembles a raggedy tangle of yarn. When I pressed her again for more actionable feedback,
she waved the Smallogep toward the part of the whiteboard where I
had bulleted some more forward-leaning measures and told me that
these were utter folly because they ran the risk of producing something that sounded like "near osh." I requested an explanation of the
seemingly undesirable phenomenon of "near osh." This only produced
more laughter from the Asset, who, once she had recovered her composure, assured me that if I were the sort of person who needed to
have it explained, there was no point in explaining it to me.

The conversation, if it could even be called that, was cut short when
Dr. Stokes emerged from her office carrying what I later understood
to be a briefing document that she had prepared for Blue Team Leader.
She summoned the other members of the team and led a pre-mission
briefing session, short on actual operational detail and heavy on historical trivia. Blue Team Leader seemed distracted and unfocused. At
more than one point during the meeting I observed him gazing fixedly
at the whiteboard on which I had drawn up my bullet points. When it
was time for the mission to begin, Dr. Stokes had to snap him out of

his reverie and inquire as to whether he felt ready to venture once more into the ODEC. While I cannot read his mind, I interpreted this as suggesting that my intervention and my suggested bullet points had impacted his thinking. This gave me some hope that during the DEDE that commenced a few minutes later he might take more direct and aggressive action to resolve the logjam that has developed around Sir Edward Greylock's investment strategy.

SLIDE 11: CONCLUSION TO INTERIM SITREP

- DODO Site Prime in state of general disarray
- Corrective measures under way; some personnel resistant to change
- Abundant grounds for HR proceedings against several members of existing Blue Team staff should that be desirable from tactical standpoint
- Smallogep requires further analysis
- Recommend wait and see approach but only for brief window

LETTER FROM

GRÁINNE *to* GRACE O'MALLEY

A Sunday of Late-Harvest, 1601

Auspiciousness and prosperity to you, milady!

It's in a dozen Strands that Tristan Lyons has tried to sway Sir Edward Greylock to put his money into the East India Company, and in each one Sir Edward seems on the verge of doing so, and yet Tristan returns from the future with word of no success. He has now amended his strategy, so that he appears to Sir Edward twice in a week, that they may have an unfolding conversation and he may twice impress upon him, without seeming to do so, the wisdom of entrusting his fortune to the East India Company.

The German with the sharp yellow beard is present in all of these conversations, though according to Tristan he hears much and says little. At least we know his name now: Athanasius Fugger. Himself pronounces it "Fucker," in the German style, but it's "Fugger" they spell it when abroad in England. He is some manner of third cousin thrice removed to Sir Edward's German mother. Like all of his clan, he is a banker, and 'twould seem he has Sir Edward's ear. Tristan complains that this Athanasius has "a poker face that would make him a million in Vegas," which means naught to you and me, but to him what it signifies is that it is impossible to make out what the fella is thinking—whether he favors the plan of investing in the Boston Council or the East India.

Nor is it much Tristan can glean from Sir Edward himself. For each time, doesn't Sir Edward claim he is "seriously considering moving his investments"? And yet each time, when Tristan goes off to spy upon that factory, isn't the factory still there?

So I made Tristan an offer, and it's sorely tempted he was to accept: if he would but tell me plainly everything, the whole of his schemes and their necessity—why magic declines, why he wants to save it, and with whom, and by what means—I would find others who might also prevail upon Sir Edward, and I would find other witches for him to talk to, should our witchiness somehow be helping his efforts in the future. Most tempting to him, of course, was when I offered to introduce him to the Court Witches, as they be the only witches with the standing to turn Sir Edward's head.

Tristan is eager enough to be meeting the Court Witches, once I allowed that there were some. Especially it was the younger ones he wished to meet, for he has a most ambitious plan that is somewhat mad, and yet 'twould amuse me to see it come to pass: he wishes to create a broad constellation or "net-work" of witches who might overlap in time, if not in space, so that he and his brethren, having traveled to some particular time, might freely move about the globe with the assistance of these witches, in any era of their choosing. So if our young witches here can be brought into his fold, then when they be old, they will be alive at the same time as the witches in the New World who are helping him there already, and thus he and his brethren can be moving between the New World and the Old with ease, as Breda and myself move Your Grace's agents between Ireland and London when the need arises.

A mystery it is to me, why anyone would want to do this in some era not of their own living. 'Twould be exhausting. The complications are legion and you would need an áireamhán so large that it would fill a room, and months it would take to work through all the twigs and stems to guard against the lomadh. Himself seems to understand this, and yet will not be dissuaded. He will not explain more to me, but it's arrogant he is in believing I should give him everything he wants anyhow. "It's for the sake of magic's preservation," has quick enough become his new rallying cry, and I believe him to a point but 'tisn't enough to keep me his ally if he will not tell me more. Sure I've played enough people in my time that I do not like being played my own self.

Although sure it's gorgeous shoulders he does have.

So I have told Tristan that until he confesses more of his strategy, he would not be meeting any Court Witches or even being introduced to others who might help change Sir Edward's inclinations as to his inheritance. But I did agree to introduce him to one other witch, should something ill befall me before his work here is complete.

A wealthy merchant's daughter she is, fixing to be married by her ambitious father on the Feast of St. Ethelburga to a country gentleman. Rose is her name. I met her when first I came over from Eire, years back. Her father loved the theatre and took her and her brothers to the comedies, where I met her and knew her for a witch. It's often enough I cross paths with her, and have watched her grow to be a lovely lass. She makes it a habit to go to the plays of a Wednesday, and since Tristan has now taken to returning for a second visit, to "follow up" with Sir Edward, I suggested he come then, and I could introduce them.

So we met up with Rose just outside the Globe gates, because of all the entertainment to be had in London, she always has a yen to see that Stratford Gobshite's latest. There were mobs of folks streaming in and the chatter was loud, so it was, and not a few of them stank as bad as the backstage fellas. Rose is a wee thing, plump and round-faced, with blue eyes and black hair, almost pretty enough to be Irish. I'd already explained to her all about Tristan.

Tristan was, of course, wearing one of Ned Alleyn's costumes. Recognized it right off, Rose did, and feigned more interest in it than in our visitor. Tristan doffed his cap and bent his knee—far more honor than a lass of her rank demanded, but he's a chivalrous type—and Rose instantly said to me, in a tone of delight, "That's half of Dr. Faustus he's got upon him, isn't it?" (For wasn't Faustus the play of Kit's at which Rose and I first met.)

Tristan straightens up, frowning a bit, and Rose gives him a brief courtesy, hardly more than a dip of the head. "God ye good day," says she to us both. And to Tristan, "You must be Gracie's new friend."

"She's been very kind to me," said Tristan.

"I'll wager she has," chuckled Rose, more to me than him. I shook my head no; she shrugged (she doesn't take to the lads much, does our Rose). Tristan either truly did not understand, or chose to counterfeit ignorance.

"I am on a mission that requires the aid of many of you," he continued. "I hope that you will support my cause as generously as Gráinne—as Grace has."

"We could have met inside the gates," Rose said to me, as if Tristan was not even there.

"If we'd gone inside, we'd have had to pay a penny each, just to watch Dick Burbage recite lines Will Shakespeare probably nicked from Raff Holinshed," I retorted. "Including his usual insults 'gainst the Irish."

Rose smirked and said to Tristan (as if she'd never been ignoring him), "Has Gracie been bending your ear with her rant about how Will Shakespeare hates the Irish? She'll go on all day if we let her. So then. What is it exactly that you're asking of us? You may safely call me a witch here, nobody's listening and anyhow they wouldn't care, not here."

"My brethren and I are seeking witches who would be willing to align themselves with us, so that if we come here on certain quests, we might be Sent to other places or times, and most especially, that we might be returned to where we came from."

"Gracie says you're doing this on account of centuries from now, magic is lost from the world and you are trying to restore it."

"Aye."

"How does it come to be lost?"

He shook his head a wee bit, looked exhausted for a heartbeat. "That would be a very long discourse," he said.

She shrugged. "I am in no hurry, the worst that will happen is that I miss the players today."

"I will tell you more if you agree to help."

"You've got it backwards, sir. I will agree to help you after you tell me more. For instance, how does your romping around through space and time bring magic back? What exactly is it you be doing?"

He grimaced briefly. "I cannot tell you all that yet," he said. "If you work with us, and it is a fruitful relationship, then I can reveal more."

She frowned at him. "Do you perceive yourself to be doing me a favor? What do I care what happens to magic a thousand years from now? I'll be dead and gone. I'll help you now only if you make yourself interesting to me, and prithee pardon me but you are failing mightily to accomplish that."

"I swear in God's own name that I will tell you more just as soon as I can."

"Will you?" She gave him the friendliest of smiles. "That's lovely. Let me know when you're capable of doing so and we can continue this discussion. God ye good day, sir."

And off she sallied into the Globe, reaching into her pocket for a penny.

There's many better a thing I can think to do with a penny.

But at least the two have met, and under circumstances that make Tristan's situation here plain to him.

Tristan, so unlike his usual stoic self, seemed dismayed as he watched her flounce off into the theatre yard to join the other groundlings.

"It's nothing worse than anything I've said to you, lad," I said, with a comforting hand on his shoulder because I do so like the curves on him.

"I must get home," he said. "If you will not help me directly, I must get back to my time. 'Tis difficult there now. They need me."

"You look like you could use some relaxing, Tristan Lyons," I said with a smile, and put my hand on his arm. The gates closed to the theatre and the trumpet sounded within. "Come back to the Tearsheet." I smiled invitingly.

He moved away from me, but I noticed it was in the direction of the Tearsheet he was walking anyhow. "That's right," I said, purring. "That's the way you want to be going." I walked past him toward the tavern. I heard a little irritated sigh as he followed me. "What's making it so very hard back home?" I asked in a sympathetic voice, looking over my shoulder.

"There's a new man where I work," he said in clipped syllables. "We have different . . . methods. He is more forceful, and I am more strategic."

"I like forceful," I said, smiling. "I pray you, do tell him he's welcome any time." Tristan made the briefest expression of dismay, and kept walking.

We got back to the brewery and marched right up to my closet, as always. By now our established method was that we stood in the room together, he in Ned Alleyn's stolen costumes, and I Sent him away and then just folded up the clothes and locked them in the chest. But he really did seem so distressed, and I love the scent of a man under pressure. Playful I decided to be, and so I said, "Tell me everything in detail, or I won't be Sending you home at all."

The look of shock on his face was so fetching, I couldn't keep myself from laughing.

"I'm codding you, Tristan Lyons—what would I gain by keeping you here when you won't even kiss me? You'd scare all my customers away and I'd die of starvation, so I would."

'Twas both relieved and annoyed he looked, briefly, then said, "I don't believe that. You do not make your living as a bawd, as much as you want it to seem so."

I raised my eyebrows at him. "Do you know that, or is it guessing you are?"

"Common sense. If a witch can evade torture, as you mentioned, she can evade poverty and degradation. The harlotry is a cover. For what, I wonder?"

I leaned in closer to him. "I'll tell you my secrets if you tell me yours," said I, and gave him the sweetest smile in my broad collection.

His eyes narrowed a touch and he looked sideways at me. "I'm not an idiot. Make me that offer without the smile and I'll consider it."

"What if I keep the smile but drop the offer?" I said. "Is it a smile I get from you in exchange? Perhaps a little something more?"

"We are in league together," he said, holding up his hand as if I were the devil and he a priest. "I cannot do that with a colleague."

"Delighted I am to hear we're colleagues!" I said. "Pray tell me what scheme it is, in which it's colleagues we are? And don't be saying classified because if we're in league, then we should be pooling our secrets, not keeping them from each other. It's a waste of your time to be asking me for help if you're not willing to take me into your confidences."

He sat a moment considering, then nodded grimly. "I under-stand your position, yours and Rose's. And it is reasonable. Send me home and I shall talk of this with my brethren in my era. I must not act without their knowledge."

"That's grand, but do not come back here unless you are pre-pared to tell me everything."

"So be it."

And off I Sent him, once again, and now there's naught to that but seek out other Strands where he might be carrying on in like manner. Meanwhile I've naught else to report to Your Grace, so once again it's off I go to meet my sweetheart.

Whether I be near or far, may I hear only good things of you, My Lady! Yours ever, Gráinne in London

Diachronicle
DAYS 380-389 (AUGUST, YEAR 1)

In which we meet the Fuggers

ANOTHER VENTURE TO 1640 CAMBRIDGE resulted in another failure. This was duly boiled down into a series of bullet points by Les Holgate, and transmitted to Frink in Washington. I'd been doing my best to avoid the man. That said, it was unavoidable but to interact with him. My academic career had left me in pos-session of a certain toolkit. As the saying goes, when you have a hammer, everything looks like a nail.

Reader, I learned his language. I hoped that mirroring and echoing some of his speech patterns, or (those being non-intuitive)

at least inserting some of his vocabulary into my conversation with him, might put him at his ease and allow him to relax enough to behave as a human being might, should he wish to emulate one. What follows is an approximation of my first attempt at such a discourse.

LH: As I anticipated, this last insertion to the 1640 DTAP was yet another confirmed failure.

MS: It was a tactical failure in that it failed to accomplish the primary stated goal, however, it was strategically useful in that it enabled Blue Team Leader to break trail on formation of an alliance with a potential Asset in that DTAP.

LH: Try to focus, Dr. Stokes. That was not the indicated goal of this mission, nor does it move the needle according to the operative metrics. The goal of this mission is to monetize the skill set we already have on deck in the form of the Asset and the ODEC.

MS: Yes, but only after we have monetized the skill set by gathering low-hanging fruit. Blue Team's road map is to utilize the transport modalities available to us due to the Asset and the ODEC, to incept a diachronic network and exploit resulting network effects that will enable DODO to scale.

LH: That level of strategic vision is above your pay grade, Dr. Stokes. Your task is to maintain laser-like focus on Phase 1 deliverables. And the fact is that in all of your dozens of diachronic transport insertions, which have taken weeks to accomplish and have generated operating costs now far exceeding your allowed budget, you have found a total of three potential but unauthorized Assets in two DTAPS, without any confirmed achievement toward actually securing the monetizable artifact by liquidation of the blocking factor.

MS: You mean we still haven't yet secured the psalm book by
   preventing the maple syrup boiler.
LH: Isn't that what I just said?

With this example, it should come as no surprise to hear that the
other five of us got into the habit of meeting away from the office,
at Frank and Rebecca's home. I have no idea what Les was doing
most of the time, and I didn't much care, because he was just an ir-
ritant and I'm sure he was getting paid as much as all of us together.
He also slightly resembled his uncle, Roger Blevins, chairman of
my former department, only without the grey hair, and more slender. But a trick of the voice and the general body language was
enough that I had a visceral desire to simply avoid him.

And I enjoyed the ambience of my alternate workplaces: Rebecca's home, and Widener Library.

It was in the latter that I began to dig into the history of the
Fuggers. This was the third time in the short history of DODO
that the name had unexpectedly come up. And even though they
were a famous old banking family, well known to any student of
European history, this seemed like too many coincidences to me.

They had first entered the story very early, when Tristan and I
had been going through the boxes of old documents that needed
to be translated. Some of them had been marked with a logo that
looked familiar to me. I couldn't place it at the time, and it nagged
at me until a few months later, when I was leafing through a copy
of *The Economist* in my dentist's waiting room and saw a similar
logo in an advertisement in the back of the magazine. It was an
international charity announcing a job opening. When I pulled
on that thread, taking advantage of some of the secret government databases we had access to at DODO, I learned that the
charity in question was the non-profit arm of a complex of hold-

ing companies that, to make a long story short, was the survival into modern times of the medieval Fuggers.

The second incident had occurred shortly before General Schneider's brief but tragically eventful visit to DODO HQ. Tristan had asked Erszebet whether she could turn lead into gold. As I later understood, he didn't really care about gold at all— what his higher-ups at the Trapezoid really were after was plutonium. But Erszebet had scoffed at the idea and spoken about the "Fuckers"—her pronunciation of "Fuggers"—in a tone of voice that bordered on fearful. Not her usual style at all.

And now here was a real live Fugger, one Athanasius, who seemed to be directly intervening in Tristan's DEDE in Elizabethan London.

Even with the combined resources of Harvard's library system and U.S. intelligence databases, I wasn't able to find much. The medieval part of the story has been common knowledge for centuries. The Fucker family had migrated to Augsburg in 1373 and prospered in textiles. In 1459 the family had produced Jacob, the seventh surviving child in a large brood. Seeing few opportunities at home, where his older brothers were dominating the Fucker family business, Jacob had traveled over the Alps to Venice, where he had served an apprenticeship in the German merchants' warehouse on the Rialto and learned about banking. Upon his return to Augsburg, Jacob had begun lending money to broke but powerful nobles on stiff terms and, to make a long story short, become the richest person in the world.

The Fuggers (somewhere along the line, they'd switched to a more palatable spelling of their name) had become as famous and as well documented as they were rich. The research skills I'd developed while earning my Ph.D. weren't even needed; hundreds of books about Jacob Fugger and his family could be summoned up with a few keystrokes. The great man had died at the end of 1525 and handed the business off to his nephew Anton, who seemed reasonably talented, and made some investments in the Americas. But he'd been caught in the mangle of the Catholic/Protestant wars, lending money to warmongering kings who didn't pay it back. In the end he had essentially liquidated the business and distributed the proceeds among a few dozen family members who were content to live off the interest as members of the titled nobility or the landed gentry.

By 1601—the year that Tristan was visiting—the trail had gone cold. There was no one single entity that could be pointed to as the Fugger bank. The last person to wield any kind of central authority over it had been Markus Fugger, a grandnephew of Jacob, who had died four years earlier after distributing most of the remaining assets to the family. And Markus seemed like someone who would have been interesting to idle away the hours with: a patron of arts, a history buff, a collector of old artifacts, an ancient-languages geek.

Athanasius Fugger—at least, the Athanasius Fugger described by Tristan—was completely absent from the historical record.

Which was not a big deal. No one knows better than a historian how tattered that record is. But it did whet my curiosity. The obvious explanation was simple enough: he was some descendant of Markus, sharing the same family name, who had inherited a share of the money and was now hanging around in London just because he liked it there and had the freedom to live wherever he wanted.

And yet, judging from Tristan's story, this Athanasius wasn't merely a drinking buddy. He was acting as some kind of financial advisor to Sir Edward Greylock, which probably meant he was still active in the banking business.

I tried working from the other direction, getting what information I could about the modern-day organization, and working backwards. But they were discreet to the point of paranoia, running their business through a network of offshore companies registered in places like the Cayman Islands, Jersey, and the Isle of Man. They only allowed the Fugger name to break the surface when it was to their tactical advantage, as when trying to hire employees for one of their humanitarian NGOs.

So my studies into the Fuggers produced very little that Tristan could actually use. Discussing it over an Old Tearsheet Best Bitter in the Apostolic Café—served as usual by the woman with the eyebrow tattoos, Julie Lee (Professional Smart-ass Oboist)—we agreed on a plausible scenario: some of the younger Fuggers, tired of the wars and turmoil in central Europe, had moved to London and put down roots in its banking scene. Athanasius was one of those, and the business had grown since then as a private bank with tentacles all over the place.

Erszebet had told us once that a Fugger branch office was probably nearby, and indeed we were able to find that they had an unobtrusive space in an old building near Boston Common. There was a similar but somewhat larger office in lower Manhattan, and others in different financial centers around the world.

Anyway, the research kept me out of the office, which had become a disagreeable place to work. Tristan was fairly immune to ambience and had a far higher tolerance for annoying personalities than I did, but he was just as happy as I was to avoid Les Holgate.

The advent of Holgate had dramatically increased Erszebet's regard for Tristan, now that she had another by-the-book thirty-something white American male to compare him to. She became almost pleasant toward him. That said, when he expressed pleasure that the "node" for diachronic transport was developing in London, Erszebet's immediate response was suspicion.

We were in Oda-sensei's study on a drizzly afternoon, and Rebecca had just served compote of warm peaches. (At the time it seemed so quaint and tasteful—now my stomach nearly heaves at the thought of adding yet more sugar to my diet.)

"Why do we need a *node*?" Erszebet asked. "Aren't we just supposed to make money?"

"Yes," said Tristan patiently, who had inhaled all of his peaches without tasting them or possibly even chewing them. "But we're doing that *in order to* start funding the actual work that is to be done. Having a node—and later, a network of them, in various DTAPs—will help with all that future work."

She shook her head in an I-don't-know-about-*that* way. "I did not promise to do anything beyond helping you make money from the Bay Psalm Book," she said. "And that is only because I want to go spit on the graves of my enemies."

"You won't be allowed back in the ODEC unless you're doing the magic we need you to do."

"Cruel," she hissed under her breath.

"Practical," said Tristan. She turned her back on him to stare out the window in a sullenly coquettish way (we had become used to that), so he returned his attention to the rest of us sitting around the coffee table, and we continued to discuss strategy: before he returned from the DTAP, Gráinne had demanded more transparency if she were going to continue to abet him.

Frank Oda and Rebecca both sounded cautious approval of this request.

"She sounds like a worthwhile connection," I agreed. "I think you should open up to her a little more. If she is willing to introduce you to the Court Witches, they could provide another angle of approach with Sir Edward."

"Good luck with that," said Erszebet, her back still to us, knees crossed, waggling one high-heeled sandal. "You are not likely to win any witchy friends if the witchy friends knew the whole truth. I certainly would not help you if *I* had known the whole truth."

Reader, know this: I still preferred her to Les Holgate.

WE RETURNED TO the office so that Erszebet could Send Tristan back to 1601 London. Les was there, with an expensive-looking coffee-like beverage (which smelled like that awful thing I'd ordered from the Smart-ass Oboist at the Apostolic Café the day Tristan had first approached me. How peculiar, the things that summon nostalgia.). Les seemed even more smug than usual, as if he had a secret he was just bursting to share with us, but did not want to give up his privileged position of being the only one with the secret. As usual, we ignored him.

Erszebet Sent Tristan back to 1601. Although her Sending one of us somewhere was now a fairly regular aspect of our working life, we were still respectful of its significance, and generally made it a practice that whoever was in the office gathered in the control room to watch through the glass and wave to the DOer as they emerged from the sterilizing shower and entered the ODEC. This time, I noticed Les was not present. Some minutes passed while Erszebet performed the Sending. When she had finished and let herself out of the chamber, I noticed Les walking into the control room from the corridor, smiling in a self-congratulatory way as he slipped his phone into his pocket.

Not ten minutes later, the office phone rang: Frink was calling from DC. He demanded to be transferred to a video conference.

Most of the offices in the building had long since been demolished, but in recent weeks a couple of Maxes had built a new one from scratch in an underused corner of the building. Supposedly it had all kinds of anti-surveillance shielding and other top-secret electronic gear built into its walls. On the inside it looked like just another corporate meeting room, dominated at one end by a flat-panel screen without which Les Holgate would have been effectively deaf and mute, since all of his communication took place through PowerPoint decks. It could also be used for secure, encrypted video conferences with the Trapezoid or other nodes in the dot-mil world. We all gathered around the conference table while Les Holgate connected us.

"I especially need to speak to the Asset," Frink said as soon as he appeared onscreen.

"I have a *name*," said Erszebet. She slithered into a slumped position on a rotating office chair and, like a bored, fidgeting schoolgirl, began to push herself back and forth through a wide arc, chin practically resting on her sternum.

"Glad you're there. And everyone else? Sound off."

"I'm here—Mel—but Tristan has just gone back to the Tearsheet DTAP," I said.

"Here," said Frank and Rebecca at the same moment, since it was already clear Frink hardly registered their presence.

"Here, sir," said Les Holgate. He remained standing.

"Okay, good, here are your orders," said Frink's voice. "Elizabeth, Send Les back to the Tearsheet DTAP."

"Who is Elizabeth?" asked Erszebet, without interrupting the arc of her fidgets. "How wonderful you have another witch to boss around. I would like a vacation. Elizabeth can fill in for me."

"Erszebet, please," I said.

She stopped twisting the chair. "I am Sending him back exactly where Tristan goes?" she said, sounding wary.

"Yes, exactly."

She sat up a little straighter. "Why do we have two DOers in the same DTAP?" she asked. "This is a complication. It is hard enough to keep one person on the right Strand. Two is very tricky."

"It's time to get fresh eyes on the problem. We need to think outside of the box."

Erszebet said, "This is a terrible idea, and I do not want to do it."

"Yeah, I had a feeling you were going to be difficult," said Frink. "Les, show her the goods."

Les smiled complacently, opened a manila folder he'd been holding, and pulled out some documents. "Look at these," he said, as if speaking to an eight-year-old. "Erszebet, it has your name on it."

He laid it on the table directly in front of her: a British Airways itinerary for Erszebet Karpathy to fly from Logan Airport to Budapest three days hence. Despite herself, she gasped audibly, and on reflex her hand slammed down on the paper so that he could not pull it away.

"Look what else I have," he said, and from the inside pocket of his blazer he pulled out an American passport. He opened it. There was a photo of Erszebet—I still don't recall any moment in time when we subjected her to an official government-issued photo, so I don't know how he'd got it. But he'd got it.

Erszebet reached out for the passport with a rare display of physical impulsiveness. He let her grasp it, but did not let go his own grip on it.

"Once you have Sent me back there," he said.

I got a terrible feeling in the pit of my stomach. Glancing at Frank and Rebecca, I could see they felt it too. All three of us turned our attention to Erszebet.

For an endless moment her eyes flicked between the passport and Les Holgate's face, whilst her other hand continued to press down on the British Airways itinerary. Some fathomless gulf inside of her survived a change of moral tides, and then with a look of genuine pain on her face, she released her grip on the passport and crumpled the British Airways page into a ball, hurling it away from the table.

"You are bad men," she said in a husky voice, and looked away. "You are very wrong to tempt me this way when it is not safe to say yes."

Les appeared slightly taken aback that his plan had met resistance, but he rallied. "There's nothing *dangerous* about this. It's not like I'm taking a *gun* back there with me," he said in a cajoling voice.

She gave him an incredulous look. "You say that as if it were a *choice* you were making," she said. "Do you know *anything*?"

"Don't overthink this, honey," said Les. "Do you want to go to Hungary, yes or no?"

At the word "honey," a look flashed across Erszebet's face that made me relieved, for Les's sake, that she could not do magic outside of the ODEC.

"Of *course* I want to go to Hungary," she said fiercely. "But not enough to risk performing bad magic at your demand."

"You're saying you need stronger motivation," said Les, in an arrogant yet maddeningly agreeable voice.

"I am saying I need to calculate on my számológép, before anything," she corrected him. "But I suspect those calculations will tell me not to do it."

Les's eyes flicked to the computer screen. I watched Erszebet follow his gaze. Les Holgate and Frink exchanged meaningful looks.

"Do you know what," Erszebet amended, sounding almost nervous, "you are so undeserving of my trust and cooperation, I must say no, absolutely I will not Send him. It is a terrible idea. I don't even need the számológép."

"Well that's good at least," huffed Frink. "Since you no longer have it."

A hardwired reflex sent Erszebet's hand clutching for her bag. "What?" she cried. She began to frantically grope around in the bag.

"I removed the Asset's personal computational device for security and analysis," Les Holgate explained to the rest of us. All the blood had drained out of Erszebet's complexion as she dumped the entire contents of her large handbag onto the conference table, then began to shove things—hairbrush, tissues, cough drops, lipstick, vintage perfume atomizer—off the edge in her frantic search for the számológép. "Sir," Les continued, to the face on the computer screen, "I believe this move will now also work as a negotiating tactic."

"Where is my számológép?" Erszebet demanded, almost voiceless with panic. I had never imagined she could look so vulnerable.

Briskly, Les Holgate pulled out a shipping bill from his other inside pocket. "While you were Sending Tristan, I secured it and shipped it to the Trapezoid."

"Where *is* it?" Erszebet repeated, wide-eyed. "I must know this."

"It's in transit," said Les Holgate.

"I need it," said Erszebet, struggling to maintain her dignity. "I must have it, here, in my hand. There can be no diachronic magic without it."

"Permission to negotiate with Asset?" said Les to the computer screen. I barely repressed the impulse to throw something at him.

"Granted," said Frink.

Les turned to Erszebet, tucking the shipping receipt back into his pocket. The glib, aggressive positivity he radiated was the social equivalent to fingernails down a chalkboard. "You obviously don't need the zamlagip"—(he never once pronounced this correctly)— "for every transfer, since you didn't have it on you just now when you Sent Lieutenant Colonel Lyons back. Ergo, you don't need it to Send me back. Just one DTAP, one time, one DEDE."

As usual, he pronounced it wrong: "dee-dee." Rebecca rolled her eyes and blurted out, "Deed!" He wasn't expecting the correction, and faltered for a moment before winding up to the big finish:

"Trust . . . just . . . trust me on this. It's only going to take one time, because *I'm* going to *crush* this!"

I saw her almost answer him, and then restrain herself. She had recovered some color, but only in an unhealthy way, in that she was now slightly green. "You are saying that if I Send you to the Tearsheet DTAP, I will have the számológép returned to me immediately."

He smiled. "Send me to the Tearsheet. Once I have returned, I'll issue a recall code to have the zamaligope returned to you."

"And if I don't Send you? What happens?"

He shrugged. "The ODEC's not much good to us if it's not helping us to accomplish our stated goals. The team members will be considered redundant and their employment terminated."

"You will fire me?" she said, struggling to regain her derisive demeanor.

He shook his head. "Negative. But your zamlogap is almost certain to get lost in the reallocation of physical resources. That would be a shame."

"I'll do it," she said, looking grimly at the table. "I'll Send you."

Everyone pushed their chairs back to go.

"Dr. Stokes," said General Frink, "if I could have a private word with you."

It sounded like more of an order than a request, so I scooted my chair forward again and doodled on my notepad while the others filed out of the room. Les was the last to go, and pulled the door closed behind him. He tried to make eye contact as he did, but I wouldn't give him that victory.

It was just me and General Octavian Frink now, or rather me and a flat-panel screen displaying an oversized rendering of his face from some secure videoconferencing facility in Washington.

"Yes, General Frink?"

"You're an intelligent woman," Frink said. "You have to have realized that this is an incredibly expensive and roundabout way to raise what amounts to pocket change, by the standards of the Trapezoid."

"The thought had crossed my mind," I admitted.

"Nevertheless, what Les just said to you all is an empty threat. DODO is not going to get shut down. Its management may be changed but it will keep on going."

"Why?" I asked. "Is it because you want cheap plutonium?"

"I won't lie to you. There is certainly a lot of interest in that. But even if we can never get the Asset to turn lead into plutonium, this project keeps going. It is *distressing* that you have bungled this bucket-burying project to the extent that you have. There is no way that this passes a cost-benefit analysis even if you get the bucket and sell the book tomorrow. But we are learning, Dr. Stokes. Painful as this trial-and-error phase may be, DODO is building institutional knowledge of how we can conduct diachronic operations in the future—and how our adversaries may be conducting them even as we speak."

It wasn't the first time that someone in my chain of command had dropped a hint that foreign powers might have their own equivalents of DODO. It explained a lot about how willing Frink and others were to keep backing such an unlikely enterprise.

"Well, I am glad that we are making progress, however haphazardly," I said.

"It's the haphazard part I would like to work on," Frink said. "There is far too much unpredictability and randomness in these . . . DEDEs . . . for my taste." I had to give him credit for nailing the pronunciation. "It is for that reason that I am going to bring Roger Blevins into this in a more serious way."

The general paused, and I could tell he was awaiting some sort of reaction from me.

Which wasn't something he'd have done if he'd been expecting a *negative* reaction. No, he was expecting me to jump out of my chair in transports of joy. He was expecting it because his old school chum Blevins had prepped him for it—told him of the superb mentor/pupil relationship we had enjoyed, or some such ~~bullshit~~ malarky.

Instead I was frozen. Like a deer in the headlights. Not one of my more admirable qualities. Later, when I was going through hand-to-hand combat training with military experts, I heard a lot about the predator/prey relationship, and how it was the natural instinct of many to freeze up when in the grip of a more powerful animal. It turns out you can train yourself to fight, or to run away; but I hadn't been through such training at the time.

"I've been discussing it with Roger," Frink went on. He seemed a little nonplussed by my reaction, but soon enough worked himself back up to his usual brute intensity. "He speaks highly of you, but we have arrived at a consensus that it might not hurt to have a couple of greybeards in the loop—people who know their way around history and dead languages and such. Constantine Rudge is still following along, but he's busy and can only put so much time into it. So I have asked Roger. And he has expressed a willingness to take a leave of absence from his position at Harvard so that he can throw himself into DODO with a higher level of commitment. It'll take a few months for him to disentangle himself, but he's on it. I wanted you to be the first to know, Stokes. Given your warm relationship with him, I expect this will be a load off your mind."

"Thanks for letting me know, General Frink," I said. "Will there be anything else?"

"I look forward to hearing good news from your end in a few hours," Frink said. "Les is a good man. When he says he's going to crush it—it's time to pop some popcorn and pull up a chair."

"I'll get popping, then," I said.

LETTER FROM
GRÁINNE *to* GRACE O'MALLEY

Your Grace—pardon me the rude beginnings, but it's a terrible, terrible thing that's happened, I must write quickly to tell you all and I warn you now, it may be the last letter you shall ever receive from me, for reasons that will become clear as you are reading.

Tristan Lyons returned again, still without success, but with a willingness now to be honest with me. But the truth he shared was foul enough to kill an ogre, and that was just the beginning of the woes.

As I told you before, he comes from an era in which magic has been blotted out entirely. Sure he and his brethren are attempting to resuscitate it, but it's only one witch he has to work with, and it's a horrible situation she's in from the sound of it. Lives like a prisoner, she does, under their watch all the time for they want her kept safe else their work comes to naught. So very limited her life sounds. And the worst of it is the work itself! They instruct her on all the magic she may do, and 'tis only ever Sending they want her for, which as you've heard myself and my sister Breda tell you, is exhausting and often frustrating, for there are so many particulars to be kept in mind, and the risk of Iomadh—and you haven't the satisfaction of accomplishment, for by its very nature, the results are not where you are.

And even worse than that, 'tis a strange mechanical chamber she must spend her time in, the only place magic will function in their age. Tristan described it somewhat to me and for all the pride in his voice—'tis his creation—it sounds a right horror, so it does. So this poor witch is living under nasty circumstances, and more than that: she is nearly two hundred years old! Magically preserved she is. So for all those years she survived, aging slowly, in a world with no magic, making friends and then watching them die of old age . . . while she waited patiently for the time to come for her to spend her day in a horrible little room doing unpleasant tricks on demand for a secret government.

For that's the other part of his confession: Tristan and his lot aren't bringing magic back for the good of the world, or for magic's own sake, but because his government (what rules over the nation full of Irish who speak English) wants to use magic to spy upon and check the power of other kingdoms. Now I've nothing against that, sure we're doing it ourselves, right now, and who doesn't? But it's nothing to the glory of magic, it's nothing to the artistry or craft, and worst of all, it's a horrible life they're giving this witch, by the sound of it. I asked Tristan was she happy, and he said not especially, but he thinks that is due to she's Hungarian and they're not a merry race. And he has a point. Still, very sad I was to think of the state of affairs. Not at all as I'd imagined it, when first he told me their aim was to bring back magic.

But all of that is nothing compared to the horror to come. For Tristan's crew is an evil one, and never was there more evidence of that than the story of Lester Holgate. 'Tis a fell tale I'm about to impart to you, so I hope you are nursing some potent spirits to get you through it.

Tristan was giving it a rest with Sir Edward. As soon as he arrived and told me and Rose all (for didn't I summon Rose to be a witness to his story too), he went from the Tearsheet Brewery with Rose. She was friendlier to him now, given as how he had spoken with us more openly, as he'd promised. In fact, she had offered to introduce him to other witches around, of whom she knows more than I, having family here. She is about to be married off to a gentleman, pleasant enough, but very dull, and it appealed to her sense of adventure to be assisting a handsome fella from the future, especially in the name of magic. The plan was that Rose would take him to meet her mother and aunts, as they're a whole family of witches (like Breda and myself), with the grandmother out on the Fulanham estate by the Sheppards Bush Green. So it's an overnight trip he had left on, and didn't I feel like a mother seeing her son off to the wars?

No, in fact, I didn't. A bit of a relief it was.

So there I was on my lonesome upstairs at the tavern, taking the rare chance to air out the closet and the bedding, when suddenly there was a shimmer in the corner of the room and there's *another* naked fella, with his hair cut in a peculiar way. He's about as tall as Tristan but thinner, less imposing (good teeth though), and he falls to the floor moaning like they do. He most certainly does *not* seem familiar, telling me he's only on this one Strand—something strange is afoot here, one of those things that Tristan would call an Anomaly.

As soon as he could speak, he looks around the closet like it's Newgate Prison and he's no idea how he got condemned to be there. "Have a seat," I say, and pat the mattress beside me, but Mr. Anomaly looks nauseated and stays where he is, covering his shaft but feigning not to. I give him a moment to collect him-self, chuck an extra set of drawers and shirt at him and wait for him to dress himself (he's not so much to look at, a wee bit soft around the waist like a bride he is). As it happens we've collected some of Ned Alleyn's fancier costumes from Dick Burbage, should Tristan ever have occasion to chat up the Court Witches, or courtly associates of Sir Edward, in nicer places. But Tristan was wearing his regular costume that day, so the fancier one was at hand, and I gave it to this new fella. Such a mess he made of putting it on, you'd think he was from the Indies. "Can't you lace a doublet?" I asked in amazement, and he doesn't even seem to hear me as he's trying to figure out what the devil to do with the codpiece. I barely keep myself from crying with the laughter, but finally we get him dressed, and then for the first time, a quarter hour after my hands have been all over him to help him dress, he looks at me directly.

He's not a bad-looking fellow but it's city air he breathes a lot, I'm guessing, not like our Tristan, for his complexion is sallow like a hatter's (although fashionably pale) and he squints a bit like a tailor. He carries himself well enough but unsteady he seems to be, as if a permanent amazement he is trying to hide. And his hair,

Your Grace—'tis a thing best not spoken of, but I'll speak of it anyway, as there is much worse to come, and as it enters into the narrative in a small way. The whole time we were struggling with the doublet his colorless limp hair kept straggling down over his brow and nervous he was in tucking it away.

And didn't I then remember a thing that Tristan had told me, concerning his unlovable colleague, Les Holgate: "He employs a surfeit of Product." I'd no idea what he meant by it, but he'd said it as if revealing it was, of something important concerning the man. So I had pressed Tristan for an explanation and didn't he say, "That means his hair is gelled until it's hard and shiny as a beetle's back. It is a kind of pomade that some in my time use." Tristan, understanding that none of this "Product" or pomade would be Sent with him, had grown out his own hair and had it trimmed in accord with our fashions, so that conspicuous he wouldn't be. But this fellow hadn't done so much. And since his Product has stayed behind in the chamber whence he'd been Sent, wasn't his hair now all over the bloody place and a court fool he seemed to be.

"Les Holgate," I say.

"The same," he says, and he holds his outstretched hand toward me. I look at it, wondering if I am expected to kiss it, which I've no intention of doing. So I wait. After a moment, he drops it onto his lap. "You must be Gráinne." He pronounces it wrong and he knows it.

"Why must I? And what business is it of yours if I am?"

"I'm a colleague of Tristan Lyons. You know, from the future?"

"I know."

"I'm here to help him with his deed." He pats his hands on the bombast of his hosen, then crosses his arms, then puts his arms akimbo, as if arms are something he's just acquired and hasn't yet worked out what they're good for.

"A colleague, are you now?" I ask. "Let's have you prove it. Tell me a bit about his deed, and why he would be needing your help, and what kind of help you're intending to give him."

"We have no time for that," he says, frowning. To be honest he looks almost confused that I would be questioning him. Quite peremptory he seems to me.

"I have no time for foolishness," I retort. "These are dangerous times and I dare not take a stranger at's word. I'm needing evidence you're Tristan's fellow. Tell true."

Mr. Anomaly harrumphed a bit at that. Then he pushed his hair back, rubbed his hands together, and said briskly, "We are try-ing to disincent Sir Edward Greylock from investing in the Boston Council. Tristan has tried speaking to him on multiple occasions but the results we seek have yet to eventuate."

"And those results are?" I asked.

Irked he looked, as if it were an imposition to speak of it. "The removal of a certain building forty years from now in Massive Shoe Hits."

I continued to question him in this vein, with his impatience and irritation compounding, until, despite his queer language and displeasing attitude, I had satisfied myself that he was indeed on Tristan's crew, and served the same masters, with the same ends in mind.

"So what exactly are you here to do?" I concluded my questioning.

"We've figured out a better way to change Sir Edward's mind about where to put his money," he says. "Since Tristan was already here, in 1601, we couldn't give him the new instructions, so we've called an audible and made an unplanned insertion. I've got some specific plans to enact, and I need your help just like you've been giving it to Tristan."

"As long as you understand what I have *not* been giving to Tristan," I say, for his talk of insertions was putting me on my guard. He was not near so comely as Tristan and I didn't want him to be making any insertions on my person. But he gave me a strange look, as if he hadn't the faintest idea what I was referring to. "Certes," I said, letting it go. "I am in league with Tristan so by association I am in league with you. Be stating your intentions, O man from the future."

"I'm going to put Sir Edward between a rock and a hard place. Make him an offer he can't refuse. Turn up the heat."

"All right," I said cautiously.

"Yeah. Here's the plan. The Constable of this parish? St. Mildred's?"

"I know what parish we are in," I told him.

"He's poor. Easily corrupted," he tells me. I reckon he must know this from his history books—and don't I know it from my own life! "Introduce me to that Constable. And then, separately, introduce me to one Simon Beresford—the father of Sir Edward's fiancée."

"Why's that, then?" I asked.

"Well, Sir Edward uses this whorehouse, right?"

"Once or twice," I said.

"There's a girl here he likes, Tristan told me."

"That would be Morag. Bit of a gymnast she is."

"We have to get the Constable to inspect the whorehouse while Sir Edward is here with her—and Sir Edward's future father-in-law is with him on a ride-along."

"On a what?" I asked. I did not like his attitude or his strange accent or queer way with words and phrases.

I did not like the notion that Tearsheet would be inspected, but in truth, all the bawdy-houses are targets occasionally and isn't Tearsheet overdue for it, on account of my magic fending it off so long. Often's the time a parish constable will squeeze a whoremonger for money. Constables are given power but no money at all, and so usually held by somebody with a high enough opinion of themselves, who happens to be short on coin. "Well enough," I said. "But Simon Beresford? The father-in-law-to-be?"

"Yeah, I don't know where to track him down. He's a lord or something. Knows the Queen. We have to get him to go with the Constable on the inspection."

"And why would he do such a thing?"

"So that he can report to Queen Elizabeth which of her courtiers was caught in the whorehouse." He seemed chuffed with himself for this idiot scheme. His arms—when he wasn't using them to push his hair out of his eyes—hung more casually at his sides now, as if he'd grown accustomed to them. He was finding his sea legs, as Your Grace's men might say.

"Hardly seems like something a gentleman would care to do," I pointed out.

"Good way to win points," himself said confidently, in that tone that says: he has made up his mind about it, and therefore any new information or suggestion has the weight of mist. "Also, if we drop a hint that his future son-in-law might be one of those in the brothel, then Simon Beresford will have a pressing need to see for himself who comes out of the brothel door during the raid."

I shrugged. "There are hidden exits on every floor for the customers to leave unnoticed," I said. "Constables have sought them out for years and never found them, it's a matter of great pride at Tearsheet. Morag knows those exits same as any of us, she'll take Sir Edward out of there to safety."

"No she won't," said Les Holgate. "I'll be blocking the exit on that floor. Sir Edward can only get out if I let him."

I wasn't so sure about trusting this fellow now, he had such a different sensibility to him than your man Tristan.

He goes on: "I'll show up at the same time as Beresford and the Constable. You should be in the whorehouse and protest, make a fuss, follow us around. When we find Sir Edward and Morag, you make enough of a fuss to distract the Constable, and I'll pull Edward aside and offer him a get-out-of-jail-free card: he can run out the front door and be seen by Simon Beresford, and kiss his social-climbing marriage goodbye forever. *Or*, I'll get him out safely and Simon Beresford will never know he's there—but I'll only do that if he signs his name to an oath, that he will never fund the Boston Council, no questions asked. Got it?"

Absurd, I thought it. Dull-witted. Absolutely mental. But I nodded, grimacing.

So: that was the plan. That is not what happened.

This scheme—this accursed scheme!—was easy enough to begin because of how the stars were aligned. I spoke to Morag, and explained a little of what we were up to—not about Les Holgate being from the future or such details, just that we needed to blackmail her newest customer and she'd be recompensed for her cooperation. Pym the owner has a strict no-blackmailing policy at Tearsheet, but it only applies to blackmail that he knows about, and Morag (being Scottish) is resourceful. To my request, she laughs and says, "Well, Sir Edward and I do have a special little romp planned for tomorrow afternoon. If you want to catch him in the act, this will be the act to catch him in. This will be an *act* for all the ages to speak of." And she laughs with such abandon that I can't help but be a wee bit curious, suspicious even, of what she's on about, so I ask her.

"What are you on about?" I ask her.

She sobers right up, although her eyes look like the laughter will still come spilling out of them. "Ach, I might have no morals, but I certainly have manners," she says. "I'll not reveal a gentleman's *pro-clivities*." (For doesn't she like to show off her schooling with these fancy new words.) "But I know he'll be arriving here just as the bells toll two, so come at half-two and you'll get at least as much as you're seeking." And we'd have to pay her well for that, for it's true her lips are generally as tight as her character is loose. She's the one the fellas ask for when it's especially secret they need to be. She valued her reputation that way, so hard up for money she must have been, if she was willing to play our game with us. Now I'll always wonder about that.

'Twas easy enough to find the Constable, as he's also the manager of the bear-baiting pit, so he's always around Southwark. The Constable is a funny enough fella, perhaps on account of his line of work. His assistants, who feed the bears and file down their teeth, are large fellas, and fierce, but he's entirely different. Mild and obsequious at once, he is, and doesn't he smile deferentially even as he regrets to inform you that he'll be taking advantage.

I did him a good turn once. The bears don't take to himself or his lads much, yet he's the one keeps them alive and healthy, for isn't a bear a terrible expensive thing to come by? Anyhow, I reasoned with a bear whose wounds he was salving, and the bear stopped trying to smack him. So he owed me a favor for a couple of years now. This turned out to be useful.

Les Holgate believed the Constable would leap spurs-first at the opportunity to intimidate Pym, the Tearsheet brewer. He did not take into account that the Constable was less inclined to upbraid brewers than bears, for an upbraided brewer is less likely to pass you a pint. It's a good thing the Constable was under a compliment to me, for he only agreed to Les's scheme as a kindness to myself. So in the end, he did agree to put on his constabulary cap and go inspecting the "tavern" the next afternoon.

Les Holgate next wished me to go with him to find this Simon Beresford and induce him to come along with us, but 'twould take more of my time than I'd a wish to give it. So I declined, but (believing I was still abetting a scheme that Tristan was a part of) I did offer to find out Simon Beresford's location, so that Les might go and fetch the fellow his own self.

This I did, the next day (Les Holgate having slept on a tavern bench overnight and whinging all the next morning). Simon Beresford was on London Bridge seeking to purchase a new hat.

As soon as Les Holgate had set out for the Bridge, up to my own closet I went, and sought out Tristan by scrying, as I knew he and Rose should be on their way back through the city, headed my way. It seemed to me they were by the Paris Gardens. I sent to Rose as much of this message as I could, which was hard to communicate since she wasn't expecting me to try to reach her: "Your man Les Holgate has arrived and plans to use extortion to accomplish the task at Tearsheet." So I hoped Tristan would have at least a notion that mischief might be afoot.

Then I went back into the tavern and sat back with a mug of Tearsheet Best Bitter, the finest ale you can find outside of Ireland, and waited to see who would return first. It was quiet in there for the time of day, perhaps half a dozen drinkers. I had no personal need to see the scheme succeed, and guessed it would be a lark to watch. But I did feel the slightest bit of unease deep in my gut, and I hoped Tristan would return, as he had a gravity to him that put me at ease, while this Holgate fella made me a bit squeaky-bummed.

No surprise it was that Les Holgate returned first, with a confused-looking older fella who had to have been Simon Beresford. He was dressed in the old style, all in elegant black, prudish but not quite Puritan (for then his daughter wouldn't have been one of Elizabeth's ladies, of that I'm confident). His ruffle was pretentious—as if his head sat on a fancy platter that just happened to be balanced right on the top of his neck. Hard to imagine a fellow like that shopping for himself on London Bridge, but it takes all sorts. I heard his voice out in the street, old enough for childish treble. He was asking someone for an explanation. Answers were coming both from Les Holgate and from a third voice I recognized as belonging to the Constable.

In the tavern I was, as they approached, and wasn't the doorway open to let in the glorious autumn day, so they stood in the door backlit. Proprietor Pym recognized the Constable by his silhouette, and cursed under his breath. He went out the door, shooing at them, and made a fuss about letting them in, even as the old fella protested he had no interest in setting foot in such an establishment. I followed Pym out just to keep an eye on things.

So, here we all are standing on the gravel street, just outside the brewery door, with throngs of people pushing by us going to the theatre or from the bear-baiting. We were myself, the Constable, Les Holgate, Simon Beresford, and Proprietor Pym. Inside upstairs, of course, were Morag and Sir Edward, carrying on blissfully unawares.

The Constable shoulders Pym out of the way and strides into the tavern, where right off all the customers make a bit of a fuss, like hens in a coop when the farmer comes in after dark.

"Stay outside, sir," says Les Holgate to Simon Beresford. "It's not a proper place for a gentleman like yourself to be seen. Stay here and note who comes out." And then he rushes in after the Constable. I follow after him. And so leaving Master Pym and Simon Beresford outside on the street (with Simon Beresford so dismayed and perplexed to find himself here at all), the trio of the Constable, Les Holgate, and myself are rushing through the tavern to the steep steps that lead to the rooms. We're not making noise ourselves, but the tavern regulars are making noise enough to surely alert everyone on the floor above. The wenches in the tavern duck under tables, until they realize the Constable isn't after them at all, then they either return to their work or scurry out the hidden door, just to be safe.

Now up the steep stairs it is we're going: Constable, Les Holgate, myself. It isn't too dark at all on the landing, not on a Harvest-season afternoon with unwonted bright sun outside shining in through a small open window. The upstairs, as perhaps I've described to Your Grace, has a narrow corridor with rooms off either side, first a couple of rooms big enough for private conferences, and then beyond them, four wee curtained-off closets for more intimate congress. It's Morag's closet we're wanting, and that's the first curtain to the right after the meeting rooms. It's the largest of the lot, some three strides square, with a mattress on the floor, and a curtained window what looks out over the street.

We rush past the two meeting rooms, both with doors ajar letting light through the windows, both empty (it's day, and these are the sorts of rooms more used to candlelight). Following Les Holgate's, commands, aren't I tugging at the Constable's sleeve and complaining of his being here.

We come to Morag's curtained doorway. Les Holgate tugs open the curtain. And there's the unglazed window with the afternoon sunlight tempered only slightly by a linen kerchief, so we can see clear as if we were standing in a market square. The Constable, Les Holgate, and myself fill the cramped doorway, with me cackling like an angry hen—until I see what is happening inside the wee room, and then my voice does fail me.

Your Majesty, I can scarce bring myself to write what we do see there. For it is *not* Morag there with Sir Edward, but Sir Edward with a third party altogether. From Morag's tone the day before, I confess I had expected a surprise. But I had assumed it might be another wench.

It is not. 'Tis a man, and he and Sir Edward are at it with each other, which is a hanging offence here. Morag is not even present. She was but a cover for them to be together. The two men freeze and stare up at the three of us crowded at the doorway so, and quickly part.

Les Holgate looks very surprised, but I ken he doesn't under-stand how dreadful this situation is. Tristan told me that in their age, it's only the most religious of zealots (belonging largely to sects of churches that do not even exist in our day) who are much both-ered about buggery. In his day, 'tis lawful and unremarkable—even in London! So I'm thinking Les Holgate does not understand that he is looking at two dead men. Unless we can bribe the Con-stable with a lot of money straightaway.

But I'll be honest, that's not the only thing that shocks me. It is the fellow Sir Edward's buggering that shocks me more. For a famous bloke it is. A very famous bloke.

There is a commotion back down the corridor, of somebody climbing up the stairs in a hurry, clear enough to hear due to our amazed silence. The Constable is goggle-eyed, and finally he says, "I cannot believe what I am seeing. The heralds and the chronicles will never let us hear the end of this. Never." Myself, I can't stop staring at the two men. At the one man in particular. For that man—the famous man—is my lover. Who I believed until that moment hadn't a secret from me in all the world.

The scuffling on the stairs has turned into footsteps beating their way down the short corridor, and suddenly there's a heaving Tristan Lyons, who grabs Les Holgate and shoves him back down the corri-dor toward the steps. "You fucking moron," he says, but then imme-diately turns his attention back into the room. Pushes the Constable out of the way, he does, and sees the two on the ratty mattress. He

points to my darling, sitting there staring at me wide-eyed and naked beside Sir Edward, and asks, "Who is *that*?"

I could barely make myself speak the words. "That," I said, "is
Christopher Marlowe."

Tristan frowned in confusion. "Christopher Marlowe is dead.
He died in 1593 in a pub brawl. It's almost the only thing I know
about him."

Kit and I are staring at each other with a shared look of stu-
pidity I did not think either one of us capable of. "A counterfeit
death, it was," I say, my chest tight. "Staged, for convenience sake.
He was a spy, so he was—"

"Gracie," says Kit in a quiet, warning voice.

"Sure it came out after, everyone knows you're a spy by now
anyhow," I said. And explaining to Tristan: "I had just been Sent
from Ireland, and so in love with him I fell, and him with me, we
would do whatever we asked of each other." Those huge, beautiful
brown eyes of his bored deep into mine as I spoke, as I gave away
the secret I had kept for years, kept even (I pray you forgive me)
from you, Your Majesty: "'Twas the greatest bit of magic I have
ever done. He told me they needed to counterfeit a wound that
would give him the freedom of seeming to have died, but it must
be so thoroughly accomplished that even a physician examining
his body would reckon him dead. So they claimed there was a pub
brawl, and a spell of protection didn't I put on him, that when he
was stabbed, he seemed dead but wasn't, although he was close to
the shadows for awhile. Then I spirited him away and nursed him
back to health in secret." And still those eyes how they looked at
me, and how I looked at them. "And for these eight years gone," I
went on, "in secret I have loved him and he's loved me. I knew he
had other dalliances and I was not jealous of him. But the secreting
of it—oh, Kit—the *concealment*, in my own *home*—"

Before Kit could respond, or I could say anything else, Tristan pushed me aside into the room and grabbed the Constable by the back of his collar. The Constable had been staring at the two men all this time, and while I hadn't been listening to him on account of my own confessions, I realized now he was muttering over and over again how all of it—their impending deaths as well as this revelation—would shake the city, would shake the nation, to its very roots.

Tristan lightly slapped the Constable's cheek to get his attention. "The two sodomites must be released unconditionally at once," he said. To Sir Edward he said firmly, "Get your clothes on. While you're at it, open your purse. You will reward the Constable handsomely for this act of mercy on his part, and in exchange, the Constable"—and here he released the Constable's collar but only to grab his shoulder and turn him squarely to face him—"the Constable will never speak a word of anything that has happened today."

"But that is Kit Marlowe," repeated the Constable in awe, gaping still. Then turning to Tristan, does he offer up this: "He was arrested for heresy just before his death. Did you know that?"

"Atheism," clarified Kit promptly, for sure he hates it when people think *heresy* suggests he was a believer in some sect.

"They meant to put him on trial," said the Constable. I realized from his obsequious tone that he was collecting his wits now, and expecting Tristan to reward him for this information. "All of England was waiting to hear what he said at the trial. There was no pub brawl. He was assassinated to keep from spilling state secrets, secrets all of London was waiting breathlessly to hear. He can finally spill them, now he is alive!"

"No he cannot," said Tristan very firmly, as my da used to speak to me when I was a wee lass throwing a tantrum and he needed me to shut it. "You are about to be given a lot of money to agree, for the rest of your life, that Marlowe died in 1593."

The Constable had recovered from his amazement, and was ready to see reason. "I've certainly heard that rumour," says he. "If you'll show me where it's written in gold, I'll happily swear to it."

"I have no gold with me," fretted Sir Edward. "But I do have plate enough back at my lodgings. If I am allowed to dress, and somebody shows me the back-exit, the Constable may follow me—"

Listening to him, I felt something beginning to move in my chest. Nothing good, nothing pleasant. Jealousy was a foreign thing to me, I'd no experience of it ever in my life, not that I could recall, and so a moment it took me, to realize the name of this horrible feeling. Sir Edward must have sensed my gaze on him. He glanced in my direction, and then casually away again, as if I counted for nothing. Jealousy at once bred with rage inside of me, and made such an inward clamour that I heard the next bit of the conversation as through a hailstorm.

Les Holgate, having recovered from being shoved down the corridor, now pushed back in, stepping between me and Sir Edward and shouldering Sir Edward down onto the mattress. He then stumbled over Sir Edward's flailing legs and was obliged to steady himself at the far wall by the window. He spoke to Tristan. "Stay on task. This other guy's not important. All that matters is making sure Sir Edward doesn't give his money to the Boston Council. The rest of it, these other people, it's a sideshow. You," he continued, to Sir Edward, "your future father-in-law is standing outside. You do as we say, or he's going to know you're a sodomite and you won't get to marry your rich girlfriend."

"And what is it you want of me?" asked Sir Edward, scrambling to stand.

"Swear on the Bible not to give any of your money to the Boston Council."

"Abort," said Tristan crossly, as Sir Edward gaped, perplexed. "This is not the time or the way, Les. You've royally fucked this up. For now, for today, we pay off the Constable and everyone disappears out the back way. You and I go straight back to the ODEC. But first, you need to go downstairs and tell Beresford there was nobody here. You've botched this."

"I haven't!" Holgate said. "You've been totally ineffectual for all the times you've come here. I've come here once, and look: results!" He gestured round the wee room.

"Abort," repeated Tristan. He reached to a peg on the wall and threw the clothes that hung there—shirt and drawers and a very fine vest it was—at Sir Edward, and spoke to him: "You, sir, go out the back way with the Constable, and pay him whatever is required for your own good. You"—Tristan turned his eye on Kit now—"will vanish. Disappear. Wherever you've been hiding, go back to hiding there. Sir Edward will keep your secret. Will you not, Sir Edward?"

"Naturally," said wan Sir Edward, looking ever so much more wan.

"This is the *perfect* moment to demand submission," said Les Holgate to Tristan.

"Shut up," said Tristan, almost fatigued he sounded, and not bothering to look Holgate full on. "Don't you get this situation? If these two men go outside and are revealed to Simon Beresford, there will be such a scandal—"

"Exactly!" trumpeted Les Holgate. "That's why this is the perfect moment to make demands of Sir Edward! That's our leverage—their wish to avoid that scandal!"

"That scandal *cannot* happen," said Tristan, in a low, quiet growl. "*We*—you and I—*we* cannot let it happen. The consequences are too great for us to allow it to happen. It's on us, it's not on him."

Exasperated Holgate looked. "You *idiot*, by saying that in front of him, you've just lost our best bargaining chip. If he even under‹ stands what you're talking about."

"Oh, I do, sir," said Sir Edward, as he dressed with shaking hands. He was trying to calm his breathing, and his color was re‹ turning somewhat. "You yourselves do not want this to be revealed. Therefore I need not pay you to prevent you from revealing it."

"You do have to pay *me*, however, milord," the Constable re‹ minded him, with a neighborly chuckle, and waving a finger at him all affably‹like. "As *I* have no hesitation to reveal it."

"Neither do I," said Les. "This man"—it's Tristan he means— "does not speak for me."

"Yes I do," said Tristan. "I have operational command here."

"He doesn't," Les assured Sir Edward. "Listen, Ed, I don't want your money, I want your compliance. I'm revealing you to Simon Beresford unless you agree to my demands. He's right below this window." And he called at once: "Simon Beresford! Lord Simon Beresford!"

"Shut up," Tristan commanded of Les Holgate, and immedi‹ ately stepped right over Kit, snatched Sir Edward by the arm, and hauled him back toward the door, while the poor fool sputtered in amazement that he was being trundled about so.

Shutting up was not of interest to Les Holgate, who continued to call out: "Lord Beresford! There's a fellow up here who looks a heck of a lot like Sir Edward Greylock."

"Sir Edward Greylock? Up there?" cried the older man's voice from below, and horrified it was he sounded. "Sir Edward! Pray reveal yourself, sir!"

"Of course he won't reveal himself," called Les. "You'd better come up here and see for yourself."

Moving with the swift and sleek efficiency of a wolf, did Tristan now fling an arm around Les Holgate's neck and get Les's throat nestled in the crook of his elbow. With his other hand he pressed forward on his captive's head, shoving him deeper into the trap. Les's voice dried up into a squawk. His eyelids fluttered. And then he went altogether limp. Tristan let him down onto the mattress like a sack of grain, and devoted a moment to arranging him on his side.

"What have you done!?" the Constable demanded.

"He's fine. I put him to sleep with a vee choke. Now I'm putting him in the recovery position," Tristan explained. "He'll wake up in a few minutes." He stood up and turned to face Sir Edward, who by now was sufficiently dressed that he could move about in the streets without drawing overmuch attention to himself. "Go with the Constable out the hidden exit," Tristan commanded. "Give him a lot of money and do not set foot in this building again. Never speak to anyone in this room again, except for me when I come to find you at the Bell. At that time you will agree to obey my further instructions to make sure there is no further scandal. Do you understand?"

Sir Edward nodded, looking ill at ease. Tristan stepped back to the window and showed himself at the casement. "Pray pardon us, m'lord," he called down. "There has been a confusion. There is no Sir Edward anyone up here."

"Who are *you?*" came the agitated voice from below. "What in the name of Heaven is going on up there?"

"'Tis nothing to do with you, milord," Tristan returned, and gestured at me. I understood at once and joined him. This took me past Kit, who reached out a hand toward me, but I slapped it away. I had a score to settle with him; but there'd be time for that later.

"Is that Milord Simon Beresford?" I asked, using my best London accent. Tristan backed away into the room, leaving me to hold Beresford's attention. Like Juliet with Romeo. Not an easy performance, what with the jealousy and rage in my heart and the squabbling behind me: Tristan again commanding Sir Edward and the Constable to leave by the back way, the two of them protesting they didn't know where the back way was, Kit scrambling to collect and don his drawers and shirt, offering to show them the back way as soon as he was dressed. He only knew the back way because of all the times he had visited *me* here and taken such delight in *me*. And now he was using the knowledge he had of me to save that ponce of a so-called gentleman? Why should he care if Sir Edward be saved or not? 'Twas the shock he was causing upon myself that should be chief amongst his worries!

"And what shall we say when the likes of you are seen loitering about a bawdy-house?" I meanwhile asked down to Beresford with a smile.

"'Tisn't a bawdy-house," Pym shouted up at me in annoyance. "'Tis a respectable establishment and you know well!"

"Politely waiting your turn, is it?" I grinned at Simon Beresford. "Don't be shy, come on up!"

The man's face reddened. "I will not set foot in a place of ill repute."

"Oh, but milord, it's *marvelous* repute we have," I informed him cheerily. "Sure nobody's got better repute than the girls of Tear-sheet Brewery. It's the talk of London, so it is. Just ask the proprie-tor, that's him beside you."

Pym was scowling up at me. "What mischief are you up to there, Gracie?"

I give him a playful smile. "A bit naughty I'm being," I sing out. "Pardon me, and I'll stop it now." I turned away from the window.

"Show them the back exit," mutters Tristan to me. "Take Mar-lowe too."

So now I'm to be saving Kit *and* the fellow he betrayed me with. As I again brush past Kit, he has finished donning his undergarments, and he reaches his hand for mine again and this time I grasp it, tight, so tight as if I will never release him, for in truth all I care about is getting him to safety.

Him, yes, but not Sir Edward. For what benefit is there in securing Sir Edward's safety? It keeps him free to continue his dalliance with my love, *and* it keeps him free to pledge his money where Tristan doesn't wish it. Suddenly as clear as day, I see the single stroke that will bring succour to both Tristan and myself.

As Kit and I approach Sir Edward so that I may lead us all from the building, I bend over a moment, rise up quick, and then quicker still, I make that stroke.

Sir Edward puts both of his hands to the close of his velvet vest. A dizzy spell takes him and doesn't he reach out with one of his hands to steady himself against the doorway. The hand is red, and makes a bloody print on the wall.

Tristan takes this in, his face a handsome study in consternation, and his clever mind soon arrives at the only possible explanation. He looks at me and sure I show him that bloody dagger still in my hand. 'Twas the very weapon he himself had wrested from my dim fella on his first arrival, and kicked across the floor to me. I'd snatched it up then to prevent further violence, and hadn't its owner stormed out of the place without reclaiming it. Since then, I'd got in the habit of carrying it. Its sheath was bound to my leg under my skirts. It had found a home, just now, in Sir Edward's heart.

Tristan's amazed to learn it's capable of murder I am (not knowing a thing of my life back home, and the uses Your Grace has put me to over the years), and so silent he is, as we watch Sir Edward settle to the floor, looking a bit like Juliet at the end of that detestable tragedy. He hardly has as much of a beard as Saunder Cooke himself.

"Well there," I say to Tristan, "he won't be funding the Boston Council any more, will he?"

I see in the corner of my eye that Kit—more concerned than heartbroken, and a good thing too!—is ushering the Constable out of the room. One of Sir Edward's legs has kicked out near me, so I wipe the dagger's blade on his drawers and slide it into the sheath on my leg, just to keep it handy. Then I get up, stepping well clear of the pool of blood that's been burbling out of Sir Edward, and follow them out.

In the shuffle of bodies in the corridor, Kit arranges himself to be beside me. "I'd sooner slay myself than break your heart, dearest," he whispers urgent in my ear. "That man was nothing to me, I was just using him to get some information for Her Majesty. I'll explain my secrecy and make it up to you as soon as we are out of here." He kissed my cheek and I confess, Your Grace, it made me wobbly. Never was there a lovelier set of lips to be kissed than my dear Kit's.

Pardon me for that distraction. Back to the events now.

For a moment, every one of us wants the same thing: to get down to the ground floor. For different reasons everyone wants it, but still there is a cooperation that wasn't there before, and so in very short order we are there. The tavern is deserted; people left when all the shouting started and the blood began sheeting down 'tween the floorboards. A crowd it is now gathered in the street just outside. Although the front door to the street is open, we can't see out into the glare, so no way to know if Simon Beresford is there. This hardly matters now, for the most important thing now is that Kit Marlowe is recognized by nobody.

The secret door for which we're headed is in the back corner behind the bar, meaning we must cross by the front door to reach it. Tristan is in the lead, then the Constable clutching at him, so he won't be separated from the man in charge, who, in the absence of Sir Edward, is the likeliest one to pay him off. Just behind them comes myself, clutching hands with Kit.

Now enters Proprietor Pym through the front door, blinking in the unaccustomed darkness. I turn to greet him, to assure him that—as mad as it might seem to say it—all this chaos is about to be resolved, with the one unfortunate detail that the Constable will be learning of one hidden exit. But certain I am that Pym will prefer this to his establishment being revealed as a trysting place for sodomites.

As I watch Pym's face, his eyes adjust to the dim, and land upon the half-dressed Kit Marlowe. Kit's not-being-dead was as much a shock to him as it was to the Constable. But he collects himself almost at once, turns to me and says, "Gracie, do you have this in hand?"

"I do. We're taking them out the below-exit. None will ever see him."

I think he will be pleased, but he shakes his head. "Know you not that in Deptford, at the alehouse where Marlowe staged his death—"

"It weren't an alehouse," I said. "It was a gentlewoman's private home, who rented out rooms. What about it?" I ask, with a queer worried feeling in my innards. I glance over to Tristan to see how he is faring with the door.

The hidden door here hides perfectly in plain sight, for it cannot be detected by the eye, only by touch. Tristan is running his hands over the paneling, trying to find it. And as he does, Pym finishes his thought: "They say business in Deptford quadrupled on account of people going to see where the famous Christopher Marlowe was murdered. So imagine what this will do for *us*!" And he grabs for Kit, meaning to push him outside into the curious Southwark crowd forming around the door of the tavern—most of whom will know him by sight.

Now, Kit knows his way around a fight, but he's not expecting this, and so before he registers it, Pym's fist, big as a hamhock, has closed around his arm, just above the elbow. Kit looks like a boy who's been caught in the middle of some mischief by a fat school-master.

Tristan has opened the hidden door. The Constable has lost no time in scurrying through it; I can hear him rattling down the narrow case of wooden stairs beyond it. That'll take him down a short tunnel—an expanded kitchen-sewer, to call it by its proper name—to a ditch that runs along the side of the brewery. 'Tis what remains of a creek that, I fancy, used to wind through a field to the Thames; now it is imprisoned between narrow vertical banks that have been built to either side as the city has grown up round it, and it's been half covered over with platforms and bridges. It matters not whether the Constable turns left or right along that ditch; ei-ther way he can slosh for some little distance through the nameless collection of fluids that oozes through it, and choose his moment to clamber back up to the level of the street. So he's sorted.

Having seen to that, Tristan is turning back around into the room. He sees how it is with Pym and Kit. And he sees, as I do, that there is no earthly way he can reach them before Pym drags Kit outside.

"Pym. Yer mad," I say, "don't make me use this." And I let him see the dagger as I draw it out from beneath my skirt.

That stops him, for a moment.

"No," Kit says, "don't go to the gallows on my account, Gracie." A pleasant thing to say, but it has the unfortunate effect of bol-stering Pym's confidence a bit. Pym gives me a sneer as if to say "you wouldn't dare," and drags Kit one step closer to the sunlight. I follow, closing the distance—just in time to be slammed to the floor by one who's just come flying down the stairs. Before I know it I'm face down on the boards with a knee in the small of my back and my arm's being twisted the wrong way.

"Got it!" announces Les Holgate as he pries the dagger out of my fingers.

And that's all he has time to say before he's cut down by a meaty punch from Tristan. Les Holgate has awakened from the "vee choke" only to be rendered unconscious again by a more *kinetic* approach. Feeling his knee come off my back, I spring up onto hands and knees and turn to look at the exit, just in time to see Kit, still firmly in Pym's grip, silhouetted in the bright light of the sun.

It is now impossible to keep Kit secret. Christopher Marlowe is about to be exposed to the world, and it's as a direct result of magic being used to Send someone. If there be a hundred men standing outside the tavern, I warrant at least three score will know his face. And I know what that means, with a profundity Tristan surely lacks. Voices outside the tavern begin to cry out in amazement, "Christopher Marlowe! 'Tis Christopher Marlowe!"

As Tristan steps toward them, in a bootless attempt to avoid calamity, I reach out and catch his hand to pivot him around, even as I'm making for the secret exit. He understands, and follows. As we stumble down the stairs, we can hear voices in the crowd calling Kit's name.

A wee, dank tunnel conducts us to the edge of the sewer-ditch-creek. Tristan's doubled over from the stench, which is a good thing since there's not enough headroom for him anyway. I lead him toward the Thames. As we scurry along, I note we are being accompanied by an impressive number of rats who seem to have the same idea. Their squeaking is drowned out by the rumble and clamour of the coming lomadh. I knew it was coming the same way you know when lightning's in the air.

I knew that this could happen, Your Grace, have always known it, in my bones; sure every witch knows it as well as fish know

swimming. We see traces of it in the everyday glamour that accom-
panies our spells. But isn't Iomadh compared to glamour what the
firing of a cannon is compared to a wee candle flame?

There are certain changes that must not be made through magic,
and while this is true—has always been true—with even the most
benign of entertainments, it is far more true and far more dire with
Sending, for then you've put one person in a place where they don't
know the way of things, and are like to make some dreadful change,
and it takes an áireamhán plus common sense to guard against.
When the worlds cannot bear the weight of one Strand suddenly
altering that abruptly from the others, it is Iomadh, as if you've
snapped off a twig upon a hearth broom: it is broken, gone, and
cannot be redeemed. So it was that moment.

As soon as the public saw Christopher Marlowe alive, this broke
the twig. But that image is too soft. For it wasn't a snap, rather the
very world seemed to erupt.

It's news you'll hear soon that there was a fire at the Tearsheet,
leading to the collapse of it and the neighboring buildings too,
with many lives lost. 'Tisn't wrong, that. But 'tisn't complete either; 'tis but a story they are telling to be making sense of what
they cannot understand. Fire there was, or something akin to fire.
But cold there was too, bitter cold, and bursts of wind that struck
like fists, and inhalations that made stout buildings shrink into
themselves like a dried leaf crumpled in the hand. But this was
more than a mere trick of the air. The very fabric of the world was
misbehaving. Think of how 'tis when vomiting, in the moment just
before the muck in your stomach rushes up your gorge, when 'tis
as though your entire body is clenching itself, trying to turn itself
inside out like a stocking. Now in your mind's eye see the Tearsheet and the neighboring buildings—the entire neighborhood—
the ground itself and the air above it, the very ether, all doing

likewise. Tristan and I were thrown down so hard that we skidded, and drew ourselves up to our feet only when the river came after us as if 'twere alive.

Those fortunate enough to be outside the lomadh could save themselves by running fast enough, and never looking back. Nearly knocked down we were, by several who'd tried to get clear by leaping off the embankment and into the ditch. Those on the inside, such as my poor Kit, and Pym, and Les Holgate, were quickly snuffed out with barely time to scream—or so I tell myself, as I don't like to imagine what worse fates might have befallen them. But didn't those in between—neither to one side nor the other of the lomadh, but caught in the fringes of it—suffer in the most dreadful ways. Impossible monstrosities their bodies became, like two-headed calves you sometimes see stillborn at home (not among Your Grace's cattle but often enough around Lough Swilly or Killybegs), and then out of that impossibility, decaying like rotten fish in sunlight, flesh coming off so quickly it fizzed and sprayed, and those it sprayed on caught it like leprosy and went down to fates of the same nature. A mercy it was that flames consumed what remained.

Milady, never have I believed in the priest's tales of Hell, discounting it all as a load of bollocks. But if the lomadh has occurred in other times and places, surely it explains where stories of Hell originated. Any soul unversed in magic, who wasn't knowing the true nature of what they witnessed, would try to explain what Tristan and I saw by claiming that the mouth of Hell itself had, for a moment, opened upon this mortal coil.

But only for a moment. After that, just a fire it was. And who's to say whether 'twas a ravage or a blessing, for it burned to ashes many an abomination spawned of the lomadh. So it seems to me now, upon reflection. But in the moment I could not help thinking of Kit and Morag and Pym and the other wenches of the Tearsheet. No sooner had we got clear of the catastrophe than I wished to return, in case any of them might be saved. We were down in that filthy ditch yet and I began looking about for a handhold I might use to climb up to the street. I saw none, and it's more and more exasperated I became, until all of a sudden there's a hand right in front of my face, reaching down. It's a hand in a white kid glove, expensive, immaculate. My gaze follows the arm upward until I'm looking into a man's face. He's above me on the pavement, squatting down, offering his hand to pull me up. A yellow beard, waxed and groomed to a sharp point, and the fanciest and most fetching hat, with a gorgeous plume on it. It's for the first time now that I'm seeing both of Athanasius Fugger's eyes, for doesn't he have the queerest habit of keeping his hat pulled down low and cocked to one side. I'm struck, in the midst of all the chaos and lamentation of the lomadh, by a peculiarity of the man's face. The pupil of the left eye—the one he prefers to hide behind his hat—is larger than the other. Stuck open, as it were. You might say it were an odd thing for me to attend to in such circumstances, but for some reason it struck me clearly in the moment.

I reached up and lay my palm upon his and felt his strong grip. Putting his legs and his back into it, he drew me up out of that ditch and got me safe up to the street. For the first time now I could see the fire and smoke burgeoning from what was left of the Tearsheet. That held my attention while he squatted down again, and helped Tristan just as he'd helped me. For which Tristan thanked him, in that clipped and wary manner that passes between men who are not sure of each other's intentions.

By the time we worked our way back round to the Tearsheet's former entrance, there was nothing left of tavern or of brewery. People had scattered, coughing, bleeding, dazed, gibbering like madmen. I saw old Simon Beresford staggering confusedly down the street.

Not one other member of our party was to be seen. Les Holgate was no more. No more Morag, or Pym. The other wenches of the bawdy house. And worst of all, at least for me although of no note to another soul: no more Kit Marlowe.

And of course, no more Tearsheet Brewery, the only place in London where ever I was safe.

Diachronicle

DAY 390

In which—finally—we seem to learn from experience

TRISTAN STAGGERED OUT OF THE ODEC in a terrible state. He was bruised and his hair disheveled, his eyes bloodshot and his skin almost grey. I felt a little sick seeing him: whatever happened, it could have been worse, and thank God it wasn't. I reached for the intercom button, then drew my hand back. He did not look in the mood for a conversation. We could only chew our thumbnails and speculate as he put himself through decontamination.

When he emerged, I did not resist the impulse to embrace him. But he caught me up short as my arms reached around him, and politely pressed me away from himself. He gestured gingerly to his left forearm. "Hairline fracture," he whispered hoarsely. "Possibly."

"Let's go to the emergency room," I said, reaching for his good arm, but he shook his head.

"Debrief first. Call the Odas."

"They can meet us in the ER—"

"Here. Now." He staggered down the hall toward the toilets.

I telephoned. Rebecca said they could be there in ten minutes. Erszebet came with them, for Rebecca had been soothing her after the drama of the morning.

Tristan sequestered himself in the conference room, on a video conference to Frink, until the others had arrived. When finally it was the five of us, and the video screen, so long the bane of our existence, had been shut off and unplugged, he glanced about the table at us, then looked down briefly, then back up and said in a heavy voice, "Les Holgate is dead."

"Excellent," said Erszebet immediately, before the rest of us could so much as draw breath. "He deserved it."

Tristan gave her an angry look. He seemed about to say something but then contained himself.

"That's horrible," I said. "Who killed him?"

He shook his head. "It wasn't a *who*, it was a *what*." He took a moment, briefly pressed his good hand to his forehead, and began again. "He arranged a scheme that had elements he hadn't considered or thought out. I tried to foil it but there were unforeseeable complications. And then . . ." He looked at a lost for words. "The brewery blew up. Everyone inside of it was killed."

"There was an explosion?" Frank Oda asked.

"No!" Tristan said firmly. "Something I can't describe. Explosion, implosion, turning inside out, being put through a blender, fire, ice . . . worse things too."

Erszebet looked solemn, and sighed. "*Diakrónikus nyírás*," she said quietly. "Diachronic, mmm . . ." She made a broad, sideways chopping gesture with both hands. "*Shear*. Diachronic Shear. There is a separating." She shook her head. "I even tried to warn Les Holgate because his ideas were so extreme. Very bad. I have heard of it but never seen it."

"What does it mean exactly?" asked Frank Oda.

"And what do we do about it?" Tristan followed.

"Can we go back on another Strand and fix it somehow?" asked Frank Oda.

Her eyes widened slightly, and she shook her head. "Oh. No. No, it's over. His existence—the existence of everything caught up in the Shear—it is gone forever, across all Strands. You cannot even go to look for him. He is gone. Full stop."

"That's horrible," I said again.

"Why? He was a terrible person," said Erszebet. And then, softening: "But I am sure there were innocent people destroyed too. It is very sad for them and their families." She looked thoughtful. "I thought perhaps this was apocryphal because I never met anyone who had experienced it. The last one in Europe was Paris, 1777. I suppose by my time everybody knew better than to risk it."

"Who else was lost in this Diachronic Shear?" Rebecca asked. "Gráinne must have survived or you could not have gotten back here."

Tristan looked as if another hundred-pound weight had settled upon his shoulders. "She's not the one who Sent me back," he said. "After the chaos, the young English witch named Rose found me and offered to return me here."

"We've lost Gráinne?"

He grimaced. "She's not dead. She's not even physically injured, but I think there's other damage. As well as killing Les, the lomadh took Gráinne's lover, and her boss, and of course destroyed the Tearsheet itself, which has been her home for ten years. She's an unwed Irishwoman in Elizabeth's London. The Tearsheet was her sanctuary. When I last saw her she was hysterical."

"Of course she was," said Erszebet quietly. She had gone quite pale and still. "It is a horrible thing to be torn from your security. This poor woman."

Something didn't add up. "How could you leave her in that condition?" I asked. For all of Tristan's mysterious ways, I knew him well enough to know that he would not simply abandon Gráinne.

"She's being looked after," Tristan said, "at least temporarily."

"Who's looking after her?"

"Athanasius Fugger."

There was a long pause while we absorbed that.

"You left her in the hands of a *Fucker*!?" Erszebet exclaimed.

"Why would he, of all people—" I began.

"I'll tell you what I know," Tristan said. "He was there. On the scene. Close enough to see it, far enough away that he didn't get—involved, or whatever you call it—in the Diachronic Shear. He must have followed me and Gráinne. He helped us up out of the ditch. He accompanied us back to the scene of the fire. Gráinne was losing it. Fugger puts an arm around her shoulder, draws her in, she's sobbing on his shoulder. He looks up at me—there's something very weird about his gaze—and says, 'I believe it's time for you to go back to where you belong. You know another witch who can do it. Go and reflect.' And he nodded at the fire, then looked back at me in a very serious way. 'I'll see to her,' he added, nodding at Gráinne, and then he turned his back on me. That was the last I saw of them."

"'Go back to where you belong . . . go and reflect . . .'" I repeated. "He knows."

"They all know," Erszebet spat. "All of the Fuckers. They always have. How do you think I have survived all these years without my own means? The Fuckers knew I was temporally indentured and saw to it that I remained alive and functional. They know everything."

"Well, this particular one knew *something*, that's for damn sure,"

Tristan said. "In a weird way, I trust him to look after Gráinne, at least temporarily. It almost felt like Athanasius Fugger came to the Tearsheet to clean up my mess."

"Our mess," I corrected him.

"Les Holgate's mess," Erszebet said.

"Anyway, Gráinne's part of that mess and Fugger's overall vibe was like *I got this, fool, get out of here.* So I got out, with Rose's help. I don't know what Rose really thinks of this project either now, but she at least was calm enough to realize that there was no benefit to anyone, for me to remain. That's why she Sent me back. I wouldn't call it a working relationship yet." Tristan sat back in his chair, wincing from the arm injury, and sighed. "Anyway, so let's avoid 1601 London. Maybe go to early 1602 and see how Gráinne has recovered and if she's still willing to work with us."

Frank Oda had been gazing thoughtfully into space. "If Sir Edward Greylock's existence has been obliterated across the multiverse," he said, "that should mean the maple syrup boiler does not come into existence in any Strand."

Erszebet considered this. "There is possibly some other Strand where another investor might be approached to fund it, but I would say you are most likely correct."

"How long will it take you to calculate that likelihood?" Tristan asked Erszebet.

Immediately the standard look of contempt. "How can I tell you?" she said. "I have been tricked. Les Holgate stole my számológép." And then a look of horror came over her face just as it occurred to myself and to the Odas: "Now we may never recover it."

Tristan looked weary. "I missed that—what?"

"Your rude boss in Washington with the big table, he forced

me into sending Les Holgate back to that DTAP by stealing my számológép, and now it is lost." She was so distressed by this realization that she was enervated, and so seemed oddly calm. "This means I will never perform magic again."

Tristan, exhausted, misread her meaning. "Are you saying you quit?"

She clearly had not been thinking that—until he said it. "I cannot work without my számológép," she said harshly. "It is gone. Because of very bad people. So yes, I will quit. This is all *hülyeség.*" She rose from the table.

"Where are you going?" asked Tristan, not even turning to look at her. "Where do you intend to live and work and pass your time? You're an immigrant without a legal identity and pretty much no marketable skills."

She paused at the door. "Your boss is a terrible man," she said, sounding on the verge of tears.

"He did a terrible thing," Tristan agreed unhappily. "And a terrible price has been paid for it."

"But your walking away right now does nothing for you," I added.

"I cannot Send anyone without my számológép!" she said. "It is too dangerous!" For a moment, I could see the very-very-very old woman peering out from her stormy, youthful eyes.

"I might be able to help you with that," said Frank Oda. "I was starting to get the hang of it. Give me a few days and I might have something to show you."

Erszebet gave him a wearied, disbelieving look.

"Meanwhile," I said, treading gently, "you do not need the számológép to Send me back to the 1640 Cambridge DTAP, and we are so very close to accomplishing this thing. Please do not abandon us quite yet. You will get your share of the money. We'll find your passport in Les's things. We'll buy you new plane tickets to Hungary, if we must. You'll never have to speak to Frink again."

There was a long moment as she stood in the doorway, troubled. Then whatever was going on inside her resolved itself, and she nodded once, decisively. "All right," she said. "I am not happy to be doing this, but I will help you complete the mission with the psalm book. But let us do it now, and be done with it already."

I have already described the events of my DEDE enough times—for indeed, I had lived through them enough times!—that I need not recount them now in detail. I now knew what to expect so well, knew the nuances of all these people who thought that they were meeting me for the first time (although as usual Stephen Day, the printer, commented that there was something very familiar about me).

Having been clothed by Mary Fitch, hauled by Goodman Griggs, ferried by the handsome brothers, having conned Hezekiah Usher and Stephen Day, having avoided the lechery of the cooper . . . having done all of these things as efficiently as possible, I headed out on the Watertown Road in the soggy August air, sealed bucket under my arm, using the shovel as a walking stick . . . praying that this time, I would not see that ~~fucking~~ boiler-foundation.

I did not. The erasure of Sir Edward Greylock from Elizabethan London had likewise erased all his possible investments, including this one.

Heartened by this, I measured out the length of my arm away from the boulder, and dug the length of my arm in depth. The clam and oyster shells seemed like old friends as I unearthed them. I settled the bucket in the hole, shoveled all the soil back in, stamped it down with unwonted exuberance, and headed back, a final time, toward Cambridge.

And then as ever, returning through the town, across on the ferry, back along the oxcart path, to the home of Goody Fitch. A final conversation with her and her young daughter Elizabeth about working with us. And then home.

Journal Entry of
Rebecca East-Oda

AUGUST 22

Temperature 89F. Dusty, dry. Barometer steady. Lettuce bolted. Kale ready to harvest but will be too bitter. Perennial herbs in fine form. Asters magnificent.

It finally happened today. In the former vegetable garden, which had been dug up so often earlier in the summer but lately lay unmolested while Tristan went to the London DTAP. We gathered around it. Mel dug a hole. Tristan has one arm in a homemade sling he had fashioned from two T-shirts tied together, and could not dig; Erszebet was in stockings and heels; Mel insisted Frank and I are age-exempted. So she dug it all herself. No doubt it gave her satisfaction, for all the times she had to bury it before.

And there it was. The barrel. Quite small, and very old, and soft around the edges where damp had found its way into the wood. But *not* rotted away. That cooper knew his business.

I have not been to a DTAP. I was not in residence during Erszebet's first few weeks exploring her powers in the ODEC. Other than seeing her transform herself, this was my first concrete experience of magic. I have seen that plot dug up a dozen times, and it has never contained a small well-sealed barrel containing an unspeakably valuable seventeenth-century hymnal.

Until today.

Diachronicle

DAYS 391–436 (SEPTEMBER–OCTOBER, YEAR 1)

In which we sell a book

THE CATASTROPHIC DEDE FROM WHICH Les never returned, and the recovery of the Bay Psalm Book from Frank and Rebecca's backyard, occurred at the beginning of the final week of August. Not until early October did we actually bank the money. In the meantime, General Frink continued to sign our paychecks, for our recovery of the book had saved our bacon politically. As with General Schneider, Les Holgate's death was deeply and sincerely regretted, but apparently considered to be just one of those things that happened when patriots went into harm's way for the defense of their homeland.

So, September was a month of unruffling all the legal feathers, getting the i's dotted and the t's crossed. Frink's brain trust concocted a story to explain Les Holgate's disappearance. It wasn't a very convincing story, but it didn't need to be; friends and family of people who worked in clandestine service knew that mysterious, unexplained death was something that happened.

There was a no-casket memorial service for him. This was attended by his family—including his uncle, Roger Blevins, who, like Tristan and myself, flew down from Boston. There was (obviously) no interment, but at the solemn reception afterward, in a bland conference room with recessed fluorescent lights, we were fortified with bad institutional coffee and Royal Dansk butter cookies. Tristan and I were there to represent the Cambridge office; the others had sent cards and flowers. I had hoped to avoid Blevins. Our turbulent past included two incidents of sexual harassment that would have sufficed to get any other man fired. Somehow, however, he cornered me at the hazelnut-flavored-cream dispenser, all smiles and smarm.

"I'm sorry for your loss," I said, refraining from direct eye contact.

"It's terrible," he said, slightly hurried, as if to get the formalities out of the way. "But I must say, Mel, it's good to see you've landed on your feet. I don't need to tell you how concerned I was when you left the department so suddenly. I was afraid your head was turned by, let's say, non-professional considerations." He gestured vaguely toward Tristan. Tristan pivoted and took a stride in our direction. I hadn't told him about the harassment, but he knew how to read me, and he seemed to have an overdeveloped damsel-in-distress radar.

"I have no regrets," I said, deciding to skip the creamer.

"Oh, neither do I," Blevins said. "It's a far better fit for you." The insult didn't need to be spelled out: *You were going nowhere in academia.*

"It's an excellent fit," I heard Tristan say from over my right shoulder. Blevins's eyes rose to see him. Tristan rested his hand on my upper arm and squeezed gently. "This woman is the most talented linguist, translator, scholar, and researcher I've ever encountered. And a brilliant team player. Worth her weight in plutonium. Thank God we ended up with her." Reader, I do believe I blushed the slightest bit with pleasure.

Blevins gave us both a forced smile, as if somebody were tightening his belt without his consent. "I've been a mere advisor until now, as you know, and my involvement is to be ramped up, or so I'm told," he said, with a glance across the room at General Frink, who was offering his condolences to Les Holgate's mother. It was a classic Blevins move—making it seem as though he was being drawn unwilling into the project, affecting a sort of patrician befuddlement.

Tristan's hand almost imperceptibly tightened around my arm. "So I'm informed," he said.

"I've been working with General Frink and Dr. Rudge for years on the precursors to DODO, always on the assumption it would peter out. Never saw myself as the cofounder of a new department. But life takes us to surprising places!"

Tristan's grip now tightened considerably. *Shut up, Stokes!* "When I approached you, sir, you refused involvement in DODO," he said.

"Not exactly, Colonel Lyons," said Blevins, always happy to seem wiser than anyone else. "I was just making it clear that I wasn't right for that *particular* role. Which"—and here he had the audacity to reach out and pat my left arm—"clearly was the right move, as it left a space open for our Mel here to fill. I knew my skills would be better applied elsewhere, as is proving to be correct." He smiled. "I look forward to working with you. Just like old times, Mel."

WE HAD MADE no preparations whatsoever for actually selling the book. We'd hardly even thought about it. Once it was in our hands we realized that this was going to be complicated. The mere existence of DODO was a highly classified secret, so we couldn't very well sell it openly. To make a long and tediously legal story short, we ended up establishing a private trust to act as a front operation for DODO. It was called the East House Trust, and the story was that it was the legal owner and custodian of Rebecca and Frank's house, with the two of them being its trustees. As such, the trust now became the legal owner of the book, which had, after all, been discovered on the property. Rebecca and Frank named Tristan and me officers of the trust, with authority to conduct certain business operations, and on that authority we opened an account at a bank in Harvard Square and rented a large safe deposit box where we placed the book for safekeeping while we entered into negotiations with various auction houses. Expert advice was that we would get the highest price in New York or London, and that we should wait for a few weeks so that the auction house could advertise the book and spread the word to collectors around the world.

So it was that in the first week of October, Tristan and I flew down to New York, he carrying the book in a locked metal briefcase. Sitting in the window seat, I gazed out at the fall colors sweeping down across the countryside from the north. The forests of Connecticut were nearing their peak in a glorious carpet of fiery red. I couldn't help thinking of Goody Fitch, who had been dead for over three hundred years, but who to me was every bit as alive as Rebecca and Erszebet and the others. After all, with the assistance of Erszebet and the ODEC, I could go and visit her anytime I wished, and so, to me, she really was alive. How would she and the others in the colonial Boston DTAP look upon the changing of the leaves? Probably as a warning of bitter cold and hard times to come.

The auction house was on Fifth Avenue, across from Central Park, and not too far from the Met. The neighborhood was, of course, where the richest people lived, and had been living for a long time, and so as we walked into the establishment and conducted our business with the proprietors, I had the comforting sense that we had come to the right place.

Our copy of the Bay Psalm Book was the fourteenth and last item on a list of high-priced antiquities that were auctioned off over the course of a couple of hours. I'd grown up in a family that respected books and old things, but I'd never experienced anything remotely like this auction. Sitting there in my new skirt suit from Lord & Taylor and my mom's best strand of pearls, watching the rich people and their representatives bid millions of dollars on various ancient artifacts, was a view into another world as strange to me as anything we could have visited through the ODEC.

The Bay Psalm Book had clearly attracted the attention of several well-heeled, highly motivated collectors, and so the bidding was intense. In moments it had blown through our expected price of five million dollars and shot upwards from there. Not until we got above ten million did bidders begin dropping out. It came down to a bidding duel between a collector from Los Angeles, who'd been sitting in the front row the whole time, and a man who had walked into the auction house and taken a seat at the back only moments before the bidding had started. In the end, the latter won, calmly nodding to the auctioneer whenever the man from LA raised his bid. The entire process had lasted less than a minute. The book sold for fourteen million dollars.

I assumed that payment, and the physical handover of the book, would be taken care of later, with the buyer and the auctioneer involving lawyers and bankers and so on. But after the auction finished and the room cleared out, the man who had bought the Bay Psalm Book walked up the aisle, pocketing a phone on which he had just finished making a call. He was dressed in an impeccable dove-grey suit, with a vest under the jacket that gave it a distinctive look—either retro or fashion-forward, I had no idea. He was in his fifties, well built, trim. He was groomed meticulously but a bit oddly, with sideburns that were longer than the norm. He wore rimless eyeglasses with tinted lenses. This detail had been noticeable when he had first walked in from the street. I'd guessed at the time that the lenses were those photochromic things that darken automatically in sunlight, and that they would lighten over the course of a few minutes indoors. But they had not changed; his eyes were still just barely visible behind a grey screen of tinted glass.

Tristan and I were standing in the aisle as this man walked by us. "If you would just give me a minute," he said, on his way by. We were too surprised to answer, so he looked back over his shoulder with a slightly bemused expression. "I won't be long."

"Of course," Tristan said, just to be polite. But I sensed he was a little uneasy. We were here under cover, pretending that DODO didn't exist, that we were just representatives of the East House Trust. Our job was to hand the book to the auctioneer, watch what happened, and get out. Not to socialize. We had a flight back to Boston in a couple of hours, and a dinner date with our colleagues. But it would be bad manners to bolt out of the place, ignoring a man who had just handed over fourteen million dollars, and so Tristan and I drifted to the back of the room while the buyer conducted a discussion with the auction house staff. We looked out the windows at Central Park, which was glorious, approaching peak color. Strollers and bicyclists were out enjoying the crisp autumn day, and park employees were out in force, raking up leaves and fallen branches.

"Beautiful day, isn't it?" said the buyer, as if reading my thoughts.

Tristan and I turned away from the window to see him approaching us. He was holding the Bay Psalm Book on which he had just spent fourteen million dollars. "My name is Frederick," he announced. Then he casually tucked the book under his left arm, as if it were a paperback he'd just bought in an airport bookstore, and extended his right hand to shake.

"Mel," I said, since it seemed we were operating on a first-name basis.

"Tristan," said my companion. We shook hands with Frederick. Still keeping the book tucked under his arm, he pulled a nice pair of gloves out of the pockets of his overcoat and pulled them on while moving toward the exit. Tristan held the door open for him, and for me. A fortuitous gap in traffic enabled us to cross Fifth Avenue, and a few minutes later we were strolling in the park together.

"Where on earth did the East House Trust find this remarkable specimen?" Frederick asked. He moved briskly. Tristan kept up with ease; I had to step lively in my borrowed heels.

"Respecting the confidentiality of the trustees, I'll treat that as a rhetorical question, Frederick," Tristan answered.

Frederick slowed to a stop and turned toward us. "It's new," he remarked.

Both of us must have looked goggle-eyed. This amused him. "The trust, I mean. Only established a few weeks ago. Oh no, I wasn't referring to the *book*. The book is obviously quite old!" He pulled it out from his armpit and opened it up, flipping curiously through a few pages.

"You are correct on both counts, Frederick," I said. I found it strange to be looking at those pages, darkened and mottled with the passage of hundreds of years, which I had seen fresh from the printing press only a few weeks earlier. To be quite honest, it gave me a feeling of satisfaction that bordered on smugness. DODO had come together, as I've explained, in a crazily haphazard and chaotic fashion, with many twists and turns, and a few tragedies, that we'd never foreseen. But *it had come together*. I had traveled back in time, on many occasions. I had achieved my mission. Proof of that was right in front of me, in Frederick's gloved hands, and in the enormously swollen bank account of the East House Trust.

Frederick turned his back on us, a bit rudely, and resumed walking. He forked off the main path onto a smaller trail that rambled off through a wooded section of the park. We followed him, kicking through fallen leaves. He said, "I suppose you're going to tell me that this was discovered squirreled away in the attic or something, and once the East-Odas understood its value, they decided to form the trust in order to manage the financial ramifications. I suppose that story hangs together reasonably well."

Lagging half a pace behind him, Tristan and I exchanged a glance. It was a bit difficult to hear him, because we were approaching an area where some groundskeepers were cleaning up fallen branches and leaves, tossing the debris into a gasoline-powered chipper that reduced everything to confetti and hurled it into the back of a truck. It was noisy. Frederick drew to a halt not far away from this machine and turned to face us again.

I understood. Or I *thought* I did. He wanted to speak to us privately, without fear of surveillance microphones picking up his words, and so he had moved to a noisy environment.

"Do you know anything about markets?" Frederick asked. "Given your professional backgrounds, Dr. Melisande Stokes and Lieutenant Colonel Tristan Lyons, I'm guessing not really. Oh, you've read the odd article in the business section of the *New York Times*, and, as educated persons, you have some general background on which to draw. I like to think I'm a bit more up to speed on such things, as being related to my profession."

"What profession is that, Frederick?" Tristan asked.

Frederick had tucked the book under his arm again—a habit I found quite annoying given the rarity and fragility of that artifact. No book collector would have treated it so cavalierly. This had freed his hands. Turning slightly away, he reached up and removed his shaded eyeglasses, folded them up, and slid them carefully into the breast pocket of his overcoat. For a moment he squinted against the bright golden sunlight of the New York autumn, showing creases around his eyes. He blinked a couple of times and then turned to face us. "The sort of profession," he answered, "that places me in a position to spend fourteen million dollars on a book."

"Touché," Tristan said. Then his face went slack with amazement. He was staring at Frederick. I turned to look in the same direction, but didn't see anything to explain Tristan's reaction. There was something odd about Frederick's eyes, which took me a moment to process. They were asymmetrical. His left pupil was dilated to the point where the blue iris could scarcely be seen, but the right pupil was constricted, as you'd expect when outdoors in broad daylight.

"It's simple," Frederick said, "but it's not. Supply, demand, individual transactions, such as the one we have engaged in today—child's play, on the level of a sidewalk lemonade stand. But when billions of them are integrated over centuries—not so simple at all. The resulting flows of information, encoded as fluctuations in prices, shifts in markets, are far beyond the ability of any one human mind to comprehend. Which is why such things are best left in the hands of professionals with the requisite training and, if I may say so, lineage. Good day."

Frederick turned his back on us and walked directly toward the wood chipper. The crew members, distracted by their work and rendered deaf by their hearing protectors, didn't see him coming until he was just a few yards away. Then, sizing him up as a gentleman of a certain bearing, well attired, they straightened up and regarded him with a kind of wary curiosity. Frederick acknowledged them with a polite nod, then took a step closer to the roaring maw of the machine while reaching under his arm. Suddenly I knew what was about to happen, but I could not believe it.

Glancing back over his shoulder to make sure that Tristan and I were watching him, Frederick pulled the Bay Psalm Book out from under his arm and gave it an underhand toss into the chipper. The machine made a brief coughing sound—as did I—and we saw a spume of white confetti spray into the back of the truck.

Frederick walked away into the park.

"There goes one strange fucker," Tristan remarked. "Let's go home, Stokes."

THE APOSTOLIC CAFÉ had expanded its offerings to include Euclid's Grill—casual buffet by day, fine dining by night, served in the former nave. Tristan and I went directly there from the airport that evening. Waiting for us were Frank, Rebecca, Erszebet, and the newest member of our little band, Mortimer Shore. Mortimer was the historical swordfighter whom Rebecca had recruited from the park, and who had trained Tristan in the use of the backsword. He was a tall, rangy Californian with a mop of wavy dark hair and a bushy beard that as often as not framed an easy smile. He was double-majoring in metallurgy and computer science at MIT, but Tristan had talked him into putting his academic career on hold so that he could go full-time as DODO's systems administrator and in-house swordfighting expert. These four had already grabbed the big booth in the corner of the restaurant, reserved under the name of the East House Trust. Resting in an ice bucket nearby was a magnum of champagne that looked expensive. To judge from the high fives and hugs with which they greeted us (yes, even from Rebecca), they were already well into it. We hadn't told them the weird story about Frederick yet, and it wasn't clear that we needed to.

Julie the Smart-ass Oboist (who always seemed to be our waitress) uncorked the magnum and came to our table to pour flutes of champagne for Tristan and me, and we went through several rounds of toasts. Erszebet, looking like she'd been born with a glass of bubbly in her perfectly manicured hand, was determined to teach everyone how to toast properly, in the traditional European style: you had to look each person straight in the eye as you clinked glasses with them. She was looking more cheerful than I'd have expected, given that her precious számológép was still locked up in some vault in the Trapezoid. I said as much to her. She allowed as how she was so very (grudgingly) chuffed by the success of the venture, and her role in it, that she had decided to delay her relocation to Hungary until we were able to replace her, by bringing forward through time more witches to work in the ODEC.

Tristan got to the bottom of his champagne glass pretty quickly. He still had a haunted look about him, as if he'd seen a ghost in Central Park. Not really the champagne type, he raised one hand and hailed the Smart-ass Oboist.

"What can I get you?" Julie asked.

"The usual," he said, his attention already on the dinner menu.

She faltered, her face pinkening slightly. "I'm sorry," she said. "I feel like I should know what that is, but the memory escapes me . . ."

"Old Tearsheet Best Bitter!" he said, glancing up.

She frowned. "I don't think we have that," she said. "Is it an import?"

He gave her an Eagle Scout smile, but his tone was firm. "You know. I've been ordering it since this place opened. You definitely carry it."

"All right," she said with a skeptical smile, writing. "T-e-a-r-s-h-e-e-t? Bitter?"

"That's right," said Tristan.

We all perused the menu, until she returned a moment later with the announcement that they did not carry—and had never carried—Old Tearsheet Best Bitter. Tristan half stood up and looked incredulously over at the barman, who shrugged broadly, indicating he had never heard of that ale. That ale he'd been pouring Tristan for years.

Erszebet tugged at Tristan's sleeve, pulling him back down into his seat. "This is the Diachronic Shear," she said quietly. "There is no Tearsheet Brewery. After September of 1601, there never was."

"That's almost as big a tragedy as losing Les Holgate," Tristan muttered under his breath.

IT WAS ODDLY intimate yet oddly formal, the six of us sitting around a proper dining table that was not littered with coffee cups, whiteboard markers, handheld devices, and notepads. That we were holding actual silverware, and napkins larger than a coaster. That we allowed a stranger to approach us and do something exquisitely mundane: serve us a meal that was not delivered in to-go containers or rewarmed in a microwave. That we ate slowly, savoring our food and relaxing in the hum of conversation around us, and feeling a part of the human race—or at least, that fraction of the human race that frequented the Apostolic Café.

As we ate, we reviewed our lessons learned about the use of time travel, all of which Erszebet felt the need to point out she was already aware of.

"Very well," said Tristan, setting down his fork. "If you know everything, save us the time and aggravation and tell us what we don't know yet."

She made a *tch*'ing sound and shook her head. It is fair to say her condescension toward him was softening now—a little—into something more resembling big-sister exasperation. "What you do not know is almost everything. Quite literally. Except what my számológép could anticipate on any given Strand."

"Clearly we're still in the learning process there," said Tristan. "We need to think in a little more depth about how to master the Strands."

"You cannot *master* the Strands," said Erszebet. "It is like a doctor with medicine. You can only *practice*. And you cannot do even that without the számológép."

"It does seem to me there are discernible algorithms regarding the Strands," said Frank Oda. He touched his wife's wrist gently and she reached down to the floor for a bookbag, which she raised and handed to him.

"There is always, what is the term, wiggling room," corrected Erszebet.

"It is a complexity theory problem—a branch of what mathematicians call graph theory," said the professor.

"Graph? As in graph paper?" I asked.

"Math geeks use the term differently," Oda said, "to mean structures of nodes connected by branches. Like a számológép, or Gráinne's broom, or Rebecca's heirloom."

"Or the many forking Strands of history," Rebecca said.

"Point being, a lot of progress has been made in recent decades around just these sorts of problems," Oda said. Anticipating an objection from Erszebet, he added, "Which isn't to say there's no more 'wiggling room,' but we can tackle these questions now with well-tested algorithms, and graphical UIs." He opened his bag and reached inside.

"We are better than any other humans at extrapolating from what the Strands tell us."

"That's true," said Oda. From the bookbag, he withdrew an iPad. Rebecca took the bag from his lap and returned it to the floor as he set the iPad on the table before him. "However, computers can enhance and sharpen the abilities you already have. With all respect, even witches can benefit from an app."

Erszebet looked at the iPad. "What is this?"

"It's a present," said Frank Oda. "I would not insult your history with the missing számológép by calling this a replacement számológép, so let us say it is your quipu."

"That is a computer," she argued. "It is a piece of machinery. It does not even have moving parts."

Oda smiled at her, undisturbed by her attitude. "I took the premise of the quipu, and what you had shown me of your számológép, and I designed a program to do algorithmically what you do intuitively. Plus a graphical user interface to go with it!" He held up the iPad so that everyone could see it. On the screen was a branching diagram that might best be described as a mathematician's attempt to reproduce the structure of those devices used by the witches. Call it a quipu, a broom, or a számológép if you will; they all had the same many-branched structure, and so did the thing that Oda-sensei had rendered on this screen. It was a constellation of small gleaming figures in various shapes and colors, like a Christmas tree; the structure that held it together was a snarl of fine colored lines. He dragged his finger on the glass, and the thing rotated around, showing that it was three-dimensional; he swiped, he zoomed, he tapped, and things happened. "It's a work in progress," he said shyly, "but with time and resources, we should be able to build it out."

Erszebet looked profoundly insulted. "You are saying you can replace me with a machine?"

"Not you. Your számológép," he said. "Except even better."

Every so often, Frank said exactly the right thing. This was one of those times. Erszebet's face softened. She reached out for the iPad. He handed it to her. She pulled it into her lap and gazed at it in fascination. Her fingers began to move across the glass, halting at first, but quickly gaining fluency.

"Dude, that's sick," said Mortimer reverently.

"That's beautiful," said Julie the Smart-ass Oboist, pausing at our table with a pitcher of red ale and a platter of onion rings. "That looks like my grandmother's *Yao Jìsuàn qì*"—and before any of us could think to question her, she had moved on to deliver her burden to a table of bearded ~~CS nerds~~ scholars.

Oda-sensei went on: "If we'd had something like this in place, fully realized, for the Bay Psalm Book gambit, for instance, it might have predicted the possibility of the maple syrup boiler being there if we didn't first go back to the earlier DTAP and deal with Sir Edward Greylock and his investment schemes. It might have predicted the danger of Christopher Marlowe being in the Tearsheet Brewery that day."

"It would take forever to imagine all such possibilities!" I objected.

"It's not just about imagining," he replied. "We can integrate this with historical databases, and we can improve those databases as we go back in time and learned what actually happened."

"I don't know," I said. "We have all just had a very sobering lesson as to why nobody should rely on diachronic travel, ever, and instead you respond by saying, 'Oh, let's find a way to rely on diachronic travel.'"

"I'm pretty beat up," Tristan admitted. "But I'll bet the first person to survive an airplane crash, a hundred years ago, was pretty beat up too. You can limp away from the crashed airplane saying, 'Man wasn't meant to fly, I am done with this,' or you can be saying, 'I just learned how to do it better next time.'"

"What's the point of it? Why even bother?" I asked. "We went to all of that effort, and people died, so we could make fourteen million bucks. We'd have been money ahead if we'd just founded a tech start-up instead."

"There are other powers in this game too," Tristan said, "who can do what we can do, and who most definitely think there's a point. We can't let them have a monopoly on this kind of force."

"So it's back to the Magic Gap argument."

"In a word, yes."

Erszebet had been oblivious to the conversation ever since she had seized the iPad, but now she broke in with a question for Frank. "So many different colors and shapes of little blobs! What is this one? The little white cloud with the question mark?"

"That's where the system is telling us it needs more input."

"Input?"

"Information about something that happened in the past."

"It knows about known unknowns?" Tristan asked. I gave a little snort, thinking he was making a joke at poor Les Holgate's expense, but it seemed he was serious.

"Yes," Oda-sensei responded, "this is a case where we would have to send a DOer back to collect information."

"Holy crap," Tristan said. "How much computational power—"

"More than can fit in an iPad," Frank answered, cutting him off. "This is linked to a small cluster running in the cloud. But it's still just a toy. It needs to be scaled up radically. To be really useful, it will take an immense amount of computing power." With an almost impish smile, he added, "We're gonna need a bigger quipu."

PART THREE

SENATOR HATCHER: Professor Oda, I draw your attention to this rather large document that was produced by DODO staff during the post-mortem analysis phase from the Les Holgate tragedy. Are you the author of the section of the report entitled "Diachronic Shear: A Layman's Guide"?

FRANK ODA: Yes, I am.

HATCHER: To be frank, as a confirmed layman, I found that your explanations only made me more perplexed than I was to begin with. I have some questions about this.

ODA: I'll try to be of service.

LIEUTENANT COLONEL LYONS: Senator Hatcher, if I may just insert a brief remark—

HATCHER: You may.

LYONS: This phenomenon isn't well understood by anyone just yet. All we know is that it exists. We've seen it ourselves, and witches have attested to it. So any scientific hypothesis should be regarded as preliminary.

HATCHER: Thank you for that careful hedging, Lieutenant Colonel Lyons. I'm sure that your subordinates appreciate your paternal concern for their well-being. But I wish to address Professor Oda if that is fine with you.

LYONS: Of course. Thank you, Senator Hatcher.

HATCHER: Professor Oda, would you be so good as to explain the relationship of Jell-O to Diachronic Shear?

ODA: Excuse me, Senator. Jell-O?

HATCHER: Yes, it says here on page 793, third paragraph, that the properties of Jell-O, as in, Jell-O brand gelatin desserts, have something to tell us about the structure of the universe. And I found that to be a somewhat unusual statement from a man of science. I was wondering if you might elucidate it.

ODA: Yes, I remember that section. Traditionally we have tended to think of the past, present, and future as parts of a single continuous line—a thread, if you will.

HATCHER: And if I may just interrupt you there, Professor Oda, we have already been over this topic of quipus and so on ad infinitum, so we don't need to belabor any more the idea that it's not just a single thread but a whole network of them. I think that I understand it as well as any non-scientist can understand such a thing. Just as I felt I was achieving some level of comfort with that idea, you jumped to Jell-O. My great state happens to be home to no fewer than three different state-of-the-art industrial facilities that are part of the supply chain for Jell-O brand gelatin desserts and so naturally my interest was piqued. But I'll be darned if I can follow your reasoning here.

ODA: If you have ever observed the properties of Jell-O, such as a molded dessert made of that substance—

HATCHER: I have, Professor Oda, on many occasions on the campaign trail.

ODA: You'll know that it is flexible and deformable, up to a point. You can tap it with your spoon and it will jiggle. You can stretch it. But if you overdo it, the material will rupture. A crack will form, just like a crack in a block of stone. Later on, the crack may heal itself—the gelatin can knit itself back together.

HATCHER: Especially if you reheat it.

ODA: Exactly. Which is not true of cracks in granite and other brittle materials.

HATCHER: It is truly a marvelous property of Jell-O.

ODA: You could say so, yes.

HATCHER: But what is the relationship to this dreaded phenomenon of Diachronic Shear?

ODA: Viewed from the standpoint of the many-worlds interpretation of quantum mechanics, you could think of the past as being not a single thread but—

HATCHER: A quipu, yes, we've been over that.

ODA: When the quipu becomes sufficiently vast, it becomes instructive to transition, in our thinking, to a different mode, a continuous as opposed to discrete model, in which all of the threads effectively merge into a block of stuff that I am likening to Jell-O. When we send DOers back in time to carry out DEDEs, it's like tapping the Jell-O with a spoon and making it jiggle a little bit. It creates internal stresses that the material is capable of withstanding. But if we try to change too much, too fast—

HATCHER: It cracks?

ODA: Yes.

HATCHER: It just splits wide open.

ODA: Just for a moment. But unlike a Jell-O dessert on your plate, the space-time continuum cannot simply fall apart. It is self-healing. The cracks must be sealed immediately. If you are far away from the crack, then you are safe—it's like being far away from an earthquake. But if you are unlucky enough to be right along the crack boundary, then you are in for a bad time. The universe needs to decide whether you are going to go on existing or not.

HATCHER: You're referring here to the so-called Tearsheet Brewery. What happened in that scenario?

ODA: You might think of the Tearsheet Brewery as like a lettuce leaf embedded in a Jell-O molded salad. Because of the unfortunate chain of events, this piece of lettuce was yanked out of the Jell-O and ceased to exist. A vacancy was left in its wake, which self-healed with the most terrible consequences for those unlucky enough to be near it.

HATCHER: Terrible consequences, indeed. Thank you, Dr. Oda. Madame Chair, I yield my time.

CHAIRWOMAN ATKINSON: Are there any further questions for Dr. Oda at this time? No? Very well, you may step down, Dr. Oda.

SENATOR COLE: Madame Chair, in light of Dr. Oda's remarks I would like to call Lieutenant Colonel Lyons back.

[REDACTED]

SENATOR COLE: . . . the descriptions of the Tearsheet Brewery event are, in sum, so bloodcurdling, and the benefits of this mission so trivial in comparison—the recovery of an old book from a cask in Dr. Oda's backyard!—that it must call into question why we are being asked to spend the taxpayers' money on this sort of undertaking at any level, to say nothing of the exorbitant requests embodied in this proposed budget.

CHAIRWOMAN ATKINSON: I would like to thank my distinguished colleague for that impassioned, eloquent, and thorough statement. Was there a question for Lieutenant Colonel Lyons?

COLE: Why should we spend the taxpayers' money on building a device that will only expose this great nation to additional risk?

LIEUTENANT COLONEL LYONS: Thank you, Senator Cole. For high-level strategic questions I might refer you to General Frink, but I'm happy to address your question on a more nuts-and-bolts level. As you point out, we need to keep the costs as low as possible while minimizing risk and maximizing benefits. From a cost point of view, I'll remind the committee that the only work being actively funded right now, and for the next few months, is CRONE: Chronodynamic Research for Optimizing Next Engagement. We have cut back the number of

DEDEs to the bare minimum needed to sustain progress and we have limited those to missions of an exploratory or experimental nature. Most of our current budget is devoted to pathfinding work on the Chronotron, a device whose entire purpose will be to minimize risk.

COLE: To minimize risk, you say.

LYONS: Yes, Senator. That is its purpose.

COLE: Both Dr. Oda and General Frink in their earlier testimony praised the Chronotron as a tool that would enable DODO to plan future missions. Would you concur?

LYONS: Yes, it duplicates the functionality of the quipus or other similar devices used by witches to navigate the different Strands of history, and combines that with a colossal database of historical facts. If we'd had it earlier, we'd have planned our first DEDEs differently and gotten results more quickly and more safely.

COLE: Or perhaps chosen some different DEDE altogether?

LYONS: Yes, it's quite possible that with a functioning Chronotron we might have been able to identify something both easier and more profitable than recovering a Bay Psalm Book.

COLE: This is precisely what concerns me about building the Chronotron.

LYONS: I'm sorry, Senator Cole. Why would you be concerned about DODO having a tool that would enable us to make more informed choices? As opposed to just winging it?

COLE: When you just wing it, you are aware of the risk and the uncertainty, and inclined to be more cautious. When you have a high-tech tool giving you an illusion of omniscience, I am concerned that it will lead to greater risk-taking.

LYONS: I would argue that more information is always better. I would make an analogy to using computers to predict the weather. Back in the days when all we had was a weathervane and a barometer, a ship's captain had to make his best judgment about what the weather was going to do, and trust his gut. Now that we have weather satellites and computerized forecasts, the captain can make informed decisions.

COLE: It is an attractive analogy, but it's self-serving, since we all know that those satellites and computers actually work most of the time. You're likening the Chronotron to familiar technology that we trust. How close is the Chronotron, really, to deserving that trust?

LYONS: As of today, about halfway through the CRONE phase, we have the individual processing units—the QUIPUs, or Quantum Information Processing Units—running according to spec, and we're developing the manufacturing capability to produce them in larger numbers. By linking just a few of them together we've been able to achieve more accurate results than the quipu-like item Erszebet was using—

ERSZEBET KARPATHY: My számológép, which has now been lost because of the incompetencies and manipulations of this government.

ATKINSON: Ms. Karpathy, you are out of order.

COLE: Yes, thank you, Ms. Karpathy, we have already noted your remarks on this topic several times.

KARPATHY: My comments have not yielded results.

ATKINSON: Order! Order!

[REDACTED]

(NEXT DAY)

SENATOR EFFINGHAM: . . . moving on to Line 539 of the proposed budget, unless my eyes deceive me, you wish to allocate twelve full-time positions to historians?

MELISANDE STOKES: In order for the Chronotron to do its job it has to have a vast database of historical facts in memory. Going back to the weather analogy from yesterday, you can build a computer that's really good at performing the mathematical calculations needed to predict weather, but it's going to be totally useless unless you can feed it real-time information about actual weather conditions. Which is

why we need weather balloons and satellites and so on—to supply
that data. In the case of the Chronotron, we have these QUIPUs that
know how to do the math, but they're useless without historical data.

EFFINGHAM: I believe we covered this in Lines 420 through 487, which
describe a program to extract this information directly from digitized history books already in the Library of Congress.

STOKES: Yes, that covers ninety percent of it, but some books contain
ambiguous material that confuses our natural language processing
algorithms. When that happens, the offending passage can be sent
up the line to a human reader who can try to parse it. For obvious
reasons we think that historians will do the best job.

EFFINGHAM: Very well, but it appears that their cost is being split with
another subprogram called . . . DORC?

STOKES: We should probably come up with a different name for it, but
DORC is the Diachronic Operative Resource Center. Colonel Lyons
and I had to improvise our own training program when we learned
how to speak, dress, and behave in colonial Boston and Elizabethan
England. As DODO's scope of operations expands to other DTAPs . . .

EFFINGHAM: Ah, yes, thank you for jogging my memory, Ms. Stokes.
DORC is like the Starfleet Academy, if I may indulge myself with a
reference to *Star Trek*.

STOKES: The Hogwarts.

EFFINGHAM: Yes, the training ground where DOers will acquire the requisite skills.

STOKES: Those budget entries begin around Line 950.

EFFINGHAM: Yes, my aide has found it for me.

STOKES: It makes sense to split the historians' time so that they can
help out with DORC activities.

EFFINGHAM: This is quite a large section of the budget and I may need
additional time to go through it . . .

[REDACTED]

SENATOR EFFINGHAM: Line 1162 jumps out at me. Why do you need to spend so much money on swords?

LIEUTENANT COLONEL LYONS: It turns out that they are more expensive than you might think. They have to be hand-made from special kinds of steel.

EFFINGHAM: You are missing the point of my question, Colonel Lyons. Let me rephrase: this seems to imply that you are assembling a squad of warriors and assassins.

LYONS: Probably not assassins per se because of the risk of Diachronic Shear.

EFFINGHAM: You can't just go back and kill Napoleon.

LYONS: It would be a terrible idea.

EFFINGHAM: Renewing my question . . .

LYONS: People back then—people of the upper classes—carried swords and other edged weapons all the time. And they knew how to use them. Any DOer, at least any male DOer, who went back pretending to be such a person, but who had no skill with using a sword, would be as conspicuous as someone who couldn't mount a horse or speak the language.

EFFINGHAM: Are you expecting some of your DOers to engage in sword-fights?

LYONS: I had to do it several times during my DEDE in London.

EFFINGHAM: But that was before you had the Chronotron—it was an improvised DEDE.

LYONS: Wars, battles, and duels are important events. In some cases, depending on what the Chronotron tells us, we may need DOers who are capable of effecting that kind of change—or at a minimum, staying alive in such environments.

EFFINGHAM: It sounds dangerous.

LYONS: It is, by definition. Only a small minority of DOers will be fighters. They make a big splashy impression in the budget because we have to buy them training equipment.

EFFINGHAM: But the majority will have other specializations?

LYONS: Yes. As an example, during the current CRONE phase, our efforts are focused on making discreet insertions into certain DTAPS, trying to develop and nurture our relationships with KCWs—

EFFINGHAM: With what?

LYONS: Known Compliant Witches.

EFFINGHAM: Ah. Yes. This takes us back to, er, Line 345 or thereabouts. Developing the witch network. The subway map.

LYONS: Yes, like the subway map that tells us how we can route our DOers from one DTAP to another and eventually get them home safe. Obviously, this relies on having friendly relationships with witches.

EFFINGHAM: Who tend to be, shall we say, peculiar individuals.

ERSZEBET KARPATHY: I find your tone offensive, Senator.

CHAIRWOMAN ATKINSON: Order!

EFFINGHAM: Go on, Colonel Lyons.

KARPATHY: Are you ignoring me? I said I find your tone offensive. I do not even want to be here, I am here only out of the goodness of my heart, but all of you, all of these millions of dollars and plans to rule the planet and all that, do you understand that all of it depends on me? And yet you use that tone with me? Who do you think you are?

EFFINGHAM: It's all right, Madame Chair. Now, Ms. Karpathy—

KARPATHY: Don't "Ms. Karpathy" me. Apologize for your tone.

EFFINGHAM: I apologize, Ms. Karpathy.

KARPATHY: I do not accept your apology.

EFFINGHAM: Why not?

KARPATHY: You do not sound at all sincere about it. It does not count if it is not sincere. I am going to leave this room and I want you to think about what happens if I do not return. Then when I do return, I expect you will apologize appropriately.

MELISANDE STOKES: Tristan, shall I—?

LYONS: Yeah.

ATKINSON: Let the record show that Ms. Erszebet Karpathy has left the hearing room without authorization at 1723 hours accompanied by Dr. Melisande Stokes.

EFFINGHAM: Colonel Lyons, you were saying?

LYONS: Erszebet has just given you an excellent example of why we require very specialized agents to win over witches. They don't want money. They're not the sort to join us on behalf of Truth, Justice, and the American Way. Every witch has her own agenda for why she might or might not help us. So we need to be able to find witches, but then also to win them over. Sometimes that can be a complicated undertaking, involving a series of actions that require various sets of skills.

EFFINGHAM: I suspect I'm not the only one in the room who would appreciate an example of what you mean.

LYONS: Okay, recently we wanted to establish a foothold in the Balkans for reasons that General Frink can explain if you need to know, so we did research to anticipate where a witch was, and then we Sent back one of our agents to find the witch. Well, he found her, and she did agree to Send him back here, but she wasn't interested in being on call for us, so to speak, unless we made it worth her while. Her husband was imprisoned, so she told our DOer that if he could get the husband out of prison, she'd work with us.

EFFINGHAM: Why didn't she just, you know, use magic to get him out?

LYONS: With respect, magic isn't the same thing as omnipotence, Senator. It's a hereditary skill set, really, that's all. Anyhow, our fellow who we Sent back there, his language skills are first-rate and he's a tremendous athlete and good at problem-solving, but he's not much of a schmoozer and he doesn't have the skills that would assist in a jailbreak. So the witch Sent him back here, but said she didn't want to hear from DODO again unless we could get her husband out of jail. If we'd had somebody who specialized in picking locks or was a general escape artist or whatever, we could have Sent that person back. We didn't have anyone like that, so we had to try bribing the prison guard, but we did not succeed.

EFFINGHAM: Bribe them with what? According to this document, you can't take anything back in time with you.

LYONS: That's correct.

EFFINGHAM: So what did you try to bribe him with?

LYONS: Um. Mel—Dr. Stokes—she went back because. She was willing to try. Bribing him with. What she brought with her.

EFFINGHAM: Her body?

LYONS: Yes.

EFFINGHAM: You're saying she

[REDACTED]

LIEUTENANT COLONEL LYONS: The utter failure of this effort led us to conclude we needed an actual sex worker, or at least somebody capable of passing as one.

SENATOR EFFINGHAM: I yield, Madame Chairwoman.

CHAIRWOMAN ATKINSON: I recognize Senator Villesca.

SENATOR VILLESCA: Colonel Lyons, I hope you appreciate that prostitution is illegal in this great country of ours, except in certain rural parts of Nevada.

LYONS: The prostitute would be plying her trade in sixteenth-century Balkan territory, sir. Or possibly his trade, based on Dr. Stokes's reception. Anyhow, we haven't found one yet.

VILLESCA: You're saying you want to use taxpayer money to recruit prostitutes.

LYONS: That's not a typical example, sir. We need people with specific skill sets like masons and soldiers and people with specific athletic abilities, and we need people who can blend in—like I said, schmoozers. Actors. Whatever it takes.

GENERAL FRINK: Madame Chairwoman, if I may?

ATKINSON: Proceed.

FRINK: With all due respect, Senator Villesca, it's not like taxpayer money has never been used to hire prostitutes before. I know you're aware of that.

[REDACTED]

(NEXT DAY)

GENERAL FRINK: . . . an ongoing theme in the last few days' deliberations has been the need for wisdom and discretion in future DODO operations. Senator Hatcher has reminded us of the need to avoid any future incidents such as the one in which Les Holgate sacrificed his life for his country. Senator Cole has expressed concern that a fully functional Chronotron may lead us into taking risks we might not otherwise consider. With Senator Effingham, we've had an illuminating discussion of the importance of learning from the wisdom of experienced professional historians. Finally, Senator Villesca has spoken with great passion and eloquence of the need to maintain moral standards that we can all be proud of. It is for all these reasons that I am pleased to introduce Dr. Blevins of Harvard University as the new acting head of the Department of Diachronic Operations. He replaces Lieutenant Colonel Lyons, who is being reassigned to command of DODO's "boots on the ground" operational unit, and who will henceforth report to Dr. Blevins. Though the academic world knows Roger Blevins as a peerless scholar, those of us with security clearances are aware of his long service to his country as

[REDACTED]

SENATOR HATCHER: . . . even for one of your distinguished credentials, this is an important career transition, Dr. Blevins, and so I would like to be the first to congratulate you. Frankly, I am pleased to see that you are being moved off of the Advisory Board. I myself am on more advisory boards than I can even remember, and not one of them ever asks me for advice.

DR. BLEVINS: I've had similar experiences, Senator, and this is why I took the unusual step of establishing an office within DODO headquarters in Cambridge, and spending time there on a regular basis. I'll now hand that off to Dr. Rudge, who I most certainly will be asking for advice on a regular basis.

HATCHER: How do you see that facility developing as we transition out of the CRONE phase? What does it look like in a year? Two years?

BLEVINS: As a very special hybrid of tech start-up, liberal arts college, and Special Forces base. Our present thinking suggests we'll need about a dozen kinds of specialists, divided into classes, such as tracker, fighter, entertainer, and so on. All of them will need immersive training in the language and ethos of whatever DTAP they go to. Meaning we also need to hire people to train them in those things—manners, customs, how to put on and take off clothes, fighting styles. All of that falls under the heading of the Diachronic Operative Resource Center, whose acting director will be my student, Dr. Melisande Stokes.

SENATOR EFFINGHAM: The budget and head count envisioned for DORC are impressive.

BLEVINS: The personnel expenses add up as quickly as the technical expenses. That's why the budget is as large as it is. We obviously can't outsource any of these services, given that there is evidence that the governments of **[REDACTED]** and **[REDACTED]** are already engaged in this kind of training program. Whoever works for us has to be kept very close to the mothership, as it were, and that kind of loyalty doesn't come cheap.

EFFINGHAM: How do you know that [REDACTED] and [REDACTED] are ahead of us in this?

BLEVINS: That's classified, Senator, even for the purposes of this hearing.

EFFINGHAM: Be that as it may, I question whether a linguistics student with no management experience is equipped to manage a department of that size.

BLEVINS: Yes. Most of the day-to-day burden of HR, facilities, and so on will fall under the Conventional/Contemporary Operations Department for which we have been fortunate to recruit a very able manager in Macy Stoll. With those managerial and administrative tasks out of the way, Dr. Stokes will be free to concentrate on the historical and linguistic research that is her specialty.

HATCHER: Well, I'm in no position to assess the technical requirements and their associated costs—I'll leave that to my honored colleagues on this hearing committee with more expertise in this field, such as Senator Effingham—but having compiled different staffs, for different purposes, over the years, I certainly feel capable of assessing your personnel hiring goals. So I will be submitting my opinion that the budget you seek is tied into your laying down very clear goals for who exactly you wish to hire, and why. That includes reports on all potential witches you'd be working with in other DTAPs. Can you do that for me?

BLEVINS: I'll see to it that Dr. Stokes writes up something specific, as soon as she has calmed Ms. Karpathy.

HATCHER: Out of curiosity—a curiosity I suspect is shared by other members of this panel—how exactly does one calm Ms. Karpathy?

BLEVINS: It always seems to help to listen to her spend a few uninterrupted minutes besmirching the reputations of certain people, with Colonel Lyons being a particularly frequent target of abuse.

HATCHER: Is it accurate to describe her, then, as a truculent and abusive team member?

LIEUTENANT COLONEL LYONS: If I may, Madame Chair, it is accurate to describe her as the only witch available to us at the present moment. That pretty much trumps any other description.

GENERAL FRINK: What Colonel Lyons is trying to say, Senator, is that unlike politicians, her job security does not depend on other people's approval.

BLEVINS: Not that General Frink is suggesting there's anything inappropriate about politicians having that dependency.

FRINK: Yeah, that's right. Thank you for clarifying that, Dr. Blevins.

BLEVINS: So to get back to the point, you're asking us to create two things. First, a personnel profile of our most desired hires. We're happy to do that. I can create a template as soon as this hearing is adjourned. Colonel Lyons and Dr. Stokes can help me out as their schedules allow. Second, a template for recording how we determine who to approach as a potential KCW.

HATCHER: That works for me. I yield the floor to my colleagues for further questions.

FROM LIEUTENANT GENERAL OCTAVIAN K. FRINK
TO ALL DODO DEPARTMENT HEADS
DAY 581 (MARCH, YEAR 2)

After several grueling days of congressional hearings, I am pleased to announce that DODO's budget has been approved and sent on to

POTUS for signature. All DODO staff are to be thanked for their hard work over the difficult months since the tragic and heroic demise of our friend and colleague Les Holgate. During that span of time DODO has been stripped down to the bare metal, as it were, and rebuilt into a new kind of organization that we can all be proud of.

New resources and responsibilities naturally bring organizational changes in their wake. Effective immediately, Dr. Roger Blevins is the overall head of the Department of Diachronic Operations, reporting directly to me, with a dotted line to Dr. Constantine Rudge at IARPA. To him will be reporting the heads of various subdepartments, as bulleted below:

- Dr. Melisande Stokes, acting head of the Diachronic Operative Resource Center.
- Macy Stoll, head of C/COD (Conventional/Contemporary Operations Department).
- Dr. Frank Oda, head of Research.
- Lieutenant Colonel Tristan Lyons, head of Diachronic Operations, which for obvious reasons will be organized and run along the lines of a military unit.

With Dr. Blevins's change in status, the Advisory Board is reduced, at least temporarily, to one member, that being Dr. Constantine Rudge.

I hope that the rest of you will join me in welcoming Ms. Stoll to the organization. Her long experience managing operational matters in various civilian and military environments will no doubt prove of enormous value to DODO during the coming era of rapid expansion.

Top-level direction on DODO's mission will be supplied during a meeting within the next few days at the Trapezoid.

Best wishes to all of you and may God bless America.

Gen. Octavian Frink

· ·

ABOUT ME

NAME: Mortimer Shore

OFFICIAL TITLE: Systems Administrator

UNOFFICIAL TITLES: What's-his-name, the Tall Guy with the Beard, the Sword Geek, the IT Guy, Hey, What the F*** Happened to my Email?

BIO: Hey all, as DODO keeps expanding there seems to be a lot of colorful rumor floating around about how I came to work here and so I thought I would tell the whole story.

TL;DR: I got recruited out of a park to prevent Tristan from getting his ass kicked in a swordfight and they found out I was a CS major.

EDIT: This is mostly about computers. If you are visiting this page because you are a DOer and you think you might be about to get into a swordfight, scroll to the end.

So, as you can probably tell from my appearance and mannerisms, I am California born and bred, my father and his father before him (heh) worked in commercial building construction in SoCal, punching out Home Depots and parking garages and making enough money to put me in a private school when I turned out to be kind of a screw-up academically. Turned out I was just bored and over-medicated LOL so they cut off my Adderall and put me on the robotics team where I made the mistake of telling them I knew how to weld (because of my dad's company) and so then I was just the welding slave for a long time until they finally let me start writing code. Long story short, I ended up at MIT doing both, which is to say, metal and code. The code part of it is pretty self explanatory: an MIT CS major can pretty much always get a job, a fact that was important to my dad who was paying a lot of money to put me through school.

As you have probably noticed if you work at DODO, I hang out near the server room. During my first six months at DODO I spent most of my time setting up ODIN, the Operational DODO Intranet. If that sounds like a long time, let me just say that getting a full-featured wiki to run under Shiny Hat is no picnic! I still put out IT fires and help people with their email, etc. when not working with Dr. Oda on the Chronotron. We're recruiting more IT staff to keep our systems stable and secure, so pretty soon I'll hopefully be a full-time Chronotron geek.

A word about metal. The substance, not the genre of music (though I like both!):

This is the part of my story that seems to cause the maximum amount of confusion and rumor among new hires at DODO and so this is the part you'll want to read if you are having trouble understanding why a newly minted MIT CS major is helping people with their email for a small gov't agency instead of making a zillion dollars in a start-up LOL.

My dad was a civil engineering major with a minor in metallurgy and so this runs in the family—a lot of commercial buildings are made out of steel, and in California where earthquakes are a problem there are a lot of rules around what kinds of steel to use, how to weld it properly, etc. I picked a lot of this up through osmosis when I was a kid, and when I was doing robotics in high school, and the smart kids wouldn't let me write code, I ended up doing a lot of industrial art: robots with flame throwers, rotating blades, etc. So, I ended up doing a double major in Comp Sci and metallurgy.

At this point I could say a lot about steel. A LOT. But I'm not going to. If you want to talk about steel FOR A LONG TIME, come by my desk with some beers LOL. Point is, I am a steel geek.

When you are a steel geek you inevitably end up talking about swords. Sort of like when you are a climber you end up talking about Mt. Everest.

I got interested in swords when I put some crappy homemade blades on one of my robots and they kept breaking/bending and I couldn't understand why.

My interest in swords led to an interest in swordfighting. Not modern fencing, which is cool and everything but totally different. I mean historical swordfighting with actual things that look like swords.

As a freshman I joined a LARPing group that did foam fighting on the Esplanade, but that was just a gateway drug to a real HEMA (Historical European Martial Arts) group that fought with real steel blades (blunt obviously) using documented historical techniques.

During one of our practices I was approached by Rebecca (East-Oda) who asked me a lot of questions. Not the usual dumb questions like "is that a real sword?" but like super nitty-gritty questions that clued me in something weird was going on. She took me back to her and Frank's house and NDAed me, and like ten minutes later I was with Tristan teaching him the Four Grounds and the Four Governors of George Silver, the Elizabethan backsword master who hated Italian rapier fighters with an unquenchable fiery hate LOL.

Later I found out I had passed a background check, and after I had peed in a jar and all the other stuff I was sworn in and have been working for DODO ever since—I guess seven or eight months now. I am responsible for having set up most of DODO's basic IT infrastructure such as the intranet, the wiki, etc. but don't hate on me because it was all supposed to be temporary LOL.

Dr. Frank Oda was also kind enough to take me under his wing and get me in on the ground floor of the Chronotron project. DISCLAIMER RE THAT: I am not a physicist and so all of the quantum mechanics underlying the chipset of the QUIPUs (the Quantum Information Processing Units) is totally incomprehensible to me. All I know about it is that it runs really, really fast and solves problems that would take forever using traditional non-quantum computation.

Fortunately for dumbass computer scientists like me, at one end of each QUIPU unit there's a connector where you can jack in a plain old Ethernet cable, and from that point onwards it just looks like a traditional computer, albeit a really fast and weird one, to the outside world. All of the cables from all of the QUIPUs (as of this writing, 128 of them—soon to be 256) feed into the Chronotron itself which, never mind what people say about it, is JUST A BIG OLD COMPUTING CLUSTER that happens to be tied in to a lot of historical databases, etc. Which is more my speed.

In layperson's terms: if it has to be dunked in liquid helium to work, I don't understand it. If it's in a rack with fans blowing on it, that's a different story.

—IF YOU ARE ABOUT TO BE IN A SWORDFIGHT—

This comes up a lot and I am working on upgrading the relevant wiki pages, but people seem to end up here anyway LOL.

My basic advice: DON'T DO IT! It is ridiculously, fantastically dangerous. Modern people are calibrated for a whole different level of danger acceptance.

Admittedly, an unfortunate precedent was set by Tristan's getting into a rapier-vs.-backsword duel in DTAP 1601 LONDON. This is fully documented in the relevant after-action reports, which, as our roster of DOers has expanded to include others in the "Fighter" class, have achieved somewhat legendary status within DODO. But this IN NO WAY suggests that swordfighting works as a standard operating procedure.

If you're in the process of getting "trained up" to carry out a specific DEDE (Direct Engagement for Diachronic Effect), you'll know that each DTAP has a highly localized weapons environment. What is true in one DTAP might not be the case in another that is fifty years or fifty miles away from it.

So, you have to start by knowing exactly what weapon type(s) can be carried by an individual of your assumed social class in your DTAP without freaking people out.

Since you're going back naked, you'll have to score weapons after arriving. If you're fortunate enough to be visiting a well-established node in DODO's witch network, there may be some weapons waiting for you there. In my copious spare time LOL I plan to visit those DTAPs to inspect the available weapons with the modern eye of a trained metallurgist and to check them for fatal flaws. But, never mind what you've seen on the History Channel, these people really didn't know dick about steel and so most of it is crap, and likely to break at the worst possible time.

If you are "breaking trail" in a new DTAP, then once you have evaded pursuit and stolen some clothes, you'll have to acquire your weapons in whatever way you can ("proceeding adaptively" LOL). This means evaluating them through visual inspection and, if possible, by subjecting them to certain simple tests which I can explain to you—eventually I'll document these on the wiki.

Assuming you have a good sword, you'll have to know how to fight with it. Which starts by defending yourself from the other guy. Which means you have to know how he fights. Which means learning the martial arts techniques prevailing in your DTAP. One day, I hope we'll have a vast library of every known historical swordfighting system, but as with so many other things at DODO we are just getting started—just scratching the surface. Here's what we are currently sort of good at:

- Late medieval backsword (a personal fave)
- Italian rapier
- Medieval longsword

Come and talk to me if you really think you need training/instruction in these. In the meantime, it helps if you're in some kind of decent physical condition and you know where your body is in space—we've had good luck with wrestlers, circus acrobats, gymnasts, and dancers. People who spend all day looking at pixels, not so good.

Stay tuned on ODIN for more relevant pages as I have time to write 'em!

Peace out
Mortimer

DODO WHITE PAPER

BRIEF NOTES ON "WENDING"
(formerly, "super-witches")
BY REBECCA EAST-ODA
Submitted to ODIN archive, Day 580

(Note to readers: Please consider this a temporary placeholder in lieu of a more thoroughly researched document to follow. I am feeling an urgency to head off the increasing use of the term "super-witch" and replace it with a more reasoned approach. —REO)

KCWs Fitch (colonial Boston) and Gráinne (Elizabethan London), while employing similar techniques in most respects, exhibited a marked difference in their understanding and utilization of Strands.

As best as we can make out, Goody Fitch had a general knowledge that multiple Strands existed, sufficient for her to conduct practical magical operations.

Gráinne, by contrast, appears to have had an additional ability that Goody Fitch didn't (and perhaps couldn't even have imagined). Namely, she had the ability to shift her stream of consciousness from one Strand to another, effectively inhabiting different versions of her body on different Strands. Gráinne jumped "sideways" from one to another as it suited her purposes. In this manner she was able to encounter and re-encounter Tristan on different Strands and thereby to collaborate more mindfully and effectively with him as he repeated the same DEDE.

"Wending" is a term used by Gráinne to describe this behavior.

Erszebet seems to be somewhere in between Fitch and Gráinne. She understands the concept of Wending and can speak about it, but seems to consider it a little beyond the pale of normal magical practice. Further conversations will be needed to better understand her misgivings on the topic. I can think of two possible explanations: (1) it is somehow dangerous or disagreeable, so Erszebet doesn't want to do it, or (2) Erszebet simply lacks the required degree of magical power and skill; understandable given she came of age as magic was waning.

The second hypothesis has led some within DODO to posit the idea that Gráinne is a "super-witch" with a degree of magical power that places her head and shoulders above other witches.

The "super-witch" concept is now beginning to influence DODO's planning process, as some members of the staff have begun looking for others of this type. It is supposed, for example, that Winnifred Dutton (1562 Antwerp) may be another "super-witch."

The purpose of this document is to discourage further use of the "super-witch" idea for which we really have no firm evidence yet, and instead request that DODO staff use the terminology "Wending" to describe the specific behavior we want. The ability to Wend will undoubtedly make a Known Compliant Witch (KCW) a more effective collaborator, and so let us seek out KCWs who know how to do it, rather than making the "super-witch" distinction which is not supported by evidence and which is pejorative to Erszebet Karpathy—the one witch we actually have to work with in the present day.

Diachronicle
DAY 584 (EARLY MARCH, YEAR 2)

In which everything expands

AS DODO EXPANDED, THE ORGANIZATIONAL hierarchy, and its
attendant bureaucracy, evolved accordingly. It was both electric
and irritating to witness a corporation blooming around us, leaving us sometimes marooned in the middle of it. I was grateful for
Mortimer, the IT ~~geek~~ specialist, who brought a touch of whimsy
to the chunks of that bureaucracy he managed. Even more grateful than I was Rebecca, whom DODO decided to hire given that
she was frequently underfoot anyhow, not only asking lots of intelligent questions but frequently answering them. She was also
very good with Erszebet, and that could be said about nobody else
except myself, who was increasingly beleaguered with procedural
developments. Once Mortimer got the intranet (ODIN) up and
running it began to take up ~~too much fucking bandwidth~~ a lot of
my time.

It also altered how we did things. Within a matter of months
Tristan and I went from being almost Siamese twins to actually
seeing each other in person only at the (snazzy new) snack bar or
the occasional lunch out; most of our engagement was via ODIN
channels. This had an odd effect on our friendship: after the electricity of first meeting, there had been a frisson between us that
we never acknowledged (although it was strong enough for others
to comment upon)—but we certainly enjoyed it. (Or at least, I
confess to enjoying it, and to perceiving within him clues that
he did as well.) Then, spending so much time together, we grew
accustomed to our closeness, so that we went from not-quite-first-
date to old-married-couple almost seamlessly.

Until ODIN came along.

Once Tristan became just an icon on the nearest screen, I often forgot that he was a living, breathing, winsome Male, and so when we would encounter each other—in the copy room, grabbing a handful of grapes, waiting for a meeting with Blevins . . . that initial electricity, that exquisitely repressed well-*hello*-there energy, erupted all over again, and never quite settled because we were never in each other's presence continuously for quite long enough.

THE ONE EXCEPTION was in early March of the second year. Tristan and I flew to DC for a meeting with General Frink and Dr. Rudge at the Trapezoid. I will only detail the mental takeaway, but the emotional and visceral takeaway was that I got to spend two entire plane rides alone in a private plane with a ~~hot bad-ass dude~~ handsome gentleman, who crossed his legs carefully when I looked at him too long and who could make me grin inwardly (only inwardly, I assure you) merely by uttering my surname in a particular tone. Now that I know there will never be such plane rides again, I wish to state that despite the violation of DODO's baroque sexual harassment policy, it really is ~~a fucking shame~~ regrettable that we did not make better use of that privacy.

But I digress. Back to the mental takeaway:

Based on Oda-sensei's most recent estimates, the goal became to have a fully functioning Chronotron by the end of the year, at which point we would be able to undertake formally planned DEDEs—DODO's chartered purpose. Meanwhile, we would postpone any outcome-oriented missions. No more moneymaking gambits, etc. After the Chronotron was online, we would be able to run such missions far more safely and efficiently.

In the meantime, those of us on the payroll would not be idle.

Do not think it, reader! As well as the office-speak mumbo-jumbo to become familiar with, there were still certain diachronic jaunts it was deemed safe to undergo, those being:

First and above all, to seek out and convert witches and other abettors, thus creating a network of Known Compliant Witches (KCWs) and safe houses.

Second, to fill in the data gaps the Chronotron noted as it was uploading digitized information from primary and secondary historical material—in other words, factoid-finding missions (what did a particular intersection in Rome look like in 44 BC; how large were daikon in pre-modern Japan; where *did* George Washington sleep the night of 11 January, 1779, etc.). Not only was this useful for the Chronotron data workers, but it would also help us to break in new recruits with low-stakes missions.

Third (in a similar vein), to make reconnaissance missions to DTAPs we knew would be important for future work. Chief amongst these was Constantinople circa 1203 (more on that in a moment) and Renaissance London, both of which would be major hubs within the KCW network.

Fourth, we were free to rove for the purposes of counter-intelligence: to keep an eye on potential diachronic activities of our strategic rivals. Not that the identity of those rivals had been shared with us.

As to Constantinople. That jewel in the crown of the Byzantine Empire. That continent-straddling stronghold of the Eastern Orthodox Church. That famously inviolable walled city ruled by ~~generations of interbred usurping nut-jobs~~ a pantheon of families so tortuously intertwined as to be the basis of our modern adjective *byzantine*. This was a fantastically complex city with a wide range of languages and cultures, so it was required to build up a large database including not just linguistics but maps, etiquette, cultural practices, weapons, and other things that our DOers would need to know in order to function in that time and place—the time being circa 1203, the Fourth Crusade (not, for the history buffs among you, the siege a few days later, or the occupation, or the ~~final shitstorm~~ destruction of the city, but Galata Tower). A lot of that research fell into my lap, in my role as head of the amusingly named Diachronic Operative Resource Center.

The DNI (that would be Frink) wished to stabilize certain national and ethnic frontiers in Eastern Europe, the Balkans, and Turkey that had begun to show considerable GLAAMR—an indication that Someone Else might be conducting diachronic operations in an effort to shift them. Between Erszebet's iPad Quipu (her IQ, as it were) and Frank Oda tapping into the elemental quipus of the Chronotron, we were able to calculate backwards that our best counter-action was to move a particular Orthodox relic from one tent to another in the Byzantine Emperor's army camp when his army fled from the Crusaders after the siege of Galata Tower.

Regarding the developments of the witch network: as well as Constantinople 1203, we also sought KCWs in a range of intermediate eras and locations where we perceived it would be easier for us to conduct operations (or, as I might have said before I learned to talk the talk, "do things"). New ODECs were being built, but as we had only one witch—who was temperamental on the best of days—we had to "leverage" (General Frink's term) Erszebet by having her Send DOers to familiar locations: pre-1851 safe houses where we had KCWs who could then forward our agents onward through the network.

The "trunk line" of the network, so to speak, was to be anchored at one end in 1203 Constantinople and on the other in 1602 London, where we had re-established connections with Gráinne and her friend Rose. Thanks to Rose's intercession, we now had access to a secure safe house on the outskirts of the city, equipped with clothes, weapons, and other DOer resources. The other major stop on the line needed to be Antwerp circa 1560, for reasons beyond the scope of this narrative. I had attempted to cultivate a relationship there with one Winnifred Dutton, an English witch resident in that DTAP. Knowing her own worth (she had admirably influential family relations and appeared capable of Wending), she was standoffish toward my initial queries; eventually she decided she would assist us in exchange for a certain hard-to-find herb known as kalonji.

Rather conveniently for us, kalonji grew in profusion in the palace garden of Blachernae . . . in thirteenth-century Constantinople.

Post by Dr. Roger Blevins to Dr. Melisande Stokes
on private ODIN channel, 15:32:37
DAY 584 (EARLY MARCH, YEAR 2)

Dr. Stokes:

...

Post by Dr. Roger Blevins to Dr. Melisande Stokes
on private ODIN channel, 15:32:59
DAY 584 (EARLY MARCH, YEAR 2)

Dr. Stokes:

...

Post by Dr. Roger Blevins to Dr. Melisande Stokes
on private ODIN channel, 15:33:07
DAY 584 (EARLY MARCH, YEAR 2)

Dr. Stokes:

...

Post by Dr. Roger Blevins to Dr. Melisande Stokes
on private ODIN channel, 15:52:34
DAY 584 (EARLY MARCH, YEAR 2)

Dr. Stokes:

Disregard previous posts. I had to find Mortimer Shore (on the roof of the building engaging in what appeared to be a sword duel) and get him to explain to me the proper usage, in the modern world, of what I call the "return," and he denominates the "enter," key.

I'm losing track of the different types of DOers. Could I trouble you or Lieutenant Colonel Lyons to post a canonical taxonomy?

Cordially,

Roger

DODO MEMORANDUM

CANONICAL TAXONOMY OF DIACHRONIC OPERATIVE TYPES
BY LTC TRISTAN LYONS
POSTED Day 585

For clarity in internal communication and record-keeping, please employ these terms, and these terms ONLY, when referring to different types or categories of DOers. If you think of some other new category that needs to be added, please see me or Dr. Stokes before editing this list.

FORERUNNER

(deprecated synonyms: SUICIDE BOMBER, DEAD MAN RUNNING, SCHNEIDER)

One who is Sent to a DTAP in which DODO has no Known Compliant Witch, safe house, or other contacts/infrastructure whatsoever. Considered the most elite and difficult-to-recruit subclass of DOer, Forerunners must possess all the skills of a STRIDER (see below) combined with those of a FIGHTER, LOVER, or CLOSER.

FIGHTER

(deprecated synonyms: CONAN, WARRIOR)

One who specializes in missions where, to put it politely, martial attributes are of the essence. Since every DTAP has a unique environment surrounding weapons, fighting styles, and martial culture, competence in fighting is only a part of the skill set required to be a successful Fighter. It is equally important to know how and when to fight.

LOVER

(deprecated synonyms: REDACTED)

Seems self-explanatory. But to counter some misconceptions, actually having sex is not part of the job description. We prefer to focus on the unique combination of personal charm, appearance, and social skills needed to influence historical decision makers who have been identified as "libido-motivated."

CLOSER

A new category best described as LOVER without the carnal element. One who is highly skilled at changing someone's mind without hurting or seducing them.

STRIDER

(deprecated synonyms: SNAKE EATER)

Wilderness survival expert.

SPY

Specialist in stealthy, unobtrusive observation and (since we can't bring notes/sketches home with us) memorization.

SAGE

Subject matter expert, such as a historian or linguist, sent to a DTAP to investigate a specific question of interest to DODO.

MACGYVER

Typically a biologist, chemist, materials scientist, or engineer with exceptional aptitude for building devices, concocting medicines, etc., using natural and man-made substances available in a given DTAP.

MEDIC

Medical professional with additional training required for practice in pre-modern conditions.

A final note: the above are not mutually exclusive. More often than not, a given DOer will fit into more than one of these categories.

Post by LTC Tristan Lyons on "Recruiting" ODIN channel
DAY 620 (EARLY APRIL, YEAR 2)

As has been noted repeatedly by Dr. Blevins and others higher up the chain of command, recruitment of DOers has proceeded more slowly than we would like. Finding people with the right combination of security clearance, skill set, and physical attributes is a very demanding challenge. I've lost track of the number of promising candidates we've had to reject because of dental work alone.

As DORC continues to staff up new HOSMAs (Historical Operations Subject Matter Authorities) and trainers, we'll increasingly be able to "grow our own" DOers by selecting promising candidates and training them in the requisite languages and skills. We've already seen progress in that area with new HOSMAs coming online almost daily, specializing in the languages and cultures of late medieval Europe and the Byzantine Empire. But a DOer can only learn a language so fast.

In the meantime, we are therefore going to have to rely on a small number of extremely exceptional people who just happen to walk in the door with all the capabilities we need—needles in a very large haystack. Fortunately, General Frink and Dr. Rudge have been active in connecting us to the existing recruitment networks that the United States Government and its allies have established in the military and intelligence sectors, giving us broader access to the aforementioned haystack and enabling us to search through it more efficiently.

I'm pleased to announce that today we have signed our first two DOer recruits: Chira Lajani and Felix Dorn. Both were recruited specifically with an eye towards the upcoming kalonji DEDEs, which as you all know is the linchpin of our plan for establishing a really solid safe house in 1562 Antwerp. Because of her unusual linguistic skill set, we also believe that Chira will be DODO's pathfinder in 1200 Constantinople, which is projected to be the focal point of many diachronic operations in the first year or two of DODO's operations.

Chira and Felix came to us through very different recruitment pathways. Chira first came to the attention of U.S. Intelligence talent scouts active in the Syrian refugee community. Considered too physically conspicuous for conventional intelligence work, she was brought to our attention as someone fitting the "Lover" profile. Felix, by contrast, is an old friend and mentor of mine whom I recruited over a beer. Their dossiers are available on the ODIN system for those of you curious to know more about our newest colleagues. Please join me in making Chira and Felix feel welcome in the Department of Diachronic Operations!

—Tristan

DODO HUMAN RESOURCES

PERSONNEL DOSSIER

FAMILY NAME: Lajani

GIVEN NAME(S): Chira Yasin

ALIAS(ES): Cyl

AGE: 24

CLASS: Lover

HEIGHT: 5'3"

EYES: Brown

HAIR: Brown

COMPLEXION: Medium/olive

DISTINCTIVE FEATURES: Mole near left clavicle

ETHNICITY: Kurd

NATIONALITY: Syrian

LANGUAGE FLUENCY RATINGS:

   Kurdish: 5

   English, Zaza-Gorani, Turkish: 4

   Farsi, Syrian, and Iranian Arabic: 3

   Bulgarian, Greek: 2

   NOTE: Following immersive training in medieval Hebrew as
   preparation for kalonji DEDE, subject scored 2.5 fluency rating in
   that language, however the score is at best speculative given our
   uncertain knowledge base.

RELIGION: Non-observant Muslim

CITIZENSHIP: Stateless, being fast-tracked for U.S. citizenship

BIOGRAPHY: Upper-middle class secular Muslim from Kobani (Ayn al-
   Arab). At the age of 16, lived in United States (Issaquah, Washington)
   for 9 months as part of a foreign exchange program. Attended Cornell
   University. Psychology major, Dance minor. Dropped out in sophomore

year when parents publicly decapitated by IS forces. Pretended to be
ISIS sympathizer on social media, flew to Istanbul, traveled overland
to border region with intention of crossing Syrian border. En route, fell
in with and entered into sexual relationship with male MI6 agent also
masquerading as ISIS recruit. With him, crossed border into Syria
and returned to Kobani to protect younger sister (15) and brother (13).
During subsequent military operations, escaped from Kobani with her
siblings and crossed back into Turkey, made way overland to Bodrum,
crossed over to Greek island of Kos in inflatable boat, joined refugee
community on Kos. There recognized the body language of American
DODO recruiter who was posing as a refugee. Approached him. Her
story cross-checked with accounts on file from the MI6 agent. Agreed to
work for DODO in exchange for her and her siblings being fast-tracked
for American citizenship.

SKILL SET: Besides languages (above) and keen assessment of body
language (above), extremely fit, hardy, able to stay calm in high-stress and
physically challenging circumstances; dancer (modern, jazz, bellydance);
history and affect suggests aptitude for emotional/psychological
persuasiveness and manipulation. Well-spoken with broad Western-
style liberal arts education. Appealing face and figure by most cultures'
metrics.

LIMITATIONS: Minimal self-defense or martial arts experience. Incapable
of being inconspicuous or subtle, even when wearing burka. Do not send
on missions requiring stealth or delicate negotiations. Comfortable in
cosmopolitan and suburban settings; rural and slum settings not so
good.

DODO HUMAN RESOURCES

PERSONNEL DOSSIER

FAMILY NAME: Dorn

GIVEN NAME(S): Felix John

ALIAS(ES): N/A

AGE: 31

CLASS: Strider

HEIGHT: 5'9"

EYES: Hazel

HAIR: Brown

COMPLEXION: Light

DISTINCTIVE FEATURES: Appears to squint (actually has 20/15 vision); slight stutter on the letter L

ETHNICITY: American of Austrian/German/Dutch heritage

NATIONALITY: U.S.

LANGUAGE FLUENCY RATINGS:

  American English: 5

  German: 4

  French, Spanish: 3

  NOTE: As part of preparation for kalonji DEDE, underwent immersive training in medieval Hebrew (fluency rating 1.5), Byzantine Greek (2), and medieval Dutch (2).

RELIGION: Non-observant Lutheran

CITIZENSHIP: American

BIOGRAPHY: Raised in middle-class home in CT, father owned auto shop, mother a nurse, formerly for Médecins Sans Frontières. Dyslexic. Majored in PhysEd at UConn, emphasis on cross-country and wilderness survival skills. Former USA Olympic track & field team, took bronze in Marathon. Worked at Outward Bound, involved in various "extreme sports" activities including cliff jumping, rock climbing, Parkour.

RECRUITMENT: Personal contact by LTC Tristan Lyons, whom he met while leading a rock-climbing expedition (Lyons 14 at the time). They became friends, and continued to engage in wilderness-oriented athletic activities together.

SKILL SET: Extremely fit, hardy, capable of functioning under punishing physical circumstances (natural or man-made). Physically nondescript enough to "blend into crowd" in most Caucasian populations. Decent MacGyver-like capabilities. Loyalty unshakable.

LIMITATIONS: Dyslexic, not comfortable in conversationally dependent situations. More comfortable in rural than urban/suburban surroundings.

Post by Mortimer Shore
on "General" ODIN channel
DAY 622

Hey all,

In the wake of yesterday's incident in the cafeteria line, Macy Stoll has asked me to post a few safety tips that y'all should keep in mind until such time as we can print up posters, establish training programs, etc.

Just as background, the requirement for Fighter-class Diachronic Operatives (DOers) to achieve and maintain proficiency in various historical martial arts styles entails wearing, transporting, storing, and using a wide range of historical weapons and weapon simulators on premises. No single, blanket policy can cover all such cases, but here are some general rules:

- Scabbards are trip hazards! Glance down before stepping behind a swordfighter.
- Assume all blades are razor sharp.
- If you see something falling out of a scabbard, don't try to catch it.

DODO WHITE PAPER

UDET: OR, DIACHRONIC MISSION DURATION

BY REBECCA EAST-ODA

Submitted to ODIN archive, Day 622

The recent influx of funding and new personnel has led DODO staff to look more deeply into certain aspects of how diachronic operations are conducted that hitherto we had just taken for granted. In particular, the need to schedule complex missions, such as the upcoming kalonji-related DEDEs, has forced us to think in greater detail about the duration of missions and how many can be scheduled in a given span of time.

Most of DODO's experience has centered on the colonial Boston and Elizabethan London DEDEs conducted last year by Dr. Stokes and LTC Lyons respectively. Both of these were of relatively brief duration. Dr. Stokes was able to accomplish her tasks in the course of a single day. With the exception of the first repetition, LTC Lyons's DEDE was a "sleepover" in which he had to spend one night at the DTAP. In all of these cases, the responsible witches (KCWs Karpathy, Fitch, and Gráinne) acted in a way that preserved "Unity of DOer-Experienced Time," hereinafter UDET. The idea of UDET is simple and can be quickly explained: if Dr. Stokes experienced eight hours of elapsed time during her mission in colonial Boston, then the same span of time separated her being Sent by Karpathy from the ODEC to the DTAP and her reappearance in the ODEC upon being returned home by KCW Fitch. Likewise, when LTC Lyons spent approximately twenty-four hours in the 1601 London DTAP, the same amount of elapsed time occurred between his being Sent there and his being "Homed" by KCW Gráinne. UDET means that from the point of view of the DOer as well as observers in the facility, it is as if the DOer walked through a door into another room, spent eight or twenty-four hours there, and then walked back through the same door.

This does not pose a serious inconvenience for short missions. By contrast, however, the nature of the kalonji DEDE is such that it cannot be accomplished in less than approximately two months. For those unfamiliar with the premise of this DEDE, a short explanation follows: we are attempting to recruit Winnifred Dutton, a potential KCW in Antwerp circa 1560. The only way we have found to motivate her is by supplying her with samples of an herb called kalonji, which is rare and nearly unobtainable in her time and place. We have found a source for kalonji seeds in Constantinople circa 1200, which is a DTAP of interest to us anyway. The current plan of record is to send one DOer to 1200 Constantinople to obtain the seeds. She will then hand them off to a wilderness survival expert (Strider class) who will carry them overland to Belgium and sow them in a known location where we think that they will thrive. It should then be possible to visit that location circa 1560 and harvest the herb in the wild. The plan's primary drawback is that the overland journey from Constantinople to Belgium is projected to take two months, and it will have to be repeated on at least three Strands in order for it to "take." Our Strider will therefore have to experience a total of at least six months of (our) elapsed time in that DTAP.

If the mission is performed in a way that preserves UDET, then the Strider will indeed be absent for a total of six months.

If, on the other hand, we can arrange for the Strider to be "Homed" from 1200 Belgium only a few minutes after he is Sent to 1200 Constantinople, then the entire series of missions could be conducted in less than a day, as time is perceived by those of us here in modern-day Boston. The Strider would still be six months older at the end of it, and would have six months' worth of memories from his journeys, but the clock, as far as DODO is concerned, would only have advanced a few hours.

The latter procedure is obviously a more efficient use of time as far as DODO is concerned. Moreover, to the extent DODO is engaged in a competition versus the diachronic operations agencies of foreign powers, we must assume that our adversaries are making use of such optimization wherever possible and are getting their jobs done that much more quickly.

This is a topic that has been on several people's minds for some months now and that has been brought to the front burner, as it were, by the kalonji DEDE planning process. Initial attempts to raise the question with KCW Erszebet Karpathy proved unavailing, as the very idea of it made very little sense to her and could seemingly gain no purchase on her mind; she could not make heads or tails of what it was that we were asking her to do, much less express an opinion on it, and repeatedly accused us of being demented or insane. As the overall emotional tone was becoming counterproductive, I was asked to work with her on the topic, since I have known her for longer than most DODO employees, and she trusts me on the basis of the belief that I am descended from witches and that I have some latent magical ability. The results of my inquiry are detailed below. A top-level summary is that **DEDE time compression does not appear to be a practical option**, largely because witches have great difficulty even understanding the idea, and consider it to be reckless, far-fetched, and childish. The best analogy I can think of is how a modern physicist would react if you approached him and proposed to travel at greater than the speed of light. Mixed with this is a little bit of how Chopin would react if you proposed to play a piano by striking it with a sledgehammer.

Detailed Analysis

Witches' objections to DEDE time compression (to the extent they can even fathom the idea) can apparently be broken down into two general categories: one, the asymmetry between Sending and Homing a time traveler, and two, the risk of something akin to present-day Diachronic Shear.

1. SENDING/HOMING ASYMMETRY:

Non-witches are apt to think of "Sending" (moving a DOer from an ODEC back in time to a DTAP) and "Homing" (the reverse process) as the same thing, but it turns out that from the witch's point of view they are entirely different spells. The contrasts are explained in the following table.

SENDING	HOMING
Back in time	Forward in time
Once Sent to the past, the DOer can take actions that might affect the present-day reality of the Sending witch, the DOer him/herself, etc.	Once Homed back to the present day, the DOer's actions cannot affect the past reality of the Homing witch, etc.
The DTAP is terra incognita to both the Sending witch and the DOer, must be extensively researched beforehand from historical documents, maps, and scrying.	The destination is perfectly familiar to the DOer but unknown, and nearly unimaginable, to the Homing witch, for whom it is in the distant future.
The DOer is moving from their natural time and place to one where they are an unnatural intrusion.	The DOer is moving from a place where they fundamentally do not belong, back to their natural time and place.

For these reasons, witches think of Sending and Homing as asymmetrical, and fundamentally different, spells. Sending is much more difficult, first of all because it entails more advance prep work if it is not to produce a random result, and secondly because it means working against the natural flow of time.

An analogy might be made to a rubber band connecting the DOer to their natural time and place. When the DOer is Sent to a past DTAP, the rubber band is stretched, which requires more effort and more focus on the witch's part if the DOer is not to end up in the wrong place. When the same DOer is Homed, it is as if their connection to the DTAP is simply severed by the Homing witch. The "rubber band" yanks the DOer unerringly back to the ODEC from which they were Sent. Indeed, if this were not the case, diachronic operations would not be possible at all. In the case of Dr. Stokes's colonial Boston DEDE, how could KCW Fitch possibly have returned Dr. Stokes to the ODEC in modern-day Boston—a time, place, and environment beyond her imagining—if not for this "snap-back" effect?

The "rubber band" feature of Homing is therefore fundamental to DODO's ability to do anything at all. But there is a catch: if the DOer has experienced eight hours, or seventeen days, in the DTAP, the "rubber band" yanks them back to the ODEC eight hours or seventeen days after they departed.

Compressing mission time by returning the DOer to an earlier moment is, therefore, not simply a matter of using the Homing spell in a different way—turning the knobs to different settings, as it were. It would require a different spell altogether. And the witch performing it would have to have some prior familiarity with the future DTAP in order to "aim" the DOer in the correct "direction."

2. SHEAR RISK:

Witches appear to have a nose for situations apt to produce Diachronic Shear. Mission duration compression seems to be one of those. If a homebound DOer can be Homed back to the "wrong" time (i.e., earlier than the natural snap-back time) then they could just as well be sent home *before they departed*, which would lead to a situation in which two copies of the same DOer were existing in the same time and place.

Other absurd or paradoxical situations could be imagined. Let us say that a twenty-year-old DOer were Sent back to a DTAP where they lived for sixty years, then Homed to a point in time only a fraction of a second after their departure. From the point of view of an observer in the ODEC, it would be as if the twenty-year-old were instantaneously replaced by an eighty-year-old.

Such possibilities are deeply distressing to witches, who seem to see in them a kind of moral and aesthetic abomination.

To sum up, it appears that the idea of compressing mission duration is a non-starter. From the witches' point of view, it requires getting a compliant witch in the distant past to undertake an unfamiliar spell of extreme difficulty, all to achieve an end result that is viewed as both insanely risky and viscerally repugnant.

We are, therefore, stuck with UDET for the foreseeable future, and it seems safe to say that our adversaries are in the same boat. DODO personnel planning the kalonji seed DEDE, or other time-consuming missions, will have to take that reality into account. Fortunately, we have the luxury of time at the moment since we are awaiting the completion of the Chronotron.

DODO MEMORANDUM

POLICY ON OFFICIAL JARGON AND ACRONYM COINAGE
BY MACY STOLL, MBA
POSTED Day 623

Now that I've had time to settle in to my new role as head of C/COD (that is DODO's Conventional/Contemporary Operations Department, for those of you who have been tucked away in exotic DTAPs during the recent organizational upgrades), I'm beginning to see opportunities for optimizing and perfecting the way DODO operates on a day-to-day basis. In coming weeks we're going to be challenging ourselves to implement new procedures and policies that will help ensure that the taxpayers get the most for their hard-earned dollars, even though hopefully none of them will ever know of DODO's existence.

Communications becomes all-important in a large organization. Informal practices that worked well when it was just a few friends sitting around a table at the Apostolic Café may no longer be well adapted to a large agency that spans not only the globe, but most of recorded history as well.

In that spirit I would like to take up the subject of jargon and acronyms.

Now, before any of you old DODO hands beats me to it, I'll stipulate that jargon and acronyms are a staple of many large modern organizations, especially in the military and intelligence sectors, where documents sometimes look like a bowl of alphabet soup. I know that perfectly well from my twenty years of experience in such environments.

Even so, I was taken aback when I first came to the Department of Diachronic Operations and began to experience a whole new world of exotic terminology and funny strings of letters. Diachronic Shear, Strands, ODECs, QUIPUs, DOers, and more! Now, some of these I think are clear and good terms to use, such as DOer, which is self-explanatory, and DEDE, which I now understand is just an alternate spelling of "deed." But in some cases I do sort of get the idea that a very clever person, perhaps someone from an advanced academic background where wordplay is a kind of sport, is trying to have a teeny little joke at my expense. And maybe also trying to poke fun, in a sly way, at the military world that has brought us so many brave defenders of our freedoms such as LTC Lyons and the late General Schneider. For example, lately we have begun to see DORC for Diachronic Operative Resource Center and DOOSH for Diachronic Operative Occupational Safety and Health. Perhaps those of you who have been putting so much of your creative energies into dreaming up these hilarious acronyms might consider putting yourselves into the shoes of Dr. Blevins when he has to give a tour of the facility to a senator or a general, or a foreign visitor from one of our allies, and finds himself having to explain why such terms are stenciled on doors and bandied about on official letterhead. It certainly doesn't send the message that all the brainpower we've gathered together under this roof is being applied in the most productive manner, does it?

To impose a little order on all of this creative chaos, and to ensure that none of the taxpayers' money is wasted as the result of inefficient communications, I'm putting into place a new Policy on Official Jargon and Acronym Coinage. You'll find full details and procedures in the attached PowerPoint deck, which I encourage you all to peruse at your leisure. Existing acronyms, where widely adopted, can of course be "grandfathered in," but those of you seeking to add new terms to DODO's specialized lexicon will need to abide by the procedures spelled out in the deck.

Exchange of posts between Dr. Melisande Stokes
and LTC Tristan Lyons on private ODIN channel
AFTERNOON AND EVENING, DAY 623

Post from Dr. Stokes:

Re: POOJAC (Policy on Official Jargon etc. . . .)

Tristan—do you want to break the news to her, or should I?

Reply from LTC Lyons:

Stokes, I know. Everyone's talking about it. Shut up. The first one who calls it POOJAC to her face is going to come off either as a malcontent or a snitch. If it's the former, you're going to end up on a PEP.

From Dr. Stokes:

PEP?

From LTC Lyons:

Try to keep up, Stokes. PEP = Performance Enhancement Plan. It's what you get assigned to when you are in trouble.

From Dr. Stokes:

First I've heard of it. Has "PEP" gone through POOJAC?

From LTC Lyons:

What you're not getting is that THIS IS ALL PUBLIC. It doesn't matter how secure the Shiny Hat operating system is, Stokes, when the subpoena comes through from the Inspector General, all of what you're writing ends up in public.

From Dr. Stokes:

Just making an observation.

Post by Macy Stoll, Head of C/COD,
on "General" ODIN channel
DAY 623

All, there seems to be some confusion brewing in the wake of my memorandum concerning the Policy on Official Jargon and Acronym Coinage. While I am aware that the letters spell out POOJAC (a non-sense word—don't waste your time Googling it!), this is *not* an approved substitute for the full name of the aforementioned Policy. Remember, the entire point of the Policy is to establish an approved procedure for coining new terminology, and so to refer to the Policy as POOJAC is in and of itself a violation of the Policy.

You can easily spell out the full name of the Policy, or copy-paste if you are in that much of a hurry.

I realize that it's something of a mouthful to use in conversation. Around the office, we have taken to calling it the Jargon and Acronym Policy, and I encourage the rest of you to follow suit.

Follow-up from Stoll, two hours later:
In the wake of a very respectful and sensitive exchange of feelings with Dr. Oda, I would like to amend the above to "Acronym and Jargon Policy." Please refer to DODO's Diversity Policy for more on these matters, which we take extremely seriously.

Follow-up from Stoll, one hour later:
I have been made aware that our Diversity Policy is still being drafted. I assumed we had one in place already, but the unusual operational environment of DODO apparently makes it more complicated. In the meantime let's all just use common sense, please.

AFTER ACTION REPORT

DEBRIEFER: Dr. Melisande Stokes

DOER: Chira Yasin Lajani

THEATER: Constantinople

OPERATION: Antwerp witch recruitment

DEDE: Obtain/secure viable kalonji seeds for later p/u

DTAP: Blachernae Palace, Constantinople, August 1202

STRAND: Fourth and last repetition of this DEDE

Note: Will avoid undue repetition of physical details, etc. from previous three Strands.

Erszebet Sent Chira via ODEC #2 at 11:15 of Day 626, without incident.

Chira materialized in the unlit brick bathhouse of the women's apartments of Blachernae Palace. We had already confirmed a witch in Blachernae on previous Strands: Basina, illegitimate granddaughter of Empress Irene (née Bertha).

Chira arrived in the dark hours of the morning but moonlight shone in to give illumination to the room. (She has drawn detailed diagram of bathhouse, scanned and converted to 3-D renderings; refer to DORC Cartographic and Architectural Database.) General setting: large striated-brick hall with marble baths heated from below, running water available via lead pipes.

From prep research combined with past Strand experience, she knew that for efficiency in plumbing, the laundry was beside the bath-houses, and a connecting room between the two held cabinets with clean shmatas/drab shifts to be worn by women working in either chamber. After waiting in the shadows to ensure that the coast was clear, she moved quietly to this cabinet and donned one; it would pass as a servant's nightdress.

Chira found a small amphora, filled it with water, and carried it from the bathhouse to the stairs for the Empress's apartments. Nearing the foot of the stairs, she encountered two armed Varangian Guards (for more on what we know of the arms and armor of this class of fighter, refer to Mortimer Shore's MARS [Martial Arts Research Summary] #12). She approached them carrying the amphora. They challenged her in accented Greek; she identified herself as a new servant of Basina's, sent to fetch her mistress scented water for a headache. The taller guard was about to let her go, but the shorter one expressed skepticism and proposed accompanying her back upstairs.

Speaking in what might have been a Norman dialect, the taller Varangian rebuked the shorter one. Chira cannot understand circa 1200 Norman, beyond some ability to pick out French and Anglo-Saxon loan words. Having been on this DEDE several times now, she is fairly certain that the topic of conversation was a woman named Candida. Body language, facial expression, tone of voice, and one unmistakable Anglo-Saxon word all suggested that the short Varangian was seeking an excuse to visit Candida in the middle of the night for the purposes of sexual intercourse, and that the taller Varangian disapproved of it.

The short, horny Varangian disagreed with this assessment and, as proof of its inaccuracy, suggested he remain below while the tall one accompany Chira upstairs to Basina. Tall one agreed to this and marched Chira up three broad, shallow flights of marble steps, finally arriving at tall, decorated double doors, visible as a tangerine-colored sunrise was coming in through windows overlooking the stairwell.

At this point, more Varangian Guards challenged them, speaking in Anglo-Saxon, which Chira also does not speak. After a brief conversation, during which Chira's physical endowments were obviously being closely assessed, she and the tall Varangian were allowed into the antechamber of the apartments, made of marble with serpentine inlaid heavily in patterns on the floor; high ceilings; eunuchs in abundance. Chira was handed over to one of them, and tall Varangian was dismissed. The eunuch took her into a chamber with windows overlooking a courtyard.

This room had golden-tiled ceilings and smelled of incense. A woman in her early thirties (Basina) was in the central, extremely ornate bed; there were smaller beds along the walls, and four younger women dressed in long silk gowns were preparing Basina's jewelry and wardrobe for her. They looked startled by the early morning intrusion. The eunuch presented Chira to Basina saying, "Your Ladyship, this woman was found by guards at the bottom of the stairs, claiming she was your handmaiden."

Basina stared at Chira with a slightly mocking air, as if she could not believe an assassin had been stupid enough to approach from such a direct route. Chira met the look calmly, held out the amphora, and said, "The scented water for your headache, m'lady." She spoke with a small reassuring smile, and then winked at Basina.

Basina showed no reaction at all to the wink. After a few more heartbeats, she instructed the eunuch, "Leave her here and wait outside." The eunuch released her and left.

Before the door had closed, the four young women had surrounded Chira at a distance of perhaps a yard, each with a hand on the eating-knife at her belt (see Mortimer Shore's MARS #19 for more on these; they are short blades, nominally for cutting food during meals, not considered weapons, but obviously capable of being used as such).

"What are you wearing under that?" asked Basina of the shift. "That's from the bathhouse. I would never dress my servants so poorly." She had a low voice and spoke slowly, sounding sardonically amused.

Chira set down the amphora and in one smooth gesture pulled the shift over her head; it dropped to the ground at her feet, leaving her nude. Basina continued to stare at her, now a little appraisingly. "I see," she said. Her attendants sniggered slightly but she made a harsh, word-less noise of disapproval and they all instantly went silent. Finally Basina asked, "Are you a gift? Who sent you?"

"Someone who would be your friend," said Chira.

Basina smiled, then chuckled like a contented hen. "Everyone wants to be my friend," she said. "Most of them bore me."

"I am sent from someone who will not bore you," Chira said. "But I am under instructions to reveal more only when we are alone together."

"We're alone," said Basina comfortably. "My women are nothing but an extension of me."

Adopting a very gentle tone of voice—almost sympathetic—Chira said, "I have reason to believe that might not be true." Basina frowned and sat up, throwing the sheets off of herself. The clutch of attendants stepped in closer and brandished their eating-knives.

"Who says so?" demanded Basina. Chira met her gaze and said noth-ing. After a long moment, Basina ordered her women, "Check her."

Chira then submitted to a body cavity search, which was unpleasant but brief. Once they found nothing on/in her, Basina ordered the four of them out of the room. They protested, shocked and angry, but she grunted at them and they left.

When Basina and Chira were alone, there was a long pause. "I detect some glamour," said Basina at length. "Who has Sent you?"

"Nobody you know, milady," said Chira. "A company of good men and women who seek your aid. We are from far away, in every possible sense."

Basina listened, took a moment—in general her movements and words were slow and languid—and then said, in a bored and long-suffering tone, "What is desired of me?"

"A clandestine introduction to a member of the court."

"It is a rather large court, girl, can you be more specific?"

"There is a court apothecary who is also responsible for the mainte-nance of the herb gardens."

"Let me guess," Basina said with a throaty laugh. "Somebody wants kalonji. It's always kalonji."

Chira suppressed surprise and asked, "Who else wants kalonji?"

"Everyone. Every witch I've ever met, especially Franks, since nobody can seem to make it thrive in the north. Cyril Arcadius—the apothecary—would be a very wealthy man if he sold it. Then he could *buy* himself as many ladies' favors as he liked."

"He prefers the barter method," guessed Chira.

"He finds it romantic." Basina laughed.

"I'm prepared to barter," said Chira. "This should be simple."

"Honey-bee," Basina said in a knowing voice, "nothing is ever simple."

Although she was already fairly certain of what was coming, from her experiences on the first three Strands, Chira kept a blank look of innocence on her face and asked, "What isn't simple about Cyril Arcadius?"

"He likes a witch to be performing magic—any little spell, nothing dramatic—while he is taking her. Makes him feel like he's somehow part of the magic-making. It's pathetic."

This is not what Chira had expected, as on previous Strands Basina had simply alerted her to various peccadillos of the apothecary's, none of which fazed her. This variation posed a serious problem, however:

"I am not a witch," said Chira. "I can't offer that."

Basina shrugged. "Well," she said after a moment, "I suppose I could be your proxy. If you will be my proxy for another matter."

"Meaning?"

"I am expected in His Majesty's chamber this evening," said Basina.

Chira knew from DORC-prep that the Emperor—Alexios III Angelos—was married to Euphrosyne Doukaina Kamatera, a first-class Alpha Bitch who, despite being famously adulterous herself, would eviscerate anyone found fiddling with her wussy husband's tackle-box, especially since she'd only given him daughters. That is not what surprised Chira about the news of this dalliance. Rather it was this: "Aren't you . . . a kinswoman . . . of his?"

"Honey-bee," said Basina, "it's the imperial court, we're all each other's blood-cousins. Why do you think everyone fights so dirty? I would prefer to be in someone else's bed tonight, that's all, so I need somebody to distract His Majesty, and I need it to be a stranger so she can vanish before Euphrosyne hunts her down and gouges her eyes out."

"Is the Emperor expecting you?"

"I was summoned by his cupbearer, so *somebody* is expecting me," she said. "But it might be his wife trying to entrap me."

"Ah," said Chira.

"Yes," said Basina. "If you open that wooden cabinet over there, you'll find my summer gowns. Help yourself to any but the purple one. I'll have the maids oil and dress your hair to resemble mine, but I will not trust you with my jewelry."

"Very well," said Chira, wishing DORC's curriculum included a mandatory anti-assassin workshop.

"Spend the day in here. You'd be underfoot anywhere else."

Chira dressed herself in the most modest of the several gowns—all garish by modern standards, with tremendous amounts of small garnets and turquoise sewn onto the fronts, as well as decorative stitching in silver and gold thread. She then received (grudging and ungentle) ministrations from Basina's attendants, who attempted to goad her into revealing her identity until Basina told them to shut it. Chira was left alone in the chamber for approximately five hours, until Basina and her entourage returned, the entourage tittering, Basina looking pleased with herself. In her hand Basina held a black silk drawstring bag, half the size of a human fist.

"That was painless. Here are your kalonji seeds," she said, and tossed them onto Chira's lap. "Keep them tied to your belt, or better yet, your wrist."

"When am I to go to the Emperor's chambers?" Chira asked.

"After nightfall," said Basina. "One of his eunuchs will come with a summons. Have you eaten today?"

When Chira said that she had not, Basina sent two of her retinue down to the kitchens to bring up fruit and nuts and cheese, further cementing the attendants' resentment. A mediocre lute-playing eunuch came in to entertain them, until Basina got tired of him and sent him away, and finally after the sun had set, Basina excused herself to go to her other lover's bed.

"Do not abuse her," she ordered her sulking retinue. "If I hear of any bad behavior on your part, I'll have you flayed by that Genoan His Majesty keeps in the cellars."

She departed, leaving Chira alone with the seething attendants. All efforts on her part to gather intelligence from them met with complete failure as they were barely able to contain themselves from tearing her garments off her à la Cinderella's stepsisters.

Finally the Emperor's eunuch came in search of Basina. When the attendants presented Chira in her stead, he blinked a moment, then sighed, then rolled his eyes, shook his head, and lugubriously gestured her to follow him. The attendants were pleased by this response, and one of them whispered, "Surely he is leading you straight to what should have been Basina's death. Ha!" Followed by a Greek term with no perfect translation but meant in essence, "Sucker!"

The eunuch led her through such a maze of torch-and-lamp-lit stairwells, corridors, halls, and yards that she became disoriented and is not able to reconstruct the route for us (shown as, literally, a gray area on the DORCCAD rendering). But eventually, she was brought to a grand set of copper-faced double doors with intricate gold chase-work as decoration. The eunuch rapped on one of these with a particular staccato rhythm, and in response the doors swung outward toward them. Ahead of them was a very small vestibule, candlelit, with one door to the right and one to the left. (We know from old maps—digitized and cleaned up in DORCCAD—that these led to the Emperor's and Empress's respective bedchambers.) The eunuch, giving her a mournful look, literally shoved her into the vestibule and turned his back. As the door began to swing shut, a smooth, strong hand grabbed Chira's arm and she felt a slender blade press against her carotid artery. As her self-defense skill set is of the flight-not-fight variety, she froze.

"Finally, Basina," said a woman's voice, harshly happy. "Finally I have caught you in the act."

"I am not Basina, Your Majesty," said Chira. "I am simply an entertainer obeying a command from my Emperor."

There was some cursing, the knife blade was removed, the hand loosened its grip, and she turned so that her back was to the wall and she could face her assailant in the candlelight. The Empress Euphrosyne was considerably older than her but still, in a ravaged, cougar-esque sort of way, definitely pretty hot.

"Who are you? You can't go in there," said Euphrosyne. "I know what happens when a whore gives an emperor a son. If he doesn't get one from me, he doesn't get one from anyone. Nobody is going to rob my daughters of the throne."

"I'm Jewish," Chira said. "No son of mine would ever be allowed on the throne, no matter who his father is."

Euphrosyne looked surprised. "He would never bed a Jewess," she said.

"He saw me dance at a feast a fortnight back and made inquiries. We've never spoken in person, but he has already paid a great deal and I am tardy. Given I am no threat to Your Majesty, may I attend to my Emperor's wishes?"

Everything about Euphrosyne's demeanor changed as this sank in. She gestured to the door that led to the imperial bedchamber. "Go on, then," she said. "I don't care if you fuck him. In fact, fuck him thoroughly so I don't have to worry about his fucking anyone else tonight."

With these words of encouragement she opened the door herself. It was a very large room, marble floors, and panels of marble for walls, ceiling of glassed gold-leaf tile looking burnished in the flickering light from a dozen beeswax candles. One entire wall opened on to a balcony that overlooked a garden.

In the middle of the room was the single piece of furniture: a large bed that appeared to be carved out of solid turquoise, and on this sat a sickly pale, dark-haired man who did not look at all what Chira expected of an emperor. He was wearing a nightshirt, which was thick white silk with gold thread sewn into the collar, cuffs, and hems. He looked up expectantly when he saw her, and then pulled his head back like a surprised turtle.

"Where's Basina?" he demanded, standing nervously.

"Basina was ill tonight, Your Majesty," said Chira, with a reassuring smile. "She sent me to entertain you in her absence."

"You're an assassin," said His Majesty.

"Of course not, Your Majesty," said Chira pleasantly. "I am here entirely for your pleasure."

"No, you're an assassin, you must be an assassin, I've never seen you before and you came in here without my eunuch."

"Your honored wife sent the eunuch away in the antechamber," said Chira. "She wanted to speak to me in private before I came in to you."

"Did she tell you to assassinate me?"

"Your Majesty," said Chira, looking graciously shocked. "Of course not. She herself is so solicitous of your safety that she would not allow me in until she had reassured herself of my benign intentions. She has deigned to allow me to enter your bedchamber."

"Prove that you are not an assassin," he said, not moving from his defensive stance by the side of the bed.

Chira continued to smile at him, adjusting the tone of the smile to try to reassure and calm him. She shimmied easily out of Basina's long royal-blue robe, which she had not fully secured specifically so that she could remove it easily. Because of all the jewels and stiff metallic thread, it landed inelegantly, but she stepped out of it with a sinuous grace, presenting as much of herself as possible directly to him. She slipped the drawstring of the kalonji-seed bag over her wrist and palmed it. Entirely unclothed, she smiled invitingly at him, crossed to him, and took his hand with her free one. He stared at his hand in hers as if this was an experience he had never had before. She examined his face. He seemed on the verge of a panic attack.

"Would Your Majesty like to examine my person himself, to see that I have no weapons?"

She ran his hand across her breasts, and then down her belly and between her legs. "Please inspect as carefully as you would like," she whispered into his ear, and closed her lips over his earlobe. He began to tremble.

"If you're not an assassin, you must be a spy," he said, pulling his head away. "You are from that navy of so-called Pilgrims that are wintering in Zara, aren't you?"

"I do not know what you speak of, Your Majesty," she said, and squeezed his hand between her thighs. He made a confused moaning sound but tried to pull his hand away.

"You're from Montferrat, aren't you?"

"I have never heard of Montferrat, Your Majesty," she whispered, and again closed her lips upon his earlobe. Then she licked the back of his ear.

A moment later he was naked atop her, bucking away, and a few moments after that, with a loud sob of relief, he finished and lay panting on top of her.

Immediately the door to the chamber pushed open, and Empress Euphrosyne stormed in with two large Varangian Guards behind her. The Emperor did not bother to raise his head.

"Thank you," said Euphrosyne briskly. "Alexios, get off of her, we're sending her home."

Without further acknowledging Chira, the Emperor rolled over on the bed and lay staring up at the gold-tiled ceiling with a morose expression. The Empress picked up Basina's blue gown and Chira held her hand out for it. "I don't think so," Euphrosyne said with a laugh, and tossed it into a corner. "Alexios, I'm giving her your nightshirt to wear."

The Emperor was already asleep.

Euphrosyne picked up the garment and tossed it to Chira. "Put that on quickly, Jewess. These men are taking you back to Pera."

This was convenient enough, as the second part of Chira's task was to get across the Golden Horn to Pera, to leave the kalonji seeds with another witch (KCW from previous Strands, but still a stranger in this one) in the Jewish section of the city. Getting an armed imperial escort was not how she had done it in previous Strands, but this would take less effort on her part.

One of the guards offered her a woolen cloak and she wrapped it round her shoulders. She allowed them to take her down various flights of stairs and across yards and gardens and halls and down corridors, until she was once again disoriented. Eventually the smell of briny water began to waft past her nostrils, so she was not surprised when they came to an enormous wooden gate that opened onto a street at the edge of the water. There was a boat with two oarsmen who wordlessly rowed them across the Golden Horn—the deep protected harbor, less than two bow-shots wide, that led to the hilly northern suburb of Pera, in the shadow of Galata Tower.

Upon landing at the foot of the steep hill (not an official dock, although there were several in either direction), the oarsmen secured the boat, and the two guards got out and then hoisted her directly to the shore. Throughout this she had maintained her firm hold on the kalonji-seed bag and now was mindful not to let the harbor water touch it.

"Where's your home?" asked one of the guards, with the clumsy, angry-sounding accent of the Britons who made up such a large percentage of the Varangian force.

Suppressing a mischievous urge to address him in modern English, she responded in Greek. "It is directly behind the synagogue," she said. "My father is Avraham ben Moises. I will show you."

The three of them marched up the steep hill along the street, which was not very broad but paved with stones and well maintained. About halfway up was the synagogue, a large building with a fenced garden.

Chira directed them to the rows of neat wooden homes behind this, all dark as it was now about midnight. In the middle row of houses, set on leveled-off stone foundations, Chira pointed to one house in particular.

One of the guards took her by the shoulder and the other pounded on the door.

After a confused moment, there were voices within both this house and the surrounding homes, and candlelight appeared in windows. Eventually the door opened and a man barely old enough to be Chira's father opened the door. He sported a long beard, longish hair covered by a felt cap, and dark robes. A woman, obviously his wife, stood behind him, and behind her were the shadowy forms of several children ranging in age from approximately seven to full-grown.

"What do you want?" asked the man in Greek, fearful, staring up at the Varangian Guard.

"We've brought your daughter back," said the guard, sounding bored.

"Our what?" the man said, amazed.

"Your daughter," repeated the guard, in a warning voice.

"All of our daughters are here with us already," the man said, looking alarmed and confused.

The guard took a step forward to tower over him in the doorway. "To disown your daughter because she has been with the Emperor is to disown the Emperor himself," he said warningly. "Either you receive her into your home or I will bring you back to answer to His Majesty for the insult directly."

Looking mystified, and a bit spooked, the man stepped back into the house and somewhat robotically held his arm out in a gesture of welcome. The other guard pushed Chira through the doorway.

"*Abba*," said Chira in a happy voice, throwing her arms around him. And then turning to his equally mystified wife, "*Eema!*" The woman very woodenly put her arms around her.

Then Rachel, the oldest of their daughters (late teens?), and Chira's connection, gasped as if remembering or realizing something, and said,

"Oh, my dearest sister, I'm so glad to see you safely home!" She threw her arms around Chira with a bear hug. To her younger siblings, she said emphatically, "Is it not wonderful to have our sister home again?"

They gave her strange looks.

"Pretend you know her, and welcome her home," Rachel whispered fiercely in Hebrew.

The children immediately surrounded Chira and hugged her with feigned enthusiasm.

"The Emperor thanks you," said the senior guard to the father. "But the Empress requests that you keep your daughters closer to home from now on."

"Yes, of course, sir," stammered the father.

The other guard added, "I'd marry this one off as soon as possible. If nobody in Pera wants her, I've got some connections in town who would be happy to take her off your hands. Get a great price with those tits."

"I . . . I'll take that into consideration, thank you," said the father.

This man pulled back his helmet to give Avraham a clear view of his face. "Name's Bruno. Bruno of Hamlin," he said agreeably. "You can ask for me via the imperial kitchens, the head cook's a kinsman through marriage." He winked at Chira and then turned his attention back to the father. "I'll take fifteen percent commission. Think about it."

The guards left.

As soon as the door was closed, the younger children pulled away from her and scurried behind their mother, as Chira turned to face the family. Rachel looked delighted, but the father and mother were frowning unhappily and the younger children took their cues from this.

"Thank you," said Chira in Hebrew, in her most winsome smile. "I apologize profusely for the alarm and confusion I've just caused you. Please allow me to explain the peculiar circumstances of our meeting."

She then revealed herself as working with a witch network. She shared as much as she safely could, and requested their permission to leave the kalonji seeds with them until her associate came to collect them, which she anticipated would be within a day or two. Persuasive narrative is one of her specialties; due to her innate charisma and agreeable demeanor, by the time she'd finished, the entire household had relaxed and adopted a more welcoming air. The family (as we knew from previous Strands) has a commitment to protecting fellow witches, and agreed readily to assist her. In fact, the daughter Rachel pressed her for more information about the witch network she was working with, and expressed a desire to go adventuring with Chira in other times and places, despite Moises's quiet disapproval.

"When my associate Felix comes to collect the bag, you may speak more with him about it," Chira suggested. "In the meantime, please be kind enough to send me back to my own home."

"I shall do that," said the mother.

"Oh, *eema*, please let me try," said Rachel. "I would love to know I can help such interesting people to have such marvelous adventures out in the world."

The mother was about to agree but Moises interrupted. "Your mother will do it," he said. "You are too eager."

Chira smiled at Rachel. "I was like you at your age," she said. "Except I did not have the powers you have. You will certainly be a remarkable force for good in the world if you make your mind up to be so." Rachel looked rapturous.

"You are welcome to invade our home but not our daughter's mind," said Moises curtly. "Sarah, send this woman back where she came from, before I decide to follow Bruno's advice and sell her off."

At 05:10 the morning after her departure, Chira was Homed to ODEC #2 uninjured.

Post by Dr. Roger Blevins to Dr. Melisande Stokes
on private ODIN channel
DAY 627 (MID-APRIL, YEAR 2)

Have reviewed your After Action Reports on Chira Yasin's series of DEDEs in the Blachernae Palace. All are too long, editorialized, and frankly tawdry. Revise to reflect the professional standards of DODO, and see to it all future reports remain within department guidelines (brief, containing salient facts only).

Allowing a chatty tone, personal timbre, etc. to seep into your reports is unprofessional, Dr. Stokes. As such it is, by the letter of DODO policy, grounds for being placed on a Performance Enhancement Plan, which I need not remind you may culminate in demotion or dismissal.

It might behoove you to review the transcripts of the recent congressional hearings during which we were raked over the coals by various Red State senators for even suggesting that sexual activity might be involved in diachronic operations. In the future, any DOer actions of this nature are to be downplayed to the greatest extent possible that is consistent with accurate record-keeping. This is not a Nora Roberts novel.

—RB

AFTER ACTION REPORT

DEBRIEFER: Dr. Melisande Stokes

DOER: Felix Dorn

THEATER: Constantinople/Late Medieval Europe

OPERATION: Antwerp witch recruitment

DEDE: Retrieve and carry viable kalonji seeds across Europe for sowing

DTAP: Pera, Constantinople, September 1202; Peerdsbos Forest
(Antwerp), Belgium, November 1202
STRAND: First (out of a projected three) repetition of this DEDE

Erszebet Sent DOer Felix Dorn from ODEC #2 at 08:10 of Day 627.
DOer landed safely in Pera, retrieved kalonji seeds without incident, traveled for two months by foot, river, and stolen horse from Constantinople
to Belgium. Many adventures. Did not die. Arrived in Peerdsbos Forest,
sowed kalonji seeds, was Homed by Goedele, our KCW of that DTAP.

Note: Witch Rachel in Pera volunteered for diachronic engagement
but father disapproved.

Dutifully submitted,

Dr. Melisande "Reads Less Nora Roberts Than Dr. Blevins Does"
     Stokes

INTERNAL MEMO

From: Dr. Roger Blevins
To: General Octavian Frink
Re: Melisande Stokes
Day 688, 14:12

General Frink—
[REDACTED]

...

INTERNAL MEMO

From: LTC Tristan Lyons
To: General Octavian Frink
Re: Dr. Blevins's recent statements re: Melisande Stokes
Day 688, 15:02

Dear General Frink:
[REDACTED]

...

INTERNAL MEMO

From: Dr. Roger Blevins
To: General Octavian Frink
Re: LTC Lyons's response to my (somehow leaked) memo re:
Dr. Stokes
Day 688, 15:39

Okie—
[REDACTED]

...

INTERNAL MEMO/EMAIL

From: General Octavian Frink
To: Dr. Roger Blevins and Lieutenant Colonel Tristan Lyons
Re: Leaked memos, etc.
Day 689, 10:19

[REDACTED]
. . . Coming from an academic background, Dr. Blevins, you
should know better than to consign anything to writing. I will
have to redact most of this correspondence not due to security
concerns but from sheer embarrassment.
So you will let it rest there, gentlemen.
General O. K. Frink

Post by Felix Dorn
on "Recreation" ODIN channel
DAY 617

As some of you have noticed, I am not much of a talker, but I just wanted to mention that if anyone wants to join a barefoot running group, meet me at 0430 tomorrow at the Harvard Bridge, on the Cambridge side.

Reply from LTC Tristan Lyons, Day 619:

Well, everyone, maybe this isn't much of a surprise, but response has been muted to Felix's "dawn barefoot running" group. Heavy spring rains, darkness, and muddy conditions have been cited as an excuse. I just wanted to remind everyone that when you are Sent, you arrive naked—which means barefoot. Your feet are probably larger than average for the DTAP, so stealing shoes isn't as easy as people make it sound. And we do prefer nighttime arrivals because there's less chance of being noticed. Participation in Felix's dawn barefoot running group is a breeze by comparison, and will help you develop skills, grow calluses, and build up a tolerance to pain that will serve you well when sprinting away from an unsecured DTAP (or, worse yet, getting clear of a possible Diachronic Shear event). Cardio: it's not just for knights!

DODO MEMORANDUM

CRITICAL UPGRADE TO JOB TITLES
BY MACY STOLL, MBA
POSTED Day 629

As those of you in management positions are already aware, it is essential that we move over to ISO 9000 compliant job titles for all current and future DODO staff. It is beyond the scope of this memo to enumerate all of the benefits that will accrue to DODO (and, by extension, the taxpayers) as a result of organization-wide ISO 9000 compliance, but those of you who are curious can find plenty of information about it on the non-classified Internet.

Making this especially urgent is that we are getting pushback from concerned parties in the Trapezoid about having a staff member whose job title is "witch." The word simply looks bad when it shows up in a spreadsheet or official report. Moreover, since it is gender-specific, it is a violation of our Diversity Policy (or at least it will be when that policy is written!).

It's time to nip this in the bud, since it will only become that much worse when/if we recruit more staff to perform the same function.

After lengthy consultations with Dr. Oda and others, we have settled on a new job title, which has been fast-tracked through the Policy on Official Jargon and Acronym Coinage. That title is . . . (drum roll) . . . MUON, for Multiple-Universe Operations Navigator. We believe that this acronym encapsulates the essential functions and duties of this all-important role without any of the backward and sexist connotations that have raised hackles within the Trapezoid.

Later on we may establish additional gradations such as Junior MUON, Senior MUON, etc. but for now this is unnecessary as we only have one of them on payroll.

This title applies only to paid staff members living in our timeline. Terms such as KCW may still be employed when referring to individuals in past or alternate timelines.

Exchange of posts by DODO staff on "Recruiting" ODIN channel

Post from LTC Tristan Lyons, Day 630:

I've been reading Stokes's After Action Reports on Chira's Blachernae Palace DEDE, and I want to start a conversation about Varangian Guards. For those of you who might not be up to speed on context, these are fighting men from Scandinavian or other Northern European countries who were recruited to serve as palace guards and elite troops by the Byzantine Empire. I had read of them in history books, so I knew of their existence, but reading these After Action Reports really drives home how pervasive their presence was in Constantinople circa 1200. Best of all, they tend to show up in important places like the Imperial Palace and key fortifications like the Galata Tower, city gates, etc.

Why is this of interest to DODO? Well, it's no secret that we are having difficulty recruiting DOers capable of blending in in 1200 Constantinople. The required combination of physical appearance, cultural literacy, and language fluency needed to "pass" in that DTAP is difficult to pull off—occasional miracle recruits like Chira notwithstanding.

The ubiquitous presence of Varangian Guards suggests a different strategy, at least for male DOers: don't worry about trying to pass as a native Byzantine. Instead, hide in plain sight. We can recruit DOers who can pass for Northern Europeans, then Send them back and look for ways to infiltrate them into Varangian Guard units. Their lack of fluency in the Greek language, ignorance of contemporary customs and etiquette, etc. then becomes a natural fit with their cover story.

This strategy presents two main challenges that I can think of:

1. We don't know much about how the Varangian Guards were actually recruited. If we're lucky, there's a sort of labor market in this DTAP,

such that big, healthy-looking Northern European males who show up in town with no past history or connections can get recruited into these units without going through the Byzantine equivalent of a background check. Now that Chira is finished with the kalonji-seed DEDEs and has established some familiarity with Constantinople, maybe we can Send her on some scouting missions to learn more about how this works.

2. Even if it works for a DOer to show up in Constantinople from parts unknown, with no connections or background, he's not going to be able to pass for a Varangian Guard unless he speaks the language. Leading to the question: What is the language that these guys speak, and where can we learn it? Stokes?

Reply from Dr. Melisande Stokes, Day 630:
Tristan, the Varangian Guards were drawn from all over Scandinavia, Northern Europe, and Britain over a span of centuries, so it depends. In our era (1203) the majority were speaking Anglo-Saxon. But some of the ones Chira encountered were apparently speaking Norman, which is a transitional dialect, not a stable language as we normally think of it. As you probably know, the Vikings invaded France, were bought off with Normandy, settled there, then used it as a base for invading Britain and many other places. The most bad-ass Normans crossed the Channel with William the Conqueror; the ones that stayed behind in Normandy spawned the generations who mostly enjoyed jousting and courtly love, etc. . . . This + Normans and Anglo-Saxons obviously detesting each other = surprising to find Normans in the 1203 Anglo-Saxon-centric Varangian Guards. But actually, we can use it to our advantage:

If we train DOers to speak Anglo-Saxon, they will *probably* blend in just fine no matter their accent, but they do run *some* risk of being called out—Anglo-Saxon had a limited geographical spread and thus a limited number of dialects, most of which are probably represented in the 1203 VG cohort. Someone speaking an eccentric variation might arouse curiosity. Small chance, but a chance.

However: Variations of "*Norman*" were spoken from Greenland to the Volga and from Sicily to the Arctic Circle. If Normans were accepted into the VG, then a DOer could learn any kind of mash-up passing as some variant of Norman, and never run the risk of being called out for lack of fluency—they can just claim they're from some other clan over the mountain. There would be too many variations of the language, and too few native speakers in residence, for anyone to get wise.

From Dr. Roger Blevins, Day 631:

I have been monitoring this exchange with some interest. LTC Lyons's idea seems to merit further development.

LTC Lyons: please see me about deploying Chira Yasin on scouting missions to Constantinople so that we can better understand procedures for recruiting Varangian Guards. I only wish that she were less conspicuous. Can we put her in a burka? There must have been some Muslim presence in the city in that era.

Dr. Stokes: the obvious failure mode in your linguistic analysis—for Norman *or* Anglo-Saxon—is that our DOer, claiming to be a native of some specific region, might happen to cross paths with another Varangian Guard who actually was from the exact same location, and who would detect faults in our DOer's accent, knowledge base, etc. and become suspicious. Agreed: less likely with Norman than with A/S, but not impossible. We can minimize the chances of that happening by developing a cover story according to which our DOer is from an exceptionally remote and obscure part of the Norman world. Please move this to the top of your priority list.

DODO REPORT

POTENTIAL KCWs, NORMANDY, 12th Century
BY MELISANDE STOKES, PH.D.
Submitted to ODIN archive, Day 645

OBJECTIVE: Identify potential Known Compliant Witches (KCWs) in remote settlements in Normandy during the approximate span 1050–1200, as a preliminary step toward establishing a DTAP there/then. Proposed function of that DTAP: to serve as "Language Camp" for Fighter-class DOers, giving them linguistic and cultural proficiency needed to pass as (Norman) Varangian Guards in the 1200 Constantinople DTAP.

GENERAL BACKGROUND: Normandy in this era had been colonized by transplants from both Scandinavia and Anglo-Saxon-Danish-influenced regions of Britain for well over a century. It had not yet been incorporated into France but had been expanding its borders at France's expense for some time. The linguistic environment was accordingly complicated and fluid. The population was largely Christianized, at least in name (nobility very much so by 1200). Since most were illiterate, essentially all of the available records fall into three categories. The first two are (1) legal records and (2) chronicles/accountings kept by the feudal lords' stewards, but these rarely refer to women independently of their marital status. The more fruitful source therefore is (3) church documents, typically written by priests, friars, etc. in Latin or, less frequently, medieval French.

METHODOLOGY: Review medieval church documents for points of convergence per following criteria: (A) references to heretical leanings per church fathers; (B) family trees featuring illegitimate but non-ostracized daughters over the course of several generations; (C) recorded activity suggestive of magic, particularly pertaining to crops, livestock, weather, and ease of pillaging nearby adversaries; and (D) perceived non-conformity in local female individuals, especially those as found in (B) above.

RESULT: POTENTIAL KCW THYRA OF COLLINET

A: *"And in June of this year (1027) was Thyra delivered of a girl-child of no known sire, as Thyra herself had been twenty-two summers earlier, and her mother Wilmetta before her, and yet was Emma the aunt of Thyra joyful to receive Thyra and her bastard child to her hearth, and the child was christened Beatrice." (ref 2876)*

B: *"And in April of this year (1046) was Thyra again deprived of those villainous and Satanic objects with which she adorns her cousin's chamber, and scorned to replace them with an image of Our Lord. For this she was given a penance of ten Hail Marys which she was loath to perform, but said she would rather receive a lash, at which the priest hastily did declare her free of all sin." (ref 3486)*

C: *"And in this month (August 1050) did Thyra of Herb-lore cause great sorrow upon the (mayor?) of the village of Collinet and the (lord?) of (? Illegible) for her scolding at their crossing her when she wished to forage upon their lands for select herbs."*

D: *"And in this month (January 1061) died Thyra of Herb-lore, and the valley wept at her passing for fear of the famine returning that they credited her for keeping at bay." (ref 6584)*

Further research recommended, as incidental accounts in 1002, and throughout the 1100s, suggest an uninterrupted lineage of witches in Thyra's family, all with strong local and familial authority. (Rec search words: 1137 Collinet:Maneld, 1191, 1192, and 1195 Collinet:Rikilde, and 1193 and 1197 Collinet:Imblen)

Exchange of posts between
Dr. Roger Blevins and Dr. Melisande Stokes
on private ODIN channel
DAY 650 (MID-MAY, YEAR 2)

Post from Dr. Blevins:

Dr. Stokes, I am hereby directing you to proceed with the recruitment of the potential KCW known as Thyra, circa 1045.

As much as we need your energies behind the expansion of the Diachronic Operative Resource Center, it is clear that you are the best qualified of our existing roster of DOers to undertake this mission, and so I suggest that you delegate some of your present responsibilities to others as you undertake the necessary training. Macy Stoll is an obvious candidate to shoulder routine administrative and managerial tasks and has expressed a willingness to do so.

Reply from Dr. Stokes:

Understood. As busy as I am here, I can't dispute that I would be the best person to act as Forerunner in this DTAP, barring some recruiting breakthrough in the next couple of weeks.

I anticipate that getting up to speed on local languages and customs will occupy me for most of the summer, with the actual DEDE slated for August. Meanwhile Erzsebet can be putting in the usual research needed to Send me to that DTAP with reasonable temporal and positional accuracy.

One thing about your message surprised me, and so I wanted to double check to make sure there was no misunderstanding. You specified Thyra, 1045, as the target of the operation. This means that our DOers would be learning a dialect of Norman, and a set of customs, that would be 150 years out of date by the time they show up in Constantinople circa 1200.

My research indicates that Thyra's descendant Imblen is also a witch.

I propose we have a higher chance of success in this endeavor if we send our "Varangian Guards" to 1190s Collinet to study with Imblen. They will stand a better chance of both comprehending and being comprehended if they've got 1200 Norman French.

From Dr. Blevins:

Thanks for your illuminating feedback. For classified reasons, 1045 works better for us than the 1190s do. Assuming language immersion will indeed work for Tristan, let's send him back there ASAP.

From Dr. Stokes:

What are "classified reasons"? How could they be so classified that neither Tristan (the probable DOer in question) nor myself (the linguistic historian expressly in charge of determining these matters) is being told about them?

Can we CC in General Frink and Dr. Oda to this thread in case they can shed light on either Chronotropic or top-level-strategic reasons for not doing the sensible thing here?

From Dr. Blevins:

Mel, thank you as always for your spirited commentary. There is no need to trouble either General Frink or Dr. Oda in this case. The answer is straightforward: training our "Varangian Guard" candidates close to the time of the Constantinople DTAP is dangerous because, however remote their "hometown," they could still be recognized. That is why to choose a spot not only temporally but also geographically isolated from 1200 Constantinople.

Other issues in this decision are above your pay grade so you don't need to know.

DODO MEMORANDUM

CLARIFICATION TO DRESS CODE
BY MACY STOLL, MBA
POSTED Day 653

The distribution of DODO's newly minted dress code has brought in a flood of requests for clarification. Until such time as this document can be reworded, here is a useful rule of thumb: DOers on active missions are exempt from all dress code provisions, including the requirement to wear anything at all.

LETTER FROM
GRÁINNE *to* GRACE O'MALLEY
Winter Solstice, 1601

Auspiciousness and prosperity to you, milady!

I pray Your Grace will forgive my few months of silence, for wasn't it in a terrible way I found myself, trying to secure safety and security after the disaster of the Iomadh. Rose it was sent Tristan Lyons back to his era, and wasn't I glad to see the back of him for a while.

But only for a while, Your Majesty. For I've landed on my feet, and determined I am to learn the truth behind what Tristan be up to. When he "told me everything," truly 'twasn't everything at all, or else why would that right arse Les Holgate appear and make such a muck of everything? There are things going on in the future, and it's to do with magic, and 'tis the least Tristan Lyons can do but be fully honest with me at last, now that he and his like have robbed me of all I cherish in London.

But as I said, it's safety I've found for myself, and at the merest cost. I've told Your Majesty in years past of Francis Bacon's society of Good Pens ('tis a pun on the male member, is what I'm thinking, given what I know of Sir Francis). This group meets at Gray's Inn, and composed of the brightest of menfolk it is, them being intelligencers and counterfeiters, not to mention secretaries, physicians, poets, theologians, apothecaries, and the occasional natural philosopher, and of these last few, doesn't Sir Francis love to debate with the nature of the universe, in ways that seem like conversations witches might have with each other, if witches were wont to waste their time putting into words things which go without saying. There are no witches in their discourses and indeed no women at all! Like a bunch of turtles trying to discuss flight, they remind me of, and not getting all of it correct, neither.

But sure it's entertainment enough. Don't I keep my mouth shut when I'm near them and pour the ale; they are the best minds in London, and one of them natural philosophers with a mystical bent, one Jacques Cardigan (a mad enough fellow with a mad enough name!) has taken me in as a servant, and Your Ladyship will understand that I warm his bed when he asks for me, but it's an easier life than posing as a bawd, so it is. Himself is a wealthy enough fella, although an obvious Catholic (what with a French name and his surname coming from a Catholic shire in Wales, he can hardly hide it, can he?), so he keeps out of politics and that may in the end mean I must move on to other quarters, for to be of use to Your Grace. But for now it's safety and security and no questions asked—sure he thinks he's landed in it, here's a pretty Irish refugee who will give him pleasure in exchange for room and board, and not be questioning his religion neither!

He's a summer house in Surrey, in Norwich, and we'll be retiring there come spring, if I'm still under his roof then, but through winter we're near enough to Gray's Inn. Rose knows my circumstances and conveyed them to Tristan, so I've let him know I'm pleased to continue to help him knot his network of witches, and it seems to have grown with breathtaking speed, so it has. I've stopped asking him questions directly, though, and it's trying to learn a bit by observation I am now. For it seems to me that he knows precisely what it is that brought magic to its knees, and it seems to me that if I might know it too, I might hoist him by his own petard (to quote that poxy playwright)—I could be using his own strategy of moving around through time and space, not to bring back magic but to prevent its cessation in the first place. I've no idea how to make that so, and it's cagey enough he's being with his information, but I've naught else to do with my time now that I'm away from Whitehall circles, so I mean to figure it out.

The one thing I'm knowing for certain is that in his ever-expanding fellowship of witches, Tristan occasionally runs into an ornery one who needs to be coaxed into the congregation (and sure why shouldn't they? I would have been demanding some coaxing, if I didn't foolishly think I could benefit from him as much as him from me.). At this moment of time, himself and some other DOers are romping about the universe trying to please some Wending woman in Antwerp who lived some fifty years back (and who had some connection to that banker fellow, Gresham—and therefore somehow-or-other to my new friend Bacon, for didn't Sir Thomas Gresham's bastard daughter marry Sir Francis's half-brother? Is right she did. And of course I'm sure the Fuggers are involved in all of this somehow, they always are.).

Truth be told, I don't even know if I should be taking the side of Tristan. What does he need do in Antwerp fifty years back? Especially requiring magic? Was there something about that time and place that contributed to the corruption of magic? And why make use of a witch who knew the forebears of the menfolk I now brush elbows with? A pure coincidence is it, or with his future-knowledge does Tristan plan to make use of me somehow, and my new friends? So many questions, Your Grace!

So it's learning about all that I intend to do, but not so's Tristan would notice my efforts. In fact, I intend to make myself excessively useful to him, in the hopes that he includes me in his confidences. (Perhaps even finds cause to have me Sent to his own time! Then I can see for myself what's what.) He's a grand lad, when he's not scheming on behalf of his overlords, and I've a fondness for him, so I do.

With all good wishes to ye, milady, Gráinne formerly of London

DODO HUMAN RESOURCES

PERSONNEL DOSSIER

FAMILY NAME: Overkleeft

GIVEN NAME(S): Esme Claire

TITLE: Doctor (Ph.D., Bioinformatics)

AGE: 34

CLASS: Closer/MacGyver

HEIGHT: 5'10"

EYES: Blue

HAIR: Chestnut

COMPLEXION: Light, freckled

DISTINCTIVE FEATURES: Crooked nose, bent left clavicle (results of sports injuries)

ETHNICITY: Northern European

NATIONALITY: Belgian

LANGUAGE FLUENCY RATINGS:

    Dutch, French: 5

    English, Walloon: 4

    German: 3

RELIGION: Atheist, from historically Catholic family on mother's side, historically Dutch Reformed Church on father's

CITIZENSHIP: Belgian (EU)

BIOGRAPHY: From an academic family that moved among various university towns (mostly Low Countries) while she was growing up. States that this nomadic lifestyle forced her to acquire social skills she might otherwise have neglected given a generally introverted/ intellectual personality. Participated in various sports, with emphasis in field hockey and track & field. Hobby: sewing and textiles. Attended University of Antwerp, majored in biology. While at school, became involved in local chapter of Society for Creative Anachronism with emphasis on making period-correct clothing. Later obtained Ph.D. in bioinformatics, focusing on plant biology, from Leiden. Obtained security clearance, and thereby found her way into Defense Dept. personnel databases, as result of a NATO project to design upgraded military camouflage patterns in response to projected botanical shifts resulting from climate change. When approached by DODO, was in London seeking investors in an apparel start-up that was a spinout of the camouflage project. Agreed to put that project on ice in order to accept the DODO job.

SKILL SET: Athletic, hardy, uncomplaining, with a winning personality and ability to adapt to various social milieus. Keen eye for clothing, textiles, needlework of the late medieval/early Renaissance era. Exceptionally strong knowledge of botanical matters, especially in Northern/Western Europe.

LIMITATIONS: Her unusual height will make her conspicuous, particularly in medieval populations.

AFTER ACTION REPORT

DEBRIEFER: Dr. Melisande Stokes
DOER: Dr. Esme Overkleeft (Closer)
THEATER: NEER (Northern Europe Early Renaissance)
OPERATION: Antwerp witch recruitment, Part C: Harvest kalonji as incentive to potential KCW Winnifred Dutton
DEDE: Recruit Dutton as KCW
DTAP: Peerdsbos Forest (Antwerp), Belgium, 1562

Note: A previous unsuccessful recruitment attempt had been made by Dr. Stokes circa Day 500. The encounter ended awkwardly. Dutton had demanded kalonji, which Stokes knew nothing about, so recruitment was abandoned until a new gambit could be established for obtaining some. The series of DEDEs conducted by Chira Yasin and Felix Dorn circa 1200 had the effect of sowing kalonji in known locations in the Peerdsbos Forest where conditions were right for it to thrive and remain available centuries in the future.

Thanks to the earlier DEDEs by Dr. Stokes, Winnifred Dutton was already aware of us, and Overkleeft knew how to obtain clothes, make contact with Dutton, etc.

MUON Erszebet Karpathy sent Dr. Overkleeft from ODEC #3 at 08:21 of Day 818.

Having retrieved clothes stashed from Stokes's previous efforts, Overkleeft went without incident to fortress at which DOer Felix Dorn had sowed seeds in 1202. Discovered that 360 years later, a small but hardy patch of kalonji had survived in one south-facing exposed courtyard. Esme uprooted one plant and took samples of leaves, removing viable roots and seed-buds so that Dutton could not simply establish her own patch of kalonji. Carried these to the home of Winnifred, wife of Thomas Dutton (Thomas Gresham's Antwerp factor).

It is now known, and was an open secret even then, that Winnifred had been married off to Dutton only to get her out of England, where she had been Thomas Gresham's lover and had borne him a natural daughter, Anne (twelve years old at time of this DEDE).

Consequently Dutton was living in a comfortable home with a disinterested "spouse," in a foreign country, deprived of her lover, and except for the task of raising her daughter was very restless. She allowed the servants to bring Esme into the home at once and was delighted to receive the kalonji plant, the merits of which she immediately began to describe to both Esme and young Anne. Without further obstinacy, she pledged herself to being a KCW and made her residence available as a safe house. Furthermore she encouraged her daughter to do so as well, which Anne agreed to eagerly.

Esme Overkleeft returned without incident at 18:45.

Note: It is already marked in DODO archives, but for ease of reference, here is additional historical context (not told to Winnifred or Anne, of course): Anne Gresham/Dutton will go on to marry Nathaniel Bacon (half brother of Sir Francis), with whom she will live in Norwich, England. Her three daughters, all witches, are roughly contemporaneous with Gráinne in London. Accordingly, our next DEDE will be to reach out to them for recruitment.

Diachronicle
(CIRCA DECEMBER, YEAR 2)

In which Tristan has a working vacation

THE VILLAGE OF COLLINET STRADDLES a tributary of the river Dives, which empties into the English Channel a few miles downstream. The actual DTAP was a copse of trees both leafless and evergreen, some half-mile from the center of the village proper.

DODO now had a small operational group called TAST: the Tactical Archaeological Strike Team. As the name implied, they combined the skill set of traditional archaeologists (digging holes and finding stuff) with those of covert intelligence operatives—they knew how to get in and out of potentially hostile locations without drawing attention, and how to find what they were looking for in a hurry. You might not think of Normandy as a hostile location. But because of France's ancient and secret laws banning diachronic operations, it was hostile to *us*. Anyway, TAST, zeroing in on a powerful GLAAMR centered on this copse of trees, had been able to carry out a couple of midnight digs and verify that it had been the homesite of the lineage of presumed witches we'd seen mentioned in various church documents. It was classic witch real estate: close enough to the village to allow commerce and social contacts but sufficiently remote to afford separation and privacy.

Erszebet was admirably on the mark: I materialized unobserved right at the copse, where the ground was mercifully dry, and after recovering from the usual disorientation, I followed the scent of woodsmoke to a hut some fifty very chilly strides away: the home of our potential KCW, Thyra of Collinet. I had landed, by design, in late afternoon in midwinter; in spite of the risk of hypothermia, I elected to arrive now because Thyra would likely be holed up in front of her fire.

As we'd come to expect, Thyra—a handsome woman of some forty years, brown hair gently greying—was not surprised by the arrival of a naked stranger, although I cannot say she was particularly pleased by it either. She grudgingly allowed me to enter her hut and warm myself by the fire. She muttered to herself.

"Pardon? Please repeat," I said politely in Latin—the educated traveler's language of the time.

Thyra appraised me a moment, then turned back to the fire. "I said"—now in slightly stiff Latin—"I sensed a glamour in recent days. But I did not expect somebody Sent. I cannot imagine why anyone wants to visit such a remote location."

"Would this language be easier?" I asked in Anglo-Saxon; she gave me a confused look. "Let it be Latin, then," I hastily amended. "Are you fluent?"

"Too fluent for the priest's liking," she said with a reluctant little chuckle. "If you speak slowly I can probably understand."

I was able to convey to Thyra our proposal: namely that young men, apparent warriors, would come and stay with her from time to time, with no other purpose than to become familiar with the local language and customs. They would be disciplined and well-behaved. After a few weeks she would Home them.

"Pah," she said, turning her attention back into the fire. "I do not like young men. Why not Send young women?"

"The men could be your house-help while they are here," I said, looking around. "Chop firewood and bring it in. Fetch water. Fix that leak," I added, pointing. "Is that roof-beam rotting? Do you think it's safe to wait until spring? What kind of snow-load do you get here?"

With a dismissive wave of her hand, she grunted. "I have magic for all of that."

"Magic can be tiring," I said. "If the young men were here, you could rest all the time. Order them around."

Thyra made an exaggerated expression of hmm-maybe-I-should-think-about-this-after-all, and after a moment nodded her head. "You say they are warriors?"

I nodded.

"I have no weapons for them, only some small knives and an axe for the chopping of wood."

"They are not here to act as warriors," I clarified. "They are here only to learn the language."

"What if we require them to act as warriors?"

That brought me up short. "Why?" I asked. "Are you at war?"

She shook her head. "No, but there has been some concern in the village about maybe raids from boat-thugs who have been using the Dives estuary to get to the interior from the seacoast. If these young men could protect the village, this would make them more attractive guests."

"I can't promise protection," I said, "since there is no guarantee they'll be here if such an attack happens. But you must surely agree that having a strong young man around is better than not."

Thyra shrugged. "It's not bad," she said. "Not as good as a strong young woman, though."

Over the course of the next few minutes, I could see her warming to the idea, and eventually, without actually having said yes, it was clear she was amenable.

"How might you vouch for these visitors?" I asked. "Their presence will be noticed in the village."

Thyra shrugged and gave a dismissive wave of her hand (a sort of early medieval variant of Erszebet's body language, now I think of it) and said, "That is easy. Much trade across the Channel, there is nothing strange about cousins, friends of friends, and that sort, showing up from Britain and Ireland. I shall say my guests are such people, from such places."

A few minutes more conversation, and she was willing to actually speak the words, "Yes, I will take them" (which put my fledgling Inner Bureaucrat at ease). She even invited me to share her meal of rabbit stew with root vegetables, and to stay the night before she Homed me the following morning.

Back at DODO HQ, I delivered my good news. Tristan and I sat at the same computer (be still my heart, I suppose) to pore over the feudal, judicial, and church chronicles of the area, seeking references to raids circa 1045. We found nothing, except one possible indirect reference to villagers who perished during altercations with bandits. It did not match Thyra's description, nor was it chronicled officially anywhere—it was an ancillary comment in testimony given during a property dispute.

"Well, that's good, anyhow," said Tristan. "Probably means I won't encounter anything while I'm there."

I entered notes about Thyra's dialect into the relevant linguistic databases, and sat with DORCCAD personnel, giving them sketches of the area for entry into their systems.

There was some chatter about timing, conducted over ODIN— and occasionally in person, since we tried to dine with the Odas every couple of weeks. To make a long logistical issue short, it was determined that Tristan would go back to stay with Thyra four different times, for a fortnight each time (rather than going back twice for a month each—Frank Oda determined this to be stabler with Chronotron calculations, and Erszebet agreed with him).

Tristan already knew Anglo-Saxon, and I'd been prepping him on Latin almost since we met (how can anyone with Western language interests not know Latin, ~~FFS~~?). So he needed very little prep. Erszebet Sent him. Thyra had secured clothes in anticipation of his coming (he was Sent in spring).

Thyra had also already communicated to curious villagers, priests, etc. that Tristan (her supposed kinsman) would be sojourning with her for a fortnight so they might exchange news, and that he was of mixed Danish/Anglo-Saxon descent originating from a remote part of England (Tintagel—or as they called it then, Dintagel), journeying to Normandy to seek his fortune on the tourney field. This would explain why his accent was unfamiliar and why he tended to use Britannic, Cornish, and Anglo-Saxon vocabulary. Since no one in the settlement had been to that part of England, they accepted the cover story.

I KNOW THAT in the bowels of ODIN, there is an official DEDE report of Tristan's time there, for I wrote it myself; I know also that there is an "incident report" that the well-intentioned but insufferably officious Macy Stoll required him to write as well. But I have just come into an extra measure of whale oil, and there is ink enough, and I cannot sleep from my growing anxiety, so it pleases me to recall Tristan's telling me of his time there, and one element in particular.

When he arrived, he was made welcome by the settlement at large, and all manner of gifts and entertainment pressed upon him. Once a level of trust was established, he asked to learn their combat styles, and the men of the settlement were pleased to show off and practice with him. It was generally limited to stick-fighting arts, as the locals were rural villagers. These sessions also allowed him to work on language immersion more fluidly, imitating not only the vocabulary but the cadence and pitch of able-bodied young males. He was not in danger of "talking like a girl," which would have been the case if he'd mostly stayed under Thyra's roof.

He was Homed after two weeks (yes, it was dreadfully good to see him, and yes, I did try to catch a peek of him before he disappeared into the decontamination shower). After about ten days of downtime, he went back; another two weeks, another ten days; a third fortnight, a third rest period. During the rest periods, he was fully debriefed (usually by me) and all lessons learned were inserted into DORC's linguistic database, so that future "Varangian Guard" candidates could bone up on their Norman prior to visiting Thyra, and learn the language that much more quickly.

Then came the fourth and final repetition. This is the part I most like to remember him describing.

One morning, shortly before dawn, Tristan and Thyra were awakened by suspicious noises. Tristan arose, went outside, and saw a longboat moving up the tributary toward the village center, with six men in it. He grabbed a peeled tree branch, at least an inch thick and about his own height, which he had been intending to use to build Thyra a drying rack. He ran to the village, entered the church through its narthex, and rang the bell urgently to alert the villagers. And then he stayed in the church, realizing the strangers must be coming there to steal the only thing of value in the area: a reliquary of a wrought silver cross, about a handspan across. Embedded in a decorative gold rosette in the center was a flake of white enamel, alleged by local clerics to be a fragment of a molar formerly belonging to St. Septimus of Pontchardon, an early missionary who had been martyred by the Gauls. Obviously this was of value to the would-be thieves for the metal, not the relic. They were startled by the bell as they approached the church entrance, more so because they found themselves unexpectedly face-to-face with a large man brandishing a stick.

Three of the men, armed with an axe, a steel-tipped lance, and a seax (knife)—held Tristan at bay in the narthex while the other three ran up the aisle of the church to nab the reliquary, which lived on the altar. While there, they snatched up a few other odds and ends that had caught their eye—the candelabrum, the communion cup, etc. These booty-carriers emerged from the church first, only to find some villagers—alerted by Tristan's ringing of the bell—waiting for them with shovels, rakes, pitchforks, and knives.

These first intruders were lightly armed but their hands were full of loot, and they were obliged to drop the valuables in order to defend themselves. The more heavily armed men, who had been menacing Tristan, came out to join the fray. The last of these was the one with the lance. He backed toward the exit of the building while keeping the weapon leveled at Tristan . . . then pivoted toward the open door to make a fast departure.

However, the lance got hung up in the tiny doorway, in a manner reminiscent of an early-twentieth-century slapstick film comedy, or so it always seems when Tristan is acting it out for new recruits. Seeing an opening, Tristan advanced and delivered a "pool cue" style shot to the head of the lance-man, catching him by his ear with the butt of his staff. The man sagged toward the floor and dropped his weapon. Tristan grabbed the lance, but he himself was the next person to fall victim to the cramped dimensions of the doorway, as he tripped over its high threshold on the way out and sprawled across the pavement outside (it is a hoot to see him re-enact this moment). The lance was lost (it was still dark, the sun not having risen yet), but in groping for it Tristan found himself grasping a boat oar that had apparently been carried up to the site by one of the intruders, perhaps to use as a weapon.

The melee was moving in the general direction of the river-bank. This was a long stone's throw from the church; the intruders struggled to fight their way through the mob of a dozen or so villagers who were haphazardly beating at them with farm implements, as though not sure if the point was to prevent them from getting back into the church or to prevent them from escaping.

Tristan collected himself from his unintentional vaudeville routine, and caught up with the intruders as they were attempting to board the boat to make their getaway. By now, they had dropped all their booty, but nobody could see that in the dark yet. A villager grabbed the gunwale of the boat with both hands in a bid to prevent them from getting away (presumably with the reliquary). The axe-wielding intruder raised his weapon high, clearly with an eye toward cutting the villager's fingers off.

Tristan lunged toward them, swung his oar in a wide arc, and caught the axe-man in the gut, knocking the wind out of him and sending him sprawling back into the boat. At the same moment, the villager holding the gunwale did a belly-flop into the river. (I am trembling with suppressed mirth even now as I write this, recalling the many times I've seen it all acted out at office parties when Tristan's had a few.)

The intruders got away in their longboat. Five of the villagers sustained very superficial wounds (Thyra healed them in an hour), and Tristan strained ligaments in his shoulder when he slammed the oar into the axe-man. It was nothing serious, but as I said, Macy Stoll ordered him to write an incident report about it. (And this was before DODO's bureaucracy had bloated up out of control. I wonder what would happen if he did that now . . . Well, I'll never know. Get used to it, Stokes.)

Once the sun rose, all of the artifacts were recovered, cleaned, and restored to the church, and the village had a shared breakfast, during which the children imitated the more absurd physical moments of the brief raid. What could have been a tragedy was transformed into a playful morning.

But if I told you the consequences of this minor skirmish, reader, you would absolutely not believe me.

Post by Macy Stoll to LTC Tristan Lyons on private ODIN channel

DAY 872 (MID-DECEMBER, YEAR 2)

LTC Lyons, as a rule I don't keep tabs on all of the After Action Reports on the various DEDEs, since Diachronic Operations is your department and not mine. Medical benefits, however, ARE my department. In that vein, I note that you consulted an external physician upon the conclusion of your most recent visit to the 1045 Normandy DTAP. In order for this expense to be approved, I'll need details on the nature of the injury, whether it was sustained on the job, and why DODO medical staff were unable to deal with the problem in-house.

Reply from LTC Lyons:
NVM I will just eat the expense.

From Macy Stoll:
Your selflessness sets a brave example, but it's not just about the money. By tracking these incidents and expenditures, we are able to optimize the planning and budgeting process, unlocking the ability to

hire additional medical staff to meet the needs of our growing organization. Also, for legal reasons we need thorough documentation of
all on-the-job injuries.

From LTC Lyons:

I came back with a tweaked shoulder. Dr. Srinavasan checked me
out and suggested I consult a physical therapist to get it worked on.
The PT doc did some myofascial work and sent me home with some
exercises. Everything is fine now. To the extent that this is relevant to
budget and staffing, we might benefit from having a physical therapist in the medical section.

From Macy Stoll:

Thank you for the explanation. I still need to know whether the shoulder injury was contracted in the workplace.

From LTC Lyons:

If by "workplace" you mean Normandy a thousand years ago, yes.

From Macy Stoll:

Thank you for that additional clarification. Given the unusual nature
of DODO, that does indeed constitute a workplace injury. As such, you
are required to file an Incident Report crosslinked to Dr. Srinavasan's
outside medical specialist referral paperwork.

FROM DR. ROGER BLEVINS TO LTC TRISTAN LYONS
CC: LIEUTENANT GENERAL OCTAVIAN K. FRINK
DAY 874

Lieutenant Colonel Lyons:

I am in receipt of an Incident Report, filed yesterday, describing events that took place during one of your DEDEs in Normandy in 1045. The account is sketchy and appears to have been written in haste, or perhaps you are simply accustomed to taking a casual attitude toward such matters. In any case, if this document is to be believed, you voluntarily engaged one or more "historicals" in potentially lethal combat during this DEDE. For the benefit of LTG Frink (CCed for the record) this DEDE was strictly for the purpose of gaining fluency in the local language. It did not call for a Fighter-class DOer, and engaging in combat was not part of the mission scope. During the unscheduled and unauthorized tussle, you sustained injuries that later required expenditure of DODO funds on an outside medical specialist lacking security clearance, with possible risk of exposure of top-secret information.

Please consider this a formal reprimand. As the head of the operational wing of DODO, you set an example for the ever-expanding staff of DOers who serve under you, and as such you must be held to a higher standard of professionalism and conduct than you exhibited in this case.

While this is technically grounds for being placed on a Performance Enhancement Plan, or even outright dismissal, I am willing to make an exception just this once. Please consider yourself on notice, however, that further such lapses in judgment will be treated with the utmost gravity.

With that disagreeable task out of the way, I would like to consider the matter closed, and wish you the best returns of the season.

Sincerely,

Roger Blevins, Ph.D.

Director, Department of Diachronic Operations

FROM LTC TRISTAN LYONS TO DR. ROGER BLEVINS
CC: LIEUTENANT GENERAL OCTAVIAN K. FRINK

DAY 875

Dear Dr. Blevins:

Concerning yesterday's letter of reprimand, I would like to point out the following circumstances that may help clarify matters for you and General Frink.

- The "injuries" that I sustained consisted of a sore shoulder. The "outside medical specialist" is a local physical therapist. I told her that I had sustained the injury while practicing jiu-jitsu. She accepted the story. There is no risk of leakage of classified information.
- The "potentially lethal combat" consisted of swinging a boat oar into the stomach of a drunk and disorderly Norman

who was about to chop off a man's fingers. To describe this as potentially lethal is about like saying that I got up this morning in Boston and took a potentially lethal train ride in to work.

- When we go on these DEDEs, we have to blend in, and behave as the locals expect us to behave. I was the biggest and strongest man in the village and had been practicing stick-fighting with the locals for weeks. For me to have stood by passively during this disturbance would have raised more questions than taking the minimal action that I did.

Merry Christmas,
LTC Tristan Lyons

**Annotation, handwritten by General Frink at the bottom of
above letter, scanned and delivered digitally**
DAY 876

Gentlemen,

Xmas is four days away and we should be focused on (a) brotherly love and (b) turning on the Chronotron at the beginning of the new year. Please consider this matter closed with no further repercussions, and trouble me with it no more.

Happy Holidays

O. K. Frink

Exchange of posts between
Dr. Melisande Stokes and LTC Tristan Lyons
on private ODIN channel
DAY 879 (CHRISTMAS EVE, YEAR 2)

Post from Dr. Stokes:

Subject: Chinese take-out?

My turn to pay, but can you get the usual and I'll reimburse? Meet at my place. (Trying to get Erszebet out of here before she goes nuclear on Blevins again.)

I know you're on the outs with Blevins, but we should talk to him about fast-tracking another resident witch. E has stayed far longer than she agreed to; she's being a good sport (by her standards), but I'm tired of running interference every time Blevins is a jackass to her. There's three or four who expressed interest (Rachel in Constantinople, etc.) and they're all in DTAPs with multiple KCWs. Talk about it over dinner?

—MS

PS: Merry Christmas.

Reply from LTC Lyons:

STOKES!

1. Bad form to call your boss a jackass on a company messaging system.
2. Merry Christmas.
3. I thought you were heading out of town to spend time with family.
4. We've never brought a historical forward in time before. Can we even do that?

From Dr. Stokes:

Tristan,

1. If we get to the point where said jackass is reading my personal

messages to you, then we have bigger issues and we're all done here.

2. And Happy New Year.

3. Canceled the trip. Mom's showing up late tonight, we'll hang out at my place. Too much going on here, and Erszebet gets a little nutty around the holidays.

4. You're right that Sending a historical forward is different from Homing a DOer back to their "natural" time and place, but Erszebet says it can be done. Especially if the Sending witch has developed familiarity with the ODEC by Homing a lot of people there. We have, as of today, run fifty-five DEDEs in 1200 Constantinople. We have used three different KCWs to Home all of our DOers. One of them (Rachel) has done it thirty-two times and Erszebet feels she has our ODEC strongly dialed in. We should consider it.

—MS

From LTC Lyons:

OMW with the usual. Break out your finest chopsticks!

From Dr. Stokes:

OK but setting a knife and fork for E. She won't eat otherwise.

—MS

Post by Mortimer Shore on "General" ODIN channel

DAY 887 (NEW YEAR'S DAY, YEAR 3)

Happy New Year, everyone! I'm still a little buzzed (heh) from the festivities at Oda-sensei and Rebecca's, but now that we are almost FOUR

WHOLE HOURS into the new year I wanted to buckle down to work and send this out.

As we prepare to power up the Chronotron for real (T-minus four days and counting, huzzah), Dr. Oda recommended that I send out some informal layman's language on What Exactly Is a Chronotron. I'm pretty amped about this (so to speak) and really grateful that I've been able to move away from the SysAdmin role (a big hand to the staff who's running all the stuff I used to manage, especially Gordon Healey, another MIT CS'ist who now gets asked all the questions about email servers, but hey, Gordie, I'm proof this place is all about job growth LOL).

So just a reminder, I'm not qualified to explain WHY this works, because that's the physics part where I'm a bonehead, but here's a simplified take on HOW it works:

The Chronotron is based on a theoretical model, which proposes that for the present-day universe that we all live in, there's not just one past, and not just several alternate pasts, but an infinite number of them. Similarly, this one single present also has an infinite number of possible futures. But our relationship to these infinite pasts and futures isn't random—plausibility throws its weight around, per some freaky quantum mechanics stuff that Dr. Oda calls Feynman Diagram History Pachinko. If you're really interested in the details of that, check in with him in his spare time (heh) and he will be happy to expound.

The QUIPUs (Quantum Information Processing Units) that make up the Chronotron are capable of dealing with the infinite-pasts-as-weighted-by-plausibility calculations in SLIT (Something Less Than Infinite Time). They know how to "renormalize" per plausibility quotients, so that irrelevant pasts can be ignored and high-leverage pasts can be zeroed in on. Thanks to all the input from our fine team of in-house historians, it can sort out what leads to what (and what DOESN'T lead to what) with more accuracy than Google directing you to NSFW porn sites.

Diachronicle

DAY 891 (EARLY JANUARY, YEAR 3)

In which the manifestly obvious takes us by surprise

THE CHRONOTRON WAS READY TO be turned on and used for the first time.

During the year and a half that DODO's R&D division, under Frank Oda, had been developing and testing the Chronotron, the rest of us had been slowly building out the witch network through many DTAPs, and recruiting HOSMAs (Historical Operations Subject Matter Authorities—what any normal person would call professors) for DORC. We hadn't been conducting full-blown diachronic operations per se, but we'd been laying the ground-work, recruiting new DOers with painstaking care, training them in languages and other skills, Sending them on dry runs to various DTAPs just to break them in.

The ODEC had gone through two complete redesigns. Four copies of that design had been constructed in the basement, with two others roughed in and ready to be finished as soon as there was a need for them. But there was no need, for we still only had a single witch—or, in the jargon of the agency, MUON.

The exact numbers have flown from my memory, but on the day that we booted up the Chronotron, our head count looked something like this:

DORC (of which I was in charge, and, reader, how often does one have the opportunity to say one works for the DORC of DODO?) comprised about twenty full-time HOS-MAs, five support staff, and one hundred part-time consultants, all security-checked and sworn to secrecy, not to mention five full-time DORCCAD technicians (this being our Cartographic and Architectural Database). One of the more colorful and active sub-departments was DoVE, the Department of Violence(s) Ethnology, which was responsible for instructing DOers in historical martial arts as well as related skills such as riding, armor, and making improvised weapons. This had expanded far beyond Mortimer Shore's early training sessions in the park. Under the leadership of Dr. Hilton Fuller, an Ivy League academic with a passion for historical martial arts, it now operated an in-house dojo as well as a larger training and riding center outside of Boston.

C/COD (headed up by Macy Stoll) had a head count of nearly a hundred, many of whom seemed to be busy setting up other DODO facilities around the world. The department had five full-time medical professionals, as well as the usual complement of janitors, HR people, finance, IT, and the like. Its largest single sub-department was the redundantly named Diachronic Operations Security Operations, under Major Isobel Sloane, who had been recruited "sideways" from a military police unit based in the Middle East. People in the know pronounced it "doe-seck-ops," but its acronym, DOSECOPS, inevitably led to new hires pronouncing it "dose cops" and referring to individual members—who did actually resemble police officers—by the same name.

R&D (in Frank Oda's purview) was the smallest department, some dozen computer scientists and physicists, a few programmers, and an administrator. Until this point it had worked on the Chronotron to the exclusion of all else, but Frank had some other ideas he was itching to work on.

Finally there was Diachronic Operations, under Tristan. This was the unit that employed all of the actual DOers and Sent them on missions. By this point I think we had about twenty DOers who were "good to go"—fully trained and checked out—plus a dozen more in the pipeline. More than half of them were Fighters or Striders. Those classes were easier to recruit, in a sense, because the military's Special Forces units had already done the work for us of combing through the entire population and picking out the ones who were suited for the job. We just had to sift through their personnel records looking for ones with the right combination of good teeth and unusual language aptitude. Lovers, Closers, Spies, Sages, and the rest were under-represented simply because finding them was harder. But we had a few of them in each category— enough, we felt, to "make a dent in the universe" once the Chronotron came online and started telling us what we should actually do with them.

All told—once General Frink's entourage from DC had been bundled in—some two hundred people were present at the ceremony where we booted up the Chronotron. And, by extension, the Department of Diachronic Operations in its fully operational form. It was An Event—the sort of thing Macy Stoll excelled at organizing. Erszebet persuaded me to get a haircut and borrow one of her skirts. Tristan wore his dress uniform. Frank Oda put on a suit, then threw a white lab coat over it to conceal some moth holes that he didn't notice until he put it on. Even Mortimer found a necktie and a pair of leather shoes.

Merely getting all of those people into the building without causing a public spectacle required some planning. We were still operating out of the same dingy, nondescript industrial building in Cambridge. Outwardly this hadn't changed at all; it still sported the same graffiti tags and vinyl window shades as when I'd first seen it two and a half years ago. People in the neighborhood, when they noticed it at all, shook their heads and wondered when some real estate developer would snap it up and turn it into a high-tech office building. To hide the fact that more than a hundred people were going in and out of it every day, Macy's facilities team had built half a dozen secret entrances connected to neighboring structures by tunnels. We were about a block away from the river and so we also made use of some utility passages connecting to public works facilities in the green belt. When General Frink arrived, he was in the backseat of a small SUV that was completely nondescript save for the fact that its rear windows were darkened, lest some pedestrian at a stoplight look in and recognize the face of the Director of National Intelligence.

The Chronotron itself was not physically that large, but the space in which Frank and his team had built it was obstructed and complicated by the requirements of ventilation and power. Between the ODECs in the basement, which still had to be jacketed in liquid helium, and the QUIPUs on the second floor, which also ran at super-cold temperatures, this building was one of the largest cryogenic facilities in New England. A large fraction of its interior volume was set aside for tankage, insulation, ducting, and safety equipment.

Consequently, we didn't have anything like enough room for two hundred people in the actual Chronotron room, which was up on the second floor. The only people physically present were General Frink, Dr. Rudge, a few of their top aides, Blevins, the department heads—including yours truly, as the head of DORC— and some of Frank's senior geeks. Everyone else watched it from their offices or the cafeteria via live stream.

We'd actually had a small celebration of our own at the Odas' beforehand—just the original quintet, plus Mortimer Shore, of whom both Odas were very fond. By unspoken agreement we had always shielded Mortimer from too much information about DODO's high-level political dysfunction, though I often wondered if he used his sysadmin privileges to eavesdrop on some of our internal disputes. On this particular morning, as I looked at his beaming face, it didn't seem likely. Mortimer just thought it was cool that the big kids had invited him into the sandbox.

Then we'd all piled into Frank's Volvo and gone to the office. General Frink showed up twenty minutes later, right on schedule, and toured the facility with Blevins at his elbow, ending up in the Chronotron control room where there was a great deal of fuss over the powering-on and the booting-up of the machine. As we had actually been beta-testing it for several weeks, this was largely ceremonial, but Oda-sensei still looked flushed with pleasure and I did not begrudge him the moment. He "switched on" the Chronotron. Actually it had been on more often than it had been off over the past several weeks. And it was in fact already running, so all he was really doing was turning on a fancy workstation that was connected to it. But that's ceremony for you. As a grid of flat-panel screens came alive with scrolling text windows and dancing infographics, everyone clapped and some of the coders hooted. Frink congratulated Oda-sensei heartily, Blevins almost as heartily, and then Tristan, Erszebet, and myself with little more than civil courtesy. We were getting used to this, although in truth it ~~pissed me off~~ saddened me.

Adjacent to the control room proper was a secure conference room, equipped with all manner of screens and VR and AR displays, where the results of its analyses could be reviewed and cross-correlated with maps, historical timelines, and diagrams of DODO's network of safe houses and KCWs. We filed into it once the Chronotron had been turned on, and received a briefing from Blevins on the projected first few months of DODO's operations. These focused on what we were calling the Constantinople Theater.

The Constantinople Theater was a broad canvas of safe houses and planned DEDEs, all having to do with limiting Russia's power in the Balkans and the Black Sea. This was not to be done in an invasive manner that would alter any of that area's endlessly turbulent history, but in a subtle way to ensure a lack of Russian hegemony in the future. This included, of course, massaging the boundaries of the East/West schism of the church. But there was far more to it than that. Hundreds of discrete DEDEs were encompassed in this plan. We did not yet have all the resources required to accomplish them. But we knew what the first four or five gambits were supposed to be, and so today, we would move en masse directly from the Chronotron down to ODEC Row to send Tristan off on the first one.

I say "supposed to be" because Robert Burns was right on the money about best-laid plans.

As if in a medieval street festival, our clutch of officials, aides, geeks, and department heads followed Blevins, Rudge, and Frink down the hallway and staircase to the basement, and were joined along the way by additional historians, DOers, office workers, and techies emerging from the spaces where they had been watching the live stream. The basement level had room to accommodate a few more spectators. Erszebet, decked out as only she could deck herself out, awaited us.

ODEC Row looked more like a medical facility than a magical teleportation center. This was because of the need to preserve strict epidemiological precautions. We'd improvised a working decontamination suite around the first ODEC, of course, but the more recent influx of funding and expertise had given us the resources to do it right.

The entire basement was cut in half by a wall of glass. On the other side of it, as we came in, was the bio-containment zone, subdivided into discrete isolation zones for each of the ODECs. They all shared some plumbing in the form of the sterilizing showers—"human car washes" in Tristan's description—that all DOers passed through en route to and from the ODECs, and the air filtration systems that ensured not even a virus could pass across the barrier. A fully equipped medical suite—sort of a compact trauma center—was tucked away in one corner. It was equipped with x-ray machines and an operating room so that injured DOers could be treated on-site, immediately and secretly. Next to that was a two-bed recovery ward. Compared to all of that, the ODECs themselves—the four that were up and running, and the two that were only roughed in—occupied only a small footprint. They were cylindrical rooms, just big enough on the inside for the Sending witch and the DOer, larger on the outside because of the thickness of the cryogenic jackets and electronic systems.

Tristan—who was en route to 1203 Constantinople on Varangian Guard duty—had slipped out of the conference room early, come downstairs, and passed through the airlock into the bio-containment zone. By the time we arrived, he had gone through the showers and was undergoing other decontamination procedures that my current Victorian sensibilities forbid me from discussing on the page.

The crowd of dignitaries and support staff tumbled like unmilled corn into the space on the "dirty" side of the glass wall. General Frink was positioned in direct view of ODEC #3 and the pre- and post-DEDE bio equipment surrounding it. Oda-sensei was just off to Frink's side, checking the ODEC's status through a touch-screen interface.

We'd used all four of the finished ODECs sporadically, just to make sure they all worked. It was expensive to keep them running because of the need for liquid helium and electrical power. Until today, DODO hadn't had the budget, and we hadn't needed them frequently enough to justify leaving them on. With the new year and the powering-on of the Chronotron, this had all changed. Over the holiday weekend the technicians had been chilling the whole system down to just above absolute zero and running tests on the electronics. From now on, it would stay on 24/7. This meant keeping the doors shut to limit heat loss and the excess usage of energy and cryogenic fluids. When we arrived that morning, the door to ODEC #3 was decorated with a red ribbon tied into a bow. For the schedule called for us to kill time with another ribbon-cutting ceremony as Tristan completed his preparations. Blevins droned on while Erszebet went through the airlock and changed into a disposable bunny suit and surgical mask—these were standard procedures, needed to prevent re-contaminating Tristan during the moments that they would be standing together in the ODEC. She emerged in the space between the glass wall and the door to ODEC #3 and picked up a sword that was waiting for her on a table. It was a sharp one—a Hungarian saber. Mortimer had sourced it from eBay and honed it until it could slice through a handkerchief in midair. Erszebet had been training with it, enough that she could swing it without killing herself. At a signal from Frank, she raised it above her head and drew it down through the ribbon, severing it in one quick motion. At the same moment, Frank whacked the "enter" key on his keyboard, executing a command that made all the lights come on.

ODECs #1 through #4 had been officially powered up. A round of applause swept through the crowd on the "dirty" side. At the same moment Tristan finally emerged, wrapped in a sterile paper jumpsuit. This created the amusing impression that he was a character in a sitcom who had just made his entrance on the set and was getting a round of applause from the audience. He saluted General Frink through the glass wall. Frink saluted back. Tristan and Erszebet moved toward the ODEC door. The crowd on the "dirty" side pressed forward, trying to find space along the glass wall. For many of these people, it would be the first time they saw the ODEC actually in use. There'd be nothing really to see, of course, except that two people would go in and only one would come out.

Frank had switched on an audio link so that he could talk to Erszebet and Tristan. Standing near him, I could hear their voices through the tinny little speakers built into the monitor.

Tristan turned toward ODEC #3 and reached for the button that would cause it to open its door.

Just before his hand touched it, there was a pounding from within, and a muffled scream.

Tristan and Erszebet glanced at each other with concern. "*Open it*," I said urgently, but Tristan was already mashing the button.

As the door hissed open, a naked young woman tumbled out of the ODEC, clutching her head and wailing with fear. As she curled up protectively, her wordless hysteria was interspersed with a few hyperventilated phrases of medieval-era Hebrew.

Tristan sidestepped and pulled a hospital gown from a rack of them hanging nearby. He tossed the gown on top of the hysterical girl, like a man throwing a blanket on a fire. Erszebet elbowed him away and adjusted the gown for modesty.

Nudging Frank away from the control panel, I spoke firmly in Hebrew: "You're safe. You are among friends. There is no need to be frightened."

Relief at hearing her own language made her catch her breath. Pulling the gown around her body, she rose to a kneeling position and stared about the place, wide-eyed. Tristan dropped to one knee and pointed toward me. I waved to her and caught her eye.

"You are safe," I repeated, and then, rifling through my mental roster, maintaining eye contact: "Are you Rachel? From Pera? Constantinople? Daughter of Avraham? Is that who you are?"

Clutching the gown to her front, she rose to her feet and padded over toward me. For a moment I was afraid she'd walk straight into the glass wall, but Erszebet put a restraining hand on her shoulder, and Tristan darted ahead and rapped on the glass with his knuckles. She slowed as she approached, and stopped with her face only inches from mine.

"Yes . . ." She turned her head and glanced around the space—not to the ODEC itself, the open door of which was just behind her, but around at the control panel and the scores of curious faces, in what must have been extremely curious forms of dress. She gasped. Electric cables, fluorescent lights, plastic chairs . . . every single thing in that room, other than the biological reality of other human beings, was utterly alien to her. Her eyes opened so wide I could see the whites all around the iris. I thought for a moment she would faint.

Instead, she erupted into giggles.

"Ladies and gentlemen," Tristan announced, "looks like we've got ourselves another witch."

PART
FOUR

INCIDENT REPORT

AUTHOR: Rebecca East-Oda
SUBJECT: Rachel bat Avraham—unauthorized ODEC use
THEATER: C/COD
OPERATION: Ribbon-cutting ceremony
DTAP: Cambridge, MA, present day
FILED: Day 896 (early January, Year 3)

Summary: At 11:21:16 of Day 891, the subject, Rachel bat Avraham, a KCW from the circa-1200 Constantinople DTAP, was Sent from there to ODEC #3 and materialized in normal physical condition. She was issued clothing and placed under observation in the medical isolation facility adjoining ODEC Row. She was debriefed in Hebrew and in Greek by Dr. Stokes (head of DORC) and Dr. Lingas (in-house Byzantine Greek HOSMA) respectively. Initial briefing focused on two topics of immediate concern, namely (1) whether any more surprise visitors from 1200 Constantinople were to be expected, and (2) the importance of immediate medical procedures needed to protect subject from our diseases and vice versa. As precautions in the meantime, Dr. Oda had shut down all four operational ODECs, and ODEC Row had been placed under bio-containment lockdown.

Upon receipt of verbal consent from subject, medical staff began administration of inoculations required to protect subject from modern diseases to which she is not likely to have immunity, and collected samples (swabs, blood, urine, feces) for analysis of possible historical disease agents. Upon examination, subject had fully healed scars indicative of a past encounter with smallpox, suggesting that no active, virus-shedding infection was in progress. Subsequent laboratory analysis detected low levels of intestinal parasites and gut flora of a potentially contagious nature; these were eradicated through orally administered medications and the subject given a clean bill of health following four days of analysis and treatment. The inoculation protocols are scheduled to continue for another two weeks, whereupon subject will be cleared to emerge from biocontainment and mingle with the general population. Psychologically, subject appears normal, other than some natural disorientation.

Results of debriefing: Subject is a seventeen-year-old resident of Pera, the Jewish neighborhood lying across the Golden Horn from Constantinople proper. She is one of a small network of KCWs recruited by DODO and used extensively for DEDEs conducted during the last two years while laying the groundwork for full-scale diachronic operations slated to commence immediately. She is well known to our DOers, who from the very beginning have commented on her marked curiosity about our time and place and her frequently voiced desire to travel into the future and join us. She was able to reach ODEC #3 through the assistance of her mother, another KCW in Constantinople who agreed to carry out the Sending.

Until this incident occurred, we had not envisioned that a security breach of this nature was a realistic threat.

1. Sending by a historical witch into her own future was considered extremely difficult.
2. There was no place in the present day where magic worked, save in the confines of an "up and running" ODEC. Since we didn't leave the ODECs up and running, the Sending witch had no fixed target to "aim at."

Obviously, these two assumptions are no longer valid.

1. Our KCWs in 1200 Constantinople have had so much practice Homing our DOers that they seem to have developed a feel for how to access the modern Boston DTAP.

2. The policy just inaugurated of leaving the ODECs running 24/7 has given the Sending witch a much broader and more stable target to "aim at."

During her debriefing, subject admitted that she had become aware of the new ODECs and the "always on" policy slated to go into force at the beginning of the new year. This leakage of information was not the result of one specific disclosure by one specific DOer, but rather a pattern of information that she had assembled through numerous conversations with various DOers. In addition, it appears that subject, along with many other witches, has the ability to extract information from nearby persons through non-verbal techniques. That combined with subject's intense curiosity and drive to escape what she sees as the stifling confines of a traditional medieval Jewish household led to her devising the plan that led to her materializing in ODEC #3.

General remarks: Subject is beginning to learn modern English and is rapidly becoming familiar and comfortable with modern technology, conveniences, etc. It will be some time before she can move about freely in modern society without supervision, however, nothing in principle stands in the way of her doing so. It should go without saying that she carries in her head classified secrets that can never be divulged to the modern world at large. Likewise, if she were to return to her place of origin and divulge information about the future, or attempt to alter the reality of that DTAP in a heavy-handed manner, Diachronic Shear would likely result.

For her own protection, she will remain in biological isolation for another two weeks, but after that, top-level direction will be needed in order to determine her fate.

FROM LIEUTENANT GENERAL OCTAVIAN K. FRINK
TO DR. ROGER BLEVINS

DAY 900 (MID-JANUARY, YEAR 3)

Blev,

I was perusing Mrs. East-Oda's report on the recent incident and came across something toward the end of it that, to put it mildly, startled me: Ms. bat Avraham "has the ability to extract information from nearby persons through non-verbal techniques."

Am I to understand that she is a mind reader? And that other witches have the same ability? If so, then this document is an extraordinary example of what is referred to, in the journalism business, as "burying the lede."

Yours in consternation and amusement,

Okie

FROM DR. ROGER BLEVINS
TO LIEUTENANT GENERAL OCTAVIAN K. FRINK

DAY 902

Okie,

I too noticed the passage you referred to in your letter, and was doing some investigation before reporting further. I would recommend against use of any such pulp-novel terminology as "mind reading" but, in short, it does appear that many witches have enhanced skills around sensing others' mental states, and manipulating same. Of course, like any other magical technique, it can only be used in an ODEC, or in a pre-1851 DTAP.

In a larger sense, this is not a surprise. For reasons I needn't belabor to you, DODO has focused on one, and only one, form of magic: Sending people to other DTAPs. But magic has many other possible uses. Making an analogy to electricity, it's as if Thomas Edison devoted his entire career to the development of washing machines but never put any effort into light bulbs, elevators, or the myriad other applications that surround us today. We know perfectly well that witches could perform other kinds of magic; we just haven't put any resources into it yet.

Blev

Post by LTG Octavian K. Frink
to Dr. Roger Blevins on private ODIN channel
DAY 903

Blev, I'm moving this over to the secure messaging system for efficiency's sake. I got your letter. To put it bluntly, exploitation of the Sending type of magic has ballooned into an enormously expensive and cumbersome operation. All worth it, I'm sure—not suggesting that the taxpayers' money is in any way misspent on ODECs and so on. But now that we have all of that apparatus up and running we need to look for other opportunities to make the most of it.

It didn't escape my notice that you mentioned the possibility of manipulating others' mental states as something witches could do. Let's drill down on that.

Reply from Dr. Blevins:

In a sense it's almost common knowledge, Okie. Historically, witches were feared and mistrusted for just such abilities; where do you think the term "bewitched" originated from?

We haven't put much effort into this because it only works in an ODEC, and it's hard to imagine a practical application of such techniques, which depend on getting the subject into a cryogenically isolated telephone booth in a basement in Cambridge, Massachusetts. Also, we only have one witch.

From LTG Frink:

Now we have two, and we pretty much own Rachel bat Avraham; we can't very well just let her wander around free. If she came forward, it means others can do likewise. Let's get more witches, and let's put 'em to work.

I take your point about the ODEC. Why can't we make these things smaller? More portable? That would make their use for psy-ops far more feasible.

From Dr. Blevins:

As to your first point, we've been contemplating such a program for a long time—which is why we built so many ODECs. I'll put my foot on the gas, and I'll spread the word to the department heads.

As to your second, my understanding is that they are impossibly cumbersome because of the cryogenics. But Dr. Oda is now surplus personnel, since he finished the Chronotron. I'll try to draw him out on the topic, without tipping our hand.

Follow-up from Dr. Blevins, a day later:

Okie, I had coffee with Dr. Oda, framed as a conversation about his future at DODO. We had contemplated moving him to "emeritus" status to get him out of the way without sending his troublesome wife into a rage. In that capacity he would have the freedom to explore independent research projects as long as they were relevant to DODO's mission. Without any prompting from me, he mentioned that he had ideas on building an ODEC capable of working at non-cryogenic temperatures. The technical details are over my head but apparently it has to do with room-temperature superconductors and certain advances in computer processing power that he has been tracking. Sounds like this could possibly lead to a portable ODEC—and if so we could redirect resources from diachronic travel to psy-ops.

Unless you say otherwise before COB today, I'll slide him over to the new role and encourage him to pursue the idea.

Blev

Post by Macy Stoll
on "All Employees" ODIN channel
DAY 905

Everyone, Dr. Blevins is extremely busy just now but has asked me to reach out in this forum and shine a light on some of the confusion and resulting rumors that have surrounded the recent arrival of Rachel bat Avraham.

To clarify, Rachel's arrival was a PLANNED event—NOT a security breach.

There was indeed some surprise and confusion around the exact timing, which is why some of you may have noticed startled expressions on the faces of LTC Lyons and Ms. Karpathy. Rachel was scheduled to be Sent forward to ODEC #3 on a different date in the near future as part of a planned program of activities for which Dr. Blevins has been laying the groundwork for some months now. Because of some understandable confusion around calendars (Julian vs. Gregorian), the Sending KCW in 1200 Constantinople did it on the wrong day and so Rachel showed up ahead of schedule.

Now that the cat's out of the bag, Dr. Blevins has asked me to let everyone know that Rachel is just the first in a series of "Anachrons," which is a term we will be applying to colleagues from earlier historical epochs who will be coming forward to present-day Boston and other DODO sites to collaborate with us. The exact policy is still being formulated, but we anticipate recruiting Anachrons in the following general categories:

- KCWs, such as Rachel, who can help Erszebet handle the anticipated uptick in demand for Sending personnel to various DTAPs.
- Subject matter authorities, such as people who know how to speak a particular dialect or fight in a particular martial arts system for which we don't have modern-day expertise. These can serve as valuable adjuncts to the existing DORC staff.
- Evacuees who must be brought forward for tactical reasons, typically to avoid the possibility of Diachronic Shear. This might happen in the event of a security breach leading to a situation where someone knew too much about their future.

The above is not the definitive list—the full policy document is still being drawn up.

Soon Rachel will be cleared by our medical staff to mingle with the general population, and when that happens I know you'll all join me in making her feel as welcome as possible in her new home and era.

EXCERPT FROM TRANSCRIPT OF INTERVIEW
BETWEEN DR. MELISANDE STOKES (MS)
AND RACHEL BAT AVRAHAM (RBA)
DAY 904 (DAY 13 OF RBA'S MEDICAL QUARANTINE)

NOTE: Conversation took place in Hebrew, translated into English.

MS: You're looking stronger today. Dr. Srinavasan told me you ate all of the chicken soup.

RBA: My shoulder [vaccine injection site] is no longer hurting and the chills have stopped. Yes, I feel better, but still weak.

MS: Would you like me to tell Dr. Srinavasan about your feeling of weakness? Perhaps he should know about it.

RBA: No, he cannot help.

MS: Why do you say that? Modern medicine can do things that would surprise you.

RBA: This I understand. I have seen it with my own eyes. But my feeling of weakness is not the kind of thing that a doctor would understand, or know how to fix. If you let me go into the ODEC, I would feel strong again.

MS: Because you could do magic there?

RBA: Yes, of course. You [non-magical persons] don't understand. You think that witches do magic only at certain times, when we perform a spell, such as Sending. Actually we are doing it a little bit every moment, even when we are sleeping.

MS: I have heard similar things from Erszebet. Only when she is in the ODEC does she feel completely herself.

RBA: I can't wait to learn better English so that I can talk more to Erszebet.

MS: The computer can help you learn some basic parts of the language, and when you get out of quarantine you'll learn faster.

RBA: I have been reading the computer.

MS: That's what Mortimer told me.

RBA: Who is Mortimer?

MS: You haven't met him, he is one of the people who helps make the computers work.

RBA: How does he know that I have been reading the computer?

MS: Do you remember our conversation the other day about how the computers are linked together in a network?

RBA: Yes, of course. A little bit like the network of Strands.

MS: A little bit, yes. Well, because of this, it's possible for someone like Mortimer, who is on a different computer in a different place, to see what you have been reading. And he tells me that you have been looking at Wikipedia in both Hebrew and Greek.

RBA: The Hebrew hasn't changed as much. There are many new words, of course, but I can learn those. The Greek has changed more. I can read both of them, anyway.

MS: What have you been reading?

RBA: The future of Constantinople.

MS: You mean, the history?

RBA: (laughs) To you, yes. But to me it is the future. I was reading about the Fourth Crusade.

MS: To you, that would be only a few weeks in the future.

RBA: You know about it?

MS: Yes, as you know we have been quite interested in that DTAP and so I have read many historical accounts.

RBA: Then perhaps you can tell me what happens to the Jews of Pera, after the Crusaders cross the Bosporus and attack Galata Tower? We live right in the shadow of the tower!

MS: There is no written documentation about that directly, but related documents point to the Jewish community having dispersed without incident, probably in response to the Catholic presence.

RBA: (agitated) In the Levant, Catholics slaughtered legions of us! Are

they going to slaughter my family? I must go back and warn them
and tell them to leave before the trouble starts!

MS: I'm sure they don't slaughter your family, Rachel. Something else
happened. Your family, and everyone else, they must have just chosen to leave—without incident, or it would be recorded somewhere,
right? With the Jews, everything bad is always recorded.

RBA: So is everything good.

MS: No, just the miracles. So there are no miracles, but there's no
slaughter.

RBA: I should warn them.

MS: You chose to leave them, Rachel. You cannot leap back and forth
between DTAPs.

RBA: Why not? From how you have described DODO that is the whole
point, leaping back and forth.

MS: We follow instructions on what to do and not to do, and never for
personal reasons. It is always in the interest of the work. Otherwise
things get complicated. When we started speaking, two weeks ago,
you had to agree to stay in this DTAP before I could tell you anything. You remember that, don't you?

RBA: Oh, of course, and I'm very happy to be here, it is so much better
even than the most exciting magic my grandmothers ever did. It is
amazing. And all of you seem to take it in stride! Even Erszebet! It is
all so wonderful, and everyone is kind to me, and it's such fun to see
how everyone is clothed and I cannot wait until I can try all the food,
and this medicine is *better* than magic, if I were this sick at home I
would never be so recovered in three days! All these, what are they
called, innocuvations—

MS: Inoculations, and vaccinations. And that bag up there that's attached to the tube that goes into your arm, that has some medicine
that's making you better faster.

RBA: Yes! Easier than magic! I do not like the hum of the electricity but Erszebet says I will get used to it, and so I cannot imagine even Heaven would be so wondrous as this.

MS: Then I hope you are at peace with staying here. And helping us. Please trust that your family will be safe without your assistance.

RBA: Very well. How can I help? Once I have adjusted to being here?

MS: The role of witches, here and now, is to Send agents back in time to different DTAPs.

RBA: I remember. I had no idea the world was so enormous!

MS: Yes, even for us, with all our knowledge, it is a remarkable thing to contemplate. So you Send us back in time, and we do things, very subtle little things, to prevent undesirable situations from happening. You don't need to worry about what those are. That's somebody else's responsibility. You just need to perform the magic of Sending them back in time.

RBA: Very well, that's easy enough. What else?

MS: That's all.

RBA: That's all?

MS: Yes.

RBA: You mean that's all Erszebet does every day? She just Sends people? Why don't you use her other magic?

MS: We have not found other useful applications for magic in today's world.

RBA: What?! How is that possible? It's *magic*! Magic is always useful! That is like saying you have no useful application for the sun because you found this electricity thing.

MS: You yourself noted how remarkable life is now, that in many ways it is even better than magic.

RBA: It's better in a different way, it's not better than not having magic at all.

MS: Because magic stopped in 1851, we became accustomed to living without it.

RBA: So Erszebet, all she ever does is Send people?

MS: Yes.

RBA: No wonder she's so grumpy. That must be very, *very* dull after a while.

MS: It's her work.

RBA: I have never heard of a single witch in the history of the world who just had to do the exact same thing over and over and over again. That sounds terrible. The Lord would never subject anyone to such treatment. Even when we were slaves in Egypt we had more variety to our tasks than that.

MS: Are you saying you do not wish to have the work?

RBA: I want to have something else to do as well. I am an excellent witch but I am also skilled at many other things. I can bake bread, and I am a superb seamstress. Perhaps I can spend some time Sending people and some time baking challah.

MS: I will talk to Dr. Blevins about your suggestion. I like it. Perhaps it would help Erszebet if she also had a pastime.

RBA: No, not a pastime, something real, something useful. I have met many people in this fortress now but not a single baker.

MS: We don't have enough observant Jews on staff to require that we keep challah on hand.

RBA: Forget challah, then, I wish to learn how to make those delicious sweet round things that Tristan has brought into the fortress, with the brightly colored bits on them. If I could spend some time baking those, then I would not mind if my magic work consists only of Sending.

MS: I'll talk to Dr. Blevins.

Post by Dr. Roger Blevins
on "Announcements" ODIN channel
DAY 915 (LATE JANUARY, YEAR 3)

Effective immediately, Dr. Frank Oda has been promoted to Scientist Emeritus. In this new role, Dr. Oda will be unburdened from the day-to-day responsibilities of running DODO's R&D department, and will enjoy the freedom to pursue advanced research projects that have been back-burnered until now during his months of hard work on the Chronotron. Please congratulate him if you should encounter him around the facility.

Macy Stoll has already tasked HR with recruiting or promoting a replacement for Dr. Oda as head of the R&D department. In the interim, Dr. Oda will remain in place as acting head and assign department staff to various tasks as appropriate.

Journal Entry of
Rebecca East-Oda
JANUARY 30

Temperature 29F, damp, slight NE breeze. Barometer steady.

More firewood delivered and stacked (using area of garden that was dug up for Bay Psalm Book—eighteen months later soil has still not recovered). Expecting snowdrops soon.

Yesterday afternoon Tristan, Melisande, and Erszebet drove to the house with the new witch, Rachel, who will be lodging with us until appropriate quarters can be determined for her. A tiny, wide-eyed thing, looking like a rag doll in a dress that Erszebet picked out for her during a raid on Newbury Street. Predictably, there was disagreement about logistics. Tristan wanted Erszebet to return to the office to continue to Send people—they have quite the schedule there now, and are working her almost to exhaustion. He argued that Melisande is the only one who speaks medieval Hebrew and therefore Mel should stay with Rachel.

"We will both stay with her," said Erszebet. "I was 'on hold' (*with air quotes*) for more than a century, you can be 'on hold' for overnight."

"Erszebet, you can't even talk to her, what's the good of your staying?"

"I will talk to her through Melisande," Erszebet said in her *so-there* tone. "Do you know how long it has been since I have had another witch to talk to?" Erszebet made a mock-surprise face. "Why, of course you do. You know *exactly* how long it has been. So you will give me this. If you refuse, I will understandably go on strike, which I would have done months ago if I were not so exceptionally generous and patient. I am giving you an opportunity not to force me to go on strike." (Have been coaching her on her communication skills. Clearly mixed results.)

Tristan nodded. "Fine," he said. "You'll return at 1300 hours tomorrow."

She rolled her eyes. "This is not an army barracks. I will return at one o'clock in the afternoon."

"Major Sloane has vectored a couple of DOSECOPS to the house, to keep an eye on things," said Tristan, to me now. "They're on their way here."

"Absolutely not," I said. "She's not a criminal or a fugitive."

"It's about security," said Tristan.

"Felix," Mel suggested quickly. "Rachel knows Felix from her native DTAP. He's between DEDEs. He's not technically a guard, but he's qualified—in fact he's overqualified. Surely you can arm him and have him bunk in the dining room." A glance at me. "Would that be all right?"

"Only because Rachel knows him," I said. "Being a den-mother to wayward witches is not in my job description, and I will not play along if it requires armed men in my living room."

Tristan's jaw worked silently for a few moments. I knew what he was thinking: *It's not your living room anymore—it belongs to the East House Trust.* But he had the good grace not to say this out loud. He called off the two guards, placed a call to Felix, and left.

I confess I was surprised and touched by Erszebet's cosseting young Rachel. Speaking to her through Melisande, she insisted Rachel spend the time giving vent to how very different and disorienting it is here. Melisande translating, most of the English-to-Hebrew being some form of "I know, isn't it awful? I don't know what's worse, to have it happen all at once as with you, or to have it happen with gradual inevitability as with me."

Diachronicle
DAY 1800 (SUMMER, YEAR 5)

In which the zenith becomes our new normal

I HAVE BUT EIGHTEEN DAYS left before the solar eclipse and there is far too much to cover in what time is left to me. I am more desperate than ever not to be stuck here for ~~fucking~~ ever. Therefore I shall resort to a compendious depiction of the next phase of DODO's existence.

Two and a half years passed. Every day I rose and went to work. Many times I was Sent back to various DTAPs to perform missions. A lot happened, in other words. And yet those two and a half years flew by so quickly that when it was over it felt as if some witch had Sent me into the future.

The value of the Chronotron exceeded all expectations. With it at our disposal, we were close to gods in our omniscience. Over the course of those dazzling years, DODO expanded beyond anything even Tristan could have imagined that afternoon when he took me to coffee. We expanded both in our own DTAP and also throughout history. In the twenty-first century, we built training and research centers all over the globe, with ODEC-equipped facilities in Europe, the Middle East, and Japan. To guarantee the most authentic training, we lured experts in certain fields of importance to us forward through time. Our Fighters scrimmaged in top-secret dojos with Roman legionaries, Viking berserkers, and samurai. Their training gear was wrought by armorers of ages past, brought forward to toil in air-conditioned smithies. Per Tristan's early joke to me years earlier, I did indeed have a chance, once, to practice my conversational Sumerian—with an actual Sumerian.

We could not bring people forward from the past willy-nilly, of course. Strict principles around Anachrons were codified, with each one being personally approved by Blevins. Generally it was safer for a DOer to train in a DTAP and bring that knowledge back to us, than it was to bring somebody forward, which would then oblige us to spend time, energy, and medical and psychological resources on keeping them from ~~losing their shit~~ having a difficult time adjusting to modernity, however carefully we tried to shield them. Our epidemiology unit ran around the clock checking samples and improving our vaccination protocols.

Most of the early Anachrons were witches. Erszebet, to our surprise, did not fly the coop once she had been made redundant. She rather adopted the air of Cleopatra, and made it clear—to them and to us—that she was now the Alpha Witch. None of the other witches could ever possibly know as much as she did, about the twenty-first century or about DODO's real missions; likewise, none of us could possibly know how to behave appropriately with the new witches. She maintained all of her ~~charismatic narcissistic bitchiness~~ prepossessing fierceness, but she became, in effect, the Den Mother of Weird Sisters. Frank and Rebecca's home couldn't hold them all, so DODO purchased a big old house elsewhere in Cambridge, rigged it up with all kinds of security hardware, and turned it into a kind of sorority for Erszebet and her brood. Vans with blacked-out windows shuttled back and forth between it and DODO headquarters, ferrying witches. They had come from all times and places, but they mostly followed Erszebet's lead when it came to fashion choices.

There was also a very small cohort of contemporary witches. Erszebet could smell them, and found it perfectly ordinary to approach strangers on Mass Ave and inform them of their latent abilities, to the despair of everyone who cared about security clearance. Those rare few who responded positively were immediately told it was a joke by me (or Rebecca, or whoever was Erszebet-minding that day); meanwhile the attendant DOSECOP (our version of the Secret Service) would capture an image of the woman's face, and send it electronically for identification and background check. If the DOSECOP got a green light, they would signal the Erszebet-minder, who would backpedal on the "just a joke" line and surreptitiously invite the newfound witch to an interview near (not *at*, not at first) HQ. There were only three contemp witches at first (there are now about eight). One of these was Julie Lee, aka the Smart-ass Oboist with the tattooed eyebrows from the Apostolic Café. Apparently Erszebet had known her for a witch from day one but did not bother to mention it until the mood possessed her. Another was Tanya Wakessa Washington, a legal clerk in City Hall who was a regular at the café.

The third was Rebecca East-Oda.

She was a grudging convert. I think she agreed to be recruited more for the sake of supporting an endeavor Frank loved than out of any eagerness of her own. That said, she was quite chuffed with herself the first time she turned an apple into an orange. And, with her Congregationalist studiousness, she was apt. Erszebet worked with them every day in one of the ODECs, displaying a patience and good humor she revealed nowhere else, teaching them basic magical spells, but it was slow going. Raised in a civilization from which magic had been eradicated for a century and a half, they all suffered a kind of atrophy of the faculties needed to perform it. Erszebet had told me in private that even Julie—the best of them—was probably years away from being able to Send a DOer with any degree of spatiotemporal accuracy.

Our budget seemed limitless at that time, in no small part because there were multiple variations of the Bay Psalm Book gambit—famous works of art, rare artifacts and antiques, treasure troves of all sorts . . . we made them ours and sold them all for cash. Tristan and I had ethical qualms about this, but Blevins was in charge. The Fugger Bank ~~became our frenemy~~ was neither friend nor foe to us; at some times they checked our strategems, at other times abetted us, according to some larger plan of their own that eluded our understanding. It became increasingly obvious that Dr. Cornelius Rudge, who'd been in on the project from the beginning, had deep connections to the Fuggers, and was basically serving as their man on the inside.

But acquiring treasure was no longer DODO's primary goal. Oh no, reader, do not think it.

Frink and Blevins had an uber-mission (I wonder, shall it seem antiquated or inconceivable, if these words are ever brought to light?). I can only guess at what this might have been, and at when they conceived it: at the very beginning of the project, or at some point during the years when DODO was growing to the zenith of its power? Only in the last few weeks have I gained an inkling of their true motives. I shall say what I know of these as quickly as I can, because my hand is cramping up ~~like a mother-fucker~~ most pitiably; but en route I must explain what happened in the Constantinople Theater.

Yes, DODO had several distinct theatres of operations, of which Constantinople, circa 1200, was the first, the biggest, and the one that most concerned Tristan and myself.

The official rationale for what we were doing there was as follows:

At the time of our great thriving, there were amongst the powers of the globe multiple entities that caused our government concern. These included China, Russia, and certain nefarious elements in the Middle East.

DODO was tasked with discouraging China and Russia from becoming ~~geopolitical BFFs~~ close allies. We were to do this by subtly, retroactively shifting the historical soul of Russia away from the Eastern Orthodox Church and toward the Roman Catholic one, starting just after the Fourth Crusade.

The Fourth Crusade was

~~an epic clusterfuck~~

~~a comic-opera misadventure~~

a tragic saga with farcical elements. It never even reached its intended target in the Holy Land. Instead the Crusaders—Catholics from Western Europe—invaded the Byzantine Empire, which was a Christian land, and sacked Constantinople.

Its domino effect throughout history is a remarkable lesson in cause and effect that I will return to at another time, if writer's cramp and leisure time allow it. What matters here is to note the consequences. With the help of the Chronotron and of various Spies and Sages we Sent back to serve as its eyes and ears, we planned out a long interrelated series of DEDEs. Any one of these would seem innocuous unto itself—stealing a pitchfork in some small town in the Urals, digging a trench in the city of Zara, moving a sleeping dog from a hut in a back alley in Budapest to another hut fifty feet away. Collectively, these slight alterations pushed our agenda, shifted the quantum tendencies of reality to allow us to form what we ultimately desired: that Catholicism would spread its wings over more of Christendom, and the Orthodox Church over less of it.

Catholicism unchecked would mean disaster for both the colonizing of North America and the development of science, and so every bit of strengthening that happened on the church's eastern flank had to be offset on its northwestern one, to maintain within Europe the tensions and conflicts that would lead to a successful Protestant Reformation. That too is a story for another day, but it is important to note here that it involved the collusion of influential bankers, in particular the Fuggers. Gráinne had indirect connections to that family owing to her post-Shear circumstances, and in sundry ways, she greatly assisted us in bringing her generation of Fuggers into the fold, in such manner that subsequent generations were raised to be our natural allies. As I have recently and painfully learned, she had her own reasons for becoming cozy with the Fuggers, but now I am getting ahead of myself.

Back to the uber-mission—or, to be precise, what Frink and Blevins *claimed* was the uber-mission.

Because the 1204 fall of Constantinople is what brought Catholicism so far east, most of our DEDEs set off little chain reactions, quiet little tributaries that met up in the central artery of the Fourth Crusade.

This meant several things: first, that young Rachel was invaluable to us, not only as a witch, but as a source of information far exceeding all our documented knowledge. Furthermore, we could rely on her to Send a DOer to that DTAP with uncanny specificity. It also meant that most of our Fighters had to be trained to have at least a basic grasp of Greek (spoken by the native Orthodox Christians of Constantinople), Latin (spoken by the crusading Catholics who were besieging them), and Anglo-Saxon (the most common tongue of the Varangian Guards). They also learned to fight in both the eastern style employed by the conscripted army and the northern style of the Varangians, as well as the various continental styles employed by the wide variety of soldiers from Flanders down to Sicily. There were few actual battles over the two-year course of the Fourth Crusade, but every one of them had been quite the mishmash of styles. I speak from listening to Tristan, who was one of our frontline Fourth Crusade DOers.

While we were growing and thriving in the twenty-first century, the witch network was being built out with astonishing rapidity in many DTAPs. Gráinne, who had taken up with an acquaintance of Francis Bacon (and of the Fuggers, per above), was worth her weight in diamonds, as (rather like Constantinople) late Elizabethan London is, within the time-space continuum of recorded human history, akin to Grand Central Station, especially given that we needed to have KCWs of both Catholic and Protestant backgrounds. Within eighteen months, every DTAP we'd targeted had a Known Compliant Witch who knew Gráinne, or a witch who knew a witch who knew a witch who knew Gráinne. We could safely move DOers from DTAP to DTAP in ways unthinkable before the Chronotron came online. Gráinne—whom I had never met—seemed to enjoy her position of prominence. Unlike most of the other witches working with DODO (whom, it must be said, we spent a not inconsiderable amount of time placating), she asked nothing of us. She was generous and earnest. Our one great blindness, our tragic flaw, is that we never questioned that.

But again, I am getting far ahead of myself.

INCIDENT REPORT

AUTHOR: LTC Tristan Lyons
SUBJECT: Chira Lajani
THEATER: Constantinople
DTAP: Blachernae Palace, 1203
FILED: Day 1787 (June, Year 5)

Sexual assault and repercussions (weregild)

Chira Lajani was on assignment in 1203 Constantinople. Her DEDE put her in the royal wing of Blachernae Palace after sunset. This wing is guarded mostly by the mercenary Varangian Guards of which I (LTC Tristan Lyons) was one, being there for a separate DEDE. Under normal circumstances our paths would not cross.

Chira reports that having accomplished her DEDE she was returning to Basina's quarters so that Basina would Home her, when she was accosted by a Varangian Guard speaking Greek to her with an accent she has come to recognize as Norman/French. He propositioned her as she was descending a flight of steps leading down from a raised terrace toward the bathhouse entrance in a courtyard below. She turned him down. She is used to being propositioned, especially by the Guard, who consider themselves outside the normal social constraints of the local culture. However, she is also used to being respected when she says no. This VG did not accept her no. He grabbed her as she reached a landing in the stairway and pinned her against a stone balustrade. She resisted. He ripped her robe off of her shoulder so that it fell to the sash at her waist. Although he was stronger than she was and did not require a weapon to overpower her, he reached down with his right hand and drew a seax (long knife) from a sheath on his belt, presumably considering this the easiest way to terrorize her into silence.

Her assailant was suddenly holding her with his left hand only. In the period combat training that is a requirement for all DOers, we are taught to be extremely conscious of when the opponent makes a move for his knife, since that is the single most dangerous moment in hand-to-hand combat. Chira reacted with a wrist-lock technique that forced her assailant to drop the knife. He reached down for it, giving her the opportunity to spin away from the stone balustrade. Now furious and no longer content with merely terrorizing her, the assailant aimed a wild slash at her that produced a shallow but bloody wound on the outside of her right thigh. In so doing he became imbalanced. Chira stepped in and took advantage of this to throw him, planting her left hip under his buttock and shoving hard on his chin. Spinning away from her, he sprawled over the balustrade, balanced for a moment, then fell, plunging approximately five meters onto a wrought iron fence which impaled him. As this was happening he screamed in a way that drew attention all over the courtyard.

Various other Varangian Guards came to investigate, then, seeing the wound on her leg, summoned female servants to come and attend to her. The incident was singular enough that word of it spread through the royal wing of the palace within a quarter hour, and through the entire palace compound in an hour. I heard of it from fellow guards, who were reconstructing what move Chira must have used to get him to drop the knife. On the excuse of needing to relieve myself, I made my way to where she was being comforted.

This was a small antechamber outside the bathhouse. One of Basina's attendants was there, holding Chira's torn and blood-soaked dress. Chira was by this time in a fresh robe. She had been washed clean of the blood and her thigh had been bandaged. She appeared shaken. (Although when I spoke to her later, she said she just wanted to get on with her DEDE in hopes of preventing a repeat of the assault in another Strand.)

A contingent of four Varangian Guards appeared in the doorway. Naturally, given what had just happened, I assumed their intent was hostile. I interposed myself between them and the women and placed my right hand on the handle of my seax.

Their leader was Magnus, who was known to me by reputation, being one of the most senior and respected of all the Varangian Guards in the city despite his relative youth (early thirties?) and outlier status as a Norman (most of the VG are Anglo-Saxons, and in this era the Normans and Anglo-Saxons are frenemies at best). He may have recognized my face, but we had never conversed. Magnus is a tall, lean, broad-shouldered bearded man with long brown hair and blue eyes. He entered first, displaying both hands, palms out, in a gesture of peace. Behind him were three other men, I would guess of the same kinship group. They muttered together in what I recognized as Norman French. One carried a pile of men's clothes; one carried an ornate wooden box; the third carried a small leather bag. All four were unarmed; they must have checked their weapons outside.

"It's all right, brother, I am here to make this right, as best I can," Magnus said, speaking in Anglo-Saxon. I nodded and stepped out of his way.

Magnus stopped just in front of Chira. The other three approached, went down on their knees, bowed their heads, and held up the objects they were carrying.

"I am Magnus of Normandy," began Magnus in stilted, accented Greek. "The man who assaulted you is my distant kinsman. He has no other family and so it falls to me to offer you the weregild for his offense. He did not have much but now it is all yours. There are clothes, ornamentation, and money. You will receive it, please." He gestured and the men held the items closer to her.

Chira could not hide her surprise. She glanced at me briefly, and I nodded, so she accepted the offering with thanks. Basina's attendant and a young servant woman relieved the men of their load—and then gave them a look suggesting they should leave now. Magnus saluted Chira with a fist to his chest. His men rose, turned on their heels, and marched out.

Since I had seen for myself that Chira was safe, and it would have been awkward for me to remain as the sole male, I left with Magnus's group.

As soon as we were outside the bathhouse, Magnus turned to me to ask my cause for being here.

Seeing an opportunity to forge a connection, I said, "This woman has done me a kindness in the past and I am concerned for her well-being"—and I said it in Magnus's own dialect of Norman.

He was pleasantly surprised to hear his mother tongue spoken. "What is your name?" he asked. "You have a familiar accent."

"My name is Tristan of Dintagel," I said. "I spent a year of my youth in Normandy seeking my fortune, before coming east to join the Varangian Guard."

He gave me a peculiar look. "Tristan of Dintagel?" He glanced over his shoulder at one of his men, who was simultaneously exchanging looks with the other two men. "Are you a man of great exploits?"

"You must ask the Emperor his opinion on the subject," I said, "as his is the only opinion that matters to my salary."

Magnus stared at me a moment longer and then laughed along with his men. "It is a pleasure to meet someone who speaks as we do," he said, and held out a hand to exchange peace with me. I returned to my post having agreed with him that we would break bread together the next time our duties allowed it.

Later that day I found access to Chira again, to find her resolute to finish her DEDE on this Strand, and as I had finished my own DEDE I returned here while she was still in Constantinople. She should be home within a day. The wound on her thigh will probably require modern medical treatment and leave a permanent scar, but seems unlikely to cause permanent disability.

Respectfully submitted,

Lieutenant Colonel Tristan Lyons

Exchange of posts by DODO staff
on "Constantinople Theater" ODIN channel
DAYS 1790–1797 (LATE JUNE, YEAR 5)

Post from LTC Tristan Lyons:

Gang, I wanted to raise a topic of interest in case anyone else being Sent to C'ople can confirm what I just saw, or gather more info.

Long story short is that I was hanging out there with Magnus of Normandy, whom many of you will have heard of as one of the more senior Varangians. Not so much in terms of formal rank as the respect in which he's held by the other VGs, which is saying something given he's a Norman. I had crossed paths with him a couple of days earlier and he had taken an interest in me and suggested we dine together.

As everyone knows, it's against SOP to make casual social connections with historicals, since only bad things can come of it (unless you're a Lover or a Closer, in which case it's part of your job description). So I was hesitant to accept Magnus's invitation. But as I said, he's a respected leader in the VG ranks, and I'm pretty junior. So the invitation was an honor, and it would only have raised more questions and suspicions if I had just blown him off.

Further complicating the scenario is that Magnus (who, for all his status in the Guard, has a vaguely manic "ah, WTF" aspect) decided we should dine not in the VG mess hall, nor even in the taverns the Guard tended toward, but that we should head down to the Venetian neighborhood because he "liked the smell of maritime industry" or something.

I went with him, just the two of us, and we got a lot of freaked-out looks from the Venetian traders and their families because we were, you know, *the Emperor's Guards*, coming into a Venetian neighborhood while the Venetian navy was parked across the Bosporus threatening to attack the Emperor . . . but obviously nobody was going to mess with us. We sat down at an outdoor table overlooking the harbor, and had a conversation that on the surface seemed like just polite "get to know you" stuff. My cover story was designed to stand up under exactly this kind of testing. It is that I came from a pretty obscure location in England, that I had family connections in Normandy, and had spent some time there when younger, which was how I came to speak the dialect. He probed me a little on that. This made me a little nervous since I'd been in that part of the world (Collinet, specifically) 150 years earlier and so I couldn't cite specific names or incidents to back up my story. But "my" village and his are some fifty kilometers apart, which is enough separation to blur things quite a bit, and he had left when fairly young, so there weren't any smoking guns. Basically, the cover story seemed to pass muster and we moved on to other chitchat about the day-to-day workings of the VG and rumors about the Crusaders and what they were up to.

After we'd had a few drinks and a good dinner we stood up and began to head back to the barracks. But we'd only gone about a hundred strides when he turned to me and said, "Would you like to go see your namesake?"

Having no idea what he was talking about, I agreed. We were near the border of the Venetian quarter, but now he led me back into the heart of it. We walked for about a hundred yards through winding streets. The sun was setting (time of year was midsummer, sunset was late). We came to a Roman Catholic church where vespers were under way. This is the Church of St. Bartholomew for those of you who would care to visit it. Later it was destroyed on all of the Strands I'm aware of, so it doesn't exist in our present. Point being, for purposes of this story, its west entrance was lit up by the sunset when we arrived.

He led me into the church, both of us crossing ourselves in the traditional manner as we entered (I doubt Magnus is a practicing Christian of any stripe, and when the VG guards the Empress at religious services, it's an Orthodox church, so he must have vestigial muscle memory from childhood re: how to behave in a church).

We went inside just far enough that we could turn around and look at the stained glass windows in the west front without drawing the attention of the congregants or the priest. There's a big round window in the middle and some smaller ones to the sides. As is typical of churches like this, the big one depicts scenes from the life of Jesus, with emphasis on St. Bartholomew (one of the twelve Apostles), and the peripheral ones depict various other saints.

One of the stained glass windows depicted a knight with yellow hair holding what appeared to be a boat oar. Scattered around him on the ground were the supine forms of what I took to be defeated enemies.

Behind him was a crude rendering of a church. A scroll above his head identified him as St. Tristan of Dintagel.

As you can all imagine, I was astonished and speechless for a minute. I became conscious of the fact that Magnus was studying my face intently. When I finally came to my senses, I said, "I had no idea that my saintly namesake had been commemorated in a church so far from home!" and thanked him for making me aware of it. I fell to my knees in a show of piety, offered up a prayer to St. Tristan, and purchased a candle, which I lit and placed beneath the window in question.

Magnus and I then walked back up to the barracks without further discussion of this incident. As far as I can tell, he accepts my story, which is that I was named after a saint who dwelled in my part of the world 150 years ago.

But until this incident I had no idea that there was such a thing as a St. Tristan of Dintagel recognized by the Catholic Church. Since I came back I've found traces of him on the Internet, but it's all pretty sketchy and obscured by GLAAMR. I'm guessing that St. Tristan became a thing on certain Strands but not others. Any ideas, people?

Reply from Dr. Melisande Stokes:
On it. Will get back to you with any findings.

It kinda sounds like Magnus set you up. Any worries on that front?

From LTC Lyons:
He didn't call me out. But I won't BS you, Stokes, it's worrisome and I think he senses something's weird about me. On the other hand, it's only two weeks until the Crusaders storm Galata Tower and then we'll be going our separate ways, so I intend to go back to the DTAP on schedule tomorrow. For me to just disappear would confirm any suspicions he might be harboring.

From Dr. Stokes:

Can you delay your return to C'ople? A bunch of us are working this and coming up with spotty/fluctuating results. There is heavy GLAAMR around St. Tristan of Dintagel and so we're seeing entire Wikipedia articles warping in and out of existence. Some risk that merely Googling the name is tending to make it more real.

From LTC Lyons:

So what is the point of my delaying return to C'ople? Shizzle's about to go down, you know this. We've been working toward it for three years.

From Dr. Stokes:

We can get better answers by sending some Sages back to other Strands where we think that the St. Tristan legend is more firmly entrenched. We need to know more before Sending you into a potentially messed-up situation.

And by "messed-up situation" I mean "alternate universe in which you are a two-hundred-year-old warrior saint."

From LTC Lyons:

No research needed. St. Tristan is damn well entrenched in the Strand I'm working—I already told you he has at least one stained glass window. So we have to stick with the story I told Magnus, which is that I'm simply named after him. Stokes, this is ubiquitous—almost everyone back then is named after a saint.

LETTER ON PARCHMENT, HANDWRITTEN IN LATIN
BY PROFESSIONAL SCRIBE, CONSTANTINOPLE

JUNE 1203

Brother Ando:

May the Lord find you and our mother well. Upon receiving this letter please respond as swiftly as you may. I have met a valiant warrior here in Byzantium, a Varangian Guard like myself, but of a name too familiar, that is Tristan of Dintagel, which lies in England. The rantings of the Frankish priests are gibberish to me, so I care not for their saints. Nor was I ever one to listen to the songs around the hearth, but I know you were. Do you not recall a song about a great hero who hailed from a remote part of England and who had appeared suddenly in our region and fended off a tribe with whom we feuded? He was credited with saving the village and made a saint by the Christians. It strikes me as a remarkable coincidence to meet another man with such a name. There is some quality to this man that I cannot quite describe, but he seems like a man apart, as belonging to some other race.

I wonder if there be miracles and if so, how may I make use of this one— that a hero of legend has seen fit to manifest himself within my ken, just at the moment when we are under siege by the Franks! Please respond to tell me if my memory is correct, and say as much as you can of the old legends concerning this hero. Also send news of our mother and the village if there is any.

YOUR BROTHER,
Magnus

Exchange of posts by DODO staff
on "Constantinople Theater" ODIN channel
DAYS 1798–1805 (EARLY JULY, YEAR 5)

Post from Historical Operations Subject Matter Authority (HOSMA)
Dr. Eloise LeBrun:
I'm just back from 1232 Paris with some results concerning "St. Tristan of Dintagel," which I will post on this channel as I've time to write them up, but the executive summary is that I don't think LTC Lyons should go back to C'ople. Has he been Sent yet? I can't make heads or tails of the DEDE scheduling app.

Reply from Dr. Melisande Stokes:
He was Sent eight hours ago, and isn't expected back for two weeks—this is where we complete the DEDE, during the Crusaders' attack on Galata Tower @ Constantinople. What did you find?

From Dr. LeBrun:
Ugh, I just missed him:(
    Well, it's all academic now, I guess.
    What I found is that on some of these Strands an oral tradition developed in the vicinity of Collinet in which the story of Tristan got inflated into a bigger and bigger yarn and eventually turned into a *chanson de geste* sung by various troubadours. Apparently it was popular enough that the church decided to capitalize on it by trumping him up enough to canonize him (even though there are no miracles or martyrdom attributed to him)—which is how he found his way into a stained glass window.

From Dr. Stokes:
On multiple Strands? But he only hit the burglar with the boat oar on one Strand!

From Dr. LeBrun:

Crosstalk between Strands apparently.

From Dr. Stokes:

Is that a thing!? Would one of our magic experts please enlighten me?

From Rebecca East-Oda:

We've seen it before in creative arts settings, especially storytelling. If you think about what is going on in a storyteller's mind when he or she spins a fictional yarn, what they are trying to do is to come up with a story that did not actually happen, but that seems as if it might have happened. In other words, it has to make sense and to be plausible. Typically such a story makes use of real places, historical events, characters, etc. but the events of the story itself seem to take place in an alternate version of reality.

The conventionally accepted explanation for this is that storytellers have a power of imagination that makes them good at inventing counterfactual narratives. In the light of everything we've learned about Strands at DODO, however, we can now see an alternate explanation, which is that storytellers are doing a kind of low-level magic. Their "superpower" isn't imagining counterfactuals, but rather seeing across parallel Strands and perceiving things that actually did (or might) happen in alternate versions of reality.

I think you can see where this is going, Mel. Even if Tristan smacked the burglar with the oar on only a single Strand, it's possible that storytellers in other, nearby Strands were able to sense it or perceive it and tell the story in a compelling, convincing way. From there, the story could propagate to other Strands—including ours, where just this morning I found an entry on St. Tristan of Dintagel in Alban Butler's original (1759) edition of *Lives of the Saints*, which is in our library.

From Dr. Stokes:

Holy crap he's on Wikipedia now too.

NVM he's gone now.

From Dr. LeBrun:

I don't have time to translate all of the documents from Latin and medieval French into English, but I'll post a few snippets.

From Dr. Roger Blevins:

Just became aware of this thread and am skimming it.

Am I to understand that changes have occurred, recently, on the pages of a 250-year-old book in our library!?

From Dr. Stokes:

Yes. There are faint traces of GLAAMR around it, according to Erszebet.

From Dr. Blevins:

I see. That is troubling. Not the first time diachronic magic has been troubling.

From Dr. Stokes:

How so, Dr. Blevins? The entire point of DODO is to change the present by doing things in the past. History books and Wikipedia entries are naturally going to change accordingly.

From Dr. Blevins:

Dr. Stokes, I am taking this offline, as the expression goes. Please see me in my office.

From Dr. LeBrun:

Here for example is a translation of a letter in clerical Latin from a village priest in Normandy to his bishop, dated 1063:

The struggle against pagan beliefs and practices in this parish is never-ending, and tests my faith every hour of every day. Of late some of the village wives have been filling their children's ears with a story that has spread like a grass fire from one household to the next. It is nothing more than an old saga of the Vikings, so far as I can discern. Its hero is one Tristan, a roaming Anglo-Saxon warrior of enormous strength and stature who comes to sojourn in a Norman village for a time. Peaceable by nature, he is roused to action when the village is raided by brigands, and makes an heroic stand on the shore, laying about him with a boat oar until all of the attackers have been slain. Then after accepting the gratitude of the villagers he wanders away to pursue other adventures. As you can see it is just the sort of lay that appeals to the simple minds of the common people and as such is nearly impossible to eradicate.

There is a response from the bishop in which he says that he has heard the same story from other villages in the area, but that in some versions Tristan is a Christian man who is defending the parish church from pagans who have come to defile it and steal its reliquary. He goes on to suggest that rather than trying to stamp out this popular story, the priest should instead co-opt it by re-telling it to his flock as a tale about Christian virtues.

Jumping forward a hundred years I found a fragment of an obscure *chanson de geste*. I'm dating it by its form, which fluctuates between the early style (ten-syllable assonant rhyme, in this case on short "i") and the later one (twelve-syllable monorhyme, in this case long "i"). Here's a few stanzas just to convey the flavor of it, although of course I'm translating for meaning not nuance. Stanzas are of variable length and most of them too water-damaged to make out. Can go back and do a more careful translation if required, including seeking possible encoded messages/references, not unheard of in this tradition:

By the banks of the peaceful Dives Tristan reclines,
Broad-shouldered with noble carriage and proud spirit,
Flaxen-haired knight of Tintagel, new-pledged to Charlemagne.
He's come to serve our king, the servant of Jesus Christ . . .
(about six stanzas illegible)
Look! From the loins of his enchanting mistress at dawn he leaps
To the alarms of the invading baleful-eyed heathens
Who come to steal the village's beloved relics of St. Septimus
To dishonor its Christian spirit, a woe much worse than sin . . .
(two dozen unreadable stanzas)
. . . And now does noble Tristan, Charlemagne's new paladin,
Clap hand on oar and calling upon Our Lady's virtues
Use the humble oar as staff, to smite the unsanctified chins
Of seven pagan warriors in buckram suits,
While their gleaming wicked swords no target hit
On Tristan's manly, bold, courageous side . . .

There's about another nine hundred verses, but most are too water-damaged, and at a glance, the rest seem to be about Tristan's service at Charlemagne's court and later his adventures against the Moors, which presumably would justify his canonization. Will now peruse that section and let you know if anything leaps out that might click for Magnus.

From Dr. Stephen Moore:
Sorry to be a johnny-come-lately to this thread, but the Bodleian Library was closed yesterday and so I've only just been able to visit the rare books room. I was able to find traces of the Tristan legend in a letter written in 1071 to William the Conqueror. The original is, of course, in Latin but I have supplied a hasty translation, copy/pasted below, with apologies for infelicities in language.

Greetings to my beloved monarch and cherished brother William, by the grace of God King of the English and Duke of the Normans.

As I circuit the many manors you have seen fit to bestow upon me for my assistance at Hastings, I remain profoundly grateful for your beneficence and generosity. All are bountiful with crops and livestock, the serfs healthy and none excessively aggrieved. In all, I receive it as a tremendous boon.

However I am sorrowful to inform you that my search for the hero-colony of Dintagel has come to naught. Dintagel, from which sprang that most renowned and admired knight Tristan, who is featured so valiantly in the Song of Collinet in its defense of the holy reliquary of the martyr St. Septimus of Pontchardon against the incursions of the heretics of Lisieux that enthralled us in our youth, has proven to be nothing but a spit of land with a ruined Roman fortress. In the nearby village of Bossiney (Boskyny), my men have asked after the fellowship of knights from which Tristan sprang, and are met universally with stupid looks from the villagers.

There is however an abundance of sheep, which may be exploited to the profit of your majesty and the greater glory of God.

Yours in great love and all homage,
Robert, Count of Mortain and Earl of Cornwall

Post by Dr. Roger Blevins to LTG Octavian K. Frink
on private ODIN channel
DAY 1805 (JULY, YEAR 5)

Okie, this is just to give you a heads-up on a possible situation that is developing. You'll recall a bit of unpleasantness two and a half years ago when Lieutenant Colonel Lyons went off half-cocked during a DEDE in 1045 Normandy and got into a brawl with the locals. I said at the time, and I still maintain, that this was a serious error in judgment that called his qualifications for the job into question. Well, now it looks like the chickens are coming home to roost. LTC Lyons has gone back to 1203 Constantinople to finish out the big DEDE we have been working for the last three years. That's fine as far as it goes. Unfortunately his actions in Normandy, 160 years earlier, have had incalculable reverberations, with the result that he is now revered as some combination of a romantic folk hero and Christian saint by people all over the Nordic and Christian worlds. One of the Varangian Guards at the Constantinople DTAP seems dangerously close to putting two and two together.

No action needed or requested at this time, but I wanted to put this up on your radar just in case it blows up in our faces in a few days or weeks.

I just finished a rather unpleasant meeting with Dr. Stokes who is reflexively defensive of LTC Lyons and doesn't seem to appreciate the magnitude of the problem.

Reply from LTG Frink:

Blev, I've read this a couple of times and don't see why you are so excited. I've spent my career running operations in places like Fallujah and Jalalabad and I've never seen anything go off without glitches. But you have a better grasp of these diachronic operations than I do and so I'll take it under advisement.

Are you doing anything to mitigate the problem?

From Dr. Blevins:

We have a young MUON here who I am sure you will remember since she is the one who crashed the ribbon-cutting party by materializing in the ODEC. Rachel is her name. She is now one of our most experienced witches, and is obviously an expert on 1203 Constantinople since it's where she was born and raised. I have a meeting scheduled with her in which I will explore some options for cleaning up the mess that LTC Lyons has left in his wake.

From LTG Frink:

How's it going with the portable ODEC and so on? Knowing how your mind works, Blev, I can see where all of this is leading: a de-emphasis on diachronic operations per se, in favor of C/COD psy-ops centered on witches in mobile units.

From Dr. Blevins:

You know me well, Okie. Yes. The ATTO, as we call the portable ODEC, is shaping up quite well. To develop the psy-ops wing of the organization, we are getting ready to bring forward Gráinne, who is, after all is said and done, still the most powerful witch we have ever encountered.

From LTG Frink:

The Irish super-witch?

From Dr. Blevins:

That terminology is deprecated. We have been calling them Wenders' for their superior ability to navigate between Strands while maintaining an unbroken thread of consciousness. In the entire history of DODO we have only encountered three of them. Gráinne has been by far the most loyal and it's time we rewarded her with a promotion.

LETTER FROM
GRÁINNE *to* GRACE O'MALLEY
A Tuesday of High Summer, 1602

Auspiciousness and prosperity to you, milady!

It's a brief but timely warning I'm writing you with, Your Grace, and no action does it require on your part, but only alertness. Sir Francis Bacon, the gentleman whose demeanor does command this fleet of thinkers and doers of the age, including Monsieur Cardigan my benefactor . . . he urges the nobles of the court to redouble their efforts in Ireland. He would have the crown take over our entire island as a means to "honor." Therefore if any courtier from England do come courting you, it's wise to be testing the waters of their acquaintanceship with Sir Francis. If they are even indirectly under his sway or in his circles, then surely it's disingenuous they're being.

And meanwhile merely to keep you apprised of my circumstances, they continue apace with some fascinating developments (more fascinating to myself than to you, I warrant). It's Norwich we're spending the summer in, and here I've come to know three witches, something older than myself, and sisters to each other . . . all of them half-nieces of Sir Francis Bacon himself! For isn't their father Nathaniel his half-brother. But this isn't the only peculiar thing about them, there being three other facts of note:

First, being that they know of Tristan's guild and likewise work to abet them on occasion (not so oft as I do). Of course I knew that there are many other witches working for them (their term for us, collective, is KCW), but I had not realized I had contemporaries.

A second and stranger fact of note being that they were never recruited, but rather raised in a tradition of service to Tristan's crew, for sure their mother Anne and before that her mother Win-nifred worked with Tristan's people, although there is nothing in the family history of working with Tristan himself. 'Twas Win-nifred was won over to the work by an agent named Esme, forty years ago. Here again, a minor detail Tristan's not telling me about how his guild be doing their business.

But here's the final and most interesting note, and might even be of direct interest to Your Grace: besides their connection to Sir Francis, these weird sisters are the granddaughters of none other than Sir Thomas Gresham, who as you know was an associate of the Fugger banking family . . . who, despite their unholy religion, have long financed your resistance on occasion, for the sheer joy of causing headaches to Queen Bess. I'm thinking it must be no coin-cidence that all of these particular lineages and associations twine together through time in some way that Tristan sees more clearly than I do, and surely it's use he's getting out of it in ways that I'm not seeing yet. But I will. Oh yes, Your Grace, it's soon enough I'll see as clear as he does.

Whether I be near or far, may I hear only good things of you, My Lady Gráinne! Your Gráinne now of Norwich

TRANSCRIPT (EXCERPT)
INTERVIEW CONDUCTED BY DR. ROGER BLEVINS (RB)
WITH MUON RACHEL BAT AVRAHAM (RA)
11:00, DAY 1807 (10 JULY, YEAR 5)

NOTES: Video recording was made automatically by a motion-activated security camera system in Conference Room #2 at DODO HQ, Cambridge, MA. In the wake of subsequent events, the file was salvaged from a secure server by DODO personnel and transferred to the ad hoc GRIMNIR backup system, where it was later transcribed. Excerpt below begins at approximately 11:15 local time.

RB: In preparing for this meeting, I took the routine step of reviewing your file. I see you have once again started asking the DOers you Send back to your native DTAP to get word to your family that you're safe.

RA: Yes, I am sure they are worried about me. It has been nearly three years. I want to reassure them.

RB: You signed a nondisclosure agreement. That means nothing can be disclosed. To anyone.

RA: Except God, you mean. You cannot tell me to keep anything from God.

RB: Ask God to tell your family how you're doing.

RA: I do, of course. But I am a good daughter, and so I must make the effort as well.

RB: No, you mustn't. In fact, you signed a paper swearing you would not.

RA: The commandments come before any pledge I make to a worldly regime, and the commandments say honor your father and—

RB: You ran off. You abandoned them.

RA: No, my mother is the one who Sent me! [weeping] I had her blessing! She said she would make it all right with my father. I am the

fastest Sender of all the witches, and the most precise. I am a benefit
to you because my mother sent me here. It is okay that I send reas-
surances to her.

RB: You can't. If you insist on attempting it, we will assign you to other
DEDEs and you will never Send anyone back to Constantinople.

RA: Will you lame yourselves out of spite? I am the best witch for Constantinople.

RB: Security is our first priority. If you will not cooperate with us, then
we cannot cooperate with you. I will have to reassign you to the Antwerp and London DTAPs. We will need additional help there when we
bring Gráinne forward.

RA: But I am Tristan's preferred Sender for Constantinople.

RB: Lieutenant Colonel Lyons is subordinate to me and all of his decisions are subject to my review.

RA: I understand.

RB: In any case, his habit of disappearing into remote DTAPs for
weeks at a time leaves an operational void, obliging colleagues to
fill in for him.

RA: Constantinople is not remote, it is the most cosmopolitan city in
the world!

RB: Not for long.

RA: What does that mean?

RB: After what happens next, everything looks so different that it
doesn't matter how well you know the city, it'll be completely rebuilt.

RA: What do you mean by these words, "what happens next"?

RB: I have reason to believe that by going back to 1203 Constantinople,
Tristan has blundered into a trap of his own devising. Unwittingly,
of course. But he is still culpable, because of his arrogance, his lack
of accountability.

RA: What sort of trap?

RB: The details are complicated. There's not time to explain them here. The point is that he needs to be evacuated. If he were a commando on some kind of raid, we'd be sending in the helicopters right now, the SEAL team, to extract him from the mess he has made. But since he's a DOer and he's been deployed to a DTAP, instead we need to Send someone who knows the territory and who can get to him and Home him with extreme prejudice, as the saying goes.

RA: You want me to Send another DOer to rescue him?

RB: You're not listening, Rachel. The person we Send back on this rescue mission can't just be any ordinary DOer. It must be a MUON, a witch who has the capability of Homing him as soon as he is found. One who is intimately familiar with every byway of the city, every nuance of its languages.

RA: You're asking . . . me to be Sent back?

RB: ODEC #4 has been made ready for action. One of our other MUONs is there waiting for you. I have provided her with cover—with plausible deniability. You can be back home in ten minutes, if that is what you really want. But you can never come back. You must decide now.

URGENT BULLETIN

MISSING: RACHEL BAT AVRAHAM
MISSING SINCE: TODAY, 11:25, July 10
MISSING FROM: Conference Room #2, top floor
DETAILS: During interview with Dr. Blevins, became combative, removed pepper spray device from purse, discharged it toward Dr. Blevins, fled the room; when he had finished washing the residue from his eyes, she was gone. Security reports she has not exited the building, however, her whereabouts are unknown.

APPEARANCE: Long dark hair, pale skin, dark eyes. Dressed in gray sweater-dress and jodhpur boots, lots of eye makeup and bangles. Late teens. Speaks heavily accented English.

Security is currently searching the building, which is in lockdown. Rachel lives in the MUON residence. We have contacted or left word with the off-shift MUONs there. Also sending word to local precincts and hospitals. Likeliest that she is hiding in the building somewhere waiting for somebody else to leave so that she can sneak out.

Journal Entry of
Rebecca East-Oda
JULY 10

Temperature 79F, dry, still. Barometer steady.

Faring well: cucumber, squash, chard. Starting to harvest basil leaves. Re-seeding salad greens.

Frank called from the DODO offices to say he will not be home for dinner: the building is in lockdown because the witch Rachel assaulted Blevins (how very satisfying that must have been) and disappeared. Surprised it took this long for somebody to snap.

Exchange of posts between
Dr. Melisande Stokes and Mortimer Shore
on private ODIN channel
DAY 1807

Mel: Where's Rachel?

Mortimer: idk. Checking her calendar . . .

Mel: NVM. Calling her. 1 sec.

Mortimer: looks like she had an 11:00 with Blev.

Mel: Went to vm.

Mortimer: Conf rm 2

Mel: I know but something crazy happened, Blev called security—
    medics are there. No Rachel.

Mortimer: Where r u?

Mel: OMW down to ODECs. WHT Rachel?

Mortimer: CU down there.

Mel: Bio breach!

Mortimer: ?

Mel: Rachel ran through decon area, didn't follow protocol.

Mortimer: ICU through glass wall now.

Mel: FUCK. Whole place will have to be scrubbed. Going in to check
    ODECs.

Mortimer: Someone's in #4. Check that first.

Mel: OK

Mortimer: Not on calendar.

Mel: It's Nadja.

Mortimer: ?

Mel: New MUON.

Mortimer: Rachel?

Mel: Gone.

Mortimer: Never there? Or . . .

Mel: Nadja's confused, says she just Homed Rachel.

URGENT BULLETIN: UPDATE

OK, everyone, Mortimer here, there's a lot of confusion and so I've been asked to post a temporary status update:

- Rachel bat Avraham was Homed back to 1203 Constantinople from ODEC #4 at about 11:25.
- This was an unauthorized operation. The MUON who performed the Homing was using the ODEC for routine training when Rachel showed up and demanded to be let in to the ODEC. Once inside, Rachel employed psy-ops [magical] techniques to induce the other MUON to effect the Homing spell.
- Unless you hear otherwise, RIP Rachel bat Avraham.
- There's going to be a lot of wiki confusion over the next hour or so. Please just stay away from all Constantinople-related entries until end of day tomorrow or you'll get even more confused. Tomorrow you may find references to a conflagration or explosion or firestorm around Galata Tower in Constantinople July 1203. If you are one of the Byzantine DOers or historians, it might not match your memories of the battle for Galata Tower. Those memories are now out of date.
- Lieutenant Colonel Tristan Lyons remains on active DEDE in that DTAP.

Meanwhile I've also been asked to share a little bit of information about Diachronic Shear since most of us weren't on the scene yet the last time it happened. What I've got below is a helpful mnemonic to bide you over, until one of the real pros has time to write up something more detailed. Feel free to print this out and post it in break rooms, etc. More TK soon.

Peace out, Mortimer

DIACHRONIC SHEAR
YOU CRINGE, YOU SINGE!

RAFSTIQUORDOT!

Run

A common mistake at the onset of a Diachronic Shear event is to
reflexively shield oneself from eruptions of bodily fluids and flaming
gobbets, thus losing precious moments that could be spent putting
distance between yourself and the epicenter. A rift between universes
is no place to be fussy—you can always clean up later.

Amputate

Body parts that unfortunately found themselves on the wrong side of
the rift may seem to remain attached. Intense GLAAMR and general
disorientation may hide their misshapen form. Many victims will be
unwilling to believe in the reality of what has happened to them. The
temptation may be strong to leave these attached and hope for the
best. Don't do it! Think of it as being like gangrene, except faster.

Fires (extinguish)

Most Diachronic Shear events are recorded in the history books as
epic fires of unknown origin. That's because, after the Shear itself is
over and done with, fires remain, and find plentiful fuel in destroyed
structures. Nipping these in the bud may prevent enormous loss of life
in the coming hours.

Shore up crumbling structures

Buildings may have lost primary structural members during the
Shear. Ones that haven't collapsed already may be prevented from
doing so with stopgap measures. When in doubt, get out!

Tourniquets (apply as needed)

This is an elementary first-aid procedure that may save the lives of some who were caught along the boundary of the Shear.

Intimidate witnesses

Rumors spawned by a Shear event may trigger a cascade of aftershocks, as well as compromising your cover story. Do whatever it takes to discourage witnesses from saying anything to their friends and loved ones about what they have seen. Given the nature of what goes on during a Shear, this will commonly involve some sort of appeal to whatever gods, demons, or other supernatural forces figure in to the locals' belief system.

Quell civil disturbances

Panicked bystanders may react in a way that will only inflict further human suffering—as well as making it difficult for you to get Homed.

Use your pre-established alibi

As part of Standard Operating Procedures, DOers should always have alibis and explanations handy for any discrepancies that may be called to their attention by curious and meddlesome locals. Anything you can do to place yourself far from the scene of the Shear will help you get home.

Observe

This one's far down the list because it's a lower priority. But it's still a priority! DODO is always eager to gather more data on what happens during a Diachronic Shear, and so any observations that can be committed to memory will be welcome once you get home.

Return to the twenty-first century

This is self-explanatory! Find your KCW and get Homed as soon as possible—if a Shear has occurred in your DTAP, it means that your operation has been "blown" and there is no point in your staying around.

Document

Get to a debriefing room as quickly as possible and record everything you remember while it's fresh in your mind.

Opiates

Medical research conducted during the Iraq War has confirmed that immediate administration of morphine following a traumatic event can prevent post-traumatic stress disorder (PTSD). Our medicine cabinet is well stocked and we have personnel standing by trained in the prompt and proper administration of this therapy.

Therapy

As all DOers will be aware from their HR portfolios, the benefits package includes state-of-the-art health care, with no arbitrary distinctions made between physical and mental health. These benefits are your right—don't hesitate to use them!

Post by Dr. Roger Blevins on "Department Heads" ODIN channel
DAY 1808

cc: LTG Octavian K. Frink

General Frink has asked to present an account of the confusing and re-grettable events preceding and following the disappearance of one of our MUONs: Rachel bat Avraham. Please note that this is a confidential and privileged communication for senior management only. You may disseminate relevant facts to your subordinates on a need-to-know basis.

I must begin by emphasizing that none of these events were within my power to alter, in large part due to the somewhat decentralized nature of our current org chart and the inherent limitations of managing Anachrons, MUONs, and other personalities who are not a good match for modern organizational discipline.

Having said that, below is a summary of events courtesy of Macy Stoll after interviewing all relevant witnesses. I believe at this point you are aware, at least anecdotally, of most of what happened, but you may consider the following account definitive:

Per established HR procedures, Dr. Blevins was interviewing Rachel bat Avraham in Conference Room #2. This was a quarterly review, of the sort normally conducted by Lieutenant Colonel Lyons, but since LTC Lyons was away on a DEDE, Dr. Blevins had decided to conduct the review himself.

Under normal circumstances this interview would have been unremarkable. Rachel's personnel record indicated a few areas that were in need of improvement, which Dr. Blevins brought up in the conversation as a matter of course. Dr. Blevins reported after the incident that Rachel showed signs of being under considerable emotional distress, presumably related to the upcoming climax of our 1203 Constantinople operations and possible repercussions for the family and friends she left behind in that DTAP.

Rachel became highly emotional and announced her intention to return home at once. Dr. Blevins reminded her that this was forbidden. A confrontation developed and Dr. Blevins informed her that he would summon DOSECOPS if needed to prevent her from gaining access to an ODEC. She reached into her purse and drew out a small canister of pepper spray which she discharged in Dr. Blevins's general direction. He did not sustain a direct hit, but the cloud of spray drifted into his face and created intense irritation of the eyes and nasal passages, forcing him to leave the conference room and grope his way down the hall to the men's washroom where he washed his face in a sink for several minutes before recovering to the point where he could summon DOSECOPS. By that time, Rachel had long since fled the room.

Subsequent review of security camera footage shows that Rachel proceeded via the back stairwell to the cellar level where she entered the bio-containment area and passed directly through it without performing any of the required decontamination procedures. ODEC numbers 1 through 3 were vacant, but ODEC #4 was occupied by Nadja Cole, a MUON in training, recruited only three months ago. She was using the ODEC to do "homework" related to her training program; she was not there to Send anyone, nor does she yet have the seniority or training required to do so.

Because of Rachel's seniority, Nadja did not question her when she requested entry to the ODEC. Once the two of them were closed up together inside of ODEC #4, we lose the thread of the story, since our only witness is Nadja, and it appears that Rachel employed magical techniques of some sort to cloud her judgment and induce her to Home Rachel back to 1203 Constantinople. Nadja's account of what happened is fuzzy and clearly unreliable. Since Homing is a much easier spell than Sending, apparently Nadja, with Rachel's assistance, was able to accomplish it.

We will likely never have the complete story of what Rachel did upon returning to her home DTAP. The historical record is, at the moment, clouded by GLAAMR and impossible to make sense of. LTC Lyons is expected to be Homed three days from now and may be able to supply some further details.

Dr. Blevins was examined by Dr. Srinavasan in-house and discharged with oral and topical medications to control swelling and discomfort from the pepper spray. No permanent injuries are anticipated.

Nadja has been placed on administrative leave pending the outcome of a more formal investigation.

The bio-containment zone is still being scrubbed down as per protocol and is expected to be back in working order in time for LTC Lyons's scheduled return.

AFTER ACTION REPORT

DEBRIEFER: Dr. Melisande Stokes
DOER: LTC Tristan Lyons
THEATER: Constantinople
OPERATION: Galata
DEDE: Relic relocation
DTAP: Pera, Constantinople, July 1203
STRAND: Fourth and last repetition of this DEDE

(Note to readers: Refer to the reports on the first three repetitions of this DEDE for general background. The specific DEDE was to enter the abandoned battlefield tent of the Byzantine Emperor, secure a religious relic of importance to Orthodox Christians, and move it to a different tent so that it would be found by the Bishop of Halberstadt. —MS)

As I [Lyons] knew going into this, the battle for Galata Tower took place over the course of two days, and my DEDE had to be accomplished the first day. But I had to remain until the end of the second day before I could connect with our KCW to Home me.

This was my fourth Strand prosecuting this DEDE, so at this point I knew, or thought I knew, what to expect.

I'm passing as a member of the Varangian Guard. I've attained enough seniority and respect by this point that I'm working as part of the Emperor's personal guard. In peacetime that means standing near him when he goes to church or whatever, but in wartime it means being near him on the battlefield.

The battle strategy for both sides of this conflict is all over the wiki, so

I don't need to explain that. The Emperor's so-called navy is in appalling shape, it's just a handful of ships literally rotting in the harbor, and the Emperor's army is an embarrassing joke except for the Varangian Guard.

We were camped out on the steep hillside that's north across the Golden Horn from the old walled city.

[The Golden Horn is the inlet that serves as the city's harbor. —Mel]

Across the Bosporus from us, so on the Asian side, is where the Crusaders had been camped since they arrived a few weeks earlier. The Emperor had sent emissaries over there to them, with bribes and threats, telling them, "I'm the Emperor, why are you trying to replace me with this punk kid nobody wants?" and the Crusaders' response had been, "Actually, no, we've got the real king right here in our pocket, and we're putting him on your throne." They didn't want to attack the city, they just wanted to get rid of the "tyrant."

There's two notable things about the hillside where we are camped with the Emperor. First, there's Galata Tower, which is a huge stand-alone structure right at the top of the hill. It's one of the best-sited strategic defenses I've ever seen. Archers can shoot at anyone approaching from the Bosporus, or the Golden Horn, or even the Sea of Marmara, or from inland. The single most important thing they're guarding is the chain that goes across the entrance to the Golden Horn. That inlet is so deep and narrow that it feels like a river mouth, more than a harbor. The chain is enormous, it's held up by a series of barges, and the only way to undo the chain is through a mechanism at the foot of the hill where Galata is. So the archers in Galata Tower, more than anything else, are there to keep invaders away from the mechanism that releases the chain. That's the defensive mantra of Constantinople: nobody can scale the walls, nobody can break the chain, so what matters is, don't let anyone near the mechanism that *releases* the chain. If you're invading, if you want to get near the mechanism, you first have to take Galata Tower. Which is pretty much untakeable.

The other thing of note on the hill is Pera, the Jewish neighborhood.

On a map, you could draw a line east from Galata Tower across the Bosporus to the Asian shore, where the Crusader army was attacking from. You could also draw a line south from Galata Tower that would cross Pera, then cross the Golden Horn to the old city. We were camped outside the tower, close to Pera.

That explains why the Emperor and his army were in tents—knowing that the Crusader attack was going to be directed against the Galata Tower, they had been deployed on the north side of the Golden Horn to protect it.

On the morning of July fifth, it's no secret that the Crusaders are about to attack. We—the Emperor's army—are fully geared up, the tower full of archers. On the hillside going down to the Bosporus are thousands of Byzantine soldiers fully armed and ready for the Crusaders to attack. None of them were really worried, because when you're looking at that intense Bosporus current, it seems obvious that the Crusaders could not cut directly across in those particular ships—those ships weren't built for the Bosporus, they were built for Alexandria, they were never supposed to be anywhere near Constantinople. Even if they could get across, they would have to anchor in that current, which would be extremely challenging, and then disembark without first being picked off by our archers. That was not going to happen. They were sailing into their own destruction. Of course, I knew better, but I kept my mouth shut and just let it all happen.

So the Crusader ships approach us. The Emperor gives the order for my contingent of VGs to reinforce the archers up in the Galata Tower. By the time I and my guys are up to where we have a decent vantage point, the archers in the tower are barraging the ships with fire-arrows, regular arrows, stones, we're so sure we're going to annihilate them and litter the Bosporus with their shit-stained armor.

But then something happened: the sides of the Crusaders' ships broke open and thousands of knights on horseback came leaping out of the holds, straight into the water. In that moment of the Byzantines' amazement, the archers on the boats began to shoot at us. After loosing one flight of arrows, they jumped into the water, ahead of the horses, with their bows and quivers held up over their heads, and as soon as they were in water shallow enough to keep their bowstrings dry, they began to shoot up the hillside. In full chain mail and some plate armor. As I said, this was my fourth Strand so I'd already seen it three times, but it was an astounding thing to watch. Makes footage of the Normandy landings look like nothing special.

Then the same thing happened that had happened on every Strand: the Emperor turned and fled, and most of his army fled with him. There wasn't a battle, it was just them getting chased by the Crusaders along the shore of the Golden Horn, about a mile inland, where there was a bridge across the water that the Emperor's army crossed over and then burned behind them.

The only part of the Emperor's army that didn't flee was the tower garrison, which was largely Varangian Guards but also partially local conscripts. I was still there. The whole hillside, including the imperial camp, was emptied. I knew I had about an hour and a half before the Crusaders returned. So I fulfilled my DEDE—went into the Emperor's abandoned tent, got the relic, put it into the other tent so that it would be found by somebody we need it to be found by. So the DEDE was accomplished without incident just as on the other Strands.

Now I just had to wait to rendezvous with a KCW, and since I know how things pan out, I know there will be a KCW in the Crusaders' army who can Send me back tomorrow. That's what I had done the first three Strands. I just have to survive through the rest of what's to come, without accidentally telegraphing anything to any of my cohort.

So I re-enter the tower. Approximately one hour later, as I knew, the Crusader army comes back and tries to get at the mechanism releasing the chain, but we have shitloads of arrows and, more important, fire-arrows. More specifically, fire-arrows made with Greek fire, which burns more when it touches water, so we're making them weep down by the casing to the chain-release. Their squires are holding shields over their heads to protect them, with water-soaked hides over them, and we're lighting the fucking shields on fire.

Their leader, the Marquis, finally calls them off. They pillage the Emperor's camp (and the right guy finds the relic I moved, so my DEDE is officially a success despite what happened next) and spend the afternoon and evening hollering up to us in every language they can think of, trying to bribe us to just give up the tower. Obviously we don't. So eventually they get drunk and squat in the Emperor's camp for the night, celebrating. They know there's only a couple dozen of us in the tower, and once they take us down, then they'll have Galata, which means they'll get into the harbor, which means they'll get into the city. They know tomorrow is theirs.

But what they don't know is that all through the night, what looks like regular ferry traffic across the harbor is actually thousands of armed soldiers, disguised like ragmen and coal sellers and Jews and fishermen, sneaking across from the walled city, up the hillside by Pera and into the tower. By dawn we are all packed in like anchovies. It's a miracle nobody accidentally castrates anyone else, and the stench of all those bodies is so intense, it's almost psychotropic.

The Crusaders think there's approximately thirty soldiers inside, when it's now nearly a hundred times that. In the morning, we wait for the moment when the Crusader knights are getting geared up with their squires' help, and the grooms are saddling the horses—they all do it at the same time, which is ill-considered, because right at this moment, when they are all vulnerable, we hurl open the gates of the tower and a thousand soldiers burst out and rush the Crusaders, swords and axes swinging, spears flying—and at the same time, thousands more are shooting fire-arrows down the slope at everyone on the ships, who thought they weren't even in the game today. We had a catapult on the roof of the tower that hurled boulders down into the Bosporus—they didn't hit any of the ships but they made waves big enough to capsize the smaller ones. The whole Crusader army was almost literally caught with its pants down.

Half of the Crusaders just fled because they were unarmed, or because they were servants whose pay grade didn't include armed combat. They scattered immediately into the woods beyond the camp. Meanwhile there are hundreds of thousands of citizens of Constantinople sitting on the walls of the city, watching this from across the Golden Horn like it's reality TV. Most of them don't actually care who wins because they understand it's just about who sits on the throne, they know the Crusaders aren't here to try to actually harm the city itself. All the potential emperors are assholes, and they're all related to each other, it hardly matters which one wins. So the citizens are literally picnicking and placing bets on who wins the day.

Finally the Crusader knights were mounted, and their foot soldiers got their heads together enough to finish armoring and grab their weapons, and we finally had full engagement. We still had the advantage of topography, because we were coming from the top of the hill and they were down the slope. Two Greek soldiers ran right up to the Crusader army, grabbed a lord, slashed him across the face, and began to drag him back toward the tower, but one of his knights went after him and hacked the heads off both of the Greeks, and brought the lord back to the safety of the crusading army. The whole thing happened in about thirty seconds.

That shifted everything—suddenly the Crusaders rose to the occasion, cheering and catcalling, and Christ, talk about a counterattack. None of our men had horses, and most of them were conscripted—they didn't want to be there, they had essentially no military training. So as soon as things got really heated, they deserted their stations. Some of them ran down to the harbor chain to try to pull themselves across the

Golden Horn on it—it could take the weight, those links were nearly as big as I am—but the Crusader archers picked them off easily. Remember, there's a quarter of a million people watching this for their morning entertainment. It was surreal.

Abruptly, there's only a couple hundred of us left, and we start to realize (of course, I knew this all along) that we better close the gates of the tower before the Crusaders come charging in.

To be more precise, *they* have to close the gates; *I* have to get my butt out the gates and away from there. As much as it insults my military instinct, I can only meet my KCW if I get away from the tower, because all the Varangians in that tower are going down. So—just like the three times before—I push my way out during that moment of confusion, when the Varangians and Greeks are trying to close the gates while the Crusaders are trying to force them to stay open. I'm wearing Varangian lamellar armor, relatively lightweight, so I have more mobility than the Crusaders whose ranks I have to break through. I jab at a couple of armpits and groins to encourage bodies to get out of my way, but my goal isn't to terminate anyone, it's just to get out of there. I know how it ends. My job is not to stick around for it. It's hard because I know some of those men pretty well now and leaving them to their doom while I slip away to find a witch to Send me home . . . we should consider getting counselors to help soldiers deal with that, it could fester into PTSD.

The only other Varangian I see fleeing the tower is Magnus. He follows me out of the place. He's got his eye on me. I think he's expecting me to grab a boat oar and single-handedly mow down a few hundred armed knights or something. But in all of the confusion it's easy enough for me to elude him.

So I get out, away from the tower, and I watch. I watch the Crusaders barely manage to pry the gates back open, and I watch them stream into the tower, and I hear the carnage inside, and I know what it means.

That's when it happened.

I knew what was *supposed* to happen next. The Crusaders were supposed to go down and open up the casing for the chain mechanism, release the chain, and sail into the harbor, to the astonished horror of their quarter million spectators. Then they send across the Bosporus for the rest of their camp—especially the women and the cooks. There's a KCW in the Crusader army, and she's supposed to Send me back here. Meanwhile the Jews of Pera are frantically packing their bags and hightailing it out of town to start the well-documented Byzantine Diaspora. All of that is what happened three Strands in a row.

But this time something happens that has never happened before: there is a massive flash of light and an explosion on the harbor side of the hill, right exactly where Pera is. The entire hillside—all of Pera, which was built of stone—is flaming. This has never happened before, I have no idea why it's happening, obviously at the time I didn't know that Rachel had come back to 1203 and meddled by telling people what was coming. I realized from the 1601 London DTAP that this has got to be Diachronic Shear and I knew I had to get as far away as possible. So I run toward the woods and wait to see what happens when all the fire and explosions die down. That happens very fast, actually—just like in London.

I come back toward the tower for reconnaissance, and I see at once that two things are different from how they've always been. First, because of the explosion and fire and all that hell that broke loose, there's no way to release the chain mechanism. It's fused. That thing is never going to open. Ever. And just as I'm thinking about what a massive fuck-up that is—because without the chain being lowered, the ships cannot get into the safety of the harbor, and then literally, history cannot move forward—and then the second thing I notice is that . . . Pera is gone. Gone. Not even any foundation stones. It's obliterated—a black charred spot, acres of it—on the hillside, as if there was never anything there. And that awful smell I remember from the Albigensian DTAP, that noisome smell of charred bones after an execution. The whole area, which had been walled and locked, went up so fast that nobody there had time to escape. Horrible.

A quarter hour later, while half the army is still walking around in a daze, something incredible happened: the *Eagle*, the largest and heaviest iron-prowed Venetian ship, rammed into the harbor chain and broke it. They broke the harbor chain of Constantinople! That's not how it was supposed to happen. Invaders tried for five hundred years to break the chains guarding the Golden Horn. Every generation of that chain was unbreakable. Something about the Diachronic Shear must have had a molecular effect on the metal and weakened the chain. I think the multiverse required the Crusaders to get into the harbor and so made sure it happened, even if they couldn't do it the way they did on every other Strand.

Anyhow—neither side lost many men to the Shear, but it freaked the hell out of everyone. Even being aware of the Shear, I'm already feeling confused about what happened, so I'm sure all kinds of crazy things will end up getting said about it. I'm willing to bet everyone will say that Pera must have been made of wood to go up in flames like that, and the flames must have come from the fire-arrows—something like that, even though I know Pera was made of stone and tile, and I also know the angle the fire-arrows came from would never have landed in Pera anyhow. So lots of weird crap is going to get said.

In conclusion, it appears Rachel was reunited with her family and warned them. This changed everything.

Clearly Rachel's information moved quickly out of the Jewish settlement. There is no way we will ever know what Rachel said, or to whom, or what that person attempted to do with the information. We know only that the multiverse could not bear such a change of course, and eliminated its possibility.

Post by Dr. Melisande Stokes
on "All-DODO" ODIN channel
DAY 1812

All,

Mortimer has requested that everyone please stop checking the wiki for updates on Constantinople, it's slowing the servers down and it is a waste of time until the GLAAMR dissipates. Lieutenant Colonel Lyons and I believe that over the next few days, history will literally rewrite itself, as the oral accounts of that day's Diachronic Shear make their way into written testimonials and then eventually history books, and finally the Internet.

Rachel bat Avraham almost certainly died in the Shear. Although she died in defiance of our regulations, it is important to be sensitive to the grief of the many DODO workers—especially her fellow MUONs—who had the fortune and pleasure to have worked with her for the better part of three years.

Respectfully submitted,
Melisande Stokes

Exchange of posts by LTG Octavian K. Frink,
Dr. Constantine Rudge, and Dr. Roger Blevins
on private ODIN channel
DAYS 1810–1813 (MID-JULY, YEAR 5)

Post from LTG Octavian K. Frink:

Blev, (cc Rudge):

I've been following the traffic on this system as my schedule permits. Relieved to hear LTC Lyons made it back in one piece. Somewhat confused otherwise. He accomplished the mission on all four Strands? So, how do we know whether it worked?

Reply from Dr. Roger Blevins:
Okie, that is the fundamental question of all diachronic operations— how can we know the success or failure of a campaign such as this one, where the objective is to shift national borders a few kilometers, or even a few meters, to one direction or the other?

In the present case, as you know, what we are trying to achieve is to pry Crimea loose from the Russians and get it back into the full and undisputed possession of Ukraine, all without firing a shot or engaging in military operations as that term is normally understood.

If the project succeeds, then our present-day reality changes; we wake up tomorrow and Ukraine owns the Crimea free and clear. Not only that, but history will have changed as well. We'll have no memory and no records of Russia ever having marched into Crimea in 2014. So how do we know that anything even happened?

The answer is that the alteration of history doesn't happen in a flash; it takes a little while to propagate through all of the Strands and what- not, and during that time there is this thing that Dr. Oda terms GLAAMR (Galvanic Liminal Aura Antecedent to Manifold Rift), which even non- magical people can sense if it's strong enough.

From Dr. Constantine Rudge:
Just jumping in here with a note that DODO's R&D division has invented ways of measuring GLAAMR. That's why we had three spy planes in last year's budget; we mounted the GLAAMR detection systems in their bel- lies, and even now they are flying routes over Ukraine gathering data.

From LTG Frink:
Yes, I remember the spy planes now, and the ruckus they caused in the budget hearing. Glad to know they are getting some use.

Why can't we just draw a map or something, and store it, and then compare it to a current map a few days later? I know you're going to tell me it would change and there would be GLAAMR, but is there no way to just store a document in such a way that it wouldn't change?

From Dr. Blevins:

That is being worked on too. Apparently if the map were stored in an ODEC, your idea might work. But because space in ODECs is so scarce and expensive we have done very little of this.

From LTG Frink:

Seems to me we could get a hell of a lot of thumb drives into an ATTO. Give me a sitrep on those.

Oh, and I noticed that when Rachel bat Avraham flew the coop, she used mind control on the witch who Homed her. Obviously psy-ops is a common ability among the historical witches.

From Dr. Rudge:

Just a gentle reminder, General Frink, that we try to avoid using loaded terms such as "mind control."

From LTG Frink:

Connie, you can call it whatever you want, psy-ops has got to be simpler than what we just went through to get Crimea back.

From Dr. Rudge:

Yes, General Frink, Crimea is part of the Ukraine today. You may share with me a vague memory, rapidly fading, of a Russian invasion that never happened. As if we dreamed it, and the memory of the dream is being dispelled by the more concrete realities of the new day.

Without disputing your opinion that the operation was anything but simple, I'll point out that to achieve the same result through conventional military operations would have been infinitely more complex and risky.

From LTG Frink:

I'll give you complex. Risky I'm less sure of. Hard to know what the real risks are.

From Dr. Blevins:

To answer a question earlier in this "thread," the first ATTO is proceeding through its testing routines more or less on schedule, but it is a device of many subsystems and there are endless delays and complications around procuring special parts, debugging "code," and so on. We are looking at bringing Gráinne forward in mid-September, once we're certain the device works. In the meantime we could certainly try some experiments with thumb drives or other forms of document storage, as you suggest.

   In the meantime, Okie, I would like to draw your attention to a question we were kicking around earlier, namely what to do with the surplus personnel in LTC Lyons's department—including LTC Lyons himself— now that the big push in the Constantinople Theater is over. Do we wish to throw them into another colossal operation, or sit back and assess?

From LTG Frink:

Will give you a call in five, Blev.

**FROM LIEUTENANT GENERAL OCTAVIAN K. FRINK
TO ALL DODO DEPARTMENT HEADS**
DAY 1825 (LATE JULY, YEAR 5)

First of all, I would like to congratulate all DODO personnel for the successful conclusion of operations in the Constantinople Theater. That is not to gloss over the tragic story of the late Rachel bat Avraham, however, to the best of our ability to assess these things, it would appear that DODO was able to "undo" a Russian takeover of the Crimea that, on our Strand, never successfully happened. To have achieved a similar result using conventional Trapezoid-style operations would have been immensely costly in both dollars and blood and would have raised the possibility of opening a wider war.

One of the measures of a successful team is the ability to adapt to unexpected complications that inevitably crop up during the course of a complex operation—the "fog of war," as it were. Our glitch for this mission was the unexpected advent of "St. Tristan of Dintagel" as blowback from earlier operations in Normandy. While this made it seem touch and go for a short time, the situation seems to have resolved without further repercussions.

Before many of you depart for well-deserved vacations during August, I wanted to supply an idea of top-level direction during the rest of this year, and the year following. The Constantinople Theater has proved that with the help of the Chronotron we can conduct large-scale operations that will reshape history to our advantage without the expense and bloodshed of conventional warfare. As you all know, DODO is also conducting significant operations in five other theaters at this time. All of these are scheduled to wind down over the course of the autumn and early winter. Our general plan is to stand down, stand back, and appraise the results and lessons learned before plunging into additional theater-scale operations.

With that, I wish you all a restful August.

Sincerely,

Lieutenant General Octavian K. Frink

Post by Dr. Melisande Stokes to LTC Tristan Lyons on private ODIN channel

DAY 1825

I didn't think Frink could be that smooth.

Reply from LTC Lyons:

Don't go there, Stokes.

From Dr. Stokes:

No, seriously, that was the nicest "fuck you" letter ever.

From LTC Lyons:

He's a general. He fights wars. When the war's over, he stops fighting and puts his army to work training to fight the next war. That's all this is.

From Dr. Stokes:

Hmm, I think being turned into a saint may have affected your judgment.

From LTC Lyons:

So you're going to be the little devil on my shoulder?

From Dr. Stokes:

:)

From LTC Lyons:

I'm outta here. Time for some R&R. See you in three weeks.

From Dr. Stokes:

Where you going again?

From LTC Lyons:

Probably shouldn't divulge this, but I'm going to Normandy.

From Dr. Stokes:

Collinet?

From LTC Lyons:

You got it. It's a nice place now. There's a B&B practically right on Thyra's homesite. Going to go get drunk on cider and light a candle at the chapel of St. Tristan.

From Dr. Stokes:

Light one for me.

From LTC Lyons:

Roger wilco.

LETTER FROM
GRÁINNE *to* GRACE O'MALLEY
A Wednesday of Late-Harvest, 1602

Auspiciousness and prosperity to you, milady!

So at last, the time 'tis for me to reveal my plan to you in full. As good as all these fellas have been to me both in London and in Antwerp, there's naught of use that comes of my remaining a spy for Your Grace when I've lost the chance to dawdle around Whitehall, and it's all these natural philosophers and bloody intellectuals I've got around me. And the Fuggers, of course, but they at least are clear-eyed, so they are, about how to get things done in this world. I know Your Grace grows weary of the world, and sorrowful I am to think of your moving past us to the realms beyond. I've no premonition at all of what shall come of Ireland once you've left us, and I fear the English will renew their bloody conquering schemes, especially with the urging of Sir Francis feckin' Bacon.

So I hope it's understanding that Your Grace will be, when I tell you that I've vowed to myself to look out for my own cause now: that being magic, and the fate of my sister witches. Sure Tristan Lyons trusts me as a sibling, and yet isn't he always refusing to tell me what stymies all magical abilities in future. So I'm thinking the best way for me to be learning such a thing is to go forward into the future myself, and be looking at things from his vantage point. Glad I am to hear from within the net-work that Tristan's bosses think to bring me forward anyhow, to help them with a thing they call an Atto, which is apparently exactly like the horrid little chambers their witches be spending all their days in, only not quite so little, and on wheels. As if wheels would make it any better.

I intend to use the resources of Tristan's own guild, what calls itself DODO, not to *restore* magic, but to *prevent its destruction* in the first place, as soon as I ken what is the cause of such destruction. A brilliant plan this is, to my mind, and so obvious and straightforward, I wonder what bollocks excuse Tristan's superiors have for not be doing likewise. I know not how long a stretch of time there is, between the death of magic and its rebirth, but that stretch is surely a boil on the face of history, and if it can be avoided, then it is my duty to see that happen. For surely the destruction of magic is not only bad for witches, but bad for Ireland and such like nations that are relying heavily on magic for self-defense from oppressors.

So here then is my plan: oft enough have I listened to Tristan and the other DOers lament of a certain officer whose name is Roger Blevins. This gentleman, although little enough he seems to do, yet has more power than all the others put together—even including Tristan Lyons himself! Rose is of a mind with me, and it's Sending me forward in time she's agreed to, so that I may ingratiate myself with this Blevins—and yourself knows well enough how easily I may ingratiate myself when it's ingratiating that is called for! And then won't I be in a position to be learning things Tristan wouldn't have me learn. And won't he be helpless to prevent my learning.

And so, my dear beloved Pirate Queen, I pledge my loyalty to you forever, and to the Irish cause, but it's off to the future I'm now bound.

Whether I be near or far, may I hear only good things of you, My Lady Grace!

Yours ever, Gráinne No Longer in England

INCIDENT REPORT

AUTHOR: Esme Overkleeft
SUBJECT: Magnus
THEATER: Northern Europe, Early Medieval (NEEM)
OPERATION: Botanical Infrastructure Ops for Magical
Enhancement (BIOME)
DTAP: Collinet, Normandy, 1205
FILED: Day 1857 (late August, Year 5)

Having completed my DEDE in Normandy 1205 DTAP (*Iris germanica* rhizome grafting along La Vie River), I went to KCW Imblen of Collinet to be Sent back to DODO HQ. I have worked with Imblen on several occasions and my Norman French allows us to have reasonably fluent conversations. As others who have visited this DTAP can attest, she is a calm, unflappable, good-humored woman.

However, on this occasion she was on edge. Magnus of Normandy, known to several of our DOers from DTAPs 1202–3 Constantinople, returned to his home village (some 50 km from Collinet) after many years gone, which was a cause of celebration. However, Magnus was excessively preoccupied with querying everyone about their memory of a local song or folktale, about a great hero who had, several generations earlier, saved the village from attack by a feuding tribe and later been canonized by the Church. The hero was named Tristan of Dintagel, an unremarkable enough name—except that Magnus met somebody named Tristan of Dintagel in Constantinople, 160 years after the events of the story.

Magnus called the village elders into council and described this remarkable coincidence to them. They did not share his obsessive curiosity. He then traveled to Collinet to query Imblen, formally seeking her advice and assistance as a witch to make sense of this. He was excited and aggressive and supplied many details about Tristan's recent activities in Constantinople, making it obvious that he had observed Tristan closely and recruited other members of the Varangian Guard to keep an eye on him.

Imblen feels she said, "I can't help you," a little too quickly and firmly, because he became even more intrigued, and declared that he would go to Dintagel directly to seek the (parish? Church? Hundreds?) records and establish if "his" Tristan was a descendant of the hero . . . or if something stranger was happening.

For the record, this is the fourth Strand on which something like this has happened. Each time, Imblen seems more shaken and Magnus appears more clear-headed and determined. This time—given what he understands of witches' powers—he hypothesized directly to Imblen that given Tristan's archaic speech patterns, perhaps another witch had Sent Tristan forward in time, and if so, "he would hie himself back to Constantinople to learn more of Tristan's doings, in case there could be profit for himself made from it."

Respectfully submitted,

Esme Overkleeft

Exchange of posts by DODO staff on "Anachron Management" ODIN channel

DAYS 1862–1870 (EARLY SEPTEMBER, YEAR 5)

Post from Dr. Melisande Stokes:

Welcome back from vacation, everyone. I am assuming you have all seen Esme Overkleeft's incident report. It sounds like Magnus knows too much. Should we consider bringing him forward?

Reply from Macy Stoll:

Please keep in mind that the Anachron Management Team, which bears the brunt of looking after all of these people who are brought forward, is currently operating at capacity. Some Anachrons are easier to handle than others. If this Magnus is so burning with curiosity that he would traverse half the known world to pursue this matter, then he'll cause just as much trouble for us here if we bring him forward.

From LTC Tristan Lyons:

Respectfully, Macy, if we bring him forward we will at least have some oversight re: his troublemaking. If that requires additional resources for the Anachron Management Team, then there are channels for requesting same.

From Dr. Roger Blevins:

Magnus's psych profile suggests he will probably be considered a "nut job" (possessed by demons, etc.) by anyone in his era. While he might cause problems, they don't warrant us spending the resources on housing him here for the rest of his life. He isn't sophisticated enough to figure the whole thing out—or to be useful to us if he's here. It's not worth the resources to bring him.

From LTC Lyons:

Respectfully, I can vouch for Magnus's abilities, having fought beside him on several occasions in Constantinople DTAPs. Contrary to Dr. Blevins's assessment, I cannot think of a better soldier to help train DOers who will be operating in the Viking/Norman world. I should have proposed recruiting him already. My department has a number of physically active DOers who are currently in turnaround. If we bring him forward I'll be his minder until we've taken proper measure of him.

From Dr. Stokes:

Just bumped into Esme in the cafeteria—she had to do one more Strand on DTAP 1205 Collinet, and says Imblen reports that Magnus has now advanced his theory.

Given that Tristan of Dintagel of legend came to Normandy as a fortune-seeker, and then (as Magnus sees it) almost certainly came forward in time, he is evidence that time travel is an excellent way to seek one's fortune. Apparently Magnus would like to employ the same method. He is asking Imblen what fee she would accept to Send him in one direction or another. She has reverted to typical witch maneuvers of requesting impossible-to-get things (in this case myrrh from the cradle of Baby Jesus). He threatened her—highly unusual behavior toward a witch—and she had to render him mute for an hour to put him in his place.

Esme hasn't had time yet to file a full report, but I'll link in this thread when she does. Please reconsider bringing Magnus forward.

From Dr. Blevins:

Anyone stupid enough to threaten an active witch will never get his head around what is really going on here.

But since he is now a threat to one of our human assets, and Tristan seems to think he can contain him, I'll (dispassionately) second Melisande's suggestion to bring him forward.

From LTG Octavian K. Frink:

Have been monitoring this thread.

Bring Magnus forward. Even if he doesn't figure anything out, we're dealing with the specter of Diachronic Shear if he says something to somebody more clever than he is. If we keep him busy as a combat instructor he'll probably think he's died and gone to Valhalla.

Private message from LTC Lyons to Dr. Stokes:

Don't correct him about Valhalla, Stokes. I know you want to. Don't.

GRÁINNE'S
FINAL LETTER
to GRACE O'MALLEY
PART 1

Summer Solstice, 1603

Faith and Auspiciousness to Your Grace!

It's a very long letter I'll be writing you this day, and the last one ever, for certain this time. I've been to the future and back again, so I have, and am about to go again—and this time, I am quite certain there'll be no returning. So you'll never know the end of my story, Your Grace, but now in your closing weeks, before you cease to draw breath, it's a remarkable adventure I'm leaving you to dwell upon, that you might not forget your little Gráinne as the veils lower between the worlds to receive you.

So to get on with the telling:

Rose Sent me forward, to the same place we have both so oft sent Tristan and the others. I arrived in a place so shocking that I doubt our fair language has words harsh and perverse enough to do it justice. As Tristan had already revealed to me, in this future day there's only a small, airless chamber where magic's working, with just enough room for two people, barely larger than a garderobe it is. The walls are slick and peculiar, like tiles made of painted wood. And no smells in it at all, not a one. How can that be?

But 'tis nothing compared to what happens when the door of the chamber opes. 'Twould take me half a lifetime to describe to you the wonders and the horrors of the future world. The garderobe, what they call the ODEC, is housed within a large chamber—a strange room with mechanical monstrosities and a dreadful buzz in the air as if lightning were always just about to strike, a sound they are all indifferent to, much as I became indifferent to the odors of Southwark. And this chamber in turn is inside a vast building, which is on a street full of vast buildings, in a city of streets with vast buildings. Larger than cathedrals some of them, but without ornament or even shape. Like building blocks for giants, so they are. No imagination or love of beauty at all.

Everything functions without human or magical assistance, but I confess most breathlessly that whatever power keeps humanity and its many mechanical servants humming . . . it is far more dazzling than any magic I have ever seen performed.

And I tell you straight out: suspicious this makes me, for what is the cause to bring magic back when it has been replaced by something clearly more serviceable? So the first riddle I put my mind to was this: in a world where carriages travel without beasts to pull them, and food is effortlessly abundant, and there is ample light to sunder any darkness, from all manner of peculiar torches, none of them given to burning down a place even if it is all wood, and where all and sundry wear grander clothes than most anyone in London and an astonishing variety what's more . . . something there must be, some commodity or advantage, that magic can attain but mankind cannot yet. Nothing material can it be, for no magic I ever knew summoned such luxuries for royalty as everyday folk here take as commonplace.

The environs are not the point of my tale so I shall omit most of the gobsmacking details, but please know I will happily discourse upon it if you're requesting it of me, Your Grace. To the Kingdom of Heaven I know you are bound soon, but it might not contain half the wonders of yon twentyfirst century.

So to get to the telling at last:

Greeted I was by the ladyinwaiting of the ODEC—the first woman ever I met of that time, in that time, and wasn't she strangely dressed! With teeth every bit as fine as Tristan's. When I gave her courtesy, why, she was astonished, for isn't my name one of glorious renown in the future? It is, sure. She proffered me a thick white cotton shift with a belt sewn into it, from a pile of them beside the door, and then a set of absurdly short stockings from another pile (socks, she called them), instructed me to don it all, and asked me to wait—as if I'd anywhere to go now that I'd arrived. Then she spoke directly to her desk, so she did, asking it to send her Lieutenant Colonel Lyons on account of Gráinne had arrived from London.

Within moments there he was, my handsome fella, looking at me through a wall made of the most perfect glass that can be imagined—so smooth and flawless as to be invisible. He looked ever so bizarre in the weeds he must wear in that future time, monotone and snug but shapeless, not glorifying his marvelous shape and yet neither hiding it for modesty as priests are wont to do. 'Twas incredibly dull he looked. After giving me a look up and down, he nodded as if to say "Sure that be Gráinne" and then went to a door in the glass wall, out of my view.

Meanwhile I was hustled away by another young man with gorgeous teeth, who smelled like something I might like to lick (but refrained), escorting me out of the room of the ODEC, he did, under horrible illumination that buzzed fiendishly and made everyone look dead, along a corridor covered in some kind of short, stubby pelt, very firmly set upon the boards, and then into a room tiled with a marvelous substance such as my stockinged feet had never felt before—it both gave way and yet slightly gripped the stocking. This room was blindingly bright and cold, everything made of metal like an armory, but even brighter somehow, as if everything were the color of a new sword—whole walls like silver. Most peculiar it was. At this point, Your Grace, I wouldn't be lying to say that I was that fatigued and weak, as if all my humors were being slowly drained from me. It occurred to me that a good slumber would be most agreeable. As if he were reading my thoughts, the young man led me to a peculiar piece of furniture, something between a couch and a throne, a sort of upright divan I suppose it was. 'Twas soft and padded and strewn about with blankets and in other ways most inviting for one about to swoon.

But then Tristan came into the room, and that brought me back to my senses.

"God ye good morrow," myself said gaily. "There's no need to be looking so surprised, Tristan, sure Rose is attending to my duties in Southwark, and I'd a mind to see for myself the Great Work I am helping build with my journeyman's efforts. I know you were wanting me to come, so I thought I'd better leg it to you quick as I could."

"You're two weeks early," he said.

"'Twas a change of scene I was wanting, all them natural philosophers were growing dull enough to dry snot. Isn't it right glad you are to see me, so? Sorry my togemans are so homely, they're all your maid had to offer me. 'Tisn't even my knees these stockings reach to, I never knew how tawdry your costume was in this era."

"Listen to me," Tristan said in the stoic soldierly way of his, which was grand with me as the whole point of coming here was to hear what he had to say. Besides which, I was growing weaker almost every minute. "There are things in the air here that can kill you just from what you breathe or touch. There is an entire protocol you must go through," and then he went about using lots of words what sounded Latin and of many syllables, and I wasn't especially interested in them as I was suddenly fain to sit in the divan. Happily 'twas exactly there he placed me, and talking without pause he was, saying he would have to talk to his superiors while I was going through the ordeal he was about to put me through.

A woman dressed all in white appeared in this room, like a religious acolyte of some pagan creed, and didn't she and the young man begin to work with some alarming mechanical objects, the which seemed to be alive all on their own, with mysterious eyes and lights and noises and movements, full of hoses and tubes they were, transparent like fine glass but bendable like straw, most confounding. And they were bringing these monsters close to me, and I saw all manner of needles at the ends of the tubes. The woman was introduced to me as a physician (truly! A woman physician!) and the young man as her "nurse," and they explained in a most unmusical and peculiar kind of English that they had to pump me full of medicine to prevent the invisible airborne humours from imbalancing my own. They had nothing practical there, no leeches or poultices or charms or herbs, nothing but these strange mechanical curiosities. The fellow explained they had to stick needles into my arm to fill me with the medicine—in the form of potion it was—and sure it was the closest I have ever come to panicking. Only Tristan's familiar presence kept me from something near hysteria, and Your Grace knows I am not easily unnerved.

Things were so clean, you could smell the cleanliness, cleaner than soap it was, and very cold to the spirit. The needles did not hurt, and were bound to my arms and the backs of my hands with some kind of sticking tape, and I felt a cold drowsy feeling in my veins, as if someone were binding me with a spell of lethargy. These first moments of my arrival, to speak true, were not even the slightest bit resembling what I imagined.

"You'll be getting treatment over the course of the next few days," says the physician, "and you'll be quarantined in this room for two weeks."

"And I'll have to bring Blevins in to see you," says Tristan, as if aggrieved he were, although of course secretly Blevins was exactly the man I wanted. "Gráinne, I'm shocked you did this without consulting me first."

"Sure you haven't been back to see me in weeks," says I. "How could I consult you if you weren't there to consult?"

"There have been plenty of agents back in your time," says he. "You could have given one of them a message."

"But then I'd miss seeing that look on your face." I grin. "'Tis all grand, Tristan, we'll have a grand time of it."

Unconvinced he looked, and none too happy, but away he went anyhow. Now I was alone. Or so I thought.

The light, which shone impossibly steady right out of the ceiling, was dimmed so that it was perhaps as bright as a cloudy morn—before that it had been as bright as midsummers at noon—and then it dimmed even more so that it resembled nearly sunset, but without the proper kinds of shadows or color. All wrong and strange it was. It's quite overwhelmed I was finding myself, Your Grace, and I was not at all sure after all that I was really prepared for my adventure. Wasn't I certain I would need to be finding someone who had my back.

And suddenly I realized I was not alone. As far as one might spit (well, as far as I might spit anyhow, which is farther than some) was a curtain dividing the room, suspended cleverly from a sort of track attached to the ceiling. A hand reached out from its other side and swept it out of the way, revealing another divan-throne, and upon that didn't there sit a man now with long brown hair, dressed in the same ungainly togemans I was wearing—white robe and insensibly short stockings. And needles sticking out of his arms, so he had, attached to tubes. A sinewy strength he had, rare amongst the city folk of London, even the soldiers, and honestly even Tristan, who is quite the specimen, looked merely bulky in compare. Every visible inch of skin on this fellow's body was taut. Handsome he was, but not so handsome as Tristan. There was no way to know his rank as he had nothing about him but what I did, that being what we were given to hide our nakedness. He held himself like a soldier and a leader. Common sense declared he, like myself, had recently arrived from elsewhere. Looking him over, as much as I could be seeing of him, it seemed clear to me that he would offer excellent protection, not to mention an excellent fuck, and so I took it upon myself to make friends with him.

"Good day to you," I said. "Do you speak English?"

It was a queer look he gave me, and then didn't he answer not in the Queen's English but in a peculiar patois of Anglo-Norman French. I'm knowing enough French to get along in a whorehouse, but that is the French of our day. His was of an earlier age. But plenty of time we had, and little else to occupy it, and so as the hours went by we explained ourselves to each other.

He is Magnus, from a village in Normandy. He had spent much of his life a-roaming, fighting for the Emperor's guard in Constantinople. 'Twas all the way forward from the year 1205 or so Magnus had come (he wasn't much for calendars, he was more of a map fella), and he had been Sent hither to his great surprise and without his leave, as he had begun to sort out that something peculiar was happening with the world. Lest his understanding trigger Iomadh (he had a different word for it, but understood it perfectly, as he'd seen it with his own eyes), Tristan and his company had brought him forward, so they had, for everybody's safety. He had arrived three days before me.

Now this fella, I thought, was one to have on your side if you were feeling weak as a kitten, which I was, being deprived of all

magic. So chat him up I did, and between us didn't we share nug/
gets of information. He had little to add to my knowledge, of
course, as he was no part of Tristan's company. He hadn't a strat/
egy as I did, given he didn't know he would be coming here until
moments before it happened. I kept my counsel but was friendly
enough. Surely he's not so evolved as we, in that it's obsessed he is
with gold and such, like all those accursed Norman/type peoples
who have run riot over our fair island . . . but he's canny, that lad.
Straight off I sensed that.

The next day the weakness came over me something terrible
and I had fevers and aches. As Magnus and I lay there getting
potions pumped into our bodies to balance our humors, another
physician/type woman came into the room and went straight to
Magnus and let him know, by pantomime gestures, that he should
be baring his left shoulder. This he did, and immediately she took
exception to something on it. It seemed a simple birthmark to me.
He looked askance at her interest, and no wonder, for perhaps here
as ever people are eager to see marks of the devil upon a body,
and especially upon a stranger. He tensed, but the woman did not
seem to notice.

"I see why they called me in . . . that does look a little suspi/
cious," she said, off/hand as all that.

He tensed more.

From her breast pocket the woman removed an object no larger
than a playing card. Colored light shone from one face of it, as if
'twere a stained glass window. She let her fingers play over it for a
few moments, then spoke: "I'll be removing that mole for a biopsy."

After the briefest of pauses, the object—which I later learned is
called a phone—spoke to Magnus in his own dialect. Or tried to,
anyway, as "biopsy" ain't a word to those people, any more than it

is to you and me—but as best I could discern, it strung a few words together that approximated the idea, which was that she was going to lop the thing off for a closer look.

I could see well enough that this wasn't Magnus's first phone-chat, for he was in no way as astonished as I. He rattled something off, and after a few moments the phone translated: "Going to cut it off me?" Magnus was wary but not worried.

To her gentleman attendant she said something about "lie doe cain" which the phone dutifully attempted to translate, but botched it somehow—forgive me, Your Grace, but I was half de-lirious, and this bit was a sort of comedy of errors involving the phone and the various dialects. Magnus had a lot of questions—not of a suspicious nature, you'll understand, but simple hunger to know. It was laboriously explained that "lie doe cain" is a potion, not magical in nature (since magic has no purchase in this time and place) but once injected into his shoulder with a wee needle, deadened the pain so that the woman sliced that birthmark off Magnus's shoulder without him even needing a swig of whiskey! He watched this in fascination and wonder, like a child seeing a magician at his tricks. The assistant bandaged it neatly enough, and said to him, through the phone, "That might hurt after the lie doe cain wears off."

Utterly baffled was Magnus, and he reached across to prod the bandage. "No pain?" he said.

"Don't touch it," she said with brisk compassion. "No touch."

"No pain," he repeated. "No nothing!"

The doctor had been dousing her hands with a sort of ointment they use, scented like bad gin. It is a ritual with them.

"Anesthetic," she said slowly, and repeated it several times, sylla-ble for syllable. "Makes it numb."

"But how? Is it magic?"

I shook my head. "There is no magic in this time." He looked astounded at this news, so now I knew I had some insight to offer him that sure would bind him to me.

The physician now turned her attention to me, and said she'd like to have a look at my skin, all over, as a precaution—for my freckly complexion was of a sort prone to just the sorts of moles she'd lately sliced off of Magnus, and it's superstitious they are about such things. The assistant shot the curtain across to afford me a bit of privacy, and I pulled up my shift and let the doctor look me over.

"So the lie doe cain is a numbing agent, is it?" I asked the female physician. "Where does it come from? Seems a remarkable ointment."

She shrugged. "It's very commonplace in this era. You can buy it at any pharmacy. Do you know what a pharmacy is? You might know it as an apothecary, or chemist."

"Aye I know it surely, but I doubt he does," I say. "I'll explain."

No eldritch freckles were to be found on my person and so the lady and her assistant packed up their potions and bandages and absented themselves. This was only one such encounter, for don't these people have a thousand varieties of doctor, each keen to inspect a different bit of you with a different contraption, and it's shocked you'd be, my lady, if I told you everywhere they looked.

When they were leaving us alone, I brought Magnus up to date on all I knew (besides my own schemes, of course). His pale blue eyes were round as platters a fair bit of the time.

"But you must know," I told him when I'd said all I knew, "I've never left my own age before. Well, not by more than a year or two, for sport. I've nothing left to explain, for all the rest will be as new to me as to you."

After a few days of this, my fevers broke, and my vigor returned as I was growing accustomed to an existence without magic. When it seemed I was fit for conversation, Tristan returned. He had company: one older gentleman and two women, a bit younger than myself. The younger of the two was very beautiful and wore a dress; the other, plainer, and dressed similarly to the men, and the bearing of a scholar did she have about her, like an abbess.

"This is Gráinne," said Tristan, looking tense about the mouth.

I smiled my charming smile and held out my hand to the gentleman. He stared at me. He was a dignified-enough looking chap, clearly of higher birth from Tristan by the way he carried himself. He had a short, thick mane of grey, swept back as if posing for a statue he was. He reminded me a bit of that right arse Les Holgate who triggered the lomadh and ruined my life. "This is Dr. Roger Blevins," Tristan says to me, in a heavy-handed sort of way.

"Well met and God save you, milord," I say, leaning forward from the divan to clasp his hand gingerly (as the back of my hand had all the needles still).

"It is good to meet you—but you have defied protocol in coming here," he says sternly, with great anger in his eyes. So as usually is the case, I begin to cast a spell to soften him to me . . . and at once I realize, with a dreadful feeling in my guts, that it will not work! Tristan spoke true, there was no magic here at all. No wonder I felt at once so heavy and dull.

"I cry pardon," I say, trying not to show my dismay. "Things do work best free and easy-like in London, I did not realize how regular in your habits you are here. Isn't it good I came and learned that?"

The two men exchanged glances and each sighed, in different keys. Blevins made a gesture with his head, and Tristan nodded as if understanding a secret code he was.

"Mel," he said, a bit wearily, to the plainer of the women. "Meet

Gráinne. Gráinne, here is Doctor Melisande Stokes. And here is Erszebet." That being the fine-looking one in the skirt, with the painted face.

Melisande, without a smile of greeting but a look of some checked amusement in her eye, held out her hand and shook mine. "It's an honour to meet you, Gráinne. We are very much in your debt. Welcome to America."

Much quieter is Melisande than I was anticipating her to be. She must be clever in hidden, subtle ways, not the way of educated women in Elizabeth's court who are falling all over each other to outshine one another. Her light is a secret that she uses as a tool, and sure there is something tough there underneath it, which I do respect well enough. 'Tis clear enough from watching her and Tristan that there should be fire between them, certainly some congress, but just as clear that admitting to it is something you'll find neither of them doing. Still the attraction hangs in the air almost visibly. I believe when I go back there—now that I have a plan, which shortly I shall tell you of—I must find a way to use that.

And as for Erszebet, their original witch, she is fair indeed, but she is not a happy lass. Her discontentment fairly radiates from her fiery dark eyes, and her face is fashioned, as if from birth, to have a bit of a pout or sneer. And yet strangely charming (excuse the term) I found her to be at once.

Rather than taking my proffered hand to shake, she took it and kissed my knuckles. "I greet you as a sister," says she. "As I greet all the witches who dwell in my house, and come under my aegis."

"Now wait a moment," says Tristan. "We don't know we'll be keeping her on as an employee."

"And I don't know I'll be staying," says I, "if this is how I'm to be spoken of—like as if I weren't even in the room."

"Gráinne, don't you understand, you can't leave," said Tristan with some irritation. "Once an historical agent has come forward, they cannot go back, they have too much knowledge of what is here to safely take back."

"Then staying's what I'll do," I said agreeably.

Now the Blevins is watching all of this back-and-forth with what I'm sure he imagines to be a canny and knowing mien. Ever so stern he was in the beginning, with his talk of protocols, but now doesn't he change his tune and become the friend and protector of poor Gráinne.

"Did you have in mind making the poor woman a *detainee*?" says the Blevins, taking a wee step closer to me, as if he's going to ward off the others' wicked assaults. "No, we need her abilities in the ATTO. This has been in the works for months, Tristan. Perhaps you missed it, when you were off becoming a hero and a saint, and watching Diachronic Shear in Pera, and vacationing in France; but Gráinne, though she showed up early, came here to work for me. And once we have matters sorted out, she'll enjoy the same freedoms and privileges as any other anachronic employee."

During the ensuing silence, while Tristan and Mel are rolling their eyes at this peroration, Erszebet steps in.

"She's not an employee," says Erszebet. "She has not signed your nonsense papers. She has only helped you from the generosity of her heart. You have no hold on her. As I know the story, you are deeply in her debt and have made absolutely no attempt to recompense her." To me, she says, "This is a terrible world and I would not stay if I could leave, but I have obligations I must honor. You do not. If I were you, I would leave at once. If you want to stay, I will do all in my power to make things less wretched for you than they have been for me."

More sympathy's what I'd be feeling, if these words came from an unkempt beggar, but here she is wearing a gown as fine as any at Bess's court might wear, although scandalously short of length the skirt was. So I do wonder a wee bit about how easily she finds things miserable. But she is offering me a place at her table, and I accept with graciousness.

"I will show you everything you need to know to survive in this strange world," she says firmly, as if in defiance of the men, whom she does not waste even a flicker of her attention on now. "These people think they have set up an initiation into these times, for Anachrons who come forward. What they offer is feeble. I will give you my own attention, as I do every witch. You will be comfortable and safe, and most important, you will *understand* things. These men do not think witches need to understand much, as if we were just cogs in a bit of machinery, they have no regard for our human rights."

"Our what?" asks I, as I see it's Blevins's turn to be rolling his eyes a bit.

"I will show you how to order take-out and flush a toilet and use Instagram. Although you are older. Perhaps you would prefer Facebook." A sly smile of pleasure. "I will take you shopping. For clothing. The other Anachrons are not allowed this, but the witches I take whenever I wish. I think you will enjoy that."

None of the others disagreed with her, which I took to mean that this was Erszebet's role in greeting all new witches. She'd made a gesture on the word "clothing," gracefully smoothing her hands down either side of her bodice, so that her meaning would be obvious even to those with no modern English.

Such as Magnus, who had been watching all of this from his divan silently, as a cat gazing into a garden from an open window.

"Clothing," he echoed, and they all turned toward him. Clearly he had already been introduced before I arrived, as none of them rushed to shake his hand. "Clothing," he repeated, imitating Erszebet's gesture upon his own body.

Tristan nodded, and fluently enough he spoke to him, in Magnus's native tongue. I could make out a smattering of familiar words—*chemise, pantaloons, cap.* Magnus frowned and unconvinced he looked. He responded to Tristan with a growling answer and sure didn't that answer include a word we had just learned from the physician: *lidocaine.*

Tristan looked taken aback. They spoke briefly and then Tristan turned to the others. "He's curious about the lidocaine Doctor Andrews gave him. Wonders if we are going foraging or raiding for clothes, if we can obtain some."

The Blevins made an appalled sound in his throat, which developed into a chuckle. "Foraging or raiding?" Then he laughed out loud.

"He's a medieval Norman warrior, sir," Tristan said. "There's no word for 'shopping' in his language."

"Nonsense," Blevins said. "He's from circa 1200 and he lived in the most sophisticated city in the world. Even if he was illiterate."

"Almost everyone was illiterate," rejoined Melisande. "That's why being an historical linguist is such a challenge, Dr. Blevins, or don't you remember? Oral tradition was—"

"Oral tradition is why he got into trouble in the first place," says the Blevins, and to Tristan he says it, not to Mel. "By recognizing you from such an old story."

"He put two and two together, and became suspicious that we were time traveling," Mel agreed, "and that fired his imagination."

"I'll give him that much—he has a vivid imagination," said the Blevins, "and that he imagines himself a Viking." And over the lovely face of Tristan don't I see a look of annoyance flare for a moment, then fade away.

Magnus knows perfectly well that they're talking about him. He can't make out one word in ten, but "viking" he knows. He's favoring Blevins with an innocent look that I did not for one moment believe was really innocent. I saw at once what Magnus was about: for his own reasons, whatever they be, he was gulling them all into considering him dull-witted. Seeing he now has the Blevins's attention, he taps his shoulder, and says with deliberately (it seemed to me) child-like delight, "Viking! Viking!" and makes a fist as if he's holding an axe, and goes into a little pantomime of laying about himself as if in a battle of legendary times. And then doesn't he laugh like a toddler.

At this, the Blevins smirks, and says to Tristan, "He's like that Korean guy we brought from the Silla dynasty."

"Who, Yeon Hyeokgeose?" says Melisande curtly. "He was developmentally challenged. He was simple."

"This guy's pretty simple," says the Blevins with a quick laugh, and gestures to Magnus as if he was a piece of furniture. And then quick as you like, I realize that Magnus has looked round at the rest of us to see our displeasure at whatever Blevins said (and he might, in hindsight, have even recognized the word *simple*)—and then realizing he'd just been insulted, doesn't he smile and chuckle at the Blevins as if they were old friends.

"He is not simple," Tristan said. "I've fought in battle beside him, he is quick-witted and I know his worth."

"Battle's not about brains, is it," says the Blevins. It's not Magnus he's looking at when he says it, but Tristan, and I can see well enough from that what sort of history lies between these two men. "Tristan, we're done here. Gráinne needs to be shown every kindness—whether by Erszebet or the rest of the Sea Cod Staff, it's no concern of mine—or of yours. We'll get her into the ATTO as soon as we can. As for Hagar the Horrible here, I suspect he'll end up a useless drain on our resources and our hospitality. But he seems an amiable sort. Once we're satisfied he has a decent level of impulse control—enough that we can take him off premises without causing an incident—I'll wager he'd be susceptible to a shock and awe sort of treatment."

"It's going to take a lot to shock him or awe this dude," Tristan demurred.

"Viking!" echoes Magnus, and wasn't his face beaming.

"Wait until he gets a load of modern video games," the Blevins insisted. "We'll get him some toys to play with, settle him down a little, and then see what he can do for us as a trainer."

INCIDENT REPORT

AUTHOR: MAJ Isobel Sloane
SUBJECT: Magnus and Gráinne
THEATER: C/COD (present day)
DTAP: Bio-containment ward
FILED: Day 1880 (late September, Year 5)

Pursuant to the Sexual Harassment Policy, information is hereunder presented about a series of incidents in the bio-containment ward involving recently arrived Anachrons Magnus and Gráinne (no last names provided). Technically these do not constitute sexual harassment per se since all activity took place between consenting adults in what they believe to be a private setting. However, DOSECOPS personnel, part of whose job is to continuously monitor the video and audio "feeds" from the room in question, have raised a number of complaints that need to be addressed.

Without getting into overly lurid details, the basic situation is that after a few days during which she complained of fever, chills, aches, and low energy (all typical for newly arrived Anachrons going through the inoculation protocol), Gráinne has bounced back and returned to a level of vitality and vigor that, though it might be normal for her, is exceptional by our standards. Magnus, of course, had a three-day head start on her in this department, and the inoculations never seemed to make much of a dent on him anyway. They are in adjacent beds, separated only by a curtain, twenty-four hours a day. No one else is in the ward, and they are blissfully unaware of the existence of modern surveillance technology. Beginning three days ago and building from there, the two of them have been engaging in a wide range of sexual activities, as often as four times a day. These activities are quite obviously consensual, so there is no issue where that is concerned. Gráinne, as it turns out, exhibits a pattern of loud, prolonged, and repetitive vocalizations while engaging in such activities—in the vernacular, she is what is known as a "screamer." All of this comes through in full Dolby 7.1 on the security consoles that DOSECOPS personnel are expected to monitor as a condition of their employment. While it may have had some novelty value at first, it is now to the point of posing a serious distraction at best. At worst it is creating an actively hostile work environment, particularly for female employees and for those whose religious convictions make such viewing problematic.

Accordingly, I have muted the audio feeds from the bio-containment ward and encouraged security personnel to leave the cameras off most of the time, making occasional spot checks only. Since Gráinne and Magnus are locked in, escape is physically impossible, and since our long-suffering medical personnel are on the other side of a door, only a few yards away, with access to the no doubt spectacular bio-monitor readout infographics, there is zero chance of either of these two Anachrons suffering any kind of medical emergency without our knowing of it immediately.

These measures, which I unilaterally placed into effect this morning after stumbling into the ops center during a particularly egregious transaction between Magnus and Gráinne, have already lifted morale among security staff and eased a tense situation. Lieutenant [name redacted], who first drew my attention to the problem, has been placed on medical leave and assigned to a counselor.

Exchange of posts by DODO staff on "Department Heads" ODIN channel
DAY 1881

Post from LTC Tristan Lyons:
Not to nitpick, but Gráinne's not a "screamer" in my experience.

Reply from Dr. Melisande Stokes:
Could you clarify that please?

From LTC Lyons:
Hahaha, yes, happy to clarify (thanks, Stokes!). During various DEDEs in settings where Gráinne was engaged in sexual activity WITH OTHER PEOPLE, I did not observe the vocalizations mentioned in Sloane's incident report.

From Dr. Stokes:
Maybe she simply wasn't enjoying herself—there's no reason a sex worker would.

From LTC Lyons:

Can someone tell me how to retreat from this minefield? All I'm saying is: archive the recordings even if they're not being live-monitored.

TRANSCRIPT (EXCERPT)
CONVERSATION BETWEEN GRÁINNE (G) AND MAGNUS (M)
DAY 1884 (LATE SEPTEMBER, YEAR 5)

NOTES: Video recording was made automatically by a motion-activated security camera system in bio-containment ward at DODO HQ, Cambridge, MA. In the wake of subsequent events, the file was salvaged from a secure server by DODO personnel and transferred to the ad hoc GRIMNIR backup system, where it was later transcribed. Excerpt below begins at approximately 14:12 local time. Subjects are engaged in "missionary position" style coitus with faces in close contact and so audio is of low quality. Dialog is in a mishmash of languages; this is an approximate translation into modern English.

G: I asked Erszebet about "shock and awe."

M: The words the Pigeon used?

G: (slapping Magnus on the buttock) *Blevins*, lad. His name is Blevins.

M: What is their meaning?

G: 'Tis a phrase used by soldiers. From one of their sagas. A tactic to break the will of the enemy, so it is.

M: I understand this tactic well and moreover have used it. In fact I am using it now!

[REDACTED]

G: Oh, there's more. In one of their wars, didn't they face an enemy that was poor, ill-equipped, with bad weapons and low morale. To make the war be over fast, they used many of their best weapons in a great show of force. This was shock and awe.

M: So Erszebet thinks that the Pigeon means to use this tactic on me. To fuck my mind like I am fucking your pussy.

G: You're fucking my pussy? I hadn't noticed.

M: Notice this!

[REDACTED]

G: Be getting your mind off of Erszebet, now.

M: That is difficult.

G: Then close your pretty eyes and pretend it's her you're fucking.

M: Okay. Mmm, that's very nice!

G: (pinches Magnus's nipple)

M: Bitch!

G: Be paying attention, I'm trying to tell you something important about Blevins.

M: I understand. But if you pinch my nipple again I'll flip you over and give it to you up the ass and then I'll be pinching your nipples and pulling your hair and you won't be able to do a thing about it except moan like an alley cat.

G: That, and reach up underneath to be grabbing you by the ball sack which is what happened when you tried that yesterday.

M: Yes, I remember . . . or was it the day before?

G: In any case the K-Y Jelly is right over there if you mean it.

M: Kind of them to leave that there for us. I was going to kill that doctor when he shoved his finger up my ass but then I realized the possibilities of that substance.

G: Yes, you could fuck me in the ass and not be seeing my face so you could imagine I was Erszebet.

M: She makes me hot.

G: She makes me hot and I'm not even a woman-fucking kind of woman.

M: I'd like to see the two of you doing it!

G: Maybe soon. Growing close aren't we, she and I. She has much to say to me.

M: About shock and awe?

G: And other things. She saw the death of magic with her own eyes. Lived through it, so she did, poor lass. So we don't just talk about your concerns, Magnus, but matters of interest to us witches.

M: I know that, I'm not stupid.

G: You just act that way.

M: Yes.

G: Keep it up.

M: I will.

G: Oh, and be keeping *that* up too!

[REDACTED]

Post by Dr. Roger Blevins on "Announcements" ODIN channel
DAY 1890 (1 OCTOBER, YEAR 5)

For fear of "putting a jinx" on it, we're not having a formal ribbon-cutting ceremony this time, but I wanted to announce that ATTO #1—the first of our new, fully mobile ODECs—went "hot" this morning at

0900 sharp. I'm assured that all systems are working normally, and Gráinne—who is now out of quarantine—reports that she is able to perform magical activities inside of it as effectively as she ever could in Elizabethan London.

Please join me in congratulating Dr. Oda on another major achievement. It is going on three years since he shifted to "Emeritus" status in the wake of the successful Chronotron launch, and some of you may have mistaken that for a dignified form of retirement. In truth his work on this project has been tireless and relentless, and a testimony to what may be achieved by a gifted mind when given the freedom to pursue its own interests unfettered by bureaucratic restrictions.

Post by Dr. Frank Oda on "Announcements" ODIN channel
DAY 1890 (1 OCTOBER, YEAR 5)

Thanks to Dr. Blevins and to all those of you who have sent me congratulatory messages and greeted me in person today. In truth it is a bittersweet day, for I actually am now transitioning to full retirement after three years of work on the Ambient Temperature Tactical ODEC (ATTO). My full departure is still a few months away. In the meantime, here is a little more information for those of you who haven't been following this closely.

"Ambient Temperature" simply means that this ODEC is capable of functioning without being connected to large, expensive, finicky cryogenic systems. To make a long story short, we have achieved this by replacing the traditional superconductors with higher-temp superconductors that can be kept at the required temperature through a combination of clever insulation and solid-state Peltier coolers.

"Tactical" is a reference to the fact that these ODECs, unlike the ones we are used to, are capable of being moved about. For simplicity's sake, we have constructed the first production run of ATTOs in conventional, unmarked shipping containers. So this finally answers the question that has been on so many people's minds during the last couple of years: Why is there a shipping container in Loading Bay 3 with technicians in bunny suits going in and out of it?

Finally, "ODEC" simply means that, despite the innovations mentioned above, this is, at the end of the day, just another ODEC, i.e., an environment in which it is possible for MUONs to conduct MAGOPs. On the inside it is somewhat larger than our stationary "strategic" ODECs in the basement, but as far as the MUON is concerned, it is functionally the same.

As to what uses the ATTOs might be put to, I'll allow readers of this message to use their imaginations. Let's just say that when we fired up the first ODEC some four years ago and let Erszebet go to work in it, we learned very quickly that most of the things witches are capable of were not actually that useful, from a practical standpoint, as long as they were confined to a fixed volume the size of a phone booth. We settled on Sending and Homing as the two most useful functionalities, and as you know we have constructed a large organization around that. The new ATTOs (of which we have one up and running, three in final production, and six more in the works) can do everything the old ODECs can do, but our ability to move them around the world and disguise them should enable our ever-growing staff of MUONs to practice their craft in a greater diversity of operational modalities, broadening the palette of force projection options available to our strategic leadership team as they consider how most effectively to project American soft power across time and space.

Journal Entry of
Rebecca East-Oda
OCTOBER 2

Temperature 65F—warm, fair, and dry, with slight breeze from the west. Barometer steady. Foliage turning; about nine days from peak (will be a little early this year).

Didn't make a journal entry yesterday because feared I couldn't keep emotions in check.

The day comes for every man when he has to retire. There is little point in pretending otherwise. For Frank that day was yesterday; he has already dropped to fifty percent and will taper to full retirement at the end of the year. I am a little apprehensive as to where he will find outlets for his energies when he is spending all of his time at home again, but the East House Trust can certainly put him to work on innumerable repair and improvement projects, at least for a little while.

For the most part, he is going out on a high note with the ATTO. During the years of his first retirement, when he was living in exile from the scientific community, we were both in denial about how bad things were. Going back to productive work at DODO was the best thing in the world for him. All the politics and the mishaps tempered his enjoyment to quite a degree, but the honors he has received within the secret world of black-budget defense technology have meant the world to him.

He announced his retirement yesterday, but his message to his colleagues was butchered by someone in Macy Stoll's department who heaped on a lot of gibberish at the end. I can only trust that his treasured colleagues saw through it and found it amusing.

**LETTER (HANDWRITTEN) ON PERSONAL STATIONERY OF
DR. ROGER BLEVINS TO
LIEUTENANT GENERAL OCTAVIAN K. FRINK
DAY 1905 (MID-OCTOBER, YEAR 5)**

Okie,

Hope you're enjoying the cooler weather down in DC, up here fall is on the way and the colors are starting to peak. Great football weather.

Just wanted to drop you a note letting you know progress with our two newest Anachrons.

Gráinne bounced back from the inoculation protocol in fine form and seems to have picked up an additional infusion of energy and high spirits from spending hours each day in the ATTO, where she has access to magic again. As you know we had a challenging battery of experiments lined up for her, all more or less in the realm of psy-ops, and after a rough patch at the beginning when she didn't quite see the point of it (systematic experimentation not being a natural fit for a witch!), she buckled down to work and has been generating all sorts of interesting results. Yesterday I went into the ATTO while it was up and running and sat in on some of these procedures as an observer. There is the usual "ODEC mind fog" which nearly all modern people complain about to a greater or lesser extent, but I came away immensely impressed with Gráinne's talents and her dedication to DODO's mission. In retrospect, it's a shame we kept her tucked away in Elizabethan England for so many years. She is clearly our most capable MUON, and if I may say as much without stepping over the boundaries of the sexual harassment policy, a real ornament to DODO. She doesn't have Erszebet's drop-dead looks but rather a kind of presence that grows on you.

Anyway, that's probably enough on that topic—the R&D boffins are working up some numbers on the results of our experiments that you should be able to share with all of those senators who are badgering you for the latest news on the Trapezoid's so-called "mind control" experiments.

Sometimes it's a shame you're not up here in Cambridge with us, as you miss the human side of things. Today I introduced one of our other new Anachrons to some of the wonders of the modern world. This is Magnus, whom you'll remember as the troublesome Varangian Guard who had to be Sent forward. To judge from the alarmist reports that were flying around prior to that decision, you'd imagine him as some kind of dangerous predatory mastermind. Of course, now that he's here, he turns out to be nothing of the sort. He's a simple, amiable chap with a wide-eyed appreciation for everything we share with him. Don't get me wrong, I wouldn't want to get on his bad side, but we think he could be a fine trainer in the Violence(s) Ethnology Department.

To whet his appetite a bit, and air him out, I took him up to Andover for the homecoming game, which as you'll know from the alumni newsletter we won in a fine come-from-behind effort. This was an excellent fit for his overall mentality. He isn't the sharpest knife in the drawer, but he is enthusiastic, and after some initial confusion he understood the basics of the rules—which he likened to shield-wall combat among the Vikings. He cheered lustily for our side all the way through the game and seemed genuinely moved by the last-minute heroics. I'm able to converse with him in a mixture of Byzantine Greek, Old French, and modern English (knowing lots of half-dead obscure languages continues to have its plusses, even if it doesn't put me in your pay grade).

This is all somewhat calculated, I'll admit: since arriving in our age, Magnus hasn't seen modern people engaged in any sort of rough-and-tumble, and I wanted to impress upon him that we as a people have not gone entirely soft. Message delivered; after the game we went down to the field and chatted with some of the players (I am introducing him as a recently arrived exchange student from Dagestan), and afterwards in the car he made appreciative comments about their size and strength and grit.

Having got that message across, I then proceeded to take him to Walmart en route home.

Imagine a man from the thirteenth century suddenly plucked into the twenty-first . . . and introduced to Walmart of all places!

Beyond the total astonishment of modern life in general, the cornucopia of goods clearly left him gobsmacked, as the Brits say. He has had a childish fixation on lidocaine ever since the dermatologist used it on him, and was delighted to find that there was an entire section of the store stocked not only with that but many other magical potions as well. I showed him a cordless drill—and then the expressions on his face! He almost tired me out with his naive enthusiasm—we covered the entire store. Not just the obvious things like furniture and clothes, but sports equipment, dinnerware . . . He was delighted with things we take for granted—insect repellent! He loved the insect repellent! As well as canned goods; chili mix; hairspray. A refreshing reminder of how amazing the world we live in really is.

If you ever want to be reminded how extraordinary modern life is, if you ever need to slap yourself out of the complacency of taking electricity or Teflon for granted . . . come take an Anachron out on an orientation tour.

Love to Bess and the family. Get your butt up here some time soon for a round of golf. Don't worry about the bugs—we have insect repellent!

Cheers,

Blev

Post by Macy Stoll on "Announcements" ODIN channel
DAY 1920 (31 OCTOBER, YEAR 5)

To all employees and contractors:

This is just a final reminder that we are closing early this afternoon at 3 p.m. to make preparations for the annual Halloween party. For those of you who've joined DODO in the past year—and I know there are many of you—this is traditionally our biggest social event of the year, comparable to what the Christmas party would be in a less culturally and spatiotemporally diverse organization. In accordance with our usual protocols, we need to make special preparations to welcome your family members and SOs without inadvertently leaking classified information. Thanks to all who have volunteered to help out with that work—by now you should know your assignments.

On a practical level, this means that all access to the basement biocontainment/ODEC complex will be sealed off at 3 p.m. sharp, and a rotating security detail assigned there (we want to make sure DOSECOPS gets to enjoy the festivities too!). The main site for the party will be the cafeteria. Please be sure you have removed all documents of a potentially sensitive nature from that area. We'll also be allowing visitors to tour the Chronotron on a half-hourly basis, and so IT personnel need to make sure that all documents are stowed away in locked drawers—this includes Post-it notes on monitors and desktops, etc.

Halloween decorations will go up in the cafeteria starting at 4 p.m. and we'll have the usual trick-or-treat facilities for the little ones.

Also at 4 p.m. we'll have a briefing in the big conference room for Anachrons who are unfamiliar with our traditions around Halloween and may need some guidance as to what is and is not appropriate behavior—I know this has been a concern in the past, based on some of the anecdotes and incident reports that have been shared with me. Remember, our medical staff would like to enjoy the evening too— let's not make them work!

Doors open at 5 p.m. for families and SOs.

As you choose your costumes, please try to keep in mind everything our Diversity Policy has to say about stereotypes surrounding witches. Most of you who work here don't need to be told this, but every year it seems we have some children who show up in costumes that are offensive to certain members of our staff. Remember, the following costume elements are expressly forbidden:

Pointy hats
Green skin
Warts on nose
Brooms

Anyone who shows up in a potentially offensive costume will be gently redirected to Conference Room 12 where we will have a range of alternative costume choices to choose from.

With your assistance I'm sure we can all look forward to another enjoyable and memorable Halloween party. Have fun, everyone!

TRANSCRIPT
SELECTED RADIO TRAFFIC
ON DODO SECURITY FREQUENCIES
DAY 1920 (HALLOWEEN, YEAR 5)

NOTES:

All content transcribed from recordings made during the evening of Halloween and auto-saved to DODO archives. In the wake of subsequent events, files were salvaged from a secure server by DODO personnel and transferred to the ad hoc GRIMNIR backup system, from which they were later decrypted and transcribed. Repetitive content such as routine comm checks has been redacted for clarity.

OTHER NOTES:

—"BACKHOE" is Secret Service code name for Lieutenant General Octavian K. Frink.

—"STYLUS" is Dr. Roger Blevins.

—"DOSECOPS C4" is the communications officer on duty in the Diachronic Operations Security Ops (DOSECOPS) Command, Control, and Communications Center, the hub for security operations beneath DODO's Cambridge, MA, headquarters.

—"DOSECOPS C4 ACTUAL" is the ranking officer on duty there (at the time of these recordings, Major Isobel Sloane).

—"DOSECOP 1," "DOSECOP 2," etc. denote specific security officers on site.

—"USSS 1," USSS 2," etc. denote United States Secret Service officers visiting the site as part of BACKHOE's personal security detail.

15:00:00 DOSECOPS C4: All units, this is a reminder that the facility is now officially closed for the day and transitioning to off-hours security protocols. We're expecting a number of delivery vehicles in the next two hours at Docks 1 and 2, these will be bringing party supplies. Normal screening procedures apply for all incoming cargo, drivers, and entertainment personnel. Doors open for civilian guests in two hours.

15:37:12 DOSECOPS C4 ACTUAL: This is C4 Actual. I have just received confirmation that Backhoe is coming to the party. He'll be coming in from Hanscom, exact arrival time TBD. We will be integrating with his Secret Service detail as needed. Officers on duty at Dock 1 should stand by to close it to all civilian traffic and make it ready to receive Backhoe and his entourage; please acknowledge.

15:37:38 DOSECOP 1: Acknowledged, standing by.

16:05:56 DOSECOPS C4: Two vans are now inbound from MUON Residential Facility carrying a total of nineteen MUONs and three support staff, ETA 16:30. We'll direct them to Docks 1 and 2. Any officers on patrol in that part of the building should stand by to help check credentials, just to avoid a backup and a lot of annoyed MUONs.

16:23:32 DOSECOPS C4 ACTUAL: This is C4 Actual. I've received confirmation from Backhoe's Secret Service detail that he is on the ground and in a vehicle. ETA is about 17:30 depending on traffic, will update as I have further information.

16:30:00 DOSECOPS C4: All units, this is a reminder that doors will open for civilian ingress in thirty minutes. Officers on internal patrols, now is the time for you to inspect all surfaces for potentially classified documents. All monitors are to be switched off or placed in secure locked mode with Infosec-compliant screen savers.

16:31:45 DOSECOP 1: Dock 1 here. MUON vans have arrived and are backing into the grade-level ramps at Docks 1 and 2.

16:31:55 DOSECOPS C4: Acknowledged. Have officers standing by the side doors of those vans to offer a hand to disembarking MUONs, we have been warned to expect an abundance of high heels, and some of the ladies are new to that kind of footwear. Don't want to kick off the party with an injury.

16:32:02 DOSECOP 1: Acknowledged. Standing by with stepstools and strong arms.

16:36:38 DOSECOPS C4: Loading dock detail, sitrep please? Looks on the cameras like there's quite a bottleneck and some hurt feelings.

16:36:54 DOSECOP 1: Roger that, C4. If you're watching this on the feed you may have noticed that some of the MUONs' costumes are, uh . . .

16:37:00 DOSECOPS C4: Stop right there before you get into trouble, officer. Yes, the costumes have been receiving close attention from C4 staff and we are aware of their nature. What is the issue?

16:37:10 DOSECOP 1: Some of them didn't bring their lanyards and badges because of compatibility issues of an aesthetic or stylistic nature with costumes. Procedures dictate . . .

16:37:20 DOSECOPS C4 ACTUAL: Understood. This is Actual. I am authorizing you to waive procedures and treat the MUONs as civilians for now. No need to write up incident reports or any of that. Visual ID is sufficient. The one in the red shimmery um . . . whatever you call it is gonna have to take her mask off whether she likes it or not.

16:37:31 DOSECOP 1: Roger that, Actual. Speaking of visual ID, we have two in violation of the diversity policy regs.

16:37:40 DOSECOPS C4 ACTUAL: Come again?

16:37:46 DOSECOP 1: Pointy hats and brooms, sir.

16:37:50 DOSECOPS C4 ACTUAL: So, two of the MUONs are attired in a manner that is culturally offensive to MUONs?

16:37:57 DOSECOP 1: According to the regs issued yesterday, yes, sir.

16:38:02 DOSECOPS C4 ACTUAL: That's Ms. Stoll's problem. Let them in without further delay.

16:50:00 DOSECOPS C4: All units, doors open in ten.

16:50:15 DOSECOPS C4 ACTUAL: This is C4 Actual. Just an update before all hell breaks loose. Backhoe is still inbound, ETA has been pushed back to 17:45 because he has decided to swing by Stylus's residence and pick up Stylus and his wife en route. They will all be arriving together. At that time we'll be clearing Dock 1 for the vehicle carrying Backhoe and Stylus, as well as Dock 2 for the war wagon with Secret Service detail.

16:51:20 DOSECOP 2: Reporting in from Door 1 where we have now two separate minivan loads of costumed rug rats with moms in a high state of combat readiness. They are taking exception to our holding the line on the 1700 hours opening time. Request permission to let them in early.

16:51:30 DOSECOPS C4: Hold the line. We see the moms and concur with your threat assessment. As diversionary tactic we are sending out a juggler on a unicycle. You might want to open the door for him.

16:51:59 DOSECOP 2: Acknowledged, I have unicyclist on visual.

17:00:00 DOSECOPS C4 ACTUAL: Okay to open doors to civilian guests. Officers on patrol, divert to entrance zones and help with any bottlenecks—all credentials need to be checked, no exceptions.

17:01:11 DOSECOPS C4: Door 2 personnel, our audio systems picked up a loud bang followed by a scream, please report.

17:01:25 DOSECOP 3: Roger, that was the guy making the balloon animals. Wiener dog underwent explosive decompression, scared a baby.

17:01:34 DOSECOPS C4: Acknowledged.

17:15:00 DOSECOPS C4: All door units, report with numbers.

17:15:15 DOSECOP 3: Door 2 has admitted 41 with approximately three dozen still waiting for credentials check.

17:15:31 DOSECOP 2: Door 1, 79 in, a dozen waiting.

17:15:40 DOSECOP 4: Door 3, 56 in, maybe two dozen outside.

17:16:02 DOSECOP 1: Uh, C4, no one yet except the MUONs but we are expecting two full buses from the SARF [Supervised Anachron Residential Facility] with an estimated total of 70. Should be here in ten.

17:16:12 DOSECOPS C4: Weren't they supposed to be in the building by 1600? For the Anachron briefing?

17:16:17 DOSECOP 1: Anachrons and their sense of time.

17:16:26 DOSECOPS C4 ACTUAL: This is C4 Actual, I want those buses processed fast so we can clear the docks for Backhoe's vehicles. Any officers on internal patrol, if it looks like the surge is abating at the doors, redirect to the loading docks.

...

17:27:43 DOSECOP 1: Here come the SARF buses. Brace for weirdness.

17:50:15 DOSECOPS C4: Patching Secret Service voice frequencies into local DOSECOPS VOIP network. We should all be on the same channel now, literally.

17:50:21 USSS 1: Backhoe vehicle 1, comm check.

17:50:25 DOSECOPS C4: Acknowledged.

17:50:30 USSS 2: Backhoe vehicle 2, comm check.

17:50:35 DOSECOPS C4: Acknowledged.

17:50:42 DOSECOPS C4 ACTUAL: This is DOSECOPS C4 Actual welcoming our Secret Service brothers and sisters to Boston. We are tracking you with an ETA of sixty seconds. Officers in civilian clothes are waiting on the street to wave your vehicles in. Loading docks are clear.

17:50:59 USSS 1: Thank you, C4 Actual, Boston drivers have made quite an impression on us, and we are looking forward to working with you and your staff on a safe, sane Halloween party.

17:52:15 USSS 1: C4, I'm out of the vehicle and having a look-see around the dock area. Everything looks nominal but there is one gentleman wearing a Mongol costume having an argument with your door staff . . .

17:52:25 DOSECOPS C4: It's not a costume.

17:52:29 USSS 1: Come again?

17:52:33 DOSECOPS C4: He actually is a Mongol.

17:52:40 USSS 1: Oh.

17:52:43 DOSECOPS C4: We've patched him into an interpreter over a voice link but the conversation is proceeding slowly.

17:52:53 USSS 1: Is that a real archery set he's carrying? That is my only concern. That, and the fact that he seems agitated. Is it safe for Backhoe to get out of the car? Oh, never mind, Backhoe just got out of the car.

17:53:01 DOSECOPS C4: Who is the Indian chief? Hard to make out on the security feed.

17:53:09 USSS 1: That is Stylus. Repeat, Stylus is dressed as an Indian chief.

17:53:20 USSS 2: On another note, C4, has the shipping container in the adjoining bay been cleared and secured?

17:53:27 DOSECOPS C4: The rusty green one over in Dock 3?

17:53:31 USSS 2: Roger. Just part of our SOP to check and secure any of those within our perimeter.

17:53:40 DOSECOPS C4: Understood. It's not a shipping container.

17:53:44 USSS 2: Come again, C4?

17:53:52 DOSECOPS C4: The thing in Dock 3 that looks exactly like a rusty green shipping container is something else. Will explain later. It is extremely secure.

17:54:02 USSS 1: As you can see, Backhoe's entire delegation is out of the vehicle and waiting behind the Mongol, can we have the interpreter tell him to stand aside please so that we can wave our people through?

17:54:07 DOSECOPS C4: Will pass your request on but it might be more prudent to . . .

17:54:11 USSS 1: Never mind, C4, Stylus is gesturing toward the shipping container, telling the others about it.

17:54:17 DOSECOPS C4: ATTO. It's called an ATTO. The shipping container.

17:54:31 DOSECOP 1: Genghis Khan has cleared door security, we are open for business to welcome Backhoe. Apologies for delay.

17:54:36 USSS 1: Copy that. Stand by.

17:54:42 DOSECOPS C4: As you can see, Backhoe's delegation is wandering over toward the ATTO.

17:54:55 DOSECOP 1: Is that Backhoe's costume?

17:54:59 USSS 1: Affirmative.

17:55:06 DOSECOP 1: He's dressed as . . . a lieutenant general in the United States Army?

17:55:16 USSS 1: Affirmative. He says it's the only night of the year when he can wear it in Boston and not be recognized.

Diachronicle
DAY 1920 (HALLOWEEN, YEAR 5)

In which witches will be witches

I SHALL NEVER KNOW IF the Halloween party was, from the start, a monstrous distraction created by Gráinne. It's true that the higher-ups had offered such a masque the previous two years . . . but now I wonder if perhaps Gráinne, in Year 5, did not use an ODEC to go back in time to the same ODEC two years earlier, slip out and work her wiles on Blevins (i.e., induce him to make the Halloween party an annual event), and then return to the present day—I mean to say, what was the present day before I was marooned in 1851.

In any case, there was a Halloween party and she used elements of it to her advantage. More specifically, she relied upon it as a diversion so that she could begin to use the ATTO to her advantage.

Have I mentioned the ATTO in these scribblings? In simplest terms it was a portable ODEC. Oda-sensei, with his unending genius, sorted out how to make it both portable and larger than the stationary ODECs in the office: it was the size and shape of a shipping container. Blevins was obsessed with it, a cat with catnip, and grew preoccupied with all the great psychological ops/ warfare that could be accomplished with a movable magic machine. Both Tristan and I were obviously hesitant (if the reasons for hesitance weren't obvious then, they ~~sure as shit~~ are by now!).

Erszebet's attitude toward the ATTO, and the work that could be done in it, vacillated wildly. After five years she was ~~really fucking sick~~ bored with doing no magic but Sending, and so the possibilities offered by the ATTO intrigued her; on the other hand, she resented going through another series of parlor tricks to demonstrate its capabilities, as she had done with us when we first sprang her from the elder-hostel. I wish I could remember now what Gráinne thought of it—I realize with rueful retrospection that she was playing her cards very close to her vest.

But to the events of that evening: Gráinne and Erszebet had both chosen to ~~get all ironically meta about things~~ mock the contemporary image of witches by wearing green body paint and pointy hats (they claimed they were groupies of *Wicked*, but I know for a fact that neither of them has ever seen it). Anyhow, put off by the extreme security measures, they failed to show up at the loading dock as the rest of us did, to pay political homage, as Blevins and Frink arrived.

Roger Blevins was dressed like a Native American tribal chieftain, lest any of us forget that his cultural insensitivity was boundless. Frink wore his own dress uniform. Macy Stoll, Blevins's Girl Friday, dressed as a sexy librarian, or tried to, anyhow. Erszebet had costumed Tristan and myself to resemble Boris and Natasha from *War and Peace*. (Tristan, never having read *War and Peace*, assumed he was going to be dressed like the Cold War spy from *Rocky and Bullwinkle*, and was speechless when presented with the garb of a nineteenth-century Russian aristocrat. He did look quite splendid, I confess.) Frank dressed like the George Takei character from *Star*

Trek, and Rebecca dressed like Rebecca, with a lavender wreath or something. Mortimer and Julie Lee were non-human bipeds.

Of course, Blevins immediately wanted to show off the ATTO to Frink. Isobel Sloane, the smart and tough head of DOSEC-OPS, prudently suggested that they come back in an hour, allowing them to make sure everything was "shipshape."

Blevins agreed gaily, requesting they then be joined for a demonstration by some witches (whom we were supposed to call MUONs, a term Erszebet found onomatopoetically bovine and thus offensive. Of course.). As most of the witches were in party dress, Major Sloane could not identify them, and asked to solicit Erszebet and/or Gráinne, who were the easiest to find.

Once the two were located they grudgingly agreed to this. Erszebet had thrown a hissy fit when the DOSECOPS approached her, but Rebecca and I found her in the women's restroom and convinced her this was not a return to the humiliating parlor tricks of the late 1840s. Gráinne was ~~totally shit-faced~~ quite merry and trying to molest Mortimer in the coat closet, which we discovered because Julie had been tracking her all evening in anticipation of just such an event. Gráinne had a thing for Mortimer (or more likely for whatever could only be accessed from his computer. Ah, the sad wisdom of hindsight.).

Anyhow, an hour later, Oda-sensei ceremoniously opened the door to the ATTO, ushered the quintet (two witches, Blevins, Frink, and Mrs. Blevins) inside, and closed the door on them.

The Secret Service detail that had arrived with Frink immediately grew agitated that they could not maintain a radio connection to him while the ATTO was in operation. I rather thrilled at Major Sloane's attempt to explain the decoherence/multiverse premise to them—it was very satisfying to know that everyone on the DODO team takes an interest in what we are actually doing. The Secret Service official did not grasp it, concerned only with losing contact with the general.

"Don't worry," said Isobel Sloane. "Gráinne is so drunk that Erszebet's the only one doing any magic, and knowing Erszebet she'll come flouncing out of there in about twenty minutes, bored with all of them."

And a wry sense of humor to boot? How I wish I'd ~~had the bandwidth~~ taken the time to get to know Major Isobel Sloane a little better. When I think of where I am now, I cannot but wonder if she either contributed to my situation or could possibly have prevented it.

To continue: Erszebet did not, in fact, come flouncing out after twenty minutes, or even after thirty, or even forty-five. The Secret Service folks were beside themselves with anxiety. Major Sloane, and Tristan, and Frank Oda, and myself all attempted to quell their misgivings.

Reader, we should not have quelled them. For there were things happening within that ATTO that can never be undone. If only we had known to be suspicious.

20:08:00 USSS 1: C4, get me Actual.

20:08:10 DOSECOPS C4 ACTUAL: C4 Actual here.

20:08:13 USSS 1: It's been an hour and not a peep. I am beginning to get concerned messages from people in the Pentagon wanting to know why Backhoe is incommunicado.

20:08:22 DOSECOPS C4 ACTUAL: The Pentagon?

20:08:27 USSS 1: The Trapezoid. Was my transmission garbled?

20:08:33 DOSECOPS C4 ACTUAL: Sorry, I was distracted. I thought you said Pentagon.

20:08:40 USSS 1: I'm a little foggy myself with all of the weirdness around here and I may have said the wrong thing. I am referring to the [GARBLED]. The very large building across the Potomac River from DC that is the headquarters of the United States military. Does that help clarify matters?

20:08:51 DOSECOPS C4 ACTUAL: Sure. The Pentagon.

20:08:56 USSS 1: That's what I'm saying! The [GARBLED]! People at the Pentagon are worried about Backhoe being out of touch for a whole hour.

20:09:12 DOSECOPS C4 ACTUAL: The door locks from the inside. We could force it. It would be expensive to replace and might ruin the evening for our guests.

20:09:30 USSS 1: It is uncharacteristic of Backhoe not to touch base.

20:09:37 DOSECOPS C4 ACTUAL: The environment inside of an ODEC is a little weird and can mess with people's perception of time.

20:09:44 USSS 1: Oh, that's reassuring!

20:09:51 USSS 3: Lights on the ATTO door are changing color.

20:09:53 DOSECOPS C4 ACTUAL: We see the door in unlock mode.

20:10:01 USSS 3: Visual on Backhoe. Visual on Stylus. They seem nominal.

20:10:10 USSS 1: Tracking device back online. Informing the Pentagon, they'll be happy to hear it.

20:10:16 USSS 3: Stylus's wife now coming out. One witch on her six.

20:10:22 DOSECOPS C4: Any DOSECOPS personnel near the ATTO, that looks like Erszebet. Do we have visual on Gráinne?

20:10:40 DOSECOP 5: Talked to Ms. Karpathy at the base of the ATTO steps. She says Gráinne is inside, feels unwell.

20:10:45 DOSECOPS C4: Copy. A reliable source earlier described her as drunk off her ass and sexually aggressive. Sending a medic.

20:10:58 DOSECOP 5: Ms. Karpathy concurs with that assessment. Says medic unnecessary.

20:11:11 DOSECOPS C4: It is SOP. Even if all she's doing is lying on the floor unconscious, we need to get her in the recovery position and keep an eye on her.

20:11:15 DOSECOP 5: Copy. Ms. Karpathy is blocking the entrance. Says Gráinne wouldn't want to be seen in her current condition.

20:11:21 DOSECOPS C4: Copy. Stand down and wait for the medic.

20:14:32 DOSECOP 5: I have visual on the medic.

20:14:40 DOSECOPS C4: We see her too. We see her talking to Ms. Karpathy. Sitrep? Audio garbled.

20:14:50 DOSECOP 5: Ms. Karpathy is reluctantly allowing the medic to enter the ATTO.

20:15:00 DOSECOPS C4: We see that. Why is Ms. Karpathy closing the door?

20:15:05 DOSECOP 5: Too late to ask, but she seems very protective of Gráinne's privacy. Must be quite a scene in there!

20:15:12 DOSECOPS C4: We'll send Facilities to clean it up in the morning.

20:18:51 DOSECOPS C4: We show the ATTO door cycling

20:19:02 DOSECOP 5: Door confirmed open and medic coming out with Ms. Karpathy, as you can see, C4. Will get status.

20:21:14 DOSECOP 5: Medic reports Gráinne passed out and in recovery position, vital signs normal. Ms. Karpathy has volunteered to sit in the ATTO with her until she comes around.

INCIDENT REPORT

AUTHOR: Macy Stoll
SUBJECT: ATTO procedure violation
THEATER: C/COD
OPERATION: Year 5 Halloween Party
DTAP: Cambridge, MA, present day
FILED: Day 1921 (November 1, Year 5)

The ATTO was left powered up overnight. No harm and no casualties are known to have resulted from this incident. This appears to have been an oversight resulting from an impromptu demo that was staged during the party for LTG Frink. Some of our personnel remained in the ATTO following the conclusion of the tour and there seems to have been confusion as to who was responsible for powering the system down at the conclusion of the demo and placing it in a safed condition.

Dr. Oda assures me that the system is designed to run for an indefinite period of time without harm and so I'm sure you'll all be relieved to know that the ATTO has passed a thorough systems checkup in the wake of this incident.

So, no harm, no foul—but I am writing it up anyway as a "lessons learned" document. Remember, we don't yet know everything about what can happen inside an operating ODEC and so it is never approved procedure to leave one turned on and unattended.

Post by Macy Stoll to Dr. Roger Blevins
on private ODIN channel, 10:30
DAY 1923 (3 NOVEMBER, YEAR 5)

Dr. Blevins, Gráinne failed to report to the ATTO for scheduled psy-ops research activities this morning at 0900. Keycard records show she did not report for work this morning, and she did not call in sick or otherwise advise us as to the reason for her absence. Normally this would be handled as a routine HR matter but because of her special status I felt it best to bring it to your attention directly. Shall I check in with the staff at the MUON residence?

Reply from Dr. Blevins, 15:49, same day:

Macy, apologies for the belated response, but I wanted to let you know that I just saw Gráinne in person, looking a little the worse for wear after her activities at the Halloween party, which have already become the stuff of internal DODO legend—all classified, of course. As you can appreciate, the concept of calling in sick is unfamiliar to Anachrons and so I think we can overlook her failure to do so this morning.

GRÁINNE'S
FINAL LETTER
to GRACE O'MALLEY
PART 2

And so, to make a short tale of it, when they were through pumping me with the potions, Erszebet brought a gown like her own for me to wear, the most brilliant colors, I felt like a lady of the court, so I did! And she brought me out into the world of Cambridge (not England's Cambridge, of course) and showed me the many many things I referred to earlier, which as I said would take half a lifetime to describe proper-like. So in the interest of finishing this before you die, I'll be staying with the part of this story that's to do with my plans.

The place is full of rules and regulations, and doesn't Erszebet just ignore every single one of them, and what can they do about it? There is a reverence that is paid her, and no rules apply to her. She has explained many wondrous things to me, but the most important, of course, is why magic finally stopped working. Without going into the minutiae of it, as I'm sure Your Grace has no patience for it, it comes down to this: those natural philosophers and the rest I have been keeping company with in the shadow of Sir Francis? It is their doing. Those curs and their ilk as the centuries progress. These "scientists" make the world extremely technical in innumerable ways, and it's not only that science is a new kind of magic that makes ours seem feeble by compare, it's that their powers' waxing *causes ours to wane*. And there is particular a kind of art called *photography*, which as I guess from the name means "light-writing," or the setting down of light on paper. The effect is an image like a painting or a drawing, but as real as the real image being copied. It is wondrous—and everywhere. And the cause of magic's end, so it is.

This means that for magic not to end, there must be no photography. Sure I am there's other things as well, but that is where it ended, and so that is where the undoing must begin.

The greatest risk of my tenure in the future was to expose my intentions to Erszebet, on the strong suspicion she would care to join me in my endeavors. And so she was, Your Grace—gleefully, almost greedily, did she agree to join my ranks.

"How appalling that I was so beaten down by these horrible

Yankees," she said (not certain am I, what a Yankee is), "that I never thought of doing this thing myself. You are a witch after my own heart, Gráinne, a woman of integrity!" And then we pledged ourselves each to the other in the way of witches, which I must not share even with Your Grace.

And now doesn't Erszebet Send me back, a few hours or a day at a time, so that I can be seeing to various matters of our mutual interest?

I am in London just now, to set some things in motion. But having done so, and having writ this very long letter to Your Grace, I will be returning to Tristan's lair, with a plan to undo the undoing of magic. It must be done slowly and cautiously, to avoid Iomadh, or as they call it in that era, Diachronic Shear. But it shall be done.

And here be my plan, which is of three parts.

First, I must be getting the money on my side, because after magic wanes money is the most powerful thing on earth (followed by weapons that destroy whole cities in a go, and religion—that never goes away, damn it!—and lastly, female actors who do not wear much clothing). Having little enough need for money in London, I have been but passing familiar with some men of the banking world, but by now I have corrected that, sure. The Gresham family seems to me already to be a waning force, but the Fuggers are savvy enough. I have arrived at an understanding with Athanasius Fugger, the man in our time with the sharp yellow beard. And in the future I have made the friendliest of connections with one Constantine Rudge, who is an important member of the Fuggers' high councils, and who has been in on DODO from its very beginnings. And in other times and places as well, as Erszebet finds opportunities to Send me, I have sought out other Fuggers. In short, haven't I predisposed the whole clan to be of assistance to me—or to "any comely Irish witch named Gráinne," as it is likely to be their descendants that I deal with. They have been told now that an immortal witch has pledged herself to aid the family. And whilst I was in the future, with Erszebet's assistance haven't I made a study of whole eras of what happens between then and now, and coming back here, haven't I whispered into the Fuggers' ears where they should be adjusting their interests to keep the money flowing their way? Is right I have.

So I have secured myself access to money ahead.

The second necessity of the plan is to be getting rid of human obstacles. Chief among these are Melisande and Tristan. The Blevins is now my poppet, and sure I am he'll be easy to dispatch in time. Tristan and Melisande I must somehow maroon. Tristan I've affection for and cannot bear to hurt directly. But seeing Erszebet's animus for him, I asked her would she kindly get him out of the way, and she did heartily agree. She herself is warmer toward Melisande, and so we arrived at the conclusion that it's myself shall be dispatching Melisande.

So that's the second piece. The third is the Great Undertaking itself. Using the wisdom of the Chronotron and the power of the ODEC, I must send their agents (what they call DOers) back in time to gently unweave that which has led to this madness called photography. In order to avoid lomadh, I must dismantle things gently. But persistently. I will start at the end and unweave backwards through time.

Your Grace, please know that I do all of this not only for magic but for Ireland and love of yourself. I suspect it's never again that I'll be on my native soil, and sure my heart is aching for it, but it is a far better thing I do now, than any magic or even spying I have ever done.

My heart is with you as I leave for this great battle.

Yours, Gráinne

Post by Macy Stoll to Dr. Roger Blevins
on private ODIN channel, 23:49
DAY 1923 (3 NOVEMBER, YEAR 5)

Dr. Blevins,

  Sorry for the late-night post, which I understand you are unlikely
to see until the morning. I've been burning the midnight oil here at the
office, collating some records from our internal security systems over
the last few weeks, and have uncovered something you need to hear
about as soon as possible. Headed for home now to get some shuteye,
but I'm hoping that by the time I show up for work tomorrow you'll have
made time in your schedule for a private face-to-face.

LETTER ON PERSONAL STATIONERY OF DR. ROGER
BLEVINS TO LTG OCTAVIAN K. FRINK
DAY 1925 (5 NOVEMBER, YEAR 5)

Okie—

  *Can't say how pleased Bess and I were to have you up here for the
Halloween party. As the years go by it's the old friendships that seem to
matter most.*

  *What good luck it was, to boot, that we were able to spend a bit of time
in the ATTO watching the two MUONs ply their trade. For years I've been
bending your ear about all of the things that these women can do beyond just
Sending our agents to faraway DTAPs, but there's nothing like a practical
demonstration.*

  *In that vein, I'm writing to recommend we shift the hierarchy of
contemporary witches. Now that Gráinne has been here a couple of months,
and I've had a chance to see her in action, I realize that my earlier misgivings
about her reliability are completely unfounded. She is sincerely devoted to our
work here. I recommend she be given seniority right below Erszebet—and
frankly, if she could keep off the sauce, she might one day replace Erszebet.*

She's very gifted at what she does, since she is from an era when magic was strong and she practiced it regularly, which is not true of Erszebet.

More important, however, she is remarkably agreeable to work with, and has none of Erszebet's attitude—which after nearly five years continues to make her a pain in the neck. It was one thing when Erszebet was the only means to our performing magic, but she's just a cog in a machine now and yet continues to carry herself as if she were the queen bee. Gráinne has none of that attitude—she's a terrific team player. She is all about the bigger picture.

I think perhaps because (as she has confessed to me) she worked as a spy for Grace O'Malley in her era, Gráinne understands strategic thinking and even personal sacrifice in a way that Erszebet (and most of the other witches) just don't.

Of course, demoting Erszebet would have a lot of unfortunate repercussions, so we'd have to finesse this a little by creating a new position for Gráinne—a parallel branch, let's say, devoted to MAGOPs other than Sending. In ranking based on merit, Gráinne is by far our best witch, and we need to recognize and reward excellence wherever it flourishes.

Just wanted that on the record before the Christmas bonuses get calculated;-)
—Roger

Post by Macy Stoll to Dr. Roger Blevins
on private ODIN channel, 11:12
DAY 1925 (5 NOVEMBER, YEAR 5)

Dr. Blevins,

Sorry for the repeated pings over the last few days, but I'm frankly a little surprised you haven't responded yet. I AM NOT KIDDING—it is a matter of the highest urgency that we have a private face-to-face as soon as possible. In the meantime, I suggest in the strongest terms you cancel further sessions in the ATTO with Gráinne.

...

Post by Dr. Roger Blevins to LTG Octavian K. Frink
on private ODIN channel, 11:50
DAY 1925 (5 NOVEMBER, YEAR 5)

Okie,

I just sent you a "snail mail" letter on a personnel matter. This message will probably overtake it—sorry for the confusion.

It has to do with one of our employees whose behavior is causing some concern. Nothing that we can't handle here, but I wanted to give you a heads-up in case you hear anything from the woman in question.

As you know I've been working with Macy for two decades now, and she's always been my right-hand woman. Loyal and reliable to a fault. Well, it grieves me to tell you that she has been under some considerable stress of late, and has not been herself. I think she's having a hard time with the way our MUONs outshine her on so many levels, and her self-doubt has been gnawing away at her and made her vengeful and frankly a little paranoid.

In short, if you receive any communications from Macy, please take them with a grain of salt. I'm looking for a way to land this plane, as it were, but there may be some turbulence during the descent.

•••

Post by Macy Stoll to Dr. Roger Blevins
on private ODIN channel, 22:51
DAY 1927 (7 NOVEMBER, YEAR 5)

Dr. Blevins,

I am here late again, beside myself. I can't get over the fact that you won't talk to me.

The least you could do is pay some attention to my warnings. Looking at tomorrow's ATTO calendar I see you have a block scheduled with Gráinne at 1000 which segues right into a Gráinne/Erszebet block at 1100.

WHAT IS GOING ON?!?!

I have canceled those ATTO blocks. I consider it a security matter and I have plenty of evidence to back up my decision.

...

Post by Macy Stoll to Dr. Frank Oda on private ODIN channel, 08:32
DAY 1928 (8 NOVEMBER, YEAR 5)

Dr. Oda,

Sorry for the irregular communication but I know you are frequently in the building early, and obviously you are one of the people with the know-how required to power up the ATTO.

I'm making a unilateral decision to restrict access to the ATTO until we get certain important matters sorted out.

If anyone—ANYONE—shows up while I'm not around, requesting even brief "experimental" access to the ATTO, the answer is "no." If they have a problem with that, send them to me.

Don't worry, I'm sending the same message to all the other key-holders.

Reply from Dr. Oda, 08:56:

Macy,

I received your message about ATTO access and will comply. As you know, we're getting ready to move ATTO #1 out of the dock and get it out in the field for mobile tests, beginning just after Thanksgiving. Its place will then be taken by ATTO #2.

From Macy Stoll, 09:01:

Thank you, Dr. Oda, but I'm not sure if I follow your point—remember I am an operations person, not a physicist.

From Dr. Oda, 09:03:

Today was the last day scheduled for normal ATTO research anyway—tomorrow we hoist it onto the tractor-trailer rig and begin prepping it for mobile operations. I can move that schedule up if you are telling me it's not going to be used today for scheduled research.

From Macy Stoll, 09:07:

That's exactly what I'm telling you and it's fine with me if no one uses it today. Shut it down.

Have any of the MUONs been by today?

From Dr. Oda, 09:10:

No, just Magnus, he has a boyish fascination with trucks and equipment and likes to hang around on the loading docks watching in his off time.

...

Post by Dr. Roger Blevins to Macy Stoll
on private ODIN channel, 10:15
DAY 1928

Macy, I arrived in the office half an hour ago to find my ATTO schedule canceled without my say-so, everything in disarray, Gráinne and Erszebet up in arms, and according to the security cameras you are camped out in front of the ATTO doors wearing a hard hat and watching them put the thing on some kind of hoist. Your arms are crossed in what seems a very irritable frame of mind. I'm writing you this message because this is a serious matter and I feel we need to establish a paper trail in the event of any subsequent disciplinary action that might be called for.

Follow-up from Dr. Blevins, fifteen minutes later:

I have been talking to Dr. Oda who informed me about your communications with him earlier this morning.

Security is en route to escort you from the premises.

Reply from Macy Stoll, thirty seconds later:

Dr. Blevins,

Hitting "send" on a message I have been keeping in "Drafts" for a few days. Getting this on the record before you lock me out of the ODIN system, which I suspect will be your next move.

I'm sorry it's come to this.

DRAFT MESSAGE

TOP SECRET

PRIVILEGED AND CONFIDENTIAL

This message documents what I believe to be a CLEAR AND PRESENT national security threat.

I have incontrovertible evidence that two MUONs, Gráinne and Erszebet, have been colluding to circumvent essential security procedures.

My suspicions were first aroused on Halloween, when (as shown on security camera footage) Gráinne and Erszebet entered the ATTO with Dr. and Mrs. Blevins and LTG Frink. An hour later, all of them emerged except for Gráinne. It was explained that Gráinne had been taken sick, but this was not verified until a DODO medic arrived and entered the ATTO with Erszebet WHEREUPON ERSZEBET CLOSED AND LOCKED THE DOOR! After a few minutes in the FULLY POWERED UP ATTO the medic emerged and confirmed that Gráinne was there, unconscious but stable. Erszebet then went back into the ATTO "to look after Gráinne" and remained in the ATTO until after the conclusion of the party.

Our security system automatically logs all arrivals and departures by means of RFID badges. The system recorded Erszebet and Gráinne departing the building together at 03:37 on 1 November. Gráinne did not show up for work the next day, nor the morning after that (3 November), though Dr. Blevins gave a verbal report of her being on premises the afternoon of 3 November.

Following subsequent suspicious activity I checked security camera footage timestamped 03:37 of 1 November and observed Erszebet leaving the ATTO alone and proceeding to the exit where she waved TWO RFID badges over the sensor—hers and Gráinne's. Repeat: GRÁINNE DID NOT LEAVE THE ATTO. Her next appearance anywhere on the premises was during the afternoon of 3 November—almost 72 hours after she entered the ATTO during the Halloween party!

All of this evidence supports the theory that Erszebet Sent Gráinne to some other DTAP on Halloween and that Gráinne spent three days on a COMPLETELY UNAUTHORIZED AND IRRESPONSIBLE DEDE OF HER OWN CHOOSING.

Following this lead, I have made an exhaustive study of all of Erszebet's and Gráinne's comings and goings since Gráinne emerged from quarantine. I have checked their entrances and exits from the building, tracked their movements on the security cameras, and cross-correlated this with the calendars and logs for the ATTO and the other ODECs. To make a long story short, what happened on Halloween is not a one-time anomaly, but part of a pattern. The evidence clearly supports the following allegations:

- Gráinne has made brief, unauthorized visits to unknown DTAPs on half a dozen occasions in addition to the lengthy absence spanning 31 October–3 November.
- Erszebet has Sent her on all of these occasions, and has covered for Gráinne's absence by committing ID card fraud.
- Most disturbing of all, I believe that Gráinne and Erszebet have used the ATTO to manipulate the memories and the mental

states of non-MUON personnel who were in there with them, using the very "psy-ops" techniques that Gráinne is allegedly "researching."

– Those who have been so victimized include Dr. Roger Blevins.

This explains the extraordinary and unilateral actions I have taken in changing the ATTO schedule and shutting it down until the conspirators can be apprehended. I realize that these actions will appear shocking to some, but I am confident that I will be vindicated.

Post by Dr. Roger Blevins on
"Announcements" ODIN channel
DAY 1931 (11 NOVEMBER, YEAR 5)

To all employees and contractors:

I know that some of you have noticed and remarked on Macy Stoll's recent unplanned absence from work, and so wanted to make a brief announcement before rumors and speculation get out of hand.

As you know I have worked hand-in-glove with Macy for many years. We could not have built DODO into its current form without her loyal and tireless work on the operational side of things.

It is with a heavy heart, therefore, that I announce Macy has decided to resign her position, effective immediately. I realize that this will come as a surprise to many of you, but that's the way Macy wanted it. She wanted to work at full power and effectiveness until the very end and then make a clean break, rather than slowly fading away over a period of months. She plans to take a few well-earned months off and then seek less stressful opportunities in the non-profit sector.

Needless to say, given all that Macy does for us, this is going to leave a void that will take some time to fill. I'm stepping in for the time being as acting head of C/COD while we recruit a replacement.

In accordance with the usual security procedures, her DODO email and ODIN channels have been "turned off." Those of you who would like to write personal notes to Macy should leave them in the box at the front desk—we'll deliver them in a few weeks, once Macy gets back from a long and restful vacation.

Journal Entry of
Rebecca East-Oda
NOVEMBER 13

Temperature 40F, no wind. Barometer rising. Garden: mulch, mulch, and more mulch.

Mei has sent us a cellar-conversion specialist to see about converting the cellar into a "hangout room" for the grandkids so they can be antisocial when they visit during their adolescence. Pointed out that her bedroom worked just fine for her antisocial purposes, but she says they want to set up some kind of gaming center.

Frank has been sulking around the house, as he has been placed on a "time-out" by Blevins, who suddenly informed him that somebody higher up insists he takes his vacation time immediately, because his not taking it is confusing the HR system. Apparently Macy had been covering for him, but now that she has abruptly resigned, the bean-counters are having their way. Never thought I would miss that woman.

While Frank is "on vacation" he is not legally supposed to be on site. He takes phone calls from trucking companies—something to do with acquiring a semi-trailer rig on which to mount the ATTO. Otherwise, he is very much underfoot here again. I like it, now that I'm here more often myself. He is pensive, spending a lot of time by himself. He spent ten hours yesterday in front of the computer in his office, and when I came by later to dust I found evidence of business as usual—incomprehensible sketches and equations on graph paper, and industrial supply catalogs piled on the floor, sticky notes hanging out of them willy-nilly.

It's probably too late already for Mei's "hangout room" in the cellar. If I read the signs correctly, by the time she can draw up the plans and mobilize the contractors, Frank will have claimed the space and begun a new experiment there—something to keep him busy in his retirement.

Threw a dinner party last night. Frank brought the leaf down from the attic and put it into the dinner table and we got the second-best chairs out of the basement. Tried as best as possible under these very peculiar circumstances to be all Emily Post about it, inviting people as couples, and setting out place cards.

Frank and I: seated at opposite ends of the table as host and hostess.

Melisande and Tristan: *still* not a couple, remarkably enough, but resigned to being treated as if they were. Tristan on my right, Melisande on Frank's left.

Mortimer and Julie (my fellow modern witch, and occasional DOer): very much a couple. Something about her heavily pierced and inked look appealed to Mortimer somehow (although her tattoos evaporated when she was Sent the first time; she has since grown her real eyebrows out). Once I'd gotten past her looks and her language I found her a reasonably good match for Mortimer; she seems to make him happy.

Gráinne and Erszebet: thick as thieves. Erszebet has been the den-mother to all the witches from the start, even her elders, but Gráinne is the first one she has treated as a peer. She seems almost—*almost*—content in Gráinne's company. Had never considered Erszebet capable of contentment. Gráinne extremely personable with everyone, so perhaps not a surprise that she can wrest a smile from Erszebet.

Magnus and Constance: I think Magnus had some sort of dalliance with Gráinne when he first arrived, but this seems to have cooled down, and he has lately taken up with Constance Billy, a peaches-and-cream sort of Norman witch from the fourteenth century who was brought forward last year to get her out of some predicament related to the Hundred Years' War and the Black Death. Anyway, she is lovely, she speaks Magnus's language, and she also speaks modern English now well enough to get along at dinner. I seated him across from Tristan and (breaking Emily Post protocol) next to Constance so that he would be in earshot of two people who could talk to him.

As with all such events it was more work than I had expected and I ended up wondering why I had got myself into it. I was reminded of Frank's early MIT days when an expectation of a faculty wife was to throw such affairs and extend a welcoming hand to foreign graduate students and their wives and children, who were naturally feeling isolated and lonely. The only difference in this case being that the visitors are foreign not only to our place but to our time. Constance showed up two hours early to help with the cooking, which she understands well. She is younger than I had appreciated, and all aflutter about Magnus, who shows her a lot of attention.

Frank was a bit dubious that I had invited Magnus, whom he saw as a sort of man-child who would require a lot of management at the dinner table. I was therefore braced for all sorts of Asterix and Obelix hijinks when he showed up, but this could not have been further from the case. During his stint as a Varangian Guard at the court of the Byzantine Emperor, Magnus obviously learned how to behave in formal social situations. He was on his best behavior, taking everything in with his quick blue eyes, asking intelligent questions of Tristan and Constance, showing me a degree of courtesy that was almost comically formal. I put the Thanksgiving decorations up last week—the usual kitschy stuff that has been in the family forever—but he took it very seriously and asked many questions (through Constance) until Tristan mercifully took over and gave him the whole download about turkeys, pilgrims, cranberries, the Wampanoag tribe, etc. I don't speak Norman French, of course, but this apparently segued into questions about DODO's vacation policy (Magnus understands that no one is expected to work on that Thursday) and Black Friday and Yuletide shopping and all the rest.

During dinner Magnus and Gráinne kept sizing each other up across the table, as though they'd taken each other's measure and were circling warily, but they seem to have arrived at a decision to stay out of each other's way. Constance observed apprehensively, Julie was fascinated, Mortimer cheerfully oblivious as usual. Erszebet was down at Frank's end, seated to his right in the position of honor, a detail she, and only she, would appreciate. She still views him as a sort of highfalutin techno-butler, and patronized him with questions about the plans to mount the ATTO on a truck and drive it around while conducting various experiments. These are now scheduled to begin immediately after Thanksgiving— Blevins has announced that "Black Friday" will not be a holiday for DODO personnel, and everyone is expected to show up for work as usual instead of participating in TV set riots at their local Walmart. Frank answered patiently and thus caught the attention of Magnus, who doesn't have much modern English vocabulary but does respond to "truck" and "Walmart" and a few other terms like "touchdown," "iPhone," and "Google." Like most other male Anachrons he views the latter as a near-miraculous way of viewing pictures of naked ladies. Between that and his fascination with trucks I suppose I can see why Blevins and others see him as a bit of a simpleton. But it is quite obviously a matter of male jealousy. Magnus is ludicrously hyper-masculine in ways that have been bred and trained out of modern-day men and so they have to deprecate his intelligence.

In any event we got through the evening without any sword- or cat-fights. There was the usual fuss trying to get people to leave so that I could tidy up alone, which I prefer. I had Frank summon the MUON van to get rid of Erszebet, Gráinne, and Constance, and leaned on Mortimer and Julie to give Magnus a lift back to the SARF. I shooed Tristan and Frank out and they went to the basement to drink scotch and speak of Deep Dark Things. Melisande stayed to help clear dishes. She has seemed a little distant lately, and uncharacteristically wistful, so I asked her directly what was going on. Knowing as she does that I've decided to step away from DODO in all capacities except witch-work, she confessed she was thinking of leaving too—entirely—sometime in the new year. She attributed this to (a) Blevins's unending denigrations of her competence and (b) more significantly, the growing shift away from diachronic work (where her expertise is clearly valued) and toward psychological operations (which she not only is not expert on, but which she finds more ethically problematic, as do I). I think however there is also (c): she and Tristan have teetered at the edge of a relationship for *so* long, and never yet fallen into it, and she is tired of that balancing act. Men are always better at compartmentalizing these things. I don't especially say that in a laudatory way.

Exchange of posts by DODO staff
on "Anachrons" ODIN channel
DAY 1937 (17 NOVEMBER, YEAR 5)

Post from LTC Tristan Lyons, 08:30:

FFS where is Magnus? He was supposed to be here on the 0800 bus from the SARF for a seminar in Violence(s) Ethnology. This is the third time he's been late.

Usually he's a morning person.

Reply from officer on duty at SARF (Supervised Anachron Residential Facility), 08:41:

He was out the door at 0800 sharp but apparently did not get on the bus, which was waiting outside. Will check cameras.

Follow-up from officer on duty at SARF, 08:52:

Front-door security camera footage is ambiguous. We see him exiting the door and going down the front walk toward the bus, but just as he is exiting the frame he appears to juke sideways.

Magnus has always been fascinated by the security cameras and so he probably knows where the coverage areas are. Evidence suggests he proceeded down the walk until he believed he was out of frame, then made his move.

From LTC Lyons, 08:56:

Alerting DOSECOPS and Dr. Blevins (acting head of C/COD). Anyone who sees him or learns anything, pipe up here so we can cancel the alert.

From MAJ Isobel Sloane (ranking DOSECOPS officer on duty), 09:12:

We've activated the protocols for AWOL Anachrons. These have been worked out in advance with local police departments and transit police—obviously we want to find the missing Anachron, but we have to treat it as a sensitive matter. We don't want someone like Magnus ending up in the slammer with a random assortment of criminals.

Currently checking all bus and T routes in the vicinity of the SARF.

From LTC Lyons, 09:20:
Respectfully, MAJ Sloane, Magnus isn't going to hop on a bus. He can walk faster than most people can run, and he can run faster than cars and buses are capable of moving in Boston traffic. He has been missing now for eighty minutes, and with his level of physical fitness could be anywhere in a ten- or twelve-mile radius of the SARF by this point.

From MAJ Sloane, 09:32:
Acknowledged and understood. Also putting out feelers to local PDs and social service agencies for reports of weird or threatening behavior.

From Dr. Roger Blevins, 10:05:
Just became aware of Magnus's disappearance. May I suggest sending officers to check local gridirons, sports bars, any place connected with football. I took him to a game last month and he seemed quite interested.

From MAJ Sloane, 10:16:
That's a useful lead, Dr. Blevins. Anything else in that vein?

From Dr. Blevins, 10:23:
I also took him to Walmart, which he quite enjoyed, but (a) he would have no way of locating a Walmart, and (b) even if he did, the closest one is many miles away.

From officer on duty at SARF, 10:56:
[Redacted], who frequently takes the night shift at the security desk

here, told me the other day that Magnus had "borrowed" his iPhone and apparently used the map application. Magnus was also seen using a pen to draw on the palm of his hand.

From MAJ Sloane, 11:01:

Need to wake up [redacted] and have him check the search history on his phone. Sounds like Magnus drew a map.

From Dr. Blevins, 11:05:

Suit yourself, Major Sloane, but I believe you are grossly overestimating Magnus's mental capacity. He cannot even speak English, much less type search terms into a navigational app.

From LTC Lyons, 12:00:

He's been gone for four hours. Sitrep?

From MAJ Sloane, 12:01:

Just writing one up. Nothing yet. [Redacted]'s phone didn't preserve any search history.

From MAJ Sloane, 13:27:

Bingo. We have a report from the Walmart Supercenter in Lexington that a man matching Magnus's description has been using a computer in the electronics department for a couple of hours. It's only ten miles— he could have Paul Revere it on foot. Sending all available DOSECOPS units.

From LTC Lyons, 13:30:

Please advise Walmart rent-a-cops not to engage Magnus. I can't even . . .

From MAJ Sloane, 13:31:

Neither can I. Have already emphasized this to them.

From MAJ Sloane, 14:10:

Plainclothes DOSECOPS personnel made peaceful contact with Magnus and escorted him from the Walmart without incident. Interviewing witnesses. Magnus is in the SUV, should be back in DODO HQ soon. He's calm and relaxed.

From Dr. Blevins, 14:15:

Any indications Magnus might have divulged classified information to civilians?

From MAJ Sloane, 14:23:

All eyewitness reports so far agree that he said nothing—which stands to reason since he doesn't speak English! Sounds like he'd brought a Sharpie from the SARF and was using it to draw on his hand and forearm—that's what freaked out the store management and caused them to call it in.

From MAJ Sloane, 14:39:

Magnus is in the building, being escorted to conference room for debriefing.

From LTC Lyons, 14:42:

Don't you guys have a lockable room down in DOSECOPS land?

From Dr. Blevins, 14:45:

No need to escalate by placing Magnus in something that looks to him like a prison.

From LTC Lyons, 14:47:

It won't look to him like a prison—he's never seen a prison!—it'll look to him like the nicest, cleanest room he'd ever seen in his life until a few weeks ago.

From MAJ Sloane, 15:05:

Still waiting on the Norman interpreter so we can interview him.

From LTC Lyons, 15:08:

FFS I can do that. No need to wait.

From MAJ Sloane, 15:11:

We are observing him in the meantime. As part of a psych eval. He's scratching himself with a paper clip.

From LTC Lyons, 15:12:

???

From MAJ Sloane, 15:14:

Just superficial scratches. Not enough to draw blood. Maybe the ink irritated his skin.

From Dr. Blevins, 15:23:

Why are the alarms going off?

From SGT Jones, 15:25:

Major Sloane asked me to notify everyone that we got a report from the Walmart that Magnus has a knife. Apparently they reviewed their security camera footage and saw him taking it from the kitchen section and hiding it in his trousers. He's had it the whole time.

From LTC Lyons, 15:25:

OMW

From CPT Gomez, 15:26:

Need medic conf rm

From SGT Jones, 15:26:

Facility is in lockdown. All personnel following active shooter protocols.

From CPT Gomez, 15:28:

Need medic Stairwell 2

From LTC Lyons, 15:28:

He's on ODEC level.

   He's in ODEC 2 with a MUON.

   It's Constance Billy.

   He's gone. Constance shaken but unharmed.

From Dr. Blevins, 15:30:

Gone where? To what DTAP?

From LTC Lyons, 15:32:

Constance says he threatened her with a knife and demanded to be Sent to 912 AD Svelvik. It's a DTAP she knows pretty well.

From Dr. Blevins, 15:34:

Isn't that three centuries before his time?

From Dr. Melisande Stokes, 15:40:

912 Svelvik is like Grand Central Station for old-school Vikings.

From LTC Lyons, 15:45:

Magnus has always been fascinated by that era, it doesn't surprise me that he would choose to go there. He knows he can't come back, ever, after what he's done. So he picked the one place where he could live out the rest of his days as his fantasy of a classic Viking.

From Dr. Stokes, 15:48:

Maybe he'll go discover America:)

From LTC Lyons, 15:50:

Not actually that funny, Stokes.

Magnus's search history
(recovered from computer on display in
Walmart electronics department)

TRUCK
BOOBS
FREE BOOBS PIX
LIE DOE CAIN
LIE DO CAIN NUMM
NUMB
LIDOCAINE
TOPICAL ANAESTHETICS
SCAR
HOW MAKE SCAR
SCARIFICATION
BLACK FRIDAY
BLACK FRIDAY WALMART
TRUCK BOX
METAL TRUCK BOX
BIG METAL TRUCK BOX PIX
BIG TRUCK PICTURES
TRUCK WITH BIG STEEL BOX
SHIPPING CONTAINER

SHIPPING CONTAINER IMAGE
SHIPPING CONTAINER WIKIPEDIA
SHIPPING CONTAINER DOOR
SHIPPING CONTAINER TRAILER
TRACTOR TRAILER
SEMI TRAILER
18 WHEELER
NAKED WOMAN
NAKED WHITE WOMAN
[redacted]
FUGGER
FUGGERS WHERE LIVE
FUGGER BOSS
GUN
BEST GUN
GUN SHOOT HOW
GUN HOW SHOOT YOUTUBE
REVOLVER HOW SHOOT
SEMIAUTOMATIC HOW SHOOT
SHOTGUN
SHOTGUN HOW LOAD
BULLET ARMOR
GOLD
GOLD WHERE
AMERICA WHY RICH
AMERICA WHY RICH HISTORY
CONQUISTADOR
CONQUISTADOR GOLD MAP
EL DORADO
CIBOLA
TENOCHTITLAN
TENOCHTITLAN MAP
TENOCHTITLAN HARBOR
TENOCHTITLAN CLOSEST PORT
VERA CRUZ
VERA CRUZ HARBOR
VERA CRUZ MAP
VERA CRUZ NAVIGATE EUROPE
GOOGLE MAPS

THE LAY OF WALMART

TRANSLATOR'S NOTE: "The Lay of Walmart" comprises two parts. Handwriting analysis confirms that both were written by the same author, self-identified as Tóki Olafsson, a skald originally dwelling in the village of Sverðvík (modern-day Svelvik) on the Oslofjord in the early tenth century. Part 1, written on sheets of birch bark using oak-gall ink, was recovered from a peat bog outside of Sverðvík by a covert DODO archaeological extraction team in the wake of Part 2's discovery.

The overall style is typical of Norse epic verse of Tóki's era, though somewhat rough-hewn as many parts seem to have been written in haste. Not all skalds were literate. Tóki was, and seems to have used written documents as an aid to composition and memorization. Of note here is his use of modern English loan words such as "Walmart" and "ditapp," which is his transliteration of DTAP (Destination Time and Place), a common acronym in the Department of Diachronic Operations.

PART 1

A hearing I ask. A skald am I.
A witch woke me, hurried to my hut,
Summoned me from sleep,
Beseeched me to bear witness,

Record in runes a traveler's tale.
Tailing her out of town, I heard tell
Of what had happened: a man Sent
From distant time and place,

Magnus, mighty one, subject of sagas,
Treasure-taker, ship-shaker, ring-bearer.
Yet when he came, not as well clad
As the cats the witch kept.

To her home we hastened.
Magnus, blanket-bundled, on a bench,
Sat by the sparking fire, staring
Amused at the flames' antics.

"Say nothing," he said, stretching out a hand.
"Hear only, heed me, memorize my words,
O skald, story-stretcher, keeper of epics.
Write them in runes on the morrow."

"Sent hither was I, just now, naked.
A witch-friend, fair Frankish girl,
Got me away in good order
From a far place, a fat land.

"Walmart is where the thralls
Of that land store up their wealth.
A fat fool took me there,
Thinking he would make me quail,

"Cock-shriveled, cuckolded,
Shamed by the sight of such treasure.
While the memory of that mart remains mine,
I'll make it yours too, tale-teller.

"We'll wend our way to other times,
Tell the tale, hiring a host of heroes,
Return as raiders to plunder that place
And carry on viking thenceforward.

"Of the fat land I'll say little now.
Too many tales to tell of its weird wonders.

Walmart is what I have just seen,
Not so long ago as when you lay sleeping.

"Greater than any Goth village
Is the width of its walls, sheer and strong.
Thrice-gated, though, with glass:
Frail fencing for a treasure-trove!

"For in Fatland, visits from vikings
Are few and far between;
Fear rules fellows, makes men meek,
Glass gates are good enough.

"That barrier breached, all the land's luxury
Lies ready for reaping.
Here's what my memory holds
Of how it is sorted.

"Long lanes, laden with loot
Wide ways, well made for waging war
Like the roads of the red-crested Romans
Ordered just so, as warp and weft.

"Too many for merchants to memorize,
Marked, therefore, with runes they can read.
Romans wrote them first. The fat ones stole them,
As well as Arabs' numerals, arranged below.

"For each district of the treasure-town,
A Roman rune written, raised high
For each lane lying below it,
An Arabic number to know it.

"South face the glass gates; the fat fool
Northward led me, shouldering them aside
Greeting a guard, vested in blue,
Scarcely strength to stand had that old ogre.

"To our right, ranks of clashing carts
Waiting to be wheeled and weighed down
By Fatlanders too frail for fardels.
Sight-seers only, we spurned these.

"Till-keepers' tables cluttered our view.
Beyond them, still north-questing,
Kiosks and cairns covered the place,
Towers of trifles.

"From there, to the west, lies all the food in the world.
North, a cornucopia of clothing, all colors.
Doubling back south, white witches
Doling out drugs, physicians' philtres.

"Eastward, though, lies victory for vikings.
Counting the cairns, the merchandise-mounds
Standing in the center of the wide east-west way,
Stop at the sixth. Atop it's an image:

"A fair lass, tresses flowing,
Like the lush Linndalsfallet,
Where it rushes over rocks,
Teeth shining like Snæfellsjökull.

"Cradled in the lass's hands, a bottle,
Bewitching brew, beautifying the hair.
Below it, many more such, stacked like soldiers.
That is the landmark that leads you to the left.

"A long lane, laden with loot.
Its rune is like Berkano: the Beginning.
Its number, one score and five.
Let it lead you north. Little more to say,

"For in fewer than five paces
Is what your hand has hungered for

Since you found yourself in Fatland,
Alone and naked: Numberless knives, new and needy."

Thus the blanket-wearer, who now bated,
Hefting a horn, whetting his whistle.
"More mead, if you are willing, witch.
There's riches in this tale."

Ingibjörg was the witch's name.
South of Sverðvík, alone she abided
Here in this hut, cozy, kept clean,
Cats her companions, dogs her defenders.

"Let none say I don't serve a guest sweetly.
Here is your horn, more mead for Magnus.
Gladly I'll listen to more of your story
But the riches you rave of mean ruin for me.

"Here in my hut I am happy.
Grief-bringing gold, land needing labor,
Swords, slaves, silks, swag: to what end
Should, I, Ingibjörg, buy into this business?"

"For that there's an answer," said Magnus.
"Gráinne's grief made her great with rage,
Drove her to desolate ditapps,
Reddened her hands with friends' blood.

"To you, welcoming witch, I'll have more to say
When the sun sheds its light on the shore
And cocks crow. Now is night-work,
Telling the tale to Tóki, the skald."

Drinking deep of the mead, whetting his whistle,
Magnus made the most of it then,
Telling to me, Tóki, tales of Walmart,
Where the weapons were, how to find food.

When the sun shed its light on the shore,
When the cocks crowed, home I hied,
Wrote it in runes, left nothing out,
Then slept soundly.

"Tóki, time to depart!" were the next words I heard.
Magnus and Ingibjörg stood staring.
"Distant ditapps await us. Hardy heroes
Restless to ramble, we'll sway them to our side!"

Blanket-bound was he still, blowing on blue hands.
"Furs I will fetch you, friend," said I. "No need
To ride so rude-clad, cold and uncovered."
"We won't ride," said he, "naked will both of us be

"When the witch has her way, and we're at the ditapp."
"Sending it's to be then," said I, "travel through time,
Dark and dangerous. Ingibjörg's will
Isn't what it was when last I heard tell."

The witch was fur-clad, fierce-faced,
Fingering her skein, but half in this world.
"I have heard tell from the man Magnus
Of a future that is to be feared.

"Alchemists and astronomers, addling
The wits of witches, stripping us of our strength,
Helpless hags they'd make of us. I'll not have it.
Put away your pen. In a peat bog, bury the bark.

"Let it lie there, a legend
For our friends in the future to find.
The story will stay in your mind, son of Olaf.
Tell it true, when you get to the ditapp."

Exchange of posts by DODO staff on "Diachronic Ops-misc" ODIN channel
DAY 1943 (MONDAY BEFORE THANKSGIVING, YEAR 5)

Post from Dr. Melisande Stokes:

Checking on a DEDE assignment I just got that confuses me. In two days I'm supposed to go to San Francisco 1850 to recruit an immigrant Chinese witch there. It's listed as a one-day DEDE, so I'll be home in time for Thanksgiving dinner, supposedly.

Chinese is my weakest language. We have five DOers who are fluent, three of them ethnically Chinese, at least one of those (Julie Lee) not only currently available but also (FWIW) a MUON. I'm curious why I was assigned this DEDE?

Also, regardless of who goes, I'd like to see the Chronotron data on why we need to recruit this witch so close to July 1851. Whether the goal is to bring her forward to work as a contemporary witch, or to do some final magical adjustments in those last few months . . . why not go back several years earlier and recruit her directly from China? I'm sure that data has already been crunched by the Chronotron (cc'ing Dr. Oda and Mortimer for confirmation), but I find this puzzling.

Reply from Mortimer Shore:

Dr. Oda is still "on vacation" (read: getting ready for the ATTO move on Friday). I will look into all this ASAP but I am a little overwhelmed with work right now. My understanding is that Gordon Healey and Mary Case are our data-whisperers there at the moment and they're both cool. They're not great at communicating in regular English though. I can ask them to summarize stuff for me and I'll get back to you about it.

From Dr. Roger Blevins:

Dr. Stokes,

I understand you have reservations about your Wednesday assign-ment, and out of respect for your senior position within DODO, I am willing to respond to them, although it is against protocol for a DOer to question their mission. While I understand that you would like an explanation, you do not require one to do your job.

I've told Mortimer Shore that—as he already knows, of course—he needs to focus his time and energies on projects that actually require his attention, so please do not expect him to follow up on his last offer to you regarding Chronotron data.

Mel, I do realize it must be unnerving to go to a DTAP that is so close to the very end of magic. As Erszebet has recalled on innumerable occasions, she was hardly able to perform magic at all for the last year or so before the eclipse. So I have a proposal that I hope will reassure you: when you go to the San Fran DTAP, Gráinne has offered to go with you, and as soon as you've accomplished your DEDE (which if I recall correctly is to recruit a witch from that era), Gráinne will Send you back here immediately. She will then get back here with the help of the KCW—she's not nearly as unnerved about the timing as you are, and is happy to make the journey if it will help you feel more secure about returning.

So, in short: Don't worry about it. Just do it. After all, it's your job.

Exchange of posts by DODO staff
on private ODIN channel
DAYS 1943–1944
(MONDAY AND TUESDAY BEFORE THANKSGIVING, YEAR 5)

Post from Dr. Melisande Stokes to LTC Tristan Lyons and Mortimer Shore:

Any thoughts on this DEDE? Gráinne seems awfully cozy with Blevins lately. Also, Mortimer, are you being blocked from Chronotron data?

Mel

Reply from LTC Tristan Lyons:

It's fine, Mel. Gráinne's resourceful, she'll get both of you back here safely. She's hardwired subversive when it comes to authority (I heard the coders classified her Chaotic Neutral)—she's playing Blevins, survival instinct, force of habit. Erszebet genuinely likes her and Erszebet would *not* like her if she took the Gráinne/Blevins thing seriously. Gráinne's got your back.

If you're still gone on Friday, I'll have Erszebet Send me back to help you out.

Tristan

From Mortimer Shore:

Hey, Mel, not being blocked, really am swamped with a sudden wave of mundane coding assignments that came unexpectedly from Blevins. Nobody else (except Oda) has the security clearance to do it and he's busy on ATTO moving.

I agree with Tristan. But heads-up Tristan, you can't go back to help Mel out because you are about to get a whopper new DEDE—earliest era witch-recruitment we've had yet: 20,000 BC Germany. I only know because Erszebet has been surfing the wiki doing research—she needs some kind of reference point to Send you to. I turned her on to the Hohle Fels caves in the Ach Valley. Have fun! LOL

From LTC Lyons:

I haven't heard anything about that, but I'll start brushing up on my cave art. Wonder how the hell they expect me to recruit a witch who can Send me back here.

From Mortimer Shore:

That's why they pay you the big bucks. See you both when you're back from your Extreme DTAPs lol

Peace out
Mortimer

PART
FIVE

Diachronicle

DAY 1945 (DAY BEFORE THANKSGIVING, YEAR 5)

In which the road to perdition is paved with gold

GRÁINNE AND I HAD ARRIVED in San Francisco without benefit of the level of research to which I was accustomed. Blevins,
clearly smitten with Gráinne, had allowed—one might even say
encouraged—her to learn all manner of Internet searching, and
she assured me that she had done all the background work for this
DTAP. There were no particular skills required, it was argued, as
San Francisco in 1850 was such a madcap swill of different cultures (and so extremely under-populated by women) that even if
I wore pants and chewed gum I would not stand out as irregular,
while no matter how prepared I was, I would still stand out for
being female. Because we were so close to the end of magic, the
intention was to get in and out quickly.

As arrival was always in the nude, and this was San Francisco at the start of the Gold Rush, it was sensible to arrive in a
brothel. Gráinne had chosen the Golden Mounds, right on Portsmouth Square, which was so new (having been rebuilt twice in
the past year due to monstrous fires) that it still smelled of pine sap
and paint, which stale beer and stale sweat had not yet masked.
Imagine whatever tawdry image of Gold Rush whorehouses you
like; this one was surprisingly well-appointed, despite the slapdash construction. Somebody, somewhere, had come into massive
amounts of gold leaf, and the whole place glittered. You've surely
seen the photographs of prostitutes of this era, I need not spend
the ink describing them—but I was not prepared for the loud,
rowdy, almost assembly-line attitude of the place. Curtains, at

best, separated nooks for ~~nookie~~ sexual congress. There was nothing close to privacy. It was a madhouse of copulation. This made our arrival—in the corner of a large room with some eight beds all sectioned off by hanging "tapestries"—entirely unnoticed.

We both stumbled to our knees. I recovered quickly, for I had been Sent many times. Gráinne was a little slower to shake it off—but then she was more in her element than I, and in a trice she had pinched a couple of day-dresses. Corsets and blouses generally remained on the girls, at least at this tier of low-latency prostitutional services.

"We'll do better to find their non-work clothes," I said, as Gráinne tossed me the more modest of the two dresses. "Since we shall have to go out on the street."

"No need to dress primly here at all," she replied cheerily. "Not for the time that's in it. Here's some knickers that look clean enough"—and she tossed me some linen bloomers. (Not unlike the ones I am wearing now, although these are a much finer weave and mercifully much cleaner. I must be grateful for these small blessings now.)

We made our way downstairs and headed for the main door, when a wasp-wasted figure stepped between us and our egress. "Who are you?" demanded this older woman (dressed more as one imagines ladies dressing in the early Victorian era—so clearly the madam of the place). She aimed the query straight at me, and I, unprepared, without the usual backstory we were always careful to produce, hesitated.

"It's grand, ma'am, surely," said Gráinne, with a winsome smile. "Mary it was sent us over from the other place, there's a ship arrived with lots of new women, and they haven't the beds set up. If you don't want us we'll be striking out on our own, but we've heard such agreeable things about your terms. Will you take us, so? Shall we just be fetching our bags from the harborside? Pay my cousin no mind, she's deaf and dumb."

The woman frowned. "Mary should know we don't take Irish," she said.

"It's a surfeit of English ladies you've got, is it?" Gráinne asked in a playfully disbelieving voice. And then, in an odd accent somewhere between London and Appalachian, she asked, "What if we were English, then? Would that work for your johns? We can easily be English. My cousin here, she can be anything!"

Now the woman looked confused, but in a way that suggested Gráinne would get her way. With a brusque gesture she motioned toward the door. "Very well, then, get your things and come back, we can use the help."

"*Help*," Gráinne quoted with a snigger, and out we went to meet the city.

"Who's Mary?" I whispered as we exited.

Gráinne shrugged. "Mary's such a common name there will always be at least one nearby. 'Tis the best name to be using when you're counterfeiting."

To say that San Francisco in 1850 was a city being built on Gold Rush fever does not begin to capture the chaos, havoc, greed, and rough-hewn glamour that made up the peninsula. It had taken almost no time at all for the sharpest of the '49ers—or Argonauts, as the tens of thousands who came by sea were called—to realize that the real money was to be made not from mining gold but from selling all manner of goods to the fellows who were trying to mine it. Shops of every conceivable sort had sprung up in buildings around the waterfront and on the route out of town—freshly built wooden buildings that (I did know this much from some hasty research) had already burned in three enormous conflagrations over the past year or so.

I also knew from my abbreviated Googling that a fourth Great Fire would destroy a swath of the town just a few weeks after our arrival. This, in concert with my awareness that magic was soon to wane entirely, added a certain urgency to our DEDE—I was eager to accomplish it and get out quickly.

Between credit and gold, the town was obviously, and almost dangerously, wealthy. Grand, elegant palace-like hotels and buildings were being constructed in a slapdash manner even faster than they were burning down. The building we had just exited was three stories tall and brightly painted, facing onto a large city square. I looked to either side—the entire block was a series of theatres, saloons, and inns, bustling in the bright midday sun with prostitutes, gamblers, con men, and the occasional gentleman. Given there was no easy natural source of water or wood, I cannot imagine where all the resources to do this were being obtained.

"Amazing," said Gráinne heartily, gazing down the hill toward the harbor—in which was moored many hundreds of tall ships. "Two years ago this was a village; now this. See all them ships? Marooned there by their crews, so they are, the crews having jumped ship to go prospecting. So it's taking possession the city folk have done, and turned them into homes, inns, taverns, brothels, theatres, and I do believe a jail. And look, that's where the Chinamen are living."

She pointed to a peculiar neighborhood of unaccountably neat and sturdy wooden homes, laid out in a grid, on a slope near the harbor. "Those houses were shipped over here from Canton, in pieces but ready to be assembled. They're very popular and their owner is about to make a fortune. Can't say as much for the rest of the Chinese."

"Where's Xiu Li?" I asked, this being the name of the witch we were to recruit. "Since you did all the research I assume you have some idea? I guess the Chinese have brothels as well?"

Gráinne cut me a look. "Why are you even suggesting that? Do you think all witches are prostitutes?"

"Well, in all fairness, you—"

"Sure wasn't I a spy for the O'Malley!" she said with ferocity. "Prostitution was a front and didn't I only engage in it to suit my own purposes! Anyhow," she said, collecting herself and making a let's-put-this-behind-us gesture, "it certainly isn't the case here. There be no witches amongst the Chinese tarts, no witch would be finding herself in the straits those poor women are subjected to. No, our lady is right across the square there, in the fancy hotel— the St. Francis. Not much saintly about it from what I hear." She chuckled her distinctively Gráinne chuckle, took me by the hand, and led me across the dry dirt square.

We entered the lobby of the St. Francis—like the Golden Mounds, there was tacky, tawdry opulence everywhere, much as I imagine Vegas must look, but without the neon—and a woman unlike any Chinese witch I had expected was standing by a card table in the center of the room.

Xiu Li was tall and elegant, almost gentlemanly, feet unbound (although I noticed when she walked that she walked stiffly). Her dress was an ingenuous blend of Oriental and Western that revealed just enough flesh to make a gentleman inclined to stare, and yet concealed enough that she could, technically, pass as modest, at least here.

She was watching the card game, and at a certain point, she settled upon the arm of one player's chair. She moved with the demure grace of a geisha pouring tea, and yet at the same moment somehow with brazen confidence as well. She was beautiful and spellbinding.

Literally, spellbinding.

She was helping her companion cheat at cards.

For a few moments, we watched the card game. Xiu Li's companion was also Chinese—a gentleman with short hair, cut in the Western style. There were three other players, all white men, one young, two chubby and older. Standing back from the table were an assortment of servant-ish types, including a Chinese man with long hair in a queue.

"'Tis a weak magic here," said Gráinne under her breath at last. "She's using soft magic to influence their choices, rather than what I'd do in her place, change the order of the cards in the deck." I recalled Erszebet lamenting on the cheap parlor tricks she'd been forced to perform to earn her keep, back in . . . well, just about now, actually. What an odd thought, that at this very moment Erszebet was a young witch somewhere in Eastern Europe, innocent to all that lay ahead.

We watched the game to its completion—that is to say, to her partner's satisfaction—and then without hesitation, Xiu Li turned with radiant grace and walked elegantly directly toward us. She greeted Gráinne as if a friend she knew attended her. Not surprising, as I have come to understand that witches recognize each other in subtle ways.

"You are no witch," the tall elegant woman said to me.

"Along for the ride with me, she is. Gráinne I am by name, and this is Melisande, and you are Xiu Li."

Xiu Li smiled, her teeth small opalescent pearls. "Yes."

"We've a proposition for you," said Gráinne. "Be there a place to talk in private?"

"There is a room upstairs," said Xiu Li. "I do most of my business there."

I confess deep curiosity to know what her business was, but as

Gráinne was clearly the lead DOer here, I satisfied myself with following along quietly. We headed for a wooden staircase.

It seemed to me that somebody was following us up the stairs, and sure enough, at the top, we were stopped by a Caucasian gentleman who had been just behind us. "Hey, Shirley," he said, mispronouncing her name in a nasal voice. "Introduce me to your friends here." He had a flat accent, akin to what I would in my own time describe as midwestern.

"We talk first, and then we talk to you," said Xiu Li, with cold friendliness.

"Hi, I'm Francis Overstreet," he said, offering his hand to Gráinne, and then to me.

"St. Francis, is it?" Gráinne smiled.

"Hardly," he said, in much the same tone. "Although I am the proprietor of this fine establishment. And as Miss Shirley here knows, when courtesan services are being established, I not only get a cut, but I get to sample the wares." He turned a leering eye to the two of us, and, determining at once which was more leerworthy, he winked at Gráinne. I confess a certain relief. If he were not handsome, his demeanor would be utterly repugnant. But he was a man in the prime of life, fine looking, his face intelligent. A portrait of him would suggest a man of integrity and dignity. So the leer was more disorienting than disgusting.

Gráinne was already giving him an inviting smile. "After supper?" she suggested. "I've some errand to run before that."

"My dance card is otherwise empty." He smiled back.

"Oh good," I said, nudging Gráinne slightly, as I realized that expression would mean nothing to her.

"Oh good," she echoed. "Invite a friend," she added, pushing me slightly toward him.

He looked nonplussed: further confirmation I was the less delectable morsel.

Francis Overstreet trotted back down the stairs to oversee his glamorous den of iniquity, as Xiu Li led us a short way down the corridor to a small room made all round of sanded wooden planks, with admirably clean windows, that looked out over the square.

"Your business?" she asked coolly.

"Magic's dying off," said Gráinne matter-of-factly. "I'm sure you've felt it."

After a sober, studied pause, Xiu Li nodded once. "I have. I wondered if it was to do with being in this new world that has no history or civilization."

"It has plenty of history," I corrected her. "The native people have had witches and magic all along. But they are feeling the loss as well. Everyone is."

"In fact," continued Gráinne, "we are about to lose magic entirely."

Xiu Li's eyes opened wide. She did not speak.

"But that is temporary," I amended. "Many years from now, in the future, magic is restored and used in a very different way in society. We are here to encourage you to come forward with us to a time when magic will be strong again. There are some caveats, but it will be far better than being stuck here in this time and place, especially as a Chinese woman."

She was ignoring me, her intense black eyes studying Gráinne's face. "Why does it end? What stops it?"

"Photography," said Gráinne confidingly.

Xiu Li received this and mused upon it for a moment. "I see," she said at last—as if she really did see, although she obviously lacked the education to grasp it in the manner that we at DODO did. "How long do we have before it is gone?"

"July next year," said Gráinne sympathetically. "There's a solar eclipse, witnessed by everyone in Europe, and someone takes
a photograph of it, and that's that." She snapped her fingers. "It's
over. So you'd best consider our offer and come forward with us."

I stared at Gráinne. She was strikingly well-informed for an
Anachron. Who would have told her something that specific? It
must have been Erszebet.

Xiu Li's pale skin had paled even further hearing this. She sank
onto a stool, her heavy silk dress shifting gracefully around her
legs so that she appeared almost a mermaid. "This is dreadful
news."

"Yes," said Gráinne, with no sense of dread at all. "You take
some time to think it over. Melisande, let's be seeing the city, and
we'll return by teatime."

She took me by the hand in her casually familiar way and led
me out of the room, down the hall, down the stairs, and back out
into the square.

"Where are we going?" I asked.

"Sure I'd love to see the city," said Gráinne. "But in truth there's
a gentleman here to introduce ourselves to."

"What gentleman?" I demanded. "I don't recall that being part
of the DEDE."

"Not that DEDE as written," agreed Gráinne. "But there is
more going on than meets the eye here. Blevins set me on to him,
and explained he could not put it down into the official assignment because it is, what was that phrase he was using now? Deep
cover? Black cops?"

"Black ops," I said, rolling my eyes. "Black operations. Covert
activity."

"Covert, aye, there you go," said Gráinne, without a shred of
the sober demeanor one associates with such discussions. "One

reason he wanted us to come here together was so that you could be witness to it all, but off the record, like. In fact, this whole DEDE is a different beast than you are currently thinking."

I felt a wave of alarm but pushed it aside. This was irregular, but not dangerous. "Will you explain yourself?" I said.

"Surely," said Gráinne. "There's a Fugger here, a direct male descendant of the one I know in my generation. He knows to expect us, and he'll help us with the DEDE."

The more she revealed the more confounding it seemed. "How?" I demanded. "How on earth can he possibly know to expect us? Nobody has ever been close to this DTAP before."

"Melisande," she said in a confiding, delighted voice. "What is the one thing you can carry through time with you?"

"Information," I said.

"Indeed," she said. "And it's a wide varieties of ways, so it is, that information can be carried through time. If it's going *back* in time, the information's got to move magically. But if it's coming *forward*, it can be planted and moved through generations."

"Do you mean you told this fellow's ancestor to meet you in San Francisco in 1850? And they've passed the information along, accurately and without embellishment, for two and a half *centuries*?" I was incredulous—this was an extremely dangerous way to work with historical agents.

"It's not nearly that specific," said Gráinne blithely. "Think of it more as a mythology. The Fuggers know—all of them—that there's an immortal red-haired Irish witch named Gráinne who is an ally of the family, in any generation, and the family knows this and keeps it close to themselves. And 'tis true enough that this witch, in 1602, did recommend to the family patriarch of the time to keep an eye westward, ever westward, over the generations. It has served them well, and this is as westward as it gets. So I was not surprised, when I did my Internet research, to be confirmed in my belief that there would be a Fugger already here, opening a bank and prepared to make ungodly profits. And he is already an ally though he has never met me, nor has his sire, grandsire, great-grandsire going back many generations . . . but they know about me. It's delighted he'll be by our presence, and he'll help us, no questions asked. 'Tis a remarkable boon for our needs."

"What will he do?" I asked, struggling to keep up with all this. Did Tristan know any of this? Surely Frank Oda or Mortimer must, as they oversaw the Chronotron data and none of this could be managed without tremendous Chronotron oversight. *Why had I not been told?*

"Here's the second part you do not know," she said. "We're not actually meant to bring her forward in time."

"What?" I cried. "Then what are we *doing* here?"

"We're here to recruit her," said Gráinne. "Much as I recruited the Fuggers. If she comes forward in time, what do we have? One more witch. But if we leave her here, educated and motivated to pass a family legend down, then we can sculpt her to our needs, and seven generations hence, it's allies we'll have in all her dutiful descendants. And if we set her up so that her descendants will be people of power in America, then when we come to them in the twenty-first century, it's *powerful* allies we will have. They will have things that we need—because we will arrange *now* for them to have such things."

Again, I was utterly gobsmacked—what a very clever and extremely dangerous methodology. And shocking that I had not been told of it. Again, I wondered: Had Tristan? Was he also in the dark, or had he begun to keep secrets from me?

Three banks had already opened in or near Portsmouth Square, and the third bank was owned by the current Mr. Fugger. Gráinne wrote a note to have delivered to him, and after we waited for a few minutes in the brick lobby (brick! In that time and place! Proof these were no ordinary bankers), the gentleman appeared, in very fine and sober attire, and received Gráinne as if she were Santa Claus and he a toddler. They exchanged certain code phrases that she had planted with his ancestor, to reassure each other (or to reassure him; Gráinne had this insouciantly in hand). He was only too happy to follow us back to the St. Francis, where his duty would be to set up Xiu Li as the wealthiest Chinese immigrant in all of California.

I do not know—I suppose I shall never know now—if Gráinne offered him other incentives to fork over a chunk of his private fortune to a total stranger, and a Chinese woman no less. But determined, even eager, was he to fork it over.

"Now," said Gráinne, as we all stepped lightly across the square, "it's hopeful I am of this matter being wrapped up quick enough, but 'tis a matter of logistics that we will have a gentleman caller who must be dispatched politely. This may require you to pretend to be Melisande's companion for an hour."

Young Fugger regarded me with skepticism but was too polite to express his disappointment. His eyes, however, strayed not infrequently to Gráinne's curvier shape as we walked back toward the St. Francis.

Back in the upstairs rooms, we found a grim Xiu Li.

"I am not yet resolved to go," she said, almost pouting—if pouting can be applied to a woman of such mature and majestic bearing.

"There is another way," said Gráinne. This immediately commanded Xiu Li's attention. "Yes. There's always the option to stay here and swap out magic for dosh, if you have that phrase here. Money. This gentleman is an associate of ours, and he will happily set you up for life, and for your children's lives, and your children's children's lives."

Xiu Li's bright eyes narrowed, and she looked back and forth between them. I might as well have not been present. "There is always a condition to these matters," she said. "What is the condition here? Must I marry this Caucasian? I am already the mistress of the Celestial Jong Li."

Gráinne shook her head. "No condition but that you think well of us—myself and the gentleman here. And that you breed, if you haven't yet, but choose the man yourself, sure. Then raise your children to think well of our memory, and to raise their children to do likewise, and their children, and so on down the line. One day in the future I might be meeting one of your descendants, and I would have them very well-disposed toward me."

With a wink to me, as if I were a part of all of this unsettling collusion, she commented, "Worked a wonder with the Fuggers, might as well try it again, isn't it?"

Xiu Li thought this over. "When magic disappears," she said, "are witches gone? Do the powers lie dormant through the generations or are they entirely snuffed out?"

"Oh, the magic comes back just fine, so it does," said Gráinne. "Although it takes the witches a while to get the feel for it."

"So a distant daughter of mine—"

"—is what I'm saying," said Gráinne, nodding.

Xiu Li pursed her lips and looked out the window. It seemed to me an eternity passed, and I was not comfortable about this, as time was drawing near for Francis Overstreet to return to "test the wares," and I did not like the idea of pretending to be a prostitute with Mr. Fugger as my client.

Xiu Li finally turned to us. "I will agree to this. But I want a contract and surety."

Mr. Fugger raised his handsome leather briefcase. "I've got it all arranged here," he said. "But this is hardly a place to do respectable business, so I'd like to bring you both to supper where my cook will treat you like royalty."

"Both?" I echoed, now feeling even more invisible, in a manner that was beginning to make my hackles rise. "There are three of us here."

The gentleman turned to me. "Miss Gráinne said you'd be wanting to return home as soon as possible."

"Yes, but—"

"There's no need of you to stay here," said Gráinne cheerfully. "This was really my DEDE all along, we only needed you to come along to cover my tracks. If I return a few scant hours after you, 'tis no concern of anyone there." With a wink. "And the longer you stay here the likelier you are to be called to service, not that anyone will be too hot to hoist that skirt up off your bony hips."

I reviewed my options. Gráinne had entirely commandeered the situation—mostly because I was so unprepared for any of these developments, but it seemed clear enough that Blevins had entrusted her as a DOer. I could not see a benefit to my remaining here any longer. And frankly, it would be helpful to have some time in Cambridge without Gráinne underfoot, to suss out how all of this had come to pass.

"Thank you, yes, I'll go home now," I said.

"Excellent," said Gráinne, and turned to Xiu Li. "Do you have much experience Sending people?"

Xiu Li shrugged. "As children my sisters and I did it as a game, but as magic weakened it became very difficult, the fun not worth the effort."

"I'll be refreshing your memory, then," said Gráinne. "I shall

Home Mel, and you, watching me, will then know how to Home me after our agreeable dinner."

Xiu Li nodded.

"But I need you to be paying particular attention," said Gráinne, "as a few things will be different. In particular, the co-ordinates of where we are to end up."

"How so?" I asked. "We are both returning to the same place."

"No," said Gráinne, in an amused-yet-apologetic smile. "We're not, actually, Melisande Stokes."

Suddenly I had a terrible feeling in the pit of my stomach—a premonition, which is not, dear reader, something I am prone to. I sensed it had something to do with Gráinne's detailed knowledge about photography, and the significance of the eclipse. "Where are you going?" I asked.

"Oh, it's back to DODO headquarters for myself, sure," she said. "I've stacks to do there, and I can't have you underfoot. So it's elsewhere I am Sending you, where there will be no magic strong enough to Send you forward. God ye good day, Melisande Stokes. 'Tis been a pleasure to serve with you. Fare thee well."

Even as she spoke, the room began to dim and tilt about me, and the lovely aroma that always wafted at the edges of my attention when I was Sent—I smelled it, and then . . .

. . . And then I awoke three weeks ago, naked, cold, on the grimy pavers of a London street at dawn, frantic to know what date it was, like a perversion of Scrooge at the end of *A Christmas Carol* (which came out less than a decade ago).

To make short shrift of it: a beadle was called and I was bundled off to Bedlam, but a physician there sensed there was something different about me (thank God!) and brought me to his home, for he and his wife to try to "salvage." They have it almost right: they take me for a witch (there are witches in distant branches of his family, and he has watched with compassion as several of them have fallen into despair as their powers waned; one took her own life). So they have offered me shelter, food, the clothes upon my back . . . on the sole condition that I make no attempt to communicate with any witch in any way.

Not that I know any witches in 1851 London anyhow. And even if I did, it would be a miracle if she had the power left to Send me forward before the eclipse. Which will occur in just seventeen days.

Post by Mortimer Shore on "General" GRIMNIR channel
DAY 1947 (BLACK FRIDAY, YEAR 5)

Mortimer here, writing first entry on new GRIMNIR system from safe locale.

OK, so those of you who are into the Norse mythology might have read a story about Odin disguising himself as a regular mortal for tactical reasons. The name he adopted was Grimnir.

The old ODIN system is no longer accessible to me, they have changed the passwords and kicked me out, I'm on the outs, and on the run, with a few of the others. But I set up a new system on the dark net that we can use to stay in touch with each other and make a record of all that's happening. And I'm calling it GRIMNIR.

I'm not much of a narrative writer, but here's what has gone down . . .

Two days ago, on Wednesday afternoon (the day before Thanksgiving), after some delays, Mel and Gráinne were Sent to the 1850 San Francisco DTAP, supposedly to recruit a Chinese KCW there. The old-school ODECs don't have enough room inside of them for a Sending witch and two DOers, so this was a dual Send from ATTO #1, which has plenty of room on the interior. By that point it had been hoisted up and mounted on the back of its tractor-trailer rig, making it ready for field trials on the streets of the greater Boston area beginning Friday.

This was billed as a one-day DEDE, or possibly a one-nighter, but as I said it got off to a late start, and by the time they were going into the ATTO, Mel was resigned to the fact that it was probably going to wipe out most of Thanksgiving Day and that she'd take Friday off instead.

At the same time (Wednesday) there was a lot of bureaucratic back-and-forth involving Tristan, Erszebet, and Blevins regarding this unusual DEDE that had been planned for Tristan starting Friday morning, where he was being sent back to 20,000 BC Germany. Erszebet was all like, "I am only following orders. Like the indentured servant I have been since I met you." And so it was up to Tristan to verify and double-check the order with Blevins and interface with the Chronotron crew.

Gordon Healey, one of the Chronotron nerds, ended up staying late and missing his flight home as he tried to help make sense of the mission and dig up the background information that Tristan needed to prep for it. He and Erszebet booked a slot in ODEC #1 early on Friday morning (that's today), since the ODECs were already fully booked for the rest of the day and the ATTO would not be available. I volunteered to come in and run the control panel.

So we arrived this morning, about an hour before the rest of the staff was due in. Tristan had slept well although he still looked a little ruffled about this strange assignment (like I said: *20,000 BC*. Dude.). Erszebet had a look of sort of grim resignation to her—but that's not too unusual for her. We checked the logs to see if Gráinne and Mel had made it back, but there was no sign of them. A little unusual, but nothing that would really raise a red flag yet.

I stayed on the outside of the glass wall to run the controls. Erszebet and Tristan went through the usual protocols in the bio-containment ward while I got ODEC #1 powered up and ran the usual checks. Through the glass wall I saw Tristan come out of the sterilization suite in the usual bathrobe. He tossed me a salute and walked into the ODEC.

Erszebet began to follow him in. Then she hesitated mid-stride, and stepped back away from it. For a long moment she stared into the ODEC. She kind of looked a little queasy.

I turned on the intercom and asked if there was a problem.

"Come on, Erszebet," I heard Tristan say.

"You will come out of there," she said.

"What?"

"I say you will come out of there. Very quickly. I must tell you something."

A sound nearly a harrumph, and then Tristan came out of the ODEC. Erszebet closed the door behind him, and then visibly relaxed—I hadn't realized she had been tense until I saw the tension leave her shoulders.

". . . All right," said Tristan, bemused. "What's going on?"

"There is no real assignment to send you on this DEDE," she said.

Tristan was totally still for a moment, and then pursed his lips together until they were colorless.

"What?" he said at last.

"It is all faked. Every bit of it. It is all part of a scheme."

"What scheme? Who's behind it?"

She looked troubled, but resigned. "The scheme requires getting rid of Melisande and yourself. Melisande is gone forever and now I am supposed to get rid of you."

The look on Tristan's face was of even greater shock than I myself was feeling, which is saying a lot. "But Mel's with . . ." he protested.

"It is Gráinne's scheme," said Erszebet. "It was almost mine as well. But I have been awake all night thinking of Melisande and it is wrong to do this. So I am not doing it."

There was complete silence in the chamber except for the background hum of the ODEC.

"I do not want to do this anymore," she continued, sounding almost plaintive, which if you've ever heard Erszebet speak is a hard thing to imagine. "I am quitting. I will leave and do something el—"

Tristan had closed his hand around her wrist and was trembling with the effort of not shaking her. "What's happened to Mel? What is Gráinne doing? Explain yourself!"

She looked cowed—or at least, as close to cowed as Erszebet Karpathy could ever look. "She wants to take over DODO and use it for her purposes," she said in a strangely small voice. "From San Francisco, she has already Sent Mel somewhere else, someplace Mel will not be able to come back from."

"Where? When?"

She avoided his gaze. "We agreed not to tell each other what we were doing. Like the French Resistance—it is safer not to know."

"How the *fuck* is this like the French Resistance?" Tristan growled, looking angrier than I've ever seen him. He let go of her and walked away, muttering to himself.

Erszebet's face had flushed such a bright shade of red that she was almost unrecognizable. I'd never known until this moment that she was capable of being embarrassed. "I know, of course." She looked at Tristan. "And, if you think about it, so do you. You have always known where Mel would end up."

Tristan turned and looked at her, his anger suddenly replaced by a look that said, *Of course. I get it.* "London," he said, "1851."

"Yes. We can speak more of it later. But today . . . Gráinne will be back from 1850 San Francisco," said Erszebet. "She has Blevins wrapped around her pinkie finger. Frink too. She also has the affection of Mr. Shiny-face Gordon Healey. She tried to seduce Mortimer but she says he is too much of a nerd."

"Geek," I corrected. "I'm a geek. If I were a nerd she'd have me in bed by now."

"There are other people," said Erszebet. "I do not know all of them."

Tristan's face still showed blank astonishment. "But what's her *goal*? What does she *want*?"

"She wants magic not to go away," said Erszebet. "That is not the same thing as letting it go away and then bringing it back."

"Holy shit," said Tristan under his breath. And then, as the full implication of this hit him, he repeated it much louder: "*Holy shit!*"

"I will leave," said Erszebet, with nervous decisiveness. "It is best if you leave too, Tristan Lyons."

"You're not going anywhere without me," said Tristan. "Not until you've told me everything you know."

Erszebet's breathing suddenly seemed labored, as if it were dawning on her that she couldn't casually walk away from her aborted mission. "I have already told you almost everything. But I will stay with you until we figure out how to help Melisande."

"Damn right you will," said Tristan.

"That is *my choice*," she informed him, rebounding back to the fierce and scornful witch around whom we all love to walk on eggshells. "Do not treat me like I do not have a choice in this. It was my choice right now not to send you back to the Ice Age. I could have done it like *that*"— she snapped her fingers for emphasis. "Do *not* treat me like I have done something wrong. I have done something *right*. You will appreciate that or I will walk away."

Tristan collected himself. "Okay," he said. "You're right. Thank you for not annihilating me when you had the chance, I realize that maybe wasn't easy for you." A brief pause as he considered options. "We'll go to Frank Oda's house and bring him up to date." He turned to me. "You're logged in as being here with us right now. If we disappear they'll want to know what you know. You should probably get out of here with us."

"We have an hour," I pointed out.

"What do you mean?" Tristan asked.

I'd already punched in the commands to power down the ODEC. "Gráinne can't come back until at least one of the ODECs is turned on for her." I was checking out the day's schedule on a monitor. "Earliest that could happen is an hour from now. During that time, I'll get as much intel as I can and get it out of the building." And because Tristan hesitated: "I'm on Team Oda. I don't care about the rest of it."

"We should go," said Erszebet to Tristan, heading back into the bio-containment ward, which was the only way out. "Everyone arrives soon. Let's be far away."

They left, and I did some deep-breathing exercises to lower my heart rate back to normal, and then went about my morning as if it were just another day. Except that I also quietly plugged my biggest flash drive into my desktop computer, and began to download as much of ODIN as possible. The whole ODIN system—all of the message threads, NDAs, HR records, DEDE reports, security camera video, and other bureau-cratic junk that had piled up on our servers during the five years that DODO had been in existence—would have filled my flash drive a thou-sand times over, so I tried to be selective, searching for documents that referenced Mel, Tristan, Blevins, and other key names, and focusing on certain ranges of dates when it seemed like a lot of important shit had gone down—like Halloween. Even so I ended up accidentally grabbing a lot of stuff like the sexual harassment policy that I didn't really want or need, but I didn't have time to be more selective. Now that it's all up on GRIMNIR I can maybe go through and prune it later.

I kept my head down as people came in and the office filled up as on any other day, except that head count was low because a lot of people were taking vacation. My cube is on the edge of the R&D group area, so I saw Dr. Oda come in and do a stand-up meeting with the crew that was going to be taking the ATTO out on the road—a driver, obviously, plus a MUON and two technicians who were going to be in the back, operating the equipment and running tests. Nothing too fancy—they just wanted to verify that the ATTO's onboard power supply and comms features would operate nominally while the thing was bouncing around in real-world traffic conditions.

My cube is also in earshot of the big open stairwell that runs up the middle of the building and so eventually I heard Gráinne's voice—she had returned from the San Francisco DTAP, without Mel. I heard her go up to the floor above me and enter Blevins's office. The door closed, and there were a few minutes of calm-before-the-storm before voices were raised and people up there started looking stressed out. A couple of DOSECOPS personnel came up the stairs double-time and blew past Blevins's re-ceptionist into his office and there was a lot more jawing. I was sitting there trying to be cool, watching the progress bar on my screen, won-dering whether I should just yank the thumb drive and get out of there.

Then the decision was made for me by a DOSECOP who had ap-proached me from behind, a little bit sneaky-like, and told me I was wanted in Blevins's office immediately. I made a glance toward the stairwell and saw another DOSECOP loitering there, keeping me in the corner of his eye, so I figured they had orders not to let me just bolt. So I got up and went up the stairs into Blevins's office. He and Gráinne were in there with two of the higher-ranking DOSECOPS officers, in-cluding Major Isobel Sloane, who I kinda wondered if Gráinne had a bit of an influence over. Blevins was in his big leather swivel chair and Gráinne was standing behind him, sort of hovering, and both of them were glancing between me and a monitor on Blevins's desk.

"Where be they, then?" Gráinne demanded, eyes fixed on me in a way that made me feel like a prey animal.

"Who?" I asked, trying to look stupid, which is actually something I'm pretty good at when I have to be.

"Where's Colonel Lyons?" demanded Blevins. "We know he and Erszebet came into the building early this morning within moments of your arrival, and that they both left a short time later."

And then Blevins pivoted the monitor around and let me see some security camera footage from earlier that morning: yours truly talking to Tristan and Erszebet.

I have no idea what kind of look was on my face at that moment, but

I can tell you how *they* looked: Blevins was sort of blank-faced and un-nerved, while Gráinne was trying to kill me with her eyes.

"Yeah, I saw them, but they had a fight about something and they both stormed out. I wasn't really paying attention because I'm a little hungover and anyhow those two are always bickering. I think Erszebet said she was going home."

"It's a lying bit of treachery, is this one," Gráinne declared.

And then I glanced down at Blevins and saw a change come over his face. I know magic can't work outside of an ODEC or an ATTO and that Blevins's office was neither of those, but I swear it was like seeing a Jedi mind trick in action. Whatever Gráinne had done to Blevins dur-ing all of that time they'd spent together in ATTOs conducting psy-ops "research," it still worked on him somehow. Maybe it wasn't magic at all. Maybe it was just plain old psychological influence. But it was clear to me in that moment that Blevins had been reduced to a marionette.

But not a very precisely controlled one, apparently.

"You," announced Blevins, with a flip of his manicured gray mane, "are fired."

"Don't be firing him now!" Gráinne objected. "You want to be inter-rogating him, you're not allowed to do that if he's not yours anymore."

I caught the eye of Major Sloane, the ranking DOSECOPS officer, and I thought maybe she was taken aback a little too, so I was maybe mis-taken about thinking she was Gráinne's minion. I pointed out, "You're not allowed to do it anyway because this is a free country and we don't just interrogate people here. Maybe Major Sloane could explain some of the legalities."

Blevins thought about it for a moment, which was fine with me—I just needed time to download as much of the ODIN database as pos-sible. Major Sloane looked back at me like she was taking the point I was making.

Then Blevins called out to his admin that he wanted General Frink on the line as soon as possible, to discuss a matter of national security.

"Where's Mel?" I asked Gráinne.

"Detained in San Francisco," she answered, sort of indignant, like how dare I even.

Getting Frink on the line happened incredibly quickly, apparently he was taking the day off with family and so he just answered his phone. The admin patched him through on voice and Blevins went off on a rambling, bizarro version of the last couple of days' events, talking about how Mel was AWOL and now Tristan and Erszebet were up to no good and assumed to be on the lam with important national security secrets, and I, Mortimer, was in cahoots with them. And he couldn't just call the cops because national security this and classified that, and so he wanted to invoke special powers and procedures and basically send out a DOSECOPS squad to round up Tristan and Erszebet and just let the chips fall where they may in terms of lawyers and arrest warrants and all of those other minor technicalities. Every so often he'd pause for breath and General Frink would grunt into the phone like, *Yeah, I'm still here, I'm with you, bro.* Finally Blevins didn't so much finish up as wind down for lack of anything more to say and Frink says, "I am authorizing you to mobilize the DOSECOPS Extra-Facility Ops Team and get this done as surgically as you can."

Now, I'd never even heard of the EFOT before, so its existence must have been a pretty closely guarded secret, but everyone else in the room seemed to know exactly what it was. Major Sloane nodded and said, "Already mobilized, General Frink. When I got word earlier this morning that trouble was brewing, I sent out the call. We have two squads in the ready room fully armed and armored, deployable on short notice." As if reassuring herself this was the case, she unlocked her phone and scanned her eyes over some information.

"Well done," Frink said over the phone.

"And what is the word from our surveillance team at the East-Oda residence?" Blevins asked. I guess I shouldn't have been surprised they'd already covered that angle.

"Sir, Professor Oda is still on the premises here, of course," said Sloane, "but Colonel Lyons and Erszebet were just reported at the residence with Mrs. East-Oda. Somehow they got in without being spotted, but they got careless once they were in there, and surveillance saw them in the kitchen."

"What are the odds that if we go in quickly, EFOT can take them into custody without it becoming a cause célèbre in the neighborhood?" Blevins asked.

"Depends on whether Tristan puts up a fight," said Major Sloane, "but I don't imagine he would."

"Very well," said Blevins. "Major Sloane, I am ordering you to deploy the EFOT squads to the East-Oda residence and—"

He stopped in midsentence, a little surprised because every phone in the room had started ringing. Even mine. And there was a bit of a funny moment, just then—not "ha-ha" funny—when Gráinne clearly didn't know what to do. Because Gráinne didn't have a phone. And it was clear from the look on her face that she hadn't been expecting this interruption—whatever it was.

Everyone else was looking at their phones, so I did too, and what I saw was a text from one of the R&D crew saying, "OMG is that the ATTO on Channel 5?" And for a second I didn't even catch the reference. I thought he was referring to some internal top-secret communications channel. It took a minute to realize he was talking about *the local television network news station*.

Meanwhile there's all kinds of confusion and consternation from others in the room, everyone shouting into their phones with their fingers plugged into the other ear, Gráinne looking around with kind of a wild desperate expression. "Dr. Blevins, can that thing stream live television?" I asked, nodding at his computer.

"I haven't the faintest idea," he said. "You're the sysadmin."

"Point taken," I said. "Let's all trot downstairs to my workstation and I'll pull up the stream." And before any orders could be issued to the contrary I ducked out the door and headed down the stairs. Frankly I didn't care whether they followed me or not, but when I reached my cubicle and looked back over my shoulder I saw them all traipsing along behind me, on their phones or whatever, and all around the whole office was in pandemonium. I sat down and plucked the flash drive out of my workstation and slipped it into the little cargo pocket down on the calf section of my tactical pants, and then cleared my screen and brought up the live news feed from the local network TV station.

And what we were seeing was the front of a Walmart, and the caption on the screen said it was in Lexington, Massachusetts. The same store where Magnus had hightailed it to a few weeks ago, before he'd coerced Constance Billy into Sending him back to Viking Paradise or wherever.

The entire front of the store—the glass entryway where they keep the shopping carts—had been punched in by a huge impact, all the windows destroyed.

Embedded in the middle of all that destruction we could see the rear of a tractor-trailer rig that had obviously just been driven straight into the front of the building at high speed, and come to rest just inside the store. Looked like it had obliterated some checkout lanes en route.

The rig was a common type seen around port facilities: a steel shipping container resting on the bed of a trailer. The shipping container was green, with rust spots.

We had all seen it before.

It was the ATTO.

Before I could ask the question, Major Sloane—who'd been on the phone—looked up at Blevins and said, "Confirmed. We lost contact with it immediately after it left the facility. Obviously, it was hijacked."

"Police radio transmissions report several large naked Caucasian males have emerged from the shipping container and are taking hostages," said the TV reporter.

Gráinne was the first to put it together. "Magnus!" she hissed, and then let fly with a torrent of rage in what I assumed was Gaelic. She's always been pretty emotional, but I'd never seen her just completely lose it before. She'd have torn Magnus apart with her fingernails if he'd been in the room.

"Major Sloane," Blevins said, "get the EFOT squads and everything else you have to that Walmart immediately."

Everyone split up. I trotted downstairs and walked out the front door and around the corner. And then I ran like a motherfucker. I just had a feeling it would be for the best.

So that was the moment I went from being a geek with the coolest job a recent CS grad from MIT could ever in a thousand years hope to find . . . to being a renegade. A serious renegade. Anonymous has got nothing on me.

That's how we ended up here at the Odas' place. I'm not even sure how Frank himself got back here. I mean, there's an argument we should just GTF out of here and try to disappear, but (1) disappearing is hard and (2) we can't just ditch the Odas and (3) we haven't violated any laws and so there's no reason the Cambridge PD should give a crap one way or the other.

Rebecca is (natch) making us some tea. I'm not sure when she will relax her jaw muscles enough to ever open her mouth again, but that doesn't mean she wants to throw us out.

We're sort of expecting Blevins will be sending someone to assassinate us, at least figuratively, very soon. Which is why I wanted to get this whole story written and uploaded.

Journal Entry of
Rebecca East‑Oda
FRIDAY AFTER THANKSGIVING

Temperature 38F, and never mind about the rest of it.

Extraordinary development: Tristan, Erszebet, and Mortimer have taken up residence in the basement and we presume Frank is no longer an employee of DODO, but it's all rather disordered at the moment. The local news is airing the most remarkable story about a raid at the Lexington Walmart. Mel is stuck in 1851 London, thanks to the machinations of Gráinne. Tristan and Frank immediately preoccupied with sorting out how to build a homemade ODEC in the basement so that if Mel can find a KCW, she will have a safe re-entry point to the modern day (although since she wouldn't know we had it, how would she know to be Sent there? Never mind. Better than taking no action.). Frank suggested shanghaiing one of the new ATTOs, toward which he has a wounded proprietary pride—ATTO #1 seems to be embedded in the aforementioned Walmart with naked berserkers pouring out of it, but three others have been constructed and six more are nearly complete. Mortimer is trying to set up a secure mini-intranet in our basement, as he has a flash drive called GRIMNIR with an enormous amount of ODIN material on it and he wants to upload it someplace stable so that it can't fall out of one of the pockets of his ludicrous trousers. The cats have disappeared in the chaos.

THE LAY OF WALMART

TRANSLATOR'S NOTE (CONTD.): Part 2, written in ballpoint pen on printer paper, was found in the ruins of a Walmart in suburban Boston, Massachusetts, following a bloody siege by persons described in media reports as a gang of methamphetamine addicts connected with the Russian mafia.

PART 2

Ingibjörg and those of her ilk
Sent me and Magnus to more ditapps
Than memory can contain. Twenty and two
Were the reckless recruits, all renowned warriors.

On Sverðvík's shore they stood, steaming,
Ready for the recital. Tales from Tóki,
Told many times, from Magnus's memories.
Mead he served to the men, full horns.

Looming from a longship's proud prow, he spoke.
"The ship we sail today, fighting the Fatlanders
Is but a box, oarless, ordinary. ATTO they name it.
To it Ingibjörg Sends me. It's on a great cart.

"Vikings love to shove ships
Up onto the shores of realms ready for ruin.
Just so, I'll attack with the ATTO
The glass gates of the Walmart

"Like a dagger, driving deep, not stopping
Till the blue-vested guard, the till-keepers,
Towers of trifles, the cart crushes,
Ramming, reaming out of its way.

"Furious Ingibjörg, future-fearing,
By then will have Sent Storolf." Magnus's sword
Swung round toward he of that name,
Grizzled but great-framed, giant-killer.

Storolf recited: "Inside of the ATTO are
Oddments, weird wares, dangerous distractions.
I ignore them. Brace my body on the bulkhead.
Ride through the ruin of the glass gates.

"Silence is my signal to dart to the door.
From it I face east down a wide way.
Vexing my vision, many marvels. Ignore them.
Magnus my guide. I go where he shows me.

"Eastward, thence, lies victory for vikings.
Counting the cairns, the merchandise-mounds.
Standing in the center of the wide east-west way,
Stop at the sixth. Atop it's an image:

"A fair lass, tresses flowing,
Like the lush Linndalsfallet,
Where it rushes over rocks,
Teeth shining like Snæfellsjökull.

"Cradled in the lass's hands, a bottle.
Bewitching brew, beautifying the hair.
Below it, many more such, stacked like soldiers.
That is the landmark that leads me to the left.

"A long lane, laden with loot.
Its Rune is like Berkano: the Beginning.
Its number, one score and five.
Let it lead me north. Little more to say,

"For in fewer than five paces
Is what my hand has hungered for

Since I found myself in Fatland,
Alone and naked: Numberless knives, new and needy."

"Furious Ingibjörg, future‑fearing,
By then will have brought Brand." Magnus's sword
Swung round toward he of that name,
Berserker of Zealand, brutal and bearlike.

Brand recited: "Vexing my vision, many marvels.
Storolf shows my way. Stop not where he does.
Brand goes beyond. Count cairns thrice more.
Number nine is a doll‑dump: toddlers' toys

"Painted purple and pink, smiling like simpletons,
Box‑bound. Brand there turns right.
A long lane, laden with loot.
Shopkeepers screaming. Pay no mind.

"Clashing carts may cause trouble. Don't be deterred.
Vikings can vault them, berserkers bash them aside.
All the way to the wall goes Brand.
Heaped there are hammers. Axes also.

"Spades, saws on long shafts, all manner
Of death‑dealers, racked and ready
Or stacked like firewood on the floor.
Commandeer a cart, kill its keeper if need be,

"Fill it full of those death‑dealers, leave nothing
That might be handy for hewing heads
And severing sinews in the struggle to come."
Thus the berserker, bright‑eyed, blood‑lusting.

"Furious Ingibjörg, future‑fearing,
By then has Halfdan Sent." Magnus's sword
Swung round toward he of that name,
White‑bearded king‑slayer, lord of legend.

Halfdan recited: "Vexing my vision, many marvels.
Ignoring them, I wait. Ingibjörg sends more.
In the meantime, knives from Storolf,
Axes and hammers from Brand, harden my hand.

"All told, my band is four. My companions three
Are Thorolf, Bild, and Glama. Travel to the tenth cairn.
Turn to the left. Toys stacked to the ceiling.
Do not let them beguile the eye.

"Long lanes, laden with loot.
Wide ways, well made for waging war,
Like the roads of the red-crested Romans
Ordered just so, as warp and weft.

"Too many for merchants to memorize,
Marked, therefore, with runes they can read.
Romans wrote them first. The fat ones stole them,
As well as Arabs' numerals, arranged below.

"For each district of the treasure-town,
A Roman rune written, raised high.
For each lane lying below it,
An Arabic number to know it.

"Their runes resemble ours often.
Others are different. One's like a fish-hook.
That's in the northeast of the store,
Norsemen's native land, all the good gear.

"Forests of fishing-poles you can see from afar.
Ropes for rigging. Machetes for making way
Or bringing battle. Don't be delayed though.
Go till glass gleams on all sides. Behind those wide
    windows,

"Boxes, brick-sized, written with runes, stacked to
    the ceiling.
Glass is nothing to Glama. Hammer in hand, he has at it
Shears shelves, loots little boxes, carrying them in carts
Down long lanes to the wall of the wonder windows.

"Halfdan hastens down the glass-lined lane
Till the way to the wall's barred by a counter.
Behind it, bang-sticks of the Fatlanders
Counter-keepers looking askance.

"They're the only true foes we must fight at first.
Don't be deceived that there's no swords at their sides.
Bang-sticks instead, shooting sling-stones
Faster and more fearsome than arrows.

"At a distance they're deadly. Get close quick.
For of fighting at arm's length, axe to axe
They know nothing. Rush at them right away
If their hands are empty. Lie low otherwise.

"Hunker down, holding my tongue,
Till I hear Heid, who's the only one
Who can get close to the guards.
When the shield-maid has their attention,

"That's the time to burst in bravely."
Thus Halfdan, gray-hamed, picked out for his patience.

Magnus's sword-tip, swinging this way and that
Picked out each warrior, each shield-maid.

In turn, each told the tale, written by Tóki,
Foretelling the future of what was to come,
The doom to descend on the Fatlanders' storehouse,
What deeds each warrior would do, and when.

Under the awning of the longship, idle till now,
Ingibjörg waited, sipping stew of spotted mushrooms,
Eyes lazy, but half in this world,
Fingers fondling her broom-twigs.

Magnus met her there, sharing the shade,
Smelling the scent of eldritch herbs,
Gathered round the gunwales, we felt the glamour.
Ingibjörg had Sent him, sticks thrown, die cast.

Storolf she Sent next, blade-bringer.
Brand the berserker, Halfdan the wise,
Heid the shield-maiden, Glama, Bild, Thorolf.
Tóki was taken. Ship sank from my sight.

I beheld a big box, shiny steel.
It must be the ATTO. I darted to the door.
Vexing my vision, many marvels. I ignored them.
Magnus my guide. I went where he showed me.

North of the nose of the great cart, the ATTO-bearer,
Where it had crashed to a halt after driving deep,
A forest of fabric, as had been foretold:
Clothing of all colors, made for men and women,

Bigger than any bazaar. Beyond that, the marvel
Magnus had mentioned, too strange to speak of:
Wonder-windows, a wall of them. The great gift
Of the Fatlanders is these: panes of perfect glass

Showing not what lies beyond them,
But images, effigies, prophecies, wonders.
Painted in piercing light, melding many hues.
Bright as berries, flickering like fire.

Like the windows of Christian cathedrals
When lanced by the light of the sun.

But not frozen forever, as those are;
Images in movement, flashing and flitting.

Tóki was here to take treasure,
Reading the runes in those windows.
North went I, wandering in the wake
Of the shield-maiden Heid. Her hair

Was braided in back, hanging below
Brushing bare buttocks. Walking behind,
My gaze was beguiled. Gladly I'd go
To battle behind one such as Heid.

She raised her arms, baring herself
To a shocked shopper, a fat woman
Fondling fabrics. Heid, heedless,
Elbows bent, hands swung down behind head.

A knife she held there, stolen by Storolf,
Sheathed safely. She stuck it into her braid
Where the tresses came together at the nape of her neck.
Tucked in, held by her hair, until needed.

Remembering Magnus, Tóki took trousers,
Sacking a shelf-load, but went onward
North to the wonder-wall. East turned Heid.
Tóki's eyes tracked her. She broke into a run.

Screams escaped from her mouth. Not war-whoops
But cries of terror. Not a word of the Angle-speech
Heid spoke. No matter. The men it was meant for
Heard it, and heeded. Heid was now bound

For the bang-sticks. Kept in that corner
Were the weapons of Walmart. Three guards
Gathered there, wondering what had happened.
Cart's crash, shoppers' screams, fleeing Fatlanders

Alarm had raised. And now a lass, not a stitch on,
Screaming for succour, coming on at a run.
What harm could she do them? Into the arms
Of the first Heid threw herself.

Out from the braid came that blade,
And into the back of his neck. As he dropped,
She closed on the next, arm whirring.
The third aimed his bang-stick, ready to shoot

Till an axe struck home in his head,
Hurled by Thorolf, part of Halfdan's band,
Running round from the long lanes
Marked by the rune of the fish-hook.

The first part of the fight was now finished.
From the ATTO, attackers kept coming.
Asmund, Icelandic berserker, far-famed.
Hrani, the shipwright from Sweden.

Arngrim, Hjorvard, Yngvar, Snorri,
Mighty Thord. Magnus gave each man a task.
Sending them this way and that.
Hostages were herded and held.

Strange sheets of wood, wide and flat,
Formed the flanks of a new fortress
Wrapped and roofed in bright blue tarpaulins
Lashed down with lines.

The West-march of the Walmart
Held all the food in the world,
Bottled beer by the boatload,
Frost-kept food, milk and meat.

Setting up for a siege behind barricades
The Norsemen fetched food, collected clothing,

Turkish trousers with flies in the front
Kept closed with clever contraptions,

Tiny teeth, meshing like millipedes' legs,
Gnashing, knitting, concealing the naked.
Zipper the Fatlanders called it.
Cock,catcher it was to Hunfast, the hapless.

Chains, padlocks, ropes of wrought steel
Fetched forth from the long lanes
Curved round the captives' necks.
But all turned to the source of a sound,

A big bang, like the trunk of a tree
Snapping in a storm, making all deaf.
A Fatlander, about to be fettered
And fastened to the fortress's side,

Had pulled out a small bang,stick,
Concealed in his clothes, shot a stone,
Struck Saemundr, Yngvar's son,
Beloved brother, oar,puller, sword,swinger.

He had taken on a troll once, outside of Eiðar,
Bested him in battle, hand to hand.
But the bang,stick's stone had struck a lung,
Saemundr's life,blood gushed out of his mouth.

He fell like a tall tree. Magnus took a machete,
Held it in the hero's hand, sent him to Valhalla.
Another bang bloodied our ears. Thord cursed.
A stone had struck him in the arm.

A third bang as Thord threw down, thrashed
The man who'd murdered Saemundr,
The coward who killed from afar.
The stone struck no one, hewing a hole

In the wooden wall, tearing the tarpaulin.
Face down on the floor, the Fatlander
Rose not again. Murder-loving Magnus,
Riven by rage, grabbed an axe,

Swung it into the spine of the shooter,
Severing two ribs, just by the backbone,
Adjusted his aim, swung again,
Rending the ribcage, separating the spine.

The shooter's screams went silent
As wind whistled through those wounds.
His struggles ceased. Magnus opened the man
Like the spreading wings of an eagle, blood-bright,
Lungs loose, open to the air now.
A clashing cart was fetched, dumped out,
Making room for the murderer's remains.

Magnus shoved him out through the glass gates.
Fatlanders' fear-cries resounded, Sirens screamed.
Magnus made his way back to the fast fortress
We'd made around the wonder-windows.

Translator's note: "The Lay of Walmart" breaks off at this point.
Surveillance camera footage, combined with eyewitness accounts
compiled from surviving hostages, agree that from this point onward
the author, Tóki, was kept busy learning how to extract cartographical
data from computers in the home electronics section.

Journal Entry of
Rebecca East~Oda
NEXT DAY, I.E.,
SATURDAY AFTER THANKSGIVING

Temperature 39F.

Our dining area has been designated a "War Room" and is now matted with cables of various descriptions. Most of these have something to do with Mortimer's efforts to "boot up" the new GRIMNIR system, which is going to be his improvised ragtag replacement for ODIN. It runs on something called the dark net, of which the less said, the better. Fielded a telephone call from a representative of the cable television company complaining that we have been making all sorts of connections to dodgy servers and are in danger of having our service cut off. Played the little old lady card, feigned ignorance, requested technical support which I knew would hold them off for days.

A few years ago when we dug the book out of the vegetable garden, and made all of that money, and transferred the property to the East House Trust, and ceased to become its legal owners, it felt as if I had sawed my right leg off. But only for a few days. When it became obvious that this made absolutely no practical difference, I forgot it had happened. Since then it has only entered my awareness when we receive a property tax bill or some such, and I see the official name on the address label. Today, however, it is much on my mind, as it gives me a sort of detached emotional status from which to view all of these goings-on. SUVs, obviously belonging to some sort of government agency, are parked on the streets around us, drawing comment from the neighbors. Presumably they are spying on us, but they make no effort to cross the property line.

At two in the morning, three people climbed over the back fence and caused us all sorts of alarm before we recognized them: Felix Dorn, Esme Overkleeft, and Julie Lee. They had got together for late-night drinks at the Apostolic Café and made the decision to defect from DODO to join our little ragtag reboot thereof (Julie being the obvious instigator given her romance with Mortimer). Then they all stayed up all night talking. Now they are sleeping in shifts in Mei's old room, the guest room, and the floor of my sewing room. (Chira Lajani, they report, counts herself among us in spirit, but dares not defect openly from DODO lest it interfere with her younger siblings' immigration status. She might be able to function as a mole, but these are early days yet.)

From them we were able to get more news of what has been go-- ing on at the Walmart. Our access to the message traffic on the ODIN system was of course cut off the moment Mortimer left the building, and since then we were limited to what we could glean from television news reports and Internet rumors. The powers that be at DODO—which by this point basically means Gráinne, since she seems to control Blevins absolutely—are not even aware that Felix, Esme, and Julie have come over to our side, and may not appreciate that fact until the three of them fail to show up for work on Monday morning. In the meantime they still have access to the ODIN system over their phones.

This has enabled us to solve a riddle that bedeviled our minds from the very beginning of Magnus's siege at the Walmart.

Clearly, Magnus made the rounds of the Viking world and re-cruited a sort of all-star team of marauders who were willing to follow his lead.

And on one level it makes sense for them to raid a Walmart, which to them would be a poorly guarded storehouse of near-infinite wealth.

But beyond that it makes no sense at all. They must either stay in the present, or return to the past via the ATTO.

If they stay in the present, they will inevitably be caught, tried, and put in prison. Magnus must know this.

If they return to the past, they'll do so naked and empty-handed. Why, therefore, go to the effort of sacking a Walmart and gathering loot they can't take with them? Magnus must understand this too.

According to the "over the fence" gang—Julie, Felix, and Esme—the answer was pieced together yesterday afternoon by the DOSECOPS people who have access to surveillance camera footage from the Walmart.

As soon as they had the electronics department fortified behind plywood and blue tarps, and their hostages secured (except for the one unfortunate who was rolled out into the parking lot after being blood-eagled), Magnus raided the pharmacy section and secured a large amount of lidocaine, which is a topical anesthetic.

In the meanwhile, some of the hostages were being chained to computers in the electronics section and put to work downloading information on certain topics. To make a long story short, it appears that during his sojourn in the present day, Magnus became aware of the fact that the New World contained an amount of gold and silver that was beyond the dreams of the most avaricious Vikings. Their longships were perfectly capable of making the voyage across the Atlantic by hopping from Iceland to Greenland to Newfoundland and thence down the coast. What they lacked was *information*: nautical charts showing the way, and land maps of Mexico and Peru and other gold-rich areas. And so this is the sort of information that the hostages were put to work downloading and printing out on paper.

Magnus's Vikings then took turns lying facedown on the floor. Lidocaine was smeared on their bare backs and the treasure maps carved into their skin using hobby knives from the store's art supply section.

This procedure has apparently been going on all night. When the DOSECOPS people understood what was going on, they cut power to the building. But the Vikings were ready for that with candles and lamps from the camping section, and by then they had already printed out everything they needed on paper. The ATTO has its own built-in power supply capable of running for days; Frank made sure of that. One of DODO's spy drones has been circling above the store and has been picking up bursts of GLAAMR suggesting that some of the Vikings are already being Sent back. So they must have a witch among them who is ensconced in the ATTO doing the Sending and god only knows what else.

All of this information is several hours old, and I'm writing it late Saturday morning. The television news shows no change in status at the Walmart, which of course doesn't reflect what might be happening within the ATTO; the police haven't raided yet, no hostages have been released; it is a standoff.

It appears that what is going to happen—or already has happened, many centuries ago, on this or some other Strand—is that Magnus's band of "all-star" berserkers will end up in tenth-century Scandinavia with detailed maps carved into their backs showing them how to traverse the Atlantic and Caribbean and sack the Americas for their unimaginable wealth of precious metals, then bring it all back to Scandinavia, or anywhere else they feel like living.

It is difficult to see how this could be stopped. DODO could Send some DOers even further back in time to try to change history to somehow foil Magnus's plan, but two can play at that game—Magnus can just as well Send people further back yet to intercept the DOers, and so on.

Needless to say, any Strand on which Magnus's plan succeeds will have a very different future from the one we are living in. Tristan is of the opinion that DODO spy planes are probably flying high above Mexico City and Cuzco at this moment, looking for signs of GLAAMR indicating the temporal equivalent of a nuclear strike.

We all wish Melisande were among us to help us think it all through. Unfortunately she remains marooned. Mortimer, logging in to ODIN through Esme's phone, has been able to pull up some message traffic confirming that Gráinne Sent Mel to Victorian London in the summer of 1851—only weeks before the eclipse that marked the end of magic. By that time, the few remaining witches who could do magic at all were much enfeebled, especially in London, as that's where the Great Exhibition was, and thus there was an immense concentration of magic-dampening technology all amassed in one place. So there is great concern that even if Mel were able to land on her feet in that DTAP and make contact with a practicing witch, it would be too late to get her back. In any case, there is little we can do except try to provide a place for her to land. If she materializes in one of the existing ODECs, she'll immediately be in Gráinne's power. So we need to build or obtain an ODEC of our own. Frank, who has spent the last couple of years designing and constructing room-temperature ODECs, is of course the leading authority in the world when it comes to that. He seems to have had a premonition of what was to come (or perhaps he received a warning from the future?), for he has for the last few weeks been laying plans to improvise a room-temperature ODEC in our cellar. Many of the parts, he says, can be obtained from Home Depot, but others are highly specialized, including room-temperature superconductors that are easy to obtain with the resources of DODO at one's back but almost impossible for mere civilians to acquire.

UPDATE,
WRITTEN LATE SATURDAY

Television reveals that the siege has been lifted. The Walmart was stormed by SWAT teams after several hours had gone by with no sign of activity. The hostages were found bound and gagged with duct tape but otherwise unharmed. No arrests have been made; police are claiming that the perpetrators made their escape from the building by crawling along a sewer line, or some such nonsense.

On the television footage, which is all shot from a distance, using drones and helicopters with long lenses, it's possible to see two different groups of officers inside the Walmart: the local police SWAT team, which is roaming all over the store, and DODO's EFOT squad (whose existence we've all just learned about this weekend—sort of DOSECOPS on steroids), which has surrounded the tractor-trailer rig and is not allowing anyone else near it. Apparently the tractor and trailer were so badly damaged as to be unusable. Now, however, another tractor-trailer has showed up in the parking lot, as well as some sort of enormous forklift from Massport that is capable of picking the ATTO off of the one and transferring it to the other. I'm sure that the ATTO is about to disappear into the bowels of the military-industrial complex, never to be seen again.

Exchange of posts on "ATTO Operations"
ODIN channel
DAY 1949 (SUNDAY AFTER THANKSGIVING, YEAR 5)

Note: Posts recovered from a telephone belonging to Julie Lee, who had access to ODIN until the following day.

Post from MAJ Isobel Sloane, 00:16:
Here is yet another update—hopefully the last—from the Walmart. The obstructions that had been preventing the forklift from getting into the building were finally cleared away about an hour ago. We've had to work around the police crime scene teams. Since there is no particular urgency, we have taken a "go along, get along" approach, which is why it has been so slow. They were irritated by our insistence on padlocking the ATTO the moment we arrived and keeping people out of it, but thanks to some calls from on high (kudos to LTG Frink, I suppose) they eventually got the message that the ATTO was a no-go area on national security grounds.

The forklift is now maneuvering into position alongside the tractor-trailer and getting ready to move the ATTO.

Reply from LTG Octavian Frink, 00:21:
Thank you, MAJ Sloane, despite the late hour I am monitoring from my office at the Pentagon. What is the status of the ATTO itself? Has it suffered any damage?

From MAJ Sloane, 00:30:
It took superficial damage—one good reason for housing it in a beefy steel shipping container. From the fact that Magnus's team were successfully Sent into it and later Homed, we have ample evidence that it remains fully operational. The external status lights all show green.

BTW I don't know if you have video feed on this, but the forklift has removed it from the ruined rig now and is taking it into the parking lot. Should have it on the good rig in a couple of minutes.

From LTG Frink, 00:35:
Do we know how Magnus's personnel were Homed?

From MAJ Sloane, 00:37:
Haven't had time to do a full after-action report. Will analyze it. Presumably they had their own MUON in the ATTO and she Homed them one by one after they had the maps cut in their backs.

From LTG Frink, 00:40:
Is Dr. Blevins awake and monitoring this? I feel the need of some expert opinions. My understanding is that MUONs cannot Send or Home themselves; some other MUON must do it for them.

From MAJ Sloane, 00:45:
ATTO is now on the good rig and the truck driver is conducting routine inspection prior to departure. I'll ride shotgun with him. There is a security concern around possibility of media vehicles tailing us back to DODO HQ and so remainder of ETOF squads/vehicles will block streets and run interference until we are clear of the area.

From LTG Frink, 00:49:
I have confirmed with staff here that air space has been shut down, so you don't have to worry about media choppers. Drone frequencies being jammed.

From MAJ Sloane, 00:51:
LOL I see drones falling out of the sky all over the place. Very satisfying.

From LTG Frink, 00:52:

I have not seen a response to my query about MUONs being able to self-Send. Dr. Blevins must be out of commission.

From MAJ Sloane, 00:55:

Not an expert but my understanding is that they can't self-Send.

From LTG Frink, 00:56:

In that case, when Magnus's MUON had finished Homing all of Magnus's other personnel, what did she do? Remain in the ATTO? She would be marooned in the present day, correct?

From MAJ Sloane, 01:01:

General sitrep: truck driver reports good to go, have deployed DO-SECOPS personnel/vehicles for traffic management detail.

In answer to LTG Frink's last question, hostile MUON did not remain in the ATTO.

From LTG Frink, 01:02:

How do you know that?

From MAJ Sloane, 01:03:

Well, when we first entered the store at conclusion of the hostage situation, I went into the ATTO to check it. It was empty. We then padlocked the door. It has remained padlocked since.

From LTG Frink, 01:05:

I would like you to double-check it before departure.

From MAJ Sloane, 01:05:

Roger wilco. Stand by.

From LTG Frink, 01:15:

Has anyone on site heard from MAJ Sloane? I would like a sitrep. It has been ten minutes.

From MAJ Sloane, 01:19:

Sorry for delay, it was a mess in there. Everything is fine, proceeding to DODO HQ, will report in upon arrival.

From LTG Frink, 02:03:

It is very late and I want to turn in but would like positive confirmation that the ATTO is safe and sound at DODO HQ before I shut this damned thing off. I have not heard a sitrep in something like forty-five minutes. What is status? Major Sloane?

From LTG Frink, 02:05:

Major Sloane? Are you monitoring this channel?

   Will someone else on this channel please supply Major Sloane's phone number?

From 1LT Jesperson, 02:07:

She is not answering her phone. It went off the network after she checked the ATTO. It may have fallen out of her pocket there. ATTO is electromagnetically shielded.

From LTG Frink, 02:10:

So we have no way of tracking or communicating with Major Sloane?

From 1LT Jesperson, 02:11:

Correct.

From LTG Frink, 02:12:

Lieutenant Jesperson, where are you exactly?

From 1LT Jesperson, 02:13:
Down in DOSECOPS C4.

From LTG Frink, 02:14:
Has the ATTO arrived?

From 1LT Jesperson, 02:15:
Negative. DOSECOPS personnel standing by to receive it.

From LTG Frink, 02:16:
Patch me through to ranking DOSECOPS officer in escort vehicle.

From 1LT Jesperson, 02:18:
Escort vehicles already arrived.

From LTG Frink, 02:19:
Escort vehicles arrived without the vehicle they were escorting? How many?

From 1LT Jesperson, 02:19:
Both of them.

From LTG Frink, 02:20:
We only had two escort vehicles? What is remainder of DOSECOPS staff doing? Christmas shopping?

From 1LT Jesperson, 02:23:
Staking out the East-Oda residence, as per Dr. Blevins's orders.

From LTG Frink, 02:25:
I am pulling him out of slumberland right now. Am I to understand that we have lost the ATTO? Does anyone know where the ATTO is?

From Dr. Roger Blevins, 02:36:

Okie, unsettling news that we have temporarily lost track of the precise whereabouts of ATTO, but Boston's a small town, we'll find it in a jiffy once we get local police involved.

From LTG Frink, 02:41:

FOR FUCKS SAKE WE CANNOT GET LOCAL COPS INVOLVED! We have to track this down with national security resources.

From Dr. Blevins, 02:45:

Sorry, a bit groggy, not thinking straight. Of course you're right, Okie. But those resources are considerable as you know and how far could it have gone?

From LTG Frink, 02:49:

In an hour and a half? Approximately a hundred miles.

In case you are too groggy to remember Mr. Reinhardt's 7th grade geometry lessons, that implies a search area of 31,142 square miles.

Has it not occurred to any of you that if a MUON stayed behind in that thing, she could have played with people's minds? And that Magnus could by now have Sent more hostiles into it?

From 1LT Jesperson, 02:52:

General Frink, Dr. Blevins, all of this traffic is going out on the ATTO Operations channel which has wide distribution inside of DODO. Suggesting we switch over to DOSECOPS RESTRICTED channel. Please acknowledge.

From LTG Frink, 02:53:

Yes.

From Dr. Blevins, 02:53:

Acknowledged.   [message thread ends here]

Post by Felix Dorn on
"General" GRIMNIR channel
DAY 1949

As you all know, I'm not one for writing long reports, but Tristan is twisting my arm to jot down some notes on what I observed during my last couple of days at DODO. He wants this on the record so we can document and explain our actions if this all comes to light eventually.

During the last week or so I began to see message traffic on the "Deutsch" ODIN channel, which is simply a channel that is used by German-speaking staff members like me for general discussion.

To make a long story short, it was obvious from these messages that a DEDE to Prussia was being planned on short notice and that its date was unusually late—I could guess from some of the references that it was going to be the late 1840s or even the early 1850s.

DEDEs of that nature are extremely unusual because magic had already become very weak by that time and so there is a risk of the DOer ending up trapped in the past (as Mel seems to be now unfortunately). We don't even have any legit KCWs post about 1845 and so these DOers on the message threads were asking questions about some sketchy witches that we'd been in contact with circa 1840, wondering if they were still alive ten years later.

The DOers asking these questions were tough guys. Fighters and Snake Eaters. Not the kind of people you would send on a scouting or intel-gathering type of mission.

I started asking around, buying people beers, chewing the fat with the Chronotron staff, trying to get to the bottom of it. The whole thing just seemed weird to me, especially combined with Mel's very unusual DEDE in 1850 San Francisco and the one that had been planned for Tristan. As context you have to remember that the operational wing of DODO has been pretty much in mothballs for the last few months—

we've been winding up ops in different theaters but not starting anything new. This felt like something new, but also something very weird.

What I learned was that Blevins had been asking a lot of questions
about Berkowski, the photographer who took the daguerreotype of the
July 1851 solar eclipse that put a stake through the heart of magic. And
not just about him but about Daguerre and Niépce and Schulze and
some of the other inventors who worked on early forms of photography. Blevins had set up a small private channel on the ODIN system to
discuss his interest in this topic and had invited three of the Chronotron
geeks but was otherwise keeping it under wraps. I was able to talk to
one of those guys about it. He said it had been started a little after Halloween and that Gráinne was definitely in the loop, driving some of the
questions and the discussion.

Erszebet has come over to our side now and has confirmed, just
in the last few hours, that Gráinne has pretty much seized control of
Blevins's mind by repeatedly using some pretty hard-ass magic on him
during their many hours in the ATTO together.

What this all adds up to is that Gráinne is looking for a way to roll it
all back. She wants to change history so that photography, and other
magic-jamming technologies, were never developed in the first place.
Maybe it begins with assassinating Berkowski, which would push back
the end date by a few years, but that's just the beginning of what she
wants to do. She wants to morph our entire historical timeline into one
where science and technology never advanced out of the late medieval
age and magic still flourishes. To avoid Shear, she'll have to do it one
small change at a time. That implies a program that is going to be executed patiently over a long period of time, using the full resources of
the Chronotron and the ODECs (until there are no more Chronotrons
or ODECs because duh, to quote Mortimer). And that in turn means
she has to control the organization from the top down. Blevins she has
in her pocket. Mel and Tristan had to be gotten out of the way by other
means.

And she came close to nailing it on the first try. Two unexpected outcomes messed up her plan. First of all, Erszebet had a change of heart and decided not to Send Tristan into Gráinne's trap. And second, just at the moment when the EFOT squads were about to pounce on us and round us all up, Magnus launched his raid on the Walmart. It is obvious from the way Gráinne has reacted to this that she wasn't expecting it and she's furious.

So, the good news is that Tristan's safe and that Magnus has thrown a huge monkey wrench into whatever Gráinne was planning. The bad news is that we don't know how to get Mel back and that the full resources of the Department of Diachronic Operations are now at Gráinne's beck and call.

Diachronicle

In which I meet my final witch

TODAY I ACCEPTED A LOAN from my patrons to afford a custom-fitted corset, perhaps because I now know that I shall be wearing one for the rest of my days. The end of magic approaches and my last chance for escape has been denied me.

The Great Exhibition—that very event which had such a dreadful influence on magic's demise—provided me an opportunity to take the air at last. My patrons expressed an interest in attending it, now that the initial flood of visitors has calmed somewhat (it still bustles like a city inside), and allowed that I might go with them without any danger or embarrassment to myself.

I doubt that in the twenty-first century any gathering could marvel the general population the way that the Crystal Palace marvels today. An enormous glass building framed by iron— nearly a million square feet and more than one hundred feet high. In its sheer spectacle it rivals anything in Las Vegas. Within were tens of thousands of items and exhibits, visited by more than forty thousand people a day. It had been built essentially as a giant two-story greenhouse, leaving old-growth trees undisturbed on site and thus creating in certain open areas the quaint feeling of an antique movie set. (Except movies do not yet exist.) I was given leave to roam, with instructions to meet up at the reconstructed Medieval Court (between the Sculpture Garden and Africa) in two hours.

The wonders waiting within include all sorts of mechanical and technical marvels, and samples of the raw materials processed or created by them. Foucault's pendulum is there, hanging from a roof beam to demonstrate the rotation of the earth. There are envelope-folding machines, musical instruments, inventions from abroad and fabrics from everywhere, an elementary voting machine, at least two enormous diamonds (one pink), a rash of photographs and daguerreotypes (I avoided those, instinctively), tinned foods, a stuffed elephant or two, a locomotive, and for the price of a penny, the novel experience of—gasp!—public lavatories! And foodstuffs from all over the world, or at least the British Empire, which here in 1851 is nearly the same thing.

I had studied the catalog and exhibition layout ahead of time, naturally, and had plotted a course before we arrived. We entered via the vast, vaulted Southern Transept, between wares from China, Tunis, and India, and at the Crystal Fountain I bid my patrons au revoir and turned left. The air had the humid, peaceful heaviness of greenhouses. I hurried past offerings from Africa and Canada, Ceylon, Jersey, and Malta, past inventive labor-saving hardware for housework and industry, past sumptuous furniture and items of leather, fur, rock, paper, scissors (not a joke), and—wait for it—*hair*, then mounted stairs and continued westward until I had pressed on through the bustle of fascinated faces, all the way to the Western Nave, where I knew I'd find the telescopes and other lens-related hoo-haa items amongst the "philosophical instruments."

I had come here with the wan hope that astronomy might be of interest to witches, being as ancient as magic is. And I hoped perhaps my presence might leave a trace of glamour that only they could see—in which case perhaps I would be approached by one of them. A far-fetched wish, I realize, but I was in desperate straits (although not yet as desperate as I now feel).

My eyes scanned the crowd, wishing I knew what it was that identified somebody as a witch. Standing with a handsome older couple near one of the largest telescopes (Buron's, I believe the nameplate said) was a very beautiful young lady, perhaps twenty, who looked like Erszebet Karpathy.

Because it *was* Erszebet Karpathy.

To be honest, she did not look exactly like Erszebet in our era. While certainly grave and serious, her demeanor was lighter, her presence more buoyant. She was smiling at something the man had just said. It was a charming, unself-consciously girlish grin. She did not carry the weight of centuries upon her shoulders. She was truly, as they say, in the bloom of youth. In that first moment of recognition, I understood, in I way I could not have before, what all those decades of waiting for us had done to her spirit. For a passing moment I was pierced with guilt for what we had done by convincing her to preserve herself.

And then I realized, with a shock, that *this* was that moment. This was the moment she had referred to when first we'd met: the moment that I convinced her to stay alive into the twenty-first century.

Since she had indeed preserved herself, I already knew that I would be successful—apparently with only one Strand's effort! This suggested our encounter would be an easy one, and further—oh, the joy of it!—*she could Home me*. I was saved! I had never felt more grateful to her than I did that moment, although she had not officially even met me yet.

I took several hurried steps towards her, wondering how coy I should be, and then realizing I hadn't the time to be coy whatsoever.

"Miss Karpathy Erszebet?" I said, approaching with a polite but familiar smile.

She and the two older adults turned to look at me. As she sobered slightly, she looked more familiar, and her familiarity in that setting was so reassuring that I could barely keep myself from embracing her.

"Miss Karpathy, I am a friend of yours you haven't met yet," I said quietly, barely audible above the general hubbub. I had to risk assuming the two guardians knew her for a witch. "I have been Sent here with a very great request to ask."

She frowned, and looked confused. Then she glanced at the man and said, "*Papa, Ki ő?*" Then turned to me and said, in halting English, "Do you Hungarian? I can only some little bit English."

"*Kicsit,*" I said, wishing her native language was Akkadian or classical Hebrew or something I was more familiar with. Given how strong her accent was after at least a century in America, it should not have surprised me that she did not yet speak English, yet it was jarring to suddenly have a language barrier between us.

"I speak English," said the man. "I will be your translator." Seeing the wary look on my face, he said, with stern reassurance, "I assume you are working with a witch and perhaps somebody powerful."

"May we speak in private?" I asked.

He looked around at the crowd. "We hide in plain sight," he said. "We attract more attention if we huddle in a corner. Here nobody pays attention, we are ignored."

He had the air of a man unused to changing his mind, and for a moment I felt stymied.

"*Nem, Papa,*" said lovely young Erszebet, and gave me a shy smile. "*Én teázni vele. Azt szeretné gyakorolni az angol tudásom.*" To me: "We have tea, yes?"

With a sweetness and grace of movement, the pure fluidity of youth, she held her hand out to me with a smile, and smiled even more happily when I took it.

"*Add nekem néhány shillinget,*" she said over her shoulder to the man, whose solemnity melted. "*Én is fizetek vissza, amikor hazaérünk.*" He drew a coin from the wallet in his vest pocket, she accepted the money with a grateful smile and began to pull me through the crowd, down the stairs, to the West Refreshment Court (flanked by those exotic public lavatories). She selected a tea-cart surrounded by little tables and chairs full of flagging matrons.

When we were close to the tea-cart, she gave me a conspiratorial grin, her eyes twinkling as I had never known Erszebet's eyes to twinkle. "I speak very good English," she whispered in my ear. "But I do not want him to know that."

"Thank God," I said impulsively. "Erszebet, I am glad to hear it, because truly I must speak to you alone."

"Very well, let us speak over cakes and tea," she said, and, smiling, she held up the coin with a flourish.

When we had settled at a small table with our refreshments, she said, eyes still sparkling, "So you have been Sent from the future. That has never happened to me before and I am very happy to meet you. Please tell me about the future. Father would say it is wrong to ask that, but I am so curious. I hope it is better than the present. The present is very difficult for us, for so many reasons. Please tell me magic is repaired soon. Surely it must be, or you could not have been Sent."

I had never heard Erszebet speak so exuberantly, without an absence of rampaging insults, in all the time I'd known her. I hated that I had to be the one to give her the news.

"I am here to warn you that things will get much worse before they improve," I said, "and they can only improve at all if you will agree to the request I am about to make." I hesitated for a moment. Surely Erszebet knew many witches. Should I ask her to tell *all* of them to preserve themselves? Would that not give us more witches to collect in the twenty-first century?

And yet that would create such a muddle, and I had no Chronotron or even quipu to ask for clarity. I decided to stay within the bounds of what I knew we needed to accomplish. "And you must keep this request a secret. It is only for you."

"I love secrets," she said, grinning again. Grinning, she looked like a teenager. "I'm very good at keeping secrets." She lowered her voice to a whisper, and said confidingly, delighted with herself, "I have a secret lover my parents do not know about. Not even Mother suspects, and she's a very able witch!"

"I promise not to tell her you have a lover," I said, forcing myself to grin right back at her. "If you do not tell her this. But, Erszebet, this is something you cannot even tell your lover."

"That is easy, we do not actually *talk* very much," she said slyly, with the tiniest blush of a recent ex-virgin. She giggled.

Erszebet Karpathy giggled. It took so much willpower to keep my face smiling, to not close my eyes and shudder a bit at what I was about to ask of her.

"Erszebet, magic is about to end completely. Totally." She blinked, and suddenly was serious and attentive, vaguely more similar to the Erszebet I knew. "It will stay extinguished for many, many years, and then we will bring it back—you and I, and some other people." She blinked again, doe-eyed and speechless. "But, Erszebet, this is the most important part: it does not come back for such a long time that you would have died of old age first. So I have come here to tell you to cast a spell upon yourself that will prolong your life as long as possible. To slow your aging enough that you can live for two hundred years."

She looked almost in a state of shock. "Who are you?" she asked. "Who are you that would ask me to do this?"

"My name is Melisande Stokes, and I am your friend," I said. "I wish I did not have to ask this of you, but you, and only you, will be able to save magic someday—as long as you cast that spell upon yourself."

She gave me a distressed look—not the haughty irritation of my Erszebet, but a childlike confusion. "Why me?" she asked.

"I don't know," I admitted. I had never stopped to think about this, since my experience of our relationship was that she had reached out to me. "Perhaps it is because fate has placed me here at this moment in time, when magic is about to end. It is perhaps that random. I don't honestly know. What I do know is that it is your destiny to fix it. Extend your life, and Send me back to my own time, and we will meet there eventually and work together."

Her dark green eyes darted from side to side as she considered this. "If this news is true, then I would prefer," she said, "that I extend both our lives and you go through this journey with me.

Then when the time comes, we will meet your colleagues and work together."

I believe my heart actually stopped for a beat. "That's not possible," I said, thinking fast. "I already exist in that time period, I will be an old woman and a young one simultaneously on the same Strand. Surely that will cause *diakrónikus nyírás*."

She thought this over, her mouth setting into a harder line now, a foreshadowing of the Erszebet to come. "This is a terrible thing you are asking me," she said. "A very, *very* difficult thing."

"I realize that, Erszebet," I said. "But so important. And you choose to do it. And it is the right thing. You are there with me, in the future, and—" I hesitated. It would be a lie to tell her that she was glad of making that choice. She had only ever expressed regret and bitterness. But I had to convince her to do it. "In the future you know that it's the right thing to have done."

She stared at me levelly a moment. "Am I happy?" she asked. "Am I joyful? My lover tells me I am joyful. It is my favorite thing to be these days." I stared at her like a ~~deer in headlights~~ startled fawn, and she knew the answer before I could prevaricate. "I see," she said. "Not happy. Not joyful."

"But . . . satisfied that you have done the right thing," I insisted. "This makes you the most significant witch in the history of the world."

"And if I say no?"

"Magic will end forever, completely, seventeen days from now, and it will never return." I realized that was likely a lie, that some agent from some other nation would still manage to recruit some other witch—that I was asking this not for the good of magic but only for the good of the United States' ability to close the Magic Gap. I chose not to clarify this point.

"So," she said, "magic will end in seventeen days no matter what I do, but in the next seventeen days, if I put this spell on myself, I will bring it back someday."

"Yes."

"What do I do for all the many long years that I am alive? How do I make my way? I am trained only to do magic."

"I don't know," I said, taken aback. "But I know that you land on your feet. When we meet, more than a century from now, you have been staying somewhere for many years where all your needs are taken care of, so somehow you must stumble across money. Perhaps you marry a wealthy man and inherit his fortune. Perhaps you become a schoolteacher or scientist or take up with the Fuggers—remember that name, Erszebet, and ODEC, and Facebook, and—" My mind whirled: What else was I supposed to tell her? What else had the ancient Erszebet claimed I'd told her? "I don't know, Erszebet. I wish I did. All I know is that if you had not agreed to do this, I would not be here right now."

"I Sent you back?"

"Not this time. But most of the times that I have been Sent places, you Send me."

She frowned. "Why do you want to be Sent so often?"

"We work for the government of the United States. It requires us to move around through time."

Her eyes brightened for a moment. "Will I do that too? Move around in time?"

"You never expressed an interest, but I suppose you could. We can discuss it—but only if you agree to put the spell on yourself and Send me forward to my own time."

She pursed her lips. "Why does magic end in seventeen days?"

"It's very complicated," I said. "Technology—like everything you see here in the Crystal Palace—it interferes with magic. In just over a fortnight, an extremely significant technological achievement will occur and that will end magic."

"Why not just prevent the technological achievement?" asked Erszebet.

"It's too important to the rest of the world."

"More important than *magic*?"

"Yes," I said, and she looked displeased in a way that made it clear this would be harder than I'd anticipated.

"Technology should not be more important than magic," she said earnestly. Very earnestly, and naively, because she was actually only nineteen years old. Not one hundred and eighty appearing to be nineteen. "I will interfere with this technology. What is it?"

"It's too far away," I said. "It's something that happens in Prussia."

"I have friends in Prussia," she said immediately. "I can communicate with them and tell them to sabotage whatever it is."

"That will cause diakrónikus nyírás," I said.

She looked terribly deflated. "I wish I did not know this," she said.

"There is no other way," I said. I had never believed much in fate, but I was shaken by how remarkable it was, that I had been sent to this DTAP as an act of Gráinne's treachery, and yet being here—it turned out—was unavoidable. Perhaps on other Strands I got here by different methods.

"I need to think about this," she said. "This is so much, so very much, to ask of anyone. Do you understand?"

"I do. I wouldn't ask if it was not incredibly important. Please let me give you the information that you need in case we are separated." Out of my reticule I took my journal and a pencil, and wrote down *ODEC*, *Facebook*, the approximate date we were to connect in the future, *Tristan Lyons*, and *Fuggers (Bank)*. Then, remembering that she had impressed Tristan with her understanding of the ODEC's mechanics, I scribbled what fractured physics-engineering babble I could remember from five years earlier, when Tristan and Oda-sensei were first bonding over developing the ODEC. I tore the leaf from my journal and handed it to her. She hesitantly took it, looked at it, grimly tucked it into her own reticule. I felt faint with gratitude. "So you will say yes?" I said.

"It would be easier if somebody else aged with me." She looked relieved. "Perhaps my lover!"

"That's a bad idea," I said. "Do you know the saying, three may keep a secret if two of them are dead? It will be hard enough for you to pass undetected."

"Then you shall stay here and keep me company until you die. By then I will have found somebody else. I will be a freak of nature if I try to remain in one community for very long. They will grow suspicious. I will need companions. You must be my first companion."

"Erszebet," I said, "I cannot do that. I must get home. I must warn my friends against some terrible things that are happening. If I do not warn them, even your sacrifice may ultimately be for nothing."

She looked very weary then, and rubbed her face with her hand. "This is far too much for me to think about all at once," she said. "I need some time."

"There is no time," I said with urgency. I glanced around and, with a sinking heart, saw her parents approaching us, her father with a scolding look on his face. "Please think about it," I said, "and meet me again as soon as possible. Tomorrow?"

"Tomorrow we go home to Budapest," she said, looking down. "I cannot help you. And I will not extend my life to help you in the future, it is far too painful a calling."

"Please," I said, "please, Erszebet, reconsider. If you do not do this, I am mired here forever."

"I would not be your jailor, but I cannot be your savior," she said, almost apologetically. Then she rose, with a forced smile on her face, as her parents reached us.

Her mother gave me a look that might shatter concrete, and then in a low voice began to interrogate Erszebet right in front of me in Hungarian. My Hungarian was weak but the sentences were fairly rudimentary: "Who Sent her? Where is she from? What does she know about magic dying? What can we do?"

Perhaps Erszebet was not the witch I should have spoken to?

"Tell your mother!" I said urgently to Erszebet, as her parents began to move her away from me. "Tell her everything!" And to the mother, in bumbling Magyar: "Erszebet can help the magic. I told her how. But I can do nothing. She must do it."

Her parents looked astonished. After a stunned moment, they both glanced at me and then back to her, and she seemed to wither under their gaze. To see Erszebet Karpathy cowed was even more disorienting than to see her joyful.

Her father took her arm and very forcefully began to lead her through the crowd. I was certain—I *am* certain—never to see her again.

In a daze, I wandered over to the reconstructed Medieval Court, which I alone of all those tens of thousands knew from personal experience to be ~~a hack job~~ abounding in solecisms. The good doctor and his wife collected me and brought me home, expressing great concern that I seemed so exhausted by the outing, and declaring that for the next week or two I must have bedrest or the equivalent. They do not perceive themselves as keeping me a prisoner. Indeed, they believe themselves to be nothing but my benefactors. They were very willing to bring me all the paper and ink I could ask for, although they had no idea I would ask for as much as all this.

For when I returned from the meeting with Erszebet, I realized I must make an accounting of everything, as there shall never otherwise be any record of it. Tristan, I suspect, must also be lost now too, and he is not the sort who would stop to record a narrative like this. So this is all that will ever remain of us.

I shall now take this sheaf of papers to the Fugger Bank on Threadneedle Street and deposit it in a safety deposit box. I have lost all hope of returning to my own time.

And so, dear reader, with these words, as the ink dries, I disappear.

Journal Entry of

Rebecca East-Oda

DECEMBER 6

Nothing good to report. Yesterday—or was it the day before?—realized, while eating Chinese take-out, that a week had passed since the events in the Walmart. Frank, Tristan, Mortimer, and the others have scarcely ventured out of the house during that time, except to run to the hardware store for parts, or farther afield to collect obscure ODEC components from various scientific and industrial supply houses. These are being assembled into a contraption that has taken over half of the cellar. For a while it seemed that this was coming together quickly, and

morale was high as the big components were being hammered
and welded together with impressive speed. Meanwhile Julie (on
her motorcycle) and Felix (in his SUV) kept making runs to the
Amazon Locker over by MIT to collect packages of various sizes
containing electronics that Mortimer has been incorporating
into the "server rack" taking over my pantry. A bundle of cables
as thick as my waist now snakes from there down the dumbwaiter
shaft into the cellar where it is connected to various devices built
into the walls of the ODEC.

So the physical changes are impressive. This had gulled me into
thinking that actual progress was being made toward getting Mel
back home. But last night, just before he turned in, Frank broke
the news to me that the entire project is futile unless he can get his
hands on a larger quantity of high-temperature superconductors.
He already had some samples on hand, which have been incorporated into the device, but he needs ten times as much of the stuff
in order to make an ODEC large enough to accommodate a person.

All of the work that the crew have been doing since Black Friday
has been in the hope that these materials could be obtained. Only
two companies in the world manufacture them. One is in China
and has been slow to deal with. Julie, who is fluent in Mandarin,
has spent many hours on the phone with them trying to cajole
them into overnight-shipping some samples, but they see us as
too small a customer to be worth bothering with. The other possible source is right here in the Boston area—they are on Route
128 in Waltham, so only a few miles away—and Frank had high
hopes that they would supply what he needs until yesterday, when
his order ran afoul of some kind of internal roadblock within the
company. I suspect some kind of meddling by Blevins.

Post by Mortimer Shore on
"New ODEC" GRIMNIR channel
DAY 1957 (7 DECEMBER, YEAR 5)

Hey all, I could just walk upstairs and deliver this news in person but I'm too tired to stand up and I know people are sleeping.

Breaking news: if you check out a couple of these links from this morning's *Wall Street Journal* and some other biz sites you will see that we have just been Pearl Harbored as far as getting what we need to finish the new ODEC. TC Materials Science Group—our erstwhile friends out in Waltham—have just been purchased lock, stock, and barrel by a hedge fund operating out of lower Manhattan. This explains why they suddenly clammed up a couple of days ago and stopped processing our order.

So as you might expect I have been learning whatever I can about said hedge fund.

We have all been assuming that Blevins had something to do with our recent difficulties in getting these supercons. That might be the case with the company in Shenzhen, which is a big DODO supplier, but what's happening today seems unrelated. There is another player, apparently.

This hedge fund has also recently taken big positions in a number of mining companies operating in Mongolia, Congo, and Bolivia, which are the only places to get the rare earths and other unusual minerals needed to manufacture the high-temp superconductors we need.

So it would appear that someone with a lot of money is making a concerted effort to corner the world market on exactly the stuff we need in order to conduct diachronic operations, or for that matter magic of any kind.

I have a few feelers out to friends of mine in the "gray hat" world who I was not allowed to have contact with when I was a U.S. government employee. They might be able to dig up more.

Follow-up from Mortimer Shore, four hours later:

I have heard back from a friend of mine who got scared straight a couple of years ago and ended up working as a programmer for a Wall Street quant fund. He knows his way around the financial systems.

It's a big data dump, but the bottom line seems to be that our adversary in this case is not Blevins or DODO.

It's the Fugger Bank.

Reply from Tristan Lyons:

Makes me wonder about the disappearance of the ATTO from the Walmart. We assumed that was Magnus's work . . . but who knows?

ENTRY FROM PERSONAL JOURNAL OF

Karpathy Erszebet

written in Magyar in a leather-bound diary on linen paper

LONDON, 13 JULY 1851

Dear Diary,

Today I was at the Great Exhibition in London, with my parents, when I was approached by a woman who, while not a witch, knew much about magic and why it has been waning. She warned me that magic will soon die and requested me to participate in its resuscitation. This required two things of me: first, that I cast a spell upon myself to extend my life out by more than a century, and second, that I Home her back to the future time from where she comes. Overwhelmed by the enormity of her request, I refused.

However, Mother, seeing the distress on my face, demanded to know what it was we spoke of, and when I told her, she said that of course we must prevent this Mr. Berkowski from taking his accursed photograph and ending magic (this is the event that completely destroys magic). As soon as we were back in our room at the inn, she began to scry in an attempt to find a sister-witch in the area of Koenigsbourg, Prussia, who might be able to deter Mr. Berkowski.

Father pointed out with some impatience that this would merely delay, by some small time, the actual snuffing-out of magic, and that if Miss Stokes was so determined, that surely I should follow her resolve and put a spell on myself to lengthen my life. I said I could not bear to do this. When Mother agreed with Father, I told her, "You are free to use such a spell on yourself if you like, then."

"I am already too old for such a spell to work well," she said. "I

had you too late in life and I am already an old woman and my health wanes with my power. It has to be you."

I dared her then to set the spell on me. She said it would be bad magic to use such a spell against an unwilling witch—especially her own daughter.

Exchange of posts on "General" GRIMNIR channel
DAY 1959 (9 DECEMBER, YEAR 5)

Post from Frank Oda, 11:17:
Has anyone seen or heard from Julie? She went off on her bike two hours ago to pick up some parts and should have been back a while ago. It's not like her to not report in.

Reply from Tristan Lyons, 11:20:
Good catch, Frank, we have been a little distracted by the sudden disappearance of the DOSECOPS SUVs from the street. They all took a powder about forty-five minutes ago.

From Rebecca East-Oda, 11:25:
Good riddance. The neighbors will be pleased too.

From Julie Lee, 14:30:
Sorry for the mysterious absence, everyone. I'm fine and I'm hanging out in a top-floor hotel room at the waterfront Westin with none other than Major Isobel Sloane.

From Tristan Lyons, 14:31:
WHAT!? Glad you are okay but please explain.

From Julie Lee, 14:45:
I was on my way back to the house with the delivery, just a couple of blocks out, when I noticed that all three of the DOSECOPS SUVs were blasting down the street, headed for the main drag. So, on the spur of the moment, I decided to follow them. Couldn't have kept up with them on the highway but of course they were in Boston traffic and so it was pretty easy to keep pace. I had to make a few illegal sidewalk runs and cut through some parking lots but was able to track them across the Mass Ave Bridge and across the South End into Southie where they ended up passing through a guarded gate into the container terminal. There's a big slip there lined with cranes where they load and unload the container ships. Thousands of containers stacked all over the place, trains, trucks, etc.

I couldn't get through the gate, so I was kind of stymied at that point. I looked around for a tall building and noticed the Westin a few blocks away—it's like twenty stories high and I could see its top floors, so I knew it had a view of the area. So I gunned it over there. The neighborhood is kinda forbidding, lots of big industrial-type buildings but no place to come in off the street. I left my motorcycle with the parking attendants and went into the lobby and asked the lady at the front desk whether there was a bar or coffee shop on the top floor where I could have a drink and look out over the harbor and she was like no, all of our dining establishments are down low and the top floors are all rooms and suites for our guests. I asked if any of those was available and she said she could get me one with a view of the harbor so I plunked down my credit card and said I would take it.

While I'm there filling out the paperwork, I see a woman approaching in my peripheral vision. She's coming from the direction of the coffee shop in the lobby, holding a latte cup. I figured she wanted to talk to the front-desk lady but instead she approached me and said, "Excuse me, this might sound very weird and I'm sorry if this makes you uncomfortable but I have the strongest feeling that I know you from somewhere and I was wondering if I could chat with you for a minute." So I look up at her and holy shit it's Isobel Sloane from DOSECOPS! She's dressed in a sweatshirt and sweatpants and some Crocs that I'm going to take a wild guess were looted from Walmart and she basically looks fine, but a little spacey and disoriented. As evidenced by the fact that she didn't know my name. We've had coffee together lots of times at the DODO cafeteria and she totally knows me.

Obviously something weird was going on so I said, "Sure, I would totally love to chat with you, hang on a sec and we can go up to my suite and get some room service and just chill out for a little bit." Which she was fine with.

So, ten minutes later we're up in this fancy suite. Pricey, but the only room I could get with a view of the harbor. I was super nervous that we'd be followed, but nothing of the sort happened, and as soon as we got inside I locked and security-bolted the door. I got Isobel settled down on a comfy chair in the living room area of the suite and then looked out the window and down into the container port area.

DOSECOPS has a fleet of half a dozen black SUVs, as you know, and all six of them were down there, clustered together like cockroaches along the side of the big slip where the container ships tie up to be loaded and unloaded. I could see people standing around them but it was too far away to make out faces. Some of them were looking out into the harbor. And right there, just a mile or two out, south of the airport, was a big container ship steaming away. Piled with hundreds of containers, of course. And everything about the body language of the people around the SUVs was "goddamn it we just literally missed the boat."

More in a few minutes but I'm gonna hit "send" on this so you get the update.

From Mortimer Shore, 14:59:

I checked the shipping records. That's the *Alexandre Dumas*. She's owned by a French shipping company. They name all of their ships after writers, I guess.

From Tristan Lyons, 15:03:

Where's she headed?

From Mortimer Shore, 15:06:

Le Havre apparently.

From Julie Lee, 15:12:

CONTINUED

So when I saw how it was down along the waterfront I turned to Isobel who was just chilling, sipping her latte and looking out the window, and I said, "So, Isobel, it's good to see you!"

"Isobel. Right. That's me," she said. Like she'd forgotten her own name.

"We have been worried," I said.

"Who has been worried?" she asked.

"People who work with you and who knew you had gone missing," I told her. "You have been missing for over a week."

"Oh, I wasn't missing," she said, and kind of nodded down toward the harborfront area below us. She seemed completely unconcerned.

"You were down there?" I prompted her.

"Yes, there's a shipping company, with an office, and a lot of shipping containers that they look after."

"Might one of those containers be green, with some rust spots and some equipment inside?" I asked.

"You mean the ATTO?" she asked without skipping a beat.

"Yeah, the ATTO."

"That's mostly where I was. It was in the warehouse. It's not green anymore, though. We painted it red."

"We? So, you were involved in this painting project?"

"Yeah, I didn't have anything else to do, so I helped out a little. It was fun."

"Where is the ATTO now with its shiny new coat of red paint?"

"They just loaded it onto the ship a little while ago. Then I found myself out on the street and so I decided to go get some coffee. That's when I saw you."

"Were you being held prisoner?" I asked.

"No."

"Was there another woman in the ATTO part of the time?"

"Yes. She was always there."

"Was it Gráinne?" I asked. "Irish accent?"

"Oh, no," she said, as if that would be preposterous.

So then I thought about what kind of witch Magnus would probably have with him and asked, "Did she look or sound, like, Scandinavian maybe?"

And she said, "Nope."

"Do you remember what she looked like?"

She shrugged. "Maybe like Italian or Spanish?"

I couldn't think of any Italian or Spanish witches on our payroll so I let that go and asked, "And is she in the ATTO right now?"

"Oh, no. They shut it down and locked it before they put it on the ship."

"So where did the woman go?"

"I don't know. She went away in a car with the shipping company guys."

"So all of them—all of the shipping company guys—they all left?"

"Yeah."

"And pretty much left you where you were standing."

"Yeah."

"But it looks like they didn't hurt you or anything."

"Oh, no. Why would they do that?"

"Just asking, Isobel."

And at about this point a change started coming over Isobel's face. Until then she'd been super relaxed, like she'd been sitting on a beach washing down Xanax with strawberry margaritas and listening to global chill music, but now it was like the circuit breakers in her brain were flipping back on. She seemed preoccupied, and sort of embarrassed. I felt a little bad for her and I didn't want to, like, jump down her throat or anything. So I just sat there quietly and let her work it all out.

"Wow," she said. "Oh, shit."

"You've been missing for a week," I said.

She nodded. "I've been missing for a week. I need to call my mom. And my boss. And the cops."

"Do you remember DODO now?" I asked her. "And DOSECOPS."

"Yeah. Sure."

"Well, they're all down there, staring at the ass of that big ship as it cruises out of the harbor," I said. "And I can take you down there if you want. But maybe you could show me the shipping company on the way?"

"Sure. Yeah, I need to get down there," she said, and by that point she was fully back to normal. The Isobel Sloane we are accustomed to. She stood up and kind of patted herself down, but she didn't have her phone or any of her DOSECOPS electronic gear, just the Walmart togs she'd been given.

So we went down and got on my motorcycle and she had me drive along the north side of the shipping channel, which is just one long, long row of warehouses with little shipping companies all over the place. It's hard to tell one from the next, and Isobel's memories were fuzzy, so my expectations were pretty low. But as we were getting near the end, where the road terminates with a view of the harbor and the airport, I was sorta hit over the head with an incredibly focused and powerful sense of GLAAMR. And it quite obviously emanated from behind the door of one company, which was unmarked except for a suite number (2739) and a little piece of paper about the size of a business card with a drawing on it, a pattern of circles, wide at the top and tapering to the bottom, with a stem and a leaf at the top. Like a bunch of grapes. It was locked, and through the frosted glass window I could kind of make out a filing cabinet and a water cooler. Normal office stuff. Isobel seemed pretty sure that this was the place she'd been hanging out for the last week. It smelled like paint. But I didn't need her help anymore to know that this was it. I'm a witch. I can tell. The GLAAMR behind that door was almost enough to knock me down.

I dropped her off on the other side of the channel, near the gates to the container port, and then came back to the hotel, where I'm now safely locked in my suite. As long as I paid for the damn thing I intend to get the most out of it!

From Tristan Lyons, 15:39:
Fantastic stuff, Julie. Glad to hear Isobel is fine. Stay safe.

From Mortimer Shore, 16:42:
BOG Container Lines Inc. is the survival into modern times of Bunch of Grapes, which is an extremely old presence in the shipping industry. I mean, it's named after a tavern in Boston from the 1600s that was named after a tavern in London that dates back to at least the 1200s. Suite 2739 is a registered business address for them. One of many. I'm still waiting for some query results to come back so that we can discover their inevitable connection to the Fuggers. I don't even know why I bother.

From Tristan Lyons, 17:03:

Mortimer, Julie, you are flying to London tomorrow. Pack.

From Mortimer Shore, 17:05:

My man, that is fascinating and I'm totally packing, but I just wanted to point out that Paris is closer to Le Havre. Assuming that is where you are trying to get.

From Tristan Lyons, 17:07:

Yeah, I have Google Maps too. Marginally harder for the bad guys to track your going into France if you're arriving from a nearby country via ferry, vs. arriving in a commercial airliner from Boston.

From Mortimer Shore, 17:44:

Tristan? You around? I can't find you anywhere in the house.

From Rebecca East-Oda, 18:19:

Tristan and Felix are incommunicado. I am giving them a lift to a helicopter charter service at Logan Airport. They have a lot of cash and a lot of equipment.

ENTRIES FROM PERSONAL JOURNAL OF

Karpathy Erszebet

ON THE TRAIN HOME TO BUDAPEST, 14 JULY 1851

Dear Diary,

Mother has been working upon me, or rather trying to, with her ever-weakening abilities, for I can feel her inside my very skull at times over the past few days, trying to convince me to put the spell upon myself willingly. I will not. I considered it, but I know I lack the fortitude to survive the endless decades to come.

BUDAPEST, 23 JULY 1851

Dear Diary,

I have resigned myself to learning a skill, to earn a proper living when magic is no more. With each passing day, I feel a diminishing of power and clarity of mind, an almost physical heaviness. I push through it. I have decided I might learn to be a seamstress, for at least then I shall spend my life around beautiful gowns (which I am fond of) even if I soon lack the means to own them.

BUDAPEST, 26 JULY 1851

Dear Diary,

As the days go by, Mother keeps to her chambers, and Father, when I see him, mostly scowls at me. The day after tomorrow is when this horrible eclipse will happen and then it will all be over.

MISSION LOG OF TRISTAN LYONS

Written in ballpoint pen on pocket notebook

DAY 1960 (10 DECEMBER, YEAR 5)

General intro: I have no idea whether the finder of this notebook is going to consider me a hero, a traitor, or a nobody, but I want to go on record stating I firmly believe my actions are (a) important and (b) based on a good-faith reading of my service oath, as well as a larger commitment to the principles of the United States Constitution and the post-Enlightenment worldview from which it sprang.

(Here's where Mel would make some crack about how I take myself too seriously, but she's stuck in 1851 at the moment.)

Furthermore, I don't know whether the reader will have access to digital electronic devices, or for that matter any post-medieval technology whatsoever, and so I'm writing this in ink on paper so that you don't need gadgets to read it.

Hell, it could be that by the time we reach France the whole continent will be nothing but smoking ruins . . .

I'm in a steel box on a big boat. I came here with my friends Felix Dorn and Rebecca East-Oda. I talked them into this adventure. Not to say they're not grown-ups or anything (for the record, Rebecca is a grandmother), but I take responsibility for this, and if there are legal proceedings to follow, they should be exonerated, because this whole thing was my call.

As general background, just to help the reader calibrate the level of weird that's going on, I believe that the building we all know as the Pentagon was called the Trapezoid when it was first built, circa World War II, and that it remained the Trapezoid all through the Cold War and the decades that followed. It only became the Pentagon a few months ago. But when it did, it wasn't only the building itself that changed, but everyone's memories of it as well. So everyone, including me, thinks it has been the Pentagon from the moment its cornerstone (vertexstone? whatever) was laid, and has memories consistent with that, and it's what you'll read in old documents and see on old maps. I have memories of the Trapezoid but they have the same surreal and suspect vibe about them as things seen in dreams, or hallucinated during LSD trips.

It was converted into the Pentagon on Halloween, just about two months ago, when a significant chunk of the United States military-industrial complex was taken over by witches in a carefully premeditated coup d'état. They remain in power—well, one does. If you, the reader of this document, are a Special Forces operative who just finished taking me and Felix down in a raid, or a Military Intelligence analyst at the Pentagon, then you actually work for her. The witch, that is. Sorry to break it to you.

The witches' goal is to roll back scientific and technical progress to roughly the late medieval period. I think they are probably okay with a Leonardo da Vinci level of tech, but once we get into Galileo or even Francis Bacon, these witches get the heebie-jeebies and want to put a stop to it. Cf. my earlier remarks about the Enlightenment.

Okay, so Felix read the above while I was peeing into an empty water bottle (we are saving it in case we end up having to drink our own urine in a few days), and he has advised me to get on with some more concrete details of what's happening. Thanks, buddy.

But I've done some stuff here that from a narrow-minded point of view looks just incredibly batshit illegal, and I need to explain that.

In retrospect, we should never have built the ATTO.

The whole diachronic operations thing was never perfect—actually we had some pretty hairy misadventures from day one—but at least it was under some kind of control as long as we just had a few ODECs that were totally locked down in secure facilities, with necessary bio-containment procedures in place, etc. We used them for one thing and one thing only: time travel, according to a clear set of rules and procedures.

Our critical mistake was the recent policy shift toward using ATTOs (portable ODECs) for psy-ops in the present day. (Note: Melisande Stokes was always iffy about the psy-ops tack, not that she had a say in policy, but given the impact this has had on her fate, she at least deserves her opinion to go on the record.) On the face of it the psy-ops redirection seemed reasonable, or at least no crazier than diachronic operations, but we didn't reckon on Gráinne and the fact that she would immediately begin using those very techniques to influence DODO's top leadership.

And Gráinne, in turn, didn't reckon on Magnus.

Who didn't reckon on the Fuggers (see below).

So lots of people are surprised.

I won't re-tell the whole story here because it can be gleaned from documents on GRIMNIR, especially Julie Lee's entry, but I do want to record (a) what's happened since then and (b) what I'm pretty sure is the behind-the-curtain truth to What's Going On. Which I will do first. I'm leaving out an enormous amount here—I'm not "showing my work" as my grade-school math teacher would complain, because I don't know how much ink is left in this ballpoint.

After Magnus finished getting what he wanted out of the Walmart (treasure maps, basically) and made his getaway, there must have been one witch remaining in the ATTO, since a witch can't Send herself. (I see empty cold cut wrappers and a whole lot of used water bottles, so somebody was hanging out here for a while.)

After the siege, when DOSECOPS showed up and Major Isobel Sloane went in to check the (still-operating) ATTO, the witch clearly used some kind of mind-influencing technique on Sloane.

The tractor-trailer containing said witch was then shanghaied to Conley Terminal, given a false identity, and sent off to France. Major Sloane was maintained in an altered mental state for a full week while that happened; eventually she turned up unharmed in Julie's hotel lobby, and I'm guessing the truck driver has turned up somewhere with a similar story.

BUT: after hashing this out ad nauseam, I need to change/add one detail:

The warehouse and all that's happened since is clearly a Fugger operation—which means it must have been a (new-to-us) Fugger witch, not Magnus's witch, who was controlling Major Sloane.

This in turn means that Magnus's witch got "jumped" by some other (Fugger) witch who manifested in the ATTO at some point post-Walmart siege and Homed Magnus's witch back to Viking-era Norway or wherever, with or without her consent.

No idea why the Fuggers stole the ATTO from DODO, or why they are getting it not just out of the country but specifically to France, which happens to have old, secret laws governing the use of magic for diachronic operations.

If this all seems even beyond the scope of the Fuggers, remember—DODO's own Dr. Cornelius Rudge is a Fugger agent (hi, Dr. Rudge!), meaning the Fuggers know whatever DODO knows. And always have. Also: they are obviously waiting to collect ATTO #1 in Le Havre.

So we decided to beat them to it, so that we have a way to get Mel home.

Felix and I packed duffel bags with all the gear we could carry and found a chopper pilot who was willing to fly us and Rebecca out to the Alexandre Dumas. We circled the ship a couple of times and identified the ATTO. Even though it has a new paint job, it has some identifying characteristics, such as the side door, that make it stand out clearly if you know what to look for.

We hailed the ship on VHF. I gave the captain the same story we'd been telling the helicopter pilot, which was that this was an "enforcement operation" related to a "sensitive national security situation" and that it would be best if he just clammed up and didn't make a fuss until I could come and talk to him. And then I requested permission to come aboard, which is the polite thing to do.

We landed on the top of the container stack and set a rope, which I used to let myself down to the door. I cut off the padlock with a battery-powered grinder and got it open. We let down a rope ladder and helped Rebecca and the chopper pilot get down and inside. I went back up onto the top of the container stack and walked forward to the ship's superstructure, which projects up above the level of the containers. The captain was waiting for me. I was in full quasi-military tactical gear, and I guess I looked convincing. The captain is Spanish, the crew is Filipino, and, at the end of the day, none of them wants any trouble. They just want to drive this thing to Le Havre and cash their paychecks. I explained to the captain that there was a situation in the red container that he needed to see with his own eyes. It took a little social engineering, which Mel always says I'm not very good at, but after a few minutes he sort of rolled his eyes and agreed to come back and have a look.

So now it's me and Rebecca and the chopper pilot and the ship's captain all together in the red container, and I can tell that the ATTO system has been turned on. The first few times I experienced the inside of a running ODEC, I came out of it deeply confused, like a kid who'd been roofied at a frat party, but over the years I've become accustomed to it. I can maintain some level of conscious awareness and come out of it a little spacey, but basically intact.

The same was not true of the ship's captain and the chopper pilot, who just became listless and generally out of it as soon as I shut the ATTO door. Felix, for his part, was smart enough to just hang out on top of the stack until this part of it was over.

Witches have no problem in ODECs/ATTOs, and Rebecca had been practicing enough with Erszebet so that she could give the captain and the chopper pilot a mild talking-to, there in the ATTO. Outwardly it just looked like a school librarian lecturing a couple of schoolboys who brought their books back a day overdue, but I could feel the GLAAMR all over the place as she made sure their memories of all this would be seriously muddled. Go Rebecca.

Then we opened the door and shut off the ATTO. The captain went back to his business without a word. The pilot climbed into his chopper and took off, headed back to Boston, taking Rebecca back with him (not that she isn't game for an adventure at this point, but she's exhausted after her first successful psy-ops mission and Frank will probably forget to eat if she's not around).

As for the ship's crew, all they know is that they saw some weird stuff happen, but it's not in their interest to talk.

Felix and I went back into the ATTO, removed all of our ropes and carabiners from the outside, and locked the door behind us.

TL;DR Magnus hijacked the ATTO, the Fuggers hijacked it from Magnus, and now we have hijacked it from the Fuggers. As long as Felix and I keep it powered down, people can't be Sent to it.

Now we wait.

ENTRY FROM PERSONAL JOURNAL OF

Karpathy Erszebet

BUDAPEST, TRAIN STATION, 28 JULY 1851

Dear Diary,

Today has been the most horrifying of my young life, although I fear it is only the beginning of many days, and weeks, and decades of woe.

This morning, Mother suddenly emerged from her room, descended the stairs, and called me into the great room, with a fierce determination on her face, but otherwise so wan as to look waxen, and so haggard as to be almost unrecognizable. "Erszebet," she said, and seemed about to say more—

—so I stood there in a wholly receptive state awaiting her words.

But she did not continue to speak to me directly. Rather she uttered ugly incantations I had never heard before, and a terrible feeling came over my body, as if I were bound with hot iron, while being frozen on the inside. I screamed in alarm and pain, but the sensation only grew more intense. It seemed to last for a very, very long time. Hours—

—and then suddenly, it stopped. And I found myself lying prone across the ottoman. My skin felt unnaturally tight on me and I felt somehow heavier. Mother was lying prostrate near me, in the doorway, as pale as death.

"I've done it," she said grimly. "Better bad magic than no magic at all. Now you will be here for Melisande Stokes."

"I will undo it," I said between clenched teeth, fighting off panic.

"I do not think so," she said. She turned away from me and tried to raise herself up but lacked the strength.

"Give me an hour to regain my spirit, and I'll undo the spell," I insisted. "And then I will leave here and you shall never see my face again."

"In an hour, there will be no more magic, anywhere upon this earth," said Mother hoarsely, sinking back onto the carpet and covering her pale face with one pale hand. "The solar eclipse has already begun. Somewhere in Prussia, this Mr. Berkowski has set up his photography equipment. In mere minutes it will all be over."

I have no words, dear diary, to express the feeling that came over me. I have refuted any connection to my parents; immediately I packed a small suitcase and left the house with no idea of where to go. Then I went to the train station and bought a ticket to Praha to stay with my paternal cousin, Dagmar, as I know a little bit of Czech.

Now even if I wished to help Miss Melisande Stokes to return to her time, I would be unable to. She is in part to blame for my *predicament, for if she had not come, I would not have heard her remedy and then neither would Mother, and now I would be like Mother, or any other witch—a normal mortal woman. Such simplicity is to be denied me. It is a very bitter fate.*

In the absence of any other remedy I suppose I must rely—as my foremothers have in the worst of their years—upon the mercy of the Fuggers.

Exchange of posts on "Ops" GRIMNIR channel
DAY 1970 (20 DECEMBER, YEAR 5)

Post from Tristan Lyons, 05:30:

Anyone there? This is a burner phone I picked up in Boston, you're just going to have to take my word for it that it's me. Seeing one bar, apparently a cell tower in Penzance.

Reply from Mortimer Shore, 05:31:

Pirates of Penzance reading you. Welcome to the English Channel, bro!

From Tristan Lyons, 05:33:

They call it La Manche where we're going, but thanks. Everything fine here in the ATTO. I think I read the entire works of Dickens and did 80,000 push-ups.

From Mortimer Shore, 05:35:

Heh I think I drank 80,000 pints in the local.

From Tristan Lyons, 05:37:
What is sitrep? Got numbers for me?

From Mortimer Shore, 05:40:
All good. BTW, I'm going to lose you in a short while but later in the morning you will come in range of the island of Jersey, which is where we registered our shipping company. Esme is hanging out there. And Julie's en route Le Havre. Rebecca's in London en route Gatwick (last I heard). Frank and Erszebet are at the house back home. Erszebet's in charge of feeding the cats LOL.

From Tristan Lyons, 05:45:
Hang on, we have a shipping company?

From Mortimer Shore, 05:47:
<grin> we do now . . . it was the easiest way to manage the numbers. Turns out that you can't just paint any old number on the back of a shipping container and have it work . . . there's an owner code, and a check digit, and some other details . . . all covered by an ISO spec that I had to get my head around.

From Tristan Lyons, 05:51:
Figured. That's why I asked Rebecca to put you on it.

From Mortimer Shore, 05:55:
So, before you get out of range, here's the number: EHTU 314 1597.

From Tristan Lyons, 05:57:
You used pi? Really?

From Mortimer Shore, 05:58:

Just an accident:) The 7 is the check digit, if that's not right the computers in Le Havre will reject it.

EHTU is East House Trust—all part of the shipping company thing—had to do it so it wouldn't cause trouble going through customs in Le Havre.

From Tristan Lyons, 06:00:

So if I paint this on the back of the ATTO, everything is going to just happen automagically?

From Mortimer Shore, 06:02:

According to our modern standards of magic, yeah:)

See you in Le Havre.

Post by Rebecca East-Oda on "Ops" GRIMNIR channel
THREE HOURS LATER, 09:21

Note: Spotty Internet so have written this in real-time commentary but will now upload all at once.

Have reached Portsmouth, which none of us was expecting. In the guise of dotty but vigorous spinster tourist (which isn't too far off, in some sense), enjoyed a gusty walk from the railway station to the harbor, where I am now comfortably ensconced at a table in a waterfront pub. Will explain what I'm doing here.

Tristan, I expect you'll be back in cyberspace by the time I upload this, and so you might be wondering what I'm doing on this side of the Atlantic at all.

Briefly, the answer is that I came over to London because we had to manage a number of legal and financial transactions related to setting up the new shipping company under the umbrella of the East House Trust. Frank and I are co-trustees and so a lot of documents needed to be signed. Our scanner was on the blink and apparently fax machines are no longer au courant. It was simpler for me to just be in this country. So I got on a plane.

Frank could not join me because he is still working on the ODEC in our basement—some parts unexpectedly came in.

I was planning to fly home today. I'd have liked that. But we've received some new information about ATTO #2 and I've changed my plans accordingly.

This is a long story, but via Chira Lajani, we received a "leak" from DODO two days ago suggesting that hasty arrangements were being made (presumably by Gráinne even if Blevins or Frink signed off on them) to get ATTO #2 moved into a cargo plane—a 747F capable of swallowing a whole shipping container.

It turns out that there are persons called "plane spotters" who have nothing better to do with their time than to keep track of the comings and goings of airplanes. They are all on the Internet, naturally. Thanks to them, Mortimer was able to identify a 747F that made a flight yesterday from Hanscom to Gatwick.

I took the train from London to Gatwick and arrived in time to watch from the roof of a nearby hotel as ATTO #2 was unloaded in plain view and placed on a tractor-trailer. I recognized it as an ATTO from the side door, which makes it different from other shipping containers. We don't know why DODO wants an ATTO over here, but here it is.

Hailed a taxi and asked the driver to attempt to follow the rig. It left the airport southbound, as if headed for Brighton, but we lost track of it. Had the driver deposit me in Brighton and paid him a frightful amount of money, but there was little to see there—it's a resort town, with not much in the way of port facilities.

On a hunch I took the train here to Portsmouth today. By hunch I mean common sense: there was a brochure about Portsmouth in the Brighton train station, complete with detailed map of its large port, with freight and passenger connections across the Channel (including a direct connection to . . . Le Havre. Maybe just a coincidence that DODO wants their ATTO directly across the Channel from where the Fuggers' ATTO is bound, but maybe not.).

My perch here in this pub gives me a direct view through a chain-link fence, topped with copious snarls of razor wire, into a huge parking lot adjoining the ferry terminal. Several score tractor-trailer rigs and shipping containers are scattered about the place.

One of them is ATTO #2. It has been dismounted from its trailer and is quietly sitting in a corner of the parking lot. I'm keeping my eye on it.

Update, forty minutes later:
I am still in the pub. Management have apparently decided I am a harmless trainspotter type. Which I suppose I am.

Here is where my story stops being about an old lady spy and adopts witchy overtones.

A few minutes ago I began to pick up a strong sense of GLAAMR from the ATTO. I can both feel it and see it (Erszebet gets credit for being a good teacher). Clearly, the thing has been turned on. Meaning there is a witch in there. Gráinne herself? Possible, but maybe she would want to stay near Blevins to pull his strings.

A white van has pulled up to the side of the ATTO, just next to its door. From it, men are unloading some kind of cargo and tossing it in through the ATTO's side door. I gather it doesn't weigh much—perhaps clothing, stuffed into garbage bags. I presume these people are from DODO/Gráinne since DODO/Gráinne caused this new ATTO to be here.

Hmm. Perhaps it is another coincidence, but the passenger ferry to Le Havre departs in one hour.

Update, twenty minutes later:
Oh dear, hang on a moment: *Magnus* just showed up in an Uber! How very confusing. I thought he and Gráinne were utterly at odds with each other re: Walmart shenanigans.

Supposition: in light of the Fuggers' stealing ATTO #1, they (Gráinne and Magnus) realized they would have to make common cause to retrieve it. Still, I wonder what each of them intends to do with it once they have it back. Are they going to share it? Neither of them plays nice in the sandbox with others.

Update, a few minutes later (10:31):
Strong GLAAMR from the ATTO, and men are coming out of it now, one by one, every few minutes. Dressed in civilian clothing. But they are Vikings. I think it's the same crew that sacked the Walmart.

Update, fifteen minutes later:
White van just took Magnus and eight of his Vikings over to the passenger terminal. They are getting on the ferry to Le Havre. I'm going to get on the ferry too, and try not to let Magnus see me. Going to click "send" on this now. Hopefully I will be able to update you all soon. If I do not, assume it is because the Walmart Vikings have gotten to me, in which case somebody please remind Frank to water the garden.

(If you had told me five years ago, when Mel and Tristan first knocked on our door, that I would find myself writing that sentence I'd have laughed you down the street.)

Scribbled addendum in pencil at the bottom of Melisande Stokes's Diachronicle, in her handwriting

After requesting a safety deposit box here at the private offices of the Fugger Bank on Threadneedle Street, and giving the agent my name, I was informed I already owned a box. Amazed, I asked it to be brought to me, and saw that it contained a sealed envelope. Addressed to me. In Mortimer's gangly penmanship (albeit somewhat ink-blotted).

I have memorized its contents and will leave it here in the box, attached to my Diachronicle, for thoroughness.

I depart the bank in far higher spirits than I arrived.

Handwritten note on Fugger Bank stationery

Came back to 1848 to leave this for you to read in 1851—trippy, huh? We're trying to Home you. If you're reading this before July 28, 1851, cross the Channel ASAP to Collinet—aka Norman Language campsite. Near Le Havre, inland, on river Dives, if you don't remember. The B&B in our era is Chez Envouteur and the family women were openly witchy (descendants of Thyra and Imblen, talk about clan loyalty wOOt!) until magic stopped so if you ask for the witch's house the locals may know where to send you. Fingers crossed witch of 1851 is cooperative—have her Send you to her own backyard in our time where (if you get this) there will be an ATTO waiting to receive you.

Keep your head down and stay low when you arrive.
Gotta go, writing this wearing nothing but Mr. Fugger's
greatcoat and he's really not amused lol —Mortimer

Exchange of posts on
"Ops" GRIMNIR channel
1.5 HOURS LATER

Post from Esme Overkleeft, 12:17:
You there?

Reply from Tristan Lyons, 12:19:
Yeah. Just got bars.

From Esme Overkleeft, 12:20:
Welcome back to the world! I'm on Jersey.

From Tristan Lyons, 12:23:
Glad there's a world to get back to. Didn't know what I'd find on the
other end of the ocean.

From Esme Overkleeft, 12:27:
It's been a little hairy while you were gone . . . lots to report. But no
major Shears as far as we can tell. In spite of Magnus's best efforts.

From Tristan Lyons, 12:28:
Yeah . . . I'm reading the message from Rebecca . . . wow.

From Esme Overkleeft, 12:36:

The ferry with Magnus and the other Vikings (and Rebecca) is going to reach Le Havre shortly before you—you might even be able to see it out the ATTO door as you're approaching Le Havre. Taking into account the time zone change, your ETA is around 5:30—a little after sunset. Then, unloading should happen as per usual.

From Tristan Lyons, 12:40:

Let's talk a little more about "per usual." Port operations isn't my strong suit.

From Esme Overkleeft, 12:45:

Actual unloading of the ship probably won't start until tomorrow morning. Your container will come off almost immediately because of where it is. The crane will set it down on the wharf. That's when you disable the radio tracking device. A straddle carrier will pick it up and take it to a temporary storage location farther from the ship. There'll be some customs formalities—we'll take care of that, but if you have any contraband you should throw it overboard now. A forklift puts it on a tractor-trailer. The driver of the tractor-trailer works for us. He'll drive it away and take it where we told him to.

From Tristan Lyons, 12:48:

And where is that? I've been a little out of the loop.

From Esme Overkleeft, 12:50:

Nice little town in Normandy. I think you have been there . . . many times as it were:)

From Tristan Lyons, 12:53:

:) What are the Fuggers going to think when their ATTO makes a wrong turn?

From Esme Overkleeft, 12:56:

We don't know their plans of course, but presumably they were going to take it someplace safe. And Magnus and his crew mean to intercept it along the way although we're not sure about the Magnus/Gráinne relationship at the moment. Neither Magnus nor the Fuggers know about us . . . hopefully. So when we get it to the farmhouse, we'll have at least a few minutes' breathing room to turn it on and open a window for Mel to come home.

From Tristan Lyons, 13:05:

Okay, here's where this time travel shit gets really mind-bending . . .

The Fuggers and Magnus might not know about us TODAY but they'll sure as hell know about us TOMORROW when they notice that their ATTO has gone missing. And they have at least one ATTO of their own, dockside in Portsmouth. So what's to prevent them from, I don't know . . .

From Esme Overkleeft, 13:15:

Don't torture yourself. The most they can do is Send a naked Viking into our ATTO when we turn it on to receive Mel. She already has instructions to hit the deck and stay safe as soon as she arrives.

From Tristan Lyons, 13:20:

Have re-read your last transmission several times, and don't understand. How is "hitting the deck" going to keep her safe from a naked Viking?

From Esme Overkleeft, 13:22:

That's your job.

From Tristan Lyons, 13:24:

????

From Esme Overkleeft, 13:26:

Keeping her safe. Got any weapons in there?

From Tristan Lyons, 13:28:

Tossed them overboard, as you just instructed.

From Esme Overkleeft, 13:30:

Hmm . . . how's your hand-to-hand combat skills?

From Tristan Lyons, 13:32:

A little rusty, frankly. Fortunately I have Felix to practice on. Or vice versa.

Diachronicle

ALTHOUGH THERE IS NO LONGER need of it, I suppose out of habit I shall write this in a tone akin to the Diachronicle, that is to say, in accordance with the literary inflections of my most recent (and enforced) DTAP.

I fell through fragrant darkness, and fell tumbling hard to ground on a painfully cold, metallic floor that shook and rumbled as if it were a truck being pulled down a country road somewhere, which meant—the ATTO! I had arrived! I was safe!

—No, I wasn't!—there were three figures grappling violently above me in the eerie amber-green glow of the ATTO. Their efforts caused the rumbling. Two were clothed, and they were fighting with a third who was naked.

And who was winning.

"Stokes! Turn it off! TURN . . . IT . . . OFF . . ."

Tristan's voice was familiar even though sounding a little strangled: as my eyes focused I saw that he was in a headlock, his neck crooked in one of the naked man's massive arms. With his free hand, the man was swatting away Felix Dorn with an almost casual air. The stranger had tangled blond hair tumbling down over his shoulders, and a reddish beard. He was immense.

Being Sent is no picnic in the best of circumstances, and being in a working ODEC is always disorienting. I forcefully tamped down the part of me that wanted to celebrate my return to the modern world, trying to focus on the fact that my friends were losing a fight to a man-mountain . . . and trying to remember how the ATTO was laid out. I'd never had much to do with the ATTOs, as they were for psy-ops and I had always remained focused on diachronic work.

Still keeping Tristan's neck in the crook of his arm, the Viking (I assumed he was a Viking) came toward me at a ponderous gait, kicking empty water bottles out of the way as he planted his feet. Tristan was flailing out, trying to grab anything that would serve as an anchor. Felix fell to his knees, staggered by an elbow to the face. The Viking's gaze was fixed on something behind me. I turned and saw the control panel at the forward end of the ATTO.

I scrambled on hands and knees in that direction, hurled myself toward the panel, and mashed the big red button that served as the emergency "off" switch.

My own momentum then sent me sprawling back to the icy-cold floor, my head clearing now that the system was shut down. I drew myself up into a fetal position, spun around, and watched the progress of the fight.

Felix's face was gushing blood, probably from a broken nose.

He was getting unsteadily back to his feet, and seemed to have his eye on a fire extinguisher bracketed to the wall at the other end of the ATTO.

Tristan had managed to reach up and get one hand on the Viking's face, and was now groping around trying to insert a finger in an eye or mouth, but the Viking kept jerking his head away. Tristan finally got purchase on a handful of Viking hair, but it was a feeble grip compared to what the other had on him.

I was struck by the Viking's calm patience. This was not a berserker—indeed, he seemed more like a parent controlling a three-year-old throwing a temper tantrum.

The door of the ATTO was flung open from without, and slanting sunlight flooded in. Backlit and framed in the entrance was a female form; the ATTO light showed her to be a middle-aged woman, wearing a simple housedress with a heavy cardigan over it. She was brandishing a long, double-barreled shotgun. Her breath came out like clouds. I smelled apples baking.

There was a long moment while we all considered matters. The woman with the shotgun was clearly as surprised by the situation inside the trailer as we were by her sudden appearance. Certainly she had a lot to take in.

Felix stopped moving for the fire extinguisher and held up his bloody hands. Tristan couldn't see what was happening. I watched the woman between the tree-trunk legs of the Viking, whose manhood hung down, somewhat obscuring my view. I do believe this organ contracted a smidge when the woman trained the shotgun at him. (In fairness, the cold winter air coming in the open door may have accounted for some of that.) Certainly the gun got his attention: this wasn't the first time he'd seen a modern firearm. This confused me, for I knew all the DODO Anachrons by sight, and he was not one of them.

The sunlight glanced off his shoulder, highlighting a red scar—fresh and angry-looking—cutting horizontally across one of his cannonball deltoids.

The woman demanded, *"Relâchez-le immédiatement!"* Then getting no reaction, she tried in English, "Leave him go!"

Tristan, hearing her voice (he couldn't see the door), said in a strangulated voice, in Norman, "She has a bang-stick!"

This was the moment I realized the man probably *was* a Viking, so I tried Old Norse (a recent, somewhat half-baked addition to my linguistic arsenal). "Whoever you are, that thing will kill you."

The Viking released Tristan so abruptly that Tristan fell to the floor. The Viking turned around to face me, then reached up and patted the scar on his shoulder. "I know it," he returned in Norse. "A coward hit me with one of those accursed weapons in the Walmart."

"Walmart?" I repeated, flummoxed. "What were you doing in a *Walmart*?"

Tristan made a brief sound that might have been coughing or might have been laughter. "Welcome back, Stokes," he said. "You have a lot to get caught up on."

THE ATTO HAD been plonked down in the yard next to the same Normandy farmhouse whence I'd been Homed in 1851. Very little about the property had changed: there were now telephone wires connected from the road; a satellite dish; a sign reading CHEZ ENVOUTEUR, a bed-and-breakfast.

The woman had run inside to fetch ice for Felix's nose, and white terry bathrobes for me and the Viking, who called himself Thord (the woman, Tristan said, was Anne-Marie).

I waited for my bathrobe to arrive while burying my face

against Tristan's chest. I never wanted to let go of him, and his arms gripped me tight. Having just been steeped in Victoriana for the past several weeks, I noted that his delight in seeing me once again (important detail: seeing me entirely unclothed for the first time ever) was reflected in every inch of his healthy and vigorous frame, not excluding the matrimonial organs bestowed upon him by the Creator for the propagation of the race. I put my arms around the small of his back and pulled him into me, just to give him a hint that I had noticed.

Pressing my head into his shoulder, he muttered, "Damn, I'm glad to see you."

"Yes," I said, then pulled away and looked right at him, eye to eye, nose to nose. "I can tell."

He reddened a little, then a lot, then he started laughing and pulled me back against him.

We had been avoiding this for five years. Time to sort it out.

BUT NOT IMMEDIATELY. This was France, so first we all had to go inside for coffee, Felix trying to avoid water from leaking onto his jeans as he iced his swelling face. Anne-Marie offered me a woolen dress, which I accepted gratefully. She was nervous about Thord until Tristan took her aside and explained to her that "our Viking friend" would be docile now.

Most of the farmhouse's ground floor was one great room, kitchen at one end, dining space at the other, the whole of it spanned with a huge plank table that looked like it was a thousand years old. We sat at one end of this as Anne-Marie prepped food and drink just beyond the other end.

Over croissants and tartine (which of course Tristan practically inhaled without tasting), Tristan and Felix caught me up on all the dazzling adventures and misadventures I had missed while I was in San Francisco and London, the chief topics of conversation being: the Walmart raid; the ATTO heist shenanigans; and word from Frank that a shipment of high-temperature superconductors had just appeared on the doorstep of the East House. (Given that the Fuggers owned the company, this put us in their debt.) To bring me up to the minute, there was this further summation: Frank was busy wiring up the superconductors in his cellar to create an ODEC; Julie had rented a hotel suite in Le Havre and was staying there to ensure a base of operations near the port; Rebecca and Mortimer were even now joining her there from their sundry deployments; and Esme was expected to arrive in Le Havre at any moment from Jersey.

Thord, amazed by the first-time effects of caffeine, was pacing agitatedly around the farmhouse (by around I mean circumambulating it barefoot despite the winter chill). Anne-Marie had fairly decent English, and as she moved from our end of the room to hers, she seemed so unfazed by what she was overhearing that I assumed (correctly) Tristan had already told her more than the average abettor would know.

"So if I've got this all straight," I said, "now that you've stolen the ATTO from the Fuggers who stole it from Magnus who stole it from DODO, the Fuggers are wondering what became of what they thought would be their ATTO."

Tristan nodded. "From their point of view, it vanished from the container port in Le Havre. They had a tractor-trailer ready and everything. They were expecting to tow it away from there and take it to . . . who knows where." He waved his hand vaguely toward the interior of France. "Someplace safe, anyway. We still don't know who their witch is."

"It's rather unsportsmanlike of us to deprive them of an ODEC on the heels of their making it possible for us to build our own."

"Sportsmanship is for sportsmen," muttered Felix, a bit nasally with the ice pack pressed to his face.

"Anyhow, it was all happening at the same time an ocean apart and we're telling you to come *here*, so we had to *be* here," Tristan added.

"What do you mean, telling me. You've already *told* me." Then I realized something didn't make sense. "Wait—how did you Send Mortimer back to tell me to come here?"

"We haven't yet," said Tristan. "Julie's going to Send him when they get here." Seeing the look on my face he added, "I know, it's pretty freaky, don't think about it too much."

"I can't even . . ." I shook my head. "Never mind. So who's Thord, and what's his involvement in all this?"

"Yes," said Anne-Marie suddenly, from the kitchen area. "Who *is* Thord?"

"He's obviously one of the Vikings Magnus recruited," said Felix. "But no idea why he's here now."

"We could just ask him. I don't think he's used to coffee," Tristan joked.

Tristan went outside to collect Thord, still clad in his terry bathrobe (which somehow simply made him seem even more naked). He arrived inside staring wide-eyed at the exotic domestication of the great room. Anne-Marie—whom he regarded with the greatest respect, even fear—gestured to the end of the bench, which he plopped down onto wordlessly and quickly, like a chastised child. I told him my name, and asked if we might interview him, explaining that Tristan and I both had limited abilities to speak his language (which had linguistic ties to what Tristan had learned in these very fields, when they were still woods, a thousand years ago). He agreed, and began by confirming Felix's assumption.

"When we returned to Sverdvik after the raid, I was the only one without the scars in my back," Thord said. "This was because I had been injured by the bang-stick. I said to Magnus, 'Fuck you and your plan, Magnus, I did not want to come in the first place and now look.' So I did not let them carve maps in my back because I knew that I would then be part of his plan forever."

Anne-Marie had cleared the coffee and pastries, replacing them immediately with beer, and now was setting out plates of charcuterie and a fresh loaf of bread, which Thord began tearing into at an impressive pace. He chewed for a few moments, gazing out the window at the sun on the trees, while I translated for Felix (and Anne-Marie, who was swapping out ice packs for Felix's nose). Thord swiveled his blue-grey eyes back to us, washed the bread down with a swig of beer, and continued: "Magnus after that began to have dreams. They were dreams of his past—of his boyhood in Normandy and his days as a Varangian Guard. But in every single one of those dreams, his life was cut short by murder. He consulted a witch who explained that he was in fact seeing other Strands, and that on each and every one of those Strands, the young Magnus had in fact been assassinated by agents sent back in time by his enemies. Magnus became like ice on a frozen river when it is being melted from below by the warming water of the coming spring, and becomes thin and brittle and you can almost see through it." Having delivered this poetic metaphor, Thord belched, sighed, and speared a slice of ham. "He understood that he would cease to exist entirely, or be turned into a mere wraith, unless he made an alliance with others skilled in Sending and Homing. Thus he had the witch Send him forward to the ODEC in Boston. There, of course, he found himself in the power of Gráinne, who was most angry with him, but also satisfied, in a way, that Magnus had come crawling back to ask for her help."

After another pause for him to eat (and belch) and me to translate, Thord continued: "Gráinne and Magnus made a pact to fight the Fuggers and get this ATTO back in their possession." He waved in the direction of the yard. "Magnus cannot do magic, but he can fight, and is a good leader. Gráinne can do magic, but only in an ODEC, and she is otherwise helpless and weak in this world of Walmarts and so on. So, they could help each other. Magnus supplies muscle so that Gráinne can get things done. In exchange, he becomes rich by raiding gold from wherever he chooses to go, back in the old days. So, Magnus came back to Sverdvik saying, 'The Fuggers have stolen the ATTO from us, now we are going to steal it back, I need volunteers.'"

Tristan nodded. "Gráinne, through Blevins of course, made arrangements to fly ATTO #2 over to Portsmouth on a cargo plane. Magnus and a bunch of Vikings manifested in that ATTO yesterday—those must have been his volunteers from Sverdvik."

Thord listened to my translation of this, then nodded. "He tried to recruit me. I repeated to him that he could go fuck himself. The others went, as you said. They would cross from England to Normandy on a big ship and then follow the ATTO from Le Havre to the fortress of the Fuggers, wherever it might be, and then slaughter them and get it back. Or perhaps hijack it en route." He shrugged. "Like we do."

"But the plan failed," Tristan prompted him, as I quietly translated for Felix.

"The plan failed, as you know, because you stole the ATTO and so it did not go onto the wagon that the Fuggers had waiting but instead departed by some other way. There was a big mess, and what it came down to was that Magnus begged me to solve his problem for him. 'When the ATTO is turned on—which it must be, so that they can save the woman Melisande—then you,

Thord, can be Sent there at the same moment. They will try to turn it off as soon as they have Melisande back. You must prevent them from hitting the red button. Then we can Send more fighters, and witches, and fill the whole ATTO with our people in a short period of time, and then it will be ours. It's just a bit of wrestling, after all, and you're good at that.'"

I saw a little grimace on Tristan's face, and a shake of the head, which I took to mean: *Actually you're a crap wrestler, you're just overwhelmingly strong.*

"This plan almost worked, as you saw," Thord continued. "But when I saw Anne-Marie with the bang-stick pointed at me, I thought to myself, 'Fuck this, I have a wife and children in Iceland, I don't need to pry any more bang-stick rocks out of my body or even perhaps die just to make everything perfect for Magnus.' So now I will just wait here in this future until someone can Home me."

At this moment we heard car tires crunching the gravel on the drive outside.

"That'll be Julie," said Felix. "She can Home Thord."

"She should take you to the hospital first," said Tristan. "So you stop bleeding all over Anne-Marie's furniture."

"It's just a broken nose," said Felix. "I can go to the local walk-in clinic."

Tristan gave him a look, which he did not see because the ice pack obscured it. "We're in the middle of nowhere, there's one car, and it has to end up back in Le Havre. Go the hell to Le Havre."

Felix was so startled by Tristan's intensity that he removed the ice pack to give Tristan a *WTF bro?* look. Tristan immediately stared at the floor. Felix glanced at me, then back to Tristan, back to me. He looked around the room, noting who else was here— just Thord—and figured it out.

"Right, I should go to Le Havre," he said. "Julie can Home Thord tomorrow."

"Right, by tomorrow morning everyone will have congregated in Le Havre and you can all pile in the car and come back out here together," said Tristan in a rapid monotone, as if needing to rationalize being alone with me overnight as nothing more than a matter of logistics.

DEAR READER: It was not a matter of logistics. But you knew that.

When you know something is going to happen but it hasn't happened yet, there is a surfeit of tension, both pleasurable and otherwise. So it was for several awkward moments, as Julie came in to greet us, registered my presence—and Thord's—and helped Felix into the car. She was about to ask if I wanted to return with her to Le Havre—Tristan alone needed to stay here, to handle Thord—but then she, like Felix, understood the circumstances, and turned her head away trying to hide a delighted little smirk.

Tristan felt compelled to see the Viking settled in for the evening, to unburden Anne-Marie of her hostess duties. She vanished into her private rooms, clearly relieved.

Other than the room where Thord was to stay overnight, there were two guest bedrooms upstairs. They both had double beds. I chose the cozier room with one small dormer window. I half-closed the door and turned off the lamp, leaving the small night-light on. I began to undress, then hesitated, feeling self-conscious, and sat on the bed, waiting.

Eventually I heard Thord's door open and shut, and Tristan's slow footfall on the landing between rooms. Seeing the dim light from my room, he entered and stood in the doorway. Ever the gentleman. Even when I did not wish him to be so.

"Just come *in*," I suggested. "Don't pretend there's anywhere else you're planning to spend the night."

He strode up to the bed and hovered beside me a moment, his arousal nearly in my face even as his own face, absurdly, attempted to remain subdued. "We should have some understanding of—"

"After five years, if there's anything we still don't understand, fuck it," I said, and ran my hand up the front of his body. Then back down it.

He grabbed me and in one smooth movement picked me up and then tossed me face up onto the bed, settling his weight carefully upon me, nudging my thighs apart with his knees. It felt so good to be trapped beneath him I almost fainted. Except—

"This generally works better when there are no clothes in the way," I pointed out.

"Jesus, Stokes, it's been five years, why the sudden rush?" he shot back, with a very rare impish grin. "On some other Strand I've probably already torn your dress off."

"I want to go to that Strand," I said at once. "Take me there."

I WAS AWAKENED by a deep, subsonic throbbing that I felt through the frame of the bed before I heard it. I rolled over on my stomach and buried my face in a pillow, but the sound didn't go away. I groped out with one hand and found a warm, rumpled place where Tristan was supposed to be.

The noise got louder. Was it a wave of Diachronic Shear cresting over Normandy? I rolled onto my side, opened my eye, and saw Tristan in the dawn light gazing out the little dormer window, watching events in the yard. He looked interested, but not alarmed.

Finally I got up, pulled a robe around myself, and went to look.

IT WAS A helicopter. A preposterously large helicopter, bug-like, with a round cockpit in the front and nothing behind it save a long skinny spar running back to its tail rotor. It was hovering over the yard. Dangling from it were four cables, which were being attached to the corners of the ATTO by men in black.

The roar of its rotors grew even louder, the cables grew taut, the ATTO rose off the ground and ascended for perhaps a hundred meters. Then, slowly, it flew off. An unmarked van pulled out of the yard and drove away, carrying the men in black.

It was just past sunup.

Tristan and I dressed and went downstairs. Anne-Marie didn't seem to be around, and neither was Thord.

Beyond the head of the table were windows looking out onto the farmhouse's kitchen garden, currently bare and dead, and rolling fields and hedgerows beyond that. Seated at the head of the table with his back to that view, enjoying a cup of café crème and reading a French newspaper, was our old friend Frederick Fugger. As before, he was dressed in an impeccable grey suit, though as a nod to the rustic setting he was wearing a turtleneck sweater instead of a shirt and tie.

"Thord's been seen to," he said. "We Homed him before moving the ATTO. Anne-Marie is in town shopping for groceries, at our suggestion."

"At five in the morning?" I said, dumbfounded.

"It's after eight," protested Frederick pleasantly.

"You own the grocers," Tristan guessed.

"Not literally. Please, make yourselves comfortable. The coffee is nice and hot and the cream is fresh."

My eyes met Tristan's. He shrugged. There was no reason not to. For a minute or two we busied ourselves pouring coffee and cream, then took seats. Frederick finished the article he was reading, then folded the paper neatly and arranged it on the cracked and weathered planks of the old table.

"I wanted to be the first to congratulate you on the rescue of Dr. Stokes," he said. "The two of you look very happy together. I've taken the liberty of ordering a bottle of 1851 Château Miqueu, to be delivered to your room—a very old vintage, obviously, but it's been well cellared and I hope it is still drinkable."

"We'll let you know if it passes muster," Tristan said drily.

"Please do," Frederick returned. "The winery has been a property of the Fuggers since Roman times and has a high standard to uphold."

"Does it?" I asked. "I've never heard of it."

Frederick smiled. "You wouldn't have. It is a private concern. Its proceeds are consumed entirely within the bank and do not appear on the retail market."

"Well, thank you for the gift," I said. And I was tempted to add something like, *It's the least you could do after stealing our ATTO*, but I held back. It wasn't really our ATTO, after all.

Frederick cleared his throat. "I'd like to bring to your attention certain perhaps unintended consequences of your recent actions that you might have overlooked, given the rush of events and given, if I may speak frankly, a certain naiveté about matters financial that is entirely understandable given that you have devoted your lives to the study of other topics. Fortunately, the world contains some people who specialize in such matters, and I happen to be one of them."

"All right," Tristan said, "let's have it."

"Briefly," Frederick said, "it's unthinkable for the ATTO to be floating around loose. Dire consequences would ensue."

"For whom?" I asked. Not disagreeing with him, just wanting details.

"Dire. Consequences."

"For us? For the Fuggers? On this Strand? Other Strands?"

"It's all the same," he said. "Surely, after all you've been through, you have arrived at a level of sophistication where this is obvious to you. You simply haven't admitted it to yourself yet."

"I've been a little preoccupied, as you pointed out," I said, "and the coffee hasn't kicked in yet."

He picked up his newspaper—one of those financial rags only read by investment types. He unfolded it, thumbed to the back pages, and then with a big dramatic movement snapped the whole newspaper inside out to display a page completely covered with numbers so tiny that they just looked like a grey fog from this distance. "Look at all of this information," he said. "Where does it come from? What does it mean? The changes in the prices of these stocks and commodities and bonds all reflect flows of information. Information about the weather, politics, trends in what consumers want, discovery of new oil fields, invention of new technologies. You grew up, like most people, believing that it was all confined to a single Strand. That there was only one copy of the world. Now you know the truth: that information flows not just along a particular Strand but between them, all the time, in subtle ways known only to a few.

"We're bankers. That is really all we are. If you've been imagining some sort of fabulous conspiracy, you are in for a disappointment. Bankers, you see, don't actually do very much. We take our percentage. That is all. We subsist on movements of money—across space, across time, and between Strands."

"How does money move between Strands?" Tristan asked.

Frederick looked a little pained. "I'm not going to tell you *everything*."

"Ooh, a riddle!" I said. "Let me think. Information moves between Strands. Prices change in response to information. Money moves in response to prices."

Frederick had a good poker face.

"And right now," Tristan said, "a big chunk of information has moved into the past, in the form of treasure maps carved into the backs of Magnus and his crew. Longships are going to be heading across the Atlantic to raid Mexico and Peru and bring their gold and silver back to Europe. The changes made to history will be incalculable. And the Fugger policy on all of this is what, exactly?"

"There's no point in getting emotional about it," Frederick said. "Money will flow where money will flow."

"And you'll collect your percentage," I said.

"The most we can really do is manage these things as best we can," Frederick said. "Magnus's ship has, quite literally, sailed. We cannot undo that. But for a legion of ATTOs to be moving freely about the world, and witches and Normans and SEALs popping in and out of them"—he shuddered—"there would be Shear all over the place, and Shear destroys things."

"And destroyed things don't make money," Tristan said.

"A burning factory cannot ship product."

"What does this mean for us?" I asked.

Frederick shrugged. "Some Strands will go the way that Gráinne and Magnus want them to go. In other Strands, their plans may be frustrated. Your level of involvement is up to you."

"Now that we have our own ODEC, you mean," I said. "In the East House basement."

He made the slightest of nods. "You're welcome, by the way."

"SO WHAT DO we do with it, now that it works?" asked Mortimer.

We were all sitting around the dining room table at Frank and Rebecca's—the original quintet, plus Mortimer, Julie, Esme, and Felix. Coals gleamed in the hearth and the air was fragrant with pine branches, frankincense, and lapsang souchong tea. It was New Year's Day.

"We figure out what Gráinne's doing and we undo it," said Tristan. "Or we prevent her from doing it to start with."

"And how do we figure out what she's doing?" asked Julie.

"You might start by asking *me*," said Erszebet. "I *was* her co-conspirator, you know."

"What is Gráinne planning to do, Erszebet?" I asked immediately.

For one breathless moment every one of us stared at Erszebet—who was now, for the first time in years, uniquely qualified to help us move forward. The hopeful tension around the table was palpable.

"She wants to undo technology," said Erszebet, in the same tone, examining her manicure. "*Tch. Obviously.*"

The hopeful tension collapsed. Tristan clenched his jaw a moment and then said, in a controlled voice, "But *how*, exactly, Erszebet?"

Erszebet waved her hand at him as if he were a bug. "I was not involved in the tactical details, my involvement was entirely spiritual."

"Thank you," said Tristan, grinding his teeth to keep his sarcasm in check. "Glad we asked, that was *really* helpful."

I pressed my hand over his as a silent suggestion to shut it. Erszebet noticed—and was immediately more interested in that intimate gesture than she was in the future of humanity. "Ah!" she said, her eyes darting between my hand, my face, and Tristan's face. "I knew it! Did I not say this would happen?" she demanded of Rebecca and Frank, triumphant. And then to me, blithely self-congratulatory: "I always knew you were a good match."

"Are you sure you have no clue what Gráinne's next move might be?" I asked, squeezing Tristan's hand now in a signal to remain quiet.

Erszebet shrugged scornfully. "Do I look like I would dirty my mind thinking the way Gráinne does?"

"Ah," said Oda-sensei peaceably. "Of course, that's how we sort it out. We think like Gráinne. We peel away the leaves of history that uncover photography. Where does it start?"

"Camera obscura?" I suggested. "Da Vinci?"

Frank Oda shook his head. "That merely redirected light in action, it did not collapse the wave function, it did not embed any given moment in time."

"Daguerreotypes," said Erszebet, with distaste. "I remember those becoming so popular so quickly. Like this social media obsession just after the turn of the millennium, or automobiles a hundred years ago."

"But what led to daguerreotypes?" asked Oda-sensei. True to form, despite the urgency of the moment, he was enjoying this as an academic exercise.

"Photosensitive paper," I said. "That's silver nitrate, right? Lenses. Mirrors, maybe?"

He nodded. "These are the things she will undo. If you kill Louis Daguerre, you trigger Diachronic Shear, but if you undermine the development of lens-grinding technology and you do it on enough Strands, then Louis Daguerre will turn his innovative brilliance in some other direction. The same with photosensitive chemicals."

"Now that you say that, it does sound familiar," said Erszebet—Gráinne's erstwhile deputy.

"But the technology behind grinding lenses applies to more than just the development of photography," said Tristan. "The development of optical technology has influenced the course of human history—it's given us telescopes and microscopes and spectacles—"

"Well, if she is successful, now it won't," said Oda—still as if this was nothing more than a most interesting theoretical problem set. "So if she is successful, human history will retroactively alter."

"And silver nitrate," said Tristan, looking a little spooked. "That was discovered by Albertus Magnus in the thirteenth century."

Oda nodded. "She can't kill him off, but she would have to interfere with his accomplishments and discoveries. And he was one of the greatest thinkers of his age, so that, too, would alter what we believe to be our heritage and destiny."

"Undoing photography from the roots up essentially undoes the development of science in general," Esme said.

"Well, I'm not going to stand by and let *that* happen," said Mortimer drily. "That would *totally* mess with my undergraduate curriculum."

No one laughed. There was a pause. A long pause. Outside, I heard someone knocking on a nearby door.

"If we really think she's going to do this, we have to stop her," I said.

"Of course she is going to do this," said Erszebet. "I would do it, in her position."

"Would you really?" I asked. "It's pretty evil."

She gave me her signature cutting side-eye. "Why? History evolves one way or another, history itself is not evil, even if there are evil people in it. I know what you are about to say," she said, as I held up a protesting hand. "You are going to say, just to name one example, slavery is evil, and to that I say, perhaps it is, but we would not have this world without it."

"That doesn't make it acceptable," I said.

"If I could rewrite the world so there was never any slavery, I would do that, yes, absolutely, but then human history would be unrecognizable to us, and you would not like what replaced what you already know, because everyone wants familiar things. You want to stop Gráinne, not because she is trying to do something evil, but because she is trying to make things unfamiliar to you. And that is inconvenient for your view of how life is to be lived, with Walmarts and cotton underwear and things for which you need this so-called rare earth. You want to have always had those things. That's all. Gráinne's plans are inconvenient to your life-style. You have no valid complaint beyond that."

"If she interferes with the development of *science*," said Tristan, "we have a *very* valid complaint."

"No," said Erszebet stubbornly. "Humanity existed without making much of science for a very long time. This is true regardless of what magic ever did or did not do. Science has brought good and evil to the table, in equal measure. I have watched that happen. To have the world without scientific developments is not to have a better world or a worse world—just a different world from the one we know."

"That's such *bullshit*," said Tristan harshly. "Come on, Erszebet, you're being . . . academic. *Obviously* science and technology has improved the existence of humanity."

"Tell that to the people in Hiroshima and Nagasaki," she said. "Tell that to the atmosphere that is choking on carbon emissions."

"I'll tell it to the hundreds of millions of people who would be dead without basic antibiotics," he retorted impatiently. "This is a ridiculous conversation." He got up from his seat and paced in the small triangular space described by the table, the hearth, and the kitchen door.

Then the doorbell rang. Everyone looked surprised except for Tristan, who invited the rest of us to remain seated while he took care of it. Through the windows we could see a FedEx truck idling in the street. A little surprising, on a holiday, but we had been receiving deliveries at the strangest times as rush orders came in for the ODEC project, and so we all assumed it was another shipment of exotic superconductors.

"Erszebet," said Rebecca, speaking for the first time. "Are you arguing *against* fighting Gráinne?" She asked it in a very neutral tone, simply a request for information, all judgment reserved.

"No," said Erszebet. "I am happy to fight her. She is too powerful. Every witch is enthralled with Gráinne, except Julie and you, who are still learning how to do good magic. I myself was in thrall to Gráinne, and I almost did her urging, even though I knew it was evil. Luckily for you, I am too good a person and too loyal a colleague to kill you off."

Tristan came back in carrying a small package that he had received from the FedEx man. He carried it into the kitchen, set it on the counter, and carefully slit it open with his pocketknife.

"Give me an ODEC," Erszebet was continuing, "and I will help you to preserve the world as you know it, which you seem to think is the best world."

"Even though you don't agree," I said.

"I do not think there is any 'best' world. *I* am not *judgmental* that way." But there was a hint of a smile in one corner of her mouth, as if she understood, and enjoyed, how maddening she was.

"With all respect, it seems to me," said Mortimer, "that the operative part of this conversation is: give Erszebet and Julie and Rebecca an ODEC and they'll help us stymie Gráinne. We have the ODEC. We have the three weird sisters. No offense."

"None taken," Julie said. "I like being weird."

"Am I right? And then if you guys want to get into philosophical bickering, you can do it on your coffee break or something."

Erszebet's face suddenly fell. "Only we do not have a Chronotron."

Frank nodded. "I can reproduce some of its functions with my old code base—the iPad app I wrote years ago. But you're right. It is absolutely no replacement for the Chronotron."

"And before you ask," Mortimer said, "there's no replacing that. We may be able to build a makeshift ODEC in the basement, but the Chronotron is a multibillion-dollar project."

"It'll be fine," said Tristan, still working on the package in the kitchen. "We're not trying to launch any new campaigns. We're not being *proactive*. We're being *reactive* now—reactive to Gráinne. We wait for her to make the first move, by sending DOers to the DTAPs we know so well. Then we go to those same DTAPs and stop them."

"Fuckin' A!" Mortimer said.

Tristan came in from the kitchen carrying a white plastic bag that he had extracted from the package. He continued, "We start by going back and talking to our KCWs, explaining how it is, asking them if they are willing to come over to our side. I think many will say yes. So we can develop our own witch network, our own system of safe houses. And in the present day, we still have friends within DODO."

"How can you be so sure?" Erszebet demanded. "Gráinne is subtle. These people who claim to be your friends may in reality be her agents, trying to win your trust."

"Then explain this," Tristan said. He reached into the plastic bag and pulled out a dingy, tangled jumble of yarn, which I did not immediately recognize because I hadn't seen it for years. Erszebet knew it before it was half-revealed.

"My számológép!" she cried, with the wide-eyed wonder of the girl I'd only ever seen in 1851. She began to scramble to her feet, but Tristan saved her the need by tossing it to her over the table.

"Merry belated Christmas! It occurred to me you might need something like this. I've spent the past month tracking it down."

"How?" I asked, amazed.

"Classified," Tristan said. "All bureaucracy, no cloak-and-dagger. It's been stuffed in a filing cabinet for five years."

"You are a good man," said Erszebet almost tearfully. She clutched the számológép to her, cradled it against her heart as if it were a delicate pet. "Thank you. *Thank you.*"

"Ask and it shall be given!" said Julie. "Tristan, your timing rocks."

"Do you know how to use one of those?" asked Rebecca quietly, to Julie. "I have no idea."

"Mortimer and I can work together to rebuild the app," Frank assured her. "It will never be the Chronotron, but it will be more powerful than the számológép and easier for those of us not used to the analog models."

"Is there enough room left in the cellar for that project?" asked Tristan, wresting his attention from the cooing Erszebet.

"We have a guest room upstairs," said Oda-sensei.

"You're all fools," said Rebecca. "This *cannot* be the headquarters for a new diachronic endeavor. Besides the fact that I want it to be safe for family to visit, Blevins will be after all of us. I'm surprised they haven't already knocked our door down."

"Actually, I've been thinking about that," Tristan said, and finally sat down again. "It's the dog that didn't bark. Why *hasn't*

Blevins sent a DOSECOPS squad to knock the door down? What's holding him back?"

"Probably not Gráinne," I said. "Gráinne's pretty hawkish."

"Let's cut to the chase: it's the Fuggers," Tristan said. "They made sure we could build an ODEC in the basement here. They've obviously made a decision that it's better to have us around as a counterbalance to Gráinne than to cede total control of history to her and her minions. And so we are protected, somehow. We can stay here as long as we want."

"Until the Fuggers change their minds," Rebecca said, in a tone that made it clear this wasn't good enough.

"I don't think they'll do that, though," Tristan said. "They'll protect us—they might even fund us, indirectly, untraceably—as long as we're holding up our end of the deal."

"Which is . . . ?" I asked, although I already knew the answer.

"To figure out what Gráinne's up to, somehow—then go wherever she's sending her DOers, and fight them. With wit and words when we can, with swords when we have to."

"Yesss!" Mortimer said

"Works for me," said Esme instantly.

"Me too," said Felix.

"I'm in," Julie said.

"Excellent," said Frank, looking pleased, as Rebecca made a *well-fine-be-that-way* gesture of allowance.

"I have already agreed," Erszebet contributed moodily.

Tristan glanced at me. "Stokes?"

"As if I had a choice," I said. "Of course I'm in."

And that, dear reader, is who we are, and what we now are doing.

THE END

ACKNOWLEDGMENTS

The authors would like to thank Ed Allard, James Gwertzman, Karen Laur, Sean Stewart, Ned Gulley, Professor Natasha Korda, Billy Meleady, Chrysal Parrot, George Fifield and Lynne Adams, Janice Haynes and Beckie Scotten Finn, the Gorgeous Group, Liz Darhansoff, Jennifer Brehl, and Marc H. Glick, Esquire.

CAST OF CHARACTERS

———

WARNING: CONTAINS SPOILERS

(* = historical figure)

Twenty-first-century Cambridge, MA (or DC)

Tristan Lyons, Major (later Lieutenant Colonel) in the U.S. Army; founder of DODO

Dr. Melisande Stokes, initially lecturer in Harvard's Department of Ancient and Classical Linguistics, then Tristan's first recruit to DODO

Dr. Frank Oda, retired MIT physicist, husband of Rebecca East-Oda

Rebecca East-Oda, his wife; a witch

Erszebet Karpathy, a Hungarian witch

Dr. Roger Blevins, chair of Harvard's Department of Ancient and Classical Linguistics, later head of DODO

Lieutenant General Octavian Frink, Director of National Intelligence and Blevins's eventual boss at DODO

Dr. Constantine Rudge, head of IARPA, advisor to DODO, intimate of the Fuggers

Brigadier General Schneider, Tristan's initial boss at IARPA

Lieutenant Colonel Ramirez, Schneider's aide

Les Holgate, Blevins's nephew and Frink's protégé, appointed advisor to DODO

Mortimer Shore, MIT student, systems administrator, swordsman, and general geek at DODO

Julie Lee, classical oboist, waitress, DODO agent, and witch

Macy Stoll, head of C/COD at DODO

Chira Yasin Lajani, DOer, Lover class

Felix Dorn, DOer, Strider class

Dr. Esme Overkleeft, DOer, Sage class

Major Isobel Sloane, officer in command of DOSECOPS, DODO's security force

The Maxes, ODEC builders

The Vladimirs, ODEC geeks

Frederick Fugger, a man of business

Senators Hatcher, Cole, Effingham, and Villesca, and Chairwoman Atkinson, members of the secret Senate committee overseeing DODO's budget

Gordon Healey (offscreen), a Chronotron nerd

Mei East-Oda (offscreen), daughter of Frank and Rebecca

Darren (offscreen), theatrical swordfighting instructor

Tanya Wakessa Washington (offscreen), DODO witch recruit

Dr. Eloise LeBrun, HOSMA

Dr. Stephen Moore, HOSMA

Dr. Hilton Fuller, HOSMA

Nadja, witch recruit

Dr. Srinavasan (offscreen), in-house physician

Sundry DOSECOPS and Secret Service officers

Constance Billy, Anachron witch from fourteenth century

An unidentified witch in collusion with the Fugger Bank

(*In France*) Anne-Marie, proprietress of Collinet B&B

1640 Cambridge, America

Goody Mary Fitch, a witch

Elizabeth Fitch, her young daughter

Goodman Griggs, their neighbor

Ferrymen (brothers)

*Hezekiah Usher, merchant and bookseller

*Stephen Day, printer

A cooper

1560s Antwerp

*Winnifred Dutton, witch

*Thomas Dutton (offscreen), her husband, factor to Thomas Gresham

*Thomas Gresham (offscreen), banker, Winnifred's paramour and father of her child

*Anne Dutton, twelve-year-old child of Winnifred Dutton and Thomas Gresham, witch

1601 London

Gráinne, an Irish witch, spy for Gráinne Ó Máille

*Grace O'Malley (Gráinne Ó Máille), "Pirate Queen of Connacht" (offscreen, Ireland)

Athanasius Fugger, banker

Sir Edward Greylock, courtier

*Queen Elizabeth I (offscreen)

*William Shakespeare, playwright (offscreen)

*Christopher Marlowe, playwright and spy, believed deceased

*Richard Burbage, actor

*Edward Alleyn, actor (offscreen)

*George Clifford, Earl of Cumberland (offscreen), cofounder of East India Company

Pym, proprietor of Tearsheet Brewery

Morag, wench at Tearsheet

Mary, wench at Bell Tavern

Rose, an English witch

Herbert, a handsomely armed young nobleman

George, his not-so-handsomely armed older friend

The Constable of Southwark

Lord Simon Beresford, Sir Edward Greylock's intended father-in-law

*Sir Francis Bacon (offscreen)

Jacques Cardigan, one of Sir Francis's "Good Pens" at Greyfriars (offscreen)

*Nathaniel Bacon, Sir Francis's half brother, married to Anne Dutton (offscreen)

*Three daughters of Nathaniel and Anne, all witches (offscreen)

1203–4 Constantinople

Magnus of Normandy, Varangian Guard

Basina, out-of-wedlock member of the royal family

*Alexios III Angelos, Byzantine Emperor

*Euphrosyne Doukina Kamatera, his Empress

Avraham ben Moises, a Jew of Pera

Rachel, his eldest daughter, a witch

Sarah, his wife, a witch

Bruno of Hamlin, a crass Varangian Guard

*The Crusaders: European warriors, Venetian sailors, churchmen, camp followers, etc. Underfunded and undermanned, but sailing first-rate ships with ample armaments, this army had been called to liberate the Holy Land by way of Alexandria in Egypt; political and financial manipulations resulted in its detouring to Constantinople, to replace Emperor Alexios III with his nephew, Alexios IV (who'd offered to pay the cash-strapped army for this service—but then failed to follow through, leading to the eventual rape of the city).

*Marquis Boniface of Montferrat, leader of the crusading army (offscreen)

(In Collinet, Normandy) Imblen, a witch

1850 San Francisco

Xiu Li, Chinese witch

*Celestial Jong Li, her paramour

Francis Overstreet, proprietor of the St. Francis Hotel

Mr. Fugger, a banker

1851 London

A physician and his wife, Mel's self-appointed guardians

Mr. and Mrs. Karpathy, and the young Erszebet

Mr. Fugger, a banker

(*In Prussia*) *Berkowski, daguerreotypist of the fateful solar eclipse (offscreen)

1045 Normandy

Thyra, witch of Collinet

Vikings

Tóki Olafsson, skald from tenth-century Svelvik

Ingibjörg, witch of tenth-century Svelvik

Twenty-two Vikings, including Storolf, Brand, Halfdan, Thorolf, Bild, Glama, Heid, Asmund, Hrani, Arngrim, Hjordvard, Yngvar, Snorri, Hunfast "the Hapless," Saemundr, and Thord

GLOSSARY

————

Acronyms

ATTO	Ambient Temperature Tactical ODEC
CHRONTEL	document label; intelligence gathered by DOers
C/COD	Conventional/Contemporary Operations Department
CRONE	Chronodynamic Research for Optimizing Next Engagement
DEDE	Direct Engagement for Diachronic Effect
DNI	Director of National Intelligence
DODO	Department of Diachronic Operations
DOer	Diachronic Operative
DOOSH	Diachronic Operative Occupational Safety and Health
DORC	Diachronic Operative Resource Center
DORCCAD	DORC Cartographic and Architectural Database
DOSECOPS	Diachronic Operations Security Operations
DoVE	Department of Violence(s) Ethnology
DTAP	Destination Time and Place
EFOT	Extra-Facility Operations Team
GLAAMR	Galvanic Liminal Aura Antecedent to Manifold Rift
GRIMNIR	neo-ragtag successor to ODIN; not an acronym
HOSMA	Historical Operations Subject Matter Authority
IARPA	Intelligence Advanced Research Projects Agency
IPOPWI	Infinite Pasts, One Present, Weighted Influence
KCW	Known Compliant Witch
MAGOPs	Magical Operations
MAGSEC	Magical Security
MARS	Martial Arts Research Summary
NEER	Northern Europe, Early Renaissance
NELM	Northern Europe, Late Medieval

NOCHRON	document label; not to be viewed by Anachrons
ODEC	Ontic Decoherence Cavity
ODIN	Operational DODO Intranet
OPIFDI	One Present, Infinite Futures, Diffuse Influence
PEP	Performance Enhancement Plan
POOJAC	Policy on Official Jargon and Acronym Coinage
QUIPU	Quantum Information Processing Unit
RAFSTIQUORDOT	mnemonic for what to do during/after Diachronic Shear
SARF	Supervised Anachron Residential Facility
SLIT	Something Less Than Infinite Time
UDET	Unity of DOer-Experienced Time

Terms

áireamhán	Irish name for broom-quipu object used like abacus by witches
Anachron	historical person brought forward in time to modern day
Diachronic Shear	infernal, catastrophic response of the universe to too-extreme changes being wrought as a result of diachronic activity
diakrónikus nyírás	Hungarian term for Diachronic Shear
lomadh	Irish word for Diachronic Shear
Shiny Hat	ultra-paranoid secure operating system
Strand	parallel universe
számológép	Hungarian name for quipu-like object used like abacus by witches
Wending	witch practice/superpower of jumping sideways between Strands

ABOUT THE AUTHORS

———

NEAL STEPHENSON is the author of *Seveneves, Reamde, Anathem,* the three-volume historical epic The Baroque Cycle *(Quicksilver, The Confusion,* and *The System of the World)* as well as *Cryptonomicon, The Diamond Age, Snow Crash,* and *Zodiac.* He is (with Nicole Galland) one of the seven coauthors of the Mongoliad Trilogy. He lives in Seattle, Washington.

NICOLE GALLAND is the author of six previous novels: *The Fool's Tale; Revenge of the Rose; Crossed; I, Iago; Godiva;* and *Stepdog.* She is (with Neal Stephenson) one of the seven coauthors of the Mongoliad Trilogy. She lives on Martha's Vineyard.